Frank Hardy was born in Southern Cross, Victoria, in 1917, the son of a milk factory worker. Leaving school at thirteen he worked in a variety of jobs: messenger and news boy, grocer's assistant, fruit and vegetable picker, factory worker and illustrator. His writing career began at the age of twenty-seven with the publication of short stories in Trade Union journals.

In August, 1950 he published *Power Without Glory*; two months later he was arrested, jailed and charged with criminal libel. *The Hard Way* was written to tell of his arrest, trial and subsequent acquittal.

Hardy was a driving force behind the Realist Writers Movement, becoming President of the Melbourne Group in 1946 and later forming groups in other cities.

In 1952, with the late George Seelaf, he formed the left-wing publishing house, The Book Society, which arose out of the interest in literature in the Labor Movement inspired by the *Power Without Glory* defence campaign.

Among Frank Hardy's many published works are novels such as *But the Dead Are Many, Who Shot George Kirland?* and *The Outcasts of Foolgarah*; collections of short stories including *Legends from Benson's Valley* and *Great Australian Legends* and a book about Aborigines based on personal travels and experience, *The Unlucky Australians*. His stage plays include *Leap Seven Times in the Air* and *Faces in the Street*. His *The Yarns of Billy Borker* appeared as a series on ABC television in 1966; *Power Without Glory* as a serial in 1975.

Frank Hardy died in 1994.

T0363441

Power Without Glory

FRANK HARDY

VINTAGE **CLASSICS**

Australia

A Vintage Book
Published by Random House Australia Pty Ltd
Level 3, 100 Pacific Highway, North Sydney, NSW 2060
www.randomhouse.com.au

First published 1950
First published by Vintage in 1994. This edition published in 2008

Addresses for companies within the Random House Group can be found at
www.randomhouse.com.au/offices

National Library of Australia
Cataloguing-in-Publication Entry

Hardy, Frank (Francis Joseph), 1917–1994.
Power without glory.

ISBN 978 1 74166 761 5 (pbk.).

A823.3

Cover photo by Corbis
Cover image selection and design by Jenny Grigg
Typeset by Midland Typesetters, Australia
Printed and bound by Griffin Press, South Australia

Random House Australia uses papers that are natural, renewable and recyclable
products and made from wood grown in sustainable forests. The logging and
manufacturing processes are expected to conform to the environmental regulations
of the country of origin.

PUBLISHER'S NOTE

During Frank Hardy's time in the army in the 1940s, one of his friends suggested that he could be a writer. 'What would I write about?' he responded. 'Those stories you tell on beer nights,' was the reply. It would be trite to say the rest is history, because the road to fulfilling this prophesy proved not to be an easy one. To begin with, back then, Hardy did not consider himself to be a writer; this writer would not be truly born until his combined powers of captivating storytelling and political conviction fused into an explosive force that would literally drive him to complete his first novel, *Power Without Glory*, in 1950. This book was to become a literary classic.

Power Without Glory was and remains an extraordinary novel for many reasons. Firstly, it was originally a self-published work and if Hardy had not had the courage to take a gamble on his book, scraping together the money to typeset and print it, it would not be with us today. Secondly, it sparked the most controversial criminal libel case in Australian judicial history; one that would imperil Hardy's freedom and pose questions about the limitations of freedom of speech and political association in this country. And finally, it is a work which illustrates the power inherent in a writer's determination to expose, interpret and understand. There is little doubt, considering the gargantuan task that Hardy had set himself in collecting the research for this book, let alone undertaking to write and then publish it, that there must have been times when he wondered at this determination. But the literary significance of this book lies in the very journey Hardy's passion compelled him to take: what began as a deliberate attack on capitalism, designed to expose the corruption operating at the very top level of Victorian politics and business, developed into a complex portrait of power and the people it makes and destroys. Hardy ultimately captured a vivid picture of an epoch in Australian political and social history in a way that has not only endured the tests of time and academic scrutiny, but retained its relevance, fascination and its powerfully Australian voice.

'Let fiction meant to please
be near to truth'
–*Horace*

INTRODUCTION

Many novelists have caused scandals or uproars by dragging out into the light of day various aspects of life which the conventional morality of the period or strong vested interests wanted to keep hidden away. Zola, Flaubert, James Joyce, D. H. Lawrence spring to mind as writers in whom the artistic urge for new ways of expression was linked with the need to deal with new and forbidden material. On a lower artistic level we meet writers like Upton Sinclair who used the novel form for a vigorous exposure of bad social conditions. But no novel has had such a violent and tempestuous career, at every moment of its writing, printing, and initial publication, as Frank Hardy's *Power Without Glory*.

Hardy's book was an epical representation of a whole phase of Australian social and political history, done from the angle of the forces behind the scenes. In treating those forces he could not but find himself up against very powerful interests, especially as he came to the conclusion that the man on whom he must concentrate was a ruler in the sporting world, with a strong underground organisation as well as his obvious empire, whom it was highly dangerous to challenge. Not that Hardy began his book with any simple idea of exposing an individual. He was interested only in the person in question, John Wren, because he felt him to be typical of the corruptions he wanted to explore; and though, as he went on, he found himself fascinated by the problem of Wren, his rise to control of the sporting world and his political role, he always sought to generalise his material, to see Wren as both a remarkable and subtle character and as an emblem of Australian political development at a crucial phase. However, the way in which he felt his purpose to be tied up with the revelation of Wren as man and as social portent was shown by the fact that he could not even disguise his protagonist with a quite different sounding name, but called him West.

We can see that the kind of book Hardy was driven to write was largely determined by his own experiences. He was born into a working-class family in Victoria, Australia, where his father moved from place to place, working in milk and butter factories.

His own youth was spent in the depressed Thirties, with all sorts and shifts and struggles necessary for the family to survive. The sort of world in which he grew up is depicted in his book of short stories, *Legends from Benson's Valley*, which excellently evokes the devious dodges and conflicts of the time – but does so in something of traditional Australian style, with the easy flow of the folk-yarn in pub or round campfires, whereas in *Power Without Glory* he breaks new ground in both material and method.

Hardy thus grew up with his nose close to the grindstone of harsh economic realities, with a keen mind that wanted to understand what it was all about and why things happened the way they did. He did not however for sometime foresee a literary career for himself. He aspired to draw caricatures and had some slight success in this vein. No doubt his powers of acute observation induced him to take this turn, while at the same time his struggles to master caricature and cartoon helped him to sharpen those powers still further and to train him for novel-writing. In 1942, at the age of twenty-five, he joined the army and was posted to the Northern Territory where he edited and largely wrote a unit-newspaper. In November 1944 he was taken on as artist by the official army-journal *Salt*. His work on *Salt* was of great importance for his future, particularly through the friendship he struck up with the artist Ambrose Dyson, a member of the Dyson family that did much to enrich Australian art and literature. Ambrose helped to deepen Hardy's understanding of the nature of literature and give substance to his ambition. Before the end of the war, Hardy had some success with short stories and had conceived the idea of a large scale novel that would attempt to set out a full picture of Australian realities, going deep under the surface and grappling with the hidden forces at play. Such a concept excited both Hardy's young and topless ambitions, and the political passion which had been bred in him by the family's sufferings. Further, it seemed the right sort of thing to come out of the war in which Hardy was involved, a tribute to his fellow-soldiers and the cause for which they fought and died. Discussions with Ambrose and others confirmed him in the idea.

Hardy had told the story of how he wrote the novel in a book, *The Hard Way*. I have also heard him narrate the stirring episodes with all his considerable skill and verve as a ranconteur. He has

Irish blood in him, I believe, and in fact the only authors I have known who were even better at spinning a yarn in the flesh than in putting it down on paper have been Irish – Liam O'Flaherty or Jim Phelan, for instance. Indeed, the compliment that launched Hardy on his writing career was one paid to his yarn-spinning. A professional writer who happened to be in the same unit in the Northern Territory said to him, "If you would write some of the stories you tell on beer nights, you'd make a fortune." Hardy replied, "What? Those! But that's not literature." The writer told him, "Literature is life." This conversation made Hardy struggle to get one of his tales on paper; the result won a competition at Sydney; Hardy turned definitely to literature as his career.

As soon as he was discharged, he set to work collecting material for the novel. His great interest in the sporting world, its seamy side as well as its public events, made the theme of Wren of special fascination to him. He knew something of his general reputation and the way he had risen in the world through illegal betting-establishments which the police had failed to shut down. Australian journalism had long been more akin to American than to English in its readiness to dare libel actions and pillory persons who for one reason or another could be held up to ridicule or denunciation. I recall John Dalley, when editing the Sydney *Bulletin* in the early 1920's, saying to me that he took the line there were certain persons who had gone so far in making themselves public enemies that considerations of libel did not apply to them; and John Norton in *Truth* had shown in a style of ferocious alliteration how far such an attitude could be carried. *The Lone Hand Magazine*, a periodical of high standing, had published about 1910 an outspoken essay on "John Wren and his Ruffians," with remarks like the following, "His near and dear blood relations, who makes himself useful about the place, is one among many of Wren's bodyguards who have been flogged or sentenced to death, or both." (The near relation was Wren's brother, Arthur, about whom Hardy later dug out much information.) We see then that Hardy was intent on following up a national tradition of journalistic audacity, though he wanted to produce a work which rose far above any level of journalistic muck-raking and succeeded in marrying a strong social purpose to a high artistic aim.

He began, in his own words, copying out in notebooks "extracts from *Hansard*, from old newspapers and magazines,

3

from Royal Commission Reports, from documents in Melbourne and Sydney libraries," gathering "material about the bank crash in the 1890's, the growth of the City of Melbourne, changes in fashion, raids on the Collingwood Tote, Federation, the war between Wren and the police and wowsers, population figures, relevant sporting events, the deportation of Father Jerger, the Conscription Referenda of 1916–17, the life stories and personalities of various politicians, criminals and others, the political ramifications of the Catholic Church hierarchy, the Mungana scandal, the police strike, the depression, the Unemployed Workers' Movement, the rise of the Santamaria secret 'Movement,' and a hundred and one other subjects." He soon compiled a list of useful contacts, people who had lived near the Collingwood Tote (the illegal betting establishment on which Wren first built himself up), enemies of the Wren machine in the political, sporting and business spheres, associates of Wren who had been cast off, and, in a few cases, even members of the Wren machines and friends of the Wren family. "One contact led to another like an endless chain. Every piece of information had to be checked, verified and put into place in a card system of events covering sixty years." A first rate piece of prolonged detective work was the first necessity of the novel.

Sometimes, as always happens with a man who never lets up on an inquiry, he had his moments of luck. He spent much time searching for a man who was said to have been cheated out of a big business by Wren; then one day in a Melbourne train he began talking with a fat jovial fellow about the Caulfield Cup, deliberately naming a favourite named *Anstey* after a well-known Labour politician. "*Anstey* won't win," declared the fat man. "No horse John Wren named after a victim of his ever did any good." In a few minutes Hardy discovered that the man was the business-man he had been long chasing after. By the time they reached Sydney he had learned a great deal more about Wren.

He joined in the fight which the trotting men were carrying on against Wren's control; took part in running the trotting paper *The Beam;* and thus gained further valuable contacts and inside information. He followed the Wren trail into the boxing and wrestling worlds, and then into the big political scandals of the earlier 20th century, such as that of the Mungana Mining Leases. All the while he was extremely hard-up. He had married and there were two children to look after. Obsessed with the sporting world, he himself gambled, lost and won, won and lost; and all the while he was afraid that Wren and his very widespread organisation would find out what he was doing. If his intentions were guessed, he was liable to come up against all forms of intimidation and violence. In Brisbane he was shadowed and received an anonymous threatening letter. Then, as on many other occasions, he thought the game was up. But he persisted, and somehow managed to evade detection. Often he used assumed names in his inquiries. He had at times to do a fair amount of hard drinking as he hobnobbed with the tough characters who held the clues he wanted to get; and that made all the more difficult his need to keep a padlock on his own tongue while noting carefully everything that the others blurted out.

The idea of using a Wren-type figure as part of a general picture of the real sources of power in Australian politics had now given way to a passionate desire to track out every detail in Wren's complicated system of power. Wren as a man had become synonymous for him with all the darker forces at work in society; and he felt his quest as one into the depths of evil as well as into the spirit of a typical man of the times. As the material grew and the scope of the book extended, he was becoming more and more aware of his lack of training as a writer. He fought to overcome his weaknesses and to grasp the nature of the problems of novel technique. Two books to which he has paid special tribute were Elizabeth Bowen's *Notes on Writing a Novel* and Stefan Zweig's *Balzac*. The latter book had the further value of leading him on to a systematic reading of Balzac as the master who was able to fuse the exploration of the human soul with that of society itself, its economic and political structures. Dickens also he read closely. At the same time he went on struggling to deepen his grasp on political economy, on Marxism, on philosophy, on problems of social development. Only by such studies could he fill out and dignify his idea as he felt it was necessary to do.

In March 1948 he was able to spend two autumnal months on a sheep station where he could relax from the quest and find leisure to digest his material and write. He found that his characters fell into three categories: real people whom he tried to make as close to the facts as possible (Tom Mann, Billy Hughes, and so on); characters based on real people but developed as imaginatively as his powers permitted (West-Wren, Thurgood-Theodore, Archbishop Malone-Mannix); entirely fictional characters used to complete the needed range of types and experiences. The place and purpose of the large number of characters thus emerging were determined by the now clear perspective of the whole. But Wren-West stood at the heart of the picture and everything depended on how he was given life and developed.

Once more hard up, Hardy returned to the *Trotting Beam* as reporter. The political situation had become difficult and he was afraid that the police might be informed about his novel, in which case it was liable to be seized and all his labour would have been in vain. He managed to get out of Melbourne to a Youth Camp at Eureka. There he was able to get down thoroughly to the novel. He was now well into the work, and the momentum carried on after his return to Melbourne. But as he neared the end, he had to face the question of what he was going to do with the unwieldly manuscript. No publisher would dream of touching such a thing; no printer would dare to print it if he knew what he was handling. The moment that its existence and whereabouts were known to the Wren machine, there would be swift and drastic action against it. The book had inevitably grown to considerable proportions; it amounted to over 700 pages when it did at last get into print. Hardy had no money to finance it in any way.

Then the sporting world which he both hated and loved came for once to his rescue. He won £200 on a trotting bet. He sounded a few printers and decided to use an old family-firm. Some of the book was set. All the while he was afraid that the firm would realise what dynamite they were playing with, and he did not dare to provoke questions by asking for credit. His £200 was soon used up on hired metal and type-setting. He found another firm ready to do some composing. His next step was to find a firm that would do the actual printing. The plan was to save money by printing 32 pages at a time, returning the metal, and then ordering some more.

He tried a few printers, but realised that he would never find one to do the job. The only course was to buy a machine. He found one advertised for £1,800, which the owner said would have to be left in the works for some six months till a new machine arrived. As Hardy had nowhere to take the thing, that proviso suited him. Borrowing £500, he paid £400 on deposit and used the other £100 for more setting. Still afraid of his secret leaking out, he started work with a more experienced friend, printing during the Christmas holidays. Then they went on for some three months, always on the guard against snoopers. The works foreman was impressed by their tidiness – they took care never to leave a single spoiled sheet anywhere about. Hardy was kept busy, printing, writing and revising, lugging type about, arguing about payments and raising more loans. The printed sheets were piling up steadily; but so far no thought had been given to the problems of folding, sewing, binding.

Wearing a new suit that he had won at the trots, he interviewed a firm and arranged about the folding. Now the workers began reading the sheets and there was excited talk; the management, uneasy, stopped work. By this time Hardy owed about £2,000. He found another firm; but in his haste, as he was transferring the sheets, the badly tied bundles fell into the gutter or blew away. Bystanders and a policeman helped, but many sheets were in a bad condition. Later, only 7,200 out of 8,000 could be assembled. Demands for money increased. At last a binder (who later turned out to be incompetent and bankrupt) was found. Friends folded the remainder of the sheets by hand. And at last, despite all the difficulties, in August 1950, Hardy was able to hold a completed copy of the book in his hands.

Now a new set of hurdles had to be taken. How was the book to reach the public? A friend commented. "Your body will be found floating in the Yarra soon after the book comes out." But, whatever the consequences were to be, Hardy was still far from bringing them down on his head; for he didn't know how to get the book around. At last a distributor was found, a new arrival from England who had little idea of what the novel was about; but he also had little means of distribution. A more effective idea was to sell copies direct to the Trade Unions. Friends organised meetings – the first at a big meat works – where Hardy spoke, read bits of the novel, tried to explain its theme. Slowly but steadily the book began to circulate. Some copies were sold to individuals, others were left at works to be loaned out at a few shillings a time. Book-sellers were totally uninterested.

From Hardy's point of view the problem was to get as many

copies around before the storm broke. But the storm was curiously slow in breaking. The Wren organisation gave no sign of recognising the threat. Apart from the literary periodical, *Meanjin Papers*, the press printed no reviews or notices. The whole thing seemed a flop. The great adventure had been pointless and misdirected.

And then suddenly everyone was talking about the novel. Booksellers were flooded with orders. Politicians scented the importance of the book's revelations. Copies were sold in pubs and the like at exorbitant rates. Hardy says that one black-marketeer even tried to sell him one for five pounds in an hotel, and, being out of supplies, he nearly bought it. The first edition disappeared. A second edition of 16,000 was got under way. Hardy had lost his machine by this time, and he had to turn to printers. Only five small firms, hard-up and badly equipped, were ready to take the risk. Warnings flew round. Four of the five firms lost their nerve. One dumped a truckload of sheets on the steps of the Trades Hall. But somehow the work went ahead. Now there were at least crowds of eager helpers.

Then Hardy, with the aid of sympathizers, tried out the boldest trick of all. He managed to get the edition printed mainly by night-shifts, at the official printer of the Victorian Labour Party, which was at that time dominated by the Wren machine. To make things more exciting, the works stood close by the Police Headquarters. But the printing was not carried out without one dangerous moment. The Wren machine got wind of what was happening, and arranged for the sheets to be removed and destroyed. Hardy however found out in time, and managed to get hold of the sheets (his own legal property) a few hours before the wreckers arrived. But there were still many imperfections in what had been printed. Once again volunteers got to work. The demand for the book was now immense.

Two detectives called and questioned Mrs. Hardy while Hardy was out. He had meanwhile been guarded by two seamen against possible attacks. Realising that the legal showdown with the Wren organisation could not be delayed, he avoided going home after seeing a car-load of detectives in the street. Next morning he went to a solicitor, who got in touch with the police and Hardy was arrested by appointment. To his great surprise he found that no charge of libel against Wren was being laid. Instead, a comparatively minor point was brought up. At one point in the book he had shown Mrs. West, frustrated by a loveless life, turning to another man; and he was now accused of libelling Mrs. Wren. Not a word was said of the multiple criminal activities he had depicted Wren as engaged in.

The tactics of his opponents in thus concentrating on Mrs. Wren and ignoring what was said of Wren were in the end to prove Hardy's salvation. A prolonged legal battle began, and everything seemed set for a long prison sentence. After strenuous debates the Crown took over the prosecution and Hardy was brought before Judge and Jury at the Supreme Court of Victoria on a charge of Criminal Libel, in which evidence could be called as in any criminal trial to prove the accused's guilt and the penalty was likely to be a long period in jail. For nine months the hard-fought hearings went on. A Defend-Hardy Committee had been set up, and Hardy himself carried on a fierce struggle in his own defence – his own campaign merging with a wider struggle for democratic liberties that was being waged. We are reminded of the English 18th century, the epoch of Wilkes, when personal issues and democratic struggles were similarly entangled; and as in the England of Wilkes the spokesmen on the popular side were to the jurymen. Hardy was finally acquitted.

The main witness for the prosecution was driven to the point of taking the position that the question of adultery had been selected as the basis of the trial because he considered it far more serious than all the nefarious activities laid at the door of West. Defending counsel pointed out that Mrs. West could be identified in the book with Mrs. Wren solely because she was represented as the wife of West-Wren. The prosecution's case therefore rested in the last resort on the extent to which West could be seen as Wren. So the defending counsel took up incident after incident from the book in which West-Wren was shown as carrying on in a criminal way: rigged pigeon-races, bribery of the police, rigged sports-results of all sorts, corrupt political activities, the murder of a detective and two other murders. If the prosecution insisted that Mrs. Wren could be recognised because West was recognisably Wren, why had no charges been taken out against Hardy for libel of Wren? Close pressed, the main witness for the prosecution had to answer, "In this case, yes." to the question, "Do you still say that an allegation of adultery is a grosser libel than an allegation of murder, cheating, fraud, and the other matters?''

There seems no doubt that that was the crucial moment of the long and involved trial, and that it convinced the jury that Mrs. Wren was being used as a cover for Wren and his system.

Now to the book itself, which has since been printed without challenge in Britain, Australia, and many other countries in translation: what of it? How does it stand the test of time? Is it merely a document of great importance for the inner history of Australian politics and sports, or is it also a work of art in its own way?

At first the critics, caught unawares by a book that was the centre of a vast political tumult, assumed that it must be nothing more than an industrious compilation which in due time would be sorted out by the social historian for its facts and its fantasies. A book that so obviously came up from a non-literary level, by an unknown author who was certainly an adept in the political world, was surely something that lay outside the sphere of serious artistic values. A rapid glance could show that it was written in a plain direct style and that there were various roughnesses; especially in the later part Hardy, working under desperate conditions and feeling that the novel was already rather long, did not allow himself time to get as fully inside the situations as in the earlier sections. The tendency therefore was to stress the political vigour more than the expressive powers of the writing.

Now, however, when time has allowed the dust of the immediate conflicts to settle and the West-Wren epoch has receded into the past, becoming an historical curiosity rather than something which arouses strong reactions, this tendency has been in many ways reversed; and *Power Without Glory* has been discovered as a powerful novel in its own rights. The arduous pressures which produced some of the roughnesses have their value in communicating the sense of urgency, of passionate search and discovery, which in the long run own a far greater artistic virtue than surface-smoothnesses.

Beyond all minor faults, *Power Without Glory* emerges as a truly epic work, both in conception and execution. Perhaps if Hardy had had more experience as a writer and known more clearly what he was tackling, he would have blenched and turned aside to lesser tasks, contenting himself with the short stories at which he already had much dexterity. His very ignorance and inexperience thus had a positive quality, setting him off on his Herculean attempt to kill tremendous monsters and cleanse Augean Stables with an ardour and courage that carried him right through to the triumphant end. Not that a keen spirit alone could have solved his problems. Hardy succeeded because he realised as he went on what he was tackling, and made strenuous efforts to educate himself to the height of his task, struggling with history and philosophy as well as with statistics and the gossip of the underworld. He was able to write his book because with each burst of writing he deepened his own understanding of the theme and developed himself decisively as a writer. Such a method might well have produced a confused scattering of the impulse that had generated the book. With Hardy, however, because of his complete devotion to the work, it operated in the opposite way and produced a creative concentration of purpose.

The novel therefore does give us a picture both of a whole Australian epoch and of a man. It has coherence and unflagging interest, not merely because of the vitality of the incidents, but because West-Wren is realised as an individual, caught up in circumstances, fighting to shape them his own way, succeeding and yet defeated. He is depicted as a ruthless man, corrupted and corrupting; and yet we feel sympathy for him. We are made to feel there were great potentialities in the man, which are warped by the struggle for survival as he sees it. This is one form of struggle in a world of corrupted power: to beat the forces that are crushing you by forcing yourself to become stronger and more dangerous than they are. We see Wren in his process of corruption, gaining a sort of evil grandeur as he rises, and yet remaining a man, conditioned at every point by the circumstances that he seeks to control. Then comes the point of tragic catastrophe. Wren is defeated, but his defeat is complex. He is cornered in part by the forces which he cannot understand, expressed by the men who struggle to change the world, not to adapt themselves to its twists and distortions; in part by the very forces which he himself has conjured up and strengthened. Wren had known well enough the world of his early years. The novel's opening episode of the spinning coin that bribes the policeman provides a perfect image of West's development. The coin hypnotises West as much as the bribed man; it represents his first moment of secure power and his key to the future. In the world of the spinning coin he moves with masterful ease, quite sure that the spin which controls the others is something magically at his service. But all the while he is himself becoming more and more the creature of what Carlyle called the crash-nexus, the dehumanised sphere where men are reduced to things, to mere items of the commodity-market. And the world of the cash-nexus, of the spinning obsessional coin, is not a static thing, an instrument tamely obeying the will of West. It is a dynamic process to which he is importantly contributing, but which in the last resort is his master, not his slave. So it grows in size and significance, and one day the point is reached where Wren no longer understands and dominates it. The very forces that he has nurtured reach out and hold him fast.

Thus Hardy succeeds in powerfully expressing the processes of social development, not as abstract things, not as a mere background of the story, but as forces imbedded deep in the spirit and the will of West, his protagonist. This is what gives a greatness to the novel.

And in managing to concentrate and focus his sense of social process in the development, the growth and final frustration, of West, Hardy has written one of the few deep-going novels of urban industrialised society. That is, a novel which does not merely have that society as its setting, but embodies in its structure, in the nature and development of its protagonist, the essential characteristics of the world of the market, of the hypnotic spinning coin. Such novels are rarer than one might think, though near the fountainhead of the modern novel stands Balzac, the master of such insights. And what one may thus call the urban novel is particularly rare in Australia, where, though the mass of the population live in cities, the cultural tradition has always laid, and even now still lays, its main emphasis on the pioneering stages, the characters of the wayback. Though urban elements can be traced in earlier Australian fiction, from Lewis Stone to Vance Palmer, it is with *Power Without Glory* that the urban Australian scene comes in full strength and range into the literary picture.

These deeper aspects of the novel are what now come uppermost. *Power Without Glory* has a secure place in the political and social history of Australia, and its remarkable story, which I have sketched out here, is not going to be easily forgotten. But it has now also begun to conquer its place in the literary history as a work of striking originality, force, and depth. The evil that Hardy has unveiled goes much deeper than the political terms in which he began by visualising it; and the image of West has tragic insight as well as social cogency. The intense devotion with which Hardy approached his task stirred his whole being and drew him spiritually into deeper waters than he had bargained for.

The novel itself and the circumstances surrounding its conception, birth, and publication, make up a singular unity; and even the reader whose political convictions are far from those of Hardy can hardly fail to be moved by such a tale of dedication and its results, both in the world of action and that of literature.

Jack Lindsay, 1968

PART ONE

1890–1907
ROAD TO POWER

*A working man who deserts his own class, tries
to get on and rise above it, enters into a lie.*
CHARLES KINGSLEY

PART ONE

1850–1907
ROAD TO POWER

A working man who is...

CHARLES DICKENS

CHAPTER ONE

*Men make their own history, but they do not make it just
as they please, they do not make it under circumstances
chosen by themselves, but under circumstances directly
found, given and transmitted from the past.*

KARL MARX

One bleak afternoon in the winter of 1893 a young man stood in
the doorway of a shop in Jackson Street, Carringbush, a suburb of
the city of Melbourne, in the Colony of Victoria. The shop was
single-fronted and above its narrow door was the sign CUMMIN'S
TEA SHOP. In its small window stood a tea-chest with a price ticket
leaning against it.

The man was of short, solid build and was neatly dressed in a
dark-grey suit. His face was clean-shaven. He wore a celluloid
collar and a dark tie. With his left hand he was spinning a coin.
It was a shiny golden coin, a sovereign. Standing on the footpath
facing him from a few feet away was a tall policeman in uniform,
whose small, unintelligent eyes followed the flight of the coin as
it spun up a few feet and fell into the palm of the young man's
hand, only to spin rhythmically upwards again and again.

The policeman said: "This shop is on my beat. I have had
complaints that you are conducting an illegal totalisator here."

A cold wind blew through the door fanning against the young
man's trouser legs, revealing that he was extremely bow-legged.
From a distance, the first noticeable characteristic was his bandiness, but, at close range, his eyes were the striking feature. They
were unfathomable, as if cast in metal; steely grey and rather too
close together; deepset yet sharp and penetrating. The pear-
shaped head and the large-lobed ears, set too low and too far
back, gave him an aggressive look, which was heightened by a
round chin and a lick of hair combed back from his high sloping
forehead like the crest of a bird. His nose was sharp and straight;
under it a thin, hard line was etched for a mouth.

He was twenty-four years of age, and his name was John West.

His brother, Joe, younger by a year, stood behind him in the gloomy little shop. Joe was of similar build, but lacked the striking personality. Like the policeman, Joe was watching the coin as it spun up and down, glinting in the dull light.

After a pause, John West answered quietly in a resonant voice: "I told yer before: this is a tea shop and we only work here." His eyes were not watching the coin; they were glued on the policeman's face. "See for yerself, Constable Brogan, a chest in the window, and tins and packages of tea on the shelves and under the counter. A tea shop. Someone has informed yer wrong. All you have to do is to report that somebody's made a mistake, and everything'll be all right."

"You understand, Mr. West, that we must follow up all complaints. Our informants say that nearly every afternoon, especially Saturdays, people stream in and out of this shop and don't buy any tea. I don't wish to doubt you, but – er, I have instructions to search the shop," Brogan said, and his eyes broke from the hypnotic effect of the spinning coin and met those of the young man. As they did so, John West, as though reading a message in them, suddenly flicked the sovereign at the policeman, who reached quickly and caught the coin in front of his chest. Constable Brogan looked around furtively, his cheeks reddened, and he dropped his head.

"I can see you realise you have been informed wrong," John West said. "This is a tea shop. Say that, and everything'll be all right."

Joe West had watched them tensely. He sighed when the policeman slipped the coin into his tunic pocket, saying: "I will report that, as far as I can see, this is a tea shop."

Constable Brogan spoke huskily. He hesitated, opened his mouth as if to speak again, then turned and walked down the street.

When he was out of earshot, John West turned to his brother and said: "I told you I could do it, but I never thought it would be so easy." His voice, steady during the conversation, was now shaky and strained. "I'm goin' down to football practice. Lock up, and make sure all them bettin' slips are taken home." He walked through the shop to the small room at the rear and returned, putting on his hat. "Tell Mum I'll be home for tea at six o'clock," he said.

As he walked briskly up the street a cable tram lumbered by. He ran beside it, then leapt aboard the open front. Cable trams had not long been running from Carringbush to the city of Melbourne, and passers-by stopped to watch this one as it went clattering along.

John West sat watching the gripman operating the driving-levers, but he was not thinking of the technicalities of cable locomotion. He was gripped by a new feeling of elation which he could not fully explain to himself. It concerned the bribing of the policeman; he knew that much. Others, including Joe, had started totalisators in Carringbush since the idea spread from Sydney, but they had been closed up by the police; yet he, John West, had now been able to buy off the police. It gave him a vague sense of power to think of it. That he could change the policeman's mind seemed to release in him a new stream of life and strength. He had once believed that the police were people to be feared, men who brought you to punishment for breaking the law; yet now he could "square" the police – one of them anyway – with a golden sovereign.

Familiar scenes of Jackson Street flitted by, but he did not notice them. The shops, many of them shuttered and empty; the old houses; the rows of newer tenements and, sprinkled here and there, incomplete houses on which work had ceased; the TO LET signs; the group of ragged unemployed men standing outside the hotel near where the horse trams had changed steeds in the days before the cable was put down; the spindly children playing list-lessly in the gutters; the old man driving the herd of cows home from the river bank where he had grazed them for their owners since morning; the silent boot factory; the carts, buggies, jinkers and hansom cabs; the long queue of despair-haunted people waiting outside the Salvation Army Hall for their daily bowl of soup; the top-hatted, side-whiskered men standing outside the closed bank building, waiting and hoping against hope as they read the notice on the door, CLOSED FOR RECONSTRUCTION. John West had heard yesterday that some of the banks had crashed, that now the "bad times," already three years old, would grow worse.

Life in Carringbush and heredity had imposed on John West the humble, the furtive and the sordid aspects of life.

His family was among the poorest in the squalid, poverty-stricken suburb. His friends were the workers, the workless, and the larrikins.

When he and his two brothers were boys, the police often found cause to call at the house; and later, when they joined the larrikin pushes, they were often chased by the police. Two policemen called, six years ago, handcuffed his older brother Arty, and took him away.

John West's mother had married the son of a ticket-of-leave convict, soon after she arrived from Ireland. She was a pretty golden-haired colleen then; but poverty and a drunken husband had broken her health, wrinkled her skin and threaded her hair with grey.

The West family lived in a shabby lane behind Jackson Street in a house that was as dingy as the others there. It was single-fronted, of weather-board, with an unkempt garden plot squeezed in between the picket fence and front verandah. A narrow path ran down the right side into the tiny backyard.

Somehow Mrs. West kept the home going on what little money she could get from her husband. In her three boys she found consolation. She gave them as much simple comfort as conditions permitted, but usually this amounted to only a bare minimum of food and clothing. On Saturday nights she tubbed them, for a bath was a luxury in Carringbush. She watched them grow, heard them learn to talk, marvelled at the way they could play games without toys. She was joyful when they were well-behaved, despairing when they were cheeky, mischievous or destructive. When they were old enough, she sent them to the State School, where they learned to read and write, and to get into mischief.

When her boys grew up she reaped a bitter harvest from the seeds sown so lovingly. Her sons grew away from her, beyond her control. Even before they had left school, she found the need to tell herself that they were not bad boys. They "played the wag" often, especially Arthur. Arty was a headstrong boy: heart-to-heart talks, even beatings, had little effect on him.

The boys had grown up during the land boom in the 80's, when Melbourne's population had grown to more than 500,000 people, when large ornate buildings sprang up to make a great city where, nearly fifty years before, tents and a few crude stone buildings had stood. In the suburbs, thousands of new houses were sprinkled among the old. Where only fifty years before bullock drays had laboured over rough tracks, cable trams and horse-drawn vehicles travelled along smooth metal roads, and steam trains ran to and from the suburbs and country districts. If a black man were seen he would probably be begging or rummaging in a dustbin for scraps of food; yet, until 1835, when the white man came, the black man had hunted and fished, built his mia-mia and held his corroboree here on the banks of the Yarra River. Those of his people who had not fled inland to be relentlessly pursued by the civilisation of the white man, had stayed to be demoralised by it.

In the 80's, the overseas price of wool was high. Land and property prices rose to fantastic levels. The speculators, with their building societies, bought and sold land and property and built houses, in deals that often did not get past the paper stage. Through their estate banks, they carried on banking with the false securities created by the building societies.

Prosperity was in the air. Melbourne became known as *Marvellous Melbourne – the Queen City of the South.*

The 80's were also the heyday of the larrikin pushes. These groups of youths roamed the streets, mainly at night; breaking windows, knocking on doors, often insulting and molesting people, particularly women and girls; sometimes committing theft and assault, and once or twice even rape and murder.

John and Joe West became members of a local push, and Arthur joined the notorious Bouvaroos, of whom he was one of the very few members who had not been in prison.

It was then that the police commenced to make occasional visits to the West home, when one or other of the boys was suspected, from time to time, of being involved in fruit stealing, window breaking or some such peccadillo.

Mrs. West always lived in dread, and always in hopes that they would heed her persistent requests to settle down in good steady jobs. John and Joe worked much of the time, but Arty never did – he managed, somehow, to get money without working.

A sense of impending calamity grew in Mrs. West, and it was justified when Arty became involved in something worse than stealing, worse than assault or even murder; he and a few other youths were arrested on the capital charge of rape.

The revelation struck terror and shame into Mrs. West's heart. Her son was imprisoned without bail. She went to see him.

"Arthur, say it isn't true!" she begged. Arthur did not answer, he didn't even look at her. He was ashamed and, at the same time, aggressively impenitent. During the days that followed, Mrs. West's imagination kept conjuring up the terrible scene. Six men, among them Arty, luring the woman to a quiet place, then . . . Yet she went to the trial and pleaded for her son. He was not really a bad boy, she said. He had never had a chance. If he could have got a good steady job he would have been a good man. The shock of the savage sentence stunned her . . . *Hanged by the neck until . . . dead.* But they commuted the sentence to twelve years and a flogging. They took Arthur West away to prison and they flogged him there, flogged him fifty times across the bare back with a cat-o'-nine-tails.

At night sometimes Mrs. West would dream of the flogging, or, worse still, of the violation that she tried hard not to admit her son had helped commit. When she visited him at the jail, she found him bitter and morose, but she determined that she would help him to begin again when he came out. She could never remove the weals from his back, she told herself, but she could help remove the weals that seemed now, as well, to have seared his brain, his very soul.

Meanwhile, she cowered at the humiliation of the malicious gossip that fevered the whole neighbourhood. Her husband drank all the more after the trial. She managed to feed him, but otherwise ignored him. She turned her attention to John and Joe, to strive desperately to keep them out of trouble.

Arthur's crime and its aftermath aroused in John West a complex reaction: humiliation and fierce resentment that his family should thus be made outcast; increased fear and hatred of the police; and something else not clearly defined and buried deep in him – a vague determination to rise out of the lower depths. Joe met the crisis in a typical manner – he didn't brood over it much. Their father displayed no reaction – flogging held no terrors for him; his own father had weals on his back.

A day or two before jail visiting times, Mrs West would say to her husband and sons: "Will you be coming to see Arty with me?" Otherwise his name was never mentioned among his own family. Sometimes John or Joe would accompany her, but her husband never did.

When the two boys obtained work in one of Carringbush's

many boot factories, Mrs. West was very pleased. Her sons were good boys, she told herself, if only they could get a chance.

Mrs. West clung to the hope that John would succeed. He had been a lovely, winsome baby, and as a little lad he had been a preoccupied, cunning little fellow, but timid and easily rebuffed. Through malnutrition he had contracted the dread rickets and his legs became deformed. At school he was the quickest of the three boys to learn. He mastered his sums and grammar easily enough, without being brilliant. And he was smart where trading was concerned: always he could make a good exchange of the little things that schoolboys treasure. He was good at marbles; he could not afford to buy many, but he usually won when he played. Then when he was about ten or eleven he made a little handcart, and would run messages for his mother and neighbours, but the neighbours had to pay in cash or kind for his services.

During his first years at school he had been a target for the bullies. Sometimes he would arrive home in the afternoon and cry in his mother's lap – cry uncontrollably; but in his last few years at school she noticed a gradual change. He had gathered around him big boys who could fight his battles for him. Through them he would protect himself and occasionally punish his enemies.

John West often told his mother that one day he would make a lot of money, that then he would look after her and she would not have to slave and scrimp and work her fingers to the bone any more. She liked to believe he would do so.

When he left school he built a larger handcart, and made money running messages, carting wood from a wood-yard, and buying and selling pigeons. He liked always to keep a little nest egg for himself. This he kept in a bag in his room, often counting it and always sleeping with it under his pillow. He neither drank nor smoked, did not spend money on girls. It seemed his only vice was an occasional threepence each way on a racehorse. He found these investments unprofitable, and came to the conclusion that only the book-maker made money from gambling on horses. This view was confirmed when he took an agency for a book-maker while at the boot factory; he took bets from his workmates on commission, and earned a few extra shillings each week.

Joe lost his job again, but didn't seem to care much. Joe, Mrs. West was convinced, was just lazy. John stayed on at the boot factory until the bad times came in 1889.

In 1889, the overseas price of wool fell, goods had accumulated far in excess of the market, land and property prices began to collapse. The inevitable depression began with the bankruptcy of the biggest building societies; then the position was aggravated when English investors, faced with a crisis at home and hearing news of a worse crisis developing in Victoria, ceased investing capital in Melbourne.

Unemployment grew to alarming proportions. Bewilderment and panic gripped the speculators, business men and bankers; starvation and despair gripped the workless. The Trade Unions resisted with a series of strikes, culminating in the maritime strike of 1890.

The weight of the economic crisis fell swiftly and heavily on Carringbush, reducing many of its 35,000 people to destitution. John West was sacked, together with most of the other boot workers. The West family sank with their kind deeper into the mire of poverty.

No wonder John West felt elated at the success of his bribe. Now he could satisfy the hunger for power that had grown unnoticed out of the years.

He had first begun to climb out of the pit of poverty and helplessness about a year after the bad times began. He could remember the occasion well. It was in the spring of 1890. He was playing cards with the others in the back shed.

Eight bedraggled young men were in the shed. They sat crowded together uncomfortably on boxes around a homemade table, playing poker.

John West was dealing. He sat behind the table in the gloom of the shed.

He had not long ended his twenty-first year, and looked more like a youth than a man. He flick-shuffled the worn pack of cards and dealt seven hands of five, neatly and quickly. His dark suit was shabby and frayed; it was the only suit he had ever owned, and he had grown out of it. He wore an old shirt but no collar or tie. His boots were broken beyond repair, but showed signs of regular polishing.

But for the inscrutable eyes and the bandy legs folded under the table, there seemed little in John West of the man who would spin a sovereign under the nose of the policeman three years later.

"How many, Joe?" he said, addressing his brother on his left.

"I'll have a couple," answered Joe, who wore dungaree trousers and an old flannel shirt.

John West flicked two cards in his brother's direction. Like the others, he seemed uninterested in the game. Poker is essentially a gambler's game, and no one had any money to gamble with. Listlessly, he decided that Joe was probably bluffing with a pair and a "swinger."

"How many, Piggy?" he asked the next player.

"Ar, gimme three," said Piggy. No one seemed to know his real name. Behind his monicker he had long since achieved that strange anonymity which sometimes comes to a member of the criminal class. He was a thief and garrotter. Only a year earlier he had completed a two-year jail sentence for robbery in company. He was a big man going to fat, with a great, snoutlike nose which earned him his nickname. His whole appearance was subhuman. Patches where hair had fallen from his head were a symptom that he was diseased in the worst kind of way. His enormous, hairy arms protruded from the short sleeves of his dirty flannel, and he held his cards awkwardly in thick fingers.

"Be givin' me another lot, Jack, for God's sake," said the next player, Mick O'Connell. "It's swearin' by the Mother a' God I am, that I haven't had the soight nor soign of a pair all day."

Mick O'Connell was a chubby Irishman in his early thirties; not given to cleanliness or to scrupulous honesty, but possessed of a sly humour, a rich Irish brogue and a reckless gambling instinct. He had been born lazy, it was said. He lay in bed until near midday every day, and could fall asleep anywhere and at any time. His face was red and round his mouth generous and set low near his chin. Mick possessed that ability sometimes found in an unemployed slum-dweller to live precariously on his wits. He even managed somehow to keep alive his wife and the four young children she had brought into the world at yearly intervals.

"I'm out," said Eddie Corrigan, the next player. "I'm sick of just sittin' round playin' cards." He threw his cards into the centre of the table. Though his clothes were tattered, his aspect was pleasing: he was an Irish-Australian in his middle twenties, tall and robust, his handsome head crowned with a mop of curly black hair.

Ignoring his remark, John West said: "How many, Sugar?" He addressed the player on Corrigan's left; a crooked-eyed, bullet-headed youth named Renfrey, who was dressed in dungarees, a dirty flannel and, incongruously, a battered boxer-hat.

"Ar, giv'us four pieces. A man might as well be on his backside as the way he is," Renfrey answered. He cocked his head on one side and half closed his squinty left eye in a ridiculous attempt to give shrewdness to a countenance which bore traces of imbecility. "Acourse, if we was playin' for sugar I wouldn't buy four against a two and three-card buy, not on yer life I wouldn't, not Sugar Renfrey."

"Giv'us three," said Barney Robinson. He was of medium height and stout build. His round, pleasant face was adorned with side-whiskers and a huge moustache which curled up from the corners of his mouth, heightening the impression that he was always smiling. He, like the others, was semi-illiterate; but possessed a thirst for knowledge which led him to read avidly but indiscriminately. Barney wore his tattered old coat undone, for there were no buttons left on it. "Me old stomach is beginning to think me throat is cut; think I'll slip down to the Town Hall for a handout of tucker shortly."

"Sure and yer want to go down to the Salvos in the mornin'," Mick O'Connell advised him. "All you've got to do is sit for an hour listenin' to some bloke praise the Lord, an' yer get a feed the like of which yer wouldn't get in the best eatin' house in old Dublin. I get enough, and some to spare for the wife and kids every mornin'."

"I'll buy three, Jack," said the last player, a thin, pallid youth named Jim Tracy, who looked like a bundle of rags sandwiched between Barney Robinson and John West.

Just as John West made to deal the three cards, Mrs. West appeared from the door of the house and stood on the tiny porch. She was short, slender and stooped. Her grey hair was combed straight back, her face was wrinkled and her mouth pinched. She had the air of a mild, homely woman slowly becoming embittered.

"John and Joseph, get me some wood at once!" she called in a nagging voice. "Is there nobody who will do anything for me in this house?"

"All right, Mum, I'll get some wood," Joe answered distract-edly. "I'll get it in a minute."

The card game proceeded, the players betting with imaginary sovereigns. John West won the hand with three aces, then Joe began dealing the cards.

Mrs. West walked grumbling to a little heap of wood in the yard, picked up the axe, which had a cracked handle, and began chopping with vicious strokes.

"In all me born days I never saw such a loafin' lot of buggers," she shouted between strokes. "It's too lazy to chop a bit o' wood y'are."

The card players turned their heads in her direction on hearing her swear for the first time, but soon went on with the game. A piece of wood leapt up from under an unskilful swipe of the axe and struck her on the cheek, drawing a little blood.

"The devil take the rotten stick and two loafin' sons that sit playin' cards while their mother chops the wood." She wiped the trickle of blood from her face with her apron, and again attacked the log of wood vigorously.

"Put the axe down. I'll chop some wood at the end of this deal," said Joe, looking in her direction for a moment.

"If it was waitin' for you to chop it I was, I'd never have a fire."

She cut a few sticks and gathered them up into her apron with some chips, then walked towards the house again.

"It would suit you better to be lookin' for work, instead of sittin' around gamblin' all day, yer lot of loafers," she called over her shoulder.

"Sure and yer must 'ave got out the wrong side a the bed this mornin', Mrs. West, the way yer be talkin'," Mick O'Connell observed.

Mrs. West stopped on the porch and faced the shed. "Don't you cheek me, Mick O'Connell, when it's at home with yer wife you ought to be. Or lookin' for a job to keep her and the little childer."

She stood, one hand holding the apron full of wood, the other on her hip.

"I thought I told you not to be comin' around here, Piggy what-ever-your-name-is. It's wantin' no jailbirds around here that we are."

"You oughta talk about jailbirds! What about your own son Arty? What about Arty?"

Piggy's words struck Mrs. West like a blow. John West leapt to his feet. He gripped Piggy by the neck of the flannel and said: "Shut yer mouth! Shut yer mouth, Piggy! Don't throw that up to Mum."

"What yer givin' me, yer little bastard!" Piggy said. Sweeping John West's hand aside easily, he stood up, glowering at him across the table. "Nark it or I'll knock yer rotten." He pushed his great hand against his opponent's chest and sent him reeling back ungracefully to a sitting position.

The other men watched tensely without intervening. Piggy made to leap across the table at John West. Mrs. West watched fearfully from the verandah. John West moved swiftly back, knocking over the box on which he had been sitting. His anger had turned to fear. Piggy upset the table in his hurry to close with his antagonist, sending the other players scattering in the dust. He grabbed John West and was about to smash an enormous fist into his face when Eddie Corrigan recovered his feet, intercepted the blow and pinned Piggy in an excruciating hold, forcing his hairy arm up his back. They scuffed in the yard while John West moved out of range and watched anxiously.

"Sit down and get on with the game," Corrigan said, releasing Piggy.

Piggy eyed him uncertainly, then turning again to John West, he said: "If ever you take a plug at me again, I'll break yer bloody neck."

Mrs. West watched until the card players had rearranged the table and boxes and resumed their seats. She returned to the gloomy kitchen and rekindled the fire. As she prepared the frugal evening meal her spirit was steeped in bitter hopelessness. The love and guidance she had tried to give her sons in the past had been replaced, of late, with futile recriminations. In her bitterness she had laid herself open to Piggy's rejoinder. It was the first time for many years that Arty's imprisonment had been slapped in her face. She had kept away from people to escape the shame that cruel tongues could arouse in her.

The past year had reduced the family to utter destitution. There seemed no prospects of work. John had sold the last of his pigeons, and his handcart had fallen into disrepair. Previously she kept the rent not too far overdue, but now the landlord was threatening eviction. She didn't know where tomorrow's food was coming from. She had so far resisted charity handouts, but would soon have to swallow her pride and beg a little soup and bread at the Town Hall, from the Salvation Army or the Methodist Mission. Oh God, where would it all end? When would the bad times finish?

The card game did not begin again. The players fell to talking idly – all except John West, who seemed engrossed in thought, and about to say something.

Mick O'Connell was telling a story. "I went to one of them land sales once. They was flash blokes there buyin' land they'd never seen, while they got as drunk as Larry Dooley on free champagne. It's all over now, and it's weepin' they are and gnashin' their teeth, or blowin' their brains out, some of the spalpeens."

"The reason there's so many suicides," said Barney Robinson, "is because these fat sows ain't used to bein' poor and shorta money. They can't stand it, so they blows their bloody brains out; see what I mean?"

"Yeah, but what about the battlers who bought houses on the strap from the Building Societies," said Eddie Corrigan, "how are they goin' to get on? If you ask me, they should put the blokes that run 'em in jail for robbery. Anyway, this big strike is showing 'em that the workers ain't going to suffer in silence for *their* sins."

"Ar, strikes is no good," said Piggy, spitting disdainfully. "We went on strike in the boot trade six years ago, didn't we, and where did it bloody get us?" Piggy, shortly after beginning the only honest bit of work he'd done in his life, had become embroiled without enthusiasm in the boot strike of 1884; but he soon resumed his former habits, and went to Sydney with other criminals, where they unsuccessfully attempted to rob a bank. "Now all the factories have been sacking half their workers."

"That would be happening with the bad times whether we'd gone on strike or not. We got a rise in wages out of their strike, didn't we, and chopped out a lot of homework?" retorted Eddie Corrigan.

"The worker's got to fight, all right," observed John West, who still appeared to be debating in his mind some important matter he was anxious to discuss with them, "but the trouble is the boss has got too much money. You've got to have a lot of money to fight the boss."

"If the worker had a lot of money he wouldn't want to fight the boss," Corrigan contended.

"Take this maritime strike," said John West. "Where's it goin' to get the workers? The boss has too much money. The worker's got to have money to fight the boss, that's what I say."

"The workers will never get anywhere," Sugar Renfrey said, not very interested. "It's every man for himself, and to hell with the rest."

"That's a bloody fine attitude, that is," retorted Corrigan. "The workers'll get somewhere if they only stick together."

"The workers should elect theirselves into Parliament, and make the bloody laws to suit 'emselves," said Barney Robinson, echoing a sentiment that was gathering support all over Australia.

Then John West decided to raise the subject in his mind: "You blokes are all out of graft, aint' yer?" he asked hesitantly.

"No," said Mick O'Connell. "It's workin' for the guverment for ten sovereigns a week we all are."

"I'm on me uppers, if you've got a scheme brewin' I'll give it a burl," said Sugar Renfrey eagerly.

"I've got a big scheme brewin', as a matter of fact. Remember once I had an agency for that bookie? Well, the way to make money is to run a book on the horses." John West was apparently trying to convince his hearers of the soundness of his proposition before they heard what it was, so as to avoid ridicule.

"Yer gotta have a few sovereigns behind yer to run a book," said Sugar Renfrey.

"I know that," John West continued determinedly, "but I think I know a scheme to make enough sovereigns to start a book, then you can all be agents for me and make a few bob."

"S'pose you gonna do up that little 'andcart a' yours and start makin' threepences and pennies agen, and save 'em up 'til yer got a bag fulla sovereigns," said Piggy disdainfully.

"No. But I know a sure way to make a bag full of sovereigns, a few sovereigns, anyway. And you blokes can make a bit a' money, if yer'll help me."

They all looked incredulously but hopefully towards John West. They knew that he had, at times, been able to earn a few shillings for himself, but a bagful of sovereigns!

John West began to gain confidence. "All of you have had a few pigeons at one time or another, haven't you?"

"What's on yer mind?" asked Joe West. He was not surprised that John had not first mentioned the plan to him. They lived in the same house, slept in the same room, but they were brothers in name only.

"Well, as I said," John West answered, "I've got a scheme to make some money to start a book on the races. There's a big pigeon race from Warragul to Melbourne a fortnight from now."

"Yes, I know," said Barney ruefully. "I had a pigeon home that could nearly 'a won it, but we had to eat him last week."

"Sure and I'd race any pigeon you ever owned, kickin' me old hat," said Mick O'Connell.

John West ignored them and continued: "Well, we're going to run a book on it; at least, you blokes are going to be agents for me when I run a book on it."

"Where yer gonna get the dough, Jack?" asked Sugar Renfrey, rolling a cigarette from some ends he had gathered in the street. He lit up and puffed out some rank smoke, much to the envy of smokers among the others.

"Don't need any dough." John West was confident now, leaning forward on the table. "I know a pigeon named Waratah that can't get beat. We'll lay all the other pigeons."

"How do yer know it can't be beat?" asked Barney Robinson.

"I know, that's the main thing."

"Is the race crook?" asked Eddie Corrigan.

"Listen, this pigeon Waratah has been over the course in record time. He can't be beat." John West lowered his voice, instinctively casting a furtive look over his shoulder. "The owners of most of the other pigeons in the race are gonna back Waratah. We'll lay every pigeon at points over the odds, except Waratah." He began to speak faster, more urgently. "It's pickin' up money. I'll give all of you blokes ten percent of bets you take for me. With the winnings I'll start a book on the races, and you can become agents."

John West could see that he was being taken very seriously. He felt a tingle of satisfaction.

"How can you be so confident? Is the race rigged?" Corrigan persisted.

"Not exactly. They're just gointa make sure, that's all. If

31

Waratah looks like gettin' beat, they've got another bird exactly the same, and another ring. They'll punch the clock and report with the other bird. We'll take threepenny, even penny bets. Everyone in Carringbush is interested in pigeons. We'll work the pubs, and go from door to door where we see pigeon lofts. You blokes get ten percent. And with the profits I'll start a book on the races. We'll work the same way on that, except you get your commission on losing bets only."

"Same as the pigeon race really," said Mick O'Connell. "All the bets'll be losing bets, seein' as we won't be laying the winner, we hope. Sure and it's a great pleasure Oi'll have in joinin' yer in your new venture, Mr. West."

"I'll be in it, Jack," said Sugar Renfrey unnecessarily. He had earned his nickname through his continued but futile attempts to make some money without working for it.

"It's a bit raw," Barney Robinson said. "Takin' money under false pretences really, but beggars can't be choosers, I s'pose."

All the others except Tracey and Corrigan signified their assent. John West glowed with pride and a feeling of ascendancy until Corrigan said: "Yer mean to say that you blokes are goin' to go round takin' money from people who've hardly got the price of a feed, on a race that's rigged?" He turned to John West. "How would you like someone to take your mother down, even for threepence, the way things are now?"

His words shook John West, who hesitated before replying tersely: "That's got nothing to do with it. Do you want to earn a few bob or not? Please yerself."

"You can count me out. Bad and all as things are at home, I don't want money that's robbed from other people who are as poor as meself."

"What about you?" said John West to Jim Tracey. "Are you too proud, too?"

"I ain't too proud, Jack, but there's a lot in what Eddie says. The people that bet will have no chance." Tracey had worked with Eddie Corrigan during the strike. Corrigan was his friend. He felt that Corrigan was right. Jim Tracey had been planning to get married when the bad times threw him out of work. He and his mother were on the verge of starvation; he wanted to be able to keep his mother, and, more important still, he wanted to get married. Absentmindedly tucking in a badly frayed cuff on his

32

coat, he added: "It'ud be different if we was takin' the dough orf the rich people; but when you come to think of it, we'd be taking food outta poor people's mouths."

"What d'yer expect us to do, just sit around and starve ourselves?" John West snapped. "Please yer bloody self, but you've got to think of yer mother, and that sheila of yours. They're the ones you've got to look after."

Tracey's thin, intelligent but weak face puckered in a frown of indecision. "When you put it that way, Jack, I s'pose it's all right. I'll take it on," he said hesitantly.

"You're a bloody fool, Jim," Corrigan exclaimed. "I'm not narrer-minded. I like a bet with the next man, and if people want to bet there's got to be book-makers, but this is daylight robbery! So help me Christ, it's daylight robbery!"

He moved out of the shed and disappeared around the corner of the house.

Tracey sat looking at the table while John West, unusually loquacious and domineering, allotted them areas to work in, and handed round sheets of paper with the pigeons' names written in his own crude hand. There was a margin for the odds of each bird, and for the name of the unfortunate gambler who would back a pigeon which could win only if a miracle occurred.

Sugar Renfrey noticed that Waratah's name was listed. "Thought we wasn't going to lay Waratah at all, Jack. Supposin' someone wants to back him," he queried; and John West explained that it was necessary to have the name Waratah listed in order to convince punters that everything was over and above board.

"If anyone wants to back Waratah, say he's laid, say we've got too much money for him already," he explained. "Or better still, say you've heard that Waratah is likely to be scratched, or give them a tip confidentially for another pigeon. Say anything, I don't care what you say. But don't lay Waratah!"

When the slow dusk came, Mrs. West appeared on the back porch again and called: "John and Joe! Come and have tea at once!"

The Wests' evening meal was simple fare; stew, bread, a little jam, and the inevitable pot of tea. The two boys and their mother began eating their stew; then a short, fattish man, of red complexion with a short stubble of beard, came in the back door

33

unsteadily, and took his plate of stew from on top of a saucepan on the fireplace.

"Stew agen," he complained in a gruff voice, as he began eating crudely and without enthusiasm.

"What do you expect?" Mrs. West snapped back.

"Yes, what do yer expect?" John West repeated, with a show of fierceness. "Suit yer better to bring your money home, 'stead of goin' crook about the tucker."

"You mind what you're sayin' or you'll get a clip in the ear. I don't see you and Joe workin'."

Mrs. West intervened. A silence fell into the gloomy room. She got up from the table and lit an old lamp. "This is the last of the kerosene," she said. "We might as well use it."

Outside the moonless night shrouded Carringbush. The gas lights came on in the streets, slowly, one by one, first in Jackson Street, then elsewhere. Soon, dull lights glowed here and there like feverish eyes.

The family went to bed early to save wood. John West lay awake for hours thinking of the proposed book on the pigeon race.

The pigeon Waratah was duly victorious, and John West won eleven sovereigns after paying commissions to his agents.

From the profits he gave two sovereigns to his mother. She had some vague idea of how he had obtained it, but cavilling was out of the question. He counted the remaining nine sovereigns several times a day, and, using them as a bank, went ahead with his plan to make a book on the races.

This plan was not as simply operated or as profitable as he had expected. There were races in the metropolitan area nearly every day. It seemed only a matter of getting entries from the daily papers, then collecting investments from his clients, but there were difficulties.

John West was a raw beginner in the gentle art of making a book, but he was alert and learned quickly. He had heard of local starting-price book-makers going broke. He had scornfully put their failure down to the fact that they started with a small bank, and did not bet within their means, but he was finding that there could be other reasons than these for a book-maker ceasing business and changing his place of abode.

34

Strangely enough, people sometimes backed winners. Sometimes enough people backed a winner to make a loss, at times a heavy loss, especially when a locally circulated 'tip' won. Sometimes people would bet in cash for a while, consistently losing their threepences, sixpences or shillings; then obtain a little credit, lose again and not pay up. Efforts to collect almost invariably failed because 'you can't take blood from a stone.' Some defaulters would immediately begin betting in cash with a rival book-maker – a very annoying thing, but there was nothing he could do about it. Also, he found that his agents were not as efficient and reliable as he would have wished. Joe was honest enough but lazy. He would work until he estimated that his commission was sufficient for his simple needs, then he would knock off and play billiards or go for a few drinks.

John West was quite sure that Mick O'Connell and Piggy were 'tickling the peter': he suspected they were failing to record and settle for some losing bets. Sugar Renfrey would lay rash odds and accept bets contrary to his employer's demand that they make a safe book. Not content with this, Sugar gambled above his means with other book-makers, and was continually asking for advances on his commissions. Barney Robinson, on the other hand, was softhearted with his clients. He gave too much credit, and most of the bad pays came through his book. He excused them by saying that you had to "give 'em a chance to get their money back." Jim Tracy was timid and self-conscious about the job. His book was small and, like Barney, he was much too softhearted; but he was perhaps the most useful of them all, for he was handy with the pen and good at figures. He was allotted the task of keeping the books and making up the sheets.

Earnings of the agents were so low that they took part time work when it was available. John West himself worked for a while in one of the boot factories during a 'bad trot,' much to his mother's joy. Custom lost through being at work was replaced by bets taken from work-mates.

John West succeeded in building his bank up to thirty-five sovereigns after a year, in spite of going broke twice and carrying on without a bank. Both times he had the good luck to have a winning day immediately.

But more hazards lay ahead. The police began to worry them in 1892. Piggy was nabbed and fined. Jim Tracey, who had just got married, lived in such dread of a similar fate that his takings fell to a negligible figure. Reassurances and promises to pay all fines could not induce him to take the slightest risk. Joe deserted for a while in the winter of 1892 to start a totalisator down on the reserve in Jackson Street where, in spite of flagrant bad management, he prospered for a while until the police stepped in. When charged, he was fined fifteen sovereigns (all he had), and warned that next time he would go to jail for six months. Carringbush had become a hotbed of gambling, and the totalisator method was popular. Tote operators took a percentage of all takings. For them there were no losing races, no losing days. But the totes had one big disadvantage. Large betting sheets listing each amount invested had to be displayed to clients to 'work out the odds.' So when an indoor or outdoor tote commenced, the police found it easy to obtain evidence when making a raid.

In the first months of 1893, John West had a "bad trot." Some of his impoverished clients started to win for a change. His beloved bag of sovereigns began to dwindle. Then he realised the wisdom of "laying off." He instituted a system whereby he met his agents on the haberdashery shop corner in Jackson Street before each race, and checked their sheets with Jim Tracey's assistance. Making a hasty calculation of the position, he would, if necessary, rush to his nearest rival and make bets on the horses which, if winners, would draw too heavily on his own bank. This method meant sure and steady profits, and soon his bank rose again until it exceeded a hundred sovereigns.

Joe had told him what a profitable scheme the totalisator method was; and, dissatisfied with the rate at which he was accumulating money, John West often racked his brain for some way to run a tote without being nabbed. Many had tried in Carringbush, but by the beginning of winter, 1893, there was not a totalisator in existence. There was no denying totes were popular with the punters. Had not most of them continued to patronise the totes even when the police regularly raided them? He had developed a reputation as a "good pay," and had many punters, but he would never get far with the book. The idea of starting a tote kept turning over in his mind. There must be some way.

John West did not know exactly what he wanted. He wanted to be rich, to be feared and respected. Since Waratah's race, something had happened to him. He noticed that his agents, even

Piggy, paid him respect. He had a grip on them, power over them. He wanted more of this power. If he could find some way to start a tote and keep it going, all the punters in Carringbush would bet with him.

He puzzled over the matter for weeks. Then, one night in bed, the idea of opening a shop as a blind to deceive the police occurred to him. He could not sleep for excitement. He arose early. During the morning, he mentioned his plan to Joe.

"It sounds risky," Joe said. "Besides, if you open, say, a grocer shop, it'll mean a lot a' work and a lot a' money for stock."

"Have to think of some business that won't take much work or money," John West replied tenaciously – and he did.

Three days later, he walked up Jackson Street with resolute purpose in his stride. He stopped in front of 136 and looked into the dusty window at a derelict tea chest.

Couldn't be better, he thought. A tea shop with a room behind and a backyard opening into the lane.

He walked another block, then entered a little draper's shop and said to the big, middle-aged woman behind the counter: "I understand, Mrs. Smith, that you own that vacant tea shop at 136 Jackson Street."

'That's right, young man. But, God knows, business was so bad I closed it last month."

"Well, I want to rent it from you. I want to start a tea business there meself."

And so it happened that John West opened his tote shop at 136 Jackson Street, Carringbush, early in the winter of 1893. The venture soon proved to be more successful than he could have hoped. He and his helpers could scarcely cope with the business.

Cummin's Tea Shop had been in existence for seven weeks before Constable Brogan called to search the shop. Rumours John West had heard about some of the local policemen were confirmed when the constable caught the spinning sovereign and put it in his pocket.

The incident marked the first big step that John West had taken along his road to power.

CHAPTER TWO

Our age is lenient with those that cheat.

HONORÉ DE BALZAC

At eight o'clock on the evening before the famous horse-race, the Melbourne Cup of 1894, Sergeant Devlin sat behind his desk in the Carringbush Police Station. He was a huge man, his flabby body bulging out of his uniform. He was saying to a tall constable who stood in front of him: "Well, Grieve, is everything ready for the raid?"

"Yes, sir," Constable Grieve replied. "The shop has been watched as you instructed. More than sixty men and boys have been seen to enter. There are men ready to move into the back lane, and others are waiting to follow us through the front door."

"Are the West brothers present?"

"I don't know, sir, but one of the constables said he thought he saw John West go in early this evening."

"Begorra, and I hope he *is* officiating. It wouldn't be a show without Punch," Devlin answered, rising awkwardly. "It's past eight o'clock. We'll be after gettin' on our way."

Curse the tote shop, Sergeant Devlin grumbled to himself, as he and Constable Grieve climbed into a hansom cab outside the station. Sergeant Devlin held no animosity against John West. Circumstances beyond his control had forced him to raid Cummin's Tea Shop. There had been complaints from Protestant ministers of religion, complaints from harassed wives of patrons of the tote whose husbands gambled above their limited means, complaints from self-righteous people who did not gamble themselves and thought nobody else should do so. Their complaints had reached the ears of "the mob at City Headquarters." Then Constable Grieve, a Methodist, a non-gambler and keen to get on in the force, had reported that Brogan and at least one other were well-disposed towards John West, and had made no attempt to close the tote shop.

The sergeant guessed that John West had bought the good-will

38

of the men on the beat, and perhaps other constables, yet he had never come near Patrick Devlin. Sure and what would a man benefit from being a sergeant if he let the constables get all the pickings? A man couldn't be expected to keep a wife and nine childer and have money over for a few whiskies and perhaps to buy a little bit of property, on the miserable few pounds he got from the force, could he, now? Young West was too big for his boots altogether. He must be taught a lesson.

Having decided on the raid, Sergeant Devlin had gone about it like the shrewd, resourceful officer he could be when he chose. He issued instructions that the constables who were suspected as friendly to West should not be told of the raid. Devlin was not deceived by the name on the door. That long skinny excuse for an Irishman, Paddy Cummin, was too mean to pay rent for a match box! He chuckled as he thought of the way he had discovered that sometimes John West, and sometimes Joe, paid the rent. How to get near the tote without being perceived by the nit-keepers, who were posted around the whole block, had been Devlin's biggest problem. Constable Grieve told him that a large crowd always gathered in the shop the night before a big race meeting, gambling on the next day's races. Raid the place at night, that was the way. And what better night than the eve of the Melbourne Cup itself? "The better the day, the better the deed!"

As the cab neared Cummin's Tea Shop, Sergeant Devlin took his pistol from its holder and checked that it was loaded. "Never know, might need it. They say West has some tough boys workin' for him!"

A motley crowd of men and youths were crowded into Cummin's Tea Shop and the room behind it. Most of them had come to bet on the Melbourne Cup and the others races to be decided at Flemington racecourse on the following afternoon. Others, who were non-betters, or who had no money, had come for the want of somewhere better to go: just to meet their friends and have a yarn. There were men of all shapes and sizes, old men and young, and a few boys of fourteen or fifteen. Most were shabbily dressed; the odd one or two who wore a neat suit seemed out of character. A confused din arose from the hum of voices and the scraping of feet on the bare floor.

Shadows played on the walls like weird ghosts in the light of the kerosene lamps. Packages and tins of tea were still stacked in the shelves behind the counter. At first, unsuspecting people had called to buy tea, but it was many months since a sale had been made.

Standing behind the counter with Barney Robinson and Mick O'Connell was the nominal proprietor of this strange establishment, Patrick Cummin himself. Cummin was about thirty-five years of age; a tall man, and incredibly thin and gaunt. He was taking bets, issuing the punter with a ticket, and recording the transaction on a large ruled sheet; while Mick and Barney, garrulous as magpies, were laying doubles and recording them on a big sheet of cardboard on the wall beside them. Paddy Cummin was John West's cousin. On hearing that his distant relative had established himself in quite a good book-making connection, Paddy had hastened to ask for a job. At the time, John West was seeking someone to accept the doubtful honour of having his name posted over the door, and Paddy readily accepted that condition.

Mick O'Connell and Barney Robinson were greatly intrigued with their new associate. Patrick Cummin was the queerest Irishman Mick had ever met. He was slow thinking and canny, he didn't smoke, drink or gamble, and made a prisoner of every penny he earned. "A mean Irishman is the meanest man in the world," Barney had declared, and they nick-named him Scotch Paddy. Scotch Paddy's slow thinking showed now in the ponderous manner with which he took and recorded the bets. The simplest addition seemed to give him trouble. "He'd get the sack if his name wasn't over the door," Mick reckoned. In conversation, Scotch Paddy would always take an inordinate time to consider every remark, Barney Robinson swearing that he had been known to enter an argument by answering a question asked half an hour before.

In the room behind the shop, John West, Sugar Renfrey and Jim Tracey were seated behind a table. John West and Sugar were taking bets, and Jim was posting these on the large sheets of cardboard nailed to the wall behind them. On the sheets were hand-printed the names of the horses in each race, and in the column the running totals of the amounts invested were written so that clients could calculate the dividend that each horse was likely to pay. Customers didn't know that John West was deducting one-third of all money handled, but, basing their calculations on past experience, they could arrive at the likely odds and fluctuations.

Piggy mingled with the crowd in the shop ready to carry out his allotted task of keeping order. In the back room an ex-pugilist known as Cauliflower Dick was acting in the same capacity. Cauliflower Dick gave an impression of apelike strength, and his ears, eyebrows and nose bore witness that, as a boxer, he had more toughness than skill.

Suddenly there came a loud thumping on the front door. Piggy shouldered his way through the crowd. A loud Irish voice from outside demanded: "Open in the name of the Queen!"

Pandemonium set in. As though in a whirlwind, men and boys ran this way and that, bumping into one another.

"Police!"

"Yow! The traps!"

"Out the back way, quick!"

Every man for himself, the fleetest and strongest made for the backyard and scrambled over the fence to fall into the arms of waiting policemen.

The front door crashed in and several constables entered, led by Devlin and Grieve. "You're all under arrest! And you you better go quietly."

John West and his helpers made some attempt to pick up their papers and rip the incriminating sheets from the walls, but there was no time. Jim Tracey's face went chalky white. His wife had been persistently demanding that he take Eddie Corrigan's advice and leave the tote. What would she say now?

Fear gripped John West. In a frenzy he squeezed through the squirming mass at the door. Instead of climbing into the back lane, he scrambled over the side fence.

He heard Barney Robinson say: "Come on, Jim and Mick. Foller Jack through Mother Moran's yard!"

Someone else shouted: "There's traps in the back lane!"

Barney Robinson and Jim Tracey managed to scale the fence in time, but Scotch Paddy and Mick O'Connell were collared in the act by policemen.

John West, Barney, Jim and three or four others made good their escape through Mother Moran's yard, while Sugar Renfrey and a few more managed to evade the policemen in the back lane.

In the shop, Piggy resisted violently, but was suppressed by three brawny policemen. Some patrons, seeing the impossibility of escape, grabbed packages from the shelves and protested that they had only called in to buy some tea, but this device was ignored by the raiding policemen.

In a few minutes more than fifty men and boys were arrested, loaded into waiting drags and taken to the Carringbush lockup. There formalities for charging the accused and bailing them out proceeded until midnight.

"For Gawd's sake, bail us out, and give us a chance to see the Cup tomorrow," some of the victims had entreated passers-by on the way to the jail.

Eventually most of them were bailed out. John West put up the money for Mick O'Connell, Piggy, Cauliflower Dick and Scotch Paddy.

In spite of the raid of the previous evening, Melbourne Cup day was a record day for the tote. A continuous human stream entered the front door of the shop and left by the back gate through the lane into Bagville Street at the rear, where they waited for John West's carrier pigeon service to arrive from Flemington with the result of the next race. When the pigeon was seen hovering above the loft in the backyard, crowds would surge around the gate to hear the result announced; then the lucky gamblers who held a ticket on the winner or had backed a placed horse "each way" would go round through the shop again to be paid after Jim Tracey and John West had assessed the dividends.

There was a secret, known only to John West and a few of his clerks, about the pigeon service. Unsuspecting customers thought the birds brought only the results of the previous race; but the scratchings for the next race were also attached to them at the racecourse, where a man, dubbed The General by Mick O'Connell, officiated on behalf of the tote.

The Tabernacle Church was situated in Bagville Street, opposite the lane which came from the rear of the shop. Here some of the waiting punters would stand in front of the sacred portals. There were a few tattered women in the crowd. Women were not allowed in the tote, so they gave their bets to their husbands or friends.

John West was supervising. His eagle eye watched the sheets and the money, and he helped to take bets at the busy period just before each race. Everyone knew him and he seemed to know everyone. He spoke jovially to the customers, congratulated lucky winners and generally had the hail-fellow-well-met bearing which stamps the gaming house proprietor the world over.

Beneath his confident bearing many misgivings seethed. Every precaution had been taken against raids in the afternoons but he had quite overlooked the possibility of a raid after dark. Could he beat Devlin?

His was the only tote shop remaining. No other bookmaker could compete with him. His riches had increased to five hundred sovereigns, and he had reluctantly decided to deposit most of it in the bank. Some of the banks were opened again after reconstruction. Previous depositors had been paid as little as a shilling in cash for each pound they had deposited, and the balance was paid in shares in the bankrupt banks. ''Never know, some of them might go broke again,'' he reasoned; so he spread his deposits in several banks in order to lessen the risk.

He had started something when he bribed Constable Brogan! A week later another constable had arrived to search the shop, and earned a sovereign. Soon Brogan came back again, and received a sovereign; then a fortnight later, yet another one arrived and was paid off. Since then he had regularly paid the trio something. He had begun to wonder where it would end. The tote had been raided and the traps who had taken his good money didn't even let him know that Devlin was preparing to strike. Perhaps Devlin would have left him alone if it hadn't been for the bible bashers who spoke from the pulpit and wrote to the press demanding action against the gambling mania.

John West puzzled over his predicament until betting began on the Melbourne Cup itself, then business became so brisk as to absorb his whole attention.

Cummin's Tea Shop was situated a few doors from Silver Street. Outside a coach-builder's shop on the corner, Mick O'Connell was leaning lazily against the verandah post all but asleep. He was supposed to be watching down Jackson Street for the police. On the other side of the Silver Street corner, Piggy was leaning against the wall of a plumber's shop looking just a little more alert than Mick. Piggy's job was to watch up Jackson Street for suspicious characters. A little further up, on the other side of Jackson Street, another side street ran off. On this corner,

43

a little weed of a man known as Jigger was standing looking down the side street in case the police should be deceitful enough to come from that direction. Jigger suffered from Saint Vitus' Dance, and was justifying the nickname given him by Mick O'Connell, by jigging about as he kept nit on the corner. First his left arm would raise itself with a jerk, then his head would shake violently, then his left leg would give a kick or two.

At vantage points around the block behind Cummin's Tea Shop other nit-keepers kept a more or less alert watch.

Piggy was disgruntled. From the honoured job of chucker-out and door-keeper he had been demoted to the common rank of nit-keeper, because John West had insisted that, if he had done his job properly on the previous night, the police could have been delayed and evidence removed. His demotion had cost Piggy five shillings a week, but the day was gone when he could defy John West. He leant against the wall listlessly; a cigarette lolled from the corner of his mouth, an old hat slouched precariously on the side of his head. He looked up and down the street at intervals.

Suddenly he moved away from the wall, shaded his eyes with one arm and swayed from side to side, then turned and ran with surprising agility and speed towards the shop. His hat fell off, but he did not stop to pick it up. He skidded to a standstill in front of the shop and rushed in.

"Jack! Jack!" he shouted between gasps. "Jack, there's two traps comin' up the street. I saw 'em."

John West came hurriedly out of the room at the rear.

"Are yer sure?"

"Acourse I'm sure. It's old Devlin and young Grieve, the nark."

"You know what to do. Get everyone out. Tell Joe to see that all the slips, sheets and money are taken away."

Piggy rushed into the backyard shouting excitedly: "Police! Everyone out! The bloody wallopers are on their way!"

The customers needed no second bidding. They surged through the open gate, swearing and shuffling and crushing, and retailed the warning to groups of men waiting in the lane and in Bagville Street beyond.

John West gathered up the money that was lying on the counter and the table in the back room. In his haste, he left a small pile of silver coins on the table; as he turned and walked into the

44

shop, Piggy dived through the door, put the money into his pocket, and fled out the back gate, shutting it hurriedly and insecurely behind him.

Within a few minutes the environs of Cummin's Tea Shop were deserted, even the nit-keepers had disappeared. Only John and Joe West remained; they were behind the counter in the shop, having a hasty conference. Joe seemed unperturbed but his brother was pale and agitated.

"Are you sure all the slips and sheets are gone?" John West asked shakily.

"Yes everything's right. Don't go to water for Chris'sake" Joe answered.

"I'll do the talking when they come" replied John West, recovering his composure. "They've got nothing on us. They can't prove we run the place. There's no evidence here." They retired to the back room and waited tensely until they heard footsteps approaching. Sergeant Devlin entered the shop followed by Constable Grieve. John West came out and faced them across the counter.

"Oh, good day, Sergeant. Nice weather," John West said. His voice quavered a little.

"Yes, the weather is nice; but it's not that I've to talk to you about, me boy." Devlin looked stern, holding himself erect, his great stomach threatening to burst the belt of his uniform. Grieve shuffled from one foot to the other behind him.

John West's eyes never left Devlin's face. "What do you want to see me about, then?" he asked. His voice was steadier now.

"I've come to place you under arrest."

"What for?"

"You know what for. For running a totalisator in this shop."

"You've got no evidence" John West's arms were at his sides, fists clenched. He was hatless, and his big low ears, long head and sharp eyes, gave him the appearance of an animal at bay. "You can search the place: you'll find nothing. This is Paddy Cummin's tea shop – you arrested him last night."

"I won't trouble you with a search. I got all the evidence I need. Where's your brother?"

"Find him."

"Are you in there, Joe West?" Devlin called out.

Joe came into the shop.

45

"You're under arrest too, me boy."

Joe said nothing.

John West's eyes roved the room as though he sought some way to escape, then they returned to Devlin's face.

"There's a thing or two you won't like, that I can spill in the court, if you bring me up," he said.

"You won't be spillin' anything in the court," Devlin replied, annoyed. Then, not wishing to antagonise John West unnecessarily, he added: "I have me instructions, so it's no use going to market on me. You and your brother run this place. You're the men we were after last night."

Devlin took a pair of manacles from his hip pocket, leaned quickly over the counter, and snapped one clamp on John West's wrist.

John West held up his arm and looked at the handcuff, and the eyes that looked at Devlin again revealed fear mixed with anger and humiliation.

"You'll be sorry for this, Devlin, yer bastard," John West snarled.

"Cut it out, Jack," Joe said quietly.

"I'll have none of your language, West," Devlin said, flushing a shade redder. "You'll have another charge against yer if you're not careful. Come here, Joe."

Joe moved over near his brother, and Devlin clamped the other arm of the manacles on his wrist.

"I'll tie you two beauties together just in case any of your mob try to take away me prisoners. Get your hat and lock up your tea shop, Mr John West."

John West had heard that Devlin was not unreasonable. "Listen, Sergeant," he said. "You've done your job with last night's raid. There's no need to carry it too far. I'm a generous man. Perhaps we could – er – come to – couldn't we have a little talk?"

Devlin seemed to hesitate, then he looked at Constable Grieve as if wishing he were absent. "Yes," he said to John West, "we'll have a little talk about how much bail yer'll be payin' when we get down to the station."

Devlin and Grieve walked on either side of the West brothers as they marched them up Jackson Street.

Just as Devlin completed laying the charges, Sugar Renfrey

arrived at the police station. John West unobtrusively gave him the money with which to pay the bail.

"Got some important news for you," Sugar whispered as they left the station. They walked down Jackson Street in earnest conversation. Sugar imagined himself to be John West's right-hand man. He was always anxious to please and impress his employer.

"I've got the tip, Jack," he said. "Devlin is dependin' on the evidence of Miss Smith, the daughter of the old battle-axe who owns the shop. She told him that you and Joe pay the rent, and seein' that he's got evidence that the shop is a gaming house, that makes you two the keepers of it, see?" He cocked his head to one side, squinting his left eye.

"I wondered why he was so bloody sure of himself. Who told you this?"

"Brogan."

"Why didn't he tell us the raids were brewin'?"

"Says he didn't know. Says Devlin never told him till after."

John West was puzzling his brain for a way out. They would probably escape with a fine, but if Devlin obtained a conviction this time he would go on raiding the place and eventually close it up.

"Supposing I can get this girl Smith to go back on what she told Devlin," John West said.

He had passed through many states of mind since Devlin had walked into the shop. When the handcuffs clamped on his wrist, he thought of the day the police had come and hand-cuffed Arty before taking him away. On the way to the police station, humiliation and shame had swamped other feelings, and turned his thoughts to his mother and the anguish he knew his arrest would cause her. At the station he had found himself falling into an apathetic calm: why worry, you'll only be fined, he had told himself.

Two alternatives now faced him. He could submit to the seemingly inevitable, and close the tote, but if he did so it might mean sinking back into poverty and helplessness. A few hundred quid would not last forever. No, he must fight this case and win it. He would carry on, and one day he would be a rich man – a millionaire even – they would see!

Stopping outside Mrs Smith's shop, John West said to Sugar: "You leave this to me. Come round to our place at eight o'clock."

Mrs Smith had heard of the arrests and was very agitated. John West was nervous, but her fears gave him a feeling of ascendancy which thrilled him. He told her she was just as guilty as he and Joe. She couldn't trust the police. She'd better be careful or she and her daughter would be in as much trouble as he was. Mrs Smith told him tearfully that Devlin had called in her absence. Her daughter had made certain statements, and had no alternative but to repeat them in court.

John West's impassive eyes searched her sullen face. She's a money-hungry old battle-axe, he thought.

"Listen, Mrs Smith," he said firmly, "if I'm put outta business, you'll have a job to rent that shop again. Tell you what I'll do. I'll double the rent if your daughter says in court that she doesn't know who pays the rent and that she didn't say that me and Joe paid it."

"That'd be perjury," Mrs Smith answered in harassed tones. "We're respectable people. We didn't know you were running a tote."

"The court wouldn't believe that, neither do I," John West answered. He took a small money bag from his pocket, slowly counted from it ten sovereigns, and placed them on the counter. "There's a little present. And I want to rent that empty house of yours in the back lane."

She hesitated, staring at the sovereigns. Her chubby hand moved slowly and picked them up.

"Susan!" she called to her daughter. "Come in here."

When John West arrived home he found his mother weeping on her bed. He hesitated at the door.

News of the arrest had soon reached Mrs West. Would they be only fined or go to prison? She wanted no cause to be visiting her three sons in jail.

John's prosperity had meant the end of insecurity. New furniture which made the old look even more shabby, new clothes, a new cooking stove, and the best of food graced the household. Some of the bitterness and rancour had left Mrs West; she felt healthier and more cheerful; but when she thought of the poverty of most of the people who gambled at the tote, she would tell her sons that they should get steady jobs. John would become resentful and explain that "people like to gamble," that "if they

48

didn't bet with me they would with someone else,'' and that "with me they are sure to get paid.'' These axioms pacified her for a while, but as the months went by she came to view the future with more and more foreboding. She worried most about the type of men John had chosen for associates and employees. There was something about John she didn't understand, something frightening.

John West tiptoed to the bed, put his hand on her shoulder, and tried to comfort her, only to be greeted with an hysterical demand that he close the tote no matter what happened in the court. She embraced him and tearfully begged him to do nothing that might bring further shame. He wanted to reassure her but he could not. He said nothing and retired to the bedroom where Joe, looking very dejected, was sitting on his bed.

"No need to worry,'' John West said tersely. "We'll get out of it."

"It's all right for you to talk,'' Joe said. "It's your first offence I might get six months. And Mum's very cut up."

Next morning John West called on a local solicitor who agreed to defend them.

John West then told Sugar, Mick O'Connell and Scotch Paddy to send the word around that he would pay all fines, and that he would refund all money wagered on the Melbourne Cup, as the raid had interrupted the wagering on the race. During the morning, a few irate punters who had backed the Cup winner, Tarcoola, called at the house. The police had seized some of the sheets the night before the Cup, he explained. In future, all bets on races before which a police raid took place would be refunded, and he would pay the fine of anyone convicted. What could be fairer than that? He didn't tell them that he had known Tarcoola would have been a bad result on the doubles sheets. The money so saved would go towards paying the fines.

In the afternoon he attended the court to hear the case against Paddy Cummin, Mick O'Connell and the fifty-three other accused, who were undefended.

It was clear to everyone in the court, even to those who did not know him, that the old grey-bearded magistrate was very hard of hearing. He kept cupping his left ear in his hand. However, he assumed correctly that all the accused had pleaded guilty. As Devlin entered the box to put the case for the Crown he was welcomed with hissing and rude remarks in undertones which the magistrate did not hear, but which caused Devlin to flush with anger. The court was crowded out with tote patrons, and curious people seeking entertainment. The atmosphere was jocular and good-humoured. Devlin's evidence and the production of tote tickets and sheets as exhibits were punctuated with humorous remarks and laughter. John West was much relieved when Devlin omitted to mention his thinly veiled attempt to bribe him.

Constable Grieve then gave his evidence in a deliberate, low voice. The old magistrate craned his neck, cupped his ear, and screwed up his face in an endeavour to follow it.

"The old beak's as deaf as the stone pillars in the Town Hall," Mick O'Connell called out. "He can't hear a word he's saying. We'll get out of it yet!" This brought roars of approval from some of the accused and the gallery. The old magistrate did not appear to hear the remark, but he heard the laughter all right, and thumped the rostrum with his hammer, shouting: "Order in the court!"

The case lasted until late afternoon. The accused were each fined ten shillings, except Scotch Paddy, who, by dint of having his name over the door, had the honour to be fined twenty-five pounds.

Next morning, John West sat tensely with clenched fists as a very scared Susan Smith entered the witness box. In a soft, trembling voice she stated that she had not told Sergeant Devlin or anybody else that John or Joseph West paid the rent for the premises at 136 Jackson Street. Devlin was non-plussed. He reminded the girl of their conversation. He accused John West of having influenced her evidence, but withdrew when the magistrate, a younger man than the one who officiated the previous day, asked for proof. Just the same, John West didn't like the look of the magistrate; his face was stern and his hearing unimpaired.

"Good on yer, Jack!" someone shouted as John West entered the box. He was nervous and trembling, but denied that he conducted the tote shop. Joe came forward with a similar denial. The solicitor then argued that they could not be found guilty because, at the previous case, Patrick Cummin had been fined much more heavily then his fellow accused, obviously because the shop was admittedly conducted in his name.

When the court adjourned while the magistrate considered his verdict, John West stood outside the grey stone building surrounded by employees of the tote and some of its most constant clients. He was impeccably dressed in a new suit and hat. His conversation and manner exuded confidence, but there were butterflies in his stomach. Joe stood on the outskirts of the crowd, pale and silent.

When the court reassembled, the magistrate commented sarcastically on Miss Smith's evidence, stated that the gambling mania must be stamped out, and informed the court that he was convinced that the premises at 136 Jackson Street had become a meeting place of undesirable persons. The last comment was most unfavourably received, being considered a flagrant reflection on the good character of many present, who gave vent to their disapproval with assorted hisses and groans, which ceased only when the magistrate threatened to clear the court. John West sat rigidly while Joe trembled and wrung his hands.

"I find the defendant, John West, guilty of the charge of conducting a gaming house on the premises at 136 Jackson Street, Carringbush. Fined fifty pounds or three months' imprisonment."

A murmur of disapproval ran through the court. John West leapt to his feet as though to protest, but slowly sat down again.

"I find the defendant, Joseph West, guilty of the same charge. Fined twenty-five pounds or one month's imprisonment. And if either defendant comes before me again on a similar charge, and is found guilty, I shall send him to prison without the option of a fine."

John West seemed in a daze as he went forward to pay the fines. He was smarting under a cultivated sense of injustice. He had been wronged, he told himself, but they'd never beat him. Outside, he answered the consolations of his supporters with a defiant air.

"The tote will open again, don't you worry about that!"

He walked away alone, deep in thought.

Presently, he came abreast with a group of ragged men breaking stones by the roadside. They worked listlessly and without enthusiasm. One stopped to inspect his blistered hands, leant on his knap-hammer, and said: "Hullo, Jack, how'd the case go?"

John West stopped. "I got fined fifty quid, Joe twenty-five."

"Bit solid, wasn't it?"

51

"Yeh, but it won't stop me. I'll open up again, somehow. How are things with you?"

"Badly, Jack. I've been out of graft for months; and now this is the best I can do. They've made a bit of work repairing the roads and fillin' the drain down Riley Street. The pay's bad and it will soon cut out. Thinkin' of going to Kalgoorlie in Western Australia, if things don't improve."

"Things look like gettin' worse before they get better. They say there's a lot of gold for the pickin' up over there."

John West put his hand in his trouser pocket and moved closer to the stonebreaker. "Here. Buy something for the wife and kids with this," he said passing over a few silver coins.

"'Struth, thanks – thanks!"

John West walked on. He heard the man say: "A ryebuck bloke is Jack West. One of the best."

His walk became a swagger. He would always help a lame dog over the stile, that was his boast. He had become quite a personality. "Jack West has done well for himself," most people said, paying grudging admiration to a battler who had got on, yet was sympathetic and generous to the poor.

As he passed a side street he looked around and saw several men carrying some tattered, shabby furniture out of a house and loading it on a four-wheeled cart. He stopped on the corner and watched.

Some poor devil being evicted, he thought. He saw a shrivelled phantom of a woman come out of the house, and heard her entreat the men to leave the two miserable beds and bedding. He hesitated, then began to walk towards the scene. He was not sure what he was going to do. He hadn't gone far when two men approached. One of them was Eddie Corrigan. They began to argue loudly with the men effecting the eviction. Two policemen got out of a hansom cab and joined in the argument. John West hesitated. Better keep away from the police; anyway, let Corrigan help the woman if he is so clever! He turned on his heel towards home.

Three months had elapsed, and there were signs of renewed activity in Cummin's Tea Shop.

The front door was locked and barred, but Mick O'Connell was sweeping out the shop, raising clouds of dust. In the back room, John West, seated at the table, black hat perched on the back of his head, was counting small change into neat piles. Seated with him were Sugar Renfrey, Barney Robinson, Scotch Paddy and a new man, named Flash Alec by Mick O'Connell.

Flash Alec had been a land speculator until the land boom burst. Since then he had managed to earn a living by any means other than working for it. When Jim Tracey returned to the boot trade after the raid on Cup Eve, Flash Alec had been recommended to John West. Flash Alec still wore spats, a frock coat and top hat as he had done in the days when he drank champagne and speculated in land. Now his clothes were tattered and frayed and his boots worn out, but he still tried to keep up appearances. He was an effeminate type, who spoke like an English nobleman.

Nailed to the back wall behind John West were large sheets of white cardboard on which the names of horses were neatly printed in red. On the table were bundles of small numbered tickets. In the backyard a small shed had been built under the pigeon loft against the fence. The shed was about twenty-five feet wide and four feet deep. It had an open front and its floor was a foot above the ground. Piggy was busy nailing large sheets of white cardboard on the back wall of the shed. The sheets were enlarged versions of those previously used to enable customers to assess the odds. Grass had over grown the yard and Cauliflower Dick was busy chipping it off with a large shovel. He was grunting and sweating profusely in the hot morning sun.

At the rear of the yard, Jigger, handy with tools despite his affliction, was screwing the hinges on to a large trapdoor which he had inserted into the fence between the tote yard and the backyard of the empty house rented from Mrs Smith. Jigger lived rent-free in this house in return for his services in the tote and for the use of the house and yards as an escape route in the event of further police raids.

Presently John West said: "Don't forget, you blokes. When you're working out the dividends, you take only ten percent out for the book, plus the odd pence. If the dividend is, say, three shillings and a penny, we pay three shillings; if it's, say, three shillings and eleven pence, we still only pay three shillings."

"Quaite clear, my deah fellah," Flash Alec replied. "That's reahlly the equivalent of very neah fifteen percent, I dare say."

John West glared at him. He didn't like this sissy, broken-down toff, but Alec looked like being a good penciller, so he'd have to put up with him. Barney Robinson said: "It used to be thirty-three and a third percent," then it was his turn to be glared at.

John West didn't want it known that he had ever charged such an exorbitant percentage. He reduced it now only because he had opposition. Two new tote shops had opened in Jackson Street a fortnight ago, their owners apparently reasoning that they would make a lot of money before the police closed them up.

"I charged a third of the takings only till I got on me feet. From now on my percentage will be easy the lowest and my dividends the highest. I'll give the punters the best crack of the whip. 'Cording to their divvies, Ryan and Cohen are chargin' at least twenty percent. They won't be able to compete with me."

"Anyway," Barney Robinson cried, "the customers have only got so much to lose. You'll get the lot before each week's out whatever the percentage is."

John West glared at him again. Easy to see that Barney had been back in the boot trade under Corrigan's influence. Business seemed to have picked up a little; Barmey, Jim Tracey and Joe West had been able to find work in a boot factory after the tote shop closed. Sugar Renfrey had found employment as a labourer in a railway workshop on the other side of the city.

"You don't have to work here, you know, if yer don't like it," John West said.

"A man's got to do something while he's out on strike."

"So that's it! You're only going to make a convenience of me while the strike's on. I s'pose I'll have Joe and Tracey comin' back lookin' for work before long."

Barney did not reply. He twirled the ends of his moustache nervously, pulled a book from his hip pocket, and began reading.

"You better make up yer mind whether you're stayin' or leavin'," John West persisted. "I can't afford to have people comin' and goin' all the time."

"I'll be stayin', Jack," Barney said without enthusiasm. Barney was courting a girl named Florrie from the factory. He was planning to marry Florrie, and his love affair seemed to be disturbing his happy-go-lucky nature. Florrie wouldn't like him to go back with Jack West, but a man had to live and dub in at home while the strike was on. Anyway, the wages in the boot trade were too low for a man with ideas of matrimony.

They were silent for a while as John West checked his piles

54

of change into small canvas bags, letting them roll off his fingers as though caressing them. When he had finished he said: "This place won't be safe until we can have a trapdoor built right here near the table."

"Missus Moran would be very pleased, I'm sure, if someone suddenly ran right through her kitchen," chuckled Mick O'Connell, who had finished his sweeping and was seated on the remaining chair, rubbing the sweat from his face with a dirty hand.

"It wouldn't be through the kitchen; it'ud be through the yard near the back door."

"Make no difference," Mick said. "She has a tongue like the fires of hell itself." Mick had bitter memories of a tongue thrashing he had received after he and Piggy had whistled at Nellie, Mrs Moran's pretty daughter.

John West ignored him. "Yes," he continued, "we could do with a trapdoor there and another one leading from the back of the shed into Moran's yard. The way it is we won't be able to get out with the evidence if there's a raid. The customers will dive through the trapdoor into Jigger's yard. The police will be on us before we can get out with the sheets and tickets."

"You are perfectly correct, deah fellah," Flash Alec observed, "victory will go to the fleetest of foot."

"It's a bloody good scheme, Jack," Sugar Renfrey said, enthusiastically, "if you can fix it with Mrs Moran."

"I'm goin' to the Catholic Bazaar tonight. Mrs Smith has promised to introduce me to Mrs Moran and her daughter, Nellie." He blushed when he mentioned the daughter's name, but the others did not seem to notice.

"Sure and you could do worse than hang your hat up to sweet Nellie," Mick O'Connell advised. "She's a bonzarina sheila, like a colleen from old Ireland. She'll make a cosy little bedmate for some lucky bloke one of these days."

John West's face reddened to the roots of his hair; his ears looked as if they were burning. "Look, O'Connell," he said savagely, "if you can't learn to shut your bloody silly mouth sometimes, you'll find yourself out of a job. You keep talkin' like old Thornton's parrot."

A silence fell, as noticeable as that in a factory when the machines are switched off. The irrepressible Mick broke it. "Did yer see in the paper this mornin' where your ole friend, Eddie Corrigan, was up before the City Court?'' His laugh seemed a little forced. ''Got fined for followin' his boss around.''

John West displayed interest, but before he could speak Barney Robinson intervened: ''There's nothin' funny about it, Mick.''

''I never saw it, what paper was it in?'' John West said.

As Sugar Renfrey pulled the AGE newspaper from his hip pocket, Mick O'Connell said, ''It's in the paper. I read it with me own eyes.''

''You never did; yer can't read,'' Barney Robinson muttered savagely, and Mick O'Connell promptly lay down on the floor.

''It's here in the AGE, Jack,'' Sugar Renfrey said. ''Old Dunn's been advertising for workers to apply by letter; then he's been goin' to interview 'em at their houses. He's opened another factory tryin' to break the strike. Corrigan and a couple of other blokes has been follerin' 'im.'' While speaking, Sugar took a small case from his shirt pocket, and put on a pair of glasses. His eyes had always been weak, but only recently had he been able to afford a cheap pair of glasses. Ever since, Mick O'Connell had been playing a joke on an oblivious Sugar. Mick would say: ''Your glasses are crooked, Sugar.'' Renfrey would invariably say: ''No they're not,'' take off the glasses and point out that one lens was thicker than the other to help his squinty eye.

As Renfrey was about to begin reading, Barney Robinson interposed: ''Yes, and then Corrigan would wait till bloody old Dunn came out, then he'd go in and talk the bloke outta scabbin'. Bloody good luck to Eddie Corrigan!'' Barney looked at John West. ''And if it interests anyone, I'm one of the blokes that went with Corrigan and helped him a few times.''

''STRANGE CONVICTION, it says,'' Sugar read gravely. *''Edward Corrigan was charged today with persistently following John Dunn. The charge was laid under the Masters and Servants Act . . .''*

John West snatched the paper from Renfrey's hands and read the article. He found himself gloating over it. Corrigan had befriended him at school when he needed friendship, but Corrigan had refused to take part in his scheme, and was undermining the goodwill of some of his employees. Corrigan was a reminder to him that there were things other than wealth to be fought for.

John West folded up the paper. "I'm going down to see if the sign-writer has finished the rest of those sheets; I won't be long."

Piggy barred the gate behind him.

When the other two totes opened, John West had resolved to reopen his own, and to reduce the percentage in order to drive them out.

A couple of times, Joe had said: "You're not going to open up again, are you? If you go to jail it'll kill Mum, you know that." He told Joe to mind his own business.

The solicitor had told him that, at each raid, the police would have to find fresh evidence, therefore, so long as some way could be found to escape with the evidence the police could not bring him to court again. It was risky. If they nabbed him it would mean prison! He must somehow get Mrs Moran to allow him to put the trapdoor through near the table in the back room. He could always be near, ready to flee. And he needed that trapdoor in the back shed through which his employees there could escape with the evidence.

John West walked along briskly, his right hand in his trouser pocket, his left swinging, when he bumped into Eddie Corrigan, who came quickly out of a side street.

"Sorry," Corrigan said. Then, recognising John West, he added: "Oh, how are yer, Jack?"

"Not bad," John West replied. He noticed that Corrigan's shabby clothes hung loosely from his massive frame, which seemed to have no flesh on it. "They tell me you've been in trouble for following old Dunn around."

"Yes, the old cow was hirin' scabs to work in his new factory."

"That'll teach you not to be worryin' about strikes and scabs."

"Won't teach me, Jack. The men are pretty solid even though there's ten unemployed men waitin' to take every striker's job."

"You'll never beat 'em. They've got too much money. You've got to have money to fight the bosses."

"They tell me you've got plenty of money these days – but I don't see you fightin' 'em."

"Bloody clever, aren't you? I do my bit for the poor, don't you worry. I'm always givin' money away to the people who need it."

"You give back a bit of what they give you. Is that it?"

"No, it's not. People like to gamble, you've admitted that, yourself. They get a fair go from me."

"All right, Jack. Have it yer own way. I gotta be goin'. We've been tipped off they're goin' to try to open at Franklin's with scab labour. We'll give the scabs a little welcome party, if they won't listen to reason." Corrigan hit his huge fist on the palm of his hand significantly.

"Bit hard on 'em aren't you? I'm against non-union labour, but yer can't blame 'em in a way. Some of 'em have been outa work for years."

"Scabbin's the one unforgivable sin. I got no sympathy for 'em." Corrigan made to walk away. "I've got to be goin', Jack."

For a moment John West's better self broke through the tough outer covering with which he was insulating himself. He found himself admiring Corrigan though he didn't agree with him. "How are the wife and nippers, Eddie?" he said in a more friendly tone.

"Oh, not bad, Jack, not bad. Havin' a bit of a battle at the moment, acourse."

John West took a sovereign from his pocket and tried to push it into Corrigan's hand. "Here's a quid to stave you over," he said. "Buy somethin' for the wife and kids."

Corrigan drew his hand away. "No, thanks all the same, Jack. We'll get along all right."

"Well, take it for the strike fund, and here's another one to go with it. If they'd come to me in the first place I'd have put in."

"Oh, all right, Jack. Thanks very much. This will help feed some of the strikers' wives and kids."

They walked away in opposite directions.

John West's mind turned to his mission at the bazaar; for the rest of the day he speculated on it even more than on the tote reopening.

Ever clean, and fastidious of dress, he was more than usually so that evening. Although he had had a swim in the morning, he went again to the river armed with a towel and soap; they still had no bath – there was nowhere to put one in the tiny house. He shaved carefully. He cogitated whether he would wear his new grey or his new dark suit, finally deciding in favour of the latter.

When he had put on his tie, he stood in front of the mirror of the sideboard in the light of a lamp and viewed himself critically, fussing with the bow. No! He took off the tie again and repeated the process three times.

The hair-combing was a difficult process. The lock of hair which he habitually combed back, as usual, would not stay in position. He soaked it with water, and after much brushing and combing it condescended to stay put. Then he put on his coat and hat and stood back, posing and turning this way and that. Yes. He was the best-dressed man in Carringbush, not a doubt of that!

As he walked through the kitchen his mother was sitting in an old rocking chair sewing by the fire.

"John," she said softly, "John, I hope you will do as I ask and not reopen . . ."

"Not now, Mum," he interrupted. "I'm in a hurry now." He was anxious to avoid a clash with his mother over his reopening the tote. After his own manner, he loved his mother. He hated to hurt her, but he knew he would defy her when a show-down came.

He walked around to Jackson Street and turned towards the hall in the St Joseph's Church grounds. He was trembling a little and his heart was thumping. John West was interested in Mrs Moran because he wanted her permission to build the two trap-doors, but he was also interested in her daughter. Nellie was a pretty girl. He liked the way she swirled her long skirts as she walked by, and the way she looked at him sometimes as he passed the house when she was standing on the little front verandah. He noticed her first about three months after he opened the tote. Since then he had seen her often, but had never spoken to her. He slyly sought information about her.

She had often gone to stay with her aunt in the country since she had left the convent. Once or twice he had seen her riding a horse from the riding school in Jackson Street. She looked very beautiful and capable in her riding habit, riding side-saddle as calm as you like. Mrs Moran conducted a small dress and hat shop at the other end of Jackson Street, and he guessed that, with the bad times, she was finding it hard to make ends meet. Apparently Nellie's father was dead.

John West became more nervous with each step. Tonight he would be introduced to Nellie Moran. For weeks he had told himself that he was in love with Nellie – that he was going to marry her. He had even dreamed about her at night several times.

John West's natural timidity still came to the surface where women were concerned. He had no sisters; he had never been taught, nor had he read, anything about sex. He had felt the first pangs of manhood early, and his timidity and ignorance had left him unable to quiet his restlessness. At first he thought that there was something wrong with him, but from things he heard other members of the local push say, it seemed that this restlessness, this physical tingling, was normal.

In bed at night, often he would think as vividly as his instinctive knowledge of sex would permit, but when it came to talking to a young woman he was timid, shy, scared!

Then at the boot factory, he had met a lusty, buxom young woman despised by the other girls, but very popular with some of the men. John West decided that with this "easy" woman he could satisfy his desires. Once in the winter, after work, he had gone with her to the backyard at nightfall. He hardly knew what to do. Her thick lips gobbled up his mouth, and he lay with her trembling and afraid. It was quickly over, and he felt ashamed and badly frightened. That night he couldn't sleep. Was he going to get the worst kind of sickness he had ever heard of? He looked up the doctor's book which his mother kept in her bedroom, but found its reference brief and unhelpful. After a week of worried days and haunted nights, he imagined he had an itch. Would he go to a doctor? He was too ashamed, and, besides, he couldn't afford to. He remembered hearing Piggy once say that it took you only a minute to get it, but you never got rid of it if you got it bad. But as the worried weeks went by the itch departed, and with it his fears.

He resolved never again to go near that sort of woman. He would wait until he met the girl he sometimes dreamed about – a beautiful, clean girl whom he would one day marry.

Leaving his hat in the lobby, John West entered the hall sheepishly, and stood just inside the door. He saw Mrs Smith, dressed up in a none-too-successful attempt to conceal her gross physique as she served at the vegetable stall.

It was a typical church bazaar – with stall and raffles and lucky dips, women buzzing about, and the chatter of voices. Among the women there was a profusion of long skirts and high hats, and among the men side-whiskers, moustaches and high collars.

John West had been baptised as a Roman Catholic. When he and his brothers were small children their mother had often taken them to Mass at St Joseph's on a Sunday morning. She taught them to go to Confession and Communion, but during their school days she went to church less frequently and hardly ever took them with her. With no religious instruction given in the State School, John West and his brothers soon grew out of their religion, and were Catholics in name only. In recent years, Mrs West had begun to attend Mass and the Sacraments again regularly; but, in spite of desultory requests, her sons never accompanied her.

"Hello, Mrs Smith," John West said.

"Oh, hello, Mr West."

He shifted his feet awkwardly and blushed. "Er – there's a good crowd, Mrs Smith. They should make a lot of money."

"Yes, a good crowd, Mr West. There's Miss Moran over there."

"Oh, yes, so she is."

Nellie Moran was busying herself selling odds and ends at a stall near the side door. She looked pretty and dignified with her long skirt, her tightly corseted waist and her auburn hair combed into a bun at the back of her head under a high decorated hat. Just like the pretty women you see in the art dealer's window in Jackson Street, John West thought.

They went over to her stall and waited a minute or two until she was free. John West's heart pounded, his stomach nerves quivered, and his big ears burned.

"Nellie, there's someone here I'd like you to meet."

"Oh, hello, Mrs Smith. Lovely crowd, isn't it?"

"Yes, Nellie. You haven't met Mr John West, have you?"

"No, I don't think I have."

"This is Mr John West. Mr West, this is Miss Nellie Moran."

Nellie answered, coyly, "Good evening, Mr West."

"Um – good evening, Miss Moran, er – big crowd."

"Yes, a lovely crowd."

"Er – make a lot of money."

"Yes, and it's for a good cause."

"Yes, my word."

Nellie Moran was blushing. John West felt sure that, for her, this had been a pleasant surprise, but this thought did not overcome his extreme shyness.

"We're running raffles, too, Mr West," Mrs Smith said. "What are you raffling, Nellie?"

"We've got two threepenny raffles going, one for . . ."

"I'll take a sovereign's worth of tickets," John West interrupted her, producing a golden coin. That should impress Nellie – a sovereign's worth of tickets, without waiting to hear what the prizes are!

Nellie Moran gushed her surprise: "Goodness me! Thanks, Mr West, that's wonderful!"

Customers again thronged around the stall and Nellie Moran excused herself and began attending to them. After promising to call back later, John West wandered around the bazaar. He saw a few people he knew who seemed surprised at his presence. Among them was Sergeant Devlin, himself, dressed in civilian clothes.

"Well, well, me boy," he greeted John West jovially, and they shook hands. "Sure and I must say I'm surprised to see you, Jack West, my boy. I'm pleased you're doing your bit in a good cause."

"I'm always helpin' good causes," John West answered brusquely. "Anybody'll tell yer that."

"Sure and there are causes and causes; and I know of no better one than helpin' remodel the House of God."

John West nodded assent. Devlin wouldn't be so bloody friendly if he knew that Cummin's Tea Shop was reopening in the morning, he thought.

Devlin called to a priest who was standing nearby. "Sure, Father, and I don't believe you know Mr John West. Mr West, this is Father O'Toole."

Father O'Toole was a fat, red-faced Irish priest, of the type that satisfies his appetites and lives an intelligently lazy and happy-go-lucky existence. His nose was mottled blue and red, his flesh was flabby, his eyes pouched, his lips sensual; yet his face was pleasant and exuded goodwill to all men, especially Catholics.

The priest wasn't long in asking for a donation towards the Church Rebuilding Fund, and when John West gave him five sovereigns, the good Father's pleasure was only exceeded by that of the good sergeant, who beamed his approval.

The bazaar chattered and fussed to its end, and, tidying up done, John West shyly but determinedly asked Nellie Moran if he could accompany her home.

"I'm with Mama," she replied, "so you'll have to take her home, too."

John West remembered the trapdoors, and was pleased. Presently he recognised Mrs Moran approaching. She was a red-haired woman with whom time had dealt kindly. She could almost have been mistaken for Nellie's sister, with her smooth skin and trim waist.

"Here's Mother now! Mama, this is Mr John West."

"Don't worry, I know him. Him and his what-do-they-call-it shop," she said cheerfully and without malice.

"My tote is fairly run; everyone gets a fair deal," John West answered.

"I know nothing about that, young man. But I wish you would stop those rough men from running through my backyard when the police come. I saw them that night."

"I'm sorry about that," John West answered. "It was done without my authority."

"Well, don't let it happen again. Your tote shop is the worry of my life. All afternoon I can hear the clatter of feet and the mumble of voices. Thank goodness I can't hear what is being said, for when sometimes they shout, the language is vile. I'm afraid some of your employees and clients are vulgar people, Mr West." She spoke in a light-hearted tone which belied her words. John West murmured something about things being quieter in the future.

Walking home slowly, they talked about the weather and the bazaar. John West mentioned his donation to the fund, reckoning on getting his money's worth in their goodwill. He decided he'd better wait a while before asking Mrs Moran about the trapdoors. Walking beside Nellie, he was strangely excited. He hoped that he might get an opportunity to speak to her alone, but when they arrived at the house Mrs Moran said: "Time for bed, Nellie. Good-night, Mr West."

Two months later, Mrs Moran allowed him to insert the two

trapdoors, in return for a sovereign per month. Her obvious reluctance convinced him that he was right in thinking the Morans were "feeling the pinch."

The two opposition totes continued in business, and great rivalry developed between the three proprietors.

John West, because of higher dividends and his flair for organisation, captured the bulk of the business, and his bank rose to over one thousand pounds. Fights between the rival mobs were not uncommon, and here, too, the West camp more than held its own, mainly through the agency of Piggy, Cauliflower Dick, Sugar and Mick O'Connell.

In a bitter scene with his mother, a week after the tote reopened, John West had lost his temper and told her that if she didn't like it she could lump it; and he would get out of the house and live somewhere else. She wept and begged him to stay. As the weeks went by, the old bitterness came back into her spirit, and the household resumed the old strained atmosphere.

The sign still graced the front of the shop and the tea chest still stood in the window like a dusty derelict, but the front door was always secured with chains and iron bars. Customers entered and left by the back gate.

Business became so brisk after three months that John West rehired Joe and Jim Tracey, who returned to work in the tote a month before the boot strike ended in a compromise. Belief that there would be no more raids led Joe to return, and sheer poverty drove Jim Tracey back.

There had been renewed protests against the gambling mania from the pulpit and in letters in the local paper; even the city daily papers, which had featured the story of the previous raids, made a couple of references to the Carringbush tote shops.

For six months after reopening, John West took great precautions against police raids, but then he came to the opinion that Devlin had been so impressed with his generosity to the Catholic Church that he was going to grant him immunity. He relaxed his precautions. Then, one Saturday afternoon towards the middle of 1895, a drag full of "civilian" passengers drove down Jackson Street into Silver Street. When the passengers began to alight at the entrance to the back lane, a nit-keeper recognised one of them as Constable Grieve himself. In the mad scramble that ensued, Jim Tracey was detained before he could escape into Mrs

Moran's yard. Unfortunately for him, he had under his arm a bundle of betting tickets and three tote sheets, which were promptly seized as evidence. Tracey was the only one arrested at Cummin's Tea Shop, but the proprietors of the two other totes were detained in simultaneous raids, one by Sergeant Devlin and the other by Constable Brogan.

Late that afternoon John West bailed out a very pale and worried Tracey. He tried to cheer him up by telling him that his fine would be paid, but Jim went home to his wife and young child in fear and trembling.

The city dailies fully reported the trials of the tote men, and great interest was aroused in Carringbush and beyond.

The stern young magistrate who had tried John and Joseph West earlier, referred in his summing up to "a guilty man who was not in the box," then sentenced each of the accused to three months' imprisonment without the option of a fine. No one was more amazed or enraged than John West. He noticed Jim Tracey turn deathly white and sag to the verge of physical collapse.

As they took Jim away, John West saw Mrs Tracey, a little shabby woman of vague, faded beauty, embrace her husband as he hung his head in sorrow and shame. The woman then stumbled from the crowded, hushed court in a convulsive weeping. John West walked over timidly to attempt to comfort her. She raised her tousled head and said, between sobs, but deliberately and with bitterness: "Now, I hope you're satisfied!"

One night about six weeks later, Constable Brogan, dressed in civilian clothes, called at the West house.

"Could I see you privately for a minute?" he said, when John West came to the kitchen door.

They walked around the side path to the front gate. Brogan said nervously: "Sergeant Devlin didn't send me, but . . ."

"You and Devlin can both go to hell, as far as I'm concerned!"

This snivelling, crawling individual, John West thought, has taken dozens of sovereigns from me under false pretences.

"Er . . . you don't understand the position," the policeman replied, flinching a little. He felt towards John West as the bribed to the briber: inferior, and conscious that always he would be despised no matter how helpful he might be.

"I understand all right," John West said. "You want to be careful I don't let out that you took money from me." This was bluff; but, smarting as he was at having to abandon the tote and step down to running a book at the hotel opposite, he felt impelled to take reprisals.

"You wouldn't do that," Brogan answered.

"Wouldn't I? Just you see."

Brogan, who gambled and drank, courted the ladies, and generally lived above his means, was feeling the absence of the regular sovereigns he used to obtain from John West, so he refused to be ruffled. "You won't when you hear what I have to say," he said in a smug undertone. "As I said Sergeant Devlin didn't send me, but I think you could open up the tote again without much trouble."

"How do you mean?"

"Well, it would only cost you five sovereigns a week, and no questions asked."

"What! Five sovereigns for Devlin, and five for every trap on the beat, I suppose. I'm tired of paying out for protection I don't get."

"Five sovereigns will cover the lot. I'm on the beat. So the only ones who can trouble you are me and Devlin. And all you have to do is to give me five sovereigns a week and I'll guarantee that everything will be all right."

"How do I know Devlin won't step in? I thought you said he didn't send you here?"

"Well, you see, Devlin really isn't in it, as I said," Brogan coughed significantly. "He couldn't afford to be. But if you give me five sovereigns every week, Devlin won't trouble you. A nod's as good as a wink to a blind man. Open the shop and find out for yourself. Acourse, you might have to cover some of the others later; yer know what they are."

"Yes, I know what they are!" John West said. "All right. Looks as if I'm going to be bled again. Come round tomorrer night; and remember, no funny business. I don't want every bloody trap in Carringbush coming around."

"All right, Mr West."

John West retired to bed in a state of great agitation. Just when he had accepted defeat, a solution had been presented to him. He had been telling tote workers and customers that he was just "lying low" for a while; now his idle boast that he would show the bloody traps something before long would come true.

Tonight's interview revived his faith in the power of the bribe. Everyone had a price, he decided. He would, in future, always work on that principle.

Tomorrow he would organise his men quickly to reopen the tote shop next Saturday. This time it would stay open. He would risk anything – even prison. No matter who interfered he would bribe them or brush them aside.

One Friday night, six weeks later, twenty or thirty men were gathered in the tote behind barred doors. They were discussing prospects, and making pre-post investments for the race meeting to be held at Moonee Valley racecourse the following afternoon. Outside, the wind was howling and heavy rain swished around the building.

John West was seated at a table in the back room with his back to the trapdoor, writing on a large sheet of cardboard in the light of a kerosene lamp which stood on the corner of the table.

There had been no interference from the police since he had reopened the tote. At first, he had been worried that Brogan might have acted without Devlin's knowledge, so he made it his business to meet Devlin casually in the street. The sergeant's manner left no doubt in John West's mind that he was receiving the lion's share of the five sovereigns which Brogan called for each Friday.

When the tote reopened, Mrs West complained, but her son had assured her that he knew positively there was no danger of police raids. She seemed to accept his word, or perhaps resigned herself to the inevitable, and now the tote was never a subject of argument in the house.

The only annoying feature of the past few weeks had been the reopening of the two rival totes during their owners' enforced absence. John West suspected that Brogan and Devlin had a finger in the pie somewhere. Anyway, his tote was easily the most popular and the most efficiently conducted; he was making profits at the rate of forty sovereigns a week.

Presently there was a knocking on the back door. It was the old code. The code knock had been changed since the reopening. John West looked up quizzically. Piggy hesitated, then took the iron bar from the door and opened it.

There was something strange about the man who entered that caused first Piggy's, then dozens of other eyes, to become glued on him. He was of medium height; his ragged, rain-soaked coat hung loosely from his incredibly emaciated frame, and his shoulders sagged around his sunken chest. His eyes were like holes in a blanket, and the hair had been shaved from his head. He looked, for all the world, like a half-drowned animal. No one seemed to recognise him. He had brought into the room with him a menacing silence.

The man took a few steps towards John West and faced him across the table. His figure was even more grotesque as it stood between the lamp on the table and the shaft of light coming through the door from the shop.

John West studied the man for a few moments, his eyes filled with wonder and his body rigid; then recognition dawned on him.

"God!" he said, huskily. "Jim Tracey!" The words seemed to relieve his tension. He gave a quick, loud laugh, throwing his head back.

"There's nothin' to laugh at, West!" Everyone in the room watched tensely. There was silence in the shop, too, and a few men crowded in the doorway between, watching and listening.

The laugh choked in John West's throat.

"There's nothin' to laugh at, you little bandy bastard!"

"I wouldn't talk like that, Jim," John West said, nervously, casting a quick glance in Piggy's direction. Piggy recovered his mobility and moved in close behind Tracey, ready for action.

"Why not? You paid me a lousy sovereign a week, then when I went to jail you left my wife and baby destitute. If it hadn't been for Eddie Corrigan and his wife they'd have starved to death." Tracey was beside himself, his voice rose to a piercing scream. "Why don't you blokes wake up to him? You can't win. And if there's a raid he'll let his workers go to jail without even giving their wives a penny."

John West did not know what to say. This was bad publicity. He had completely forgotten about Tracey. "How was I to know your wife and child were in want? They didn't come near me," he said lamely. "You can start work tomorrow, and I'll double your wages. I'll always help a man, you know that, Jim. I didn't know."

"Didn't know! You didn't care! I wouldn't work for you again for fifty sovereigns a week. I'm going to Kalgoorlie next week.''

John West smarted under Tracey's scorn. "Go where you bloody well like, if that's your attitude!''

Suddenly, Tracey struck John West a stinging open-handed blow across the cheek. "I'm going to thrash you before I go. Get up and fight!''

John West cringed and looked around desperately for assistance. Piggy leapt forward and applied a cruel grip on Tracey's right arm, driving it up his back. Tracey struggled violently, and again addressed the gaping customers. "He started this place on a rigged pigeon race. He used to charge thirty-three and a third per-cent!''

Suddenly he wriggled out of Piggy's grip, slewed sideways, and dived across the table at John West, who moved back, knocking over his chair.

Piggy quickly recaptured Tracey; and with the assistance of Cauliflower Dick, who came in from the shop, dragged him towards the back door.

Tracey tried to resist. "And I'll tell you blokes something else,'' he shouted. "West doesn't post all the scratchings, and you lose your money on horses he knows are not going to start. The pigeons bring in the scratchings and he doesn't post them on the board. That's the truth! I know! He robs you that way every day!''

Still struggling desperately and screaming abuse, Tracey was dragged to the door. Piggy opened it with one hand. They threw his dripping figure savagely into the howling night and locked the door behind him.

The following year was a period of uninterrupted prosperity for John West.

He offset Jim Tracey's outburst by announcing that in future anyone imprisoned for being on the premises would be compensated at the rate of £50 for three months or less, and £100 for over that period. He spread a false rumour that he had paid Tracey's fare to Kalgoorlie. Tote punters benefited from Tracey's exposure – thereafter all scratchings were posted.

Business rose until his profits reached over fifty sovereigns a week and his bank balances totalled over five thousand pounds. So well established had he become that gamblers beyond

Carringbush came to bet, or rang on the telephone, which had recently replaced the pigeon service. Big bookmakers from the city desirous of laying off for safety, had no hesitation in unloading their surplus investments with "young Jack West."

The only aspect of John West's life causing him dissatisfaction was his romance with Nellie Moran. When he called each month to pay the rent as agreed with her mother, Nellie was politely friendly; when they met in the street – and he contrived as many such meetings as possible – she blushed as she returned his nervous greeting. He took to going to Mass occasionally, sometimes walking home with Nellie and her mother. He soon learned that Nellie had another young man – a schoolteacher with whom she occasionally went to a dance or a music-hall show. The months increased his determination. At last, he asked Nellie to accompany him to a vaudeville show. She accepted, but, alas, her mother came too.

He wondered whether he should learn to dance, but was deterred by his shyness, and long conditioning in the push belief that dancing was "sissy".

One day he was sitting in his office pondering his love troubles when Sergeant Devlin entered the tote yard with tidings that would give him something more serious to worry about.

John West heard Mick O'Connell's voice say: "I s'pose you've come to buy some tea, Sergeant. We have a special line at a reduced price this week; or p'raps a man like yourself with a large family would prefer a seven-pound tin of Griffin's? As it says on the label, 'There's only one T in AusTralia – Griffin's Blue Label', and though I'd rather have a drop of whisky meself, I must admit . . ."

"Hold yer whist," Devlin's voice interrupted. "If it's not sleepin' you are, it's talkin' nonsense. Get up off your lazy back and tell Jack West I want to have a word with him."

"Sure and there's no need for me to be stirrin' meself. Just walk right into the parler, as the spider said to the fly. Yer'll find him in his counting house a'counting out his money," Mick's voice replied.

John West greeted Devlin with some surprise, for this was the first time he had been to the premises since the first raid on the tote. "What's the trouble, Sergeant?"

"Sure, and there's a lot of trouble for both of us. All the talk about me not trying to close your tote, and the writing to the papers, has caused headquarters in Melbourne to take an unfriendly interest in Carringbush gambling. I have it on good authority that they are planning to raid you, and Ryan and Cohen as well.''

John West sat back on his chair with hands outstretched on the table, deep in thought. He pulled a small revolver from his pocket and began toying with it.

Devlin's figure, fatter than ever, flopped into a chair. He mopped his sweating brow. ''P'raps I should have raided the totes now an' then just to put headquarters off the scent, like I suggested. I'm thinking it's never too late to mend. I'll raid the establishments next Saturday.''

John West raised his inscrutable eyes and stared at him.

''Of course,'' Devlin added, ''I'll be careful just to arrest some of your men, and leave you and Joe out of it.''

''I told you before, Sergeant. There's to be no raids. If ever anyone comes up before the court again for operating from here, it will go very bad with me. I don't mind you raiding the others, but leave this place alone!''

''But don't you see, Jack? They're saying at headquarters that I'm too friendly with you; that I'm not trying to catch you because I'm being paid. They ought to talk, the spalpeens. It's a case of the kettle calling the pot black. There was a Royal Commission into allegations of graft in the police force not ten years ago, and it revealed some pretty stories, I can tell you. But, of course, it was all conveniently hushed up.''

A hurt expression came on to Devlin's face as he added with emphasis: ''They ought to talk! They ought to talk about Patrick Devlin, who's a saint compared with most of the detectives in the city of Melbourne!''

''You say there are men in there who would take – I mean who would be prepared to co-operate. Well, what about doing something about it?''

''No! No, Jack! I've taken too many risks as it is. Don't ask me to do any more!''

Suddenly Devlin leaned forward urgently. ''Why don't you close up this place, Jack? You've done all right. It's led to too much trouble for . . .''

''What do you think I am?'' John West thrust his face

aggressively across the table at Devlin. "This tote will stay open until I am ready to close it! And I don't intend closing it now, just because you've got cold feet. And I don't like the way this protection money keeps spreading. I was paying Brogan and some of the others, and Grieve raided me. Now I'm paying you and Brogan and others, and the city police are going to raid me. Where does it all end?"

Devlin said meekly: "We'll just let things stand as they are between us for the moment. Perhaps later on I can make arrangements for you with some of the city men."

"Well, you can't expect me to keep paying for protection I'm not getting. If I'm going to be harassed by the city police, I won't be in a position to go on paying you."

Devlin had noticed this man grow more arrogant and ruthless lately. John West had him where he wanted him, and Devlin knew it.

"My God, you talk hard, and get too big for your boots. I've helped you make a small fortune. If you desert me now, I'll tell the world what's gone on here in Carringbush these last few years."

"I don't think you will, Sergeant. You respect your own hide too much for that," said John West, spinning the revolver in the air and catching it deftly. "We'll let things stand as they are; but I'll expect you to do everything you can to let me know when the raid is coming."

"All right. If I can find out anything. I'll let you know, by all means. Take no notice of my little outburst. It's just that I'm a worried man today."

John West appeared not to be listening. His lips were set hard, his eyes cast down.

"As I was saying – take no notice of my little outburst. I'll try my best to find out when they are coming, and I don't think it will be long. And something you had better watch is pimps comin' to bet here. That's the way they'll be after working. To get evidence, they will send spies in here to bet, and bring the tickets to court."

At this last remark John West raised his head.

"I see! Well, they'll get a hot welcome here. I'll have everybody checked at the gate, and unless they're vouched for by a regular customer, they won't be let in." He spoke vigorously,

72

thumping the table with his fist. 'I'll put on more nit-keepers. You keep your eyes and ears open, and your mouth shut. Leave the rest to me.''

After Devlin departed, John West sat thinking grimly. So now he had the city police to contend with!

The prospect disturbed him, yet gave him a feeling of importance and strengthened his determination.

CHAPTER THREE

The thought of all whose interests are thwarted by any law whatever is how to set the law aside in their own cases.

HONORÉ DE BALZAC

A load of hay on a four-wheeled wagon drawn by two sturdy horses came up Jackson Street. It passed some nit-keepers on its way, but they ignored it, being intent on watching for policemen.

The wagon turned into Silver Street and pulled up at the entrance to the lane. Suddenly the hay began to move convulsively, and twelve men leapt out of it – big men holding batons in their hands. And one of them was armed with an axe. Before Jigger, who was standing on the lane corner, could open his mouth to shout, six of the men dashed up the lane to the back gate. Here, Piggy and Cauliflower Dick tried to intercept them, but were brushed aside. The other six men ran quickly around towards the front of the shop. Their six companions had no sooner burst into the backyard than there came a loud banging on the front door.

Pandemonium broke out in the tote. In the room behind the shop Joe West and Sugar Renfrey quickly left their duties to fall over one another through the trapdoor into the adjoining yard. Mick O'Connell swept through from the yard, and was about to follow them when he remembered that fifty pounds awaited him if he were arrested and sentenced to three months; this thought impelled him to return.

As the six men entered the crowded yard, tote patrons scattered like ninepins. The policemen made no attempt to intercept them. The trapdoor at the rear of the shed was flung open by Barney Robinson, and he and Flash Alec scrambled through, Barney having the courtesy to call out to John West (who was in the yard on a tour of inspection when the hub-bub started): "Look out, Jack!"

Jigger rushed into the yard and shouted somewhat belatedly:

"All out! The traps are here! They come under a load of hay! All out!"

Piggy and Cauliflower Dick filled their pockets with coins from the shelf in the shed, rushed through the trapdoor into Jigger's yard, and into the kitchen where they sat down to afternoon tea with Jigger's wife.

John West made to follow them but found his path blocked by three policemen. He turned with great agility and ran swiftly towards the shed where two policemen tried to grab him. He evaded them, and ran to the back door of the shop, only to find that his path was again blocked by the six men who had smashed the front door in with an axe.

Mick O'Connell stood in the middle of the yard, hands on hips, waiting to be arrested, and Jigger was still leaping about and advising patrons who had already made themselves scarce to "get out the back way." Jigger, too, was hoping to be detained and imprisoned for at least three months.

John West stopped in his tracks and looked around like a hunted man in a dead-end street, until two policemen grabbed hold of him firmly.

"What's this for?" he said, hoping he would be mistaken for a customer.

"You know what it's for! We're the police!"

Scotch Paddy was dragged into the yard from the lane where he had been arrested after putting up quite a struggle. Mick O'Connell and Jigger were each grasped by the scruff of the neck and the seat of the trousers and tossed into the lane. Mick got up, dusted his trousers, and complained: "Sure and it's a foine country. A man can't even get arrested when he wants to be.'

Then the 'phone rang in the shop and one of the policemen answered it.

John West heard him say: "Jack who? Oh, you want Jack West to put two bob on Kirkby in the steeplechase, do you? Well, this is the police here; you won't be having any more bets at this tote."

"I have nothing to do with this case. What are you detaining me for?" John West said desperately. "I'm only a customer."

Still protesting his innocence, he was searched and hustled through the shop with Scotch Paddy to a drag in the front street in which Mr Ryan and Mr Cohen sat in utter dejection. On the way to the jail they told John West that they, too, had been visited by a load of hay.

At the Russell Street lock-up, the detectives refused to discuss bail until next morning.

That night John West could not sleep. In the seclusion of the damp, musty cell he felt the protective barriers he had built around himself fall away. He was prey to mental turmoil. As the hours crept towards midnight he vividly remembered the scene when the police had come to arrest Arty. Then he thought of his mother: the simple courage of her life, the fortitude she had displayed through the poverty, disappointment, shame and bitterness she had known. He wished he could erase the past – erase Arthur's shame and his own flouting of his mother's wishes, but he resisted the thought that he should close the tote for her sake. He thought of Nellie Moran, and his body and mind craved for her. Was she afraid of him? Did she and her mother have misgivings about him? They had moved from their house – probably because it was next to the tote. Well, they would see! He would have Nellie, and soon at that!

In the dark hour before the dawn he fell exhausted into a troubled sleep and dreamed of a police court where many judges surrounded him. They were pointing at him and saying in chorus: "You will go to jail with your brother! And your mother will die of shame!"

And then the dream changed and he was being chased down a long street by policemen; they were firing guns at him; he was getting tired and they were catching up to him. His legs would carry him no further, and he dreamed he saw Nellie Moran and his mother standing ahead weeping and telling him to hurry, to keep running. But the harder he tried to run the further away from him they seemed and the closer the policemen came – hundreds of them, all firing guns. Then he dreamed that he was seized by many hands and taken to a place where a man was tied to a whipping-post. It was his brother Arty. An enormous, evil man was bringing the lash down over Arty's thin back, and great weals were appearing across it. Arty was screaming filthy oaths at his tormentors. Blood began to stream from his brother's back and to flow across a stone floor around John West's boots. Then he dreamed that he had shouted: "Stop! I am John West! I am a millionaire! I am powerful! I will not allow you to flog my brother!''

And then in his nightmare they seized upon him and, as he struggled, he heard a voice counting: ''Thirty-nine, forty, forty-one,'' and another voice saying, ''When he gets his fifty, we will give you fifty. You are not a millionaire, you are only a larrikin from Carringbush, and you are a coward! We will give you fifty lashes, too!''

He saw his mother standing there with Joe and they were weeping as the men dragged him towards the triangle, and the voice was saying: ''Forty-seven, forty-eight, forty-nine . . .''

Then John West awakened from the nightmare screaming out; he was sweating and shivering, and the roots of his hair seemed frozen.

The pale light of dawn crept into his cell. He quickly recovered his normal senses. The dream seemed to have purged his mind of all fear and self-recrimination. He began to think of the task that lay ahead. He must be calm; he must plan. Somehow he would win this case and then make the tote an impregnable fortress. His mind investigated the possibilities until Joe and Sugar came with the bail money.

That evening he went to the little cottage where Barney Robinson now lived with his newly-married wife, Florrie.

He found Barney, Joe, Scotch Paddy and Sugar waiting in the tidy but cheaply furnished front room.

''The game is gettin' too risky for my likin','' Joe said. ''Think we orta go back to the idea of just runnin' an S.P. book.''

John West remained silent.

''Ar, I dunno,'' Sugar replied, fiddling with his glasses. ''We bought the local traps orf, who's to say we can't do the same with the city men? They say every man has his price.'' He kept squinting at John West, trying to analyse his reactions, but found his employer's face set in a stern mould.

''We mightn't find 'em easy,'' Barney intervened. ''Even if Jack defeats this case, where will it all end? The only way we could keep going would be to guard the place day and night to keep them out. That would lead to fights with the police. Piggy and Cauliflower Dick, and that new fella that's just started at the tote – what-do-yer-call-him, One-Eyed-Tommy – they all carry guns. Never know what may transpire,'' he concluded, remembering his studies in English expression. "Could easily end in altercations of a violent nature."

"You're right, there, Barney," Joe said. "Even if Jack doesn't go to jail this time, we'll all end up in jail if we keep going. Jack's got plenty of coin; he should go into business."

Suddenly John West sat forward in his chair. "Go into business? I'm in business, and not all the pimps and traps in Melbourne will put me out!" His voice rose to a shout. "You and Barney have always been a couple of weak reeds. If you're too bloody scared, get out! You can go to hell – the two of yer!"

Barney studied his feet and made play with his moustache. Joe said in subdued tones: "No need to get orf yer bike."

By this time Scotch Paddy had sufficiently worked out the drift of the conversation to make reply to Sugar Renfrey's earlier remark. "Yes," he said gravely, "every man has his price, especially solicitors. I don't care what we do after the trial; all I'm carin' about is to keep outa jail this time. My brother works for David Garside, the greatest lawyer in the world. Defended Ned Kelly, he did, that's how bloody good he is."

John West turned to Paddy with great interest. "David Garside? Do you think he would defend us? He'd be the man. These Carringbush solicitors are no good."

After due consideration, Paddy replied: "Defend anybody, if they pay him well enough. I got no dough, though, but I'll ask me brother. He's your cousin, Jack, but you don't know him. Nice fella, been edicated and everythin'."

The idea of the mighty Garside defending him seemed to mellow John West. "I'm a man of my word, Paddy. You'll get the best legal help, and if you go to jail you'll get your fifty pounds for three months or a hundred pounds for more than that."

This magnanimous promise seemed to give Paddy great satisfaction; his face cracked in a laugh which shook his bony frame as he nodded his head up and down.

"I'll go and see Garside in the morning," John West said. "We'll beat this case, then we'll show the city traps a thing or two." He turned to Joe and Barney again: "And you blokes better make up your minds what you're going to do. If you're too scared, say so!"

"I'll be with yer, Jack, you know that. Long as it's not too risky. What'll Mum say? That's what's worryin' me."

John West hesitated before he said softly: "You leave Mum to me." Then he turned to Barney. "What about you?"

Barney lowered his voice and looked furtively towards the door. "We'll see how things go, Jack. I'll probably keep on with bringing bets in from the boot factory, and working at the tote on a Saturday afternoon."

Soon Florrie Robinson came in with a cup of tea and some scones. Barney introduced her with ceremony and pride. Florrie was a buxom, attractive young woman with flaxen hair tied in a bun at the back of her well-moulded head. She greeted them cheerfully enough, but John West noted an air of hostility about her.

After each had been served with tea and a scone, Florrie Robinson sat next to Barney on the couch and said: "Listen, my love, I thought you said you no longer worked at the tote shop. I heard what was said in here; I couldn't help but hear the way some of you raised your voices." Her tone revealed injury rather than anger.

Barney hung his head like a scolded child. "Well, you see, Florrie, me love, I – that is, I didn't think it would matter just working there on a Saturday."

"Well, you know my feelings about it, Barney," Florrie continued. "The extra money is all very well; but I'd rather battle along on your wages until things improve, than to make extra that way."

Barney didn't reply. John West said: "My tote is fairly run. People like to gamble; if they didn't gamble there, they'd gamble somewhere else."

"Well, I don't care whether people like to gamble or not," Florrie answered acidly. "Barney has great ability and talent, and I'd like to see him better himself. Meantime, we could battle along on his wages."

John West was not in any humour to argue further. Paddy's mention of David Garside had opened up new thoughts – new hope that he would evade the law once again. After they had finished tea, he excused himself and left with Joe.

Arriving home they found the house wrapped in darkness – quiet save for their father's snoring. They crept into their bedroom, and John West undressed in dread that his mother might call him.

In the morning, Mrs West remained silent throughout break-fast, the old look of implacable bitterness on her face. She did not speak to him before he left the house. He walked to the city.

If there was one lawyer in the whole colony of Victoria whose advice and assistance could enable John West to defy the Melbourne police, that man was David Garside. Garside was in his fifties, and had packed a wealth of legal experience and achievement into his life. As a young lawyer, he had defended Ned Kelly, in 1878, after the bush-ranger had been captured at Glenrowan. Garside and his brother organised a petition of 60,000 signatures asking for Kelly's acquittal, but Kelly was hanged while a crowd of ten thousand people waited outside the Melbourne Jail.

Garside had been counsel for the defence when the directors of the Premier, the first of the Building Societies to crash, were arranged for trial. His wit scintillated in the gloomy court; the crown witnesses were badly ruffled by his clever, relentless cross-examination. Bush-rangers, crooked land-speculators, business men, murderers and thieves came all alike to David Garside. He defended them with enthusiasm, cunning and brilliance. He had no objection to adding the famous Carringbush tote operator to his clientèle.

John West found him in a large office on the first floor of a city building. Garside was a big, long-haired, bearded man of vital presence; he radiated self-confidence. Intelligent eyes flashed from under bushy eyebrows; the hair and beard were dig-nified with flecks of grey. As he rose from his seat behind a large cedar table, John West noticed that he was fastidiously dressed; and he saw a top hat, barrister's wig, and walking-cane hanging from the hat-stand in a corner. The table was surrounded on three sides by huge bookcases full of books, mainly about law. Garside walked around the table with agile steps and vigorously shook John West by the hand.

Whether pleading with a jury or just speaking to a client, Garside was never still. He paced as he talked, his hands con-tinually on the move; now crossed behind his back, flicking his coat-tails; now pointing a forefinger aggressively; now flung in the air; now one hitting the palm of the other.

"I presume you want to see me about the charge that has been levelled against you," Garside began. "I read of it in the newspapers. My fee will be costly, but I know that won't worry you. I am one of those people who believe that gambling should be legalised; that it should not be the preserve of the rich at Flemington and in their private homes. The law in regard to gambling in the Colony has many loopholes, Mr West. I know them well; I have successfully exploited them many times. Take this case of yours, for instance. They evaded your, er, what do you call them?"

He halted, making an impatient clicking noise with thumb and finger.

"Nit-keepers," John West explained, quite nonplussed by this extraordinary man.

"Nit-keepers, that is the word. Very interesting idiom you fellows have, very interesting." Garside continued his restless march while John West's eyes followed him to and fro. "As I was saying, they evaded your nit-keepers in a most ingenious manner, but one they will not be able to repeat with success. Remember that! They gathered sheets and betting tickets, but I may be able to prevail upon the court that these are not evidence against you and Cummin; who by the way is a brother of one of my clerks, and your cousin, I understand."

"Yes, it was he who suggested . . ." John West began to answer.

"It was a momentous day for you when he *did* suggest you should come to me, never fear. As I was saying, the court may not accept betting sheets and tickets as evidence. Experience has shown – and there are plenty of precedents for this – that the police need to have as witnesses informers who have placed bets and identified the accused. There will be one or two of those odious fellows on the scene in your case, rest assured. There is nothing more contemptible than a spy, no matter for what purpose he may be used. Our first step will be to prevail upon the spy or spies in this case to change their mind about carrying out their nefarious purpose."

John West positively gaped. He had been wondering how he could suggest to Garside that he was prepared to pay bribes, if necessary; and here was Garside suggesting bribes to him.

Garside turned to John West triumphantly. "Aah! I see that surprised you, Mr West. There are many factors in successfully fighting a law case." He commenced walking and gesticulating again. "The first, and most important, is that you obtain the services of a brilliant and experienced advocate. I shall not fail you there, Mr West. Then there are the Crown witnesses, in this case, the pimp or pimps; the police; the man or men on the bench; the Crown prosecutor; and the jury, if any. All of these people must be taken into consideration. If a man were accused of murdering the Queen of England herself, I should be confident of obtaining his acquittal, providing I knew what each of those persons was going to do, and I were able to influence what they would say, either by manoeuvring in the court or by devious means outside the court. But first of all let me explain the laws against illegal gaming in this Colony. Some dunderhead drew them up. If I had prepared them, Mr West, you should be as good as in jail at this moment, so watertight would they be. The difficulty the police are working under is that they can only raid the place, gather evidence, and have a pimp or pimps make bets and produce tickets in court and identify the person or persons charged."

He took two long paces towards John West and towered over him, his beard bristling, his eyes staring. "But, Mr West – and this is important – the gambling laws do not define a place! Aha, that is the rub! But I see you do not quite follow. I will explain it another way. They cannot declare your shop to be a common gaming house, so they cannot force you to vacate it."

Understanding dawned in John West's eyes. Garside continued: "Aha! I see you follow all right now. Until that law is amended, Mr West, you can go on conducting your, er, tea shop, until doomsday. Providing, and there is a proviso, providing you can win an acquittal in this case, or at least escape with a fine and so convince your clients that they run no great risk by doing business with you. Then you must proceed to make it impossible for the police (a) to get one or more of their spies into your establishment; and (b) to raid your establishment successfully."

By this time, John West had overcome some of his awe and confusion. "They were lucky to catch me this time. When I got the wink that the city police were after me, I doubled my nit-keepers, put men on the gate to check everyone that came in and had a bloke on a bike waiting outside the Russell Street police station to dash out and warn me if any detectives headed towards Carringbush. They tricked me this time, but you get me out of this case, and you can leave stopping the pimps and traps to me, in future.''

"So, Mr West, so! And from what I hear I shall be leaving the problem in capable hands.'' Garside sat down and leaned towards John West – elbows on the table, hands folded under his chin. "Now, our first step is to prevail upon the pimp or pimps in the case to repent of their evil ways. We must discover their whereabouts immediately. You can leave that to me. The detective in the case – I forget his name now, but it doesn't matter – is rather an ambitious fellow, and not very co-operative. Don't misunderstand, Mr West, I do not mean to infer that he is an honest man. This fellow is ambitious, and no doubt believes that closing the Carringbush tote shops will be a feather in his cap. If it had been any one of a dozen other detectives, then I should have been able to make an arrangement; though such arrangement would have increased my fee, of course. When I learn the identity of the man on the bench, I may be able to gain his goodwill, as well; but he cannot help us, unless we give him good grounds to acquit you on the evidence.''

Garside opened his eyes wide and pointed his right forefinger at John West. "Ah, you have a lot to learn, Mr West. Every police system in the world is based on the paid informer. Defeat the paid informer and you defeat the police system. The police solve murders and robberies through the network of informers they establish among the criminal classes. The average detective is a dunderhead; without his pimps he could achieve very little. A pickpocket, a brothel keeper, a garrotter or any other criminal can obtain immunity from the police for a time – *if* he informs them of the doings of his rivals. Usually these informers have been convicted of some petty crime; and the police intimidate them into becoming pimps – I like that term, most expressive! The informer is the main point of contact between the police and the criminal classes, and is usually despised by both. Many of these pimps are on sale to the highest bidder!''

David Garside arose and ushered John West to the door. "I will contact one of my, er, friends in the detective office; you ring me tomorrow morning and I may be able to give you the location of the pimp or pimps in this case. I realise that you have had experience in dealing with witnesses. I remember quite well reading how you managed to cause that young woman to change

83

her evidence in court. Yet you were still convicted. You were still convicted! There was no evidence before the Court that you were the proprietor. When I read of the verdict I said to myself: "If I had been counsel for the defence they would not have dared find him guilty!" But you fellows will brief these novices from the suburbs. Many's the time I've read a verdict and thought: just another poor devil in prison because he had not the intelligence to brief Davie Garside." He shook his shaggy head vigorously, as though in mourning for the thousands of murderers, thieves and assorted malefactors who languished in prison through lack of foresight in their choice of a barrister. Suddenly he flung the door open and grasped John West by the hand. "Good morning, Mr West. You ring me tomorrow; and don't worry, everything will be all right. Davie Garside will see to that!"

John West walked home to Carringbush, a good two miles, with vigour in his stride. He was considering the unlimited possibilities opened up by his acquaintance with Garside.

When the tote cases came before the court, Ryan and Cohen were tried first, and each given a month's imprisonment and fined a hundred pounds. They left the court resolved that the tote business, though profitable, was far too dangerous; they would be content, in future, to run a modest book in some secluded hotel.

Patrick Michael Aloysius Cummin (such was Scotch Paddy's full name) was tried separately from John West. In the witness box he gave long consideration to the many questions asked him; the magistrate threatened to declare him a hostile witness and charge him with contempt of court unless he answered more promptly.

Two men gave evidence that they had made bets at Cummin's Tea Shop and identified Paddy as one of its proprietors. Scotch Paddy was fined a hundred pounds, the absence of a prison term being attributable, John West felt certain, to the efforts of David Garside, who immediately announced his intention of appealing to a higher court.

In spite of his contacts at police headquarters, Garside had been unable to discover the pimps' whereabouts. He had suggested that John West have them followed when they left the court after the case against Scotch Paddy. Piggy and Cauliflower Dick carried out this task, and discovered that the witnesses were installed at a hotel in a provincial town, some hundred miles from

Melbourne. Next day the two pimps were approached by Paddy Cummin's brother, Danny, as thin as Paddy but very much quicker witted, and John West. The latter gave the two very frightened men twenty sovereigns each with a warning that they should "go away and lose themselves," because, "We know how to deal with pimps out Carringbush way."

An overflowing court witnessed sensational scenes when the case against John West began. He and David Garside noted apprehensively that only one of the Crown witnesses had taken the advice proffered; the other was present, sitting fearfully between two burly policemen.

The hearing hadn't proceeded far before a detective began to fire accusations of bribery at the defendant.

John West leapt to his feet. "It's a lie! A lie!" he shouted. Garside pulled him to his seat by the coat-tail, asked the Crown representative on what grounds these serious accusations were made, and began cross-examining the police witness. The informer very nervously told his story. David Garside, with admirable calm and assurance, denied the charges and asked: "You said this happened on Thursday or Friday of last week. Surely you remember which day it was."

The witness said he was not sure. He eyed John West as he spoke, and thought of the words: "We know how to deal with pimps. . ."

The case was then adjourned to enable the police to locate the other witness.

The Melbourne press reported this sensational hearing; but as to what occurred later in the case it had nothing to say, except the bare announcement of the result. The court reporters did not know the whole story; and what they did know they decided not to publish, after David Garside had suggested to John West that he "prevail upon them" to ignore the details.

The missing witness was never located. His partner was given a reminder that at Carringbush they *did* know how to deal with pimps – a reminder in the form of a bashing from Piggy, Cauliflower Dick and Sugar Renfrey. They waylaid him, appropriately enough, outside the Melbourne cemetery, and broke his arm across the iron rail fence before kicking him insensible.

After many adjournments, during which the magistrate was strangely reticent to enforce any inquiry into the peculiar reluctance of the two Crown witnesses, the case against John West was dismissed. Later, Paddy Cummin appealed successfully to the higher court.

"Three cheers for Jack West!"

"Hip! Hip! Hooray! Hip! Hip! Hooray! Hip! Hip! Hooray!"

As the drags passed Cummin's Tea Shop, the working men and women cheered spontaneously. They were going on a picnic and sports day; John West had donated the prizes for the sports events and supplied the refreshments. He often did this for factory picnics; and as often financed blackberry picking expeditions into the hills, twenty miles away. Many of the people in the drags were tote customers. He had gained a reputation for generosity among them, and thousands of other people in Carringbush and beyond.

He stood in front of the shop, arms folded, legs apart, wearing an expensive grey suit, and the inevitable black hat. He waved in response to the cheers, and the drags went on up Jackson Street.

The warmth of the afternoon sun gave him a feeling of wellbeing. The bad times had begun to lift after nearly a decade of despair. There was more employment, and the increased earnings of the workers meant increased profits for John West. He estimated that he was now worth fifty thousand pounds in property, cash and assets. David Garside should have been given much of the credit for his speedy accumulation of wealth and capital. Garside had explained to him that money would not grow while in the bank, you had to use it to get others to work for you; you had to invest it. John West, despite Garside's assurance, was suspicious of shares; he wanted to invest in things he could see and own himself, so he purchased houses – dozens of small houses, mainly in Carringbush. He bought them for as low as fifty pounds each, and many of them had already doubled in value, as property and land prices were showing signs of recovery. As well, he had invested in small businesses in Carringbush. If a man of ability wanted to go into business he would get a sympathetic hearing from Jack West, who "put up the money" in return for a fifty-one percent interest, which was "fair enough." He had even bought two hotels; one in the city itself, and one in Carringbush. These he used as agencies for the tote; their normal business was also very profitable. Dozens of barbers, in Carringbush and elsewhere, now acted as agents on a commission basis.

It pleased him to hear the workers cheer. He liked to be popular. His gambling establishment was fairly conducted; you got a fair go from Jack West, he was a man of his word and would always help a lame dog over a stile. He was a generous donor to sports clubs and charities.

When the drag disappeared over the rise he walked around the coachbuilder's corner to the back entrance of the tote. Groups of men and women stood on the corners and in the lane. He answered their greetings cheerfully. All around the block similar groups of people stood talking. The turnover of the tote had increased many times over; gamblers came from all over Melbourne and suburbs. Jackson Street trams were overloaded, especially in the early hours of Saturday afternoons.

The yard which John West entered was vastly different from the old backyard of Cummin's Tea Shop. The entrance was now through a trapdoor about seven feet in height and four feet wide inserted in a high hardwood fence, along the top of which were strung three strands of barbed wire. Above the trapdoor were the words WOOD AND COAL; and behind it were stacks of wood and piles of coal.

At the rear of this yard was another fence with a similar trapdoor and similar strands of barbed wire. This was the entrance to the tote yard itself. The yard was cunningly concealed. It had been created by shifting back the fences of the backyards of all the houses in the block, which John West now owned. The area so reclaimed was surrounded by a high fence with barbed wire entanglements along the top, and a trapdoor exit into every yard, plus three ladders reaching to the top of the fence at selected points. The houses had been "raffled" and each winning ticket carefully selected for a trustworthy tote employee, who promptly occupied "his" house rent-free.

Further ingenious measures had been taken to protect tote workers and patrons from the police. The betting establishment itself was now an elaborate affair. A long, roofed platform had been erected along the right-hand side of the yard, its floor about two feet above ground level. Three bars of two-inch piping were strung through the wooden pillars which supported the front of this shed. At the far end of the platform was a small enclosure of hardwood with a barred window in front at eye level. The back of this enclosure opened into the room behind the shop. A new trapdoor in the floor of the shop opened into an underground tunnel which linked the shop with the kitchen of a house in Bagville Street. The existence of this tunnel was known only to John West, and the tote employees who had laboured for months to complete it.

The wood-yard gate was guarded by Piggy and Cauliflower Dick, who identified every customer or had him vouched for. At the trapdoor into the tote yard itself, two repulsive-looking individuals carried out similar duties. At the right was a man named One-eyed-Tommy, whose left eye had been poked out in a street fight years before, leaving on his countenance the additional blemish of a horrible leer. One-eyed-Tommy had an assortment of criminal convictions, as had the man at the left of the gate, appropriately called The Ape; the latter's record included two years and a flogging for molesting a young girl, and two for assault and battery. Brawls were not uncommon, but these four worthies dealt mercilessly with offenders. They also took it by turns to guard the establishment at night, and intimidated recalcitrant punters who placed bets on the telephone and failed to meet their commitments promptly.

On the platform behind the bars, were four strangely attired men. They wore long black cloaks. Their heads were covered with black masks, in which holes were cut for the eyes and mouth, to make identification impossible. An Irish voice came from behind one of the masks, saying: "That double is gone, me boy, but you can have the favourite in the hurdle with Kitty in the sprint, and a mighty foine double that is. You don't want it? Well, don't say I didn't tell yer. Yer'll take Kitty with Firefly? Sure Firefly couldn't win if he started now, but I'm here especially to take yer money."

And similarly, above the hum of voices in the yard, the other masked men took bets, issued a ticket, and marked the bet on large printed boards on the wall behind them.

From the wall of the enclosure at the end of the platform, a sign looked down into the yard. It read:

A man is specially engaged to do the shouting and swearing that is required in this establishment. A dog is kept to do the barking. Our fighting man and chucker-out has won 75 prize fights and is a splendid shot with the revolver. An undertaker calls every morning for orders.

> *West's Tote,*
> *136 Jackson Street*
> *Carringbush.*

This message was written by Barney Robinson at John West's request that he put up a sign to stop some of the swearing and fighting. Below this sign was another, the import of which was clear to all:

The man who gives credit died yesterday.

The phones in the room behind the shop rang constantly. There, Joe West, Barney Robinson (working full time at the tote again; freedom from police interference having enabled him to convince his wife that he should return) and Flash Alec were taking starting price bets over the three phones.

John West still employed the cyclist to watch Police Headquarters in the city, and was spending fifty sovereigns a week protection money. In addition to Devlin, Brogan and other local policemen, he had no fewer than ten city detectives, introduced to him by David Garside, on his payroll.

Only once since these lavish precautions began had a suspected police agent got even to the gate of the tote. One-eyed-Tommy recognised him as a paid informer who worked for the police. The would-be pimp was followed home by Piggy and The Ape. That night they waylaid him and punched and kicked him to unconsciousness in obedience to John West's request that they "teach him a lesson, just in case." Only once had the tote been raided: by Constable Grieve without Sergeant Devlin's permission. He entered the tote yard one night by scaling the fence. All he got for his trouble was a tear in his uniform trouser-leg and a revolver bullet from Piggy, who was on guard duty. The bullet shattered Grieve's wrist, and he was discharged from the force on the ground that he was physically unfit. Ex-Constable Grieve departed from Carringbush forthwith, accompanied by his scared young wife. They had not been seen or heard of since; and good riddance, too, the gamblers reckoned.

The tote yard was crowded with men discussing prospects, studying the racing columns of daily papers and sporting journals and making investments. The air was charged with a tension of intermingled hope, fear, disappointment, exultation, desperation and excitement.

All are gripped by the hope of gain that prompts men – especially poor men – to gamble. Most of these are poor men; there a working man in moleskins who has come to make small bets for himself and his workmates; here a man with the wild gleam of desperation in his eyes, who pawned his children's shoes this morning to make a bet – he will lose; men as desperate as he always do. A few are not poor; that flashily dressed young man is a professional gambler here to put on an off the course commission: that sharp-featured man with the darting eyes is an "urger" who lives by attending the tote telling credulous people that he has a good tip – he persuades them to back a horse themselves and put a little on for him; as he gives a different tip to each person, he gets a few winners each day, and shows a profit. Those people in the queue, filing up to the barred window, are lucky punters who have a "divvy" to collect.

When John West came past The Ape and One-eyed-Tommy, the former said in a raucous voice with a tremor of fear in it: "I think there's a bloody pimp bettin' on the tote, Jack."

"That's right, Jack," added One-eyed-Tommy. "Says his name's Stacey. Looks like a nark, too."

"What did you let him in for?"

"He walked in the gate right next to one of the customers. I thought they were together," replied The Ape lamely. He had become lax of late, in common with the other gate and nit-keepers.

"Why can't you be more careful and do your job properly? I thought I told you not to let any strangers in, unless someone vouched for them."

"Yeh, I know that, Jack. But this bastard tricked me."

"Well, don't let him trick you again. If he comes back, keep him out!"

"He'll be back, Jack; he's got a divvy to collect."

"How do you know he's a nark?"

"Piggy recognised him when he was goin' out. Says he's been a shelf for years."

"Piggy would know. Why didn't he recognise him coming in? – that's what I'd like to know." John West was angry. "All I'm asking you to do is keep out strangers. Do it! Or you'll be out of a job. Looks like more trouble all through your bloody carelessness. If there's a raid over this, both of you will be in trouble."

John West went to his office in the shop, then a commotion began in the lane.

"You can't come in here!" Piggy shouted to a weak-faced, shabby man.

"Why can't I?" he answered, cowering back as Piggy stepped towards him, followed by Cauliflower Dick.

"'Cos we don't have police-pimps about 'ere, that's why. You're Stacey and you're a bloody nark!"

"I ain't a nark. Not me," Stacey protested fearfully, backing away. His little beady eyes darted this way and that.

They moved in closer to him. Piggy grabbed him by the shoulder. "I think there's someone who'd like to see you," he said.

"Who?"

"Jack West! He'll know what to do with a bloody pimp!"

At the mention of the name, Stacey's shifty eyes glinted with fear; he wriggled from Piggy's grip and ran headlong out of the lane.

Piggy made ponderously to follow, but Cauliflower Dick restrained him. "Let the bastard go. Let 'im go. And we betta not tell Jack, or there'll be a row."

Stacey ran into Jackson Street and rapidly traversed two or three hundred yards before he looked round and found that he was not being followed. He boarded a tram breathlessly. Bad enough not being able to collect me divvy, he thought; worse having Jack West after me. Wish I'd never let them traps talk me into this job.

After the last race, John West and several employees were in the shop finalising the day's transactions. Piggy and One-eyed-Tommy waited in the room adjoining to give him armed protection when he departed for home.

"How did them doubles get on today?" John West asked, looking up from counting coins.

91

"Matter a fact, we got hit again," answered Boney Bill, a new clerk.

"There's something wrong here. We keep some of the good doubles for ourselves and say they're gone; yet we got hit yesterday and today. Who ran them today?"

"Mick did."

"Where is he?"

"He went home early."

"Oh, did he? Let's have a look at those sheets."

He perused the doubles sheets with keen eyes.

"I think Michael has been acting suspiciously today," Flash Alec said. "I think he may depart for an unknown destination very soon."

"Don't be silly," Barney Robinson said, without conviction. "Mick wouldn't do a thing like that."

"Finish the sheets, Joe," John West said. "I'll be back in a minute. Piggy and Tommy, come with me."

O'Connell's furniture, except that from the kitchen, was stacked in an untidy heap in the backyard. Three iron bed-steads, from which the cream paint had chipped off here and there, revealing black spots; three dirty mattresses; the shabby remains of a lounge suite with horsehair showing through the leather in the chairs and sofa; a high chest of drawers with one leg replaced by a brick disguised with brown paper; a round three-legged table which leaned crazily to one side; an old suitcase and two boxes full of odds and ends; a wedding photo of Mick and his wife; sundry photos of the children and the in-laws of the family; a cracked mirror; and innumerable holy pictures – a large one of Jesus wearing a crown of thorns, prints of various saints, and one of the Virgin Mother with the baby Jesus in her arms.

Eating at the table in the kitchen sat six pallid children, all newly washed and dressed in ill-assorted garments which sufficed for Sunday best. Mick O'Connell himself was dressed in his only suit, which was too small for his rotund figure. He was pacing the floor, stopping every few seconds to peer into the gloom of the yard. The room showed shabby and smoke-stained in the dull light of the kerosene lamp. The mantelshelf was draped with newspaper in which a pattern had been cut.

Mrs. O'Connell sat at the end of the table, her back to the

dying fire, a plate of stew neglected in front of her, the baby at her breast. She was a thin little woman with wrinkled skin. Her long black hair straggled around her shoulders.

The devout practice of Catholicism seemed to compensate Mrs. O'Connell for the poverty and despair of her life. She attended Mass and Holy Communion every Sunday morning after confessing her sins on the Saturday evening – what she found in her blameless existence to report to the priest being a mystery to all who knew her. She took her religion more literally than ever the priests intended: she not only accepted all its dogmas, she also held an abhorrence for gambling and drink which was not shared by many members of the clergy or their flock. She was convinced that Mick sinned by working at the tote. Morning and evening she had offered up prayers to the Virgin Mary that Mick would reform and be saved, and on Sundays she would burn a candle for him after Mass at St. Joseph's. Through the week she constantly nagged at him – demanding, pleading that he take her and the children away where they could get a little bit of land and fresh air such as she had known as a young girl in the country.

She had become convinced that it was not God's will; then, when Mick told her, two days before, that they would go to Western Australia, she could scarcely believe her ears, or contain her joy. She knelt by the bed and thanked God and His Holy Mother. Yesterday Mick came home with fifty sovereigns in his pocket, and today with a further fifty; then her joy turned to deep suspicion. Where had he got the money? He had won it by picking a winning double, Mick told her.

In fact, Mick had picked several winning doubles, after the races were over. He had collaborated with three cronies to defraud John West. After each race, Mick would check if the winner had been coupled with the winners of all earlier races; if not, he would issue a ticket for that double to one of his friends.

"Mick! Where did you get that money?" Mrs. O'Connell asked for what seemed to be the hundredth time.

"I told you I picked a double yesterday and today, didn't I? Stop askin' questions like a bush lawyer," Mick answered as he walked to the door again and peered into the darkness which had wrapped itself around the yard and the house. "Heaven curse that carrier, said he'd be here at seven o'clock, the spalpeen. It's missing the train we'll be if he's not careful."

Jack West might check those sheets tonight, Mick was thinking and it's arrivin' here he'll be before we leave. Chalky white had replaced the redness of his face; shorn of his good humour, he was a pitiable, frightened man.

"Is everything packed up?" he asked, sitting down and picking at his food without relish.

"Yes, Mick, everything. There ain't much to take, God knows." She began to weep quietly.

"Don't cry, colleen," said Mick, with rare tenderness. "Don't cry, it's good and fine things will be, when we get to the West. There's gold there, lying on the ground, they say."

"I'm frightened, Mick, frightened! Where did you get that money?" She grasped his arm and he put it around her, trying to pacify her while the children looked on mutely.

"Don't cry, Mama," said one of the children. "We're going on a holiday. You don't cry when you're going on a holiday."

The sobs receded and she rested her head on Mick's shoulder.

A voice from the back door broke the silence: "Thinking of going away, are you, Mick?" it said menacingly.

Mick swung around. On the threshold stood John West, his face stern in the shadow under the brim of his hat.

"N – no, not me, Jack."

John West stepped forward into the room. Piggy and One-eyed-Tommy followed him silently. They stood behind him on either side, their hands on guns in coat pockets.

In a split second the atmosphere of the room was transformed. Mrs. O'Connell sat upright, covered her breast and held the baby close, her eyes wide with fear. One of the children whimpered and the others gazed uncomprehendingly. Mick's body sagged.

"Going to sleep out in the yard, then, are you?"

"N – no, Jack. No."

"N – no, Jack, no." John West imitated. "You're not going away, not much!" He stood a step forward and faced Mick aggressively. "Where's that money?"

"What money, Jack? I ain't got no money, you know that," Mick said huskily. He stood up awkwardly and moved behind his chair, his eyes glued to John West's face.

"Hand it over! Hand the money over!"

"I got no money, Jack. How could I save? – you only been payin' me two sovereigns a week."

John West walked around the table along the wall, and stood in front of Mick O'Connell, who cringed back near the fireplace.

One of the children began to cry. Mrs. O'Connell rose to pick it up. She viewed One-eyed-Tommy fearfully as she passed to and fro. His face showed like a horrible mask in the flickering light. She sat down again nursing the child and the baby.

"I said to give me the money! The money you pinched by rigging the doubles. Hand it over!"

Mick put his hands in his trouser pockets, without taking his unblinking eyes off the man who menaced him. He drew out two handfuls of golden sovereigns and handed them to John West, who passed them to Piggy.

"Count this!"

Presently there were sounds of a cart pulling into the backyard, and a raucous voice saying: "Whoa, there."

"So you weren't going away, eh? I'll give you twenty-four hours to get out of Carringbush, out of Victoria! And don't come back!"

"But I can't go, Jack. I got no money now."

"Only thirty-nine sovereigns here, Jack!" Cauliflower Dick interrupted.

"That all? I think he's got more. Search him!"

The two bodyguards closed around Mick in the corner, John West stepping back out of the way. They searched him roughly.

"Don't knock me new suit about, me boys," Mick said in a pathetic attempt to make light of the situation.

Suddenly Mrs. O'Connell said: "May God and His Holy Mother curse you, John West. You're the ruination of everyone who goes near you. It's very brave you are while your mob's around you."

John West turned towards her. She answered his gaze, then turned away. "Your husband is a good-for-nothing thief," he said.

"Mick a thief? It's you that made him a thief!"

"He's still got some on him, Jack," One-eyed-Tommy said. He handed a chinking canvas bag to John West.

"Go on, you devil, take it! Take it!" Mrs. O'Connell screamed. "I wouldn't keep your rotten money, robbed from all the poor people. Take it. Take it and go, and may God have mercy on your soul!"

Mick noticed his wife's words melting John West's rage a little. "How can I go away, Jack, if you take all the money?"

"Give him back the thirty-nine," John West said. "Let the thief keep it to get rid of him." He swung to Mick again. "Get away while you're lucky, and don't come back!"

As they walked out they passed the carrier at the backdoor. Before they had moved out of hearing, they heard Mrs O'Connell crying, and Mick saying to the carrier: "I've just had a visit from the divil himself and two of his fallen angels."

As John West walked back to the tote he said: "Keep this quiet. Not a word."

John West soon put Mick O'Connell out of his mind, and even forgot temporarily the visit of the suspected police spy for the tote, for tonight he would be alone with Nellie Moran.

He gave great care to his toilet and walked up Jackson Street tensed by a terrific physical longing; but with each stride he became less self-assured. Nellie was expecting him, he knew that; when he told her that he would bring the rent tonight, she had not objected, though she knew her mother would be out.

When he called with the rent he tried to make opportunities for friendly conversation with Nellie, but always her mother was there – friendly but not inviting intimacy. He had taken Nellie out five times, but always Mrs. Moran had accompanied them.

He was convinced by the way Nellie looked at him sometimes that she returned his love. Her mother was the trouble, he often told himself; she didn't want her daughter to marry him because of the tote. She had vacated her house next to the tote because, he suspected, she objected to it being used as an escape route. Well, she wasn't too proud to take the sovereign each month. Jack West had plenty of money; he could marry some rich, flash woman from Toorak if he wanted to. Money talked all languages. But he didn't want to marry a rich woman; he wanted to make his own money; and you couldn't control a rich woman. Anyway, he loved Nellie Moran, and he was going to marry her whether her mother liked it or not. Tonight was his chance. Tonight he would be alone with her, and he would kiss her – demand that she marry him.

Meanwhile, Nellie Moran awaited his arrival. The Morans now lived in two rooms behind a shop, further up Jackson Street towards the city, where they conducted a struggling business in ladies' clothing. Nellie sat by the fire sewing in the humble but homely kitchen. After her mother went out she had changed her dress and combed her hair. She looked most attractive with her hair swept high behind her head by two ornate combs, and her robust body tantalisingly outlined by a frock with a tight bodice.

Her heart was beating fast, her cheeks flushed. He was coming here tonight and she would be alone with him; the man with the mysterious eyes that seemed to have other eyes behind them looking at you so you couldn't look him straight in the face, or know what he was thinking. What was this fascination for John West that had possessed her in spite of her own inner voice and her mother's warnings? Was it love? Or did those eyes compel response to his silent courtship? Why shouldn't she love him, anyway? He was handsome, well dressed and rich. His body was lithe and strong. Why did something in her spirit hold back? Why did her mother tactfully but determinedly discourage the affair?

John West attracted yet repelled Nellie Moran. At times, she believed that he was the lover of whom she had dreamed since girlhood; at times she was vaguely afraid of him. She faced this evening with misgivings. She had done wrong in not telling her mother that John West would be calling in her absence.

Behind John West's shyness she sensed an indomitable force. He would make love to her tonight! Love of a different kind to that of the only other boy-friend she had had, whose subdued temperament merely demanded a restrained good-night kiss.

She waited with excitement mingled with fear and shyness. When the gate beside the shop clicked, her heart leaped in her bosom. Footsteps approached and a firm knock came to the door.

She opened the door.

"Oh, good evening, Mr. West," she said huskily.

"Good evening," he said, taking off his hat.

She stepped back and he entered the room.

"Do sit down," she said, and her voice was a whisper.

He put his hat on the table and sat down, his inscrutable eyes watching her. He took a bag from his pocket, selected a sovereign. "Here is the rent," he said.

She took the gold coin, placed it on the mantelpiece, then sat at the other side of the fire. She picked up her sewing, but her hands trembled so that she fumbled and pricked her finger with the needle.

"Oh," she said involuntarily, inspecting the finger as a ruby of blood oozed from the wound.

Swiftly John West moved to her side with a white handkerchief in his hand.

"Let me . . ." He said.

He held her hand, dabbing the hurt finger.

The warm vitality of her nearness possessed him, destroying his hesitation. He dropped the handkerchief, gripped her shoulders and pressed his lips firmly to hers.

She tried to catch her breath. Her heart pounded like a trip-hammer. She thrilled to the passion that surged from him.

At last, she pushed him away, rising to her feet.

"No, Mr. West, we . . ."

"Not Mr. West – John. Call me John, Nellie – I love you."

He embraced her savagely. For a moment she repulsed him, then her body fell limp and she surrendered her warm lips. He kissed her lips hungrily, then her cheeks, her eyes, her neck. His long-pent-up passion flooded in a frenzy. He fondled her awkwardly.

"No! No, John!" she said weakly, stiffening her body.

His lips came back to hers and she relaxed completely, returning his passion.

He was overwhelmed by a terrific feeling of love, possession, mastery, power.

"Oh, John, we mustn't," she whispered when he released her lips.

He held her head in his hands, looking at her flushed cheeks, her moist eyes, her red lips.

"I love you!" he said urgently. "I love you, Nellie. I will buy you jewels and pretty dresses, a big mansion to live in, horses to ride. You love me too. We will be married!"

"Oh, John. I think I love you. Oh, dear, this must be love!"

He embraced her again. "This *is* love," he said, and kissed her savagely.

This time she fought him off.

"John, John, please. We mustn't. We must wait. It isn't right."

He regained control of himself. He had achieved his purpose. He sat down. "I'm sorry," he said.

She tidied her dishevelled hair.

"We'll have a cup of tea," she said, shifting the kettle to the centre of the stove.

"Yes," he said. "A cup of tea. I'll wait till your mother comes home, and ask her permission for us to become engaged."

She made no reply. She was trembling and faint. Her mind was a turmoil.

There were three people in John West's new jinker which rocked along Jackson Street on the following Tuesday afternoon. John West was driving, and on the opposite end of the seat, Mrs. West sat. She was weeping. The man between them might have been old, and he might have been young. His clothes were new and of good quality, but he wore them awkwardly. His walrus moustache was snow white. His shoulders were hunched, his head was bowed so that the brim of his black hat concealed his eyes. Twelve years before he had been taken to jail where he had languished ever since. During his first week in jail he had been flogged fifty times across the back with a cat-o'-nine-tails. The man was Arthur West. His brother and mother had called for him at the jail, and were driving him home.

Presently Mrs. West took Arthur's hand and said softly: "Arthur. You are coming home, now. They can do you no more harm. We will look after you." She had spoken so, many times but John West had remained silent, gazing at the road ahead.

Arthur West raised his head, looked at his mother, then at his brother. His eyes were deep-set, and seemed to turn not gradually but swiftly, like those of a doll, and to stare after the same manner when still. They were leaden eyes, without life. They were the eyes of a man whose spirit has been frozen with cold hatred aimed at no one in particular – against nothing in particular. They reflected that insensitivity to feeling which often separates the man who has been flogged from other men, and leads him, no matter what he may have been before, to crimes of violence.

Arthur West looked again from his mother to his brother, then lowered his head without speaking. Release from prison did not bring him freedom: at the jail gates he had to resist an urge to run back and be locked in his cell again. Now he felt like a man stranded in a strange, unfriendly land.

The weals on Arthur West's back remained, and so, too, did

99

the bitter memory of the flogging. From the moment the death sentence had been commuted to twelve years and fifty lashes, he could think only of the flogging that was to come. His shame at the crime he had committed passed away. He was to be flogged! He lost his appetite and sank into a daze from which nothing could rouse him. All he could do was lie on his bed and ponder on the dreadful ordeal which lay ahead of him. He was afraid to sleep, because always he dreamed of the lash and woke up screaming, sweating and trembling with fear. The day before he was to be flogged he decided to kill himself. He made a crude noose out of his blanket, placed it around his neck and tied the other end to the bars of his cell, but his courage failed him. Life is too dear, even for a man who is to receive fifty lashes.

Next day two grim-faced warders came and took him away. He sagged between them, and they supported him as his leaden feet dragged him along the cold, stone corridor. As they passed one cell, a deep voice said: "Never mind, son, it will soon be over." Arthur West looked behind and saw the speaker's face: the face of the last man that Arthur West was ever to feel any loyalty or gratitude towards in all his lifetime.

They took him to the hospital, where a doctor examined him to ensure that he was fit to be flogged. Then they dragged him, stripped to the waist, into the yard and trussed him with leather fetters to the whipping triangle. Like a man in a nightmare he heard the jail governor read his sentence. Then a hush fell over the place, for as long as seemed forever, until a crisp voice shouted: "Look to your front! One!" The first lash seemed to cut his back in halves; and a cold hate welled up in him, that such suffering and humiliation could be inflicted by man on man.

He swore violent vengeance. The blows rained down in tune with the insistent counting voice; and his body, with each blow, slowly lost its rigid tenseness until it relaxed and only the trusses kept him from collapsing to the ground at the flagellator's feet. Then he became insensible to the terrible pain; only vaguely could he feel the blood trickle down his back and drip on to the ground. Before the lashing was finished he slipped into unconsciousness. Back in his cell he came to life numbly, and was seized with a morbid curiosity to see the result of the flogging. He slowly contorted his head back over one shoulder, and fainted at the sight of a mass of raw flesh. Consciousness returned with a realisation that a yawning gulf now separated him from his fellow men.

Twelve years in jail had not mellowed Arthur West's bitter hatred; time had driven it deep into his soul where no power on earth could seek it out and remove it.

As they neared home, Mrs. West sensed his bewilderment. "Don't be afraid, my son. You are coming home now, and we will look after you," she sobbed.

They arrived at the house late in the afternoon. Mrs. West dried her tears and hurried indoors to prepare a special meal – long planned. She fussed over Arthur as she walked to and from the stove. Joe and her husband came in and greeted Arthur with embarrassment.

As a celebration, the meal was a failure. Arthur's sullen bitterness pervaded the room, and his father's remarks about it being good to be free and home again, did not help.

The meal over, the three sons retired to the bedroom, where John West gave Arthur details of the tote enterprise which his brother found hard to understand. Arthur sat on a new bed which had been crammed into the room. He listened to John silently. Soon conversation flagged. They lapsed into an embarrassed silence. Arthur stroked his white moustache, then rubbed his hand over his close-cropped white hair. He seemed to be pondering his brother's remarks. Suddenly he said: "You've got influence. All right, Jack, you can help me get Dick out of there."

"Who's Dick?"

"Dick Bradley. He's my cobber." Arthur West seemed to come to life. "You used to know him at school. We'll get him out. We got it all planned. We'll show the bastards!"

John West was startled by the ferocity of his brother's voice. "All right," he said, "we'll get him out. But remember: you work for me, understand. Take my orders, and you'll keep out of trouble. Remember that. Take my orders, and work for me in the tote."

And Arthur West replied: "All right. Long as you help me get Dick Bradley out. We got it all planned. We'll show the bastards."

They prepared to retire for the night. His brothers noticed that Arthur West was careful not to bare his back to them while undressing.

John West was driving the jinker. The man beside him was Danny Cummin.

Their night journey was an important one. Two Saturdays before, a drag had driven down Jackson Street at headlong speed. As the two horses skidded and snorted to a halt near the back lane, ten policemen and two plain-clothes detectives alighted and dashed up the lane into the wood-yard. In the ensuing confusion they arrested Boney Bill and two others. John West heard the cry of "Traps!" while seated at his desk in the shop. A few minutes later he was sitting in the kitchen of a house in the next block, whence he had gone by way of the underground tunnel.

After the accused were bailed out, David Garside ascertained that Arthur Stacey had been the spy in the case; that he lived in a house in a back street in Carlton, where the detectives were keeping him in hiding.

John West and Daniel Cummin had first seen Stacey on the Friday night after the raid and offered him ten sovereigns to swear in court that he had never been in the tote in his life, and had never made a statement to the police that he had been. They gave a very frightened and confused Stacey two sovereigns on account, and he agreed to think the matter over. They visited him again on the Saturday and Sunday, and he had hedged suspiciously.

The horse's shoes clip-clopped on the metal road as the vehicle made its way through the city to the outskirts of Carlton. Presently John West broke the long silence: "I don't like the way he's acting," he said. "A pimp's a pimp – and he might swing back to the police."

"Yair," Cummin replied; "he's frightened of us, but he's probably frightened of the police too. He's a shifty little rat; never know what he might do."

"He'd better not try to trick me, or he'll be sorry."

"It's no use letting him stall any longer. We'd better fix up everything tonight."

"Yes, and we'll get him outside. I wouldn't put it past him to set a trap for us. We'll offer him that holiday, too."

They both laughed. John West had arranged with One-eyed-Tommy to pretend to take Stacey on a holiday to the seaside, and to "shanghai" him on to a boat bound for Europe.

While they still laughed, Arthur Stacey, dressed in a shabby blue suit, was in earnest conversation with two young detectives named Williams and Armfield. The detectives were seated on an old leather sofa, while Stacey sat on the only chair in the dim room.

"They should be here at any minute," Williams, a tall, slim man, was saying. "We'd better hide, now. No more funny business from you, remember."

"Don't make a noise, for Gawd's sake; they say West carries a gun," Stacey whimpered.

"He won't get a chance to use it," said Armfield, who was a fat man and incredibly short for a detective. "Anyway, we offered you a gun, and you wouldn't take it. Now don't forget, we'll be outside the window, listening through the broken glass."

"And remember what I told you," said Williams, "don't be too quick to agree, so we'll get plenty of evidence. If you mull this up, look out!"

The detectives retired to their chosen vantage point outside the window.

A few minutes later, Arthur Stacey answered a knock at the front door. As he opened the creaking door, he stepped to one side, as though expecting to be struck down by an irate representative of the Jackson Street tote, but all that confronted him was the benign enough countenance of Daniel Cummin.

"Would you come out? Jack West's over the road in the jinker."

"No, I can't go out, I'm too bad. This business has worried me that much I'm sick. Sick as a dog." Stacey's pallid face did not belie his words.

Cummin hesitated a moment, then went away and returned a few minutes later with John West. Stacey led them into the shabby front room where all three sat down in the light of a fluttering kerosene lamp, John West and Cummin taking the place of the two detectives on the sofa and Stacey resuming his chair.

John West looking round the room cautiously, asked: "They been here since?"

"They was 'ere last night. I told 'em I'd say what I had to say in the box."

"That's right, say what you like to the bastards," interposed Cummin.

"You look sick. You need a holiday. Why don't you go away to Queenscliff until the case is over? I'll pay all expenses."

"I can't. I can't go. I wouldn't have a hope."

"Well, have you found out if there are any other witnesses?" John West asked. He was watching Stacey suspiciously.

"No. It's hard. It's very hard."

"Well, keep tryin'. It's very important. No use you saying the right things if there's someone else giving evidence against us."

Stacey glanced apprehensively over his shoulder towards where the detectives crouched outside the window trying to take notes in the darkness. John West and Cummin were alert, the detectives were excited, and Stacey was sweating, his hands clasped in front of him. He seemed to be shrinking up with fear and trepidation.

John West then leaned forward earnestly. "Here's all you've got to do. When you get in the box I want you to swear that you were never in the tote yard – they can't prove you were – and deny that you made a statement. They can't twist you in the box, you're a good witness." The studied compliment was lost on Stacey, who was too frightened to have his ego revived. "This will give Williams a nasty knock, won't it?"

"Y-yes," said Stacey joylessly.

"Now, get this clear. You deny you've been in the yard or that you made a statement. Then say you got those two tickets from a boy at the corner of Jackson and Silver Streets. If they ask you what boy, say a boy named Joe, who said it was a winning ticket – say you gave him a shilling for it and then went down to the wood-yard where he said you could collect. Then say that when you went to the wood-yard you saw a young man who said: "There's no totalisator here." Of course the young fellow referred to will be in the court, and you can say: "Yes, that's him." They will ask you if there were any customers in the yard and you say: "Yes, there were two or three buying wood." When they question you in the box say you got into a temper because you didn't get your money and you went away and gave the tickets to Williams and made a statement to him; but you swear that the statement was not true."

"What am I going to get for all this?"

"I told you before," John West answered. "A tenner if you swear up well and twenty if you get my men off."

"It's worth more than that, isn't it?"

"Oh, you haven't got much to say. It's very easy."

Why don't they come in, Stacey was thinking. "I've only got two sovereigns up to date, when do I get the rest?"

"I never went back on my word to any man!" John West was incensed. "You can trust me; my name is a household word. I said I'll give you a tenner, and I'll give you a tenner; and twenty if the men get off." He put his hand in his pocket and gave Stacey six sovereigns – something he had not intended to do until the man had proven his 'good faith' in court. "There's six more; I'll give you the balance after the case is over."

Stacey took the coins, and John West and Cummin prepared to leave. "And there's more where that came from," said John West. "Remember what we told you. We'll be back tomorrow night with final instructions."

At that moment the window shot up and Detective Williams, with pointed revolver, leapt into the room followed by Armfield.

"You won't be back tomorrow night or any other night. You're under arrest, the two of you!"

Before the nonplussed visitors could make any attempt to escape, the detectives had placed handcuffs on their wrists.

"What's this about? What am I being arrested for?" exclaimed John West, badly shaken.

"You will be charged with attempting to suborn and persuade Arthur Stacey to commit perjury. We've been outside listening to everything you said tonight. Your reign is over, West. You'll do time for this. Five years in jail for you two!"

John West tugged at the handcuffs. "You'll pay for this, Stacey, you bloody pimp! You'll pay for this!"

"No one will pay for anything, except you," Williams said. "Give me that money, Stacey. Come on, you two."

John West and Cummin quietly accompanied the detectives into the street leaving Stacey to face yet another restless night. They were taken to the Carlton watchhouse in John West's own jinker.

Shortly after midnight Mr. and Mrs. West were rudely awakened by a loud thumping on the front door.

Mrs. West sat up in bed. "Who's there?" she called.

"The police here! Open up!"

She hastened out of bed and threw an old coat over her nightgown. Her husband stirred, rubbed his eyes and sat up. "What's the trouble?" he asked sleepily.

"It's the police, God help us!"

Joe came out of the boys' bedroom, but she hustled him back to bed and went to the door. She returned in a few minutes and said to her husband: "John has been arrested – him and young Cummin from the solicitor's office. Something about bribing a witness. You're to go to Carlton and bail him out. The money is in his room. Heaven protect us!"

She spoke in a resigned tone, as if about the death of someone who had been ill a long time.

Mr. West got out of bed, took a swig from a wine bottle which stood on the dressing table, and began to dress without commenting. He was now something of a reformed character: he drank more guardedly, and was agreeable about the house in order to curry favour with his most prosperous son.

"I'd hoped to the Mother-a-God we were free of this kind of worry. With poor Arty out at last, it looks as if John will be in jail now. Oh, why doesn't he stop this business?"

"They'll never get young Jack in jail; he's too clever."

"But this seems serious. Very serious. I want no cause to be worryin' and weepin' for a son in jail any more, after these last twelve long years with Arty away."

"Stop worryin', woman; they can't put Jack in jail; he's got too much influence. He'll be home in an hour; don't start cryin' for God's sake."

When he had departed, Mrs. West lay down on top of the bed clothes, still wearing the coat over her nightdress. She began to weep. She had tried to resign herself to John's activities. Now she found herself trying hard to be bitter against the police. Why did they harass her boys? But she answered herself with a more disturbing question. Why did her boys do things that brought them to the shadow of prison?

Mrs. West's hair was snow white. She was barely fifty-five, but she looked and felt much older. A month of worry and poverty can age the human body and spirit more quickly than a happy year, and she had known countless months of worry and poverty. Her weeping continued – the quiet, steady weeping of a person to whom weeping can bring no relief – until her husband and John came home in the early hours of the morning.

"John! John! Whatever's the matter?" she called softly to her

106

son, and she heard him answer from the boys' bedroom: "Everything will be all right. Go to sleep; it's late."

But for her, no sleep was possible – only worry, bitterness and soft weeping until dawn.

John West, too, lay awake; at times contemplating with dread the prospect of being sent to prison; at times probing the depths of his mind for a way out. Like all men who live outside the law, he despised and feared police spies. In Arthur Stacey, he now saw all that was evil and despicable. Stacey would suffer for his treachery; he must be defeated and punished. A savage desire for revenge against Stacey dominated his mind as dawn broke.

He got up early, ate breakfast silently and left the house. Arty followed him to the front gate; this was the furthest he had ventured out of doors since his release. "What's the trouble, Jack? Can I 'elp yer?"

"Me and the fella from the solicitor's office – he's our cousin really – we were arrested for bribing the bloody pimp who made bets on the tote before the raid."

"They might jug you for this, mightn't they?" Arthur said. "The pimp'll be the main evidence against yer and against the blokes that were caught in the tote raid, won't he?"

"Naturally."

Arthur West seemed to consider the matter. He was in his shirt sleeves. His white hair was beginning to grow; he was trying to educate it to comb back, but it stood up straight. He stroked his white moustache thoughtfully, then said with great intensity: "Why don't yer kill the pimpy bastard? Dead men tell no tales."

John West started, and studied him for a moment. "Oh, we'll get out of it, all right," he said, trying to affect a careless confidence. "I'm going to see Garside, my solicitor." He liked very much to refer to Garside as 'my solicitor.' "Tell Mum I'll be home for dinner."

He walked into the city, and found Garside seated behind the big desk in his office reading a morning paper.

"Well, Mr. West. We *are* in trouble," Garside greeted him. He always said "We are in trouble," or "We will win this case," or "we" this or "we" that, when speaking to his clients. He found this increased their confidence in him. "I read all about it in the press. Very clumsy, Mr. West, very clumsy, if you don't mind my thus observing. A very obvious trap indeed. You must see Stacey again and do a better job of it."

"He'll be hard to find now, I'll bet."

"Well, you'd better find him, Mr. West. Or you and my best clerk will be the guests of Her Majesty for anything up to five years."

"But I thought you said you had influence with the magistrates?"

"Aha, Mr. West, but this time we will be dealing with a judge," Garside rejoined, arising and beginning to pace the room. "This case will go from the Carlton Court to the Supreme Court. Now, judges are different. There are fewer of them and their salaries are higher. But I daresay if we are fortunate in having a co-operative judge appointed to the case, we may be able to arrange something. Of course, it will cause an even stiffer rise in my fee, than in the case of a magistrate."

His voice rose and fell musically. He raised his bushy eyebrows. "But, Mr. West, even if we are fortunate in the judge we encounter, we will need to make it easy for him to cooperate. They are not prepared to risk any scandal. Of course, Mr. West, I prefer a case where all are on their mettle – the judge, the police, the witnesses, and the jury, if any. Then it is a trial of strength, a great battle of tactics where the advocate may give full play to his powers of oratory and mastery of subtle finesse. Ah, how I wish all cases were of that variety." He shook his head sadly. "Alas, it is my business to defeat the law on behalf of my clients. But I am digressing. You can see, young man, that whether the judge proves – er – co-operative or not, you must again seek out Arthur Stacey."

"But even if we find him, he might sell us out again."

"Mr. West, a pimp almost invariably becomes what he is because he is afraid of the police. He accepts the pittance the police offer, not only for pecuniary gain, but out of fear that they will again arrest him. But, Mr. West, just as friend Stacey has been intimidated or bribed by the police he can also be intimidated or bribed by you. He is for sale to the strongest, and to the highest bidder." Garside uttered a deep sigh. "Sometimes, Mr. West, I can almost feel sorry for Stacey and his kind. But we cannot let sentiment interfere with necessity. I suggest you find Stacey, and, if bribery fails, try intimidation."

"Intimidation? I'll kill the little bastard!" John West said savagely. Garside looked at him quizzically. I believe you would, he thought.

"How can I find him, do you think? Could we follow the detectives, and get at him that way?"

"Aha, an astute suggestion, Mr. West. I shall find the address of one of the good detectives at once." Garside reached for the phone with a graceful flourish.

The long and the short of John West's serious trouble, Detectives Williams and Armfield, were up before dawn on the following Monday morning.

They had joined the force less than a year before at the request of the Chief Commissioner of Police, and although he was a reticent old man, they gathered that he could not depend on many of his detectives. They were to work under his direct instructions, and maintain secrecy, especially from certain of their associates. When the outcry against the gambling mania in Carringbush and elsewhere grew noisier, the Chief Commissioner instructed them to raid the tote.

David Garside obtained bail for the tote employees and had their cases adjourned for a month. John West and Cummin were due to appear before the Carlton Court next week.

Williams and Armfield were honest and believed that they should do their duty without fear or favour. Since arresting West and Cummin, they had shifted Stacey to the front room of an empty house not far from his previous residence. They told no one of his whereabouts except the Chief Commissioner and the reliable constables who guarded him day and night. Stacey was a stupid fellow, so they had written out the evidence they wanted him to give and he was endeavouring to memorise it. Stupidity wasn't the only drawback with Arthur Stacey: the fellow was an arrant coward – his whole being was now gripped in a palsy of fear, and the detectives were worried that, unless the hearing of the cases was soon commenced, he would be totally incapable of testifying.

As they turned into the street where Stacey was living, the early dawn glimmered. A milk cart turned into the street, and they heard the rattling of cans and billies as the driver ran in and out front gates.

109

Presently Williams looked down at his tubby associate. "Did that milkman go into the house where Stacey is? There's no need for Stacey to order milk. We supply his food and drink, and God knows he uses very little of it, the way he is."

"That's funny. He did go in there, all right. What's the constable on the gate doing?"

They walked more briskly.

Stacey was lying in bed listening to the possums in the ceiling and the rats on the floor, exhausted, afraid and cursing the day he had become a police informer. Presently he heard a knocking on the front door, and a soft voice say: "Are you there, Stacey?"

Stacey trembled in the bed, but made no answer. The knocking and the voice came again, then a silence, after which Stacey heard what sounded like someone pushing something under the door. Then he heard footsteps hurry from the verandah towards the gate. He got out of bed and lit the lantern with shaking hands. He peeped out the window and saw a milkman run out the gate, past the unsuspecting constable, as the two detectives arrived at the spot. He heard them say something to the milkman, who ignored them, leapt into the cart and drove up the street at breakneck speed. Stacey went to the front door, lantern in hand. He saw a note on the floor and picked it up.

The detectives entered the house to find Stacey standing near the bed shaking like a leaf. His dirty nightshirt hung loosely, his cheeks were like shadowy little holes, and his eyes were threatening to fall back into his head.

"Who was that?" Armfield demanded.

"I d-don't know. I heard someone knock. I got outa bed, but they ran away."

"What have you got behind your back?"

"N-nothin'."

"Come on," Williams interrupted. "What have you got in your hand?"

Stacey backed away a little. "Nothin'. Just a bita paper."

"Come on, give it to me!" Williams stepped forward and towered over Stacey.

Stacey handed a piece of paper to him hesitantly, and Williams picked up the lantern and read the few words awkwardly scrawled in pencil: BEWARE IF YOU GIVE EVADUNCE AGAINST JACK WEST YULE BE SORRY.

"Go and tell that constable he's to let no on in here," Williams said to Armfield.

"Who was it?" Stacey asked.

"I don't know. I didn't get a look at him." Williams was lying. He had seen the milkman's face; it had a horrible leer about it, and one of the eyes was a gaping red circle. "Get dressed," Williams added. He noticed that Stacey was trembling convulsively and uttering jerky, sobbing noises. "Pull yourself together, man. I'll light the fire and cook you some bacon and eggs, and, for goodness' sake, eat it. You've hardly eaten a thing for a week."

When John West said to David Garside that he would murder Arthur Stacey, he was merely using a drastic term to give vent to his anger. He had spoken without pre-consideration; but as the day of the trial of himself and Daniel Cummin came nearer, the idea grew on him. The interests and lives of other people meant little to him unless they contributed to his power. At first it startled him: that he could cold-bloodedly decide to murder a man, to snuff out a life like a candle. Then he found that the decision quieted his seething rage. Like the transgressor who finds rest from mental turmoil by deciding to confess, John West could find rest from rage only by planning reprisals against those who defied him.

He would not murder Stacey himself: proximity to violence still struck fear in him. He did not need to do it himself. Several of his 'mob' would be ready and willing to dispose of Stacey. Piggy, for instance, and One-eyed-Tommy and The Ape; yes, and Arty – he was convinced now that Arty had meant every word he said when he suggested killing Stacey.

But since One-eyed-Tommy's audacious visit, Stacey had been shifted again and they couldn't find him, let alone murder him. Unless Garside could influence the judge or achieve a legal miracle (the latter, Garside assured him, was by no means an impossibility), prison and ruin stared John West in the face.

He knew that Nellie Moran and her mother were shocked at his arrest on such a serious charge. Just as well he had got the old girl to agree to the engagement before it all happened, he was thinking when he paid them a visit the day before the trial. Since the arrest, Nellie seemed to be vaguely afraid of him, but neither she nor her mother said anything about breaking off the engagement. Nevertheless, Mrs. Moran chaperoned them wherever they went and, on the few occasions they were alone, Nellie did not renew her initial passion: it would be a sin to go any further than kisses, she told him. He chafed under his frustration, and vowed that he would overcome Mrs. Moran's objections to short engagements, and get Nellie into bed with him.

He found them in the kitchen. Mrs. Moran was ironing. The bell in the shop rang and Nellie went to answer it.

"And how is your trouble getting along at all?" Mrs. Moran said. "You must be a worry to your guardian angel."

"I'm my own guardian angel."

"My God, what a heretic you are. Have you been able to do anything with that spalpeen Stacey?"

"No. I can't get near him."

"I wonder would he be a Catholic?" Mrs. Moran said thoughtfully, then added with emphasis: "God forbid!"

John West sat bolt upright. "Yes! I wonder if he is! Might be. I never thought of that."

Mrs. Moran noted his interest. "We Catholics must stick together, you know. And if Stacey just happened to be a Catholic, surely if you saw him, or had the priest see him, he may drop the case."

"He might at that," John West answered. Whether he's a Catholic or not, he thought, a priest is about the only person who could get near him – if I could get one to do the job. John West knew little or nothing about priests. To him they were men out of this world. He held them in awe, and could not bring himself to confess his sins to them, much to the disappointment of Nellie and her mother. All he knew was that the Carringbush parish priest, old Father Logan, treated him with great deference and often obtained money from him for church charities.

Mrs. Moran ceased her work and leaned on the iron. "I am president of the Women's Sodality at St Joseph's and a friend of the Archbishop of Ballarat himself, who used to be a priest here in Carringbush. And Father Logan is often after callin' in here for a cup of tea with Nellie and me." She spoke with some pride, then continued with the air of a person who has made a doubtful decision after long deliberation. "Father Logan is a great friend of mine, and it happens that he is also a friend to Father Carroll, who is one of the priests in the Carlton parish. Now, Father Carroll is a hard case, 'tis true – he likes his little drink and his little bet on the horses – but's he's a fine and pious priest. If you were to see Father Logan, and he was to see Father Carroll, and Father Carroll were to see Stacey, then you never know what might be arranged. Stacey might just happen to be a Catholic, though God forbid!''

John West left the house immediately to call on Father Logan at the Presbytery.

Next afternoon, Arthur Stacey was surprised when one of his protectors ushered a fat, middle-aged priest into the room and departed reverently.

''I am Father Carroll, my son. I understand that you were baptised in the Church, so I have obtained permission to see if you are in need of priestly aid or guidance.''

Stacey sat on the bed and offered the solitary chair to the priest, who sat down ponderously. Although Stacey was by no means religious, the presence of a man with his collar back-to-front was an awe-inspiring ordeal. ''N-no, Father, I'm quite all right, thank you all the same,'' he said, but his abject appearance belied his words.

''You have been neglectful of your duties for many years (may God forgive you). Nevertheless, I understand that you are of the faith.''

''That's right, Father,'' Stacey said eagerly. ''And I'm goin' to start goin' to Mass and the sacraments again, when all this trouble is over.''

''God bless you, my son,'' answered the priest, turning his eyes upwards to heaven as though in thanksgiving that a wayward sinner was about to repent. ''Speaking of the – er – little bit of trouble. Did you know that both West and Cummin are of the faith?''

''No, I didn't know, Father; true, I didn't.''

The priest looked over his shoulder furtively and lowered his voice. ''Well, my son, did you know that the two detectives who have caused you all this trouble are a couple of Orangemen? – Freemasons, you know.''

''N-no. I didn't!''

''Well, they are, the poltroons. Now, is it a just thing you are doing to have helped a couple of Orangemen to get young West and Cummin, both Catholics, into such serious trouble?''

"W-well, I never thought of it that way, Father.''

"No, my son, we all act rashly at times. But, now that you know, you would be doing no more than your duty if you denied the whole story in court, and got a couple of Catholic gentlemen out of this serious mess.''

"But that'd be perjury, wouldn't it, Father? That'd be a sin.''

"No, my son. You need tell no lies. Just say that the whole thing was a conspiracy against West and Cummin, which in God's name it was. Then you'll be telling no lies. Just say that, and no more.''

"But if I change me evidence, Father, I'll get into trouble, meself.''

"No, you won't, me boy. I'll see to that,'' promised Father Carroll, rather rashly. "John West's business is not so bad, you know: it really should be legal, instead of all this nonsense about raids and witnesses.''

"You're sure I won't get into no trouble if I switch me evidence?''

"I am sure, my son. As I said before, all you've got to say is that the whole thing is a conspiracy against West and Cummin.''

"All right, Father, I'll do it. I'll just say that the whole thing was a conspiracy against West and Cummin and me too, for that matter.''

As Father Carroll walked to the door, Stacey arose and grasped his arm. "Does West know where I am?''

"He won't be troubling you as long as you do what I tell you.''

"I will, Father. You tell West I'll swear up well!''

Arthur Stacey certainly did "swear up well.'' During the preliminary hearing in the Carlton Court, he was hardly in the witness box when he blurted out: "This thing is a conspiracy against Mr. West, the other bloke, and meself. There's not four words of truth in it all!''

After a short hearing the case went to the Supreme Court. David Garside was in brilliant form. The court was packed to the walls, mainly with tote patrons who had come to hear John West carry out his promise to "show the traps a thing or two,'' and Garside treated them to great entertainment. He challenged twenty men before the jury was finally empanelled. With his wig wobbling up and down threatening to fall to the floor, he strutted, gesticulated, and declaimed like a Shakespearian actor. He cross-examined Williams and Armfield with ruthless skill.

The inexperienced detectives were soon contradicting themselves. When Garside trapped Armfield into stating that he had taken detailed written notes in the dark while he listened to the accused bribing Stacey, when only half an hour before Williams had said that they wrote out approximately what was said afterwards, he turned triumphantly to the Judge and said: "I ask you, Your Honour, to declare these men to be contradictory witnesses." His Honour didn't need to be asked anything really, for he had promised David Garside that he would do everything he could to influence the jury, providing the evidence was not too utterly damning against the accused. In return he was to get four hundred sovereigns.

John West sat beside Danny Cummin at Garside's table near the front of the court. His only worry was the jury: it had not been "fixed." Garside had assured him that he could read their minds, and that after he was finished challenging, the jury would be fit to re-try the notorious murderer, Deeming. John West kept studying the twelve men who sat in two rows listening to the proceedings. Maybe he would get a chance to bribe some of them yet, he was thinking.

When Arthur Stacey was called, he entered the witness box, repeated the oath, then said: "This thing is a conspiracy against Mr. West, the other bloke and meself! There's not four words of truth in the whole thing." That was all he had been told to say, and he got it in good and early.

The court rocked with laughter. When this had died down, Stacey added gravely: "I've been sick, I have. I've been losing weight ever since." The truth of this last statement was so obvious that a roar of laughter even greater than the first broke out, and His Honour threatened to clear the court.

The Crown Prosecutor questioned Stacey searchingly, and he started to wilt and stammer, until John West began to fear that he might blurt out the whole story. David Garside kept leaping to his feet and objecting to every second question. Stacey admitted that John West had given him the sovereigns while the detectives were waiting outside the door; but, he declared, after much stammering, the money had been paid to him in return for his promise to endeavour to find out the names of other witnesses, if any.

Cross-examining Stacey for the defence, Garside asked a question which enabled the little man to repeat his conspiracy speech. Then Garside asked if the detectives had tried to influence his evidence. Stacey said that they had, after casting a worried look in their direction.

"And did they write out your evidence for you?"

"They did."

"Then why did you not use their evidence? Did you refuse to use it because it was not true?"

"That's right, because it was not true," Stacey answered; then he repeated like a parrot: "The whole thing is a conspiracy against Mr. West, the other bloke and me."

The court adjourned until two o'clock the next afternoon. Back at his office David Garside said: "There is no necessity whatsoever to run the risk of approaching any of the jury, Mr. West. Save your money! It's bad enough that we wasted money on the judge. After my final address, no court on earth will find you guilty."

And so it proved to be. Summing up, the Judge said it did seem strange that the accused should give eight sovereigns to a total stranger to accomplish an indefinite job. But, His Honour stressed, the detectives acted foolishly. Even were they telling the truth, anything more ridiculous than the course they had pursued could not be conceived. They had made three copies of evidence and rehearsed it with Stacey. They had explained that they were merely anxious to keep to the exact truth. Either their explanation was coloured, His Honour pointed out to the jury, or the whole story was a deliberate concoction of lies. If indeed it were lies, then the motive must be that the detectives were trying to destroy the accused for the sake of promotion. If this were the case, His Honour observed gravely, then the police system was rotten to the core. However, he concluded, it was for the jury to decide for themselves.

The jury didn't take long to return a verdict of "Not Guilty."

John West left the court, surrounded by a group of admirers, temporarily grateful to Arthur Stacey.

But a few weeks later, Stacey was again the subject of his anger.

"Couldn't you hit him over the head when he arrives at the court tomorrow morning?" John West was saying, addressing One-eyed-Tommy. "Couldn't you hit him over the head, then put him in your cab and take him away somewhere and hide him?"

With them were Joe and Arty West, Piggy and Sugar Renfrey. They were in the kitchen of the house near the tote yard occupied by One-eyed-Tommy. It was a dirty room, bearing signs that an untidy bachelor lived in it.

Power of the kind that John West was amassing – power for its own sake and domination over other people for the sake of domination, presupposes the ability to take reprisals. He had become obsessed with a nagging desire to avenge himself on the men who had caused his discomfort. He issued papers charging the two detectives with perjury, under an old law, the existence of which everyone but David Garside had forgotten. But in spite of Garside's valiant endeavours in court, the detectives were acquitted after a farcial trial. Then the tote mob looked for Stacey in vain as the cases against the three tote employees went from adjournment to adjournment. This time, the detectives had successfully placed him beyond their reach, somewhere in the country.

"Cut it out, Jack," Joe West answered his brother. "No use worryin' about takin' revenge on the poor bugger. He got you and Cummin out of it. What more do yer want? Let him alone!"

"Like hell I'll let him alone. No man can betray me and get away with it."

"It didn't do yer much good suing the two detectives. You're only putting yourself to expense for nothing."

"Expense for nothing, be damned! I put the wind up them, didn't I? And anyway, the new Commissioner of Police, Callinan, takes over shortly, and he's going to transfer them to the country. That'll teach them to try and get promotion by arresting me. And Stacey won't get away with it either."

"If you start anything like this with Stacey you might get arrested again," Joe persisted. "Let him alone."

John West turned to him again impatiently. "Didn't you hear what the silly bastard said in the court today? Told all about Father Carroll visiting him. Never know what he will say tomorrow, unless we stop him from putting in an appearance."

Arthur Stacey had been brought to the city under armed guard to act as a witness in the case against Boney Bill and the other two accused. Not satisfied with saying that he had placed bets on the tote, he identified the accused as the men who had given him tickets there. They had all worn masks at the time, but that meant nothing to Stacey. He would know them again anywhere, he told the court. Now that he had obtained the acquittal of John West and Daniel Cummin, he felt at liberty to carry out his allotted task for Williams and Armfield. He looked much healthier; apparently he had been eating and sleeping much better, believing that West and his mob would now leave him alone.

This time, Stacey displayed an unexpected quality. The man proved to be a born humourist who liked to hear his audience laugh, even when they laughed at the expense of some remark which revealed his ignorance and utter stupidity. He said that the detectives had taken him to the country for the good of his health, and was grateful that the court saw the unconscious humour of the remark. Then, when David Garside asked him if he was a professional police informer, he replied that he had been one for years, in his spare time; but that, when the trial was over, he was to take a "zecative job in the Customs Department," which Detective Armfield had promised him. The very thought of the illiterate Stacey taking an executive position in the Customs Department sent the court into convulsions of laughter. This was much appreciated by Arthur, who, thus encouraged, proceeded to deliver an unsolicited speech from the witness box.

"The whole thing is a conspiracy against Mr. West, the other bloke and me," he began, then remembering that *that* case was over, hastened to correct himself: "I mean the other case was." In spite of the Magistrate's insistence that he confine his remarks to answering questions, Stacey continued: "I am a truthful man, and a Catholic. I have been telling the truth since Father Carroll came to see me on behalf of Mr. West." Uproar greeted this remark, then the court adjourned until the next day.

John West had called this meeting for the express purpose of contriving a means of getting rid of Stacey.

"We could get him that way, Jack," One-eyed-Tommy said. "It would take four of us. One to hit him over the head, two to grab him and throw him into the cab, and one to drive. I've got two very fast horses. We'd take some catchin'."

118

"Do it easy," Piggy agreed.

"Serve the little bastard right," opined Sugar.

"I'll be the fourth man. I'll clout him over the head!" Arthur West said eagerly.

"No, you won't. Cauliflower Dick will be the fourth man. You keep out of this," John West intervened.

Arthur West scowled.

"We'll have to plan it out carefully," John West added.

"We'll end up in jail if you keep this up," Joe said. "What's come over yer lately? Are yer goin' mad, or what's wrong with yer? You'll end up in jail, as sure as eggs!"

John West said contemptuously: "Got the jellies again, have you, Mr. Joe? I'll go to jail, will I? Listen, I'll go to jail if I let bastards like Stacey spill the beans on me and get away with it!"

"You're a bloody fool, Jack. You're a bloody fool!"

The others watched tensely.

"Who are you calling a bloody fool? Be careful. If you don't like us dealin' with pimps, you can get out. Get out and stay out, and see how you get on!"

Joe walked to the door where he hesitated and said: "Arty, come on home." His brother did not reply. As Joe departed he heard One-eyed-Tommy say: "What will we do with him, Jack? Put him in a bag with some stones and throw him into the Yarra?"

"No, too risky," Joe heard John West's voice answer. "Couldn't you bring him out here, tie him up and gag him, and keep him here till the cases are dismissed?"

Next morning Arthur Stacey arrived at the Carringbush Court, looking forward again to entertaining a large crowd. A uniformed constable walked on either side of him from the hansom cab to the door. As they crossed the footpath, another cab drew up and a man with a handkerchief covering the lower part of his face and a wide-brimmed hat pulled over his eyes, leapt out. It was Arthur West, who, unknown to his brother, had prevailed upon One-eyed-Tommy to take him along. He dashed up behind Stacey and brought a short iron bar smashing down on his skull. Stacey slumped to the ground. Before the police guards could recover their wits, he was picked up by Cauliflower Dick and Piggy, who had followed Arthur West from the cab with their faces similarly

119

obscured, and thrown bodily into the cab, which drove away at breakneck speed.

Three months had passed when one Saturday afternoon in the autumn of 1900, One-eyed-Tommy entered John West's office in Cummin's Tea Shop.

"What's the trouble, Tommy?"

"When are yer goin' on yer honeymoon, Jack?"

"In three weeks' time. I'm going to New Zealand."

"Well, listen, Jack, what am I goin' to do with this bloody noosance I got up at the house. He drivin' me mad, he is, fair dinkum. I ain't keepin' 'im there any longer. Now the cases has been dismissed, what are we gointa do with him?"

"I almost forgot about him. How is he getting on?"

"No bloody good, Jack. He can't seem to eat much, and vomits all over hisself. The place stinks like a skin factory."

"Does he still sing out?"

"No, not now. I told him if he did I'd slit his bloody throat. He used to try and sing out in the daytime, tryin' to 'tract attention, so I gagged him like you said. Now when I take the gag orf, he don't say nothin', just groans. He's a bag of bloody bones and keeps whimperin' and groanin', and he's crawlin' with lice. Keeps askin' for his girl friend and for a priest. I told him no decent woman or priest would have anythin' to do with him. If you leave him there much longer, I'll kick his bloody guts in, fair dinkum, I will."

The kidnapping of Arthur Stacey had been completely successful. The police cab that had made chase was soon out-paced, and One-eyed-Tommy had taken his prisoner to a pre-arranged hiding place until nightfall. Then they transferred Stacey to Tommy's house.

Stacey's bloody head was roughly bathed, and the fact that he was suffering from concussion ignored. As the weeks went by he was reduced to a gibbering lunatic.

Nothing appeared in the press about the incident except periodical announcements that the Carringbush tote case could not be heard because the main Crown witness had disappeared mysteriously. Finally the case had been struck out. The police searched without avail: Sergeant Devlin from Carringbush and a city detective known to David Garside were in charge of the search!

John West drummed the table with his fingers thoughtfully. "I suppose we'd better get rid of him. It's too risky to keep him there, all right."

"Why don't I just hit him over the head, put him in a bag with some heavy stones, and chuck 'im in the Yarra, Jack?"

"Too dangerous. Anyway, I don't want that on my conscience when I'm going on my honeymoon," John West replied. He seemed to ponder the problem calmly as if considering how most effectively to dispose of a can of rubbish or something equally unimportant and quite impersonal. "That ship that you said we could shanghai him to Europe on isn't in again, is it?"

"No. But come to think of it, a ship arrived with some "snow" the other day. I hear the captain would do a job like this."

The following Wednesday at dawn, Arthur Stacey, specially shaved and dressed for the occasion, was taken on board a ship – a little trading vessel with a cut-throat captain and crew, which travelled the world trafficking in drugs and in women for brothels of the East. The ship was a day out at sea before Stacey, shivering without food or water in the dirty hold among the rats, realised that it was not bound for the holiday port of Queenscliff, as he had been told.

In the view of the ship's captain, Stacey was quite insane. He was, as well, a snivelling nuisance who, the one-eyed man had said, was never to return to Australia, "even if you have to murder the bloody pimp." So when Stacey contracted malaria in the tropics he was promptly thrown overboard to the sharks.

The day Stacey died, John West and Nellie Moran boarded a ship, after their marriage at St. Joseph's, bound for an idyllic honeymoon in New Zealand, during which John West forgot that Stacey had ever existed.

121

CHAPTER FOUR

*The gangster exists by giving bribes and help on election
day to the politicians.*

MICHAEL GOLD

When John West returned from his honeymoon he found an
urgent message awaiting him at the tote: Mr. David Garside had
phoned and wished to see him immediately on his arrival. This
must be important: Garside had never contacted him before.

West had been nearer to happiness than ever before. His personality was in the process of breaking up into compartments;
the compartment that accompanied Nellie Moran to New Zealand
was benign and likeable enough. Nellie found her misgivings
about the marriage evaporating. They travelled to hotels in Wel-
lington and Auckland, and visited the strange hot-water springs
and bubbling craters at Rotorua. They went to both galloping and
trotting race meetings, and John West was pleased to learn that
his fame as a book-maker had spread to New Zealand.

The passionate intimacy of the honeymoon purged his spirit:
he found himself mellowing a little. Not that he repented of anything he had done; John West was not given to reverie or to
taking stock of his life. His thoughts always revolved around the
present and future.

Garside granted him an interview as soon as he arrived at the
office. "In your absence, you have had a narrow escape, Mr.
West," Garside began, proceeding immediately to march up and
down the room. "A Bill to define a place kept for gaming
purposes and to prohibit all illegal betting was brought before
Parliament by the Attorney-General. Young Isaac Isaacs, who is
a legal man, made a very good job of framing the legislation. In
introducing the Bill, he said, *inter alia*, that illegal gambling had
grown to alarming proportions in the Colony; that the Gaming
Act was inadequate. The Bill was aimed, he said, at giving the
police power to deal effectively with gambling houses and street
betting."

At this stage, John West, who had opened his mouth to speak several times, asked anxiously: "And did the Bill go through?"

"After a heated debate, it was defeated by one vote. One vote, Mr. West! And but for my good offices with several Liberal, and two Conservative members, it would have been passed. I think, Mr. West, that you had better keep your eye on the gentlemen at Parliament House. Most of the Labour men and Liberals opposed the Bill, but the Conservatives would like to have gambling kept as the preserve of the rich, and they may try again to get the Bill through. They will tell the electors: 'thousands may be starving, but, after all, we did close the Jackson Street tote.'"

John West was about to assert that they would never close the Jackson Street tote, but Garside continued to talk and walk, waving his arms like a windmill. "By the way, Isaacs gave a vivid description of your premises. Very interesting, very ingenious. I must come out one day and look the fortress over."

Garside ceased his pacing and faced John West like a schoolmaster, pointing his forefinger, puckering his bushy eyebrows and waggling his beard. "Also, young man, you will need to be wary of the gaming police in future."

"I've got ten or twelve detectives on the pay roll; surely they wouldn't have the cheek," John West snapped.

"Aha, Mr. West. It is easy to begin bribing people, but there is no end to it. Before the beloved old Commissioner finally resigns, he intends appointing David O'Flaherty as head of the gaming police. O'Flaherty would be about as easy to bribe as a statue of George Washington!"

"I warn you also to turn your attention to politics," Garside continued. "You are a moderately rich man, and daily grow richer. Though you may not be aware of it, any rich man can exert either direct or indirect influence over Parliament, which exists to serve the needs of the rich. I warn you, also, though this may not be immediately important, to tighten up your precautions against police raids. O'Flaherty was behind this Bill. It was he who suggested to the Attorney-General that the Act needed amending."

Garside walked around the table, picked up a paper-knife, and dramatically pointed it at John West. "Be warned, Mr. West. I tell you categorically that your tote shop will be under fire from O'Flaherty and from Parliament House, before you are much older. Be warned! Be prepared!"

David Garside accompanied John West to the door without giving him opportunity to comment. "I am behind time, Mr. West. I have offered to defend a poor woman who has murdered her twin babies. The poor children would have starved to death had she not, in her despair, ended their misery. Poor soul, I must win her acquittal." He stood with the door ajar and shook his head sadly. "Sometimes, Mr. West, I wish I were a politician instead of a lawyer; then I should hold an inquiry into the causes of poverty, discover who caused poverty, and hang them all. Hang them all! Ah, but those are idle words. I was a Liberal member for many years, but there seemed nothing I could do, but make speeches, very good speeches, of course, but merely words." He shook his head again, then rushed to the hat-stand and took his top hat and walking-cane. "But you are detaining me, Mr. West. I must away to this poor woman."

As John West walked towards the stairs to descend to the ground floor, Garside ran past him, his beard bobbing up and down as he mumbled to himself: "Davie Garside will save this unfortunate wretch from the scaffold!"

As he reached the top of the stairs ten yards ahead of John West, he turned dramatically and waved his cane. "Remember, Mr. West! Be warned! Be prepared!" With these few words, he fled down the stairs two at a time with his coat-tails flying, holding his top hat on with one hand and waving his cane with the other.

As John West walked home to Carringbush, breathing in slowly through his nose for eight paces, and out through his mouth for the next eight paces (he had read in THE FAMILY DOCTOR that this was most beneficial), his thoughts turned to plans to meet this new threat to his power. A threat to his power led him to spin the sovereign to Brogan, to bribe Devlin and the city detectives, to consult Garside, and bribe and intimidate witnesses. Now a threat to his power set him thinking of the need for political influence. Now, as before, he had to plan to extend his power in order to maintain and protect it.

The year of Federation, 1901, was a momentous one for the colony of Victoria. On the first day of January it became the State of Victoria in the Commonwealth of Australia. For John West, the year was to prove momentous because he turned to politics as a source of power.

Previously, he had taken little interest in politics. Voting was not compulsory, so he had not even bothered to vote at election time. He had given several donations to the Carringbush Labor League in the late nineties, as a matter of business.

Aside from horse racing, from which he derived his main income, his interests were few. He did not dance, smoke, drink or play billiards; he rarely went to concerts or variety shows. The only two books he had read in his life were his mother's medical book and a grammar he had borrowed from Barney Robinson. His literary diet consisted of newspapers, of which he rarely read anything outside the sporting pages and the "Police Intelligence" columns. He had given up playing football years before: he had not been a good player, and it was unbecoming to a man of wealth to suffer the indignity of being dropped out of the team every so often. He liked walking and swimming, but these pursuits he followed as adjuncts to health and cleanliness.

The recreations he liked best were watching football matches and prize fights. The Carringbush Football Club had no more generous patron nor enthusiastic supporter. In the winter, he would occasionally absent himself from the tote on Saturday afternoons to attend the matches. If Carringbush made the finals, he would bet heavily on their chances, usually taking the precaution to deaden some of the players in the opposing side beforehand. If a good prize-fight was on anywhere in Melbourne, John West would almost invariably be seen at the ringside. The more blood and hair that flew the better he enjoyed himself.

However, by the evening of the polling for the election of the first Commonwealth Parliament of Australia, John West had definitely added politics to his interests.

"'Ow d'yer think he'll go, Jack?" Sugar Renfrey asked him as they walked towards the city to await the results which were to be posted outside the office of the AGE newspaper.

"I don't think he'll win the seat, Sugar. Anyway, one man in the Federal Parliament is not much use. It's the State Parliament that I'm interested in; it controls the gaming laws."

The man under discussion was the independent Liberal candidate for the electorate which included Carringbush. The candidate was an estate agent with political ambitions who gambled on the tote by telephone. When John West heard that he intended

125

"going in for politics," he offered to sign his nomination paper and pay his election deposit and expenses. The man nominated against the Labor candidate, but as the campaign proceeded he appended the words "true friend of Labor" to his title at the suggestion of his backer, who soon recognised that a man needed to get the majority of the working men's votes to win in an industrial area.

"Well, Jack, why didn't yer wait till the State elections?" Sugar asked. He wore a gaudy check suit, highly polished shoes, and a boxer-hat angled over one ear, and smoked a big cigar. Renfrey possessed all the faults of men who grow up amid squalor and poverty, and none of their virtues. He had established a large connection for the tote at the railway workshops. He fawned on John West like a faithful dog. His subservience and flattery were essential to the ego of his employer. He had been chosen to become a member of the Carringbush Labor League, and turn it into an instrument with which John West could begin his drive for political influence.

"I told you before. He was keen to stand; and this campaign will get him known and give him a better chance of winning the State seat."

"I get yer, Jack. Good move, too."

Suddenly Sugar screwed up his face in pain and, grabbing one foot in his hands, hopped around like a cat on hot bricks. "Can't we get a tram, Jack? Me feet is givin' me hell in these noo shoes."

"The exercise is good for you, Sugar," John West replied, stopping and watching Sugar's antics with mild amusement. "You don't do enough walking, that's your trouble. Besides, we've plenty of time."

"I don't see no sense in walkin' when there's trams passin' all the time," Sugar persisted.

As they reached the outskirts of the city, turned into Collins Street, and walked down the hill, Sugar brightened up. "He oughta win, Jack, the way we helped 'im. We cheered and clapped at his meetin's, and heckled at the opposition meetin's. We canvassed the whole ilectrut gettin' people to vote for 'im, and spread stories that the Labor man was a Freemason that no Catholic could vote for. Today we guv out 'How to vote' tickets at all the pollin' booths. He oughta win, Jack, after all we done for 'im."

126

"He won't win, Sugar, I told you that. The Labor man will win; then he'll have to resign the Carringbush seat in the State House, then our man can become the Labor candidate. I want you to get more of our men into the local Labor League to make sure he gets the endorsement at the State by-election. Labor is the coming party."

"I'll do that, Jack, don't worry. I've got dozens of blokes all readied up to join the local League, and other Leagues around our way, too. But mosta the Labor candidates ain't no good to you, Jack. Take this bloke that's standing against our man now; 'e wouldn't take a bribe, or support the tote, nor nothin'. The Trades 'All and the TOCSIN newspaper are tightenin' things up."

"Yes, but there are some Labor men who'll support me. Take that young fella who writes for the TOCSIN, Ashton: he's a true Labor man, yet he says gambling should not be the preserve of the rich, I hear. I'm going to run him for Parliament at the State elections next year. But one candidate at a time is no good. People vote for a party more than for a man. And maybe we can get the right men standing for Labor in spite of the TOCSIN and the Trades Hall."

As John West prophesied, his candidate was defeated. The Labor man won. John West then turned to the Labor Movement as a source of power.

John West was not an imaginative man: nothing entered his consciousness until it had bearing on his rise to power, then he set out to bend it to his own purpose. He knew little of the history, policy or nature of the Australian Labor Party.

In Victoria, it was formed in 1890 under the name "Political Labor Council," during the disillusionment which followed the defeat of the Maritime strike of that year. It was set up by the Trade Unions to run separate Labor candidates at elections. Labor must win power in the Parliament because Parliament had invariably sided with the employers in industrial disputes: that was the growing opinion in the Trade Union Movement. The Political Labor Council ran candidates in industrial areas throughout the nineties, and by 1901, when it became part of the Australian Labor Party, there were fourteen Labor members of the Victorian Parliament. Their policy points were similar to those of some Liberal members: an eight-hour day, industrial arbitration, exclusion of Asiatics, early closing of hotels, etc.

But, rather than fight for the working men who elected them, these Labor politicians acted in general too much like Liberals. So disappointed was the Trades Hall Council that, in 1899, it passed a resolution refusing permission for them to attend Council meetings. Some Labor politicians were attacked as "expediency-mongers, crawling into Parliament on the backs of the working men, and then becoming independent."

In 1901, the Labor Party drew up a pledge binding all Labor politicians to vote as a bloc on issues affecting trade unionists and working men generally. No man could be endorsed as a Labor candidate unless he signed this pledge.

The first Labor members of Parliament were former Trade Union leaders, many of whom had looked on trade unionism as a career, and viewed their entry into Parliament, as well-earned promotion. But, by the end of the nineties, middle-class men with political ambitions turned to the Labor Party as a stepping stone to a seat in Parliament. In the years that followed, many shop-keepers, lawyers, farmers, estate-agents and the like, became Labor politicians.

But John West knew none of these facts. He merely set out to use the Labor Party for his own purposes.

At the end of Jackson Street, farthest from the city, a line of hills rises steeply from the opposite bank of the Yarra River. Already, in the first years of the century, rich men lived in great, ornate mansions which stood along the hills looking down across the river, as though in silent gloating, on squalid little dwellings of the poor in Carringbush.

One of the mansions was a white, two-storied building with three large pillars in front. It stood in spacious, well-kept grounds with fine, large pine trees rising behind it. One morning, as the hour approached eight o'clock, John West walked briskly through its double gate and down the hill towards Carringbush.

John West had taken his place among the rich across the river. After his marriage, he had moved with Nellie into this grand mansion, leaving her mother behind the shop in Jackson Street. But mansions cannot ensure happiness for their occupants: tension and unhappiness had entered this one.

Nellie was bearing her first child. If only she weren't so moody and complaining of the pain and suffering, John West was thinking. Anyone would imagine she was the only woman who ever had a baby!

Since her pregnancy she had become nervy and petulant, and had lost her physical attraction for him. He was fed up with her moods and complaints. He had told her so at breakfast, and bounced out of the house. She had a mansion and servants, and everything she wanted. She had better stop eternally complaining of the morning sickness and the pangs of carrying a child; and stop prying into his affairs and listening to rumours, too.

As he walked down the hill and across the bridge, he pushed Nellie from his mind. Though a tram was ready to depart from the terminus, he walked past it and along Jackson Street towards the tote. He had important business on his mind. A chance to make anything up to fifty thousand pounds, on a certainty at that; at least The General said it was a certainty.

The General was a trainer and manager of cyclists. Last week he had informed John West that the Austral Wheel Race could be won, providing certain precautions were taken beforehand, by a cyclist against whose chances the bookmakers were prepared to lay ten or fifteen to one. The famous Irish-American cyclist, Plugger Pete Manson, was to be set to win the great race. The General was bringing him to see John West at nine o'clock this morning.

Most people considered Manson to be the greatest cyclist of all time, but he was now past his prime; he was in his forty-second year, and age was sapping his speed and stamina. His sensational career was nearing its end. The sports writers were saying that Plugger was too old.

Before coming to Australia in 1895, Manson had defeated all comers in America and Europe, in races from one mile to six days. Not only had he been the speediest and strongest rider, but he knew more tricks than his rivals – more ways of "jamming" and "chopping," more ways of bringing an opponent down. In Australia, Manson had a long string of successes, including victory over the Australian champion in match races. Then misfortune overtook him. A rival cyclist "chopped" him. Plugger rode after him when the race had finished and punched him on the nose. His disqualification for two months caused him to miss the Austral of 1896, which he had set himself to win. He was disappointed. To win the world's greatest cycling event became the ambition of his life.

Everyone talked about Plugger Pete Manson, amazed at his speed, strength and daring, and his introduction of pedal clips (what would happen if he fell?) and hard-pumped tyres (they would surely burst!).

Plugger Pete knew all the devices for making money out of cycling. He had been guilty more than once of rigging a race.

In 1897, Manson was disqualified for twelve months, and again could not compete in the Austral Wheel Race. He departed for America in disgust, but returned in 1899, lured back to achieve the victory he now most wanted. But success evaded him, and the money he had made dwindled to nothing.

Manson was a gambler. He had been known to sit up all night playing poker for high stakes; then, after a few hours sleep, go out and win a big cycle race. He gambled heavily on cycling. Hardly a race was run in which he competed unless he backed himself or some other competitor to win. Wherever he went he gathered around him gamblers, touts and hangers-on.

Manson and The General arrived punctually at John West's office in Cummin's Tea Shop. Since Manson's return to Australia, The General had been his trainer and manager, and he was mighty proud to be associated with the great Plugger Pete. He introduced Manson with a flourish.

"This," he said in a deep bass voice, "is Plugger Pete Manson." Then, as if a ventriloquist were in the room, he continued in a high-pitched, squeaky voice: "We have come to discuss that business I mentioned to you."

The sudden change in the pitch of his voice sounded comical, but John West and Manson were used to idiosyncrasies of the vocal chords which had led to The General's dismissal from the tote when the telephone replaced the pigeon service from the racecourse.

John West and Manson shook hands. The cyclist was above medium height and of powerful build. He had walked from the door with a stilted gait. It seemed as if every muscle in his body was moulded for cycling. He was well rigged-up in a black overcoat but wore no hat. His light brown hair was speckled with grey about the temples, and cut short with a fringe falling down over his forehead. His was a true gambler's face, stolid and impassive.

When they were seated, John West said: "Well, gentlemen, what is the proposition?"

The General leaned forward with an air of great importance. He was a little rotund man, with a red face and a small, upturned nose. He wore a black, high-crowned hat turned up all round, and generally looked a little ridiculous. However, he was reputed to be second to none as a trainer and masseur.

"Well, it's this way, Jack," he said, this time beginning in falsetto and falling to bass as he went on. "It can be fixed for Plugger to win the Austral. The bookies are volumes open. They've got Plugger Pete at ten and fifteen to one." After this sustained effort in bass voice, The General went up to falsetto again, as he added shrewdly: "If the commission is worked properly, you'll make a fortune."

John West had learned that it paid in an interview of this kind to ask questions, to do little talking, and to take advantage of his penetrating stare, which he now focused on The General.

"Are you sure the race can be fixed?"

"As easy as fallin' out of bed . . ." The General began in his best falsetto.

"Just a minute, General," Manson interrupted in a deep sonorous voice. "This is the point, Mr. West. I could probably win this goddam race without fixing it; but I want to go in for a big kill to get my own back on the book-makers for what they did to me last year. You heard about that?"

John West nodded.

"In cycling, it pays to support the man who could probably win anyway," Manson continued, "and then make sure by giving some of the others a cut."

John West noticed Manson's insistence that he could probably win anyway, and guessed that he hated to admit, even to himself, that he was past his prime. "But you're on scratch. You'll be giving away long starts to some riders, won't you?"

"Ah, you don't want to believe all this goddam paper talk about me being too old. I can still show these mugs how to ride."

"Plugger's riding as well as ever," The General intervened in falsetto.

"All right, then, we'll assume you can win. Where do I come in?" John West asked.

Manson warmed to the plot. "The race is three months off, but they're already betting on it all over Australia. You can back me to win what you like: the sky's the limit. You'll average ten to one for your money, so five thousand will win you fifty thousand. But you'll need to spread your money. No use trying to put it on in big amounts – the price will fall too quickly. All I want is a thousand pounds if I win; nothing if I lose."

"A thousand pounds is a lot of money."

"So is fifty thousand."

"And who pays to fix the other riders?"

"You do, naturally."

"Seems to me that I'm taking all the risks. How much would that cost?"

"To be really certain, we'd need to fix a few in the heat, a few in the semifinal; and in the final, the whole field, if possible. It would cost about a thousand altogether."

"Supposing someone in the final won't co-operate, then I lose six thousand quid. That's a lot of money."

"I keep telling you, Mr. West, that I could win if they were all triers." Manson tapped himself on the chest with his right forefinger. "Plugger Pete is not a back number yet. They'll find that out."

"All right, I'll risk it. I'll send agents to every capital city in Australia, and big country towns in Victoria. I'll back you off the map. I'll want written receipts from the other riders, just to be businesslike. I'll inspect them, then destroy them. You'll get your thousand after the race. I'm a man of my word; anyone will tell you that."

"Good, Mr. West," Manson said, rising. His stolid face cracked into a rare smile. "And don't lose any sleep. I could beat these novices with one foot off the pedal. Watch out I don't set a record for the race."

"Go home, yer mug! Yer an exploiter of female labor!" Cauliflower Dick's raucous voice boomed like the roar of a bull above the din in the Carringbush Town Hall.

The heckled speaker was the endorsed Labor candidate for the Carringbush by-election. He continued his vain effort to be heard above the interjections, the shouting, the whistling. If he had been a Conservative or a Liberal, there would have been no occasion for surprise that he could not get a hearing. At the turn of the century, enthusiasm for the new Labor Party, and bitterness after the decade of despair, were so deep that any politician who opposed a Labor candidate could not hold a peaceful meeting in a working-class suburb. The situation was reversed in this contest because a West candidate was opposing the Labor man.

Silent and calm, John West was sitting in the centre of the large, crowded hall. He and Sugar Renfrey had organised the rowdy demonstration.

The Labor candidate was a big man, who wore his blue suit as though more used to moleskins and flannel. He was flushed with anger and determined to speak.

The meeting was the last in a bitter campaign, and seemed likely to end in a brawl. More than five hundred people were present, mainly Labor supporters. But dotted around the hall in groups, more than a hundred tote men kept up a continuous stream of interjections and catcalls, with Cauliflower Dick in the role of jeer leader.

"Go out, yer mug," he called again. "Yer an exploiter of female labor."

Others took up the call, including Piggy, Scotch Paddy, One-eyed-Tommy and the Ape. Sugar Renfrey himself was absent. It would have been indiscreet for a member of the Labor League to be heard interjecting at a Labor meeting; and, anyway, Sugar had left on his honeymoon the day before, after marrying a local girl who had turned Catholic at his insistence. Barney Robinson, too, was absent: he was a keen Labor supporter, not prepared to jeer at his party, yet not prepared to cheer it in the presence of John West.

As the din subsided a little, the man on the platform shouted: "The cheap labor referred to by the interjector is the fine young women who have volunteered to assist my candidature – the Labor candidature – by giving out leaflets . . ."

"And keepin' men out of a job!" Cauliflower Dick shouted back.

"These men are living on the proceeds of the illegal tote. They are raising the sectarian issue." The speaker got these phrases in amid renewed uproar. Groups of men began shouting abuse at each other across the seats.

John West was not pleased with the drift of events in the campaign. With the assistance of Sugar Renfrey and other supporters, he had obtained the Labor endorsement for his man without a ballot being taken. The TOCSIN exposed the move and demanded a ballot. A democratic ballot was subsequently held, and John West's man defeated. He then began to style himself a "selected" Labor candidate. The tactic confused many people. Sugar and his band of helpers raised the religious issue, and advised Catholics to vote for the man who "kicked with the right foot."

Then the Labor candidate issued a leaflet exposing this deceit of the electors, "the unprincipled use of bigotry" and the "boodle and bullying" of the "illegal tote operators." This seemed to have turned the tide in favour of the official Labor candidate. Enraged, John West had given an advertisement to the papers for tomorrow, election day, stating that "all who love fair play and justice are earnestly requested not to believe the statements circulated . . ."

The speaker waited for the uproar to die down a little, then began to make points of Labor policy, only to be greeted by Cauliflower Dick's voice again: "Go home, yer mug, we don't want no exploiters of female labor in Parlyment." John West had told him the main theme, and he stuck to it monotonously.

John West noticed Eddie Corrigan sitting in front of Cauliflower Dick, and he saw him lean back, and heard him shout at the jeer leader: "Stop singing out in my ear. I've come to hear Labor policy. Shut yer mouth, or I'll shut it for yer."

"You will!" yelled Cauliflower Dick, leaping to his feet and thrusting his punch-disfigured face close to Corrigan. "And who are yer goin' to get to help yer?"

"I won't need any help," Corrigan shouted.

"Well, see how yer like this!" Cauliflower Dick replied, and before Corrigan could raise his guard, a hard fist crashed on to his nose. Blood spurted over both of them.

Corrigan and his attacker became locked in each other's arms and fell headlong into the aisle. The front half of the hall became a swarming, swearing mass of fighting men. Cauliflower Dick was getting more than he bargained for. He and Corrigan were on their feet again, toe to toe, punching vigorously. John West's mob had the weight of experience on their side, and were getting the upper hand, when several policemen batoned their way into the struggling mass and endeavoured to restore order. John West moved to the back of the hall.

It took some minutes to stop the brawl. Noses were bleeding, eyes bunged, and clothes torn when the participants resumed their seats, still hurling abuse.

The speaker began afresh, but persistent interjections made it necessary to close the meeting early. Outside the hall isolated arguments started, and Cauliflower Dick, sporting a black eye, offered a bloody Corrigan out to fight. The invitation was accepted, but the police intervened. The working men stood in clusters arguing the pros and cons of the campaign, and there were a few skirmishes.

As John West departed, Eddie Corrigan pushed a leaflet into his hand. Reaching the first street light he began to read it. It called on the workers of Carringbush to close their ranks in support of the endorsed candidate, who had signed the Labor pledge. The leaflet, which claimed to be a reprint of an article from the TOCSIN, pointed out that some Labor politicians were sabotaging the local campaign and inferred correctly that John West was behind their treachery.

Persons who live on the proceeds of an illegal business, John West read, *are using all the wits learnt in long association with the nefarious side of life, to introduce Tammany Hall tactics into Victorian politics, and to keep the Labor candidate out. Men have been cajoled to promise their votes to a man who happens to be of the same religion. Beer money, personal friendship, threats, business pressure and lies of every colour have been used . . .*

He crumpled up the leaflet and threw it savagely into the gutter. "Curse the bloody TOCSIN mob," he muttered.

But in spite of the bloody TOCSIN mob, his candidate narrowly won the seat and became the first "West man" to enter Parliament.

On Saturday morning, a fortnight later, Sugar Renfrey rushed headlong into the tote yard, waving the current issue of the TOCSIN, and charged breathlessly into John West's office.

"Jack! Jack!" he shouted. "This TOCSIN's a bloody snag. Red 'ot! Listen! It says: *The Victorian Police Force, by An ex-Member*. Listen to this bit – "

He fumbled for his glasses, put them on, squinted his crooked eye and read gravely:

A constable, who had once raided West's tote successfully, received a bullet wound one night. It was reported that a burglar had shot him. The detectives who set out to arrest the would-be murderer did not, as far as we know, ever catch up with him, but the TOCSIN –

John West, who had listened with a scowl on his face, snatched the paper from Sugar's hands and began reading hurriedly and disjointedly: *Two other detectives were charged with perjury on no other evidence than that of John West and his cousin –*

Where are they getting all this information from, John West thought. This is bad!

. . . Superintendent Brown said, when handing over to Detective O'Flaherty: "I wish you luck. When you get an Act of Parliament authorizing you to enter every house in Carringbush with a pick-axe and a mortar you may be able to catch Jack West."

Act of Parliament! In a Labour paper, too. I'll have to do something about this.

. . . Rumour has it that the correspondence between the two detectives and the head of the Department would prove most interesting reading to any enterprising Member of Parliament who might consider himself in a position to enlighten both the Parliament and the public . . . They have been dealt with for having had the impertinence to catch the honourable John West, it was alleged, in the very act of bribing a witness. One of them has been transferred to the country and the other discharged on the flimsiest pretext.

John West read through the article. "An ex-member of the Police Force. I wonder who the hell it could be?" he muttered. He never discovered that the article was written by none other than Detective Williams, now stationed in a distant country centre.

John West was enraged, but as he calmed down a little, a thought which had often crossed his mind lately asserted itself. I must, in future, support only endorsed Labor candidates. And take steps to silence the bloody paper!

"We can't get Mick Laver to run dead, Jack. Says he's backed himself."

Sugar Renfrey took a butt of a cigar from his mouth and spat out a soggy piece of the frayed end.

"But he'll only have himself backed for about a hundred quid. Offer him three hundred. We can't have him mucking up the business. I stand to lose a packet if Plugger Pete gets beat, and Laver could beat him. Pete's slipped, you know that."

"It's no good, Jack; I offered Laver four hundred, but he said he wouldn't deaden hisself for four million."

"Did he?"

"Yair. Says the game is bein' ruined by the big gamblers and crook races."

John West, Sugar and The General were walking from Carringbush to the Melbourne Cricket Ground to see the final of the 1901 Austral Wheel Race.

"Does he?" John West said in the quiet, measured tone that Sugar had come to know meant ruthless measures. "Well, fix him! Fix him properly! Tip him off! Fix it with the others to run him over the fence."

"Might be trouble, Jack. There's rumours about already that the race is rigged for Manson. The bookies are moanin' 'cause he's been backed to odds on, and they can't lay any other riders."

"I said to fix Laver. See the others and fix him!"

"Don't worry, Jack," The General started in falsetto. "Leave that to old Plugger. He knows the tricks." Dropping to basso, he added: "And remember, he's riding well. His times in the heat and semifinal have been good."

"Laver is well handicapped, and he's in good nick. If you ask me, Plugger Pete will never catch him. You tell Manson to see that Laver is fixed. He can't get away with this."

They walked the rest of the journey in silence.

When they arrived at the ground. The General departed to attend to his duties. John West called after him: "Don't forget what I told you!" Then he snapped at Sugar Renfrey: "You and The General messed this up properly."

"It ain't our fault, Jack. We did our best. Anyway, Plugger Pete is at the top of his form. He could win if they were all triers, let alone with only *one* trier."

"Do you think I'd have spent a thousand quid, and laid odds

to nothing to officials, if I thought he could win with a field of triers? If the race was dinkum, Laver would win it. Plugger Pete can't give him 250 yards start. The point is you've made a mess of it, as usual. The papers are talking about bribes and race rigging."

"What do yer expect, Jack? They've woke up, but it ain't my fault."

"We won't strike trouble, anyway. I gave a donation of £500 to the Club last week. I've got most of the officials fixed. But I don't like all these rumours, and I don't like Laver being a trier."

The General ran up breathlessly and said in varied tones: "We'll fix him this time, Jack. They'll try to give him the shoulder at the start and bring him down, and if they can't they're going to pocket him. If he gets a break like he did in the heat, they're going to leave him in front on his own and take it in turns to pace Plugger Pete up to him. Plugger won't have to take a turn of pace, he'll just have to sprint home."

"But supposin' they can't catch Laver. None of this leaving him in front. Fix him!"

Forty thousand people attended, but several grandstands and a spacious outer ground easily accommodated them. The track and ground were in excellent condition, although many cycling men still argued that the grass track was dangerous, being too slippery and not sufficiently banked.

Bookmakers called the odds. The crowd seethed with excitement. The men wore all manner of clothes of the day: dark suits with boxer-hats or light suits with straw hats. There were moustaches of all shapes and sizes. The few women wore long dresses, big hats with feathers in them, and carried sunshades.

John West and Sugar took up a position near the finishing line.

At the appointed time sixteen riders for the Austral final came out on to the track amid cheers. They wheeled their bikes to the starting point and, after their photographs were taken, the pushers got ready to get them on their way. The riders wore coloured short-sleeved guernseys and black woollen shorts. A large numbered square of calico hung low on each man's back.

"We've started bad, Jack!"

"How do you mean?"

"The Test cricket. I see Trumper is out for two," Sugar

replied, pointing over his shoulder at the scoreboard, which showed progressive scores of the Test match being played in Sydney between England and Australia. John West did not even look around. He had £60,000 at stake in the Austral and didn't care who won the Test match.

The starter's gun sounded.

Before the field had gone half a lap a rider pedalled desperately from the middle of the field and pushed up inside Mick Laver, lurched, and gave him a flick with his elbow. Laver's machine began to wobble. The crowd gasped. He went back to the middle of the field, but by some miracle of skill or luck did not fall. The riders in front clapped on the pace, and before Laver gathered speed again he was back with Manson, who was being nursed along by the rear bunch.

Then came a roar of excitement as Laver, with a terrific sprint, went round the field and drew up to the leaders as they passed the finishing line the first time around.

Laver rode like a man possessed. He knew now that he must lead or be tipped over. And so for lap after gruelling lap he pedalled headlong, making his own pace. With only two laps to go, he still led by forty yards and was showing no signs of weakening. The crowd was frantic with excitement . . . the whirring wheels, the courageous man in front trying to steal the race, and the riders behind taking it in turns to pace the bunched field up to the leader. Three cyclists were beaten off by the record-breaking pace.

With a lap and a half to go, Laver was still twenty yards in front. Three cyclists emerged from the bunch, riding desperately. The two freshest men were carrying Manson after the runaway. Laver seemed to be tiring, but flashed past John West and Sugar, still fifteen yards in front.

"They won't catch him! They won't catch him! If Manson loses this, look out! You'll never get another penny out of me; neither will The General!" John West shouted at Sugar.

"They'll catch him, Jack," Sugar shouted back. "He's tirin' now."

"He's giving himself a breather. He's still got a sprint left in him."

"But Manson's fresh. He's been carried all the way," Sugar replied with more confidence than he felt.

The men pacing Manson wilted, and Plugger Pete, not satisfied with the way he was bridging the gap, went round them and after the leader, who stood between him and his ambition to win the Austral before he retired. He crept closer – within a length with half a lap to go. The Manson of five years before would have swept past Laver as though he were stationary, but only the will to win kept his sturdy legs matching those of his rival now.

"Plugger's lost his dash," John West shouted.

"He's got him, Jack, I tell yer."

"Not yet! Laver can still sprint; he's had a breather."

As John West spoke, Manson crept up on the outside within half a length and looked a sure winner. Then Laver dropped his head low over the wide handlebars, and put his last ounce of energy and courage into a sprint for the line. Manson was ready and sprinted simultaneously, but Laver rode like a demon. He seemed to gain a few inches.

John West stood rigid. The crowd yelled itself hoarse in a mighty, sustained roar. Manson came again. Plugger Pete had had the ride of the race, and he had ridden in a hundred finishes such as this. He gained suddenly – within a wheel, then almost level with fifty yards to go. Momentarily it looked as if Laver would hold him, but the strain of the gruelling ride told, and he wilted.

Plugger Pete Manson swept past him to win by a length.

The crowd cheered wildly for their idol. Hats soared in the air, and hundreds of men vaulted the fence and surged across the ground. Mick Laver was forgotten. The name of Plugger Pete was on everyone's lips. When he dismounted, several men grasped him and carried him shoulder-high to the front of the members' stand, where he was to be presented to the Prime Minister of Australia and the Governor of Victoria. The band played *Here the Conquering Hero Comes*.

The General wormed his way through the crowd, yelling hysterically in bass and falsetto. Manson turned to him and shouted: "This is the proudest day in all my career."

Sugar Renfrey leapt up and down like a jumping-jack until his boxer-hat fell off. He promptly kicked it high in the air, caught it as it descended, then so far forgot himself as to leap on John West's back and ride him to the ground.

"What'd I tell yer, Jack?" he roared.

John West scrambled to his feet. "Don't be a bloody fool all your life," he snapped, brushing his clothes and flushing with annoyance. "We'll have to keep our eyes and ears open. They might have to hold an inquiry into this!"

Late next day, Plugger Pete Manson stood beside his bed in a city hotel. He had a receipt book and pencil in one hand, a revolver in the other. On the bed was a large pile of sovereigns. The General was standing near the door. Their clothes displayed unmistakable signs of having been slept in the night before. Their eyes were bloodshot. The General was swaying back and forth a little; his cheeks were pulsating, and he kept his lips closed tight, as though his tortured stomach was threatening an eruption. His attempt at sobriety made his drunken state all the more obvious and comical; but Plugger Pete, whose cast-iron constitution was well seasoned to alcohol, stood steadily enough, though his tie was crooked, and his wispy hair dishevelled.

Presently, The General drew himself erect with as much dignity as his condition would permit and flung open the door with a crash. He squinted at a piece of paper in his hand, and shouted in his most piercing falsetto: "W. Mathieson!"

The open door revealed a group of men waiting in the passage way. One stepped into the room. He started a little at the sight of the pistol in Manson's hand; but then approached the bed as The General slammed the door behind him.

Manson said with an alcoholic fringe on his voice: "Your name is Mathieson, and I agreed to pay you eighty sovereigns if I won the Austral?"

"That's right."

"Well, sign here, and I'll give you the money."

Mathieson signed his name in the receipt book, while Plugger Pete counted out the sovereigns with disobedient fingers. Then, after The General opened the door, with much fumbling, Matheison departed.

The performance was repeated thirteen times; varied only by Thé General's tone of voice, the person called and the amount of money paid. Then the main actors in the scene retired to the bar downstairs to continue their celebration.

This was the first of a series of strange events which followed the Austral Wheel Race of 1901. The daily papers reported that one rider was prepared to make a sworn statement that the race had been rigged and that he had been approached with a bribe to ride dead.

In spite of John West's influence among the cycling officials, an inquiry was ultimately held, but not until all the bets made by him had been settled. Mick Laver, who had stated his willingness to swear that the race was rigged, was refused the right to speak at the inquiry, which ended without any action being taken.

The public followed the case with as much intelligence as the limited press reports allowed. Cycling enthusiasts became convinced that the Austral had been "a slanter," and the sport declined in popularity.

Then the press made reference to a law suit in which The General (Robert Gordon Kitchener being his full name) sued Manson for one hundred pounds for alleged breach of contract. John West managed to prevent full reports of the proceedings being published, but the public learned that The General claimed to have received only £100 of £200 promised him by Manson. It was not generally known, however, that Manson was put to the inconvenience of swearing an affidavit stating that none of the riders had received any monies from him for any consideration whatsoever in connection with the race.

During the aftermath of Plugger Pete Manson's victory in the Austral Wheel Race, John West financed an attempt to release Richard Bradley from Pentridge Jail. He did so without enthusiasm. He remembered Bradley only vaguely. They had attended school together, but as Bradley was some years his senior, he had not known him well. He gathered that Bradley had shown Arthur the ropes in jail, and to this he attributed Arthur's determination to get Dick Bradley out. To humour his brother, John West had always replied that he would assist in the project, if a suitable opportunity arose.

John West could not appreciate the strange world into which a criminal is driven by the flagellator's lash. Arthur West and Richard Bradley were members of that terrible fraternity, the emblem of which is weals on the back. Working side by side in the boot shop at the jail, a deep, sinister affinity had bound them together.

When Arthur called at the tote to say that everything was "readied up to spring" Bradley and another prisoner, John West vacillated. What use could he possibly make of a couple of escaped convicts, with prices on their heads? They would be a liability instead of an asset; not worth the risk involved.

"Dick is just the sort a man you need," Arthur said sullenly. "He's quick with a gun, and he can keep his mouth shut."

"I'll put the money – no more," John West replied firmly. "To have my men helping, and Bradley and Wood hidden in a tote house, would only draw the police around. They'd suspect you. I'm only doing this for your own good. You take my advice, and you'll always keep out of trouble."

"I ain't frightened of the police! Give us the money, then, if that's all you're game to do. I want twenty quid for Dick and his mate, and fifty quid to pay the two warders who are goin' to help 'em."

John West handed him the money without a word. Arthur took it hungrily. "I'll get them out all right. The plan can't fail. I've arranged to smuggle the swag into the jail – two suits of clothes, sergette so's they'll roll up small; a water bag; a rope ladder (they're gettin' hooks made inside to use with the ladder); and tucker."

"What do you need tucker for? You'll be able to get food for them, won't you?"

"Yes, but they're goin' to hide inside the jail for a day or two. See, when them other two blokes escaped last month, they got away before anyone knew it – they just missed 'em at tea time, see? Well, they'll miss Dick and his mate at tea time, too, and think they've got out, see? But they'll be hidin' inside the jail all the time; up between the roof and the ceiling of the woollen factory. Then when the scare blows over, the two warders we're payin' will get 'em to the first wall. They'll use the rope to get over that on to a roof, then up to the outside wall. We was goin' to have One-eyed-Tommy waitin' outside there with a ladder; but now, I s'pose we'll have to get someone else. I've got the ladder hid in the creek, just near the jail. Dick and Wood will hide theirselves on Saturday afternoon, and come over the wall most likely Sunday or Monday night."

Arthur walked to the door. Stark starin' mad, John West thought. His brother's appearance lent justification to his thought: the stooped, shabbily-dressed figure, the quick eccentric movements, the white hair and moustache, the doll's eyes.

On the following Monday morning, John West learned from the papers of the failure of the escape bid. It appeared that a well-known pickpocket, doing one of his regular terms of imprisonment at Pentridge, had been detailed to clean out the wool store on the Saturday afternoon. He heard suspicious noises coming from the ceiling, then some dust and debris fell on his head and shoulders. He reported the matter to a warder.

The pickpocket would have rather cut off his hands than turn informer; but he became an unwitting instrument in the capture of Bradley and Wood, and his life was blighted with the suspicion that he had "shelfed" them.

When John West saw Arthur at the tote yard next day, he found him bitterly disappointed and on the verge of tears, like an orphan child who had been untruthfully promised the return of its mother.

One of the successful Labor candidates, financed by John West at the State elections of 1902, was the young radical journalist and orator, Frank Ashton.

The crowd cheered wildly as Ashton stepped forward to the front of the platform, the night the poll was declared. All sitting and standing room was filled. People milled around the platform, and outside the doors others pushed and scuffed to gain entry. The windows on either side of the hall were open and too many heads for comfort were thrust through them.

"Ladies and gentlemen," the speaker began in a clear, resonant voice. "Ladies and gentlemen, and fellow workers!"

His movements and words were hypnotic in their effect. He was plainly dressed. His high collar and tie seemed out of place. His long hair was parted in the centre above a broad forehead, and curled into locks over each ear. His chin was determined, his lips thick and sensuous, his eyes sharp and intelligent: a sensitive face which mirrored a kindly, emotional nature.

The cheering abated as he stood statuesque – his hand upraised in a plea for silence. He ran his fingers through his locks of hair in a characteristic gesture, then brought to bear the powers of oratory which were to become a household word throughout Australia.

He lowered his hands slowly and allowed a few moments of absolute silence.

"This is a proud moment in the life of a man whose years

'ave been dedicated to the cause of the poor and the underprivileged – the great cause of Labor.''

In the last phrase the handsome head nodded up and down, as though in time with the words. The Labor majority cheered loudly, while the Liberal and Conservative supporters, most of them hearing the speaker for the first time, were silent, not yet under his spell.

''I remember only too well, 'ow I came to this fair land; a wretched lad, a cabin boy on a freighter, who'd fled from the poverty of the old world to seek his fortune in the new.''

The poverty of the old world! Frank Ashton's first memory of his childhood was a train journey with his mother, after which he arrived in the dead of night to meet his new father in a huge barn among bags of horse feed and rats. To guard against the rats, his mother sat up all night by the table on which he was rolled in a bundle of clothes. He learned afterwards that the kindly man with the wooden leg who had begged his mother not to come to this place because it was too rough, was his stepfather. Frank Ashton's real father had died a few months before he was born. He could recall how the new father had made the old barn fit to live in, only to lose his job there.

The trio then began to wander up and down England, the father seeking work. The ground was hard with frost, the nights were bitterly cold; and none wanted a man with a wooden leg. Once they joined an unemployed procession in some town, and marched down the street. The marchers chanted slogans asking for bread, and the father said that they should have demanded work, not charity. Just when the little money he had saved ran out, the father obtained work in a mining town near Scarborough.

Frank Ashton remembered living in the barracks with the other miners. Each miner had a garden. The father worked his plot at the back of the barracks to the limit, growing vegetables, raising pigs. The son went to school in the village two miles away, and he was happy until the strike came. A miner who lost his job, lost his place in the barracks, and his garden plot, and a miner who went on strike suffered the same fate. Yet all the miners went on strike, so they must have had good reason. Their wages had been cut, the father said. They were evicted from the barracks by the mine owners; then the family lived in a bag humpy, and the strike continued.

The father seemed to be a leader of the strike. Frank Ashton remembered the vicar coming up from the village and telling the men to go back to their work like good Christians, and to cease bringing such misery on their wives and families. He remembered his father replying to the vicar, cursing the Church which sided with the mine owners by demanding that the men return like whipped curs to their dirty, unventilated barracks, and to the mines where they worked in dangerous conditions for miserable pay.

The vicar branded the father a heathen and a troublemaker. When Frank Ashton's mother began giving music lessons to children in the village, the vicar prevailed on the parents to take the pupils away from this woman, who was the wife of an atheist. And the father defiantly composed a song for the miners to sing:

> *The parson he preach and tell me to pray,*
> *To think of my work, and not ask for more pay;*
> *If I haven't got meat, to be thankful for bread,*
> *And thank the good God it ain't turnips instead.*

The father, like most of his comrades, never returned to the mine, preferring to shake the dust of the place from his boots after some of the men gave in and went back to work.

Frank Ashton spoke under the impetus of those memories. And he remembered London. London was slums and hunger. His mother sent him to school, and to church where he sang in the choir. Then the new baby arrived. His brother, yet not his brother!

When the baby was a few years old, Frank Ashton decided to run away to sea; perhaps he ran from the hunger, perhaps because this other child was the son of the man with the wooden leg, the kind man who treated him well enough, but who was not his father. He fled to the docks and hid aboard a ship, only to be discovered and put ashore again. He walked home in the dead of night, and, listening outside the kitchen window, heard his mother weeping and the father trying to console her, saying: "Don't cry, Carrie, he will come home when he gets hungry."

Frank Ashton *was* hungry, but he left the window and returned to the docks where he fell asleep on top of some bags, only to be awakened by the pain of rats chewing at his ears and hands. He shifted into a four-wheeled hand truck in the corner, but the

146

rats crawled up its handle to bite him again. Cold and frightened, he went on board the nearest ship, where the watchman gave him tea and biscuits and promised to stow him away. He fell asleep on his feet and the watchman made him a shakedown in the galley. When he awoke in the morning he was out at sea, bound for Melbourne. On discovery he was roundly cursed, then put to work. He was taught knots and splices. At night he wept in his little bunk from fatigue and loneliness.

When the ship arrived in Melbourne, the captain threatened to take him back to England, so he deserted and spent four years on ships plying their trade between Australia and the islands to the north, only to return again to Melbourne.

"It was in Melbourne that I became involved in the battles of the workin' class. First in the Seamen's Union, then in the Tramways, I studied Union affairs and Labor politics. Later I became caretaker of the Working Men's College, and there found opportunity to read, to educate myself. At the same time I 'eard all the stalwart leaders of the workin' men speak, in the street, in 'alls, and on the Yarra bank; and I soon resolved that I would dedicate myself to the cause of Labor, to the cause of Socialism. Yes, my friends, I 'ave battled for the great cause of Labor. Well I remember the struggle we 'ad to establish the co-operatives. Right here in this electorate I 'ad the honour to be Secretary of the Victorian Labor Federation which organised the co-operatives stores . . ."

The enthusiastic crowd interrupted him with cheering.

"We ultimately failed, but much was achieved; then friends prevailed upon me to enter the political sphere."

Perhaps, while the clapping and cheering rose again, there were a few Labor men in the audience who knew that Frank Ashton and some of his comrades in the dead Federation had agreed never to stand for Parliament, because Socialism could not be won that way. But now they, as well as the speaker, were carried away by the dream of the working men that all would be well if they sent their leaders to capture the Parliaments.

"In this election no section of electors can say that they are disfranchised, because the logic of figures 'as seen to it that both sections are represented."

The Liberals in the audience moved closer to sympathy with the speaker.

"I 'ave battled for Labor and the great principles of Labor,

147

and, in the interests of all those stalwarts of Labor who 'ave struggled and fought for me, I will give due representation to those principles and opinions.''

He half-turned towards the three men in the rear, and indicated one of them, the Government candidate who had also been elected under the existing system, which allowed two Members to represent one electorate on a proportional basis.

"Your Liberal Member, on the other 'and, will give representation to opinions of a different character.''

The cheering rose again and this time the Liberals joined in. What could be fairer than that? Even the few Conservative supporters present noticed the absence of the expected attack from one who for years had flayed capitalism on the Yarra bank and on street corners, and in colourful articles in the TOCSIN.

Frank Ashton ran his hands through his hair and waited for the cheering to cease.

He had found a new ambition to become a Member of Parliament; and tonight, at least, his ill will with the opponents of Labor was cast aside, while he took a stand that would induce additional voters to swing from Liberal to Labor at the next election.

"I wish to thank from the depths of my heart those fine stalwarts of Labor who 'ave battled so 'ard to ensure my return to Parliament . . .''

A motion of the hand as though snatching something out of the air, and a pace forward.

The audience was completely captured. The speaking was not refined, the g's and h's were dropped, but the words throbbed with emotion, the voice was musical.

"On the morrow I will somehow raise the money to send a lightnin' message through the unfathomed depths of the sea to a grey-haired couple in the greatest city in the world I left so long ago. A message that the son who left their fireside in childhood to seek fortune in a far-off land was no unworthy son of theirs.''

What manner of deception or self-deception was this? Frank Ashton still had left a few pounds from the money supplied by John West, the keeper of the Carringbush tote. He was ashamed of his acceptance of West's money, but said to himself that if he won the seat he could then do all the things he wanted to do for the working class. The Labor Party had no money. West was prepared to help. What harm could it to do the cause if he assisted the tote man against the "wowsers"? What harm had it done the cause that he had stopped the TOCSIN from attacking West?

"Yes, my friends, that grey-haired couple shall know that I am not an unworthy son of theirs, and the electors, who 'ave this day placed such great faith in me, shall know that I am not an unworthy representative of theirs."

The crowd went wild with clapping, whistling and cheering, and Frank Ashton retreated slowly into the gloom at the back of the platform.

Next Sunday morning, John and Nellie West attended Mass at an exclusive church near the mansion. Nellie knelt devoutly, silently following in English the Latin chanting of the priest and altar boys. In addition to her prayer book, she carried a string of rosary beads hanging over her arm.

John West knelt casually, a handkerchief under his knees to protect his suit from the dust of the kneeling rail. The mass held little attraction for him, he did not understand it or seriously want to. He attended each Sunday to pacify Nellie and because it was good for business – Catholics were loyal to members of their own faith. If he prayed it was to ask for some material favour which he usually got by dint of his own tenacity and ruthlessness. The mystical atmosphere of the Church gripped him sometimes: the candlelight, the flower-bedecked altar, the paintings of the Stations of the Cross on the wall, and the dim-lit statues of Saints and the Virgin Mary; but today his thoughts were far away.

In the State elections he had moved closer to his goal of winning decisive influence in the Victorian Parliament. He was known as the richest and most generous supporter the Labor Party had in Victoria. As well as most Labor candidates, he had assisted several Liberal candidates who had been won over by David Garside. The Conservatives he left strictly alone; they were unspeakable wowsers bent on closing his tote.

A bell rang quietly and one of the two red-and-white uniformed altar boys walked up the steps to where the priest in Mass regalia was standing in front of the altar. The boy shifted the book. The congregation stood up. A nudge from Nellie awakened John West from his election reverie for a moment, and he slowly followed.

Of the fourteen successful Labor candidates, he had paid the expenses of eight. He could depend on them if further attempts were made to amend the Gaming Act, and he felt he could depend on most of the other Labor members, too. His political plans did not run yet to anything further than protecting the tote. The Labor Party, he had found, seemed to support David Garside's idea that gambling should not be the preserve of the rich. He was still finding opposition from a minority of Labor men. These were extremists, he was told, the socialist section. Yet Ashton was a socialist, and he had helped, and had promised to oppose any Act aimed at the tote.

Politics was a very complicated business, John West had discovered; but he was learning fast. This campaign had taught him one principle at least: you must support the man who could win both the pre-selection ballot and the seat. No use throwing your money away on a man who could not win. He had supported several unsuccessful candidates, including the Carringbush Independent Liberal who had again failed to get the Labor pre-selection, and a young fellow named Bob Scott, whom John West had known years ago in the boot trade.

Scott had become a leading member of the Melbourne Trades Hall Council. Scott gambled on the tote; he was quite prepared to protect the tote in Parliament. He won the Labor pre-selection in an industrial seat, yet was defeated by an ex-Labor man who still had wide support among the workers.

John West recalled Bob Scott's speech at the declaration of the poll. "Little Bob Scott is defeated, but the cause of Labor will go on forever." He wondered did Scott believe that sort of thing. Didn't matter, anyway, as long as he supported the tote in Parliament when he got there. "Bob Scott will fight for the cause of Labor till he ceases to draw breath; and he will fight against conservatives and the capitalistic exploiters who are ruining the State," Scott had said, yet as far as John West could gather, Scott was merely an ambitious young man seeking a seat in Parliament.

John West found it difficult to understand the revolutionary, idealistic utterances of some of his men, which were not in keeping with utterances made privately to him. Of one thing he felt certain: the Labor Party would grow; and the sooner the better, for it was still the smallest group in the House.

When the congregation sat down again he remained standing until Nellie tugged his coat-tail.

The Mass moved slowly to its end.

As they walked out of the churchyard, Nellie held his arm tightly. She was bewildered and a little cowed by her husband. Doubts she hardly dared admit to herself had aroused forebodings about him. He had been morose and ill-tempered during her pregnancy; and, obviously wanting a son, had taken little interest in her lovely baby girl. Marjorie. She knew little of his affairs except occasional press reports and rumours. He never discussed anything with her, and when any of his associates came to the house he didn't even introduce them to her. Not that she wanted to meet them; they were, to her, a frightening crew. Why had she married him? Why had he married her? The only tie between them seemed to be his desire for her body, which was already waning.

When they arrived home, John West went to the reception room at the front of the ground floor to read the sporting pages of Saturday's press; but today he could not concentrate, his thoughts turned again to politics.

Dabbling in politics appealed to him: the organisation of helpers for the candidates, the stacking of meetings with his gang, the deference paid to him by aspiring politicians.

One day he would gain control of the Victorian Parliament. He would win protection for the tote and in doing so achieve his new power. Power wielded behind the scenes, power over deliberations of Parliament!

CHAPTER FIVE

A man can inspire terror only if he has great power to do evil.

HONORÉ DE BALZAC

Early one evening in the winter of 1903, two men sat talking to John West in Cummin's Tea Shop. They were an ill-assorted pair: Paddy Woodman, short, jolly and fat; Squash Lewis, tall, grave and thin; Paddy, a Catholic; Squash, a Freemason. But they both knew how to get money from gamblers.

"Between O'Flaherty and the wowsers, you'll be out of business," said Paddy Woodman. He was gaudily dressed in a check suit, a yellow waistcoat and a flowing bow tie, and was nursing a boxer-hat on his knee. His head was bald: it shone like a china egg in the light of the gas lamp. "O'Flaherty put us out, and he'll put you out, too, unless we take over this club together. He might be Irish, but he's from the north, where all the traitors and Orangemen come from."

"Listen!" John West said aggressively. "No one can put me out, not even O'Flaherty. We might make a deal, if it suits me, but I'm not worried about O'Flaherty, or the bloody wowsers, either." John West was really very worried about both O'Flaherty and the wowsers, especially O'Flaherty.

Woodman began to massage the crown of his bald head vigorously with the palm of his right hand, as he always did when worried.

"You'll be 'appy h'if you come in with h'us," intervened Squash Lewis. "Ho'Flaherty will be h'unable to do h'any 'arm." He wore a dark suit, and was puffing vigorously at a big cigar, filling the shop with smoke. He was six feet in height: all legs, giving the impression, when standing or walking, that he was mounted on stilts. "Just think h'of it, Mr. West. You'll 'ave the Tattersall's Club h'itself as a prostitute for the tote, if Ho'Flaherty closes h'it down."

"Prostitute!" Woodman said disdainfully. "You mean substitute, Squash. He means substitute, Mr. West."

"But you can't call the new club the Tattersall's Club," John West said. "The other Tattersall's Club is still going in another premises. They restrained the police in court from cancelling the licence."

"Sure they did, me boy, but we'll call ours the City Tattersall's Club. Sounds real nice, I reckon, 'The City Tattersall's Club, Patrick Woodman, Secretary.' And all I'll be doing is running me hazards school upstairs."

In Sydney, Squash and Paddy had conducted a highly profitable business until the police drove them out. Back in Melbourne they re-established themselves, only to be driven out by Detective-Sergeant O'Flaherty. They then conceived an ambition to take over the highly respectable Tattersall's Club as a venue for a new hazards school. They succeeded in having the Club evicted from the building, and now believed that, if they entered into an alliance with the famous John West, they would be able to carry on business in peace and prosperity.

The negotiations continued for half an hour. John West haggled and cavilled, but finally agreed to share the premises with them on condition that their names appeared as proprietors of the City Tattersall's Club.

When they departed, John West rubbed his hands gleefully. Now O'Flaherty could do his worst. Devlin reckoned that O'Flaherty intended raiding the Jackson Street tote in the near future, and closing it down permanently in spite of loopholes in the law. Let him try! The City Tattersall's Club would be even harder to close than the tote.

John West took a newspaper from a drawer and spread it on the table, and read the headlines:

THE TOTE CENTRE – SKILFULLY MANAGED
PROJECT – OWNERS LAUGH AT THE LAW

———

Some Interesting Details

———

He read the article for the tenth time that day. It was a friendly article, describing the tote, the betting platform and the garb of the masked men. He felt that its publication would help him in the impending war with O'Flaherty.

Presently, a tall man about John West's age entered the room.

153

His face was long and lantern-jawed; his appearance neat but sly. His name was Bennett. He was better known as The Gentleman Thief. Tonight his self-assurance had deserted him; he was agitated and frowning.

After greeting John West, he sat down, pushed his hat to the back of his head, and took a letter from his overcoat pocket. "The New Zealand people have woke up to my brother," he said. "There's going to be trouble. Look at this!" His lower jaw worked like that of a ventriloquist's doll.

Bennett handed the letter to John West, who read it.

> *At a meeting of the New Zealand Trotting Association held last night, H. Bennett, alias Smith, and the mare Nellie W, alias Phoebe, were disqualified for life for ringing in. The meeting further resolved that the Australian Trotting Association be requested to consider the position of the Secretary, W. J. Bennett, in issuing a licence and certificate to H. Bennett in the name of Smith. This Association recommends that W. J. Bennett be disqualified for his share in the proceedings, and refuses in future to recognise registrations and other papers signed by the said W. J. Bennett . . .*

The contents of the letter occasioned no surprise to John West. When in New Zealand on his honeymoon he had become interested in trotting, and on his return purchased three trotting horses. One of them he named Nellie W, giving his wife the honour of being the first of a long line of people after whom he named his racehorses. In the hands of a leading trainer-driver, Nellie W won several races in Melbourne until her "mark" became too "hard." She was soon giving long starts to her rivals. Unable to win more races with her in Melbourne, John West arranged with The Gentleman Thief that his brother take the mare to New Zealand, after changing her name to Phoebe.

Obtaining clearance papers for the ring-in was a simple matter: The Gentleman Thief himself being, as well as Secretary of the Melbourne Trotting Club, President of the Australian Trotting Association, in which capacity it was his duty to sign clearance papers for horses to race interstate or overseas. The mare won several races in New Zealand, and John West and the Bennetts made big money. After she returned, the identity of the mare was discovered. Two New Zealand trotting men on a visit to Melbourne recognised Nellie W as one and the same with Phoebe, and reported this fact to the New Zealand trotting authorities.

"Well?" John West said.

"Well, I've lost my job as President of the Association, and I hear I'm likely to be disqualified for life."

"Why worry? We've cleaned up. You can race your horses in someone else's name."

"But everyone knows that your wife's name is Nellie, and that the mare is really yours. You might get disqualified, too."

"I don't think I will, but why worry? I'll race the mare in someone else's name."

"Anyway, the Melbourne Trotting Club is not likely to make a deal with you after this," Bennett persisted.

John West leant forward rapping the table. "You're still secretary, aren't you? Well, stay secretary!"

"I'll be able to stay secretary if you bring your influence to bear to fix this thing up."

"All right, I'll fix it up. Trouble with you is you get scared when something goes wrong. You keep working to get the Melbourne Trotting Club to sell out to me."

"It's not going to be easy, Jack. It'll cost a lot of money."

"Cost a lot of money! Everything costs a lot of money! The politicians and the police bleed me, the church bleeds me, and now the trotting club is going to bleed me."

"If you can get control of the trotting club, you'll make a fortune, and you know it."

"Well, you see that I do get control of it! Do what I said. The club's none too financial. Send it broke, and then come to me for assistance. I had a talk to young Lammence, president of the club. He's the man I want."

"Frank Lammence is all right, Jack. But you want to watch him; he's shrewd. Too quiet for my likin'. Put somethin' over you as quick as he'd look at yer."

"Don't worry. I know how to handle him. He's just the man I want to look after trotting for me later; and don't be surprised if I start running pony races, too. Conduct the races and run a book on them as well: that's my programme."

"It's a big programme, Jack."

"Not too big for Jack West, don't worry," John West said emphatically. "Did you see this write up of the tote in the HERALD?"

"Yes. You'll need all the publicity you can get to beat the wowsers. I see where the local mob of wowsers are holding another meeting tonight. They're kicking up a stink about the tote, Jack. What are you going to do?"

"Oh, I'm not worried about them. They're meeting in the Tabernacle Church tonight. I sent some of my men along just to brighten it up a bit."

The local mob of wowsers, as Bennett had irreverently styled the Carringbush Prohibition and Public Morals League, certainly were kicking up a stink. They wrote to the press; they sent deputations to the Chief Secretary; they spoke from the pulpits of the Protestant churches: they held meetings such as the one about to begin when Bennett bade John West goodbye.

The church was full as the Rev. Mr. Owen, a timid, devout weed of a man, stepped into the pulpit. He would have preferred that the band of noisy men at the back had stayed away. He began speaking in a rather high-pitched voice, and outlined the aims of the League as if he were delivering his Sunday sermon.

"My dear brethren, the aims of this organisation of prominent citizens are as follows: First, to suppress all forms of gambling; second, to secure a direct vote on all liquor licences."

The speaker looked nervously over his glasses towards the back of the hall, and gave a squeaky cough; but to his surprise no one rushed the platform or threw any vegetables. "Ahem – third, to secure a righteous observance of the Sabbath; fourth, to prevent the public sale of obscene literature; fifth, to take united action against all houses of ill fame, and to encourage a high standard of public morals."

Owen continued tremulously. "I have received a private and confidential letter telling me that a mob will endeavour to disturb this meeting and defeat its objectives. Such action would be silly. Anyone will admit, in view of what is happening around us, in our very midst is degradation of all kinds, that such an organisation as the League is needed."

He looked again towards the large group at the back of the church, but again they made no move, nor any sound above

156

earnest whispering. This gave him added courage. "As I have said before, the main object of the League is to suppress the totalisator in Jackson Street, which is a monstrosity – a reptile sucking up the life-blood of the people and ruining their homes!"

Suddenly a voice that echoed in all corners of the church roared out: "Go on, rub it in! Rub it in!"

The reverend gentleman looked up and viewed the interjector nervously. That big rough fellow with the cauliflower ears! No doubt, he and his friends are here to make trouble! This meeting will meet the same fate as those of politicians who oppose West's candidates. All heads of the League members and supporters in the front of the church turned towards the back; then the speaker marshalled all his courage and continued, with a desperate show of vigour.

"This totalisator encourages idlers and is a resort of people who prey on the public." League supporters applauded half-heartedly, almost apprehensively. The mob at the back hissed and booed.

"Personally I have no quarrel with Mr. West, the reputed owner of the totalisator. I have indeed heard excellent things said in his favour as to his charitable actions."

Loud cheers from the back of the church; half-hearted clapping from the front.

Having thus compromised with the opposition, Owen proceeded to placate his own followers with a violent attack on the tote and suggested drastic police action against it. A noisy conference was held at the back. The speaker looked around for a means of escape, but, seeing none, continued: "I hope, ladies and gentlemen, that nothing will happen in this building tonight that will bring the House of God into disrepute."

Cauliflower Dick rose to his feet. "I want to ask a question!" he shouted.

"Later on, my friend, at the appointed time."

"What! Are yer puttin' on the gag?"

A young man then rose at the front of the hall to support the League: He assured the meeting, especially the back half, that he had "nothing personal against Mr. West." It was the tote itself he was opposing, and all forms of gambling. "Why," he continued, "I was once a patron of Mr. West's tote myself, but I found a better friend in Jesus Christ."

When the man who had deserted John West for Christ sat down, Owen continued his attack on gambling.

Remembering with regret that John West had advised against violence, Cauliflower Dick said: "Ah, come on! Let 'em keep their silly bloody meetin'," and he and his mob departed.

A month later the Victorian public was greeted with the following advertisement in all the daily papers. It had been written by Barney Robinson.

JOHN WEST

begs to notify that he is doing business on the TWO
CUPS, *Epsom and Metropolitan, straightout, place or*
SP on all events.

CITY TATTERSALL'S CLUB
224 Bourke Street, Melb.
Tele. 3103
Telegraphic Address:
John West, Melbourne
(Correspondence promptly attended to)

The premises at 224 Bourke Street were quite elaborate. Downstairs was a billiard room with two big tables, a sort of café where members could obtain food and drink at a price, and a lounge room containing several big settees and armchairs. On the walls hung photos of gallopers, ponies, trotters, boxers and footballers. The sporting and daily papers were supplied for the convenience of members. A set of the Encyclopaedia Brittannmica stood rather incongruously in the corner on a stand. Barney Robinson had insisted that it "would set the place off with a bit of tone," and he was often to be seen studying its ample pages.

Upstairs, in the front room, Squash Lewis and Paddy Woodman conducted their hazards school. In another and larger room, John West conducted his book-making; behind a counter at one end he and his clerks took bets from members and answered the telephones. Members paid a shilling a year and Paddy and Squash made a pretence of managerial responsibility.

This use of the building was appropriate to its history. In the '80's, Jem Mace, an English fighting man, conducted a sporting establishment on the premises. When he cleared out, Squash Lewis and Paddy Woodman ran the place disguised as a hairdresser's shop, with a hazards school attached. The allies came to temporary grief about 1890 and went to Sydney.

Their place was taken by the more or less respectable Saqui, who styled himself a 'Turf Accountant and Cigar Importer.' Saqui rigged the place out as a cigar divan, taking the precaution of putting the prices for races in the window and having a betting establishment upstairs. His business card informed prospective clients that he imported the best cigars, bought and sold racehorses as an agent, set turf commissions and laid the odds. But the police were ungracious enough to arrest him in 1896. After serving his sentence, he went to Sydney hoping to dress his divan window replete with betting lists without police interference.

Then a young Jewish immigrant named Solomon Solomons moved into the building as manager of the Tattersall's Club. The club catered for the big men of the turf. Owners, trainers, breeders, business men and squatters obtained food and drink, played billiards and cards on the premises; but the manager, Solomons, was more interested in it as the venue of the biggest "off the course" connection in all Australia. "Sol Solomons – Melbourne" was sufficient address for his thousands of clients, large or small. No one seemed to be aware of his record, After arriving from England he had entered the noble profession of pocket-picking, and was imprisoned in Sydney when his operations were discovered. Released, he came to Melbourne, only to be imprisoned for pawning a watch: someone discovered that it was not his watch. His second spell in prison convinced him that there must be easier ways of earning a living, so he married a rich Jewess, set himself up as a bookmaker, and soon became known as The Leviathan of the Turf.

Solomon reigned in all his glory until the middle of 1903, when Squash Lewis and Paddy Woodman saw the landlord, tripled the rent, had Sol evicted, and linked up with John West.

One evening about six months after the opening of the City Tattersall's Club, the Chief Commissioner of the Victorian Police Force, Thomas Callinan, walked up the Bourke Street hill. He was a big man, six feet tall and inclined to be fat. He was fashionably dressed; a top hat covered his white, thinning hair, and he flourished a walking-cane.

Thomas Callinan achieved the ambition of his life when he was appointed Chief Commissioner. He was a conceited man, and had thrilled at the prospect of power and social status which the position promised him. But instead his life had become more and more miserable as the months went by.

Callinan had been one of the first detectives to go on to John West's payroll; and when he became Chief Commissioner West proved a ruthless taskmaster. Callinan was in West's power and there seemed to be no escape. Rumours were circulating that even the Police Commissioner was not free from West's "influence money." Questions were being asked in Parliament by Conservative members about the immunity from the law enjoyed by the Jackson Street tote and the bogus City Tattersall's Club. The wowsers were screaming for action against the gambling mania and the reign of terror being exercised by West, who was now resorting to open violence.

Only a few weeks before, a young police recruit, who had been brought into the force by O'Flaherty to act as a spy in the Carringbush tote, had been ejected suffering a black eye and severe cuts and abrasions. A few days later, another new recruit, who was to carry out a similar task in the City Tattersall's Club, was seized by six masked men when alighting from a tram near his home, and brutally bashed with an iron bar, kicked about the face and head, and left lying insensible in the gutter. This man was still in hospital and would carry marks of his experience of the rest of his life.

Thomas Callinan felt that if he could restrain O'Flaherty, West might desist from his impudent reprisals, but O'Flaherty would not be restrained. He even hinted that he was aware of the Chief Commissioner's infamous arrangement with West.

"Dave O'Flaherty is chief of the gaming squad," he had exclaimed. "And Dave O'Flaherty will end West's career in spite of his protection money and loopholes in the gaming laws!"

Half-way up the hill, Callinan stopped in front of the Royal Oak Hotel. Standing near the wall out of the glow of the lamp on the street corner, he cast furtive glances up and down the street before entering the hotel. He walked quickly up the stairs and so to the end of the passage, where he knocked softly on the last door on the right.

He stood impatiently for a moment looking this way and that, then he heard John West's voice say: "Come in!" He entered quickly, took off his hat and sat down.

The room was small and barely furnished. John West was seated behind an office table, while his brother, Arthur, sat at his right elbow in a gloomy corner. There were three photos on the wall – one of Nellie W, the trotting mare, one of a prize-fighter, and one of a footballer in the black and white guernsey of the Carringbush club. John West used this room mainly for the purpose of interviewing detectives and others of his associates who did not wish to be seen entering the club or the tote.

"I've come here at a great risk," Callinan said, juggling his hat and cane nervously.

"I have your money here. Wondered why you haven't been calling for it the last few weeks," said John West, opening a drawer in the table.

"I haven't come about money, West, I wish I'd never had anything to do with your filthy money."

John West closed the drawer slowly. Arthur watched Callinan with a sullen glint of hatred in his eyes.

"This is a private conversation," Callinan said.

"Oh," said John West, "you ought to know this gentleman."

"Well, I don't!"

"You ought to. This is my brother, Arthur. Arty, this is His Lordship, the Chief Commissioner of Police."

Arthur West nodded.

Callinan stammered: "I think I've heard of you."

"If you haven't, you will," Arthur West answered.

Callinan looked from one to the other. John: implacable, taciturn, crafty; Arthur: weak, bitter, cruel. Callinan's long dealing with the criminal class had brought him close to the worst of men; but he knew that here were two of the most dangerous characters he had ever met.

John West interrupted his thoughts. "So you're scared of the wowsers, are you?"

"No."

"Well, why don't you want the money?"

"Why? Because no one can protect you. You go too far. You shoot policemen, you bribe witnesses, you maim your enemies. That's why. From now on, the law is after you, West."

"Do you think you're wise to talk like this?"

"I should have talked like this long ago."

"You realise that the majority of detectives will have other ideas, don't you?"

"Unfortunately, yes. But there are enough wanting to put you out of business to make it very awkward for you."

"The law is not strong enough. You haven't the power."

"Perhaps I can get the power."

"If you're thinking of the Government, you're mistaken," John West said, with more hope than conviction.

"Well, law or no law, I'm after you, and so is Dave O'Flaherty."

"I'm not frightened of O'Flaherty," John West said. He took a neat bundle of bank notes from the drawer and toyed with them, waving them gently up and down. "You're sure you won't change your mind?"

"I'll never change my mind."

"You're foolish to worry about the wowsers and their deputations; or about the Chief Secretary, either, for that matter. He told them you'd have to break the law in order to catch me."

"Maybe Dave O'Flaherty *is* prepared to break the law to catch you."

John West tossed the notes back into the drawer. "Please yourself. You know I have a habit of dealing with anyone who plays the double on me, don't you?"

"Are you threatening me? Me, the Chief Commissioner of Police?"

"Take it how you like. Chiefs of Police mean nothing to me. Keep away! Leave things as they are! You can't beat me, Callinan, and I advise you not to try. You've taken money from me. How would you like that to get around?"

"You wouldn't dare."

"Wouldn't I? Try me too far, and see for yourself."

Callinan became placatory. "I'll tell you what I am prepared to do. You close the tote and I'll get O'Flaherty to leave the City Tattersall's Club alone."

"Not interested. The tote and club will both stay open, and not all the bloody traps in Australia can close either of them!"

"All right," Callinan said, abashed, "if that's the way you want it, then that's the way you'll get it. With all your precautions, and smart lawyers, and basher gangs, and paid detectives, and politicians, I'll beat you yet." He spoke without assurance, expressing a fighting spirit he didn't feel. He had come to make some kind of truce, some compromise. He had forced himself into a false position.

Callinan rose and moved hesitantly towards the door. He did not want the talk to end this way. Neither did John West.

"Why should we quarrel anyway," John West said, in a more pleasant manner, "we're of the same religion, aren't we?"

The Chief Commissioner strode back from the door and leaned on the table aggressively. "You talk about religion! All you've ever done with the church is use it for your own advantage. Why, there's not a spark of religion in your whole body. If it's influence with the church you're depending on, I think I have as much as yourself."

"How old are you, Callinan?"

"Mind your own business."

"You're over sixty, aren't you? And there's been an outcry against you raising the retiring age to sixty-five, so's you can keep your job, hasn't there? The force is up in arms, isn't it? There are a lot of ambitious men who want your job, aren't there? I think it's wrong to extend the retiring age to sixty-five; so I think I'll bring my influence to bear to have it lowered again, so's the Chief of Police and his doddery old pals will be put out of the force!"

Callinan straightened. "You're a ruthless, vicious man, West. I pray God for the strength to stand up to you." He went out, slamming the door.

John West sat pensively until Arthur stood up and said: "I'll deal with that bastard for yer, Jack!"

John West relaxed slowly. "No, you won't. Too risky. There are more ways of killing a dog than bashing its brains out."

Some two weeks later, at three o'clock in the morning, three drag-loads of sturdy men drove up Jackson Street, Carringbush. The men, who were dressed in civilian clothes, alighted some five hundred yards from Cummin's tea shop. All were armed with loaded revolvers or rifles, and some carried a lantern, an axe, a pick, or crowbar. They stood in the black night in a group around Detective-Sergeant David O'Flaherty, whose hulking figure towered over the biggest of them.

163

"Now, men," said O'Flaherty. "You have your instructions. Carry them out to the letter! And remember, if there is any resistance, shoot to kill!"

Detective-Sergeant O'Flaherty was in his element. His first assignment in the force had been to assist in overcoming the desperate resistance of the Kelly gang at Glenrowan; now he would assail the fortress of John West, beside whom, O'Flaherty considered, Ned Kelly had been a gentleman.

The violent reprisals taken against his spies had made O'Flaherty all the more determined to end John West's career, and the recent change of attitude on the part of Callinan made his task less difficult. O'Flaherty was convinced that he had found a way round the inadequacy of the gaming laws, and the Crown Law Department was inclined to agree with him. He would occupy the wood-yard, the tote yard and shop, and if West claimed his property back, he would arrest him for conducting the tote. If West didn't apply for the return of his property, the police would stay in occupation until doomsday.

O'Flaherty formed his carefully chosen squad into ten ranks of three, and they marched behind him towards the tote. All were at a high pitch of excitement. They knew what to expect if West's guard – desperate characters and expert gunmen – resisted. The marching feet crunched resolutely. There were a few faint hearts in the ranks, but Dave O'Flaherty swung along in front, hoping for another Glenrowan.

Inside the tote, One-eyed-Tommy was sitting drowsily on a box in front of a fire in the middle of the yard while Piggy, The Ape and Cauliflower Dick were asleep on the tote platform each wrapped in a few blankets. Piggy was snoring loudly. One-eyed-Tommy's head was beginning to nod, his good eye closed in sleep, his vacant eyesocket leering horribly in the dull light of the fire.

Presently the chilly air was shattered as the back gate of the wood-yard was assailed with axes, picks and crowbars. In an instant it burst open and Dave O'Flaherty dashed through, an axe in one hand and a revolver in the other, followed by several other armed men.

One-eyed-Tommy roused himself, straightened up and rubbed his sleepy eye. The Ape and Cauliflower Dick stirred slowly, but Piggy continued to snore.

When the import of the hubbub penetrated his sleepy brain, One-eyed-Tommy got to his feet. As he did so The Ape and Cauliflower Dick sat up sleepily. They heard the gate of the tote yard itself being attacked. It crashed open and they saw gloomy figures rushing at them.

One-eyed-Tommy was at a disadvantage: not only was he half asleep, but he could not see into the darkness beyond the fire. The Ape and Cauliflower Dick stood up sleepily, and Piggy, finally aroused, sat up rubbing his eyes. One-eyed-Tommy drew his revolver, but before he could use it he was overpowered by several policemen. The other guards climbed awkwardly between the bars of the platform into the arms of their captors.

Then came sounds of axe and crowbar blows on the front door of the shop. But it was not until some of the policemen in the yard smashed their way through into the shop and attacked the bars, chains and padlocks from inside that the entrance to John West's office gave way.

That task completed, the four tote guards were hustled violently into the back lane. The Jackson Street fortress had fallen.

Half an hour later, a noise penetrated the slumber of John West. Beside him, Nellie stirred and groaned softly in her sleep. She was heavy with child again, and had been tossing restlessly. John West, insisting on the need for fresh air, had had the walls of the room removed from the two outer sides to make an open air bedroom.

He sat bolt upright, drew a revolver from under the pillow, and leapt out of bed. he pulled on his shoes, threw a coat over his shoulders and walked slowly, picking his way in the darkness, out of the door through the dressing-room adjoining, and so to the top of the stairs. There was someone knocking impatiently at the front door. His heart was pounding. He was gripped by a tension of fear and excitement. Who could it be? The police? Some enemy? He descended the stairs slowly one by one. He should have a guard here at the house as well as elsewhere, he thought.

As he neared the bottom of the stairs, the knocking came again – loud and menacing.

He approached the front door hesitantly, crouched with the gun pointed unsteadily in front of him. He hoped the servants would not hear from their quarters at the back of the house. He stood in front of the ornate front door waiting for the knocking to come again. After what seemed an eternity it came. His hair was tingling at the roots. He had difficulty in speaking. When his voice came it seemed as loud as the crack of a stock-whip splitting the air.

"Who's there?"

"Me, Tommy. The traps have taken over the tote. They're there now, dozens of 'em. Come down, for crissake!"

At first the news did not fully register on John West's brain because of his relief that no physical danger lurked outside. His whole body relaxed and the gun slumped to his side. He noticed that he was shivering.

"All right," he said, "I'll come down. Wait there."

"For gawd's sake hurry," One-eyed-Tommy answered.

John West walked back towards the stairs.

"Where are you, John? Where are you? What's the matter?" It was Nellie's voice at the top of the stairs.

"It's all right. Just someone wants to see me."

She began to cry hysterically. As he entered the room, she clambered back into the bed-clothes and lay there shuddering. "What do people want calling at this hour?" she queried, terrified. "And why have you got that gun? Why do you keep it under the pillow? Why did you take it downstairs?"

John West dressed hurriedly. "Something has cropped up." he said, and left her weeping, to join One-eyed-Tommy at the front door.

They got into One-eyed-Tommy's cab and he drove headlong down the hill towards Carringbush. One-eyed-Tommy related what had occurred, and had to admit under cross-examination that last evening they had neglected to remove the ticket and other evidence from the tote yard. His fear now past, John West was furious.

In Jigger's kitchen, they found Piggy, Cauliflower Dick, The Ape, Jigger and Joe and Arthur West sitting around the table in the light of a kerosene lamp. As John West entered, Jigger arose hurriedly and gave him his chair. One-eyed-Tommy and Jigger sat on the floor.

There was an air of expectant nervousness in the room.

"Well, what did you let them in for," John West snarled.

166

After a long pause, Joe answered: "How could they stop them? There was about thirty of 'em armed to the teeth."

"They should have heared them in time. If they'd met 'em at the gate and turned the guns on them, they would've gone away. I know these johnnys, they'reall squibs!"

"We had no time, Jack," Piggy lied apologetically. "They was on us in a flash."

"One-eyed-Tommy said you were asleep. I don't pay you to sleep. And I don't pay you to leave the slips and sheets in there at night. Whose job was it to take them out last night?"

"Mine, Jack," said Cauliflower Dick, shamefaced. "But we haven't had a raid for years and weren't expecting . . ."

"I told you they would soon come. I doubled the guard. I told you to tighten up, and you'll do what you're told," John West said, tapping the table with his fingers. "It was your job to get those sheets out, Dick. All right, go in and get them out now!"

"Nark it, Jack. The place is full of bloody wallopers."

"That's your look-out. You should have removed the sheets last night. You scale the fence and make a run through the yard. If the sheets and tickets are still there grab 'em and run out again. Never mind the gowns and masks, they're not evidence."

"Why don't we shoot our way in?" Arthur West suggested.

"Don't be mad. It's too late to start shooting now."

"Ar, I can't go in there, Jack;' they'd shoot a man stone dead," Cauliflower Dick whined.

"You'll do it or get out."

The former boxer looked around the room despairingly, but found no sign of support among the shadowy faces. John West walked into the backyard. It was now daylight, and groups of people were already gathering around the tote block, expectantly, as though they thought John West would lead his men to recover the tote by force.

John West stood on a box, peeped over the fence into the tote yard. He saw several policemen and detectives standing in groups. He surveyed the scene quickly. There was just a desperate chance that a man could run the gauntlet to the platform and grab the incriminating sheets and tickets if they were still lying where they had been the night before.

He went back into the house and said to Cauliflower Dick:

"Go on! Make a run for it. If the sheets and tickets are still there, you should be able to grab them."

"Cut it out, Jack. I can't do it."

"Go on! Scale the fence! You either do it or get out!"

Cauliflower Dick walked slowly towards the back fence, mounted the box, and took a quick look into the tote yard. Driven on by fear and desperation, he scrambled over and ran half doubled towards the platform.

The others waited tensely in the kitchen. They heard Cauliflower Dick's voice screaming: "Don't shoot! Don't shoot!"

Joe West ran to the box in time to see Cauliflower Dick being hustled through the gate by three burly policemen.

Later that morning, John West saw David Garside, who warned him not to claim the tote premises, and promised to prepare a legal campaign against O'Flaherty.

That night, John West lay awake. He overcame fear and doubt. He had developed the indomitable will that arises from the exercise of power. He had learned the real laws of the society in which he lived. Victory went to the strong. If you had money, cunning and power then the courts and the police could not defeat you. Talent, honour and influence could be bought. Men could be cajoled, bribed, intimidated, terrorised! The exercise of power was a joy. He had given his whole spirit over to it.

With typical irony, he made his first moves. He sent a reluctant Patrick Cummin to claim "his" tea shop and woodyard. Scotch Paddy with an axe over his shoulder approached the back gate and demanded entry. Dave O'Flaherty scornfully told him that the police were remaining in occupation of the premises until further notice – if West wanted his tote, let him come and get it!

Next day the Carringbush tote began operations again right under the noses of the occupying police, in a house in Bagville Street.

The press in Melbourne and as far afield as Sydney spread the news with story and cartoon, at first treating the matter as a joke; but Detective-Sergeant O'Flaherty and others who sought to defeat John West found no humour in the events that followed.

To punish those who defied him had become necessity to John West. Taking reprisals was part of the satisfaction of power, and the means of taking reprisals were readily at hand: in the tote and club alone he now employed over a hundred men, and there were some desperate characters among them.

A man who kept a shop near the City Tattersall's Club began to spy on it for O'Flaherty. He was discovered. Under orders from John West, a brick was thrown through his window; as quickly as he replaced the pane, the window was smashed again and again. O'Flaherty and other detectives were shadowed day and night. Threatening anonymous letters were written to Melbourne and Carringbush wowsers who were publicly denouncing John West. The detective office was constantly watched. The police training depots for recruits was spied upon, and new constables seeking entry to the Tattersall's Club in civilian clothes were forcibly ejected.

A journalist, financed by Protestant Ministers of Religion, published a pamphlet exposing the corruption among sections of the detective force and demanding action against "West, the parasite who battens on the poor." The journalist was waylaid by two masked men. One of them, Arthur West, brought an iron bar down on his skull. A window-ledge deflected the blow and saved his life, but he was taken unconscious to hospital.

Meantime, the police remained for months in the tote premises. John West began a campaign through friendly pressmen. The AGE suggested that the tote should be legalised, quoting in justification isolated dividends which compared favourably with prices of legal course book-makers. the HERALD ran an editorial condemning the waste of public money in the futile occupation of the tote which involved sixty men in three shifts of twenty. The ARGUS, however, touted for the wowsers, giving publicity to the campaign against the tote.

O'Flaherty, baulked by the inadequacy of the law, waited in vain for John West to request the return of his property the guard on the tote was gradually reduced until only one constable remained on duty day and night.

John West decided to recapture the fortress.

One morning, just after daylight, the lone guard walked from the tote into the wood-yard. In a flash five masked figures clattered over the fence. He was stunned by a rain of blows. He felt a gun in his ribs. He struggled, but his attackers relieved him of his keys, blackened his eye and tossed him into Bagville Street.

Next morning the press featured the story. Shortly afterwards,

Arthur West, The Ape, Piggy, Cauliflower Dick and a new man named Long Bill were charged with assault. David Garside, who had recommended the re-occupation, excelled himself during the hearing. He had found an old English law, on the basis of which he successfully argued that the constable was trespassing in the sacred precincts of the tote. The accused were acquitted.

John West emerged from the campaign famous and notorious throughout Australia. The so-called wowsers who opposed all forms of gambling ranted against him; Socialists in the working-class movement and the Sydney BULLETIN, still a radical paper, denounced him as a menace to the poor; but even the BULLETIN was forced to admit that in Melbourne "more people turned in the street to look at John West than at the Governor-General."

His reputation for generosity triumphed over the propaganda against him. Wherever he went he distributed largesse. A shabby man would receive the price of a feed, another a tip for the races; punters who lost at the tote or club were sometimes given a few bob to change their luck; a tattered woman would stop him in the street and show him the arrears in her rent book and have them wiped out. He ostentatiously donated to the Catholic Church and to charities; among many people his name became synonymous with cheerful generosity.

With drive and a genius for organisation which astonished his associates, he directed his empire. He added trotting and boxing promotion to his enterprises. Bennet had succeeded in obtaining control of the Melbourne Trotting Club for him, and its secretary, Frank Lammence, entered John West's employ, controlling the weekly trotting meetings and assisting in the management of "City Tatt's."

John West also planned to rid himself of the Chief Commissioner of Police. Through friendly policemen he fanned the agitation against the raising of the retiring age to sixty-five. Even when the campaign became linked with a political programme of rank and file policemen for higher pay, improved conditions and a Royal Commission of Inquiry, he did not falter. He used the campaign to intimidate Callinan. In furtherance of this, David Garside introduced a deputation of policemen to the Premier and the Chief Secretary of Victoria. Garside was careful to emphasise only the retiring age issue, but he reckoned without the wiliness of the Premier, Thomas Bond.

Bond, as leader of the Conservative Government, was concerned only to advance the interests of business men, bankers and squatters. This sort of thing was just part of the game of politics. West had become an embarrassing political issue, and so had Callinan. Maybe he would reduce the retiring age *and* institute a Royal Commission. That would be the way to make political capital out of the situation.

"The retiring age will be reduced to sixty when I see fit," was all he said.

Afterwards David Garside reported to John West that he feared they had gone too far. Bond was crafty; he might reduce the retiring age, but he might also appoint a Royal Commission. He might even pass legislation to help O'Flaherty. John West meanwhile paid great attention to politics. In the Federal elections of 1904 only six Labor candidates were successful in Victoria, but in the vital Victorian State elections, eighteen Labor men won seats, including Frank Ashton, Bob Scott and David Garside himself, back in politics again to assist John West.

David Garside at first had refused to stand as a Labor candidate and sign the pledge. "Dammit all! David Garside won't sign a pledge, and be dictated to by the junta from the Trades Hall!"

But John West insisted. Their relationship was undergoing a change. John West was now Garside's biggest client. Garside had to do what he was told, just like anyone else on the West payroll.

John West's money was thrown behind ten of the eighteen successful Labor men. There were twelve Liberals in the new Parliament. John West had a possible thirty votes in the event of the new gaming legislation coming up; but Premier Bond led a team of thirty-eight Conservative members. The position was still dangerous.

"What's your fancy for the Caulfield Cup, Jack?" one of a group of workmen asked John West one morning as he passed on his way to the City Tattersall's Club.

"My horse, Whisper, will nearly win it," he replied, obeying a generous impulse.

"Thanks for the tip, Jack. I'll speck it for a few bob."

"You could do worse. If we can keep him fit, he'd nearly do the trick."

In fact, John West had reason to be confident that Whisper

would win the cup. He was planning to rig the race and make a betting coup that would dwarf his clean up on Plugger Pete Manson's Austral victory.

Whisper was a well-performed five-year-old galloper that John West had recently purchased and placed in the care of a leading trainer. Though the horse was an outsider, John West had arranged a nation-wide commission in expectation of being able to bribe the riders of some of the more fancied candidates. He had instructed workers in the tote and club not to lay too much against Whisper, but to send as many punters as possible to Sol Solomons with their bets for the horse.

As he walked down the Bourke Street hill, an extraordinary scene was being enacted in the lounge of the City Tattersall's Club. About a dozen of his employees were clustered excitedly around Barney Robinson, who was seated on a sofa reading to them from the ARGUS

John West had not read the ARGUS. He called it a "rotten, tory, wowser rag." It was the only newspaper not delivered to his house. The article that Barney was reading justified his hostility. It was entitled THE GAMBLING MANIA. A REIGN OF TERROR. It contained a detailed account of the methods used to protect John West's gaming business.

Barney had almost completed the article.

"... *so efficient has been this violence that no evidence such as would be accepted in court has been obtained. Men employed by O'Flaherty have again been followed to their homes, and letters containing the fiercest threats posted to them. These are the methods of men whose sole aim is to make money out of the gambling* – er – pro – er – *proclivities.*" Barney stumbled over the word, then explained: "That means habits. *The past history of some of the men who are* ... hm ... *some have served sentences, and others have been flogged in jail.*" Barney stole a glance at Arthur West, whose face clouded with a snarl.

Suddenly, Cauliflower Dick shouted: "Jees, look! They've got our records in! It says 'ere: *The records of twenty of the men.*"

"Well, what d'yer know about that," Piggy said. "There's mine there. It says: *One conviction robbery in company. Two years' hard labour.* Well, I'll be buggered."

Arthur West sat down morosely. Paddy Woodman massaged his head with great vigour and observed: "Sure and anyone would think this publicity was goin' to improve business.''

His remark was ignored as the others milled round the settee, tugging at the paper.

''There's mine. *Forging six months. Receiving stolen property eighteen months.''*

''Thirty-one convictions, one has got! Struth, who's that?''

''Where's mine? Let's have a look.''

The paper became crumpled and Barney shook himself free and stood up. ''Here,'' he said, ''I'll spread it on the floor and you can all see it. Not having a criminal record, I'm not interested.''

Although Barney Robinson took no part in the *reign of terror*, he and Florrie were both uneasy about it. Only the fact that Barney had been commissioned to do some boxing advertisements for John West had prevented him from obeying Florrie's renewed demands that he leave West for good.

Barney smoothed out the paper and spread it on the floor. The crowd surged from behind the sofa and surrounded the paper: some kneeling, some leaning on the others' backs and craning their necks.

Paddy Woodman said to Arthur West: ''Jack'll be narked about this.''

At that moment John West entered.

''That's me, I tell yer!''

''No it ain't, it's me. You ain't never been jugged for assault.''

''That's me there. Six months – larceny. Three years with hard labour and a whipping for criminal assault. That's me all right.''

So it went on, while Arthur West and Paddy Woodman sat moodily on a couch, and Barney Robinson read his beloved encyclopaedia on a chair at the other side of the room.

John West viewed the scene with his lips clamped in disgust. ''When you've finished, you might get things ready upstairs!'' he interrupted in a loud voice.

The noise ceased; the men on the floor arose like children caught playing at mud pies, and departed upstairs without a word, leaving the crumpled ARGUS on the floor.

John West picked up the paper, folded it as neatly as its dilapidated condition would permit, and was about to throw it on to a chair, when Arthur said: ''You'd better read it while you're on the job. A reign of terror it says.''

John West found the article, read it through, then crumpled the paper savagely and threw it down.

"Arty," he said quietly, "come upstairs."

Turning to Barney, he added: "Get your nose out of the bloody book for once and come up, too. I want to see you about the fight between Squeers and Cauliflower Dick."

"Righto, Jack," Barney replied, putting the book carefully in its place on the stand. "I've got the ads ready."

John West had signed up the promising heavy-weight fighter, Bert Squeers; and, for want of a better opponent, had chosen Cauliflower Dick as his first victim.

As they went upstairs, Barney said: "Funny yesterday, Jack, a bloke told me that Sol Solomons reckons his horse, Gladstone, is a good thing in the Caulfield Cup. He's sending his punters here to back it with you."

John West merely scowled and asked: "Is Frank Lammence in?"

"Yes, Jack."

"Wait in my office a minute, Barney. I want to see those ads. Must make it look as if Cauliflower Dick can make a fight of it."

He and Arthur entered one of the two offices which ran off the big gambling room upstairs. Behind the table sat Frank Lammence. He was younger than his employer, tall, sombre and slim. He stood up when the West brothers entered. Of sandy complexion, he always wore brown clothes. His manner and movements were precise, almost pompous.

John West trusted this man as no other. He had already shown himself to be efficient, shrewd, ruthless and close-mouthed. He had formed the City Tattersall's Club into a legal company with himself as secretary and Sugar Renfrey as chairman.

"Have you seen the ARGUS, Frank?" John West asked.

"Yes, Mr. West, I have a copy of it here for you." Lammence resumed his seat and passed a newspaper to John West.

"I've read it," John West said. "And I want you to find out who wrote it and get Arty and the boys to deal with him."

"Certainly, Mr. West. I was going to suggest that course. If we allowed such criticism to go unpunished, we would never have any peace."

Lammence had developed a habit of working out what his

employer would think, then fitting in with it. He had decided to make himself indispensable to John West: to become his right hand. He did not seek prominence; he liked power behind the scenes, and sinister intrigue. He would carry out John West's wishes without compunction or question.

"What will we do to him, Mr. West?" Lammence asked.

"I don't care what you do, just so long as he writes no more articles like this."

"All right, Mr. West, you leave it to me."

As John West left to join Barney Robinson in the office next door, Lammence said to Arthur West: "I'll have inquiries made at the ARGUS office, then you and the boys can get busy."

John West stood with Sugar Renfrey in front of the grand stand in the members' enclosure of the Caulfield racecourse.

The day was fine. Green lawns, brilliant flowers, the white running rails, the excited crowd, made a vivid setting for the thoroughbreds at the barrier for the start of the Caulfield Cup of 1904.

"They're off!"

"Demas is leading," a man nearby said.

"Yep. Leading against instructions, I happen to know," his companion shouted in reply. "Something wrong with this race, if you ask me!"

"Did you hear what he said?" Sugar said in John West's ear.

The horses soon covered the first half of their journey – a fast-run mile and a half. Passing the six-furlong post Demas still led, much to the consternation of his connections, who had given instructions that their charge be nursed. The big field swept on towards the four-furlong post with Demas tiring after his impossible attempt to lead all the way, and surrendering the lead to another of the most fancied candidates. As the horses galloped past the three and towards the home turn the top-weight, Emir, challenged the leader. Gladstone, Sol Solomons' entry, was sitting-in behind them, and Whisper, getting the run of the race, ridden to instructions, was lying fifth on the rails.

Spectators began to yell for their particular fancy in a tumultuous roar. "It's workin' out just like yer said, Jack," Sugar Renfrey roared. "He's sittin' in on the bloody fence waitin' for 'em to tire."

"But what about Gladstone? Why doesn't he 'go' on Gladstone? I told him to make his effort before the turn, to give Whisper the last run."

"There he goes now, Jack!"

Sugar was right: as the field began to take the turn into the straight, two furlongs from the winning post, Gladstone loomed up on the outside of the two leaders and went to the front.

About a hundred yards away from John West and Renfrey, Sol Solomons was standing near the rails at the winning post with one of his clerks. He was a strongly built Jew in his early thirties, flashily dressed, with a boxer-hat hiding his thinning hair. An outward calm belied his tremendous excitement. Solomons had considered Gladstone to be a racecourse certainty and with good reason, but he could not be expected to realise that his jockey was "riding for Whisper." As his horse led into the straight, Solomons dropped his mask of placidity, and gripped his clerk by the arm.

"What's the boy doing? What's he doing? I told him to wait till the furlong pole for the last run."

His alarm was soon justified by events. Emir fought back and the two top-weights were neck-and-neck as they straightened for the home run. As they approached the furlong post half-way up the straight, thousands of voices called the names of Emir and Gladstone. Then the little bay Whisper swept up on the outside of the leaders and, with an advantage of nearly two stones in weight, easily ran past them and, amid wild excitement, galloped past the post with a good three lengths to spare.

People thronged around John West offering congratulations.

"Great performance, Jack. The boy gave him a good ride."

"I was on him, Jack, thanks for the tip."

"Everyone in Carringbush backed him. Good luck to yer."

On the lawn nearby a policemen threw his helmet in the air and shouted gleefully: "We all backed it; Jack West told us Whisper was a good thing."

John West smiled, pushed his way through the crowd, and walked to where the coveted cup was to be presented.

During the next few days the press carried no hint that anything irregular had occurred. It gravely reported that Mr. John West had given the jockey one-third of the stake and the trainer two-thirds, and published a letter which John West had written to the

Mayor of Carringbush enclosing a cheque for £500 to be distributed among the poor and needy of the district. Then full details of a celebration held at the City Tattersall's Club were published; four Labor politicians being among the public men who drank Mr. West's health.

It was left to the BULLETIN to give the first hint of malpractice in the running of the Caulfield Cup when it wrote in the next issue: *The brilliant top-weights, Emir and Gladstone, instead of being held for a final run, were rushed to the front before reaching the turn for home, an extraordinary policy considering that they were in good positions before they put full steam on.*

The paper commented caustically on John West's charitable gestures arising out of Whisper's victory, and styled him a *disreputable citizen exploiting the poor.* It hinted that the Caulfield Cup was rigged, and followed this by telling the politicians who supped wine at the Tattersall's Club that they *should be ashamed of themselves.*

Then came a report in the daily press that the Victorian Racing Club, which controlled the four city galloping courses and all country galloping clubs, was likely to take action against a certain owner since a well-known jockey had stated that the said owner had been involved recently in rigging an important race.

"I don't think the V.R.C. will risk a scandal," John West remarked to Sugar Renfrey when he read the report. "Probably just refuse to accept my entries, that's all. Then I'll transfer the horses to someone else's name."

Soon afterwards, the V.R.C. held a secret inquiry into Whisper's victory in the Caulfield Cup, disqualified John West for life, and warned him off all courses under its jurisdiction. He managed to transfer his horses into the names of other persons, but he would never forgive the V.R.C.

During the next few months, he fought hard battles on many fronts.

His attempts to embarrass Callinan had backfired. Premier Bond had left the retiring age at 65, and set up a Royal Commission to inquire into the police force. John West and David Garside had succeeded in influencing some of the appointments to the Commission. On it were three friendly Labor politicians. Garside reckoned that there were so many men in the Conservative Government, so many high public officials, so many heads of the liquor trade and other men of wealth who had skeletons in the cupboard of the corrupt Victorian Police Department, that the Royal Commission was bound to end like most others – in an innocuous finding.

"Bond will be glad to call it off before we're through with him," Garside had remarked.

"See that I'm not called to give evidence," JohnWest replied. "From now on it's their turn to be exposed. I'll gather every bit of scandal I can about the lot of them; and I'll have it blown in Parliament, on the public platform, at the Royal Commission, everywhere! They're a lot of spineless cowards, these wowsers. See how they liked being exposed!"

With each day, John West's hatred of Detective-Sergeant O'Flaherty became more intense. O'Flaherty was still sending spies to the tote and club. O'Flaherty was still pressing for a change in the gaming laws. O'Flaherty had supplied the information for the ARGUS exposure.

Then Fate presented John West with an opportunity to wage effective warfare against the Victorian Racing Club. He learned that the manager of the Apsom Racecourse was in such financial difficulties that he had been unable to supply the owner of the winner of the Apsom Gold Cup with either the prize money or the trophy.

On hearing the news, John West called on Benjamin Levy, the owner of Apsom and two other unregistered pony racecourses.

He found Benjamin Levy, senior – Old Ben as he was called – and Benjamin Levy, junior – Young Ben – waiting for him in the office of Levy's Furniture Emporium.

John West viewed the pair across the table. Young Ben, short, fat, with curly hair and sloping shoulders, a round head, swarthy complexion; his expensive clothes somehow managing to appear untidy. Beside him sat Old Ben, a wizened, bald-headed, miserable-looking old man in his second childhood.

Young Ben folded his chubby hands on the table and said: "So you think just because the Apsom Club couldn't supply the cup or the prize money today that you will get our permission to conduct race meetings on my courses."

"Your courses?" Old Ben interrupted in a voice that crackled from somewhere deep in his bony chest. "You mean *my* courses. They're still *my* courses."

Old Ben was over eighty, but he refused to hand over the strings of his vast wealth to Young Ben, or to any of his other three sons or his daughter.

Benjamin Levy, senior, had come from England and opened a second-hand shop in Melbourne.

During ten years in this shop he accumulated twenty thousand sovereigns, a servant-girl wife and five children. Then the wife died, and Ben transferred his affections to a cut-price tobacco business, where he accumulated a further thirty thousand sovereigns and several mistresses. When the building boom began in the eighties, Old Ben entered the furniture business, and introduced the hire-purchase system to the colony. He soon gobbled up most of the smaller furniture houses and established a virtual monopoly of the trade. In eight years he was a millionaire; but when the crash in the '90's came he lost more than half his fortune.

Lately, Old Ben had married an eighteen-year-old Irish girl from the slums of Carringbush. The girl became a positive menace to Ben's sons and daughter. Old Ben lavished favours on his new bride, and his family came to believe that he had altered his will in her favour. So, a week before, they had kidnapped Old Ben and brought him back home, where he had agreed to make a new will, giving his wife only one small factory and a small sum of money, providing they allowed him to return to her.

While Old Ben endeavoured to follow the conversation through an ear trumpet, John West and Young Ben negotiated.

John West argued: the sport of pony racing was in a bad state; prize money was getting lower and lower; the whole game was corrupt from top to bottom. He had put trotting on the map, he contended, and would do the same with pony racing. He would increase prize money, cut out the crook races and get bigger attendances. He spoke as if the whole matter was cut and dried: he would take over the three courses. He would purify the sport and make a fortune for himself and the Levy family.

"Not so fast, Mr. West. There are certain conditions," Young Ben interrupted. He was shrewd, sly and ruthless, and liked to set the pace in a business deal. "There are certain conditions. You can have Apsom, if you buy a third share in the land."

"That suits me," John West said, thinking, surely he didn't imagine I'd jib at that. "What about the other two courses? You

179

own one and lease the other from the Ralstone Council don't you?''

"I might consider the other two; but you must remember there are two – er – clubs who have leases on them.''

"If I can fix things with the three clubs you will agree to my taking them all over, then?''

"Well, maybe. There is another little matter we might fix up, Mr. West. Have you ever heard of time payment? – hire-purchase, we call it, to be polite,'' Young Ben said with his sly smile. "Well, now, it is the greatest business in the world, better than totalisators, even.''

"My tote is run fair and clean.''

"So is my hire-purchase. Here's how it works. Someone buys, say, a piano. They pay a few sovereigns deposit and pay the rest at so much a week. On the balance we charge ten percent interest – at least that's what they think we charge. Ten percent flat per annum works out at over a hundred percent – see? They pay ten percent on money they've already paid back. Very clever, isn't it? Totes is chicken food, Mr. West.'' He cackled a laugh.

At this stage, Old Ben, who had been wangling his hearing aid this way and that, addressed himself to John West in a cracked, squeaky voice: "You see, Mr. West, you and me, we have both been rubbed out for life.''

"Is that a fact?''

"It is a fact, Mr. West. You are not the only one that can rig races.'' He cackled proudly, waving his ear trumpet. "I, that is, me and Young Ben, imported a horse from England, a champion horse. We changed his name. He won a lotta races in the Western District until the V.R.C. found out and warned us off for life – very comical! I used to run trots and ponies at Elsternwick till the council closed me up because the people, they complained at the swearing and the brawls and the noise. My daughter Rosie, she say to me: 'Father,' she say, 'no more racecourses; the furniture business it is more respectable.' So I say: 'All right, Rosie, all right,' I say. So I get the other three courses and I lease them to others, because my daughter say it is bad with all the noise and the language ...''

Young Ben interrupted his father impatiently: "How would you like to put a little money into hire-purchase, Mr. West. Not enough to give you any say, just enough for you to make a lot of money, eh? Things have been bad, very bad: sometimes when we take the furniture back from people that can't pay, it is worn out, and sometimes they run away with it. Too much bad paper lately; but things will improve soon and we'll make a fortune. We have control of the trade, and we are going to keep control, and out of the hire-purchase we make millions. You can have some, Mr. West. You see, our money, too much of it is tied up. And in our business you must always expand."

"Come on, Mr. Levy, what do you want me to do?"

"If you invest, say, £50,000 in my firms you can have a lease on the three courses. You buy a third share in Apsom and buy out the three managers. How does that appeal, Mr. West?"

"You make a hard bargain, Mr. Levy," John West said, thinking: Should be money in time payment; he's much easier than I thought he'd be. "But it's a deal. I'll get my solicitor to go into it."

"Mr. Davie Garside. Oh no, Mr. West, he knows too many tricks. My solicitor will draw up the deal, and he can look it over afterwards."

"Just as you like, Mr. Levy. All I want is a straight deal, and no delay."

When John West left them he was intensely elated. The V.R.C. had better look out now.

Already John West could see the advertisements in the papers with his name at the foot. He could see the posters stuck up everywhere with his photo on them, with a horseshoe around it. He could see the ponies tearing round the tracks and hear the crowd cheering. He would run book-makers, print his own race-books, have his own ponies and trotters running in someone else's name. He would conduct pie stalls outside the course, and the bars and the dining-rooms inside; and, if only he could keep the tote and club going, he would control the off-the-course betting. He would purify trotting and pony racing.

The toffs from the V.R.C. would get competition such as they'd never known before. Jack West would teach them to warn him off for life!

Barney Robinson was in high spirits. He had been promoted to the esteemed position of publicity and advertising manager of John West's enterprises. After the ARGUS exposure, Florrie had been on the verge of making Barney choose between her and John West, until the promotion came about, and now she was more content because Barney was proud and happy.

Barney sat in his own little office on the ground floor, sucking a pencil and stroking his moustache. "It's good, all right. *A sterling struggle for supremacy between strong, sound, staunch, scientific, symmetrically-shaped, skilful athletes.* Couldn't be better. that'll bring the crowd. I'll put it in all the papers."

He looked up and noticed John West and Frank Lammence pass his door. He gathered up his papers and rushed out to them.

"Jack," he said excitedly. "I've got the ads ready for the big fight and the foot-runnin' carnival. Listen to this one for the fight: TIM MURPHY *versus* BILL SQUEERS. EXHIBITION BUILDING. *From the day Squeers first appeared in this State it was apparent that a real* DYED-IN-THE-WOOL CHAMPION *was in our midst, and it became a question, after witnessing his* PHENOMENAL POWERS, *as to whether we should ever see him pitted against* A FOEMAN WORTHY OF HIS STEEL, *when suddenly, as if in answer to our queries,* A NEW STAR! A STAR OF THE FIRST MAGNITUDE *appeared on the pugilistic firmament.* IT WAS TIM MURPHY. *He had returned home armed and equipped with all the latest devices and tactics of the American ring. With phenomenal rapidity and remarkable ease, he extinguished the lesser lights, and then boldly . . .*"

John West listened impatiently. "All right, Barney, but the fight might be delayed for a while. Murphy is being difficult."

"Well, we can put someone else on with Bill."

"Who? We don't want another wash-out like the fight with Cauliflower Dick. Squeers won't carry them, so we'll have to wait for Murphy, unless I can get Jeffries from America or Mike Williams from England. I've offered them a thousand each for one fight with Squeers."

John West walked towards the stairs.

"Wait'll I read yer the foot runnin' ad, Jack."

"Read it to Frank! I'm busy!"

Barney's face dropped momentarily, then he turned to Lammence. "Listen to this. I'm goin' to put a big ad in the papers with all the entries for the West Thousand and the other events. At the top I'll put this. Listen!" Barney read like a dramatic actor: *From away back and beyond, from every nook and corner of the great land come the stalwart young Australians exulting in the hope of the victory and its rich reward at this unique sports festival. There's the* Man from Snowy River, *he of the* Overflow, *the pick of* Our Selection, *the bronzed and sinewy youngsters of a young nation, and 635 of them have signified their intention of...*

Lammence didn't seem very impressed. "Have you done the ad for the meeting at Apsom?" he interrupted.

"I got it here," Barney said, handing a large sheet of paper to Lammence, who scrutinised it impassively.

VICTORIAN PONY
AND GALLOWAY RACING CLUB

APSOM   *unrivalled*   APSOM
APSOM   *picturesque*   APSOM
APSOM   *popular*   APSOM
Monday • Monday • Monday
New Management • Higher Stakes
Better Appointment • Admirably Controlled
Strictly Supervised • Miniature Flemington

"It will do," Lammence said, his long face betraying no response. Lammence was not impressed with Barney's ideas of publicity: "Lays it on too thick," he had told John West. Barney scowled, returned to his office and began reading from the encyclopaedia.

Upstairs the long room buzzed with the voices of gamblers and the calls of the clerks who stood in front of the huge betting boards, laying the odds and answering phones.

John West walked behind the counter. One of the phones rang and he picked it up. "Hullo," he said. "All right. Go ahead."

Silence fell, and John West said in a louder voice: "They're at the barrier. Get your bets on! remember, betting ceases when they turn into the straight."

A few gamblers came forward and lodged last minute bets while John West repeated the description of events at the barrier which were being described on the Apsom racecourse. John West had recently introduced this method of broadcasting direct from the course by telephone, anticipating by two decades the practice of broadcasting races by means of radio transmission.

The crowd moved closer to the counter in order to hear the

description. They represented a wide variety of types: over-dressed, dandy gamblers; working men, without employment or taking a day off; an odd business man or white collar worker; criminals of various kinds, who spent their spare time gambling at the club by day, and at the hazards school by night.

On Saturdays the crowd was larger, but the bulk of the business came through the mail or over the phone. The club was showing a profit of over five hundred pounds a week.

"They're off!" John West said. "Dinkum is first out, followed by Katie, with Queen Bess and Prince next ..."

As the broadcast proceeded, several bets were made.

"What price is Dinkum?"

"He was two to one before the race. What's Dinkum now, Jack?"

"Cut it to even money."

"Six yards of the best on him."

"Dinkum is still leading. Queen Bess has moved up into second place two lengths back, with Prince third, and Sammy Boy is making a run on the outside." John West raised his right hand like a policeman on traffic duty. "They're turning into the straight. No more in-running bets."

The gamblers listened, some gripped by excitement, some by desperate hope, until the broadcast ended in elated shouts from the few who had supported the winner, and expressions of disappointment and despair from those who hadn't. John West hung up the phone and walked round the counter to talk to Paddy Woodman.

"Come into the office a minute, Paddy."

Paddy followed him and they sat on either side of the table.

"I've been a bit worried about the Police Commission, Jack."

"No need to worry about that. We can leave the Commission to old Davie Garside now. I'm worried about police pimps. There's still one in the club; he's been here for months gathering evidence."

This news caused Paddy to massage his head with vigour. Barney Robinson reckoned Paddy had rubbed all the hair off his head by his habit of massaging it when worried.

"What's that, Jack?" Paddy ejaculated. "Are you sure? How do yer know?"

"A certain detective told me."

"Do you know who the poltroon of a pimp is?"

"I've got a good idea."

"But how could he get in? What with our spies sittin' for the police exams, and watchin' the new recruits and all."

"He got in somehow. O'Flaherty's a shrewd man, don't worry. He's behind all this, the bastard!"

"What are you going to do about it, Jack?"

"I think it's that fellow Baddson. He's out there now. Me and Frank went to his house last night after I got the tip off, but he wasn't there and his mother wouldn't tell me anything. I think we'll have a talk to him now. We'll ask him straight out."

He walked out into the room and said to a tall young man in a long black overcoat: "I'd like to see you for a minute, privately."

The man coloured and followed John West into the room. John West called over his shoulder: "Come in here a minute, Piggy!"

John West sat behind the table with Paddy Woodman standing at his elbow.

"Your name is Baddson, isn't it?"

"Yes," answered the other, nervously, looking around in vain for a chair.

"Are you a member of the police force?" John West asked suddenly.

Baddson fidgeted with his hat as Piggy entered and stood behind him.

"Surely you wouldn't degrade yourself by joinin' the police force, would you?" Paddy asked.

"If this is a private conversation, I don't want these other men present," Baddson replied.

"I'll decide who'll be present," John West snapped.

"Why did you come to my house last night?" Baddson asked.

"I came to see if you had backed some winners the day before," John West lied. "But you haven't answered my question. Are you in the police force?"

"No."

"Are you game to let me search you?"

Baddon laid his hat on the table, and slowly took off his overcoat, coat and waistcoat and handed these to John West, who looked at him uncertainly, then went through the pockets.

A little money, a few scraps of paper, a packet of tobacco, a train ticket and other odds and ends, but nothing incriminating.

John West walked round the table, ran his hands through Baddson's trouser pockets and pulled a notebook from one of them. He flicked its pages and then opened them one by one carefully, but they were unused and blank. He threw the notebook on the table with a show of savagery and paced the room like a caged animal.

"You're one of O'Flaherty's pimps all right. I can tell you the day you joined the force. I know what's going on!"

Baddson watched nervously.

"It's no use telling me lies. I know everything. O'Flaherty has sworn thirty men into the force since this club opened; they were all recruited to spy on me. And they have all been kicked out of the force after six or nine months' service."

John West confronted Baddson, waving a threatening finger. "That's what will happen to you. O'Flaherty ought to be kicked to pieces for ruining young fellows like you." His voice rose to a shout. "And even if I was his own brother I would help kick him to pieces. Do you hear that? O'Flaherty ought to be kicked to pieces!"

"But I tell you I'm not in the police force, and I don't know O'Flaherty," Baddson answered desperately, glancing over his shoulder at Piggy.

John West banged his fist on the table. "Don't keep telling lies! I tell you I know you're a policeman and a bloody pimp!"

"W-well, w-why keep asking me?"

"Listen! You're an imposter. You're one of O'Flaherty's men. I knew you were when you first came here; I told the committee, but still we didn't block you." John West's voice was becoming conciliatory. "We'll treat you all right. O'Flaherty will use you up for a while at six shillings a day, then he'll kick you out. Take my advice and dice him. Let him get someone else for his dirty work. You come in with me. I'm a generous man. You tell O'Flaherty that this is only a social club, and that I've only got one share in it; and I'll tell you what I'll do. I'll give you twenty-five pounds and a billet at a fiver a week on one of my racecourses. How would you like that? A nice, easy job on a racecourse?"

Baddson seemed to hesitate. Twenty-five pounds and a fiver a week was a lot of money; but one stray thought of O'Flaherty was enough to make him say: "No thanks. I keep telling you I don't even know O'Flaherty."

John West confronted him aggressively. "Don't keep lying to me. I know you're a bloody pimp. Why, your own mother told me last night that you were a policeman."

"That's a lie!" Baddson answered, for the first time with vigour. "My mother wouldn't say that. She told me that all she did was to ask you for a tip for today's races. You told her three horses; and they all lost, what's more."

"Oh, mister smarty, eh? Well, it's no use you and O'Flaherty charging us. None of our judges would allow it on appeal. Don't think you can pimp on me and get away with it!"

Baddson paled. He seemed angry yet afraid. He looked around at Piggy, then at Paddy Woodman.

"You're not as smart as you think you are, West."

"We'll see all about that. Put him out, Piggy!" John West picked up Baddson's clothes from the table, threw them in his face, and walked out of the room, slamming the door. He went quickly into Frank Lammence's office, leaving Paddy Woodman rubbing his head, and Piggy saying to Baddson: "Put on your coat, and get out and don't come back. An' yer better hurry, or I'll chuck yer down the bloody stairs. We don't like pimps 'ere!"

John West shut the office door and said to Frank Lammence: "I think that Baddson is a pimp, all right. I just had a talk to him – kicked him out. See that he doesn't ever get in here again."

"Certainly, Mr. West."

"And I've decided to get rid of Baddson and O'Flaherty." John West said the words calmly. For months he had been able to find no rest from his impotent hatred of O'Flaherty. His conviction that Baddson was a spy left him in a white heat of rage from which he could only escape by planning reprisals. O'Flaherty had sent Baddson here. Both of them must be punished. He, himself, would be safe. He was all powerful!

Frank Lammence showed no surprise at the remark. "You mean – we should have them – dealt with."

"Yes, and quick. I won't tolerate O'Flaherty any longer. Did you read what he said at the Police Commission yesterday?"

"Yes. I agree we mustn't tolerate it."

"All right. Now, I'm leaving this to you. Don't let any of our boys do either job. There's plenty of men in Melbourne who'd murder their own mother for a fiver. I'm going to Sydney to buy a racecourse on Monday. I'll be away a fortnight. I want this done while I'm away. Be very careful. Say nothing. Get outside men to do the trick. Mr. Clever O'Flaherty will learn a lesson at last!''

One o'clock chimed from the distant tower as the corpulent figure of Dave O'Flaherty rolled cumbersomely towards his home in an inner suburb.

The more I walk, the fatter I get, he was thinking; these doctors talk through their hats. Need more exercise. Bah!

The night was summery – clear and warm. Big Dave was soon wiping sweat from his neck and brow with his handkerchief. Presently he heard the sound of footsteps following him. He did not look around. Jack West's boys seeing me home again. Very kind of 'em.

The problem of ending John West's career had become an obsession with Dave O'Flaherty. Usually he carried out the law without fear or favour. He had no opinions about the law, or about law-breakers. If a man broke the law you issued a summons or made an arrest, that was all there was to it. But his feud with John West had become a personal matter.

O'Flaherty felt his revolver reassuringly. He had been shadowed for months and had come to the conclusion that John West merely wished to know his every movement: that the Tattersall's Club was not prepared to risk using physical violence against its best-known enemy.

The progress of the Police Commission annoyed and disgusted O'Flaherty. It wasn't going to solve anything. All it had succeeded in doing was to make things uncomfortable for Callinan and other police officers. It would not harm West much, that was certain. Poor old Callinan had all the old dirty linen of the 1881 Royal Commission aired again, with some additional dirty linen which had accumulated since, like his wine and spirit store deal, and the time he protected that hotel of West's from prosecution. Just as well no one was game to reveal Callinan's other connections with the tote boss. More people had told lies or remained silent at this Commission than ever before. Oh, well; can't say I didn't expect it.

Callinan had got rid of the files on the Williams and Armfield case. A wily old bird is our Chief Commissioner, but an arrant coward. Instead of this Commission exposing West, he and old Garside have used it to expose others. Wonder they didn't try to get something on me. And all the haggling about leave, promotion, the retiring age and pay. Hope they do something about the pay, anyway. That would end a lot of the bribery and I could do with a rise myself. Better conditions will bring better types into the force.

Dave O'Flaherty stole a surreptitious look over his shoulder and saw two shadowy figures pass under a street light about a hundred yards behind him. They must be going to see me right to the gate tonight.

Fancy holding a Royal Commission into the Victorian Police Force without calling Jack West. No show without Punch. Well, I've got him, and under the present law, too. Dave O'Flaherty doesn't need new laws or Royal Commissions to catch West. He'll be up shortly, and will he snort?

The ghostly figures still followed at a safe distance. Don't like this! Usually they knock off when I head for home. Baddson is convinced they intend violence against him, and he's probably right. When West sends threatening letters, something usually happens. Well, Baddson's hidden away, where even West's men won't find him.

O'Flaherty fingered some betting tickets in his pocket. Constable Baddson did a good job. West is gone this time. It would take legislation to end his career; and another court case would speed the legislation up.

Dave O'Flaherty turned into a street on one side of which were narrow tenement houses, and on the other a public park. He entered the gate of one of the dwellings. He stood in the shadow of the verandah for a few minutes, then peeped cautiously over the iron gate. He saw two men standing in the shadows at the corner of the street fifty yards away.

He entered the narrow, double-storied house, lit the gas light in the front lounge room, and took off his boots. As he began to mount the stairs, he could hear the breathing of his wife and children as they slept upstairs.

Hope West's thugs are not going to start anything, he mused. Just the time they might, with their lord and master away in Sydney.

Upstairs, O'Flaherty crept into the front bedroom and

undressed in the dark. His wife's fat figure stirred in the bed.

"That you, Dave?" she whispered.

"Yes, Maggie."

"You're very late again. I was worried; tried to keep awake, but I must have dozed off. What's the time?"

"After one o'clock."

Dave finished changing into his night shirt, bumped his knee against the foot of the bed and cursed quietly. He got into bed, then arose again, took his revolver from his coat and placed it under the pillow.

Maggie was breathing heavily, apparently asleep again. He lay in the dark, and though he was tired to the point of exhaustion, sleep was far from him. Hope those two West thugs don't mean to try anything tonight. A man pooh-poohs the idea in daylight; but lying here in the dark and knowing they are out there watching, perhaps planning something . . .

They'll stop at nothing, not even at murder, he told himself. Oh, you're worrying about nothing, old fella, they wouldn't dare try anything against Dave O'Flaherty. But West's away in Sydney. Could have gone there as an alibi . . . .

Thoughts tumbled in his head. He was conscious of a confused, drowsy uneasiness, then sleep came: the deep sleep of a very tired man.

In the warm night, the house stood silent and dark. Outside two men, with caps well down over their eyes, crept towards the front fence. The light still shone through the front downstair window. Skirting the shaft of light the sinister figures crouched in the shadows.

Then came the crash of shattering glass. Mrs. O'Flaherty sat bolt upright in the bed.

"Dave! Dave!" she said, in an hysterical whisper. "Dave! Wake up! There's someone in the house!" She shook her sleeping husband desperately. He was slow to awaken, then sat up rubbing his eyes in the darkness.

"What's the matter, Maggie?"

"There's someone in the house. I heard a noise; like falling glass. And there seems to be a light downstairs."

Dave O'Flaherty grabbed his revolver from under the pillow and crept out of bed. "I think I left the light on in the front room," he said in a husky whisper. "Are you sure you heard a noise?"

"Certain, it woke me up," she answered, as he walked on tiptoe towards the door. "Oh, for God's sake, Dave, be careful!"

Dave O'Flaherty crept to the window. He saw two figures running through the gardens opposite the house. He raised his revolver to shoot, but they melted into the night.

Mrs. O'Flaherty could see him silhouetted against the dull light, the revolver upraised. "What is it, Dave; what is it?"

"You were right," he said. "Two men followed me home and they have just run across the gardens. I'm going downstairs to see what caused the noise."

As the words fell softly from his lips, the night was shattered by a thundering explosion, the whole house quivered, the floor seemed to sway, pictures fell from the walls. Mrs O'Flaherty screamed piercingly, cowering with the bedclothes over her head. From elsewhere in the house screams and cries rose like the wailing of the injured after a battle. Dave O'Flaherty stood as though petrified, then his nerves relaxed and he ran from the room to be met in the passage way by his eldest son, a youth of eighteen, who was shouting unintelligibly.

Dave heard the crackling of flames: smoke arose and crept up the stairs. Mrs. O'Flaherty ran out screaming: "Dave! The kiddies! For God's sake, get the children!"

The crackling of the flames grew louder, more fierce. Fantastic shadows frolicked through the banisters on to the walls, the smoke thickened along the upstairs passage. There was a smell of gas fumes.

Dave O'Flaherty gripped his son by the arm and steadied him. "Pull yourself together, boy. The fire is in the front of the house," he said. "Go out the back way and get the fire brigade. And hurry! Hurry!" The lad ran off, and Dave rushed to help Maggie with the younger children.

He groped his way, coughing and spluttering, through the smoke towards the front bedroom, from which he could hear the youngest children wailing and whimpering; while his wife went to the nearest bedroom and led a fear-crazed girl of fifteen to the top of the stairway.

The living room below was a blazing inferno, whose flames reached into the downstairs passage. Presently Dave O'Flaherty came back through the smoke carrying the two youngest children in a bundle, and began to descend the stairs, followed by his wife

191

and eldest girl. Reaching the bottom of the stairs, Dave said: "Out the backdoor, quickly!"

The flames licked close to them, but they managed to reach the back door, nearly suffocated by smoke.

Dozens of people, mostly in night attire, were gathered around the house. Some of them tried to pacify Mrs. O'Flaherty and the children, while Dave led a few volunteers in an endeavour to rescue some furniture and other belongings.

"Thought it was an earthquake, true as God, I did!" someone said.

Soon the local fire brigade arrived and played a weak stream of water on the flames, while others assisted Dave in salvage operations through the back door. The front of the house was now a wall of flame and smoke.

Inside half an hour, the stone outer walls were all that remained of the house. Newspaper men arrived, and sought out Dave O'Flaherty. They found him standing in the back yard in his nightshirt, black with smoke and ashes. They opened their note-books in the dull light of a lantern.

"Have you any idea why your life should be attempted in such a dastardly fashion?" one of them asked.

"I have no hesitation in saying why. This is an attempt by some betting people, whom I have had to prosecute in the course of my duty," O'Flaherty replied sternly. "They have been shadowing me. They have been watching my house. I have been expecting that they would do something. I knew my turn would come. A man who had been writing pamphlets about betting was knocked on the head. A shopkeeper who had been assisting the police had his window broken four times. Another man was assaulted and maimed for life. I tell you there is a Tammany ring in Melbourne and it will stop at nothing."

Dave's voice rose to his anger and indignation. "Legislation is the only way to break it up. This outrage ought to open the eyes of Parliament. If it does not, we are simply at the mercy of these scoundrels, who are defying the law!"

Two policemen arrived and Dave accompanied them and the leader of the fire-brigade in a search of the smouldering ruin which was once his simple parlour. They discovered evidence that the window had been broken and a bomb made of a ginger beer bottle of gunpowder with a fuse attached and thrown through.

"The light made them think I was still in this room," Dave O'Flaherty said.

"If you had been, you'd be dead meat now, Sergeant," one of the policemen answered.

Next day a startled public read details of the bomb outrage. Within forty-eight hours all the daily newspapers had written editorials against the gambling mania; the Government had offered £500 reward for information which would lead to the arrest of the perpetrator of the crime; Police Commissioner Callinan had announced gravely that he was horrified; and John West was on his way back from Sydney.

The club had an air of gloom about it on the afternoon John West was due to arrive. Flash Alec and Barney Robinson were playing billiards, but their concentration was bad, scoring slow, and conversation desultory.

A sense of guilt had smitten Barney, and Florrie said that unless he left West immediately, she would leave *him*. She would rather see him back in the boot factory than remaining with John West, no matter how much he liked the job of advertising manager.

Though they could not be certain, neither of the billiard players had any doubt about who was behind the attempt on O'Flaherty's life; nor did grey-haired Long Bill, who was listlessly sweeping out the deserted lounge next door. The cafe was also deserted, while upstairs the hazards school in the front room was not operating. Even in the betting room there was little activity. A handful of gamblers, hardened regulars, were standing yarning, and only two clerks were working behind the long counter. The phones were silent. In Frank Lammence's office sat One-Eyed-Tommy, Paddy Woodman, Squash Lewis, Arthur West, Piggy, Sugar Renfrey, the latter having recently left his employment at the railway workshops to work full time for John West. There was the mood of fearful expectancy among them that exists among men awaiting trial on a serious charge.

The palm of Paddy Woodman's right hand was working overtime on his head. He said: "If Jack's behind this, he's gone too far."

"Shoulda fixed him properly months ago, like I said," Arthur West replied, stroking his white moustache with a nervous forefinger and thumb. "Shoulda let me shoot the bastard!"

"We're in enough trouble now," Sugar Renfrey said, fiddling with his glasses. "I been expectin' O'Flaherty to walk in here and arrest the bloody lot of us!"

"We're h'apt to get fitted with this h'all right, don't worry," observed Squash Lewis, who sat leaning back in a chair with his long legs out. "H'even Jack might get nabbed. Yeh, h'even Jack West!"

"The two blokes what threw the bomb are shakin' in their shoes," Piggy informed them. "Saw one of 'em this morning. Thinkin' of leavin' the bloody country, they are."

"You know who did it, do yer?" Paddy Woodman asked.

"No," lied Piggy quickly.

"Jack orta be here any minute," said One-Eyed-Tommy, squinting at his watch.

As he spoke, John West was mounting the stairs, followed by Frank Lammence. They walked across the betting room and entered, Frank Lammence closing the door behind them.

"Squash and Paddy, I want to have a yarn to the boys," John West said.

When they had gone, he leant on the table. "So a toy bomb was the best you could do," he snarled, addressing no one in particular. They all avoided his fierce gaze.

John West had been restless and nervy while in Sydney. He watched the papers daily for news of the attempt on O'Flaherty's life. Viewing his affairs from a distance, he had begun to wish he had not issued the instructions against O'Flaherty and Baddson. It was a greater risk than he had taken before, yet he could no longer tolerate O'Flaherty defying him with impunity. He was the biggest book-maker in Australia. His accountants now estimated that he was making £5,000 a week from his various enterprises. O'Flaherty could not be allowed to end such a career. Yet a fear that he might be implicated had gripped John West. He could not sleep, and several times was on the verge of returning to Melbourne to rescind his order.

Then came the news of the bombing. He reacted to it with a mixture of rage and fear: rage at the failure of the attempt, and fear of the possible consequences to himself.

"You realise I am likely to be arrested for this. Well, don't think I'm going to go to the jug over a lot of bloody idiots!"

His eyes circled the room. His men had never before seen him in such a frenzy. Their silence intensified his rage. He thumped the table with his fist and shouted: "Don't sit there like a lot of school kids! What can we do to fix this? Frank, here, says we might be able to pin the job on to those other two bookies O'Flaherty prosecuted."

"That's what we thought," Piggy answered. "They been talkin' big 'bout what they'd do to O'Flaherty. We thought we might get them blamed for it."

"You thought! I'll do the thinking here. A toy bomb was all you could think of. You couldn't even find Baddson, and you missed O'Flaherty. If you had taken Frank's instructions you would have fixed him. Well, in future, you will take Frank's instructions. Remember that, all of you; when I'm away Frank is boss. I'll have no more of this bucking orders."

"Well, the blokes we got to do it said the bomb would fix him," Arthur West said. "If Frank had let me do the job like I wanted, I woulda fixed the bastard."

John West ignored his brother's remark. "Now listen to this, all of you. If anyone gets fitted with this job, it won't be me. Understand? It won't be me! And, look out, it might be some of you." He pushed Sugar Renfrey roughly on the shoulder. "Give a man a seat, I'm tired!"

Sugar made way for him. John West sat at the end of the table deep in thought. He must remain calm. After a while he took a large roll of notes from his pocket and handed a number to Piggy.

"Piggy, you get in touch with those toy-bomb throwers, give them a hundred quid each and tell 'em to leave the country and not come back. They're dangerous to have around; might be 'minced' by O'Flaherty and talk. Now, we'll make it look like those other bookies did this. We'll send an anonymous note to the policeman who arrested them with O'Flaherty, telling him he's next, or something like that. Tommy, you find out the trap's name and send him a note. You fools get us into trouble, and it's left to me to get us out again."

"I'll arrange that for you, Mr. West." Lammence said quietly. "If my orders had been carried out, O'Flaherty would be in a coffin now."

"I'm going to write a letter to all the papers, Frank, offering a reward or something like that," John West said. "We'll get Barney to draft it right away. Come on. And you others, listen to me. If you ever make another mistake, or open your mouths about this, I'll have you kicked to death!''

The ferocity of his manner terrified even these violent men.

Next morning the papers carried a letter from John West, written reluctantly in Barney Robinson's flowery style. The epistle denied that John West was in any way implicated in the matter, being absent in Sydney at the time; and concluded with a rather rash offer that he would pay a thousand, or a million pounds sterling to any person who could prove that he was in any way connected with the crime. John West was not quite a millionaire; but he soon would be one. Surely a millionaire could not be accused of attempted murder!

The press also featured a report that the police sergeant who had assisted O'Flaherty in a recent gaming prosecution had received an anonymous letter warning him: YOU ARE NEXT, BEWARE!

Next day a letter from a Labor Senator of the Commonwealth Parliament was published. A native of Queensland, the Senator was one of the first to come under the influence of John West, who had purchased two racecourses in Queensland, and was already gaining influence in the Labor Party in that State.

The Senator's letter ridiculed O'Flaherty's insinuation that John West was behind the attempt on his life and ended thus: "If I were Mr. West I would ask Detective O'Flaherty straight out if he means me in his severe stricture; whether he thinks Mr. West had knowledge of, countenanced or associated with the crime or criminal."

This brought responses from two different quarters: a solemn statement from Chief Commissioner Callinan that he believed Mr. West was by no means associated with the crime; and one from O'Flaherty which tore the Senator's letter to pieces. "Mr. West and his friends must have guilty consciences," O'Flaherty's letter concluded.

A further letter from John West was couched in placatory terms and concluded with the intimation that Mr. West had a theory about the crime and would make it available to Detective-Sergeant O'Flaherty should he elect to call on him.

Dave O'Flaherty elected to call late that afternoon. John West interviewed him in his office upstairs.

"You say you have a theory about the attempted murder. Well, what is it?" O'Flaherty said when he had seated himself opposite John West. O'Flaherty was in plain clothes and nursed a black slouch hat.

"Yes, Sergeant," John West replied quietly. "Did you see in the paper where a police sergeant received a threatening letter?"

"I did." O'Flaherty had investigated the anonymous letter and was convinced it was a fraud.

"Well, do you know that particular sergeant is the one who helped to arrest those S.P. book-makers in the suburbs recently?"

"I do. What of it?"

"Well, work it out for yourself."

Dave O'Flaherty's red face reddened a few shades, and he leant forward rapping the table with his fist. "Listen, West! I have worked it out. And I think it's a dastardly attempt to put the blame on innocent men!"

John West attempted to reply, but O'Flaherty continued vehemently. "It's typical of you, West. But this time you've gone too far. I'm after you. I'll close your club and tote. And, what's more, I'll have you behind bars shortly for being an accessory before the fact in the attempt on my life. Your reign of terror is ended!"

John West flinched as if he had been struck in the face. Before he could answer, O'Flaherty rose and left the room, slamming the door.

Dave O'Flaherty didn't know whether he could make good his threats, but if he failed it would not be for the want of trying.

He left behind a very frightened man. John West sat at the table as pale as a ghost. Was O'Flaherty bluffing? Like all guilty men when accused, he began to cogitate on how evidence could have been obtained against him. Who had talked? Did Piggy really send the bomb-throwers away? Had O'Flaherty got a man listening outside the door when they planned to transfer the blame to the other men? All sorts of doubts and questions arose in his mind. The arrogant self-confidence drained out of him. He must get away immediately. Leave the country. Transfer his money and clear out to where O'Flaherty could not find him.

He arose shakily and went into Frank Lammence's office. "Come out to the house tonight at eight o'clock, Frank, will you?" he said.

John West arrived home that evening in a daze. Fear had

crashed through the barriers which the years had built around his spirit. He had hardly eaten since his return, he hadn't worked, he hadn't slept, and not one word had passed between Nellie and himself. His mother had sent word that she wanted to see him, but he did not respond.

Previously he had treated Nellie's complaints with sardonic scorn, now he dreaded the inevitable clash. For days she had been frigid and silent. She seemed to be always watching him – silent, terrified, convinced of his guilt. So tense did the atmosphere become that the eldest child, Marjorie, aged six, seemed to be affected by it.

Until the news of the bomb outrage reached her, Nellie had been learning to resign herself to her marriage: to adapt herself to her rôle of wife of a leading sportsman and church patron. She was learning to ignore the rumours, and the reserve with which she was treated at church functions. She had shut forebodings out of her mind and busied herself with her household and servants. In her love for her two children she found joy and fulfilment. During the early years of their marriage, the violent side of her husband's personality had made itself felt in the house, filling Nellie with fear; but in recent years, John West had used it only to impress his associates at the club and tote, where it forced his will upon them even in his absence. At home he became a reserved and morose man; quite civil, although dominant.

Nellie had visited her mother daily since the bombing. Mrs Moran tried to pretend indifference to her anxiety, and expressed belief in John West's innocence; but yesterday, grieved by Nellie's distress, she had embraced her and exclaimed: "Oh, my darling, why ever did I let you marry him?"

Nellie broke down and sobbed pitifully.

"Be brave, little girl," Mrs. Moran said. "Be brave for the children's sake. Come again on Sunday and we'll decide what to do."

Nellie sat in the luxurious dining-room waiting for her husband to come in for dinner. She looked pale and tired, but delicately beautiful in her white dress. The youngest child, a baby girl, was asleep upstairs, but Marjorie, a charming, golden-haired child, ran into the room followed by a nurse-maid.

"Good night, Mummy, I'm going to bed now."

The child leapt on to Nellie's lap and embraced her.

"Have you been crying, Mummy?"

"Me crying? No, I'm tired, darling, that's all. I'll be going to bed myself soon. Now, off you go, and don't forget your prayers."

"Why are you sad, Mummy?"

The nursemaid waited uncomfortably. Nellie suppressed her tears and said: "I'm not sad, darling, just tired."

She kissed the child and stroked her golden hair.

When the nurse had taken Marjorie upstairs, Nellie blew her nose and wiped her eyes; then she heard John West enter the house.

Unusually, he did not go upstairs to wash. He entered the dining room with lowered head, his unruly fringe falling untidily over his forehead. His shoulders drooped; his hands hung loosely by his sides; his eyes had sunk deeper in their sockets and they were dark-ringed. Without looking at his wife, he sat at the head of the table. He seemed conscious that her eyes were on him.

Why doesn't she speak, he thought. Perhaps she knows something. Men have been given away by their own wives before today.

Without looking up he said: "Mr. Lammence is coming here tonight. And remember, if anyone asks, we had no visitors."

She stood up. "Coming here? You know I don't like those men coming here."

He looked at her. "What's wrong with them? They can come here if I say so."

She walked around and stood close to him. "Don't worry, I won't see him. I don't want to meet thieves. Thieves and – and bomb-throwers!"

The last words spurted from her mouth like spittle. He got up and gripped her by the shoulders. She saw fear in his eyes.

"Bomb-throwers? What do you mean, bomb-throwers?"

She noticed that the hands on her shoulders were trembling. He had not burst into a rage. His gaze was wavering. She pulled herself away from him, and looked into his eyes screaming: "I can't stand it any longer! You did tell them to kill O'Flaherty! Didn't you? Didn't you, John?"

She read the truth in his eyes, then he lowered his gaze and his whole body sagged. A sob came from her and she began to weep. She walked out of the room and towards the stairs, her slippered feet moving quietly over the carpetless, polished floor. Her white figure moved up the wide staircase.

John West made to follow her.

"Nellie," he called, then he hesitated, went back and resumed his seat. The maid noticed that he left most of his food untouched.

That evening, he and Frank Lammence spent an hour discussing the crisis. John West succeeded in pulling himself together in the presence of his favourite lieutenant. He felt certain of Lammence's loyalty. He could discuss his fears more frankly with him than with anyone else. If things got any hotter he would leave the country. He asked Lammence to plan his departure and look after his affairs. When this blew over, he would come back.

John West complained that he could not sleep and was suffering from violent headaches and pains around his heart. Lammence knew of his fetish for health. He believed the pains to be imaginary, but discreetly advised a visit to the doctor.

As he was leaving, Lammence said: "I really think you should see Garside, you know. He's used to this sort of thing. He'd still help."

John West's morale improved. Why hadn't he thought of old Davie?

In the morning, he went to a Collins Street doctor, who reported that there was nothing seriously amiss, but advised a sea trip. John West's tremendous vitality had been sapped by strain and long hours, and the shock and fear of the past few days.

He went straight from the doctor to David Garside's office.

Garside was unusually subdued, but before John West could make a hesitant beginning he said quietly: "I have been daily expecting you to call, Mr. West. This is a most serious situation. I am not asking whether you issued instructions for the dastardly attempt before you departed for Sydney. Before I take up a man's case, I usually demand to know whether he is guilty, but I will not press you. The perpetrators of the crime, and anyone who knows you were connected with it – that is, assuming, for a moment, that you were – must be silenced, and if possible kept away from O'Flaherty. O'Flaherty is a signally ignorant man, but possessed of common sense and craftiness. He is using an old trick of pretending he has all the evidence he needs to arrest you. You have fallen for the ruse, and are in a frame of mind that would cause you to make the error of believing he knows that which he could not know, and perhaps telling him things which you believe he already knows. Your men will, no doubt, react similarly. My advice to you is to see that none of your men talks to O'Flaherty.''

''All right, I'll have a word with them. The two who did the job are already gone overseas.'' John West said, unwittingly betraying himself to Garside. His voice was husky. Garside could see he was badly shaken. ''I was thinking of leaving the country myself. One of my fighters. Bill Squeers, has offers to fight overseas, and I was thinking of going away as his manager, until this blows over. Anyway, my doctor has advised me to go overseas for the good of my health. He says I am very run down.''

Garside laughed, trying to ease the tension. ''Run down. That's priceless. You're run down, so you go away so you won't be run down by the law.''

John West scowled. Garside swallowed his laughter and said: ''Pardon me, Mr. West. I couldn't help seeing the funny side. You must pull yourself together. You have worked very hard and the scare of the last few days has left its mark. I am not by any means certain that O'Flaherty can fit you with this crime. Announce your intention of leaving the country, but you may not have to go. I shall make some enquiries. Come back this afternoon at four. Meantime, buck up. We have beaten them before.''

There had been ominous signs that O'Flaherty was determined to fit John West with the crime. The night before, Piggy had been questioned by O'Flaherty, and the house of one of the departed bomb-throwers searched. John West announced to the press that he intended taking Squeers overseas for an attempt to win the world title.

When he returned to Garside, he found him in high spirits. He had positive information from the Crown Law Department that, because of lack of evidence, O'Flaherty had abandoned, at least temporarily, any idea of prosecuting anyone for the bomb outrage, and was going to concentrate on closing the club and tote.

In a wave of relief, John West's fear vanished. He laughed huskily.

''O'Flaherty's not so smart,'' he said, rocking his head and straightening his shoulders. ''Not smart enough to beat Jack West. Jack West is boss.''

Next morning Baddson, dressed now in police uniform, called at the City Tattersall's Club and served summonses on several members, including John West himself, Frank Lammence, and Sugar Renfrey.

CHAPTER SIX

New conditions call for new rules and a new policy.

LYSANDER

"The wowsers are saying that I am going to leave the country for the purpose of avoiding legal proceedings of various kinds." John West said at a special banquet for his supporters in the City Tattersall's Club.

"Well, then I will not go. I hold my reputation dearer than health. There is not one iota of truth in the insinuations and mysterious statements circulating. They are a pack of infamous lies! Everyone knows now that I had nothing whatsoever to do with the bombing of Detective O'Flaherty's house. Everyone knows that I have never given a shilling to influence improperly a judge or any other man."

The audience – a mixture of tote and club employees, sportsmen, a few politicians and journalists – gave John West a vindicating cheer.

"I am going to stay home and fight the wowsers and the Government."

More cheers for John West. Jeers for the despised wowsers.

"But Bert Squeers will still go overseas to meet the world's best in New York, London and Paris. Let's hope he will bring back the coveted belt."

Loud "Hear, Hear," and a bow from lanky Bert Squeers.

"With our champion, as manager, will be none other than Mr. Barney Robinson." This was a signal for loud applause. The popular Mr. Robinson arose, shook hands with himself in the manner of a victorious boxer, and launched into an oration liberally sprinkled with alliterations and halting Latin and French quotations.

Toasts were then drunk to John West's health and Bert Squeers' success. Many other toasts were honoured, and the guests drank heartily until none of the ample liquid refreshments remained.

The past two months had restored John West's health. All his energy, self-confidence and will to power returned. He worked for the present and planned for the future; his enemies again felt the weight of his ruthless determination.

The bombing episode was pushed behind him. Only on his relations with Nellie did it leave a mark: they were more estranged than ever; she had retreated behind a wall of reserve and fear.

A large crowd had gathered to hear the new trial of strength between the law and the West-Garside combination in the City Tattersall's Club cases.

"The defence will say that the City Tattersall's is a bonafide club," the Crown Prosecutor began. "An elaborate farce has been gone through to give some appearance of this. Last year, as a disguise, the club became a registered company, and scrip was sold entitling the holders to membership. Towards the end of the year it almost developed into a political institution. An intimate friend of Mr. West, a Labor politician, did not think it below the dignity of his position to disguise the objects of the club by delivering a lecture on social democracy. The persons who listened to the lecture did not attend the club for that purpose, but there was no escape ..."

Laughter greeted his words, then he proceeded to tear the defence case to pieces in advance. But he reckoned without David Garside.

"Old Davie" was granted an adjournment to finalise the defence case. John West used the three days to threaten and bribe the other police witness who had worked with Constable Baddson as a spy in the club. The bribed witness agreed to identify some other person as Sugar Renfrey, to say that he had not made bets with John West, but had seen him in the club on an occasion when it could be proven that he was absent in Sydney.

Incredibly, David Garside produced in court a man who was Sugar Renfrey's double.

"Is that the accused Renfrey?"

"He looks like him."

"Well, is it he, or isn't it?"

"Yes, it is!"

"Well, it isn't. You have sworn that, on August the fourteenth, the accused West was betting at the club, and that you got a betting slip from him – this one. It reads: 'Six shillings to two, Kismet.' Now, West was in Sydney on that date, so he couldn't have been betting in Melbourne.''

John West gripped his seat.

"It *is* West's ticket. I got a man I call Jack, who, I think, works at the Theatre Royal, to make a bet, and told him to get a ticket from West. He gave me the ticket and said West had given it to him.''

John West relaxed in his seat. It's the same old story, he thought, these police pimps are all the same: threaten to bash them, then offer them money, and they'll do anything.

"But you have sworn that West was betting at the club that day, and that you said: 'Six to two, Kismet, Jack.' Is that true?''

"The part, 'Six to two, Kismet, Jack' is true. Jack is the man who got the ticket for me.''

Dave O'Flaherty leaned forward in his seat near the front of the court, half stood, opened his mouth to protest, then sat down red in the face.

"In your report you say: 'I said, six to two, Kismet, Jack, and he, West, gave me the ticket which I put in my pocket.' Is that true?''

"Jack West didn't give me the ticket. It was his ticket, though.''

Garside took two long paces towards the embarrassed witness. "Then that is a lie. A deliberate lie! You say in some of these reports that you saw Jack West behind the counter betting.''

"I don't think I said I saw him betting.''

The fat, bald-headed magistrate looked up with a puzzled air and muttered: "The witness swore that bets were made with West and others.''

Garside then continued: "The report of September the thirteenth says: 'In a room there is a long counter, and behind it were West and some other men betting.' ''

"Did you ever see West make one bet there?''

"No.''

The Crown Prosecutor frowned. "Your worship, I'm afraid I will have to ask permission to have this witness declared hostile.''

David Garside interrupted triumphantly: "Are you going to ask for a conviction on the evidence of a hostile witness?''

"It is a question for the Bench what shall be done about this – er – witness's evidence.''

The magistrate looked more lively. "It seems that the witness has broken down under cross-examination, and you now wish to treat him as hostile."

"I would suggest that the breaking down has been arranged."

"I don't think the Bench should suffer that being said," Garside interposed.

"Unless the Crown has evidence of it, I cannot suffer it to be said."

"Oh, it is only my belief." The Crown Prosecutor shrugged his shoulders. John West folded his arms, smiling.

Albert Baddson was in the witness box most of the next day, told the story of his work as a police agent in the Tattersall's Club. He resisted all Garside's clever attempts to confuse and discredit him.

David Garside, summing up for the defence, concluded a long address by describing the case against the accused as the flimsiest he had ever been confronted with.

The magistrate said that Baddson's fellow witness seemed to have a subdued and confused mind; but he said Baddson was a "faithful witness" who produced sheaves of betting tickets. "His evidence is uncontradicted and undeniable. The defendant, West, seems to be the master mind behind the establishment. There seems some doubt about whether Renfrey was present betting at the club on the day referred to by the witness, and there is no evidence that Lammence made bets, therefore, I am going to discharge those two defendants. I find West and the other defendants guilty and fine them each one hundred pounds."

David Garside immediately gave notice that he intended to appeal to a higher court. When John West's previous convictions were mentioned there, the Judge asked gravely: "Is there no statute in regard to human forgetfulness?" After deliberating on the evidence for two hours he said that he felt he had "no alternative but to quash the convictions," which was quite true, for he had agreed with David Garside that he would do so in return for two hundred pounds.

Enraged, O'Flaherty forced Chief Commissioner Callinan to approach the Premier and Chief Secretary again, demanding that they introduce new gaming legislation.

John West's feeling of triumph faded when a very vocal wowser, the Reverend Mr. Joggins, publicly accused the Judge of having been bribed, and wrote to the Premier demanding a public inquiry before West ran away to escape the law.

In recent months, several of the weekly "Pleasant Sunday Afternoons" at Wesley Church had been anything but pleasant for John West. Joggins had used them as a forum to expose him. As well, Joggins had been holding regular meetings in the suburbs demanding action against "the twin evils of gambling and drink," and a bill to suppress illegal betting establishments.

The Judge replied to Joggins through the press, asking foolishly: "Does a Judge who is going to give a decision that has been paid for, consider the evidence for two hours?"

After that, every time Joggins spoke at Wesley Church or in a suburban hall or church, the windows were smashed the same night. Joggins began to receive anonymous telephone calls throughout each night, informing him that he would be dealt with if he persisted.

Terrified, Joggins obtained a police guard, and wrote to the Premier withdrawing his demand for the inquiry, but repeating his demand that the Gaming Act be amended.

John West had then organised the banquet at which he announced that he would stay in Australia.

"This batch is so rotten you can smell 'em through the shells," Cauliflower Dick said to John West, referring to the paper-bag full of eggs he held in his hand. With them in the lounge room of the City Tattersall's Club were Barney Robinson, Piggy, Sugar Renfrey, Squash Lewis, Long Bill, Paddy Woodman and about a dozen others.

"My wife's been keeping h'eggs for h'over two months, just h'in case something like this adventurated," Squash Lewis informed them.

"Now, don't forget. Go in one at a time and keep those parcels out of sight."

"Right, Jack."

"And don't throw the eggs until you've got in those interjections – specially that new one about the woman Joggins is supposed to have put in the family way. Get up in the left gallery with the eggs; you can get a good shot from there."

"Not me," said Barney Robinson; "I won't throw eggs. I'll throw interjections from the body of the hall." Barney was not anxious to be arrested on the eve of his departure overseas. He had left John West after the bombing, only to return, with Florrie's grudging consent, when booked as Squeers' manager.

"All right," John West said, as the others departed with paperbags and pockets full of rotten eggs. "How many tickets did you get printed?"

"A hundred, and they'll nearly all be used," Barney replied. "Joggins'll get a bloody shock when he finds we got hold of one of the invitation tickets, and copied it. A regular coup d'état, as they say in the French."

At that moment Mr. Joggins himself was walking towards the Gaiety Theatre accompanied by two tall constables. Joggins was a bundle of nerves; he walked jerkily as if he had springs fitted to the heels of his shoes. He took two strides to one of the policemen, and their height accentuated his dwarf-like stature.

Joggins was a living personification of the term "wowser." He was a little man with a thin ascetic face, and a gleam of wild fanaticism in his eyes. To him the seven deadly sins were gambling, drinking alcoholic liquor, horse-racing, telling smutty stories, hotel-keeping, fornication and young people of opposite sexes consorting together. John West was the devil himself and his mob the fallen angels. Joggins openly boasted of counting the number of people who entered the City Tattersall's Club and Madam Brussells' brothels. He unashamedly stated that he had, on many occasions, snooped around the parks and beaches on summer nights, watching the young couples from behind bushes.

He could run white hot over the evils of drink and gambling, and yet be quite cold when confronted with poverty, slums and destitution at the bottom of society, and riches, mansions and opulence at the top. He was a crusader against the sins of the poor, and a condoner of the sins of the rich. The destitution of the poor was God's will. So long as a poor man suffered humbly, he would be rewarded in the next world.

"Blessed are the poor, for they shall see God," meantime they "are always with us," and should be given the word of God, handouts of apples and soup, and a few blankets in the winter. Most important of all, the poor must be protected from the evils of gambling, intoxication and sex!

Unable to sublimate his sexual desires any longer, Joggins himself had begun an illicit relationship with a young Sunday-school teacher. In view of his denunciation of such conduct, he could not very well proclaim his relationship with the girl, and somehow he could not bring himself to say that he wanted to marry her: the world at large must continue to believe in his militant celibacy.

Joggins' narrow-minded fanaticism gave him a certain fool-hardy courage. He was developing a formidable mass movement against vice; especially against John West's gaming houses.

"My word, it appears that we will have a monster crowd tonight," Joggins said, as they approached the Gaiety Theatre and saw people overflowing on to the footpath. "And that without West's ruffians, as admission is by invitation."

They entered the hall through the back door, and the two policemen seated themselves off-stage.

The clergyman who was to chair the meeting said: "The hall is full to overflowing already, Joggins. Indeed, let us thank God that we have, for a change, a hall full of our own supporters."

They peeped through the stage curtain into the buzzing, mumbling hall. Joggins' little eyes roved the audience. Yes, there was certainly a much bigger percentage of well dressed, refined people tonight. But – surely it couldn't be! My God! It's he, all right!

"Look, Reverend," he said, "is that not the ruffian, Renfrey, sitting at the rear? Look there, smoking a cigar!"

"Good gracious, so it is! And many of his vulgar friends. How did they get tickets?"

"They must have stolen some. Oh, that such wickedness could be!"

Joggins said with an air of resignation: "They are dotted throughout the hall. We are in for trouble tonight."

The doors had to be closed before time. Joggins and the chairman walked timidly to the table on the stage, while the pressmen and a big-bosomed woman, who was to sing later on, took seats behind them. Joggins sipped water nervously as the chairman announced that Mr. Joggins was too well known to need any introduction, and that his subject tonight would be Melbourne's Sins and Follies.

Joggins opened in his strident voice, but lacked his usual fire. "We, in Melbourne, are passing through a crisis . . ."

"You'll pass through a crisis," roared a voice from the left gallery.

"It is time to make a choice . . ."

"I'll give you ten to one," Barney Robinson shouted from the body of the hall, amid laughter.

"For years the life of Victoria, politically, socially and individually . . ."

"You're a loafer, Joggins," Cauliflower Dick yelled, in tones as aggressive as his appearance. This was the signal for uproar. Policemen at vantage points waited for guidance from the platform.

"God has come down in the midst of his people."

"Praise the Lord," Barney shouted, mimicking Joggins' sanctimonious tone.

"I want to tell you the truth about the Carringbush tote," Joggins continued.

"It's a poor man's tote," roared Piggy.

"West has made a stupendous fortune out of the poor man," Joggins shouted. "I have seen as many as two thousand people enter the tote in one day, including old men and boys."

"Shows how popular it is," roared Sugar Renfrey, who led a group of interjectors at the back of the hall. He was immediately ejected by three policemen.

"Gambling is the biggest evil in the country," Joggins shouted. He faced the crowd fiercely now, but the little minister beside him was trembling.

"What about the Stock Exchange and the business people? You don't attack the rich." This from a Socialist who had obtained a forged ticket from Barney Robinson.

"Yes," a woman sitting next to this man shouted, "why don't you attack the business people who rob the workers?"

"This is the first time that I have heard a woman's voice raised in support of vice."

Uproar followed, then Squash Lewis arose in the left gallery and stood until Joggins took notice of him.

"H'I want to h'ask a question."

"What is it?"

"Why don't you pay your debts?" Squash asked gravely.

Joggins' supporters shouted: "Throw him out," while the West men roared: "Yes, why don't you pay your debts? What about that seventeen quid?"

Joggins was thrown into confusion, but quickly recovered.

"The gambling interests are trying to find out every little tale they can about me."

"Will you deny that you still h'owe seventeen pounds?"

"I saw the man this morning, and he has given me a letter to say I don't owe it."

"Throw him out," shouted the Joggins supporters.

"H'its h'all right. H'I'll go now," Squash said as three policemen closed in on him. If a man stays much longer, he might get retained by the police, he was thinking.

"What makes men gamble?" Joggins asked, while long Squash was being bundled out.

"What makes a cat drink milk?"

"You used to milk your next door neighbour's goat, Joggins."

Then the Socialist who had interjected earlier rose and challenged Joggins to debate that all gambling institutions, including the Stock Exchange and the Victorian Racing Club, should be nationalised.

Joggins refused, then Cauliflower Dick leapt to his feet in the gallery and roared: "Why don't you marry that girl, Millicent Smith?" Disorder reigned and Joggins' discomfort was obvious. How did they find out about Millicent? Marry her? My God, this is terrible! When the disorder ceased, he said, "I say . . ."

"What does Millicent Smith say?" Cauliflower Dick interrupted.

Joggins was nonplussed, but he managed to continue: "People are beginning to understand that, in the midst of Victoria, there are evils . . ."

"Yes, Joggins."

"He's a blowfly."

"Look at Melbourne at night. Then it is that evil reigns," Joggins continued without much heart while his chairman fiddled with the table cover and gazed apprehensively at the left gallery from whence the main fire was coming. The supporters of Mr. Joggins, though in the majority, began to wish they had stayed at home.

"You will have no doubt as to the extent of evil in this city. Is it not true . . ."

Joggins was interrupted by a raucous rendition of *We'll Hang Old Joggins on a Sour Apple Tree.*

Some of his supporters found a little courage and started a

counter demonstration of cheering, then one of them shouted;
"Rub it into them, Joggins!"

"We'll rub Joggins out!"

The interjectors then sang: *He's Gone Where They Don't Play
Billiards.*

Joggins stood nervously until they had finished. "As soon as
night falls a proportion of the population plunges headlong into
vice. There is an inferno, right here in Melbourne!"

"Yes, Joggins is here!"

"What about marrying that girl? Yer got 'er in the family
way!" persisted Cauliflower Dick, as usual sticking strictly to
instructions.

"You are a drunkard and a gambler," Joggins shouted, and
pandemonium reigned afresh.

Tired of trying to make a speech, Joggins addressed several
questions to the audience.

"What kind of record are you going to leave when you go to
face your Maker?"

"A better record than you left at Ballarat!"

"I am not ashamed of any record I have left anywhere. The
gamblers ought to know that, because they had detectives to help
them inquire into every year of my life."

"We found out about Miss Smith."

"Yes, and Joggins' debts."

"Has the vote God has given been cast for Him every time?"
Joggins asked.

"Yes, Joggins," roared Barney Robinson, "I vote for the
Labor Party."

The interjections and noise ceased and Joggins was able to
continue for a minute, then an egg, thrown with unerring aim by
Cauliflower Dick, hit him between the eyes. The evil-smelling
missile nauseated him. Rotten eggs rained on to the platform.
Joggins, his chairman, the reporters and the lady vocalist were
all covered with dripping, stinking eggs. One of the press-men
gallantly shielded the lady with an upturned chair, and escorted
her to the safety of the wings.

Joggins was the main target, and his tormentors' aim was accurate. Eggs exploded in his face and over his clothes. As quickly
as he wiped the dripping yolks from his eyes, face and clothes,
more followed until he fled to the wings. The smell pervaded the

tumultuous hall. Joggins' supporters pointed towards the left gallery and shouted: "There they are."

Policemen ran hither and thither trying to discover the egg-slingers. Four of the police went to the gallery and seized Cauliflower Dick and one of his henchmen.

After five minutes of uproar, during which Joggins' supporters in the audience were also bombarded with eggs, he returned to state that, "all men must go before the bar of God to be judged." He got another shower of eggs for his trouble, closed the meeting and was escorted from the hall by his own two bodyguards and three other policemen.

One night a week later John West's mother rocked in the old chair by the kitchen fire. She was knitting a pair of socks for Joe, squinting close to her work through her glasses.

The old chair afforded her much comfort. She refused to part with it, even now, when the generosity of her sons, especially John, made it possible for her to buy the best chair in the land.

The old woman looked strangely out of place. She and her chair appeared to be a last stand of old things resisting the new. A kerosene lamp stood on the table, the fire burnt brightly and she sat there, knitting and thinking, with her old shawl wrapped around her shoulders to protect her withering body from the draughts which new furniture could not prevent from coming through the walls.

She was just past sixty, yet her face was etched with deep lines marking off the score that the years had made against her. Her eyes were deep-set as if slowly sinking into her head, a creamy film was forming over them, and she was almost blind. Her mouth formed a thin line, curving downwards at each corner.

She ceased rocking at the sound of footsteps on the back porch. Joe entered, and placed his hat on the table.

"Hullo, mum," he said quietly, sitting on a chair at the other side of the fire.

"Where's Myrtle, Joe?"

"The baby has a runny nose, so she said it was too cold to bring it out."

"Just as well, Joe. Don't want the dear little mite getting sick."

Her three sons were now married: Joe to a "nice homely girl" whom Mrs. West liked very much. She didn't like Nellie Moran, with her airs and graces, who wouldn't deign to visit her lonely mother-in-law. Mrs. West had been disappointed in Arthur's choice of wife – a showy, vulgar girl, who on her only visit to the old woman had said: "Don't worry, I got no prize in Arty. On our wedding night I saw the weals on his back for the first time. I didn't know what to say, so I laughed. He grabbed me by the throat and said: 'If you laugh at that again, I'll murder you.' He meant it, too. Don't worry, I got no prize. I'm frightened of my own husband."

The old woman rocked and knitted on, and they sat in silence for a while. "How did those men of John's get on at the court over throwing the eggs?"

"They got fined a hundred pound each. Jack paid the fines."

"Do you think John will ever close the club and tote?"

"No, mum, I don't think so. Unless the Bill that's supposed to be coming before the Parliament makes him close them."

"I hope it does, Joe. It would be better. Then John would get rid of Piggy and all those criminals, and be satisfied with his other businesses."

Joe was silent. He sympathised with his mother's desire that John should end his long association with the criminal classes, but his job as manager of the tote was an easy one. Now that the police never interfered, it suited his lazy nature to earn a regular salary there. He ran the place with twenty men, including Scotch Paddy, Flash Alec, Jigger, Boney Bill and other "good blokes." The Ape, who was chucker-out, was the only violent man left.

Mrs. West liked Joe to come and sit with her, here by the fire, in the room where she had waged her long war with poverty. That war was over. John had ended it, yet somehow she liked the old days better. The days when the boys were young and the echoes of their laughter and their small quarrels rang through the dingy rooms. Before Arty got into trouble, before John started bookmaking.

She had never been able to come close to Arty since. She rarely saw him these days. He was still bitter and moody, out of her world; but while there was a spark of life in her she would worry about him and try to help him. She sometimes thought he would have been all right if he had married a sympathetic, homely girl. God knows where he would end up. She knew that, with John's protection, he would do anything. And now people were saying that Dick Bradley was out of jail!

"Joe, is it true that Dick Bradley is out?"

"Eh? I couldn't say. How would I know?"

"You know, Joe. Is he?"

"Yes."

"Has Arty seen him?"

"Yes." He studied the hearth, his hands fiddling nervously.

"God help us now! You've got to talk to John. It's bad enough now with bomb-throwers and bashers. But God knows what will happen with Bradley out!"

"John's not interested in Bradley, mum. Bradley's got no brains. John don't want him."

"But Arty does. You know that; you've heard him talk. You'll have to see John. If only he will close the tote and club, put off those criminals and give Arty a job – perhaps on one of the racecourses. You must see him, Joe. In the name of the Holy Mother of God, you must talk to John!"

Joe looked at her entreating face. Why did she still hope, still bother to worry, he thought. Too late; might as well make the best of it.

In his listless way, Joe loved his mother, but what could he do? He had long decided just to make the best of things. They could hide nothing from the old woman, and she never despaired of her hopes that Arty and John would reform.

"You must talk to John," she said again.

"He said he might come here tonight."

They sat in silence. The ticking of the clock on the mantelpiece and the flutter of the flames were the only sounds until they heard footsteps coming round the side of the house.

John West entered the room.

"Hullo, mum," he said brightly, taking off his hat and placing it on the table. "Great fire you've got. Very cold out." He turned his back to the fire, his figure fitting snugly into the neat overcoat and dark suit. He had the appearance of a man in the money who knew how to dress. Joe's cheap suit, the drab attire of the old woman, the chair, the fireplace and the smoke-stained walls were in their correct setting; but this dapper man and the modern furniture he had bought for the room were from another world. Mrs. West could sense this.

John West brushed the crest of sandy hair back from his forehead and to his mother he became again her little boy, her

215

favourite son. But this was only part of her dream.

"I can't stay, mum," John West said. "Got some business to attend to. How are your eyes?"

"Much the same, son."

"We might change to another doctor. This man doesn't seem to be doing you any good. How are the finances?"

"Oh, I don't need money, John." Joe watched her as she leant over and grasped John's arm. "John. Why don't you close the old tote and the club, like I've asked you, and get away from all those bad men?"

Joe watched his brother look into her eyes, and thought he saw his steely gaze melt.

"Please, John, for me. For your own mother." She thought she saw a glimmer of the John who had often said to her in this room so long ago when she wept if there was no meal: "I'll make a lot of money when I grow up. I'll look after you, mum. You'll be happy." But the gaze hardened again.

"You could give Arty a job somewhere, and keep him away from Dick Bradley."

John West straightened up. "So that's what's worrying you. Well, you'll have to see Arty about that. It's none of my business."

"It's no use seeing Arty, John; you know that."

"Well, it's none of my business, mum. I can't do anything. Why should I close the tote and club? The workers like to have a bet, so why shouldn't they? And, I've told you, you don't want to believe this wowser propaganda in the papers. It's all lies."

"Not all lies, John."

He took an envelope from his pocket and pushed it into her hand. "Here, mum, buy yourself something, some clothes perhaps."

She made to refuse, but changed her mind. What was the use? Even his love for his own mother expressed itself in terms of money.

They heard Arthur West's voice in the front of the house saying: "How are you, Barney?" and it eased the tension. Barney Robinson's voice answered: "Cold as a maggot on a dead polar bear."

"Is that Barney Robinson?" the old woman said.

"Yes, he's out in the jinker."

"Bring him in, John, we could have a cup of tea. I like Barney, and it's years since I last saw him. He's going to America soon, isn't he?"

"Yes. But we're running late now," he answered as Arthur West entered and they watched him take off his coat and hat.

Arthur passed a brusque: "'Night, mum."

"I've got to be going," John West said, picking up his hat and walking out.

As he joined Barney in the jinker, Mrs. West's voice came from the front door: "Hullo, Barney Robinson."

"Well, if it isn't me old sweetheart," Barney answered. "How are yer, Mrs. West?"

"Fairly, Barney."

"I got tired of waiting for you to divorce your old man," Barney said, with laughter in his voice. "Got hitched years ago, I did. Florrie ain't bad, but I'd rather have me old sweetheart."

She chuckled at this old joke. Then John West's voice called from the darkness: "Get back inside, mum. You'll get a cold." She heard the horses' hooves clip-clop away.

Mrs. West groped her way back to the kitchen, and Joe helped her into the rocking chair. Joe sat poking the fire.

Arthur stroked his grey moustache. She studied him.

"Don't have anything to do with Bradley, Arthur, will you?"
He looked up with a fanatical expression.

"Dick Bradley looked after me in jail," he said. "He's my mate, and we're gonna stick together."

The old woman shifted her gaze and the needles clicked again. Her tears welled and a lump in her throat nearly choked her.

The boys did not stay long. When Joe said he must go in case the baby was sick, Arthur left with him.

Mrs. West sat gazing in the fire, her knitting clasped on her lap. A sob broke from her as if all hope had left her soul.

John West and Barney Robinson were seated in the front room of Bob Scott's house. Bob had recently been elected to the Victorian Parliament.

"Did you see Ashton about it?" John West asked Scott.

"Yeh, but he won't come in," Scott answered. Fighting Bob Scott, self-styled, was a curly-haired handsome young man, short and stocky, possessed of tremendous vitality and a gift for sparkling oratory. He was a radical without much learning or theory, a gambler and a careerist; just the kind of man to give plausibility to John West's claim to being a democrat and a friend of the working man.

"You see it's a bit awkward," Scott went on. "The Labor men will oppose the Bill in the house, because it favours the V.R.C. and the wealthy classes, but I don't think we'll get many for this move. I've only got six to come in, but that will do for a start. We'll call the organisation the Christian Socialist Movement – there used to be one in Melbourne, years ago. We'll have a meeting next Sunday night at the Bijou. I've got a banner made with a white map of Australia on a green background. The policy will be for White Australia, and the usual things. We'll attack Joggins and say he should be made to work. And we'll say that, if they want to clean up gambling, they should start with the V.R.C."

"Righto. I only want this organisation to give the impression that the Socialists and Labor people are opposed to Joggins. I'll look after you and the others if you do a good job."

"Did you get that motion written for the meeting?"

"Yes. Have you got it, Barney?"

Barney pulled a piece of paper from his inside coat pocket and read gravely:

That in the opinion of this great gathering of free and God-fearing citizens the howling "push" of sanctimonious snuffle-busters who denounce the poor man for gambling a shilling as a child of wrath, and cringe and crawl to the gilded crooks of Stock Exchange and the V.R.C., are a standing menace to Peace, Progress and Prosperity –

Barney paused to twirl his moustache and see how this alliteration was received.

They want a piebald population under Chow-Japanese rule; free trade at ten bob a week; fourteen hours' work for one hour's pay; sweating, prison labour, and every other political and economic abomination that may add to the additional greasing of the fat sow. They should be banished from the Commonwealth in the interests of Peace, Order and Good Government.

"That'll tickle up the wowsers," exclaimed Scott.

"It'll do," John West said. "We want to get as much support from the workers as we can. The main thing is to create the impression that there are as many people in favour of my club and tote as are against them. Show what hypocrites these wowsers are. Use that argument I told you about before. Say you are not opposed to religion, but the churches promise a man good things in the next world, whereas when a working man has a bet he has a chance of getting good things in this world, where he needs them most. Attack the churches, say they build big cathedrals while the workers have no houses to live in."

"I'll attack the churches, don't worry," Scott said. "Can I include the Catholic church?"

"Don't name it. It's not opposed to gambling."

On the following Sunday evening the Bijou Theatre was packed to the ceiling. At times, the meeting seemed likely to degenerate into a farce because of excessive banter and friendly interjections. Barney's masterpiece was read as a motion and supported by several speakers, all of whom used the occasion to attack Joggins and the parsons who backed him. The banner above the platform read CHRISTIAN SOCIALIST LABOR PLATFORM.

Bob Scott made a fighting speech, thumping the table, shouting and ranting. He called Joggins and his supporters canting, political and religious humbugs who tackled the tote but were not game to tackle the V.R.C. or the Stock Exchange.

"Look at the churches," he roared, punching the table until it seemed to bounce up and down. "Millions of pounds spent for buildings while the poor people live in hovels. If Jesus Christ were on earth he would say: 'I will build houses for the poor'." Bob's voice quivered with feigned emotion. "Men like Joggins ought to be made to work."

That same night Joggins launched another tirade against John West in the Gaiety Theatre.

Next day, the Chief Secretary of Victoria, Sir Samuel Gibbon, announced that he was drafting legislation to enable the police to close the tote and club.

John West intensified his efforts to gain support in the Labor Movement. Mass backing was needed more than ever now. He had successes, but there were also signs of opposition. A few

Labor Party branches passed resolutions condemning politicians who had "publicly and morally supported gambling and gamblers." Carringbush branch was one of these. It acted against the desires of its secretary, Mr. Renfrey, who roundly abused the meeting for making such an error in policy. Later, Sugar explained to a most annoyed John West that the move was made by the Socialist extremists. He promised to redouble his efforts to stack the branch with the "right men."

On the following Monday morning, Barney Robinson was reading the AGE in the lounge of the club when he espied an article which he read aloud to John West, Sugar Renfrey and Frank Lammence.

The article described a demonstration of the unemployed to Scots Church, which had been organised by the leader of the Victorian Socialist Party, Tom Mann.

Mann, who had been a Trade Union leader in England, had come to Melbourne a few years earlier to work for the Labor Party. Quickly disillusioned, he resigned his job, formed the Victorian Socialist Party, and began publication of the SOCIALIST, a weekly newspaper.

Eddie Corrigan, who was a member of Mann's party, had told Barney about the demonstration beforehand, so Barney went to church, for the first time since his marriage, to see the fun.

The snobbish congregation did not know what was in store when they left their stately homes to worship the God with whom they were well pleased. Mann had sent word that the unemployed were coming, but the reverend gentleman conducting the service had not told the congregation, hoping perhaps that it was some sort of ill-chosen joke.

Mann led the demonstrators from the Trades Hall to the church and up the steps. He looked more like a professional man than a leader of the oppressed. Of medium height, he was sombrely dressed in a dark suit. His face was striking: the features even, the blue eyes kindly but unwavering, the mouth firm below a large black moustache.

Behind him came Eddie Corrigan, in his Sunday suit, and Mann's trusted lieutenant, Percy Lambert, a short stocky youth with a round head and wide jaws, and lips angled upwards at the corners as if he were forever smiling at some secret joke. Lambert carried a red flag. A church officer rushed out saying: "You'd better leave that flag outside!'' He took the flag and placed it in the porch.

Tom Mann entered the half-filled church and the demonstrators followed, as many as could. A church officer whispered: "The seats at the back have been set aside for you.'' Anxious eyes looked up from prayer books to view the unexpected arrival, of this neat man and his band of uncouth, ragged worshippers.

"Oh, they have?'' Mann replied. "We are not going to be stuck at the back. Come up to the front, comrades!'' To the front of the church went more than a hundred pairs of shuffling feet.

Other demonstrators entered and sat at the back, while the remainder crowded the porch and the steps. A few of the original congregation changed seats disdainfully.

"Bless the rich,'' the clergyman said, "and make them poor in spirit,'' thinking in his narrow, tory mind that this would placate the insurgents. Instead, it brought spontaneous groans. "My dear brethren,'' he continued, "if people believed that there was no life after death, there would be contempt for all authority.''

Eddie Corrigan stood and shouted: "Christ said: 'Sell all you have and give it to the poor'.'' Some of the unemployed cheered, while others looked at Mann, wondering what to do.

"There are no unemployed in Melbourne except those who do not want to work,'' the parson shouted back.

Lambert stood up from his seat beside Mann amid the shouting. He was deadly serious, but the smile still hovered round his mouth derisively. "Tell us Christ's true story and we will be quiet,'' he said, and sat down.

Tom Mann sat there, apparently calm, but he was not sure whether the demonstration was developing as he had intended. He had hoped to get the parson to address the unemployed and listen to their case. Mann saw the demonstration as part of a mass movement not only to alleviate poverty but to organise the unemployed and make them aware of their own strength.

Afraid, the minister gave the benediction and beat a hasty retreat into the vestry.

"Hundreds of hungry men are here,'' Lambert shouted after him. The organ began playing and the congregation pushed its way fearfully to the door. It departed amid sarcastic remarks from the unemployed.

221

Mann signalled to the demonstrators to remain, and tried to push his way towards the vestry past three church officers who stood on guard.

Lambert shouted: "Three cheers for the new social revolution!" and the very pillars seemed to tremble as the cheering rose, fervid and menacing.

Failing to get by the church officers, Mann said: "I want the minister to address these men and women and hear their case. Ask him and let him refuse."

"We will not ask him!" said one of the officers.

Mann endeavoured to free himself. The church officers held him, and the crowd was about to surge forward. Anything might have happened, but Barney Robinson, who had intended to be merely an observer, created a diversion by shouting with mock piety: "It is written: 'My house is a house of prayer, but you have turned it into a den of thieves'."

Loud cheers were the response, and a shouting of: "Den of thieves! Den of thieves!" The reverend gentleman quivered in the vestry and sent for the police.

The church officers released Mann, who motioned the unemployed outside, where he addressed them.

"Today you have seen a nice example of what is called following Christ. We came to tell men and women in their church that thousands of people are starving in this city while they live in riches, and they fled from us. There is nothing more to be done here. But these demonstrations will continue. The fight for Socialism will go on in all its forms."

Eddie Corrigan shouted: "Three loud boos for the money changers in the temple!"

When these were given, the crowd struck up THE RED FLAG, the English revolutionary song which Tom Mann had popularised in Australia:

> *. . . Then raise the scarlet standard high!*
> *Within its shade we'll live or die!*
> *Though cowards flinch and traitors sneer,*
> *We'll keep the red flag flying here!*

Barney finished reading the article and said: "That's the bloody stuff to give 'em!"

222

"Musta been funny, orl right," Sugar replied.

Lammence said nothing. John West had not been listening when Barney began reading, but as the article progressed he had become attentive.

Barney was very enthusiastic. "That's the sort of thing we want. The workers have got to take charge. This Tom Mann is the boy! Socialism, that's the ticket."

"Oh, I don't know," said John West. "Mann is too extreme. He advocates the overthrow of the entire system."

"So he should; it's the only hope of the workers, and the sooner the bloody better," said Barney.

"Not at all," John West replied hotly. "I believe in Socialism, in a way. But not the sort he talks about."

"'Fraid he might close the tote and club if he came to power, eh?" asked Barney slyly. He had his ticket for America in his pocket and felt secure in speaking his mind.

"That's got nothin' to do with it. But this Tom Mann must have a big following."

"'Course he has, and it's gettin' bigger every day. You orta see the hundreds that get to his meetings on the Yarra bank, and at the Bijou Theatre Sunday nights."

"Must have a big following all right. At the Bijou, eh? What are his opinions on gambling?"

"Well, I heard him say once that gambling was caused by insecurity, and that Socialism would end insecurity. He said bad housing and unemployment are bigger evils than gambling."

"H'm . . . Did he?"

At ten o'clock the following Sunday night Thomas Mann completed his lecture, and the crowd of a thousand people began to file out of the Bijou Theatre. Mann himself pushed through to the outer door and stood there speaking to people and answering questions.

"Here, take this for the movement, and God bless you," said a thin man with a little tattered woman hanging on his arm.

That man has not had a decent meal for weeks, nor has his wife. Should I give it back? Mann thought. A shilling, and the look of hunger on the bony face. And the tears in the little shrunken woman's eyes.

"Thank you," Mann said. "We will change the world with shillings like this one."

The crowd thinned. Soon everybody had left the hall and the lights went out inside. Percy Lambert joined Tom Mann on the footpath.

"Good meeting, Tom. Going home?"

"Yes, Percy, I'm going home. I'll see you in the morning at eight o'clock."

Lambert went off, leaving Tom Mann to his thoughts: thoughts of the people of the city and suburbs going to bed, of those who had no bed, those who were hungry. The thousands of jobless men, their despair, the whimpering of underfed children, the unnecessary sickness. If only I could tell every man and woman in every suffering city in the world that we Socialists have the answer, he reflected. But it will not be as easy as that. Socialism is the answer; though years of work, propaganda and organisation will be the only way to give that answer to the people. So much to be done. So few to do it. So little money to carry on the fight.

"Are you Tom Mann?" A quiet voice interrupted his thoughts. He had not noticed the man who had lurked in the doorway as the crowd dispersed.

The other man was taller than Tom Mann, but much slighter. His hat was pulled down over his eyes.

"Yes, I am Tom Mann."

"Well, I have a cheque for a thousand pounds for you to give to the unemployed."

The words seemed to take a few moments to enter Mann's consciousness.

"That's fine," he said. "Our organisation is very much restricted in the actual material aid we can give the unemployed. That's fine, very fine!"

The thin man handed him an envelope. Tom Mann peered into his face. "To whom do we owe this generous gesture?" he asked.

"To Mr. John West."

Tom Mann was in the act of opening the envelope, but at these words he hesitated.

"Mr. John West?"

"That's what I said. He said to give the cheque to you to distribute among the unemployed, and no questions asked about what you really do with it."

"H'm . . . Mr. John West. That's the man who runs the Carringbush tote and the City Tattersall's Club?"

"That's right."

Mann was uncertain what to say. No one had analysed John West's relations with the Labor Movement more clearly than he; and Eddie Corrigan had told him a good deal about the tote king.

"I'm sorry!" Mann's tone was gentle but firm and decisive. He handed the envelope back. "I'm very sorry, but I cannot accept. If Mr. West wishes to distribute money among the unemployed, let him do so himself."

The other seemed to be taken aback.

"And tell him that the Victorian Socialist Party will not accept a cheque for a thousand pounds which has been wrung shilling by shilling and penny by penny from the working people."

Tom Mann walked briskly away, leaving Frank Lammence, for he it was, standing open-mouthed.

A few days later, a deputation of unemployed men arrived at the City Tattersall's Club. They were ushered into the billiard room where John West and Frank Lammence listened to their spokesman, while pressmen took notes.

"Men of your stamp don't want charity, you want work," John West said impressively, when the man had finished. He turned to Lammence and asked: "Can we find work for any of these men on our racecourses?"

'Well, we might, Mr. West. We have no work of a pressing character," Lammence replied gravely, "but we could perhaps go ahead with some jobs which would provide work for ten or fifteen."

"Fifteen? No, thirty! We'll make it thirty!" John West answered sharply, and subdued applause rose from the assembled petitioners. "I daresay we can find room for some painters, six or eight, and some general labourers. That will relieve the pressure a little. It is a really deplorable state of things to see such fine-looking, strong men, able and willing to work, and no work for them to do. I hold that it is the duty of the Government to find work for men who are willing to work."

"If he was only Premier," said a little shabby man at the rear, in an audible whisper.

"I hold that is the duty of every citizen to enable men to earn

225

bread and butter for their wives and families. With that object in view, I will ask you to pick out thirty of your number, and I will provide work for them for about three months."

This was greeted with loud hand-clapping, and the remark: "He's a gentleman, he is."

"We will work on the co-operative principle. You men cannot work without something to eat and clothes to keep you warm; so I will devote the sum of £100 with a view to fitting you for work, and you can repay that out of your wages." Further applause greeted this philanthropic gesture.

"It is useless people saying there are no unemployed. You know it! I know it! We all know it! I have felt the pinch the same as you have, and it is owing to the bad system of government."

"Hear! Hear!" someone shouted.

"It will continue until some better form of government is established. We will pay standard rates of pay for each class of worker. And I will now give you something to relieve immediate distress."

"Ain't he a bosker?" said the leader of the deputation.

"He must have a ton of money!" said another.

The leader thanked Mr. West for his manly generosity, and accompanied him to the office where he was given a cheque.

The press gave wide publicity to the incident, the only unfavourable comment coming from the BULLETIN: *John West gave the unemployed £100 of the easily won money he had made out of them or people like them; and the money served as another glorious advertisement for his illegal business. The only difference between the other millionaires and millionaire West is that West speaks familiarly to the poor man and they don't.*

John West was very incensed with the cheek of "the bloody extremist rag."

Meanwhile the Gaming Suppression Bill had begun its passage through the Victorian Parliament. It seemed certain to result in the closing of the tote and club, and in a big reduction in the number of race meetings permitted at Apsom and John West's other two courses. The Bill defined a place conducted for betting purposes. It contained sixty other clauses, including powers to imprison persons found in betting establishments, and the owners and tenants of such premises. One clause went as far as to provide

226

that a person who lost a bet in an illegal gaming house had a legal right to recover the money. The Bill also gave to the Chief Secretary power over formation of racing clubs and the allotment of days on which meetings would be held.

During his introductory remarks, Chief Secretary Gibbon was continually heckled. Interjections rained from some Labor and Liberal members, especially from honourable members Garside and Scott. Interjections claimed class distinction against the tote and pony courses.

When Gibbon described the Carringbush tote fortifications, Bob Scott shouted: "If West had been fortifying Port Arthur it would have held out yet!"

Speaking on the adjournment motion after the first reading, David Garside defended John West. He hadn't gone far when a Government member shouted: "You are the paid representative of West!" David shook his shaggy head, feigning to be deeply hurt. "He is one of my clients and pays me for my services," he replied.

Frank Ashton struck the keynote of Labor's attitude when he asked why the Closer Settlement, and other important Bills, had been put aside for the Gaming Suppression Bill.

Labor members opposed the Bill, knowing that it would be unpopular with the majority of working people. They also knew that the Conservatives, and those of the Liberals who were supporting them, were using the Bill to divert attention from their failure to make more necessary social reforms. With some Labor men, including Bob Scott, however, the main motive was a pecuniary one: John West was paying them to do so.

The firm of accountants who handled John West's affairs had informed him that he was now a millionaire. The tote, club and racecourses were his biggest sources of income. This Bill was aimed at them. He must defeat it somehow, or at least have it watered down.

Realising that the Bill greatly strengthened the Victorian Racing Club, and still smarting under the life sentence it had imposed on him, he wrote to the Premier offering to lease the Flemington racecourse for £25,000 a year. The offer caused a sensation.

Flemington was the headquarters of the select Victorian Racing

Club, which obtained the course for a nominal rental of two peppercorns per year. The public was divided in its allegiance. On the one hand was John West, directly making a fortune out of pony racing and trotting; on the other, the V.R.C., allegedly non-profitmaking, but controlled by men who made a fortune out of galloping, indirectly through breeding and racing the best thoroughbreds. The V.R.C. Committee, like John West, sought money and power from racing; and they too enjoyed immunity from the enquiries of their own stewards.

Premier Bond rejected the offer flatly, stating that the Government was quite satisfied with the V.R.C.

Inside and outside of Parliament, John West made move after move against the Bill, but without much success. Then, as the debate dragged to its end, a bright idea occurred to him.

He summoned Bob Scott, Frank Lammence, Sugar Renfrey, and David Garside. The time was past when old Davie could insist that John West should come to him.

They met in the premises newly taken over for John West's sporting enterprises. The office was small and drab: a counter, a table and a few chairs furnished it, with the usual sporting photos on the walls.

"Well, gentlemen," John West greeted them cheerfully, "how is the great debate progressing?"

"Not too well," Garside replied. He was showing signs of wear, and his beard, eyebrows and hair had turned grey. "The best we'll be able to do is stonewall and keep the club and tote open for the big spring race meetings, as you requested."

"What do you think, Bob?"

"I'm afraid Davie's right, but we should be able to make sure the number of meetings at your courses is not cut down too much."

"Yes, that's the idea. You've got to stall until after the spring meetings. Most important of all, get me at least twenty meetings a year for each course. But, gentlemen, I've got an idea. I think we can beat this Bill altogether!"

"How, Jack?" Scott asked eagerly, while Garside stroked his white beard and squinted, as if to say: "What the hell are you up to this time?"

"This Bill is to help the V.R.C. and beat me, isn't it? Well, supposing we amend the Bill to make it unsuitable to the V.R.C.

The V.R.C. would get Bond and Gibbon to throw the Bill out, wouldn't they?"

"That's right, Jack?" Scott said.

"Well, tomorrow, one of you blokes will turn wowser, and suggest that the Bill be amended to cut out all gambling everywhere, including Flemington."

"You're a bloody genius, Jack!" exclaimed Fighting Bob, who never missed an opportunity to flatter his wealthy backer.

"You might get away with it at that," Garside said.

"We might. Think of it!" John West went on enthusiastically. "Swinton is behind this Bill, I hear. He framed it for Bond and Gibbon. He's pretending to be a dyed-in-the-wool wowser, but he's really a member of the V.R.C. committee. Don't you see, we'll have the V.R.C. on our side for once, and out the Bill will go. The bloody Conservatives won't want the rich to be prevented from betting at Flemington and the other registered courses."

"'Course they won't," said Scott. "And here's another idea. We could move an amendment prohibiting the publication of betting odds before or after a meeting. Then Sol Solomons and all the V.R.C. bookies will come over on our side. We'll beat 'em yet!"

"Jees!" Sugar said gleefully. "Even Joggins will oppose the Bill if we ain't careful!"

"I'll prepare an amendment," David Garside volunteered.

"No, I'll get Ashton to do the job. He's the man. I don't think they'll take this so well from you after what's been said up to date."

"Oh, all right, have it your own way."

"Ashton will be here shortly."

"If he's coming here, I'd better leave. The fellow doesn't like me, and it's mutual. The cheek of him to call me a traitor in the House a while back. Just because I got into Parliament on the Labor pledge, then broke it and went over to the Liberals, where I wanted to be in the first place."

John West was not interested in the differing views of his political representatives, so long as they helped him when required. He admired both Ashton and Garside. They were working well for him against this Bill. That was all he asked. He merely said: "Go if you like, but don't forget to watch for a change of tactics when the House sits this afternoon."

"Don't worry, I shan't forget."

When Garside had gone, Sugar Renfrey claimed John West's attention. "How did yer get on with gatherin' scandal about Gibbon and Swinton?"

"All right. I'll fix Gibbon. Found out all about him being the sleeping partner of a big book-maker, and about him owning Madame Brussells' brothels. It's a bloody fact! It's his turn to be exposed. See how he'll like it. Barney wrote it all up before he left for America. Going to give it to the TRUTH. John Norton is crook on the wowsers. He'll run it."

"Did you get anything on Swinton?"

"No, except he reduced the workers' wages on the big weir construction jobs. I've got plenty on Bond. He once lost the Speaker's Mace in one of Madame Brussells' brothels. But I'm leaving him alone until we see how our deputation about race dates get on with him."

"I can't get nothin' on Swinton, either," Sugar replied regretfully. "Doesn't smoke nor drink – doubt if he even sleeps with his missus."

Meanwhile, Frank Ashton was on his way. His wide brow was puckered with worry. John West had telephoned him yesterday and again this morning. Yesterday he had given him a tip for a horse: said he couldn't give its name over the phone because Joggins had the phones tapped. He would back it for me – wonder did it win? How much did he put on? I'll only have his word for it.

This morning West had rung again asking him to call at the race club offices: said the matter was urgent. Well, here I am, but I've got an idea that Mr. West and Mr. Ashton will soon part company. All right to help him with this Bill, but ...

"You want to see me, Mr. West?" he asked, occupying the seat vacated by David Garside.

"Yes. How do you think the Bill will go?"

"On present indications it will be passed and become law without much amendment."

"Supposing an amendment were moved to ban all gambling, even at Flemington?"

"Well, there are some in the Cabinet who would accept that. Swinton and others might *have* to, the way they have been talking. I hadn't thought of such a move. It may work, but I doubt it. Bond is a very shrewd man; he only has to vote out the amendment.''

"He might fall for it," Scott said.

"What about preparing an amendment, and moving it this afternoon?'' John West said. ''We could change from opposing the Bill to supporting it, providing it bans all gambling.''

Ashton seemed troubled and anxious to leave. ''All right, Mr. West, I'll move the amendment as soon as the house meets.''

As he walked to the door, John West said: ''Oh, by the way, that horse won. I couldn't give you the name on the phone. Prince Charles, it was: won the last at seven to one. I put a tenner on it for you. Here's seventy quid.'' He handed Ashton an envelope. Ashton hesitated, then took it. ''Thanks very much,'' he said, and walked out. His face was flushed with shame.

Frank Ashton knew the money was just an oblique bribe. This was going further than taking election expenses from West. Where would it lead? Not so good for a man who had just toured the State with Tom Mann, speaking of the glories of Socialism and the evils of capitalism from platforms in town and country.

The £70 would meet the most pressing of his debts. Though he had once managed to live on very little money indeed, since winning the seat he found that he could not live on his parliamentary salary. He had married shortly after his first political victory, and now had two little sons. He had developed the gambling habit, and liked to drink with his friends sometimes, and to dine at expensive cafes. But none of these was the principal reason for the parlous state of his financial affairs.

Frank Ashton could not resist requests for charity. Every member of Parliament is deluged with requests from sporting and charitable bodies in his electorate, that he become a patron – a polite way of asking for a donation. Frank Ashton never refused, nor could he refuse the ever-growing band of unemployed people who had come to know him as a man who would always give you the price of a feed. Some of the people who pulled him up in the street were genuinely impoverished, others were just touch men who numbered him among their ''bites.''

Those who knew him best had often had the experience of seeing Frank Ashton give a few pence or a few shillings to, not one, but several people, in a walk of less than half a mile. He

231

did not always wait to be asked, either. Often friends would tell him he was a mug, but he would smile and say: "I aim to help end their poverty in the long run, so I must help them now as well." His impecuniosity was a constant worry to his wife, Martha – a homely, complaining woman who did not understand her husband's temperament or opinions.

When Parliament assembled that afternoon, John West was in the public gallery. Members stood when the Speaker's entry was announced. The Lord's prayer was recited, then Frank Ashton arose to propose the amendment. He characteristically brushed the locks of hair from his forehead and began: "I wish to move an amendment to the second reading motion, Mr. Speaker: That this house is of the opinion that legislation introduced for the purposes of dealing with gambling and betting should be general in its application, and without exemption or distinction of classes, places or persons; and should, therefore, be framed to suppress betting and gambling on registered racecourses as elsewhere. Else such legislation can only be regarded as a hypocritical subterfuge, and a pretended compliance with a sentiment which it fails to serve."

Bond conferred agitatedly with Gibbon.

A long discussion on the admissibility of the amendment followed, during which Bob Scott urged members to play the rôle of a moral reform party and abolish gambling altogether.

"Perhaps stonewall would be a better word." Bond interjected sarcastically.

Finally the Labor leader suggested taking the amendment back to the Labor caucus for alteration.

"I'd take it somewhere else," Bond shouted sarcastically, living up to his name for informal and unorthodox behaviour. "I'd take it to Jack West."

Then David Garside sprang to his feet and argued that the amendment was quite in order as it was. He, as usual, claimed greater knowledge of parliamentary procedure than the Speaker or Chairman of Committees, or anybody else.

Frank Ashton arose again, and said, with satire in his voice: "I wish to test the sincerity of the Ministry. If it is desired to protect the poor man from the evils of gambling, surely there should be some protection given to the opulent rich persons

232

whom the Bill permits to degrade themselves by gambling. I demand that the Premier withdraws his insinuation that the amendment was drawn up by somebody outside. It is unfair and improper. The Clerk of the Assembly was present when I prepared it.''

"If it gives the slightest offence, I withdraw," replied wily old Bond. He had made his thrust: that was sufficient.

Outside, the Labor leader demanded to know why Ashton had moved the amendment without consulting him. The leader was intimidated by John West's influence in the Party, but this was going too far. Ashton said little. Always a good party man, he felt guilty: and when his leader insisted that he withdraw the amendment he did not resist.

Ashton came back into the house and withdrew the amendment. Bond smiled smugly. John West glared at Frank Ashton. Then Bob Scott rose and moved the amendment prohibiting the publication of betting odds. Premier Bond, so elated at his victory over his enemy Ashton, accepted it by mistake. Next day a letter signed by the Secretary of the Victorian Racing Club appeared in the press, vigorously opposing the new clause.

Premier Bond quickly had the amendment "voted out." Then John West's supporters began stonewalling to delay the Bill. David Garside excelled himself. He was on his feet making long speeches at every possible opportunity. Finally, he broke the Australian record by speaking for thirteen hours straight, quoting history, standing orders, law and classical poetry, and insulting members of the Government, each in turn.

Before the end of November, 1906, the Gaming Suppression Bill became law. The Carringbush tote and the City Tattersall's Club were legally doomed. The number of race meetings allowed for John West's courses was reduced from 152 to 48 per year. It could have been worse from John West's point of view; but he never viewed things in that light. It could have been better, that was the point, and Gibbon, Swinton and Bond must be made to pay for having persecuted him.

He chose Gibbon for his first victim, and handed Barney's article to the TRUTH newspaper. Then he sent for Frank Ashton.

"You wanted to see me, Mr. West?"

"I'd like you to put forward this material in the House tomorrow.''

Ashton ran his eye over the typed sheets handed to him. "I'm sorry," he said; "if you want Labor to handle this sort of thing, you'll have to see the party leader."

"I've seen him. He's a fool. Says he won't use it because it is in bad taste."

"Well, if he won't sanction its use, I certainly won't have anything to do with it." Ashton ran his hands through his hair; he was ill at ease.

"Don't be foolish. Gibbon is a hypocrite and a wowser. He deserves to be exposed."

"No doubt he does. But I cannot go against the policy of my leader."

"All right." Rage came from John West's gaze. "Seems to me, I might have to revise my opinion of who I should support at the next election."

"That is entirely your business," Ashton replied. He walked briskly out, his face red with embarrassment and suppressed anger.

West looked after him and shrugged his shoulders.

Sir Samuel Gibbon was a tall man with side whiskers and a parrot nose. He sat in his office trying to work, but he was too worried. John West had publicly declared his intention of exposing Gibbon's "hypocrisy and double dealing."

Presently, Gibbon's gloomy thoughts were interrupted by the Premier himself. Bond opened the door and poked his head round. His glasses were pushed back across his forehead. There was a twinkle of mischief in his eye and his beard waggled. "Have you got a copy of the TRUTH, Sam?"

"Never read the paper," Gibbon answered distractedly.

"Thought you might have a copy of today's issue."

"Well, I haven't!"

Bond grinned and closed the door.

Why the hell should he ask me for the TRUTH? Gibbon asked himself. Good God! Surely not! No! They wouldn't. They wouldn't dare!

He arose and ran from his office and out of the building to a nearby newsagent's shop.

Good God! On the front page!

He returned to his office, and sat at the table out of breath, reading hurriedly. He shuddered as if he had been stabbed in the stomach.

LECHERY AND LUCRE, he read the headlines. *An open letter to Sir Samuel Gibbon.*

Not long ago you were posing as a reformer. Frequently, as Lord Mayor of Melbourne, you have presided at public meetings and other functions having for their objects suppression of vice and crime, and the uplifting of men and women ...

In recent weeks, as a Minister of the Crown, you passed legislation against the gambling and drink traffic and against other forms of vice. Here it is that your private interests would seem to clash with, and mitigate against, your monetary interests and the due performance of your duty ...

Gibbon was clasping the paper so tightly that it seemed likely to tear apart in his hands.

... you are proprietor of several public houses, and have a lien by way of mortgage over many more. Besides this direct personal interest in the liquor traffic, you are, so I am credibly informed, the legal advisor and agent for Joe Johnson, absentee landlord and leviathan book-maker, owner of several Melbourne properties including several public houses. If rumour is not, as is commonly reported, a lying jade, this same lucre-looting leviathan is also the owner of other houses of even less repute than the lowest of the low, lambing-down side-street shaboos.

Sir Samuel groaned in mental agony as he read on.

... you have lent money again and again to the worst and wickedest woman in Melbourne – Madame Brussells – the immoral monster who for many years past has lived on the shame of her sisters in sin, and whose bagnio has been a blot on the boasted morality of Marvellous Melbourne for over a quarter of a century ...

Gibbon did not finish the article. There could be nothing more damning in it. He crumpled the paper and sat brooding. He felt a sinking feeling in his stomach, as if he hadn't eaten for several days. He was trembling.

Can't face the Labor mob in the House after this. I'll resign and leave the country. Now that his double life had been exposed, Gibbon had no desire to go on. He had a knighthood, he had wealth, and he was sick of politics anyway. The sooner he put a goodly expanse of sea-water between himself and Melbourne the better. Never know what West might do next. He didn't want any bombs thrown into his front room. This last thought struck deep, shivering terror into his very soul.

Again the Premier interrupted him.

"Have you got a TRUTH, yet, Sam?"

"What's so amusing?" Gibbon snarled. He'd never liked Bond anyway, too damn cocky. Too much of a clown. "You might be laughing on the other side of your face before long!"

"Why?"

"Well, they might expose some of your land deals and the finding of the mace at Madame Brussells'."

The smile melted from Bond's face. They might at that. His brain scurried over recent happenings. Scott called me a land shark in the House the other day. Curse the Bill! Pity I ever introduced it!

"West wouldn't dare!"

"I wouldn't depend on that."

Bond changed the subject. "The bells are ringing, are you coming into the House?"

"You don't think I'm going to face Scott and Garside, all that mob, after this, do you?"

Within a week, Sir Samuel Gibbon left Australia, never to return. He was soon followed by Premier Bond, who stayed away six months.

John West's other chosen victim proved a more worthy foe. Sir George Swinton implied that bribes had been accepted by Labor politicians in return for opposing the Gaming Suppression Bill. John West announced his intention of running an independent candidate against him at the coming elections. This spurred Swinton to further attacks. John West stated that he would attend Swinton's final election rally to answer charges.

The crowd of over a thousand people which packed the hall were surprised to see dozens of fashionably dressed young men seated on the stage in closed ranks behind Swinton and his chairman. Several policemen flanked the crowd.

John West stood at the back among a large band of his supporters, led by Sugar and Cauliflower Dick. He felt that Swinton could not prove his allegations; and was convinced he had been unjustly maligned. He was intensely excited.

236

As soon as the meeting started he was to go to the platform, take notes of Swinton's speech and challenge him to prove his allegations. Then Cauliflower Dick would lead a gang of over a hundred rough and tumble fighters to capture the platform, thrash Swinton and the chairman, and allow John West to take over the meeting.

John West walked up the centre aisle and took his seat on the platform, placed his hat on the floor and cast an apprehensive glance over his shoulder. The chairman introduced Swinton amidst cheers from the front of the hall and jeers from the back.

"Mr. Chairman," Swinton began. He was used to difficult meetings. He had been considered a radical in the nineties, but had drifted towards the Conservatives with the rise of the Labor Party.

"Three cheers for Jack West," Cauliflower Dick yelled, and the mob at the back responded.

Swinton was smiling, but nervous. "I ask you for fair play, that's all."

"You'll get more than that before you're done, ol' man," a voice shouted.

"I will say some strong things," Swinton continued. "My opponent is representing the worst elements of gambling and drink."

"Let's hear about Jack West," Cauliflower Dick shouted.

"I understand that Mr. West is trying to get control of Parliament, in order to repeal the Gambling Act." Hope these amateur boxers on the platform can fight as well as they say they can, Swinton thought.

"My opponent is not a Labor man; no one seems to know what he is, except that he receives the direct support of the director of the Carringbush tote shop."

John West was taking hasty notes. He had an air of self-righteous indignation.

"Many people ask: Why should Mr. West not have the right to nominate whom he thinks fit?"

Applause from the back of the hall.

"Mr. West is privileged to do so at an election. He is no friend of mine, and has a perfect right to nominate someone who would be friendly to him."

"You cut the wages of the workers," roared Cauliflower Dick, and the mob moved forward up the aisles.

"We want Jack West," chanted many voices.

"Mr. West had the audacity to distribute a long letter in this electorate in favour of the candidate who supports a great sport and a great industry."

Roars of approval from the West mob. Swinton's supporters were too scared now to raise their voices.

Why doesn't he repeat his bribe allegations? John West thought, glancing over his shoulder at the stalwart if dapper, figures behind him.

"The sport was pony racing, and the industry was Carringbush tote," Swinton continued, nervously.

The concerted roars of disapproval were deafening. An atmosphere of impending violence permeated the hall.

"One . . . two . . . three . . . four . . ." The gang began counting the speaker out.

Swinton tried to speak above the din for some minutes. His task was hopeless. Eventually he sat down.

John West arose, stealing a look behind him. The chairman sat him down with the assistance of three men from the rear of the platform. Cauliflower Dick's mob began to surge forward.

"Give Jack West a go! Give him a go!"

"Mr. West will not be allowed to speak," the chairman shouted, heatedly. "Let him hire a platform of his own."

Cauliflower Dick led his supporters forward through the hall, packed with Swinton's perturbed supporters. Policemen posted round the hall hesitated.

"Three cheers for Jack West!"

"Wait till we get Swinton outside."

The West men surged down to the front of the hall. Several people left, fearing violence.

The chairman quavered: "Well, Mr. West can ask a question."

John West stepped forward amid wild cheers from his supporters, who were now assembled around the platform. He was nervous, but his voice resonant and clear.

"Sir George Swinton has accused me of bribing members of the highest tribunal of this country. I challenge him to prove his allegations." John West drew a cheque from his pocket. "I challenge him with five hundred pounds."

He turned aggressively towards Swinton. The chairman placed a hand on John West's shoulder.

"Leave him alone, yer rat!"

John West thumped the cheque on the table. "Will you accept my challenge? If you are a man, stand up and repeat your accusations." He was white with anger and excitement.

Swinton's composure was ruffled, his bulbous eyes threatened to leap out of his head.

He stood up. "I made no statement that West bribed any member of Parliament," he said, apologetically.

"Yes, you did. Jack West says so!" roared Cauliflower Dick. The noise was deafening, the mob milled round the platform.

John West faced the audience again. "Did Swinton vote to reduce the wages of the workers on the Waringa Basin in 1902?"

"I can't remember all my votes," Swinton answered, nervously.

John West took a newspaper from his hip pocket and flourished it under Swinton's nose. He was thoroughly worked up – ready for anything. "Then look at this!" he shouted.

"But I raised their wages again a shilling a day, not long ago," Swinton answered.

"I want a straight-out answer!" John West shouted back.

"Yes, Jack wants a straight answer," echoed the mob.

The chairman began speaking. John West followed suit, while his gang howled and shouted. A little timid man arose in the body of the hall and called for three cheers for Swinton. One-eyed-Tommy grabbed him by the scruff of the neck and bundled him up the aisle and out of the hall. The boxers on the platform, under instructions to act only if the stage was stormed, sat waiting.

The chairman remonstrated with John West amid the uproar. Cauliflower Dick, thinking John West was about to be violently suppressed, shouted: "Come on! Come on! Up and at 'em!" Unlike John West, he had paid no attention to the packed platform. He had instructions to storm the stage, and storm it he would.

"Police! Police!" the chairman screamed, entirely possessed by panic.

The police did their best to come forward from the side aisles.

Cauliflower Dick had vaulted on to the platform. This was the signal for the amateur boxers to arise. Two of their burliest members tackled Cauliflower Dick and flung him back into the arms of his followers.

Several strong arms seized John West. Some of his supporters succeeded in mounting the platform and engaged Swinton's neat but husky band in combat.

The police were powerless to intervene. What was left of the audience stood and shouted support for the well-dressed warriors. The stage became a squirming mass of fighting men. John West's band was at a disadvantage; many of them were punched and pushed back before they gained a foothold on the stage.

The chair which had been vacated by John West was crashed on to Cauliflower Dick's thick skull and he collapsed unconscious. John West received a perfect straight left above the right eye, and blood streamed down his face. He made no attempt to fight back, but tried to free himself from the fighting mob.

Swinton and his fear-stricken chairman scrambled through the back curtains and made their escape through the rear door.

Swinton's amateurs gradually forced their opponents back, and finally off the platform.

John West recovered his battered, trampled hat. With his face blood-bespattered and his suit ruffled, he was carried from the hall on the shoulders of some of his defeated followers.

John West stood in the tote yard, in the half light of the approaching night. The air held the first chill of winter. His hands were in his overcoat pockets. Joe and the others had gone home. They had dismantled the movable property. The Carringbush tote was finished. No more voices would shout the odds, no crowds throng around to make their bets.

The barbed wire remained on the top of the fences, the trapdoors were still there, and the old shop, Cummin's Tea Shop. He chuckled at the ruse that had frustrated the police for nearly fourteen years. A rare wave of sentimentality swept over him. This was the scene of the beginning of his rise to wealth and power. Here, he and Joe, and Sugar, and Piggy and, yes, Mick O'Connell, had built the first platform. Wonder where Mick got to? Went to the goldfields in the West, no doubt. Pity about Mick. Couldn't be honest. And ol' Barney, of course. John West remembered everyone but Jim Tracey.

240

They had taken the pile of wood away, too. Same wood that's been there for fourteen years and we never sold a stick of it. Should be well seasoned for burning in mum's fire.

He walked to the fence near the rear of the adjoining yard. Have to rent these houses to other people now. He looked into the yard where he and the others had planned the recapture of the tote yard after O'Flaherty's occupation.

He had recaptured his stronghold! But now he was just moving out quietly, all because of a few wowsers. That's what it amounted to. He was just packing up and leaving without a fight. Just because they had passed a Bill. A few wowsers, and a bit of paper they called the Gaming Suppression Act, and he was walking out without a fight.

They still had to enforce it! That was it. Who said he would let them enforce it? All the boys were going crook about losing their jobs. Well, why should they lose their jobs? The application to have this property and the City Tattersall's Club declared to be places kept for gaming purposes, would soon be before the courts; and Davie Garside said he may as well close up peacefully. Yet why should he? He owned the tote building and he could buy City Tatt's building, then defy the police to enforce the law.

Yes. He'd defend the tote and the club by force! There were Dick Bradley and Arty, and dozens more who would defend them with pleasure. That's what he'd do. Let them see if they could drive Jack West out.

He squared his shoulders and walked briskly to the back gate, let himself out, drove the lock and bolt home, and walked around into Jackson Street.

The night had suddenly descended on Carringbush, and stars came up sharp and bright, where the unseen clouds parted. John West walked home deep in thought.

Next day before he could discuss his new plan with anyone, Chief Commissioner Callinan sent for him.

"You wanted to see me?" John West said when he arrived in Callinan's office. His eyes were twin flints.

"Yes," answered Callinan, lolling back in the big chair behind the polished desk, trying to appear nonchalant.

Dave O'Flaherty sat beside Callinan.

"It's regarding the tote and club, Mr. West." Callinan spoke

241

in friendly tones. What a coward he is, O'Flaherty thought.

"What about them?" The words came without the lips appearing to move.

Callinan made nervous play with his white moustache, then picked up a pen and started to fiddle with it. "I see you have closed them, since the new Act came into being."

"That doesn't say I won't open them again. Your application to have my places declared gaming houses might be rejected, on the grounds that it is not necessary because the places are not being used as gaming houses any longer."

"You realise, Mr. West, that if you reopen the tote or the club, we will then enforce the law?"

"You'd still have to get us out."

Callinan was obviously anxious to make this a final, and not unfriendly, interview. "I realise that."

O'Flaherty glared at his chief. "We'll get you out all right, Mr. West. And if you start anywhere else, we'll get you out of there, too."

John West's eyes slowly turned to O'Flaherty. They glinted with implacable hatred. "I kicked you out last time you moved in, and I could do it again, if I decided to."

"No doubt you could, Mr. West," Callinan said meekly.

John West's gaze returned to Callinan.

"You leave the tote and club closed, and we won't trouble you in any way," Callinan continued. What an open cheque to commit crime, O'Flaherty thought.

Callinan is frightened, John West was thinking. I could bluff him; but O'Flaherty ... If only that stupid bomb-thrower hadn't made a mistake. Suddenly he leaned towards Callinan, who cowered back a little.

"You realise that I am a very powerful man; and that I never forgive or forget."

Callinan coloured and could think of nothing to say in reply. Dave O'Flaherty intervened, jabbing his forefinger to emphasise his words. "Don't come here with threats, West. If anything happens to me the department will know where to look for the guilty party. There are a few unsolved crimes on our lists, and investigations may be reopened unless you're a good boy."

John West flushed. "Supposing I reopen the club and tote."

"I'll get the application through," O'Flaherty replied. "And if I can't, I'll act without it. The new law is wide enough for that."

"Supposing I defend the places. Supposing I use force to keep you and your bloody mob of pimps out."

"Do you know what I'll do? I thought you might come at this."

Callinan opened his mouth to speak, but before he could interrupt, O'Flaherty went on, his thick lips sneering: "I'm in charge of gaming in this State. If you do that, West, I'll call out the military, with quick-firing guns and mortars, and blow the Carringbush tote and the City Tatt's off the face of the earth; and you and your mob with them!"

John West sat tensely, staring at O'Flaherty. He knew that he meant every word he said.

For days John West remained in a state of agitated indecision. He told no one of the interview. His first reaction had been one of determination to fight it out, then the absurdity of so doing suddenly struck him. I am a millionaire, he thought. Must I continue being hounded by the law, the wowsers, Parliament and O'Flaherty? The law does not hound other millionaires; why should it hound me?

In the weeks that followed, his mind turned towards a fundamental change of policy. Previously, his career had been a series of obstacles overcome. All major decisions were forced upon him by circumstances, but now he was considering a voluntary change in tactics.

He thought a good deal about a remark Barney Robinson had made a few months ago. To a statement by John West that the V.R.C. had probably bribed members of the Conservative Government to pass the Gaming Suppression Act, Barney had replied "No, Jack. The rich don't have to bribe the Conservative politicians. They're all one big family. See, Jack, the big squatters and capitalists don't bribe the politicians. They don't need to, because the big politicians are in the swim. Remember during the building boom, nobody bribed anybody. The speculators just let the politicians into the swim, then it was called business. The Conservative politicians are big capitalists themselves, and they make the laws to suit themselves and their millionaire friends. They work inside the law. Their robbery is legal!"

Barney was right! Why shouldn't he work within the law? Other millionaires made money just as quickly as he did; they used different methods, that was all. The police didn't trouble them; they handled the politicians differently. He was a millionaire; why shouldn't he enjoy the same privileges and immunity from the law as they did?

A plan began to form in his mind. The tote and club were closed. Let them stay closed. His other enterprises were legal. He could become a respectable business man, inside and above the law. He would work differently, more shrewdly than other big business men. He controlled several racecourses; he would buy more, all over the country. He owned houses and hotels; he would buy more. He was a promoter of prize fights and athletics; he would extend his promotions, and drive out every other promoter. He had business interests; he would acquire more. He would go on the Stock Exchange, and buy shares in gold mines, shares in other ventures.

He would still need his political influence. He would extend it to all parties, perhaps even to the Conservatives. It was the Labor machine that would count eventually. One day Labor would be in office in every Parliament in Australia, and he would help to put them there. He wouldn't just stick to Victorian politics. Power in all States, that was what he must aim at, and in the Federal Parliament. Sugar and Bob Scott would look after matters in Victoria, and as his business interests grew he would find other men in other States. One day he would select the Parliaments of Australia.

The scope of the plan thrilled him: the wealth and power it promised. He could be a law unto himself!

He would still need the police on his side. Once he got rid of Callinan, he could have immunity. O'Flaherty didn't matter now. The police are linked with Parliament. The Chief Secretary controlled the Police Force and controlled the allocation of race dates, too! One day the Chief Secretary would be his man, a West man.

He would still need strong arm men, but he must use them differently, more discreetly. He would retain a few of them. Arthur, Dick Bradley, and that young fella. What's his name again? Runs a book at the races for me, handy with his fingers, handy with the gun. Flash little fella. Tanner, Snoopy Tanner.

And there were a few others through whom he could work by remote control.

Two bitter thrusts at John West in the press in the autumn of 1907 reminded him that he alone among the millionaires of Australia was attacked by the established newspapers.

The BULLETIN wrote: *The closing of the tote and club should have the blessed result of reducing John West to the status of a bloated fat man with an income of some thousands a year from the investment of his illegally-made wealth, and without a penn' orth of bogus sympathy for the working man – the latter's "bob" having ceased to come his way.*

The next week, a magazine called the LONE WOLF, run by the BULLETIN, published its first edition in Melbourne. Most of its pages were given to a scathing exposure of John West's career under the heading: WEST AND HIS RUFFIANS.

The article began with one of Barney's literary masterpieces – a letter to the press written when John West first took over control of trotting: *Failure has persistently followed all those who have hitherto attempted to revive interest in the noble sport of trotting and those enthusiasts who are devoted to the game for its own sake, as well as those who have invested vast sums in pure stock and splendid breeding establishments, have arrived at the verge of despair. In their dilemma they have turned to me with a request that I should adopt and introduce to my patrons trotting events, and they have tendered me assurance of earnest support in my efforts to popularise it ...*

The article continued: *The foregoing advertisement of John West is a suitable text for a denunciation of that pestilential citizen and his works. This article applies the searchlight to his offences. As a young bootmaker, Jack West began to prey on his comrades by making a book on the horse races. The needy neighbourhood of Carringbush was ever crowded with young and older men whose limited incomes tempted them to gamble. He gambled with them and acquired capital at their expense ...*

As the material was supplied by Dave O'Flaherty and written up by the BULLETIN's best satirical journalist, the article gave vivid details of all the tote cases. It was illustrated with photos of John West, of the old house in Carringbush in which he was born and of the mansion in which he now lived.

At his racing club office, John West read it with rage and humiliation. *West's crafty distribution of largesse earned him a false reputation for generosity, and his coldly-calculated appeals to religious influences served to delude the sympathies of one section of the community. Careless commentators thought of West as an amusing scandal, and mistook him for a true democrat because he was "against the Government," a fine democrat, fattening on the folly of the working man . . .*

Jack West could guarantee the trustworthiness of his employees with as much confidence as the Spider (in "The Silver King") felt in testifying to the qualifications of his domestic servants. "My front doorkeeper," Mr. West might have said, "was sentenced to two years" hard labour in 1887, my head man at the tote was convicted of larceny and other little indiscretions before he got twelve years for rape and my near and dear blood relation, who makes himself useful about the place, is one among several of my bodyguards who have been flogged or sentenced to death, or both. In his case it was both, poor fellow.

On reading this, John West stiffened and Frank Lammence noticed that his knuckles showed white as his fingers gripped the paper.

. . . during the six years since then the ill-gotten money of Jack West has talked in many State and a few Federal elections, not always on the winning side, but invariably on the rowdier side. West has become a strangely pretentious polluter of politics. Latterly he described certain candidates as "his men". When Labor member Scott held a meeting, the brute force of West's influence was expressed in a way that seemed humorous to silent onlookers. To ask an unsympathetic question of the candidate was to get a reply on the nose from the nearest Westite. A lovely mob it was that carried votes of confidence with enthusiasm at Scott's meetings and those of other Labor members.

After Thomas Callinan became Chief Commissioner of Police, the law against gambling hells in general, and West's tote in particular, became less in evidence than ever . . .

The article described in detail the occupation of the tote, the rigging of the Austral Wheel Race and the Caulfield Cup, and implied that John West was behind the disappearance of Arthur Stacey and the bombing of O'Flaherty's house.

John West sat staring at the table. After a moment, Frank

Lammence, who had read the article, said: "Well, Mr. West, we shouldn't tolerate that."

After a pause, John West looked up.

"Well, what do you expect me to do?" he snapped. "Tear my hair out?"

Lammence did not answer. He felt he had summed this little man up very well. When he's like this, wait for an order, then carry it out. The order did not come.

"You don't expect me to be worried about this rag, do you?" John West snapped.

"We could find out who wrote it, and . . ."

John West remained silent. He had been seething with murderous rage, and the calm was coming, the calm which helped him to be strong and go into attack against his enemies. But to attack now would upset his whole plan: he must wait. After a while he would bring all his enemies to heel. Wait a while and he would silence all the newspapers. Wait a while and he would run the country. But he *must* wait. It would be foolish to come out now and attack the writer, and it would be dangerous. He must wait. He would make them all pay in his good time.

"Don't stand there staring, man!"

"But I thought . . ."

"You thought I'd get off me bike, and go shooting someone. Well, you're wrong. I'm going to wait. Wait, do you hear?" He thumped the table with his fist. "Do you think this can hurt me? Well, you're wrong! I'll wait. I've got it all planned. Someday, before long, I'll silence the newspapers. And I'll run this country, do you hear?"

Lammence was flabbergasted.

John West slumped back in his chair.

After a few moments' silence he leaned towards Lammence, and said quietly: "Frank, go and get every man you can find, and buy every copy of this dirty rag that's left in Melbourne."

"Yes, Mr. West," Lammence said.

"And if they print more, buy them, too."

"Yes, Mr. West."

John West sat brooding over the scathing exposure until Lammence returned.

Lammence entered uncertainly. "I've got Sugar on the job. He'll get every available man and buy the lot."

247

"Good work, Frank."

Lammence was amazed at his employer's changed manner. John West was now pleasant, affable. "You see, we must lie low for a while and wait," he said. "I have a plan – a mighty plan! I'll tell you all about it pretty soon."

There are always a few among the most poverty-stricken and destitute people who will endeavour to amass wealth in the only ways left open to them. They may become petty thieves, police agents or confidence men; they may scrimp and save, and set themselves up in business, usually of the nefarious kind; they may become sly grog sellers, brothel keepers, pawn-brokers or starting price book-makers.

So it was with John West.

If one of these poor men be clever, ruthless and unscrupulous enough, he may rise to riches and wealth. Certainly there was opportunity for him to do so in the Melbourne of 1893; although, less than fifty years later, his task would be well-nigh impossible, because real wealth was to become vested in the hands of fewer and richer people.

John West did not understand power or the urge for it. Nevertheless, the urge for power had grown strong in him. His mind was fumbling towards an understanding of where his road had led him. He was a millionaire and was beginning to realise that his interests lay with the millionaires. His power was like their power: it was class power. He had all the sources of power held by other millionaires, and additional sources, found along the more arduous road which had led him to power.

And so a new plan for exercising his power crystallised in his mind.

This plan was discussed, a few days later, by Arthur West, Dick Bradley, Piggy and Snoopy Tanner, at Arthur West's home.

A strange crew they were. Arthur West was saying: "That's where we fit into Jack's scheme. What do you think of it?"

Piggy wiped his snout-like nose with the back of his hand and said: "Does me. We can do a few jobs, robberies and that, as well."

Tanner was cleaning his finger nails. At first glance he looked just an overdressed young man about town, but closer inspection revealed the eyes – shifty, cruel. Syphilitic from birth, he had

248

started as an apprentice in a racing stable, got too heavy, and began touting at the ponies, became a pickpocket, skilful on difficult jobs, but "rolled the drunks" as well. Began making a book at John West's courses. Did a job or two on the side, with a genius for organising the job. Affable, friendly, not without courage, a leader and organiser of young criminals.

Tanner said: "A good scheme, couldn't be a better." But he was thinking, suits me. I'll have West's protection, and I'll build a big gang of me own. I'll do West's work all right; and use him as a cover for me own work.

Bradley, slumped over the table, morose, sullen. A short man, but wide and solid. Fleshy of face, with bags under his eyes; he had a noticeably two-sided face, as if half of two faces unlike each other were stuck together up the middle. He had been made a criminal by the despair and demoralisation of poverty and by flogging. It was said that he was innocent the first time he was convicted; nobody knows for sure. No matter now, he had become the most dangerous man in Australia, having obtained leadership and protection. The others waited for Bradley to speak. He just sat there. A man who would maim or kill as a banker forecloses a mortgage: dispassionately, without any interest in his victim.

Dick Bradley said nothing. That's how it was with him: he said nothing but everybody knew that he agreed.

And so in 1907, John West set out with Frank Lammence at his side, bent on becoming the most powerful man in Australia.

That year many of the hundred men he had sacked when the tote closed complained of being dumped; but he did not worry until a few of them began to threaten him.

For months he was guarded day and night by Piggy, Bradley and Arthur West. He learned to dread nightfall, to fear dark places. He knew the terror of threatened murder. But he survived after one close call when he and his bodyguards shot it out with three attackers.

But even while his life was in danger, John West kept in mind his grand plan. He was a millionaire! He would have all the power and respect that other millionaires had, but he would be the most powerful of them all!

PART TWO

1915–1931
ABUSE OF POWER

The possession of great power, no matter how enormous, does not bring with it the knowledge how to use it ... Power leaves us just as it finds us; only great natures grow greater by its means.

HONORÉ DE BALZAC

CHAPTER SEVEN

All gangsters are patriotic.

MICHAEL GOLD

"You see, Mr. West, the war has been on for a year, and recruiting figures are far below expectations," a Cabinet Minister of the Federal Labor Government said, when interviewing John West in the Autumn of 1915.

"Well, why not introduce conscription?"

"The Party and the workers would not stand for it."

"Well, what do you expect me to do about it?"

"We want you to join the Army, Mr. West. The Prime Minister, Mr. Hughes, has asked me to approach you. We understand that you are keen to improve recruiting figures, and that you are very much opposed to Germany."

"I am. The Hun is the worst man on earth. You've only got to read the papers. They torture prisoners and boil down the dead for fat. They are barbarians. But I feel I can do more good by staying out of the forces."

"That may be so, Mr. West. I have heard of your interest in war charities. But we want you to join up, and assist in recruiting. You see, we are using sportsmen – jockeys, and boxers and footballers – on the recruiting platforms. But most of them are civilians and don't carry much weight. You have a big following. If you were to join up and go on tour you could recruit thousands. We will give you an undertaking that you need not go overseas, and that you can get out any time you want to."

"I'd like to go overseas. I'd make a good soldier. But I feel I'd do more good here in Australia."

"You've already done a lot of good, Mr. West. For instance, your giving that cheque for £500 to young Jacka's wife made a great impression."

"The least anyone could have done was to help the wife of our first Victoria Cross winner. If England goes under, we go under. The boys overseas are fighting for our homes and families."

253

"That's true, Mr. West. But there's a lot of talk about the rich not joining up. If you were to join ..."

"All right, I'll do it, if it is the best way I can help. If we lose this war, we lose all we have. Our property, homes and family will all be destroyed."

"Very true, Mr. West."

"Give me a week to fix up my affairs. And don't forget to arrange that I don't go overseas, and that I can get out whenever I like. Then if I feel I can do more good outside the army, I can get out again."

A week later, John West sat by the fire in the lounge room of his mansion. He was dressed in the uniform of a private in the Australian Imperial Forces. He was on seven days' special leave, but the uniform was a novelty, so he had left it on – all but the big army boots which were playing up with his feet, so long used to soft leather. He was reading a newspaper, and his high-backed chair was surrounded by other news-sheets and magazines. His enlistment had been hailed by nearly every paper in Australia; a notable exception being the Sydney BULLETIN. Ever since his enlistment, he had been buying every paper and magazine he could lay his hands on.

The reports pleased him: they were convincing proof that he was now widely accepted as a respectable millionaire business man; in fact little remained to indicate otherwise, except an occasional "Read the LONE WOLF, West!" hurled at him sometimes at the stadium. The report of his enlistment in the tory ARGUS pleased him most of all: *Most interesting feature of yesterday's recruiting ... Sportsman and Racecourse proprietor ... Leading part in patriotic activities ... Won the Caulfield Cup with Whisper ... regarded as a good athlete in his youth.* Bit different to the early days, John West mused. Here was proof of his great power; what better revenge could he have on the ARGUS than that it was forced to report his enlistment favourably, and on the front page, too.

A columnist in the LABOR CALL, as the TOCSIN was now called, left no doubt as to the friendliness of many in the Labor Party towards John West, when he wrote:

A small, compact figure walked into the recruiting depot at the Town Hall last week, and, after a few minutes, John West,

racecourse proprietor, newspaper proprietor, owner of consid-
erable property, emerged Private John West, sworn in to go to
the noisome trenches at Gallipoli; to shoot and be shot at, to lie
amongst a tornado of hurtling murderous shells, any one of which
might mean the sudden exit of John West ...

... If Jack entrenches himself in Gallipoli as he did in Car-
ringbush when he defied the whole police force of Victoria to
enter his tote, then the blankey Turks will have Buckley's chance
of shifting him. Here's good luck to you, John West.

John West had made his own luck. He now owned racecourses
in five States and controlled the sport of boxing in three. His business interests had developed according to plans envisaged in 1907.
These interests involved a daily newspaper in Queensland, hotels,
mines, stadiums, racecourses, theatres, cafes, houses, bookmaking,
and horse, pony and trotting racing – and, of course, his holdings
in Benjamin Levy's furniture and time-payment enterprises. He
estimated himself to be worth nearly two million pounds.

Everyone who knew him said that John West had turned into a
"rip-snorting patriot and flag-flapper." But he had forgotten one
very important factor. As the war progressed, the people who were
the basis of his power and his hopes for further power, the working
people, the Catholic minority, the Labor movement, were to
become, in the main, violently opposed to the slaughter which he
was to support fervently until the end. He had begun to cut himself
off from the people on whose backs he had climbed to power.

He sat now, reading the LABOR CALL. Behind him, hanging on
the wall, was a photo of his mother. The bitter disillusionment
of her life was painted on her face in deep lines and dull colours.
Her death a few years ago had left John West a desperate wish
that he could have been closer to her; that he could have cancelled
out the events which had built a cold, stone wall between them.
The death of his father had left him unmoved; it was as if he had
read of the death of a strange man in a newspaper; the death was
remote from him, it caused no emotional reaction.

Now his mother seemed to gaze in sorrow and longing at a
photo of her three sons on the opposite wall – her sons when
they were children, before Arty's terrible crime, before the bad
times, before the tote shop, before two of her sons had defied her
and brought shame upon her.

John West looked at his mother's photograph and he felt she

was reproaching him. The entry of Nellie and their eldest child, Marjorie, now fourteen years of age, and solid and healthy looking, interrupted his thoughts.

"I told all the children at school that my daddy's a soldier – that he's going away to fight," Marjorie said, and she ran to him, and he cuddled her in a rare manifestation of fondness.

The Wests now had four children: two girls and two boys, all unaware of their father's history and being brought up devout Catholics by Nellie.

"Your father's not going away, never fear," Nellie interrupted. "Off you go, Marjorie, and do some practising before you go out to play." The child departed obediently.

"Why do you say I'm not going away?" John West asked tersely.

"Well, you said it was only a recruiting move."

"It might interest you to know that I've decided to go away and fight!"

If he expected any marked reaction he was disappointed. "Oh, John," she said. "You're not really."

"Yes, I am, and pretty soon, too." He arose and took her in his arms. He sensed that the drama of the moment was lost on her when she said: "It's entirely your affair."

He held her passive body close. "I will come back when I've done my bit; I will come back."

Nellie could not share his mood. She had developed a passive hatred of him. To their estrangement had been added his inconstancy. Four years ago he had been involved in an affair with an actress who had starred in a show at one of his theatres. They flaunted the liaison until Nellie believed that half of Melbourne was talking. Nellie said nothing, but had frozen her husband ever since. The scandal ended with the departure of the actress. John West was glad when it ended. Such a situation had undermined his power, it had given people "something on him". Never again, he had determined.

From somewhere in the house came the plaintive strains of a violin skilfully played, and up the wide path in the grounds came sounds of running feet and the laughter of children.

After a couple of days, John West prepared to go north to Sydney, and then on to Brisbane, to arrange his affairs.

His business interests were mainly in Melbourne, where Frank Lammence could easily take over without a hitch, but it was necessary to interview his solicitors, accountants and managers in other States. He continued to collect newspaper cuttings, becoming elated to the point of convincing himself that the whole thing was genuine – so much so that he really was seriously contemplating making it all come true by allowing himself to be sent to Gallipoli.

In the train he read a poem from the LABOR CALL:

> *For malice and hatred and spleen*
> *The target you have often been*
> > *John West.*
> *But now you have shown them a point*
> *Put the wowsers' nose out of joint*
> > *John West*
> *They preached from their pulpits on war*
> *From the platforms they shouted for gore*
> > *Saintly men.*
> *But when it came to the test*
> *You showed them your way was the best*
> > *Private West.*
> *And when the great victory is won*
> *You won't talk of what you have done*
> > *Private West.*
> *But back to your kids and your wife*
> *Having done your bit in the strife*
> > *John West.*

John West had read the poem many times. He would do his bit in the strife, all right. Visions of grim battles in the mud surged through his mind. Visions of his bayonet bringing blood spurting from the chest of a Turk, or better still a hated Hun; of hand grenades hurled with unerring aim, of the trenches, of leave in London and Paris, of marching columns, with he, himself, in front proudly carrying his rifle and singing *Tipperary*. Visions of all the glamour of war, but none of its horror and destruction.

He would make a good soldier. He would rise from the ranks; that could be arranged. As always, he visualised mammoth achievement. He would become a General and conduct battles, and win the V.C.; win the war. He had said his age was forty; really he was forty-six; funny thing how he always put his age back these days. Well, a man was as young as he felt, and most Generals were more than forty-six.

Then he spied a letter to the editor which reminded him that other people in the Labor movement held other views. He read it with anger. The writer protested against the publicity given to his enlistment, and pointed out that John West had more to lose than nearly everyone else, therefore, there was more reason for his enlistment. The writer concluded: *Contemporary history in America shows that what the Labor movement has to fear is men of the type of Mr. West, and the influences which men such as he can bring to bear in the internal machinery of Labor organisations. Let us stamp the influences out in our movement before we are reduced in Australia to the sorry plight of Labor's impotent effect in American politics.*

On returning to Melbourne, John West began a round of daily and nightly recruiting meetings. He soon found that endeavouring to persuade young men to join the colours was a difficult and thankless task. At his very first meeting he received a sample of what he could expect. The meeting was held in the afternoon in front of the Melbourne Town Hall, and a crowd soon gathered at the sight of the upraised, flag-bedecked platform, and the sound of a military band.

John West was introduced as a well-known sportsman and philanthropist.

"Who's the bandy-legged bloke spruikin'? He looks too bloody short for the Army, don't he?" remarked the first of two shabby bystanders, who stood in front of the crowd.

"Oh, they're not so fussy now; recruits is hard to get. That's Jack West. I read in the paper where he joined up. Goin' away in a few days," replied his companion.

"Why don't he go then, instead of yappin' here?"

"... I am only doing what every able-bodied man should do: go away and fight for his country," John West began nervously. The experience was gruelling enough without these two sarcastic commentators.

"Well, why don't you go? We ain't stoppin' you!"

"You be quiet, you cold-footer," an old lady remarked patriotically.

"Bet you ain't got no sons to go and fight, you old witch."

"I'll put you in charge, that's what I'll do. You should be sent a white feather."

"I will be leaving the country very soon," John West continued, "but before I go I have been asked to do my bit in the recruiting campaign. There is not a moment to be lost. We are going to recruit a thousand sportsmen, and any man who joins the sportsman's thousand will never live in want, John West will see to that. Whatever we think of England, if she goes down, we go with her. Everything we have is at stake ..."

"I got nothin' to lose. You got plenty; so go away and fight and shut yer trap," shouted the second shabby bystander.

The old lady was most incensed at this unpatriotic remark. "Be quiet, you ... you cold-footer," she snapped.

An opulent-looking business man who had joined the swelling crowd, which now spread across the footpath and on to the roadway, pushed his way near to the front and said: "Give the speaker a hearing or I'll send for a policeman!" He had just received a large war contract, and was feeling most patriotic.

These asides disconcerted John West, but he managed to continue. "Andrew Fisher has said: 'We will send the last man and the last shilling'."

"Here's one darkey he won't be sendin'," interrupted the first shabby bystander, who had a most raucous voice.

"Yair," his companion stated loudly, "and I know a few shillin's in the State Savin's Bank he ain't sendin', neither. Let the pommies fight their own battles."

This remark appealed to the national sentiments of a huge Irishman in the audience, who shouted: "Sure, and yer right there, me boy. I'd rather fight for old Erin, any old day."

A murmur of disapproval ran through the crowd. The opulent business man stooped so far below his dignity as to plainly tell the Irishman to shut up. The patriotic old lady stated that she wished there was conscription, so that all loafers would be forced to fight.

John West continued fiercely: "Australia must stand shoulder to shoulder with the old country. If England goes all our property and our loved ones would be at the mercy of the horrible Hun."

"Wonder does this bloke favour conscription?" queried the

first shabby bystander, who as usual addressed his question not to John West but to his companion.

"I'll arsk 'im. Listen, mate; do you favour conscription?"

"No, I do not," John West lied. "Because I believe that all decent Australian men will go away voluntarily and fight, like I am."

"Good on yer, Jack," came a voice from the back of the crowd, which by now had expanded across the road blocking the traffic.

Amid cheers, John West shouted: "Now, I am going to call for the first of the great Australian sportsmen to join the colours, in the sportsman's thousand."

By pre-arrangement, a leading Carringbush footballer stepped forward and vaulted onto the platform. He was immediately recognised by the crowd and cheered to the echo. After John West had spoken of his football prowess and natural-born bravery, the footballer's wife gave an unexpected fillip to the proceedings by mounting the platform, spontaneously embracing her husband and sobbing: "Oh, darling! Come back to me, come back!"

"Don't worry, dear. It will be all over before I get there," he assured her. "A fine trip around the world."

When the footballer walked into the Town Hall Recruiting Depot to be medically examined, one of the shabby bystanders remarked that he should have his head read.

Several more recruits came forward and mounted the platform, including none other than Flash Alec himself, looking somewhat shabby but keeping up appearances. Fortune had not smiled on him since the tote and club had been closed. He was reduced to operating as an urger on John West's racecourses: he apparently believed that this qualified him as a sportsman.

The first shabby bystander eyed Alec critically. "That dirty toff would be a bit scraggy to pass the doctor, wouldn't he?" he asked his companion in a loud voice.

"Oh, I dunno. If he had a few more holes in 'im, he'd make a bloody good tin whistle for a military band," his companion replied, and most of the crowd responded with loud laughter.

About twenty more men came forward: footballers, boxers, horse trainers and other sportsmen. The success of the meeting seemed to rankle the two shabby bystanders, who became even more disruptive. "Did yer ever read that paper, the LONE WOLF?" the first one asked his companion.

"No, but I'll ask the speaker. Did you ever read the LONE WOLF, West?"

John West flushed scarlet, then appealed for further recruits.

"Yer better join up or he might throw a bomb into yer house," advised the second shabby bystander, and one or two people remembered and laughed, much to the discomfort of John West.

A few more sportsmen came forward, and while they were being marched off to the doctor, the two shabby bystanders displayed evidence that their attempted disruption was inspired; they began in loud tones an antiwar dialogue which was too radically political to come from casual observers.

"Do you think there'll be conscription for overseas service?" asked the first.

"The workers won't stand for it."

"Lot of 'em like me won't even stand for compulsory trainin'. There's thousands in jail without a proper trial for refusing to go to camp. Been goin' on for years before the war. The Labor Party introduced that, and the War Precautions Act, too. Watch they don't introduce conscription. But the Wobblies won't stand for conscription!"

At the mention of the word *Wobblies* a section of the audience jeered and booed and the opulent business man asked why the police tolerated loafers going round disrupting the war effort.

The patriotic old lady sniffed and waved her umbrella threateningly. "These men are Wobblies, the I.W.W. they call themselves – the 'I Won't Works.' that's what I.W.W. means!"

This statement brought a loud laugh from the crowd, and disturbed the calm manner of the first shabby bystander, who promptly mounted the platform and told the crowd that the initials of the organisation stood for the Industrial Workers of the World. He advised all and sundry to stay away from the war, which was being fought over trade. Millionaires like West were getting fine young men to go away and die, he said. He invited the audience to attend the Yarra Bank on Sunday to hear the I.W.W. and the Socialist Party tell the truth about the war, and urged all to join the new anti-conscription organisation.

He was then dragged from the platform by several policemen. He and his companion were escorted with little ceremony down to the corner of the street, from where they hurled abuse at the meeting.

They began singing the Wobblies' Doxology:–

> *Praise "Fat" when morning work bells chime,*
> *Praise him for scraps of overtime.*
> *Praise him whose bloody wars we fight,*
> *Praise "Fat", the leech and parasite* ... AW, HELL

But their efforts were drowned by the band and the crowd singing: England, home and beauty, has no cause to fear. No! No! No! No! No! Australia will be there!

This uncomfortable meeting was repeated with variations every time John West mounted the platform, and sometimes the interjections came in greater numbers and more violent mood. Feeling against the war was mounting, and John West found that his popularity was suffering from his efforts to recruit the sportsman's thousand. Life in camp was unpleasant, too: the route marches, drill and discipline soon began to grate upon him. He found the Army no respecter of persons, and the promised promotion was slow in coming – he was only a corporal after six weeks' service!

Reviewing the situation, he found that his desire to go away to Gallipoli had disappeared. He had kept his word and helped recruit the sportsman's thousand; in future he could do more for the war effort as a civilian.

The press gravely reported that "in consequence of an infection of the ear, Corporal West has been discharged by the Medical Board." The reports further declared, untruthfully, that Corporal West was in hospital; and, truthfully, that he had handed over £500 to a Board of trustees, to grant interest-free loans (not exceeding £5) to men who had suffered financial loss by enlisting.

The Sydney BULLETIN summed up the feelings of many when it wrote: PLEASE NOTE – *This is no laughing matter! J. West, Corporal, went on a twenty-six mile route march the other day, and now he is suffering from varicose veins, or a bad ear or something, and won't be able to get to Gallipoli after all, so they say. Still, West provided a good example – while he lasted.*

262

"It's no use lying to me, Arty," John West said. "I didn't come down in the last shower. I know who's doing these robberies at the Trades Hall. I'm building great power in the Trade Unions. If this business comes out, it could ruin everything. You blokes are going too far. Just because you know I'll look after you, you think you can do anything."

It was eight o'clock in the evening of the last day in September, 1915. John West was seated in the reception room of his mansion with his brother and a big man with a great curled moustache named Ronald Lassiter.

John West, in his drive to gain control of the Labor Party for his own purposes, had turned his attention to the Trade Unions. Lassiter was a member of the Trades Hall Council, Secretary of the Builders' Laborers' Union and John West's leading representative in the Trade Union Movement. He had been in the Labor movement for over twenty years. He was the counterpart of Bob Scott – a man who talked like a socialist and acted like a gangster – just the man to serve John West's purpose. Lassiter was a strange mixture of a criminal and a radical – a minority type which had grown in the Australian Labor Movement and which, in spite of John West's efforts, was destined almost to disappear with the passage of the years.

As well as working a few of his own nominees into Trade Union positions, John West had won to his service leaders of the type of Lassiter. Union executives who gambled often received a tip for the races, and a Union whose funds became depleted could obtain a loan from J.W. (at usual interest rates, of course) if the banks refused credit. With these and other favours, John West expected to obtain support for his plans in the Labor Party, over which the Trade Union leaders still exercised a good deal of influence.

Lassiter sat nursing his boxer-hat. He kept his head lowered, saying nothing. He had been worried that John West would find out about the robberies. He was glad the complaints were addressed to Arthur and not to him. He depended on John West's support, and needed his money.

Lassiter was using the Builders' Laborers' Union as a hide-out to create alibis for criminals, such as Bradley and Snoopy Tanner (as 'builders' laborers' and 'union members' they were able to defeat charges of vagrancy which the police sometimes levelled at them). Recently, Arthur West and Lassiter had decided that there were easy pickings in the safes of the various offices at the Trades Hall; often hundreds of pounds in union dues were kept overnight. Lassiter had contrived to steal the keys from various offices to which he had access, and to have duplicates made to gain entry to commit robberies.

"You only pay Snoopy and Dick and the others when they do a job for you; what do you expect them to do at other times, starve?" Arthur West argued.

"I don't expect them to rob Trades Union offices. You two, and Tanner and Bradley are behind these robberies."

The conversation continued with vehemence. Lassiter had noticed that, of late, Arty had become resentful of his brother's power and control, but this was the first time he had heard Arty talk back.

After John West had worked himself into a rage, and roundly abused both Arthur and Lassiter, the conversation took a sudden turn. "You're so bloody clever with your robberies at the Trades Hall," John West said. "Well, all right, you are going to do one more. Only one more."

"Don't be silly," Arthur said. "The police are watching the place; all the office doors inside have catches on them and some are barred; the keys we had made are no good to us now."

"Never mind. I want another robbery done. I want the books and the ballot box from the safe ..."

"I hear Dexter is in serious trouble," Lassiter intervened. "Been tickling the peter, they reckon." J.W. is cunning, he thought; he was leading up to this all the time.

"Yes, and he's lost his job at the union elections just held, as well. The ballot box and the union books are in the safe at the office. I want them got out. I want them got out tonight."

"It'll be a risky job," Lassiter said, twirling the waxed ends of his moustache.

"I want to get the ballot box out; then they will have to hold another election. Dexter says he can rig the ballot next time. Get the books out, then Dexter can burn them and draw up another set. I'm going to give him the money to square them up. I don't care whether the job is risky or not."

"It's all right for you to talk," Arthur West said. "We have to take the risks, that's the trouble."

264

"You get well paid for it. I'll look after whoever does the job, if they get caught – same as I have in the past."

"Why don't you come along yourself?" Arthur said, slyly. He sat hunched up, stroking his white moustache. Lassiter watched the two brothers. He shifted uncomfortably in his chair and its joints creaked under his heavy weight.

"I pay people to do jobs like this; why should I go myself?"

"Why shouldn't you go yourself, you get the benefit of the jobs. It's you that wants to save Dexter, not me. Not scared, are yer?"

"I'm scared of no man. Scared of nothing on earth!"

"A man who was going to go away to be a brave hero like you were, shouldn't be scared. Why don't you come along, just to prove you're not scared?"

The sarcasm of his brother's tones hacked into John West's ego. His eyes narrowed, his lips clamped shut as if he were warding off a temptation to spit in his brother's face.

Lassiter watched tensely. He had never dreamed that anyone, even Arty, would dare address the all-powerful J.W. in this manner; and he was staggered when John West replied: "All right, I'll come. I never ask any man to do what I wouldn't do myself. I'll come, it'll be child's play; but we must plan the job carefully."

Six hours later, a heavy motor car lumbered in the direction of the Trades Hall, Melbourne. It was Snoopy Tanner's car and he was driving it himself. Arthur West was seated beside him. In the back seat, with coat collars upturned, hats over their eyes, the lower portions of their faces covered with handkerchiefs, huddled Richard Bradley, Sam Wood (who had attempted to break from Pentridge jail with him, back in 1902) and Piggy.

"The safe'll be easy," Wood said. "We'll put papers and pamphlets under it, like we did on the other jobs, then just bash it open. Easy as openin' a baby's money box." Wood, a short man, was restless and on edge.

"Don't forget," Arty said, leaning over the seat towards them, "get everything out of the safe. Not only the money, but the books and the ballot box. Get the lot."

"What's doin'?" Piggy asked huskily. "Goin' to cook the ballot and the books?"

"Never you mind," Tanner replied, curtly. "I've told you before. Do your job and shut up. Ask no questions and you'll be told no bloody lies."

Piggy fell silent. Tanner's word was law in the Melbourne underworld, and no wonder. He had risen to a position of great power with John West's secret protection, and by dint of cunning, daring and treachery. He now controlled Melbourne's biggest two-up schools, had under his sway a large gang of shop-breakers, pick-pockets and murderers. He protected his position in three ways: he studiously carried out orders brought occasion-ally by Arty from John West; he paid off to many detectives and constables; and he was, unknown to his supporters, a police pimp – a shelf who would not hesitate to "can" one of his gang to save his own hide. He had no redeeming feature, no compunction or conscience. He was a liar, a braggart and a cold-blooded killer when the odds were in his favour. One exploit of which he was very proud was when, five years ago, he had gone with Piggy and dug a grave for the victim before murdering a storekeeper for a few hundred pounds in his till.

Tanner tolerated Arthur West. Arthur brought "smoke" money from J.W. if a leading member of the gang was in hiding; Arthur brought money from J.W. for legal expenses; Arthur was a bit mad – blokes who've had the cat always are – but Arthur was J.W.'s brother, bodyguard and go-between.

"Remember what I said, Dick," Arthur West said, presently. "If yer get through without interruption come out the window yer go in through into Lygon Street. We'll be waitin' for yer. If yer strike trouble, get out the quickest way yer can. The other car will be waiting in Victoria Street – go to it, if that's the quickest way out. The copper on the beat'll be on his toes after those other jobs we did."

"If he sticks his nose into that hall tonight," Dick Bradley said, "he'll be a dead man."

"Just the same . . . in case there's trouble, go to the other car in Victoria Street if your line of retreat to Lygon Street is cut off."

"Who's in the other car?" Wood asked.

"Ron Lassiter and . . ." Arthur West began.

"I keep tellin' you blokes to stop askin' questions," Tanner snarled. Long ago he had received instructions from John West

266

through Frank Lammence that none but he and Arthur were to know when they were doing a job for J.W. He was amazed that John West was coming tonight, and guessed his presence in the other car should be kept a strict secret.

"You've got your orders, you've got your tools, guns and masks. All right, that's all you want. Get in there and do the job, and stop askin' questions."

The car skirted the dark silent city and approached the Trades Hall. The night was clear and pleasantly cool. There was no moon, but countless stars twinkled.

Following Snoopy Tanner's car, some two hundred yards behind, was another; it was the Builders' Laborers' Union car and Ron Lassiter was driving it. John West sat beside him on the front seat. Lassiter wore his inevitable boxer-hat, and was puffing nervously at a home-made cigarette. His massive body barely fitted between the seat and the steering wheel. They had made the journey in silence.

The wide brim of John West's hat was pulled down over his eyes. His nerves were tingling like high tension wires, and he was cursing himself for having taken up his brother's challenge. He had made an error; he should have adhered to his policy of keeping himself several people, several stages, removed from danger. Risks were necessary to build and maintain his power, but he paid others to take those risks. Yet here he was taking part in a hazardous, dangerous robbery. If anything went wrong, his plan for fabulous power would be ruined, and he himself could, for all his influence, end up in jail.

Why had he agreed to come? Was it only because of Arty's taunting? Was it the war? The war was changing things and people. Had his short-lived dreams of glory on Gallipoli created in him a new daredevil of adventure and courage?

"You know, Jack," Lassiter interrupted his thoughts, "you and I should not be here. This job is risky, and we don't need to be here."

"I said I'd come and I'm here," he found himself replying. "This will be easy. I'm only sorry that I can't do this sort of thing more often."

But John West's calmly spoken words belied his thoughts. He had sworn that the harrowing months which followed the closing of the tote and club would be the last he would spend in fear of physical violence. Now he felt that fear again. Supposing there was shooting tonight. Supposing the police interrupted the job; in that event, he must flee quickly, for Police Headquarters were only a stone's throw from the Trades Hall.

"Snoopy's stopped. Must have seen the copper," Lassiter said suddenly, stopping the car. "He said he'd wait for the copper to pass on his way around the block."

They peered into the night until the car in front moved off again, then they followed. Lassiter swung the car around and parked it at a respectable distance from the grey, double-storeyed Trades Hall.

They saw Snoopy's car turn the corner into Lygon Street and heard it stop. They were all ears and nerves as they waited. They heard sounds made by the three intruders prising a window open, working under tension, getting in each other's way. For what seemed an eternity they listened rigidly, then from somewhere upstairs in the Trades Hall came the sound of muffled hammering.

"Jees," Lassiter said huskily, "they'll hear that at Police Headquarters."

The hammering continued for nearly five minutes.

"They shouldn't take so long on a job like that," John West said. "Why haven't the bloody fools muffled the sound better? They're making too much noise."

They were each leaning over the back of the seat watching the Trades Hall corner. They saw a policeman stop in the shadows there, then he stepped up on to the raised lawn and disappeared around the side of the building, only to reappear and run down Russell Street towards the Police Station.

"Come on," John West said. "Come on! Start the car!"

Lassiter started the engine with desperate, fumbling haste. As the car bucked into motion, John West looked out the side and saw three shadowy figures rush across the road to the Trades Hall. Before they had driven far, the crack of revolver bullets split the air.

"Jees, they're shooting it out," Lassiter said. "Bradley'll kill the bloody lot of 'em."

At the other side of the Trades Hall, Arthur West said to Snoopy Tanner: "He's come back with two more. We'll follow the bastards in, and take 'em from behind."

268

"Don't be a bloody fool," Tanner said. "They'll get out the other side to Ron Lassiter's car."

"I thought I heard it drive away just now."

Tanner started the motor, and they sat for a few more seconds, then they, too, heard the sounds of shooting.

"I'm goin' in there," Arthur West said. "I'm goin' in there to get Dick Bradley out!"

"Don't be a bloody fool," Tanner repeated. "They're probably gone in Ron's car." He shot the car away. Arthur West protested vehemently that they should go to Dick Bradley's assistance, but Tanner drove on, increasing speed.

As Tanner's car drove away at breakneck speed, Arthur West screamed: "Go back! Go back, Snoopy, you bastard. Dick Bradley's still in there, I tell yer!"

But the car sped on.

The Most Rev. Doctor Daniel Malone, D.D., LL.D., Coadjutor with the aged Archbishop Conn, of the Roman Catholic Archdiocese of Melbourne, strode the grounds of the magnificent St. Patrick's Cathedral one morning in Easter Week, 1916.

Doctor Malone had recently entered his fifty-first year. He was an Irishman. He was tall – towards six feet – slim, and sharp featured. The high cheek bones, and the long upper lip which removed his generous mouth a little too far from his upturned nose, bore witness to his origins among the fairy tales, the blarney stone, and the shamrock. His face had a happy expression; a rich Irish humour seemed to be bubbling beneath his ecclesiastical exterior. His neck was too long, but the high, reversed collar offset this defect.

His general appearance was pleasant, and he carried himself erect, with dignity. Only the closest scrutiny of his eyes would have disturbed the observer. At first sight, they were mischievous and twinkling, deepset beneath black projecting eyebrows which formed a bushy arc above them, but they were ill-matched. The left eye seemed to be half closed, giving a vague air of slyness and cunning to an otherwise even-featured, intellectual and frank countenance.

"Sure and he's a man after me own heart," one of his flock had said after first hearing him speak, "and as Irish as Paddy's pigs."

269

Dr. Malone was as Irish as Paddy's pigs, and, what's more, he was proud of it. True, he had said in his inaugural address at St. Patrick's Cathedral: "From now on I claim to be – and as time goes by I hope to justify my claim to be considered – a good Australian," but the heart that beat in Daniel Malone's breast was an Irish heart, as Irish as that of the most Gaelic of Paddy's pigs. And in absence his heart grew fonder of the Emerald Isle.

Since his arrival in Melbourne in 1913, Daniel Malone, who was to succeed the beloved old man of Victorian Catholics, Archbishop Conn, had shown no sign in his public statements or sermons that he would depart from his Coadjutor's policy of leaving the Irish Question in the background. His three points of policy seemed to be: temperance, Government grants for Catholic schools, and bitter opposition to mixed marriages and divorce.

Daniel Malone had impressed all who met him in Australia as a mild-mannered man, but today his apparent mildness had been swept aside by headlines in the newspaper he held in his hand. As he strode the well-kept lawns his step was agitated, he was both troubled and excited. However strong his belief in the justice of grants for Catholic schools; however much he opposed mixed marriages and divorce; however deep may have been his belief in the infallibility of the Pope, in the Virgin Birth, the Confessional, and the Holy Trinity, he held nothing to be more true and sacred than the justice of Ireland's demand for independence.

The headlines of the newspaper tortured his Irish heart: REBEL-LION IN IRELAND. GRAVE SITUATION IN DUBLIN. SINN FEIN RISING. POST OFFICE AND HOUSES OCCUPIED. SOLDIERS AND POLICEMEN KILLED. THE REBELS HOLD PART OF THE CITY.

The rebels held part of the City! The people of Ireland were again demanding their freedom – demanding it with rifles cocked. He was conscious only of this fundamental fact. He knew nothing of the dallying and indecision which had preceded the rising. He knew nothing of the failure of the forces of Irish Nationalism to reach unity on the eve of the struggle. He forgot about the arming by Britain of the Protestant North. He knew nothing of the treachery of the Bishops, and the desire of the Vatican to make a deal with England.

Perhaps Malone should have known the rôle the Vatican would play: that it would be fearful lest the Irish people in smashing the hold of the hated English land-owning exploiter, might have weakened the grip of Ireland's biggest landowner, the Church. But he thought only of the call of national independence. All else faded; the rebels held part of the city. Faded even the rôle he himself had played in the O'Hickey affair. When Dr. O'Hickey had defied the Bishops and the Vatican with his demand that Gaelic should be taught in the new Catholic University in Ireland, Daniel Malone, then Monsignor Malone, President of Maynooth College, had played a none too creditable part in the conspiracy which frustrated O'Hickey's request for a fair trial in Rome, threw slander and libel on his head and drove him from the Church to a lonely, bitter grave.

If Doctor Malone had been in Ireland in 1916 he might have acted differently, but he was in Australia, the rebels held part of Dublin, and his Irish patriotism stirred.

Visions of the slaughter. Fears for his old mother who was still in Ireland. Fervour for the cause of his own people. The old hatred of England. These swirled in his head in a confusing frenzy. And the feeling of frustration, and separation . . .

> Oh, Erin! Must we leave you, driven by the tyrant's
> hand?
> Must we ask a Mother's blessing from a strange and
> distant land?
> Where the cruel cross of England shall never more
> be seen,
> And where, please God, we'll live and die still
> wearing of the green.

He read and reread the newspaper reports. Presently he strode quickly across the lawn towards the Presbytery. Leaves – red and yellow, orange and brown – formed a carpet on the grass, and his feet rustled through them. It was autumn in Melbourne, but in Dublin it was springtime, and the rebels held part of the city.

He went to his study, where he sat at his desk for over an hour, deep in thought. That night he could find no rest.

Next morning. Archbishop Conn made a statement to the press deploring the outbreak of violence and expressing opposition to Sinn Feinism – the old Archbishop knew this would be the policy of the Vatican and told Daniel Malone so, when the latter demanded an explanation.

For an hour they wrangled. The senile Archbishop remained adamant, in spite of a tirade against Britain from his Coadjutor, and a plea that at least they should remain neutral and see how their flock reacted to the rebellion.

Defying the old man, Dr. Malone issued a statement to the press, giving guarded support to the rebels. "I am deeply pained by what has happened and deeply grieved at the loss of lives," he said, "but we must not lose sight of the facts. Knowing, as I do, what has been going on in Ireland before and since the outbreak of war, I am not altogether surprised ..." Diplomatically stating that "the Archbishop has already spoken on this matter, and I am sure that he has truly voiced the feelings of the Catholic body here," Daniel Malone attacked the British Government for its failure to deal with the Carsonites, and for its shifty policy on home rule for Ireland. He concluded: "I hope that those who are already calling for executions will first try to fix the responsibility for this outbreak."

Prior to Easter Week, 1916, Daniel Malone had made no public statements on the war. Many Catholics were in the Australian Army, but many also were involved in the Anti-Conscription Campaign which was developing. There was no official, united attitude on the war or conscription; the Church kept out of the controversy. But after the Irish rebellion, feeling against Britain swept through the ranks of the clergy and the Irish Catholic section of the working class. Daniel Malone sensed the mounting tempo and attuned himself to it.

John West reacted to the Irish rebellion in a vastly different manner: he saw it as a menace to the Allied war effort, and did not hesitate to say so. Lately he had become even more blindly patriotic. Only in the hours, days and weeks immediately following the attempted robbery at the Trades Hall had the war effort been deposed as his main concern.

The press carried the dramatic story. John West read the first reports over breakfast. The sounds of shooting they had heard resulted from a gun battle between three policemen and the three intruders. The first policeman had mounted the stairs and shouted: "Who's there? We are the police!" A fusillade of shots was the reply, and he was dead when he hit the floor. The second policeman switched on the lights on the ground floor and climbed the

272

stairs. Piggy and Dick Bradley slipped past him in the shadows. They rushed along the corridor intending to flee to Snoopy Tanner's car, which had already departed, only to meet the third policeman. Shots were exchanged. Bradley received two bullet wounds and dragged himself bleeding back up the stairs. Police reinforcements arrived and the three would-be robbers were rounded up. Bradley and Piggy, who were seriously wounded, were taken to hospital. Wood was arrested crouching on a narrow upstairs balcony where he had climbed in an attempt to escape to where he thought Lassiter was waiting in the second car.

Nellie's voice then interrupted John West's tense reading: "Where were you until the early hours?"

"I wasn't anywhere. Remember that. I didn't leave the house!"

That morning Arty had called at the office, desperately worried that Bradley might die and determined to help him "beat the rap." Bradley had fired the fatal shot, he said, but one of the others must be blamed. He scornfully dismissed a suggestion that there was any possibility of himself, Tanner, Lassiter or John West being implicated in the crime. But John West took no risks. When the three accused were charged with murder and with intent to commit a felony, he promised protection and payment of legal expenses as an insurance against anyone "talking." From then on he handled the case through Frank Lammence and Arthur. David Garside had died four years before, so the next best legal man was briefed for the job.

The defence developed into a diabolical conspiracy against Piggy. At the preliminary hearing, Bradley and Wood each denied firing the shot – all six chambers of Bradley's revolver were empty, but he said he merely fired to distract attention. Piggy, assured that the jury would be "squared," admitted shooting at the policeman in self-defence. Due to his admission, into which he had been lured by his protectors, he was tried separately.

Two juries failed to agree on whether Bradley and Wood were guilty of murder, whether they fired the shot or not, so they were each found guilty of the minor charge and sentenced to six and five years respectively. The juries had disagreed on the murder charges because three of their members had received substantial payments.

A bewildered Piggy was found guilty of murder and sentenced to death – he had been told not to worry if this trifling sentence should be passed upon him, because there would be an appeal which J.W. had fixed up. Piggy's childlike faith in J.W.'s magic in legal matters was not justified in his own case: the appeal was dismissed and he was duly hanged without realising that he had been framed. So ended the career of the man who had, twenty-five years before, threatened John West he would knock him rotten. His passing left John West with only a sense of relief.

Bradley and Wood were in Pentridge Jail, where Arthur West went regularly taking gifts of cigarettes and food for Bradley.

A few weeks after Easter, Nellie reminded John West that he had not made his usual contribution to the Easter dues. He grunted something about being bled, and reluctantly wrote out a cheque. When she saw the amount, five pounds, she made the complaint: "But, John! We always give at least fifty!"

"Well, that's all they're getting this time; must think a man's made of money!"

Next Sunday, accompanied by the two eldest children, they attended Mass at a fashionable church nearby. John West went to Mass nearly every Sunday, but attended Confession or Communion only the prescribed minimum of once a year. He found the confessional unpleasant: in the darkness of the box his belief in his own power fell from him.

"Bless me, Father, for I have sinned; it is twelve months since my last confession."

He always went to a church far from home to confess, for fear he might be recognised by the priest. He would confess only trivial transgressions: impure thoughts, swearing, missing Mass and eating meat on Friday. He never confessed of his bribery, his violence, or his business trickery; somehow he could not view these things as sins.

The Mass began. The red-robed priest and the altar boys in red and white uniforms went through the words and movements of the sacrifice. Nellie followed the Mass in her Missal. The girls, Marjorie and Mary, fidgeted a bit and John West stood, sat and knelt at the appropriate times. As the end of the service approached the white cloth along the altar rail was placed in position for Communion. About half the congregation filed to the altar rails, Nellie and the children with them. John West watched his wife raise her head devoutly and open her mouth to receive on her tongue the oval wafer which she believed to be the body and blood of Christ.

Communion over, the priest walked to the pulpit. He carried a notebook with him. John West heard him say the usual: "This is such and such a Sunday after Easter, and the Gospel is taken from so and so." The priest was new to John West, and, unlike his predecessor, spoke with a broad Irish accent. John West felt a little drowsy: he'd been to the fight at the Stadium, as usual, the night before.

"My dear brethren, I will now read the list of Easter dues; and, Oi moight say, the total is much lower than last year." The priest ran quickly through the list of donations, down the scale, through the fifty pound donors, the twenty pound, fifteen pound, and the ten pound. Then he paused and said: "Mr. John West . . ."

John West was scarcely listening, but at the mention of his own name, he started and straightened up.

"John West, five pounds," the priest said. "And it moight have been a lot more!"

A tingling silence electrified the church. John West gripped the seat, opened his mouth to speak, hesitated, then walked out without genuflecting to the altar. Nellie reddened to the ears and the children hung their heads as the priest continued. The congregation was nudging and whispering.

Nellie looked neither to the right nor left as she walked out. She was hurt and humiliated. Fancy such a thing being said! She was a leader in social work for the church and John had been always more than generous. As she neared the house her humiliation was replaced by a foreboding of her husband's inevitable rage. She found him sitting in a chair beneath his mother's photograph. She came to the door but walked past after one look. She knew that the rage had passed and the calm had come over him. This was a time to leave him alone, she knew that.

No word passed between them until just before lunch when he said: "That is the last time anyone from this house will pass through the door of that church."

"But, John, we must do our religious duties. The children . . ."

"If you and the children must go, you can go to some other

chapel. The church has gone mad these last few weeks. That priest was an Irishman. He insulted me because I am in favour of the war and conscription. That's why he said it. Well, let them see how they can get on without my money. They won't get another penny. And I shall never again darken the door of a Catholic church!''

News of the insult to John West was not long in reaching Doctor Malone. Archbishop Conn told him it was a further example of the irresponsible Sinn Fein spirit which was becoming rampant in Victoria, even among the clergy. The old Archbishop was worried that he might lose the church's biggest patron.

Malone, also, was worried that John West might withdraw financial aid from the church, but the incident appealed to his Irish sense of humour. Secretly, he found it possible to chuckle at the very thought of it. However, he regretted that John West had been insulted – for political reasons. Daniel Malone's main political principle was Home Rule for Ireland, but his training and experience had taught him that the Church must have political influence; and he hadn't taken long to realise that, in Australia, its prospects lay with the Labor Party. He had a long-range political plan in which John West figured prominently. The Irish priest had chosen an inappropriate time to be sarcastic.

Upon his arrival in Australia, Malone had co-operated with the Church hierarchy in other States in forming an organisation called the Catholic Federation, with the aim of pressing for grants from the Governments for Catholic schools. The Federation had gone as far as running candidates against Labor men who opposed grants. It approached other Labor candidates asking them to support the grants. The vast majority refused, then Dr. Malone made a statement which he soon regretted: he suggested publicly that Catholics vote only for candidates who supported grants.

Several Labor leaders hurled defiance at the Catholic Federation in election speeches. On polling day Labor failed to hold the gains made at the Federal Elections, and the non-Catholic majority in the Party blamed the sectarian issue. Malone then thought of forming a Catholic Workers' Association, but this, he now realised, would have further damaged the position. Already he had helped split the Labor Party without achieving his purpose. Australian Catholics were mainly working people and keen Labor supporters; he had offended most of them. The situation in the Labor Party must be retrieved, and John West could help retrieve it. With this object in view, Daniel Malone visited the West mansion on the next Sunday afternoon. He knew something of John West's history, but that did not deter him.

He hadn't far to go: his own residence was just across the road from John West's. As he crossed the wide road he thought of the successful meeting of Catholic members of the Labor Party recently held. The meeting had discussed conscription, the Irish question and, of course, grants for Catholic schools. It decided to make a drive to have more and more Catholics join the Labor Party. Add to this nucleus the support of John West's machine (so strong in Carringbush and other industrial areas and holding sway over many Labor Members of Parliament), and grants for schools would soon be a plank of the Labor Platform. This thought spurred him on to face the task ahead.

Malone had heard that Mrs. West was deeply hurt, and that Mr. West had threatened to leave the church. Sure, and we couldn't have that. It didn't pay to be too fussy or independent where such a man was concerned. Yet, as he heard footsteps coming up the long passage in answer to his banging of the door-knocker, he felt uneasy. West would be raving mad: they say he has a "paddy". He might forget he was talking to the Coadjutor of the whole State and say something out of place. For many years, Daniel Malone had not been called anything but Your Grace; no one had spoken to him with anything but the deepest respect. The prospect of insulting words, even from a millionaire, did not please him. Must remember not to lose my temper and further offend West's patriotic susceptibilities, he thought.

"Oh, come in, Your Grace. I hope you haven't been waiting long. The servants are off this afternoon." Nellie West greeted him, bustling but servile.

"Good afternoon, Mrs. West. How are the children?"

"Oh, very well, Your Grace. Do come in and sit down. I'll take your hat."

She ushered him into the lounge room. "Do sit down, Your Grace. Mr. West will be here in a moment." She seated herself on one of the big period chairs, and twiddled nervously with her handkerchief.

Presently, John West appeared, and sat down with a terse:

"Good afternoon, Your Grace." His usual lack of ease in the presence of the clergy was replaced by a feeling of hostility. I know what he's here about, he was thinking, but he won't do any good.

Malone returned his greeting. John West could see that he, too, was nervous.

"I was out for a walk," lied Malone, "and just thought I'd drop in and bid you the time o' the day."

"You're very welcome, Your Grace," Nellie said, redoubling her efforts at twisting her handkerchief. I do hope John doesn't make a scene, she thought.

They sat in silence for fully a minute. To Malone it seemed longer, with John West's eyes never leaving him. Sure and I'd better come straight to the point, he thought.

"I hope and pray you'll overlook that little incident last week, my good people; most unfortunate, most unfortunate . . ."

"I'm glad you think it's a little incident, Your Grace," John West said impassively.

"Um, well, no. I take a very serious view of it. Have I not arranged for the priest concerned to be transferred to the country?"

"I don't care if you transfer him to Timbuctoo, Your Grace. Last Sunday will be my last visit to Mass."

"Sure, Mr. West, we must never sin just because others do. If Father O'Connell burns in hell, there's no need for you to be wantin' to join him. The matter will soon be forgotten."

"I never forget an insult, Your Grace. I know I was insulted because of this Irish business. I was insulted because I am a patriot and want England to win the war."

Daniel Malone faltered, and Nellie made to speak.

John West continued: "I don't like the attitude the Church has been taking towards the war effort in the past few weeks. You and the clergy must remember that if England is beaten, we are all beaten. Anything that holds back the war effort is treason."

"Those are strong words, Mr. West. After all, England is not herself blameless. But many of the clergy and laity think as you do. They are free to do as their conscience dictates."

"You realise that I am withdrawing all financial support from the church over this matter, Your Grace?"

"Money is not everything, Mr. West," Malone said. "I give you my word that no such thing will occur again."

"It will not occur again. I'll see to that."

The British Troops suppressed the Irish rebellion, but support for the rebels ricocheted around the world. In Australia, the Irish Movement, which had bubbled beneath the surface for decades, boiled over; and Doctor Daniel Malone emerged as its leader.

Thunderous applause greeted him when he addressed a meeting in the Melbourne Town Hall, organised by a nation-wide organisation for aid to Ireland.

". . . Your generosity tonight and in the days to follow will bring comfort to these poor people who are crouching amidst the charred ruins of O'Connell Street, and this great meeting and your unbounded sympathy will give heart and hope to all those Irishmen, living and dead – because patriotism is not buried in the grave – who love Ireland, and who, even in Ireland's darkest hour, despair not of the future of their country . . .

". . . Our loyalty is freely questioned. The answer is that Irishmen are as loyal to the Empire to which, fortunately or unfortunately, they belong, as self-respecting people could be under the circumstances. I, at all events, am free to confess that down in the hearts of Irish people and their descendants is a wealth of loyalty that the British Empire has never deserved or won. And I am here to hide nothing, but rather to proclaim openly, in my own name, and I think in yours, that those depths of loyalty in Irish hearts never will be sounded, that that rich affection never will be won, until England grants that measure of self-government that we are here tonight to plead for and to demand."

Daniel Malone's eyes filled with tears. He stood erect as the great throng clapped, stamped its feet and cheered. This was his first big public meeting. He could not see where the campaign would lead: he did not care to see.

Archbishop Conn opposed him behind the scenes. John West, who loomed high in Malone's future plans, publicly stated his opposition. Malone knew that he might earn the displeasure of the Vatican: it held no brief for Protestant England, but he knew it was not in the habit of supporting popular revolutions. But Daniel Malone was acting as he felt he should, without a thought of the consequences. Even when he saw the Irish Movement merging with the struggle against military conscription he did not hold back.

When Prime Minister Hughes, not long back from a visit to England, went to the people for a verdict on conscription for overseas service – a referendum asking for a plain answer, YES or NO – the nation began to divide itself into two great armies.

Opposition arose in the cities and the countryside. Not opposition to the war – this came only from the small Socialist groups and the Industrial Workers of the World – but opposition to military conscription for overseas service. Opposition from Trade Unionists, who traditionally opposed conscription; from several Labor politicians; from farmers who feared that their sons would be called up; from shopkeepers who feared their shops would be denuded of staff; from intellectuals who saw freedom being whittled away; from the Irish minority and Australians of Irish descent.

The conscription forces were supported by the daily press. Support for conscription came from among the rich and the racketeers, who were making huge profits from the slaughter; from most Conservative and Liberal politicians; from society women who knitted socks for soldiers and worked for the Red Cross; from workers' and farmers' sons who flocked to the colours to offer up their blood that the world might be "made safe for democracy"; from Orangemen and bigoted Protestants who viewed the anti-conscriptionists as "disloyal Romans" who sought to "betray the Empire on behalf of the Jesuits."

And the leaders emerged: the occasion produced the men. The *Yes* forces needed a leader who could exercise influence over the working man. The Conservative politicians could not attempt this rôle, but Labor Prime Minister Hughes could and did. Before the war was over he had earned a nickname, "The Little Digger," but his former comrades preferred to call him "Hughes, the rat."

The *No* forces found ample leadership, from the Socialists and Wobblies, from Archbishop Malone, from the Trade Union leaders, from some of the more radical Labor politicians.

On the eve of the first referendum in 1916, the Labor Party split on the issue of conscription. Ashton resigned from the Cabinet. Hughes healed the breach with a compromise: during the referendum campaign all would be free to support either *Yes* or *No*, but all must then abide by the people's decision.

Only in such a time of political upheaval could Frank Ashton's principle and ideals triumph over his personal weaknesses. He threw himself into the fight joyfully. He would leave his personal problems behind.

Martha had complained bitterly that he never thought of her or the children. Fancy wanting to throw away his salary by resigning! Bad enough that he gambled and drank and gave away money to any old tramp who asked for it. He had tried to explain that he could not remain in the Hughes Government on principle. "Principle," she had sobbed, "you and your principles. Your wife and children should be your first principle."

"Oh, Martha," he said, "why can't you understand?"

"Understand?" she replied with hysterical venom, "Harriet would understand your principles. Oh, yes. That's what you mean. Harriet understands! Suit her better to get a husband of her own, instead of trying to deceive someone else's with her principles!"

Just before the war began, Frank Ashton, repulsed by Martha's coldness, domesticity and failure to understand his political theories, had added another complication to his already complicated life – her name was Harriet.

In contrast to Martha, Harriet was physically attractive, sympathetic and took an active interest in Labor politics. They first met at a Labor Party branch meeting, and a deep friendship was formed which he soon realised was based on more than common intellectual interests. Harriet was robust and charming – she excited him physically, and he was not the kind of man to contain such excitement. Soon they were deeply involved – the thing grew on them: they swore their love. Whether he divorced Martha or not, Harriet would never leave his side, she said; and he knew she meant it.

Divorce Martha? That was the rub: to realise to the full the grandeur of his love for Harriet, he must hurt Martha deeply, and estrange himself from the two boys. There is no satisfactory solution for such a problem: it is as old as society itself, it has never been solved, not ever, without someone being hurt. He hated scenes and explanations, and he knew if he did leave Martha, he would find no peace from self-recrimination. Martha did not understand, but she did her best, and she was the mother of his two sons. He could not give up Harriet either, so he let the matter stand. But such situations will not remain immobile: they assume a life of their own. Martha grew suspicious, and soon accused him. She lapsed into a state of brooding self-pity and predatory nagging, until the atmosphere in the house became unbearable and even the children were upset.

When Frank Ashton spoke at a Socialist Party meeting during the first referendum campaign he was greatly excited: he was being welcomed back to the fold of the militant Socialists, and Harriet would be there tonight in the front row.

When he entered the overflowing hall, someone said: "Here's Frank Ashton. Let him through. Good luck to you, Frank. Give it to 'em tonight!"

He was back in the old Tom Mann days, back among his own people.

Frank Ashton had not been free of the corrupting influences that Parliament has on Labor representatives. He had observed these influences at work on other Labor men in the Victorian Parliament, and later in the Federal Parliament, of which he had been a member since 1910. He had seen them come to the House full of determination to assist the working men who had sent them there. Then they had a fuss made of them, they were flattered, they came to think themselves a cut above the working men; he had heard some of them say that many capitalists and conservatives were nice fellows when you get to know them. Their revolutionary ardour became dampened by their social contacts, the intricacies of parliamentary procedure, and, in some cases, opportunities to enrich themselves through graft. He had seen so many of them degenerate into fashionable radicals, paying lip service to the aspirations of the Labor Movement in order to hold their seats, and setting up around themselves a wall of cynicism to keep out their old ideas. He had seen many of them, especially in Victoria, drawn into the web of the West machine, from which he himself had escaped after the debate on the Gaming Suppression Bill in 1906.

Freeing himself from West had not freed him from all the pitfalls which await Labor men in the parliaments of capitalism. For years he had felt conflict between his Socialist theories and the lack of them in the Labor Party; and he had come to need his salary, and to bask in the pleasant warmth of his social standing. But now he would tell the workers the truth about Labor's betrayal! Hughes and his clique had completely sold out to the warlords, and many others were basing their attitude to conscription on their estimate of the views of the majority in their electorates.

But he, at least, was acting like a Labor man; so much so that his old colleague, Hughes, had banned his most recent pamphlet. But he was free to write, free to organise and to fight, free to speak as in the old days. He was aware that he had a natural gift for oratory – he could spellbind an audience anywhere, at a University, in Parliament, at a Party branch meeting, in a hall, on the Yarra Bank or a street corner – and tonight he would speak as never before.

In all his turbulent career, he never made a better speech. He lashed Hughes and the Labor renegades, the warmongers and profiteers, the Conservatives and Liberals: he lashed all who supported conscription. He condemned the proclamation which Hughes had issued calling up the single men: "If all men are of the same opinion as myself, then the proclamation will be valueless."

His eyes searched the front rows of seats for Harriet. Yes, she was there! Pretty, snub-nosed, waving her gloved hand and cheering madly with all the others. The crowd was his from the start, his sentiments were their sentiments. He condemned the repressive measures being taken against the Socialists and the I.W.W.: "It is not agitators who make revolutions. Revolutions spring from the very hearts of the people; these men are the leaders of the people, and because of that the enemies of the people fear and hate them.

"The reason why conscription is advocated 'ere is because the workers are more advanced, more militant, and more united than anywhere else. The working class of Australia has become an example to the whole world. I 'ope, deep in me 'eart, that all workers will realise that the reason for the illegal call up and the demand for conscription is to lead men to the slaughter to make a fat man's 'oliday. This is a war for markets and trade and cannot benefit the working man in any way. Hughes can only march to victory over the corpses of the Unions who 'ave given him place and power, and over the bodies of men with whom he 'as worked and associated for many long years. 'E can only march to victory over the dead bodies of young Australian workers. The Australian working class will give its answer to Hughes! Hughes will fail."

Barney Robinson was at Frank Ashton's meeting. Next day, Barney was at work in John West's headquarters on the third floor of a city building. He was an enthusiastic anti-conscriptionist, but at his job as publicity man and hirer of fighters for John West's stadium he was in a hot bed of flag-flappers and yes-men.

Barney sat at a small table in the outer office behind the counter. He hadn't changed much: he looked a little older, his hair and moustache were grey-flecked and he was distinctly fatter; he still read a good deal and used alliterations in his advertisements; he was much the same old Barney Robinson.

A wooden sign behind the counter informed anyone interested that this was the Registered Office of Boxing Ltd., The Melbourne Trotting Club, and The Victorian Pony and Galloway Racing Club. On the left was John West's barely furnished room, with the forbidding word PRIVATE on the door. Under the word still remained marks where Barney had lettered in ink the word WEST, during John West's brief sojourn in the Army: the annoyance of his employer had led Barney to scratch it off, but the evidence remained.

In the centre office, Frank Lammence carried on his multi-tudinous duties. Here politicians, gunmen, boxers, journalists, cyclists, trotting and pony men, and anyone else of use to John West, were interviewed and paid for their services.

In the office on the right, a certain Richard Lamb was quickly proving himself to be a ruthless and efficient executive. Until a year ago, Lamb had been an estate agent's clerk, then he heard that John West wanted to open a permanent stadium in Melbourne. He negotiated the sale of a huge wool store to the west of the city, and so created for himself a job as manager of John West's boxing promotions in Victoria.

Barney Robinson did not like Richard Lamb. Barney believed that he, and not Lamb, should be sitting in that right-hand office. Also, Lamb was a Freemason – a bloody goat-rider, as Barney put it. Barney couldn't remember when he had last attended Mass, but he retained the animosity of the Catholic for the Free-mason, an animosity not shared by John West where valued employees were concerned. Barney's dislike for Lamb was also based on a wide difference in policy and methods: while Barney had the interests of the sport and the welfare of his boxers at heart, Lamb carried out his employer's policy of ruthlessly extracting profits by all possible means.

Lamb and Barney were continually at loggerheads. Lamb was a raw newcomer to fight promotion, but he was learning fast without any effort on Barney's part to teach him. Barney continually agitated for reforms without much success. He wanted higher fees for the prelim boys, who took a pasting for one pound; he wanted higher percentages for main bout fighters, and most of all, he wanted stricter medical supervision and an end of the practice of allowing punch-drunk boxers to fight.

Barney knew that Lamb and John West liked to match boxers who went in to be cut to pieces to make a Roman holiday for the crowds. A man going punch-drunk always drops his hands and fights back with insane courage when punched about the head: he is a crowd pleaser, a good game boy, so they matched him often, until very soon he would have to quit, and go through life with shuffling feet and nodding head, sparring up to imaginary opponents. Pretty soon, Barney reckoned, there would be more punchies in Melbourne than in any other city in the world.

But Barney remained in John West's employ. He was approaching his fiftieth year and this was his life: he had learned to love the fight game and found creative joy in his vulgar, flowery advertising copy. Yet between him and Florrie was an unmentioned disappointment, an unspoken-of regret that Barney had frittered away his talent in the West empire. Anyway, he'd got a trip round the world out of it.

His world tour with Honest Bert Squeers had been a social and financial success, but a pugilistic failure. Squeers just wasn't good enough. Barney had arranged a world title fight for him according to plan. Squeers was knocked out in the first round.

Then began a pleasure trip around the world for Barney Robinson. New York, London, Paris. Meeting all the personalities of the boxing world and the theatre, going to parties, sending postcards to Florrie, quoting halting Latin in speeches, and writing to John West promising extra profits, sometimes real, sometimes illusory, if he further delayed his return. Squeers won only a few fights, but earned big purses when he lost to more skilled opponents.

Eventually they sailed for home, where Barney found that changes had taken place: the tote and the club were closed, the old gang was largely broken up and John West was gradually achieving respectability. This suited Barney. He could settle down with his beloved ads, his encyclopaedia and his books, and earn an easy and respectable living. Time to settle down with Florrie, who, like himself, wasn't getting any younger and had put on a bit of weight in the wrong places.

Before leaving Europe, Barney had arranged for Tommy Burns, the heavyweight champion of the world, to come to Australia. Burns agreed because he wanted to get away from the Negro boxer, the redoubtable Jack Johnson, against whom he had drawn the colour line. Johnson followed Burns to Australia as Barney had guessed he would, but John West's desperate endeavours to match them in Melbourne fell down because of the stiff figure Burns demanded for what he knew would be his last fight as champion.

Barney found an opponent for Johnson in an Australian youth, Bill Long. Long was young and strong, but untutored. He fought an exhibition with the aboriginal Starlight and put up a brave if unscientific performance. He was big enough and strong enough to fight Johnson, Barney had reasoned, so he leapt into the ring and called for three cheers for Bill Long, the champion of Broken Hill, the next opponent for Jack Johnson. Long had never been in Broken Hill in his life, but he guessed Barney knew best.

In 1908 the much publicised Long versus Johnson bout was promoted by John West at one of his racecourses. The bout was fought in teeming rain. Johnson had agreed to carry Long for a few rounds. He did not suspect that he stood in danger of being betrayed. Sugar Renfrey was timekeeper with instructions to do anything he could to defeat the Negro, and the referee, who had a prejudice against coloured people, had been told by John West to put an Irishman's count or a foul on Johnson if he got half the chance.

The bout was a farce from start to finish. Johnson toyed with his inept opponent: slithering around the ring like a big, black panther he took Long's swings on his elbows, gloves and shoulders, or swayed his head to make them miss altogether. When

Johnson slipped on the greasy canvas in the second round the crowd gasped, thinking he was knocked out, but he was soon up and the one-sided match continued. Barney often said afterwards that Long was unlucky to lose the fight, because if he had stood on Johnson's chest when the Negro had slipped, the referee would have counted him out.

The crowd started to melt away after the sixth round, not prepared to stand in the rain any longer. As the fighters came from their corners for the tenth round Johnson proffered his gloves and shook hands with Long.

"This is not the last round," Long said, surprised.

"Yes, it am, Bill," Johnson replied, and so it was: before the round had progressed far, Long was on his back – out, stone cold.

Much to John West's chagrin, another promoter succeeded in bringing Johnson and Burns together for the title fight in Sydney. The game champion had no hope with his heavier and more skilful opponent. Burns cursed and swore while Johnson taunted him, and cut him to pieces. The American racial-hatred question was fought out in the boxing ring, and the Negro won.

Much water had flowed under the bridge since then. John West bought out the Sydney Stadium, and opened one in Brisbane and in Melbourne; but Barney did not get the promotion he expected. He was relegated to the background. When he complained, John West said that he had not the necessary business acumen to run a stadium.

Presently, Barney's work was interrupted by the entry of a neatly dressed young man.

Barney rose quickly.

"Here, Lou. Come here," he said in a low voice. The young man walked, hat in hand, up to the end of the counter, as Barney leaned towards him with a conspiratorial air.

"Hello, Barney," he said softly, sensing the need to be quiet. He was not tall, but wide and deep chested, his black hair was straight and wiry and his broad Irish face exuded good nature. His name was Lou Darby. His face carried no marks to indicate that he was a prize-fighter; yet he was perhaps the greatest prize-fighter ever to pull on a glove, Barney reckoned. Though not yet twenty-one, Darby had defeated all comers, including the two former world title holders from America.

Barney looked over his shoulder at the closed office doors, and whispered in Darby's ear. "Watch out for 'em in there. They're all patriotic, as you know. Regular imperialists, least that's what they say to please J.W. He wants you to join up. That's what he wants to see you about. He's not in yet."

"Everybody wants me to join the army. Old women stop me in the street. I get white feathers posted to me through the mail. Why should I go and fight? I told him before I wouldn't join up. He asked me when he was in the army on that recruiting stunt."

"Let 'em fight their own bloody war. But Jack's got recruitin' on the brain. Believes all he reads in the papers. You can't talk to him. He'll do his utmost to persuade you to join up, fair dinkum, he will."

"Well, he can go to blazes."

"That's the spirit. You're too good a money spinner for 'em to wipe you orf. Stand up to 'em. Gone mad, Jack has. Said to me yesterday, 'How old are you, Barney?' 'Too old,' I says. 'Too old in the bloody head to join the army, if that's what you mean. Besides,' I says, 'I got flat feet.' 'Cold feet, yer mean,' he said. Gor blimey, I never thought Jack West'd end up like this. Got the wind up about his millions, I think."

"Well, let him go and fight for his own millions. I've got a mother and sister to think about, and I'm certainly not going to the war until I've made enough money to keep them for life."

"Yeh, and don't go till you've won the title. That's what I said to Frank Lammence and Lamb. 'You've got a world champ in your stable and you want him to go to the war,' I says."

Sounds of cheering, singing, and music wafted through the window behind Darby. He turned and drew the curtain. Barney joined him, and they looked down on the cheering crowds and the long marching column of soldiers, and heard the military band blaring the rousing strains of *Tipperary*.

They swung around as the door of Lamb's office opened.

"Oh, hello, Mr. Lamb," Darby said. "Mr. West wants to see me."

"Good day, Darby," Lamb said. "Mr. West will be in shortly. Wait in his office. Have you got that ad ready, Barney?"

Barney scowled at Lamb and walked around the counter again. "Yes, it's here on the table."

"Bring it in," Lamb said curtly. He was youngish, under forty.

His eyes were hard, his lips thin, his chin aggressive, and he didn't smile much.

At that moment John West walked briskly into the office. "Hello, Lou."

"'Lo, Mr. West."

The office was plain and bare: table, four chairs, and the usual photos. The plaster walls were streaked with damp stains, and the windows were badly in need of cleaning.

John West hung his hat behind the door, then opened a drawer in the table. He took out a small bottle, from which he shook two tablets – he flicked his head back and swallowed them with a deftness born of long practice.

Outside, Barney leaned over the back of his chair, craning his neck trying to overhear the conversation.

John West sat behind the table. "You haven't joined up yet, Lou."

"No, Mr. West." Darby juggled his hat nervously.

"You realise there's a public outcry developing about it?"

"I've got some idea."

"You realise that the bottom is falling out of the fight game?"

"Seems like it might."

"It'll pick up again when the war's over. The main thing is to win the war; you realise that?"

"You mean you want me to join up?"

"That's right. Can't be your way all the time, you know. I've done a lot for you."

"I got big fights before you took over, Mr. West. Anyway, I don't want to go to the war till I make enough money to keep my mother and sister for the rest of their lives, in case I'm killed."

"You won't get killed."

"I'm not joining yet. That's definite. Until I have a few more fights and make some more money."

"You've done all right: you must have a few hundred put away."

"I have, Mr. West, but I want thousands. Anyway, why should I go and fight for England?"

"Because if England goes down, we go down, too. If Germany wins, our property, money, homes and families will perish." John West hit the table.

"Germany's not much worse than England, if you ask me."

"Don't talk rot. The Germans are barbarians. They burn and torture prisoners. They want to dominate the world."

"England dominates the world now. Look what she's done in Ireland. My grandmother was there; she tells me all about it. I'm not goin' to fight for England until I've feathered my own nest."

"Unless you join the colours, your next fight will be your last until the war is over."

"I don't care what you do, I'm not joining up now." Darby confronted John West across the table. "I'm ready to beat the world, Mr. West, and you can't stop me. I'll beat the world, you'll see; even if I've got to go to America." He jabbed his hat on his head and walked out, slamming the door. As he went by, Barney whispered: "Good on yer, boy. I'll come out with you. We'll have a cup of tea."

As they walked down the stairs Barney said: "Were you serious when you mentioned going to America?"

"I'm going to America, Barney. This has made up my mind."

Daniel Malone had his Irish up during the conscription referendum campaign. At public meetings, church fetes and bazaars, communion breakfasts and Masses, he made opportunity to attack the war, which he described as a sordid trade war, and to argue that a *No* vote was in the best interests of the Australian nation.

Yet he was possessed of a vague sense of uneasiness. He had entered the fight primarily to assist Ireland, but soon found himself gripped by the revolutionary nature of the struggle against conscription: he found himself drifting into alliance with the revolutionary left of the Labor Movement, with the Socialists, the Wobblies, and the more militant section of the Labor Party – forces to which the Catholic Church was traditionally opposed – forces which Daniel Malone himself had opposed before he left Ireland. For the first time he felt an affinity with these men. When he spoke from the same platform as a leading Socialist who was a self-proclaimed atheist, he found himself admiring the man. When Prime Minister Hughes censored or suppressed a workers' paper or pamphlet he found himself protesting vigorously. When twelve I.W.W. leaders were imprisoned for arson he found himself agreeing that they had been framed. He found himself relishing reports of successful violence in Ireland. He even began to despise the Roman Catholic Archbishop of Perth, Western Australia, who supported conscription.

As the campaign boiled over into the day of voting, he did not regret that he had placed himself in position for the rich and the privileged to pour hatred upon him through their press, and for the poor and the unprivileged to shower friendliness and adulation upon him. When the voting figures were released he was vehemently elated. We have won! Conscription has been defeated!

Yet the uneasiness remained. What would the Vatican say? He sensed that if the Vatican was partisan in the war at all, then it would favour a German victory; he knew, nevertheless, that many of his statements had been contrary to Vatican policy.

In the quiet after the campaign he was aware of a desire to retreat, to pursue his plan for political influence in alliance with John West. He found himself seeking some new approach to that mysterious little man who possessed the power so essential to his plans.

But history ordained otherwise. After the defeat of the referendum, the Labor Party split in halves and Hughes went over to the Conservatives to form a Win-the-War Government which was to call on the people to vote again on conscription before a year elapsed. The struggle for Home Rule for Ireland remained, too. For Daniel Malone there was, as yet, no line of retreat: the *No* majority increased the hatred of his enemies; he was to be swept along by the raging torrent of the turbulent years.

The result of the referendum enraged John West. Why had Hughes bothered with a referendum at all? Why hadn't he introduced conscription first and asked questions afterwards?

But one morning less than two months later, he was in a raging temper about a matter of a different nature. The papers carried the story of how Lou Darby had departed for America as a stowaway on a merchant ship.

John West stormed up and down his office, flourishing the paper at Lamb, Frank Lammence and the man who had last year arranged for John West to obtain control of the Sydney Stadium, one ''Snowy'' Bacon.

''He'll get no fights in America, I'll see to that. He gets cold feet and runs away. Great fighter *he* is,'' John West shouted.

''I hear he is seeking fights under Tex Rickard in America,''

Bacon said. "I know Rickard well. I'll write to him." Bacon was a tall, angular fair-headed man in his early forties. He was perhaps the most versatile athlete Australia had produced: he excelled as a boxer, wrestler, woodchopper, horseman, at almost any sport you could name. He had been equally successful as a promoter. He was manager of John West's stadium in Sydney; he had promoted the Burns-Johnson fight, and had promoted and refereed several of the big Darby fights. Sport was his god: sport organised commercially, but sport run fair and square. But Bacon had two characteristics which did not augur well for the success of Lou Darby's American adventure: he was anxious to please John West, and was a patriot who had taken an active part in recruiting.

"I'll write to Tex Rickard," Bacon repeated. "He'll take a lot of notice of me. I can tell him that Darby is an absconder from military service."

"That's a good idea. I'll teach Darby a lesson. I'll get in touch with a member of the Federal Cabinet and get the Government to contact the American Government telling them to refuse him permission to land," John West said.

"I'll ring Parliament House now, if you like." Lammence said.

"We should be able to make it impossible for him to get fights in America, if we work it properly," Lamb said.

When Frank Lammence finished phoning, John West said: "I wonder who was behind getting Darby away. Someone must have helped him." Suddenly he clicked his right forefinger and thumb. "Just a minute. I wonder . . . is Barney out there?"

"Yes," Lamb said.

"Send him in. And leave us alone for a moment."

"Barney, Mr. West would like to see you," Lammence said, as he, Lamb and Bacon retired from the scene.

Without a word Barney did as he was bid.

"Shut the door."

Barney shut it with fumbling hands, and stood twirling his moustache, and shifting from one foot to the other.

"Who were you ringing up on the phone the other day about departing ships. Some journalist or another, wasn't it?"

"Yes, Jack. Just a friend of mine."

"It wasn't anything to do with Darby going to America, was it?"

292

"Don't be silly, Jack."

"Don't tell lies! You've been putting all these anti-war ideas into Darby's head. And it's my opinion that you've had something to do with this trip to America. All right, don't answer. After all I've done for you, you do a thing like this behind my back."

Barney reddened and made play with his watch and chain and moustache in turn, but did not answer.

"You realise that Darby is running away from the call-up? That's why he's gone to America."

"Ar, you can't blame him, Jack. He's a great fighter, and the war has ruined his career. You can't blame him for wanting a crack at the world title before he goes away to fight."

"Fight? He's got no intention of fighting! Why should he be immune from the call-up of single men for compulsory training just because he's Lou Darby? It's a case of fair to one, fair to all, in war time."

"I haven't noticed the war being run on that principle."

"Trouble with you is, you're a malcontent. Anyway, get this straight. Darby will not land in America."

'He might."

"Well, if he does, he won't get any fights. I'll see to that. He'll get no fights in America, and I'll see to it that he's brought back here and put in the army, where he belongs. And don't think you're so clever, either. You're not so good that I can't do without you if I want to. Don't keep twiddling with your silly bloody moustache. Get out! If you've got nothing to do, I have!"

During this period, Nellie West made a desperate bid to escape from her unhappy, frustrated married life.

Nellie was thirty-seven years of age, had brought four children into the world, yet she looked younger than her years, and emotionally she was still a girl. She had retired into a secret world within herself, a world in which the romantic dreams of her youth still awaited fulfilment.

John West had kept his promise to give her every material comfort, but she was bitterly disillusioned with her married life. Life with a man whose reputation caused the respectable rich to snub her; a man whose one interest was the power that money could buy; a man incapable of tenderness; a man to whom marriage was a symphony of sudden, sexual crescendos, unaccompanied by the subtle preludes demanded by a sensitive, refined woman; a man who believed that all a woman could need were children, servants, a fine house, expensive clothes and her religion.

John West had killed every tender, loyal feeling she had tried to cultivate for him. She knew just enough of his affairs to conjure up pictures of corruption, ruthlessness and terror.

Nellie supposed he loved her and the children. They wanted for nothing. As far as she knew, he had been faithful to her since his affair with the actress, but she would never forgive him for his inconstancy. Apart from his temper and his puritanical assertion of authority over the household, he acquitted himself well enough when at home. He spared no expense with the children's education: he encouraged Mary to study the piano, Marjorie the violin and dancing, and proudly called on them to perform for visitors. In return, the children showed him respect and deference, but nothing more. They, too, remained outside the wall of reserve with which John West had surrounded himself in his rise to power.

Any man who sees his wife as part of his worldly possessions, and relegates her to the rôle of paid bedmate and brood mare runs the risk that she will revolt against him if the opportunity arises. Women have found many ways of taking vengeance against men for having bought them and cast them as inferior human beings. Women who take part in this vengeance are not aware of the full implication of their actions: the prostitute who takes disease to philanderers and faithless husbands is not seeking vengeance; the woman who dominates her husband through tears, petulance and recrimination is not seeking vengeance; the wife who takes a lover is not seeking vengeance, yet they are the unwitting instruments of the vengeance of nature. Nellie West was not seeking vengeance, rather was she seeking the tenderness and love that her husband had failed to give her. She was ripe for an attempt to escape from the emotional prison into which John West had banished her.

Her opportunity came in the winter of 1917. John West reckoned that the house was not big enough now that the children were growing up, so he decided to build a new wing with more bedrooms, a music room, a billiard room and servants' quarters.

In the motion pictures, Nellie West had found a satisfying

escape into melodramatic adventure, love and romance. The hero of each film was her hero, the lover of each film was her lover; and from them all she developed a fixation for the famous star of the first western or cowboy pictures: the American actor, William S. Hart. He became her adventurous dream lover – chivalrous, brave and tender.

When the contractor's men came bringing the rasp of saws and towels, the crash of hammers and the smell of woodshavings and mortar, she noticed with an involuntary thrill of surprise that the foreman bricklayer was a close double for her screen hero. Why, he even dressed like him, in a wide-brimmed, flat-topped hat, loose print shirt, thick leather belt and neat black boots! Nature and history had brought to bear one of their apparent coincidences to force their will on Nellie West.

When she first saw him she thought perhaps she was dreaming, but later she heard the other men sometimes refer to him as William S. She discovered his name – Bill Evans. It soon became her habit to stand at the kitchen window watching as he worked with skill and precision, or exercised his authority over his men with firm friendliness. She found herself transferring the dream love she had for the film star to this tall, fair-haired man who was employed by her husband's contractor to lay bricks.

At first the discovery worried her. She even thought of mentioning it to the priest in the confessional, but could not bring herself to do so. Soon she had abandoned herself to dreaming that Bill Evans was her lover. She made opportunities to speak to him. John West wished to be known as a good employer, so he had insisted on Nellie supervising the preparation of tea in the morning and afternoon, and for the men's midday meal. Three times a day a few men would come to the kitchen with billy-cans for the tea; sometimes Bill Evans came for the bricklayers' supply.

It was a strange affair. Nellie began to live her dream; with a subtle look here, and a few words quite out of keeping with their social positions there, she made it plain to Bill Evans that she was attracted to him.

Soon she became incapable of rational behaviour: like a young maiden in love she did not stop to think of the effects of her actions on other people; the servants began to notice and to talk, and the other workmen began to tease Bill Evans.

At first, Bill Evans had been puzzled at her advances, then amused, then intrigued. But as spring approached he began to wish she had never taken a fancy to him. Bill was a lady's man, and like all such he was vain and conscious of his charm for the opposite sex. It was no accident that he dressed like William S. Hart; he had done so ever since he had discovered his likeness to the dashing hero. He was one of those rare men who could be, at the same time, a philanderer and a good husband: he had his little fling sometimes, but took good care not to allow his home to be broken up as a consequence. He was in his thirties and happily married in his own way. He liked a pretty face and a buxom figure, but this was different; his wife was going to have a second child. A man had to draw the line somewhere, but . . .

Anyway, an affair with Jack West's missus was too risky even for Bill Evans; even William S. Hart would flinch from it, surely. He determined that this was one occasion when he would let opportunity pass him by; but a man had to admit she was a bloody marvel. She had four kids, yet she'd stand up beside women ten years younger and without a kid to their name. How old would she be? Nearly forty, for a moral! A bloody marvel!

One morning as Bill Evans worked skilfully near the ground, his trowel caressing each brick, he saw Nellie West come from the back of the house. His eyes followed her. You had to admit she had class, she was refined and desirable, one of them you had to treat tender and kind, whisper sweet nothings in their ears, then they melt into your arms. She's coming over here!

He pretended to be engrossed in his work, but was aware of the swirl of her long white skirt and the nearness of her scented body.

"Could you lend me your matches, please, Mr. Evans? I want to light the copper."

"Er, yes." His voice was husky, didn't seem to belong to him.

"Thank you. Isn't it a lovely morning? I do love the spring-time. Makes one feel so alive."

He was conscious that other men working nearby were watching and listening. "Er, yes," he managed to reply.

He went on with his work, but watched furtively as she walked into one of the out-houses and came out again after a minute or so. Coming towards him again!

He felt her close by, and turned. Her right hand was out-stretched and the matches were on the palm. He put down his trowel and she dropped the box carefully into his hand.

"Thank you, Mr. Evans." He noticed that her voice was faint and trembling. She turned and walked quickly towards the back of the great house.

What? A note in the match box! *Come yourself for the tea – come early before the others. Love, Nellie.* God'struth!

Half an hour later, before morning tea time, Nellie West stood by the kitchen window watching. Her whole body trembled and she kept thinking: he must come, he must understand and come. If he is coming, he must come soon – only ten minutes before the others will come.

The cook, a huge florid woman, came into the kitchen. "I'd better prepare the tea for the men, Mrs. West."

"Don't bother. I will do it. You finish in the pantry."

"Oh, it's no bother, ma'am."

"I said I would do it, Mary. Please do as you're told."

The woman started at her sharp tone. "All right, Ma'am. I only thought . . ."

"I said: do as you're told."

The woman went out again, shutting the door behind her. Nellie saw Bill Evans come round the corner of the scaffolding. He was carrying a large billy. He looked over his shoulder as he came.

She moved away from the window and stood leaning on the table facing the door. Her blood surged fast and hot through her veins, stirring up a feeling of uncontrollable passion she had never known before.

The footsteps, then the knock at the door.

She said: "Come in," in a sharp whisper, and he stood silhouetted against the sunlight, blinking a little, trying to see her in the dull light of the kitchen.

"I knew you would come," she said, leaning backwards a little over the table, wide-eyed, her body taut, her auburn hair swept back from her face, her breasts heaving above her slim waist.

"What are you standing there for?" she challenged him, in a soft, seductive voice.

He opened his mouth but did not speak; then suddenly he placed the billy-can on the floor and closed on her with two great strides. His arms circled her waist and, as their lips met savagely, her arms went round his neck, knocking his hat on the floor. They kissed with wild intensity, until breathlessness parted their lips. Nellie ran her hands through his fair hair.

"I love you! I can't help it! I love you!"

He gripped her by the shoulders, looking into her eyes. His passion was fully aroused, but he was puzzled and a little ashamed. He moved away from her suddenly, picked up his hat and the billy-can, and said huskily: "What are we doing? What are we doing? I'd better take the tea now."

She was flushed and her hair was dishevelled, stray ends falling loose from the bun at the back. She took the billy-can and filled it with tea from the urn. He took it from her and walked to the door.

"There is nothing to be ashamed of. Nothing!" She pulled a small piece of paper from her bodice and forced it into his free hand. "Be at that room at eight o'clock tonight."

"No. Not tonight. This is no good. We can't . . . it's . . . Mr. West . . . What would he . . ."

"Never mind. Everything will be all right. You must come. Tonight at eight o'clock," she replied firmly, fixing up her hair.

As he made to reply they heard footsteps approaching the door dividing the kitchen from the rest of the mansion.

"Go now," she said. "I love you. You must understand. Tonight at eight. We can talk."

He hesitated. As he opened his mouth to answer her, the cook entered the kitchen. After hesitating a moment he walked out. "God'struth," he kept repeating to himself as he walked back around the scaffolding, "God'struth!"

John West was worried, but Nellie's affair with Bill Evans was not the cause of his ill-humour. He had not noticed any change in Nellie's behaviour. He had not noticed that she went to the pictures once or twice a week without taking any of the children, nor had he noticed her nervousness or her forced conversation. She was something that was always there: a supine part of his world of power. The thought that she would choose to be unfaithful to him just could not enter his head; and, as their occasional love-making in bed lacked the subtle undertones of affection and tenderness, he had not even noticed that she responded less to his direct unadorned passion. Nor was the war situation worrying him any more than usual; in fact, his hopes for an Allied victory had received a new buoyancy lately with the news that America had entered the conflict.

It was news from America of a very different kind that was worrying him. Lou Darby was dead!

The press reports hinted at foul play: either Darby had poisoned himself, or he had been poisoned deliberately or accidentally. Why hadn't Darby joined up when he had asked him? Then he would have lived to be world champion. He deeply regretted that in his anger he had, with Bacon's assistance, done everything he could to baulk Darby. They had written to his manager, and prevailed upon him by threats and offers of money to relinquish his efforts to get fights for Darby until the war was over.

Darby had then tried desperately to get matches for himself, but Bacon's letters to Rickard and the rising war hysteria in America had frustrated him. Then a campaign was launched by the New York press, largely at the instigation of John West and Bacon, to discredit Darby as an absconder from military service. For a while, the youth who was considered by most Australians to be the greatest fighting man who ever drew on a glove, was forced to earn a living giving exhibition fights in small town side-shows. John West and Bacon were full of glee. They had taught Darby a lesson: now he would come back and join up, then after the war they would bring the champions from America to fight Darby here.

It was not at all a difficult matter for his enemies in Australia to prevail upon the American fight promoters to refuse to match Lou Darby. Darby would win the world middle-weight title, at least, and they didn't want that to happen. Prize-fighting in America was then, and has since been, a great world of money and graft. Title fights mean big gates and further dollars for the promoters; all titles must stay in America.

No fights and no friends – the disappointment and the loneliness. Soon, the press of two continents sought to represent Darby as a coward, running away from military service. Then when America entered the war in an unparalleled blaze of trumpets, the poison pens of New York sought to malign and destroy this young man who had asked for nothing more than to be allowed to fulfil his destiny.

Darby refused to return to Australia; instead he joined the American Army. But to him it was an empty gesture. He was weary, distraught and ill.

The shocked sportsmen of Australia learned that Lou Darby had died of food poisoning while stationed in Tennessee, preparatory to leaving for France with the American Army.

Could it be said that John West and Snowy Bacon were accessories before the fact in the death of Lou Darby? Apparently, Barney Robinson was of that belief, for John West arrived at the office one morning to hear Barney's voice, husky with grief and anger, raised as he addressed Snowy Bacon:

"I hope you and Jack are satisfied now!"

"This has got nothing to do with Jack and me," Bacon said, indicating the newspaper which Barney had just thrust on to the table in front of him. Bacon's face was as fair as his hair. The news was a great shock to him. He had admired Darby; he had been the means of giving him his chance in Sydney. With terrifying suddenness the meanness of his part in the conspiracy against Darby struck him, and a great sense of guilt flooded his mind.

"Nothing to do with you?" Barney repeated. His face was twitching and his eyes were filled with tears as he gripped the edge of the table. "You and Jack hounded him. I know all about it, you hounded him because ..."

John West's entry interrupted him. He turned, grabbing the paper as he did so. "Here! Have you seen the paper?" he said.

"Yes, I've seen it."

"I hope you're satisfied now."

"Satisfied? What do you mean?"

"I hope you're satisfied, now you have driven young Lou to the grave."

John West flinched. Ever since he had read the news he had been prey to self-recrimination. "Don't be silly," he managed to say. "I can't help it that he ate food which happened to be poisoned. I had every intention of making him world champ after the war, no matter what it cost me."

"No matter what it cost you," Barney imitated sarcastically. "Listen, I know that your only interest in boxing is to make money. And I know that since the war you have gone mad, because you're afraid you'll lose your millions. But you want

300

other people to protect your millions, and because Darby refused, you hounded him – hounded him to his death, I say."

Barney was quite beside himself. His words stung John West to the inevitable self-justification. "I acted in Darby's best interests. His death is a great shock to me. I had a lot of time for him."

"You had a queer way of showing it. Reading between the lines, I think he suicided, and you two drove him to it."

"Don't be melodramatic. His death was probably accidental, as the paper says. If not, then the American promoters are behind it. They wouldn't like Darby coming over there to take the title."

"The American promoters no longer had anything to fear from Lou; he was as good as on his way to France," Barney continued with a rare display of persistence. "I'm no fool, I have some idea of what's been going on since poor Lou went away. I had a letter from him recently. He was fretting for home, and in the depths of bitterness and despair about what had been done to him, I think he suicided. Think of it. The whitest man that ever lived, a man with a cultured mind, and with all the courage in the world, driven to suicide." A tear trickled over Barney's eyelid and rolled down his cheek. He wiped it away with the back of his hand.

"Pull yourself together, man. You helped get him to America, why not blame yourself?"

"He made up his own mind to go to America. What else could he do? You told him he would get no more fights unless he joined up. This war may last for years. What else could he do but go to America? It's what you did after he got there that caused the trouble – that drove him to his death."

"Don't you go round blabbing this sort of thing. I won't tolerate one of my men turning against me like this. Darby is dead, and it's no use crying over spilt milk." John West said sharply, then his manner changed. "You're just overwrought at the news, that's all. It will all blow over. Forget about it."

"Forget about it. You can forget about it. There are a lot of things that you need to forget, so you're good at forgetting. But I'll never forget Lou Darby, and the tragedy of his life. And I won't hesitate to say what I think about it either."

"You want to be careful what you say. You realise that you can be done without around here, I suppose?"

"Yes, I can be done without," Barney answered quietly. Under the impact of his deep sorrow, all his pent up disdain for John West bubbled out of him. "Yes, I can be done without, I am no longer essential, so I am due to be dumped. Of the little band of men who first started you off when Waratah won the pigeon race, only me and Sugar remain, and we will go when we outlive our usefulness. You drove Mick O'Connell and Jim Tracey out of the State, and Piggy, worthless though he was, ended up on the end of a rope, and you only tolerate Joe because he is your own brother."

As Barney spoke, facing John West sternly, Bacon looked from one to the other in rapt silence, and noticed that John West's jawbones were taut and that his eyes had narrowed in rage.

Barney continued: "Ever since you opened the tote, you have used everyone you have known for your own purposes. My biggest regret in life is that I ever had anything to do with you. I should have kept out of it, like Eddie Corrigan."

"Yes, and where did Corrigan end up? In jail! I hear he was put in jail because he is a member of the I.W.W., and burned down a factory or something."

"That was a frame-up. Eddie was no firebug. He had the courage of his own convictions, good luck to him."

"Listen, Robinson. I've always thought you were against me. Now you've come out in your true colours. You got a lot out of me, including a trip around the world. Well, if you're so smart, find yourself another job."

"Listen, West. You'll never have the satisfaction of dumping me. I'm finishing up. You can accept my resignation, right now. And you two mark my words well, the whole world will know the true story of Lou Darby. Barney Robinson will see to that. The whole world will know that he was driven to suicide by a couple of flag-flapping ratbags."

Barney was gone before John West could reply. He remained true to his word. Soon afterwards, a story was circulated that Darby had gone to America because he had been refused fights here unless he joined up, and hinted that "Australian boxing interests" were behind the debacle of his American trip.

The wrath of Australian sportsmen fell upon the shoulders of Snowy Bacon. Every time he emerged out of doors, people would shout: "There is the man who killed Lou Darby." When a film in which the versatile Bacon figured as the hero was screened in

Sydney, audiences booed, jeered, and shouted: "He killed Lou Darby!" Bacon left for America soon afterwards, never to return to Australia.

John West escaped the wrath of lovers of Lou Darby. Barney could find only one paper in Australia which was prepared to run his story, and it was not prepared to directly connect the name of powerful John West with such a serious scandal.

As Bill Evans travelled towards the city one evening to keep his tryst with Nellie in a room hired at her expense in a city hotel, he was a very worried man. Somehow he must put an end to this hole-in-the-corner love affair.

A man was a rotter to treat Myrtle like this when she was pregnant. The kid was due soon. She was suspicious and you couldn't blame her. There was accusation in her voice when she asked: "Where are you going tonight, Bill? Why can't you stay home always? I need you at home."

She was nervy and hysterical now, same as when she was in the weeks before the other kid came. God'struth, she'd go mad if she found out! Never know what she'd do – apt to lose the kid and all. Myrtle was a good wife, a man ought to be kicked to death for this. And, if ever John West found out . . . Evans shuddered at the very thought. Kill a man, he would. Not the first time he'd killed a man. Bill Evans visualised the report of his death in the papers: "The body of an unknown man was found in the Yarra last evening." God'struth.

Fancy being crazy enough to start an affair with Jack West's wife. A man must have gone mad. Nellie! His feelings for her were a mixture of sexual attraction and pity. He had no compunction as far as John West was concerned: serve West right, the way he treated her. Nellie had made many accusations against her husband – he was moody and bad tempered, she had contended, and he was a bestial lover lacking in tenderness. He was a religious hypocrite, whose Holy Trinity was Money, Property and Power. He was a bad man: he had murderers and all kinds of criminals working for him; she was sure he had killed men, or had them killed. She had told Bill of the time when her husband's life had been threatened, about his bodyguards, and her belief that he was behind the O'Flaherty bomb outrage.

Bill Evans alighted from the tram and walked furtively up the steps into the hotel. As usual, he went in fear of being recognised. Mr. and Mrs. Smith! God'struth!

He opened the door and sat on the bed. For Bill Evans the feeling of joyous anticipation no longer prefaced these meetings. He had partaken of the forbidden fruit and now wanted to avoid being cast out of the Garden of Eden. This very night he must put a stop to this dangerous affair, he kept telling himself.

She was late. Not like her, hope nothing's wrong. He walked to the dressing table and idly looked through the drawers. What was the use of her giving him presents? He couldn't take them home or use them. Shirts. Ties. A watch. Shoes. Socks. Underwear. And, in the wardrobe, a beautiful suit of clothes. God'struth! And teaching me to speak flash English. What a fool a man is making of himself.

What could a man do with her? She's not a flirt: says this is the first and only time she's been unfaithful to West, and I believe her. She's in love with me. Wants me to run away with her to Queensland or overseas. We couldn't go far enough to escape West. He'd follow us to the end of the earth. As it is she takes too many risks. Not satisfied with meeting here: must go on Sunday picnics, and to the pictures. The thing would just go on and on, until Myrtle or West found out, and then . . . God'struth!

He heard Nellie's familiar footsteps in the passage, and passion stirred in him. He knew that he could never end this dangerous affair; he knew that he would be carried along by events until someone else ended it, someone else – John West or Myrtle or both of them!

The summer of 1917 came, and still John West remained oblivious of his wife's infidelity. The Lou Darby affair had faded from his mind, the war and his business interests took up his whole attention.

He was surprised when Archbishop Malone called unannounced one Sunday in November. He was surprised but pleased, for he had lately determined that he must patch up his differences with the Church as soon as possible. He realised that the situation was all against healing the breach, but he was in placatory mood.

"A deputation from the Catholic Federation will wait on you tomorrow at your office, Mr. West," Archbishop Malone said.

"I thought I should see you first. They want one of your race-courses for the monster meeting. We have been refused use of the Exhibition grounds."

"You know my feelings, Your Grace," John West answered. "If the meeting is designed to create dissension and interfere with the war effort I will not be a party to it."

Archbishop Malone hesitated.

"You have always declared your sympathy for the Irish people, Mr. West."

"Of course, I have. My mother was a fine old Irish woman."

John West turned and looked at the photograph of his mother. He had often heard her speak bitterly against England because of its interference in Ireland. He had no doubt that she would have reacted to the present situation like most Irish Catholics in Australia, but his fear of what would happen to his great wealth if the war were lost was always in his mind.

"Your mother must have been a grand old woman, Mr. West."

"No finer woman ever lived. A descendant of the Irish King Brian Boru."

John West had heard his mother say that once when he was a boy. He had never really believed it, but now it seemed true and an important argument. "There is no one more sympathetic to Ireland than I am. But there is a war on. The war situation has improved. Victory is within our grasp. We cannot afford any further dissension. I have hundreds of letters from soldiers at the front. Men who joined the sportsman's thousand. Listen to this one."

John West read extracts from a letter which he took from his wallet.

The writer said that the Australian was the best soldier on earth, that only more Australian divisions could save the situation, that reinforcements were urgently needed.

"That's what the boys at the front are saying. I have hundreds of such letters. And yet you want me to give the racecourse for a meeting that will create dissension at a time like this?"

"It will not create dissension. It is a meeting of sympathy for Ireland."

"Sympathy for Ireland is holding up our victory. Look what's going on. Strikes, brawls at meetings. The I.W.W. are dangerous agitators; yet you allowed them to speak on the same platform

305

as Catholic Federation speakers during the last referendum campaign. I think this is really a meeting against conscription. You know my feelings; if we can't get enough volunteers then we must have conscription.''

Malone had a host of excellent arguments against conscription, but he refrained from putting any forward. He merely said: ''Conscription is unnecessary. But this meeting has nothing to do with the second referendum.''

''I believe that it has, Your Grace. I am convinced that the referendum next month will be defeated, as the last one was. You are assisting the I.W.W. and the Socialists to bring about here what is happening in Russia. I tell you, Your Grace, it's got to stop.''

''It won't happen here. We will never withdraw from the war. We will do our share, but we can do it without conscription.''

Daniel Malone had to resist an angry outburst. So strong was his love for Ireland, that anything against British Imperialism suited him. Russia's defeats and the revolt of the Russian workers would embarrass England. He was, temporarily, a supporter of the Bolsheviks, but he wasn't telling John West so. He wanted use of the racecourse now, and later he would need John West's help in the Labor Party. Archbishop Conn was dead. Daniel Malone was now Archbishop of Melbourne, and he had vast plans.

While he sat considering what next to say, John West was thinking: this is very difficult. Sugar says the Catholic Federation is sending its members into the Labor Party by the dozen – when the war is over I'll need their support.

''I'll tell you what I'll do, Your Grace. I'll let you have the course free, providing you give me an undertaking that there will be no dissension created, and providing I see the resolutions that are to be put to the meeting. Tell the deputation to bring copies of the resolutions with them tomorrow.''

''Thank you, Mr. West.''

''I am only doing this because I dearly love the race from which my mother came.''

John West accompanied him to the door. He watched the Archbishop's frock-coated, top-hatted figure disappear from the grounds. The sombre quiet of the warm afternoon gave John West a feeling of pleasant content. Some day, Your Grace, he was thinking, you and your followers will give me the extra power I need to run this country through the Labor Party.

Though Myrtle Evans was heavy with child, worried over what Bill was up to, and run down in health, she began preparing her Christmas pudding as usual on the first Sunday afternoon in December. She worked by force of habit. She completed the mixture, including the usual trinkets: a little metal money-bag, a couple of miniature horse-shoes, a little metal doll, and a kookaburra.

The Evans lived in a little weatherboard house in Carringbush less than a mile from John West's mansion. The kitchen was neat and tidy, though the wall-paper around the fireplace was smoke-stained. Myrtle was a little, frail woman and in her pregnancy her body had assumed an incongruous shape. Her face still held a faded beauty. Her hair straggled over her eyes as she worked. She accepted housework and the bearing of children as the basis of her existence. Her five years married to Bill were happy ones except when, as now, he went philandering. There was nothing surer, she kept telling herself, than that there was another woman in his life. Bad enough at any time, but now with the baby coming . . . what a fool he was. Lovable Bill, who couldn't resist a pretty face . . . but at a time like this.

What sort of a woman was this, who would flirt with her husband when she was bearing his second child? A jealous hatred of the unknown person who had led her husband astray had grown in her with the baby. She sensed that people had been talking. She did not blame Bill: she adored him and knew he would not harm her, or the boy, or the new baby that was moving in her now. Bill, who loved her in his own fashion, would not go to another woman at a time like this, unless that woman had run after him. She had never openly accused Bill, instead she complained obliquely. That he was suffering mental torment she knew: her very patience would add to his torment. She had always been aware that to hold a man like Bill, she needed to look after herself, to stem the tide of time and toil which was washing away her beauty and her sexual appetites. But how could a woman remain sexually attractive when her belly bulged with new life. Bet the hussy he's with now has never borne a child, or felt this longing for the tenderness of the man who had placed it there – bet she hadn't! Constantly the unknown woman haunted her; even in the restless sleep which she enticed in the early hours by experimenting until she found a comfortable position, she would dream of her in Bill's arms. She visualised a young, pretty woman.

Lately, Myrtle's nervous system seemed to have collapsed under the strain: she could not relax, she would scream at the boy, Bill, junior, and beat him for trivial transgressions. She managed to retain her sanity and some small measure of calm, but if ever she discovered the identity of "that woman" she would tear her eyes out – she would kill her with her own hands.

Myrtle wrapped the mixture in a pudding cloth and tied it up. I must get young Billy home from across the street. He will be as dirty and grimy as a chimney sweep, no doubt. As she walked with a waddling gait towards the door, a shadow fell across it and a plump, coarse woman entered breathlessly.

"Mrs. Evans," the woman said, between asthmatic gasps: "I don't quite know how to tell you . . . it's something . . ."

Myrtle could see that the woman carried grave tidings. First she thought of the child . . . "My God, what's wrong? Who . . .? What is it?"

The woman hesitated, still breathing heavily. "It's Bill, your husband . . . Mr. Evans. I . . . I don't quite know how to tell you . . . It's . . ."

Myrtle felt her whole body shudder – Bill – killed or something, my God! Forgetting her condition, she rushed to the woman. "Speak, for God's sake! What has happened to him?"

Myrtle's fingers sunk into fleshy arms.

"Calm yourself Mrs. Evans; nothing has happened to him. But I saw him . . . It's very difficult . . . I know it's none of my business, yet I feel it's my duty." The woman seemed confused, but suddenly she blurted it out: "I saw your husband with another woman, up in the hills, today."

Myrtle found maniacal strength and shook the woman, screaming: "What woman? Did you know her? Who is she?"

The woman flinched before Myrtle's hysteria. "Don't take on so, dearie," she stammered. "Remember your condition."

Myrtle shook her again. "Who is she? You know. Tell me!"

"It was . . . God, what have I done? It was Mrs. John West,

the millionaire's wife. People have been saying they were . . . I saw them myself, today.''

Myrtle released her. Mrs. John West. A rich woman. She had children, too. Oh, the bitch! The bitch! She had to find a word vicious enough to match her mood. She felt a calmness come over her, as though it were a quiet before a terrible storm. She found herself asking the woman questions in a quiet voice: ''Where did you see them? How long ago?'' She felt no humiliation, no hurt any more, just a volcano of hatred about to erupt upon the head of that woman – Mrs. John West, the bitch!

''Would you get young Billy from across the street and mind him till I get back?'' she asked the woman.

''Yes, of course; but where are you going?''

''I'm going to see – Mrs. John West!''

She left the house without changing her clothes or tidying herself. She half ran, half stumbled towards the tram. The journey was a nightmare – only one thought, the bitch. I hate her – I'll kill the bitch. Oblivious of her surroundings, she changed trams and alighted at the terminus. She walked, hurrying, stumbling, sobbing, up the hill towards the great white mansion which stood with the scaffolding of the new wing in the late afternoon sun.

John West sat at home reading a sporting paper. The previous afternoon he had been to the races which he always attended in the summer when football was out of season, and in the evening he had gone as usual to view the boxing from his ringside seat. He'd heard Nellie come in the front door and go upstairs. She'd been for a trip to the hills – a riding trip. Couldn't understand people who went on picnics – a waste of good time. And riding horses for pleasure: that was something people did for a living.

He had read the news which interested him most and was idly perusing the paper, seeking further items to pass the time. He heard the front door bell ring and the maid walk up the hall. Then a high-pitched, female voice betraying considerable emotion asked for Mrs. West. He heard the maid walk to the stairs and return.

''Mrs. West is changing for dinner and will be down in a few minutes.''

Soon, John West heard Nellie come down. Then he heard the hysterical woman's voice say: ''Are you Mrs. West?''

"Yes."

"Well, I'm Mrs. Bill Evans. Take that!"

John West heard a resounding smack as though the woman had slapped Nellie's face. Nellie screamed. The door slammed shut and he could hear the woman's voice screaming, but couldn't make out what she was saying. He rushed to the window and to his amazement saw the woman chasing Nellie across the lawn towards the back of the house. He hastily raised the window, climbed through, and ran to intervene.

As he crossed the verandah he heard the woman's voice yelling: "You bitch! Oh, you bitch!" He saw her pick up half a brick that was lying near a pile and throw it at Nellie's running, screaming figure. The brick fell short. The woman picked up another one and threw it with better aim and it struck Nellie on the leg.

John West stood on the verandah immobilised by his utter astonishment. Nellie stopped and rubbed her leg, sobbing; but soon began running again as the woman, who was obviously beside herself with rage and hysteria, picked up another missile and with superhuman effort sent it bouncing after the object of her insane temper. He could not comprehend the scene. The woman was mad!

He ran towards them. As he made to seize her, Mrs. Bill Evans flung another stone and it struck Nellie on the arm. He noticed the woman's bulging stomach. Good God, she's in the family way, too! What on earth is wrong with her? Myrtle Evans dodged, still screaming, and stooped to grab another brick. He grasped her and pinned her arms. She struggled violently; he had difficulty in holding her. He noticed that Nellie continued running and disappeared around the back of the house.

"Calm yourself, woman! What on earth do you think you're doing?"

Mrs. Evans ceased struggling. "Are you Mr. John West?"

"Yes. Calm yourself. Why did you attack my wife like that?"

"Because she stole my husband from me." She began to cry and he felt her body shuddering with uncontrollable sobbing. The truth dawned on him, but he could not accept it. His thoughts would not sort themselves out.

"You must be mistaken," he said.

"I am not mistaken. My next door neighbour saw them today,

up in the hills! Your wife is a wicked woman. A wicked woman. She has taken my Bill away, just when I need him most. What kind of a woman is she, taking my Bill at a time like this?''

John West was embarrassed; he felt his blood racing, but still confusion gripped his mind. Surely the woman was mad. He must get to the bottom of this. She was sobbing again.

"Calm yourself," he said. "Come inside and tell me all about it." He led her towards the front door. "What is your name?"

"Mrs. Evans – Myrtle Evans. My husband works here, he's a bricklayer." She wept bitterly.

That was right, there was an Evans working for the contractor as a foreman bricklayer. He found himself believing the woman, but his reactions were slow to crystallise. He led her to the front door and rang the bell.

When the maid answered the door he said: "Tell Mrs. West I wish to see her in the reception room. Then you may go. Take the rest of the day off."

He assisted Myrtle Evans to a chair in the reception room. She sat playing with her handkerchief: chewing its corners, wiping her eyes and blowing her nose. Falteringly, she told him the story.

John West sat rigidly in a tremendous effort to remain calm, which called on all his powers of self-discipline. The woman had no proof. He would give Nellie a chance to refute this strange tale, then he would make her pay. Punish her for the faithless, ungrateful woman that she was.

Having unburdened herself, Mrs. Evans sat like a person in a trance, and when Nellie entered the room she did not even raise her eyes. One look at Nellie removed any doubts John West had of the truth of Mrs. Evans' accusations. She slunk into the room, her hair ruffled, her eyes red, like a rebellious child who had been beaten for a shameful misdemeanour. She gripped the table and leaned heavily on it, as though on the point of physical collapse.

"Nellie," John West said. "No doubt you know that this is Mrs. Evans. She has made very serious accusations against you. In fairness, I wish to give you an opportunity to deny them."

Nellie did not speak, she did not even look up, she just stood gripping the table so tightly that her knuckles showed white. Her hair had come loose from the bun and hung over one side of her face. To John West, she suddenly looked like a besotted, disease-ridden harlot. He took a step towards her, to slap her face, to beat her, to knock her down, to kill her! He stood looking at her, his feet apart, his hands clenched; then with admirable restraint he relaxed his body and turned to Mrs. Evans.

"There is nothing more to be said here," he said. "I will drive you home, Mrs. Evans."

Nellie did not move as they walked out.

Throughout the journey to her home Myrtle Evans sat in silence with her hands in her lap. She felt exhausted and ashamed, and her thoughts turned to Bill. It was not his fault, she kept repeating to herself; it was not his fault, I must win him back. I will forgive him. She stole a look at John West. His hands gripped the wheel tightly, he was very pale, but seemed composed and tight-lipped. She vaguely knew that John West was a mysterious and dangerous man. She may have placed Bill's life in danger.

John West was an inexpert, slow driver. He didn't like motor cars. He would get rid of the car now, and get rid of the servants, too. Nellie must be punished, punished; that was the thought that kept insisting: Nellie must be punished. This was how she repaid him for all he had done for her. He had married a sinful adulltress. The mother of his children running around with a bricklayer. This was a shocking affront to his sense of power. It was worse than if someone had crossed him in business or refused to be bribed, or if one who had long done his bidding had suddenly defied him.

A power can only be maintained if transgressors against it are punished. John West had never forgiven a disservice and he would not forgive this one. It did not occur to him that he himself might have contributed in any way to Nellie's behaviour. Nellie was part of the world of power he had created; she was his, bought and paid for. She would remain his. She would be punished. He would never let her go to Evans; she would remain with him and learn the folly of her ways. And be punished, punished!

"She will be punished, Mrs. Evans," he said. "Don't worry, she will be punished. It is against my religion to divorce her, but she will be punished."

"But, what about Bill? What about my husband? You won't punish him, you won't, won't kill him or anything?"

"No. He deserves to be punished, too. But I will do nothing to him except sack him, of course. He cannot remain working for my contractor now, needless to say."

After their departure, Nellie ascended the stairs slowly. She had been overpowered by a mental and physical numbness, but now a dread of her husband's return was thawing her spirit. She had escaped into a dream world, she had made absurd plans to run away with Bill Evans, plans which she would have repudiated if she had been capable of rational thought these last few months. Previously she had been able to make the best of her life with John West: that was no longer possible, she thought. What would he do? He had so far restrained his fierce rage, but on his return?

She must meet his rage with defiance. She must justify herself by flinging back at him venom for venom, hatred for hatred, hurt for hurt. Like Myrtle Evans she found her thoughts turning to Bill; she must protect him from her husband and his hired thugs. As she reached the top of the stairs, she decided that she must send Bill away, and join him later. The affair had gone too far to contemplate any other course, yet she knew that John West would stop at nothing to prevent her leaving.

God, what can I do? No matter what happens, I must always hate him now, and hating him, defy him. Her defiance was born of the terrible fear of reprisals her husband may take, and of her own shame which she would not recognise. The defiance, fear and shame boiled within her like an inexhaustible fountain, until she could not contain it. She rushed through the dressing-room to the open air bedroom and flung herself on the bed. The fountain bubbled over, and her body shuddered in a convulsive sobbing which she could not control before John West himself walked into the room.

She did not look up. Her sobbing subsided into a spasmodic hiccoughing. John West stood panting, his fist clenched, his face contorted.

"Get up off that bed, you shall never sleep in it again."

She did not move so he leapt towards her and dragged her violently to her feet. "Get off that bed, I said. What have you to say for yourself? You, you slut!"

She faced him, her hair falling over her tear-reddened eyes, her head held high and her body erect in an exaggerated stance of defiance, but she did not speak.

John West shook his fists in front of his chest and almost leapt with rage as he shouted: "What have you to say? You have betrayed me, you have betrayed your children, and you have betrayed your religion. What have you to say, you ... you ..." He grasped her by the shoulders and shook her. "Speak! Say something!"

He was seeking some word from her that would justify his striking her, but she remained silent.

"You think I will tell you to get out, so you can go to, to your bloody bricklayer. Well, you're mistaken. You will stay here in this house with your children. You want to desert your children, but I won't let you. You will stay here. Here, do you understand? Evans will be sacked in the morning. And he'd better make himself scarce. You should go down on your knees and ask God to forgive you. Have you forgotten your religion? What will you say in the confessional?"

Words poured from his mouth like molten lava. "I suppose you have been meeting him for months, and sleeping with him like a harlot. I picked you up out of the gutter and gave you everything, and this is how you repay. Well, you will pay. You will see. You will be punished!"

Suddenly he grasped her again. "Speak!" he screamed. "Speak, I say. Say something!" He pushed her rigid body from him, and stepped back a pace, then his open hand slashed her face. An involuntary whimper escaped her lips and tears flowed, but she stood her ground.

"Perhaps that will make you talk!"

"Go on, you beast, hit me! Punch me! Kill me! You had your actress once, but that was different. Everything is in the past now. You cannot stop me from hating you. You cannot make me stay with you."

"You will never leave this house. You will stay and carry out your responsibilities, if I have to lock you up. I will sack all the servants. I will sell the car. You will stay indoors until you mend your ways. You will stay. I will teach you. I'll ... I'll tear up all your clothes, see if I won't."

He rushed like a maniac into the dressing room adjoining, opened the door of the high wardrobe, and with a strength born of frenzy, began taking out dresses, coats and underclothing, ripping them to pieces and flinging them around the room. He ripped and tore, mumbling to himself and cursing, until the floor was strewn with torn garments.

Nellie came to the door and stood, arms folded, watching him with an attempt at scorn. He became aware of her presence, and her apparent indifference diverted his attention to her again. Perhaps if she had stayed in the open air bedroom his frenzy might have subsided after he had torn the clothes, but her re-appearance served to increase it. He rushed at her.

Seeing a terrible threat of violence in his eyes, she thought of the gun in his pocket. He will kill me, she thought. She began to retreat from him, then remembered the other revolver in the dressing-table drawer where it was kept each day preparatory to being put under his pillow at night. She must get it!

They advanced towards each other, meeting on the threshold. She tried to move past him. He struck her a powerful blow on the face with his clenched fist. She reeled back and he followed endeavouring to grasp hold of her. He stumbled across her with violent impetus, and she hurtled across the room, the base of her spine struck the bedstead and she collapsed on the floor, writhing in pain.

He stopped dead in his tracks breathing in convulsive gasps, and stood watching her. With one tremendous effort she raised herself on one elbow.

"You might as well kill me," she said, her voice blurred with pain. "You might as well kill me, because I am with child. And it is *his* child. *His*, do you hear?" She slumped back and lay moaning.

John West stood rigidly, his fists clenched at his sides, his lips drawn tight, his eyes wide. Presently, his whole body slumped. He moved unsteadily to the bed, like a man walking in his sleep.

Ignoring her, he sat down, buried his head in his hands, and for the first time in forty years he wept.

And so Nellie West became a prisoner in the white mansion beyond Carringbush. From that very day she vacated the open-air bedchamber to sleep in a spare room next to the dressing-room. The door between was kept locked and a huge wardrobe stood against each side of it. There she languished, driven almost insane by turmoil of confused, bitter thoughts, and suffering great pain from her bruised spine. She rarely left the room, and only went out of doors to attend Mass each Sunday morning. John West didn't speak to her. He dismissed the servants and sold the car.

Nellie's mother had been summoned on the night of Mrs. Evans' visit, and had remained since to supervise the household. John West told Nellie's mother what had happened, and explained simply that Nellie was to be punished: she was to be treated thus until she had expiated her sins before God and John West.

Mrs. Moran avoided a crisis. She would stay and run the house with the assistance of a woman to do the cleaning. She had a little money. She closed her shop and moved into this strange, sinister household, determined somehow to solve the frightening problem which now dwelt there. The children, the eldest now seventeen years, were bewildered and afraid.

John West himself, enveloped in self-pity, humiliation and calculated revenge, became more taciturn and ruthless than ever before. He feared scandal, but few knew of Nellie's adventure, and none who had the courage to mention it to him. So strong and self-possessed was he that he went about his affairs with his usual efficiency. That he was a little more quiet and reserved was all his associates noticed, but his soul was now as hard as tempered steel.

In her bedroom prison, Nellie thought often of Bill Evans, and managed to get a little money to him through her mother, to enable him to leave the State. He went away, taking his wife and child, without even telling her where he had gone. Grief and sorrow overpowered her. When her desperate hopes that Bill might yet contact her had died, she went to the confessional and there purged her sins. This brought some relief, but the future could hold no joy for her. Only thoughts of her children and the baby that was growing in her – Bill's baby – nourished her will to live.

No matter what misfortune may befall the greatest or the least of humans, life goes on. The war-ravaged world continued its course. In Australia, the second conscription referendum had been defeated: war weariness had grown; so, too, had the *No* vote. The Allied forces at last went over to a decisive offensive, and by

316

October, 1918, rumours were current that peace was near at hand.

On the 11th of November, 1918, John West was seated in his office engrossed in earnest conversation with a well dressed big man named Thurgood.

John West had stayed in the city for his evening meal, to see Thurgood, who was on a flying visit from Brisbane.

"Red Ted" Thurgood, so called, it was said, more because of the colour of his hair than of his politics, was Treasurer in the State Labor Government of Queensland. His face was swarthy, his lips extraordinarily thick and sensual.

Presently, Thurgood threw back his head, waved the grey hat which he had been nursing, and laughed uproariously. "Haw! Haw! Haw!" His laughter – loud and raucous – was occasioned by a remark by John West that he was anxious for Real, the present Premier of Queensland, to enter Federal politics and for Thurgood to replace him as Premier.

"But supposing Real and I have other ideas. You're very sure of things."

"I never make a move unless I am sure – sure of everything. Both yourself and Real will be only too pleased, in my opinion."

The cold intensity of John West's voice startled Thurgood. "Suits me, all right; and I know that T.J. has ambitions to be Prime Minister. Just struck me as funny that you, who are not even a member of the party, should decide."

The Queensland Labor Party had been in office since early in the war. It had been the first Government over which John West could exercise complete control where his own interests were at stake. But his patriotic stand during the war had rather impeded his influence: Premier Real and many other Queensland Labor men had been rabid anti-conscriptionists. Now, with the war obviously near its end, John West was mobilising for a great drive to exert his growing political power.

"I hear Archbishop Malone said the other day that Real was the one honest man in Australian politics – sees Real as the next Prime Minister, I hear," Thurgood observed.

John West was well aware of Malone's plans for Real. They were his main reason for seeking to promote the Queensland Premier, but he wasn't telling Thurgood so.

"Is that a fact? Well, that gives Real all the better chance."

"In the Party, Ashton is thought to be the likely man to lead, if there are any changes."

"Ashton won't lead. He's sincere, but he's too much of an extremist."

Thurgood walked to the door. "I'll wait for word from you that the Mulgara Company have failed to renew their lease at Chirraboo, then I'll arrange to jump the claim. It's a great idea. We'll clean up," he said, referring to a matter they had discussed earlier. It concerned two Queensland mines in which John West had interests. They were setting in motion a conspiracy which was to cause a nation-wide scandal over a decade later.

Before John West could reply, they both became aware of a great commotion in the street below: sounds of cheering and singing.

"What's that?" John West said, as he rushed from the room into the outer office, and so to the front window.

Below in the street, the trams and other traffic had stopped, and crowds milled around shouting, cheering and singing hysterically. Men and women embraced and kissed in the street, though many of the couples were complete strangers to one another. The whole town seemed to have gone mad with joy. The song wafted up to the window.

> *Keep the home fires burning*
> *Though your hearts are yearning,*
> *Though the boys are far away*
> *They think of home.*

Other voices were singing *Tipperary* and *The Rose of No-Man's Land*. The shouting, screaming and whistling knew no bounds.

"The war is over!"

"The Armistice has been signed!"

Comprehending, John West grabbed his hat and rushed from the building, to abandon himself to the hysteria of the people. Leaving Thurgood to catch his train, John West joined the shouting, singing throng; he walked around the city in the falling dusk, talking excitedly, giving money to soldiers he met, calling them heroes. That night he sat down and answered several letters from members of the Sportsman's Thousand which had been lying in his office drawer for months. He wrote with intense feeling and

318

told each man that if ever he was in want to call on him. John West would never see him go short.

So "the war to end war" had itself ended. The millionaires and politicians stood among the millions of graves and corpses, prepared to wrangle over the spoils. Thousands of white crosses stood near the sea at Anzac Cove and among the swaying poppies in Flanders' fields, as mute evidence that a young nation had been bled white of the cream of its manhood.

John West was carried along with the tide of exultation and relief which swept over the world. For a little while, he forgot that his wife had recently given birth to a child of which he was not the father. He forgot, too, for a brief few days, the great plan which had been interrupted by the war but which must now continue.

CHAPTER EIGHT

The Papacy is never particular what the motives and methods of its allies are.

JOSEPH McCABE

"Real will get a safe Federal seat even if I have to buy him one," John West said to Archbishop Malone.

They were walking on the hill above the bank of the Yarra near John West's mansion, discussing the coming Federal elections.

Learning of the Archbishop's habitual Sunday afternoon walk, John West often went for a stroll himself and met Malone "accidentally."

Daniel Malone turned a quizzical gaze down on his companion. "Buy him a seat?"

"Yes, buy him a seat! Members in safe Labor electorates are not likely to stand aside, not even for T. J. Real. An adequate financial inducement may have to be offered."

"Sure, Mr. West, and ye'll have me believin' I'm in Tammany Hall itself."

They strolled slowly along the brow of the hill following the course of the winding river. The leaves on the trees skirting the banks were changing colour, the weakest beginning to fall before the onslaught of the autumn of 1919.

They talked mainly of politics; their old differences over conscription were not referred to. They turned towards home each well pleased with himself.

With this strange, dynamic little man as an ally, Malone thought, the Church will soon have as much power in Australian politics as she holds in many other lands. He felt himself warming to John West.

As they parted, the Archbishop said softly: "God bless you, Mr. West. You have shown yourself to be a brave and just man in your recent sorrows."

John West started, and gazed searchingly at the departing

figure, then shrugged his shoulders and walked slowly across the wide road and lawn to the gate of his home, on which the new wing had been completed.

Malone's surprise reference to Nellie's affair swept away John West's elation. His plan to win Catholic support in the Labor Party was forgotten.

As he entered the house, the sound of a young baby crying came from somewhere upstairs. He went to the music room in the new wing where it was now his habit on Sundays to sit and read. He threw his hat on the floor and slumped into the chair. He sat looking out the window, his lips tight, his eyes narrowed, the previous night's paper neglected beside him. Could he ever sufficiently punish Nellie to stifle the rage and humiliation within him?

Could he ever forget that terrible night when the alien baby was brought into the world? He had paced the dressing room while next door Mrs. Moran assisted Nellie in her birth agony. He had not uttered one word to Nellie since, not even for the benefit of the children. A sinister air of suspense and hatred now brooded over the household.

John West suspected that the older children knew something of what had happened – how much he could not guess and dared not assume. They were subdued and bewildered. The strained atmosphere would have been intolerable but for the presence of Nellie's mother: she seemed somehow to neutralise the worst effects of it. The children relied on her a good deal. With a carefully chosen word here and there she even managed to establish some indirect contact between John West and Nellie.

John West sensed that Mrs. Moran had a long-range plan to mend her daughter's broken life. She must not succeed, he determined.

A man walked down the main street of the little mining town of Chirraboo, in North-West Queensland. It was a typical "dry season" day – hot and clear.

The man was short, stockily built and of sandy complexion. He wore dungaree trousers and a short-sleeved singlet, his arms showing freckled and pink; his skin had not become bronzed, though here the sun was hot nearly all the year.

He walked briskly. His errand was obviously an important one,

321

for in Chirraboo people walked slowly as a rule, and talked and thought slowly, too. He skirted the raised wooden verandah of a hotel. He said, Good day, to an old man who sat on the verandah, but he received no answer for the old man was asleep. He nearly trampled on a wretched-looking dog which growled listlessly and moved a few inches out of his path. The fine, hot dust kicked up by his boots formed a cloud behind him.

His name was George Rand. He was on his way to set in motion the conspiracy Red Ted Thurgood and John West had begun in Melbourne a few months before.

The town looked dilapidated. Paper and other refuse had blown under the upraised buildings, around fences, and against the walls of buildings which came flush to the ground. Many of the dwellings were empty and the street was almost deserted. The town seemed to have used up all its energy and lain down to rest.

Chirraboo was the richest of many rich and promising mineral fields in Queensland. Situated just below the neck of the Gulf of Carpentaria in the Cairns Hinterland, its mineral deposits were bordered on the east and west by two other rich fields. The Cairns Hinterland had been, in the seventies and afterwards, an El Dorado rivalling Mexico. Gougers working small copper and silver-lead mines had transported the phenomenally rich surface ores by bullock waggon to the coast, before the Cairns Railway was built. In 1900, a company, consisting mainly of German investors, was formed, and erected a smelting plant at Chirraboo. Soon a home-made town spread-eagled itself beside the smelters: it attracted men, machines and buildings, willynilly, like a magnet. Nature endowed the earth with riches here, while to the north the land was ravished with bushfires, and to the west with droughts.

To Chirraboo, as it began its first hesitant growth early in the century, had come two young men carrying swags. One, named Garradi, of Italian descent, plump and jolly, with curly hair and beard; the other, half-Rumanian, red of hair and beard, a man who talked well and laughed a lot, was named Thurgood. They found employment in one of the mines, shaved their beards and began working, gambling and drinking. Then two younger men came in, this time from the North. They, too, carried swags. One was George Rand and the other a huge hulk of a youth with a great curled moustache, named Big Bill MacCorkell. They teamed up, these four, and were soon personalities in the area. MacCorkell and Thurgood became leaders among the men, the other two, Rand and Garrardi, being junior partners.

Thurgood became known as "Red Ted." At this stage of his career the reference was to the colour of his politics as well as his hair: Thurgood was well read in Socialist literature, he was fond of talking politics and economics, and of the fight the miners needed to put up against the mine owners for better wages and conditions. He told the workers that they must show the fighting spirit which the shearers had shown in the strikes during the nineties.

By 1908, Chirraboo was a flourishing mining town, as flourishing towns go in the far north. It boasted four hotels and several "sly-grog" shops and tents, a general store, a bank, a brothel, several fine houses where the smelter and mine managers lived, many smaller houses, and, on the outskirts of the straggling town, tents and improvised "humpies."

The inhabitants of Chirraboo were much the same as other people in the far north. Most of them drank too much and cursed in the same measure. They were rugged and democratic; often talk among the workmen would turn to battles of the nineties and to the men who had left them – Lane and others. Gougers still fossicked around the field like gamblers trying to "get out of it on the last race," but most of the men in the town were already wage labourers employed by the mines and the smelters.

Next to drinking, gambling was the favourite pastime. "Two-up" was the most popular form. Every night a large ring of men formed on the outskirts of the town in the light of the kerosene lamps. All heads followed the flight of the pennies up and down amid the smoke, the lurid curses, and the shouting.

"Get set on the side!"

"A quid he heads 'em!"

"Ten bob he tails 'em!"

"Come in spinner!"

Big Bill was "Boxer." He held the money for which the spinner threw the pennies. Red Ted was "Ringie." He supervised the game in the ring itself, seeing that the pennies were spun fairly, and calling the results. Garrardi and Rand assisted to run the school, and received a share in the considerable profits from the percentage charged by their senior partners.

323

In 1908, Red Ted Thurgood and Big Bill MacCorkell, with the assistance of Garrardi and Rand, organised many workers into a Trade Union called the Amalgamated Workers' Association, of which Big Bill became Secretary and Red Ted President and Organiser. These positions were at first honorary and spare time.

Realising that the Chirraboo area was ripe to send a Labor representative to the Queensland State Parliament, they organised a branch of the Labor Party. As true sons of the North, they reasoned that ballots were a city device. They decided to throw the pennies to see who would become the Labor Candidate for Chirraboo.

In the lantern light of the two-up ring they pitted skill against skill, luck against luck, for what appeared to be one of the safest Labor seats in Australia. Their clients stood around the ring and gambled on the result. When coins spin you bet: even when they're spinning for a seat in Parliament.

Red Ted announced the conditions. Whoever threw the greatest number of heads consecutively would be the candidate.

Big Bill spun first. He was considered to be one of the best "headers" in Queensland. He threw the pennies high out of the lantern glow, and three times they came down heads. He spun a fourth time, all eyes looked upwards, then down again as the pennies reappeared into the light and thudded on the canvas.

"Flat tails!"

But three heads would take beating, though it was said that Red Ted had once thrown eight and "passed the bat" without completing his spin.

Red Ted took the kip, fixed the pennies to his satisfaction, and said: "This is the new member for Chirraboo spinning, gents." Then he threw back his head and haw, haw, hawed in a raucous laugh.

He flung the coins rhythmically. "Heads," said George Rand, who acted as ringie.

Again he flung them high. They clinked in the air ominously – fatal sign for tails, some players believed – but Thurgood shouted: "Jingles for heads!" and so it proved.

Red Ted tossed the coins again.

"Two ones!" Rand said as the two pennies thudded down, one head and one tail showing. The excitement and betting were tremendous. Thurgood spun again, and once more the call was "heads." Another head and he was as good as in Parliament, he thought.

His hand was steady as the pennies again went skywards.

"Two ones," Rand said.

He spun three more times and the cool night seemed to warm with the excitement as three times the call was "Two ones!"

Thurgood took the coins from Rand again, walked away from the centre of the ring, and stood poised with his back turned.

"He's gone to water," Big Bill said huskily, stroking his moustache. "He's changin' his spin."

With a forward and backward sweep of his great torso, Thurgood flung the coins over his head and high above the lantern light. More than a hundred necks craned. At last the coins thudded down. Thurgood still stood with his back turned waiting for the call.

"He's headed 'em!" Rand yelled, and cheering went up.

"Haw! Haw! Haw!" roared Red Ted as Big Bill shook his hand. "The drinks are on me. Up to the pub and drink the health of yer new Member of Parliament."

The crowd followed, and they drank and sang and talked until near daylight, then they reluctantly dragged themselves to the mines and smelters where toil sweated the liquor from their protesting bodies.

And so Red Ted Thurgood became a Labor Member of the Queensland Parliament. Soon afterwards he married the Chirraboo school teacher – a young Catholic girl. They married in the Catholic Church in Brisbane, though Thurgood was a Protestant whose grandfather was said to have been a Patriarch in the Orthodox Church in Rumania. They made their home in Chirraboo and Red Ted came there when Parliament was not in session to assist MacCorkell with Union affairs and to ensure strong Labor organisation in his electorate. MacCorkell, Garrardi and Rand carried on the two-up school.

Red Ted became paid organiser of the Union in his spare time, and Big Bill was given a salary of £200 per year to place him outside the reach of the victimising mine owners. Thurgood visited the camps of the workers on the new railway, organised them into the Union, then called them out on strike and won a large wage increase for them.

By 1911, the Amalgamated Workers' Association had

thousands of members, and was busy recruiting more. Thurgood incorporated the Sugar Workers' Union in the A.W.A., called the sugar workers out on strike, and again won by dint of skilful leadership. The young Union became a threat to the huge Australian Workers' Union, and great rivalry developed. Thurgood and MacCorkell turned their attention to the comfortable game of politics, MacCorkell having also won a seat in 1910. They had done enough to ensure holding their seats indefinitely, so they confined their activities outside Parliament to maintaining an election apparatus and a Labor newspaper. They allowed the A.W.A. to be incorporated in the A.W.U., and bequeathed the two-up school to Garrardi and Rand.

Chirraboo continued to prosper until the outbreak of war, when the assets of the German company were frozen under the War Precautions Act. The smelters closed down, and soon the town was almost depopulated and remained so throughout the war.

Garrardi and Rand stayed on the diggings fossicking for surface ore. They had a lean time of it.

Now, as Rand opened the gate of a fine upraised house at the end of the street, he was vastly excited. A letter he had just received from Red Ted Thurgood promised a revival of prosperity.

The man who answered Rand's knock had a serious personality. Today he was sober, though he had not been yesterday or the day before. His name was Duncan. He was Mine Warden for the Chirraboo area. His duties were multitudinous and varied: he controlled mining, kept mining records, decided disputes, and granted leases; he was Police Magistrate, Justice of the Peace and friend and adviser to the local people. His white suit was crumpled, his hair dishevelled and his eyes bloodshot.

Duncan took his duties seriously, often working all night to keep his records up to date and his reports on time. Overwork and a morose temperament had turned him to the bottle these recent years. Much to the concern of his wife, he would often become hopelessly drunk for days on end. These sprees kept him continually in debt, for his wages were barely sufficient to feed, clothe and educate his five children.

"I've just received a letter from Ted Thurgood," Rand said when in the front room which served as Duncan's office. "The Melbourne company that owns the Lady Joan and Gilowell mines

326

is a week behind with its rental to the Mines Department."

"They'll pay it," Duncan said disinterestedly. He had a hangover: his head was splittting, his tongue tasted bad, his mind would not focus clearly.

"They'll pay it," he repeated. "Ever since the mines closed when the Government shut down the smelters, the Mulgara Company has paid regularly, even though they aren't working the mines."

"Thurgood said to see yer and arrange a forfeiture and for me then to stake the mines."

"Are you serious? The company has a good record; some leniency is called for. I know they haven't paid yet, but no doubt it is an oversight."

"Thurgood said for me to give yer two hundred quid, just as a present."

Duncan raised his head slowly and gazed quizzically at Rand as if unable to believe his ears. He meant to say "I'll put you in charge for attempted bribery of an official of the Mines Department," but he remembered a violent scene with his wife over the desperate state of the family's finances, only an hour before, so he asked: "Where would *you* get two hundred pounds?"

"Red Ted said he would send it, meantime I borrowed it from me wife; she's got coin, yer know."

Duncan's depressed physical state made it difficult for him to remember anything but his debts. He found himself saying: "Legally a forfeiture is in order; but I don't like it."

Rand took a roll of notes from his pocket. "I can give you the money now. All you have to do is arrange the forfeiture and grant my application for the mines. Thurgood'll see to it that everything is all right. He's State Treasurer now. He and I and Big Bill are going to form a company. We'll see that you are looked after."

Duncan buried his head in his arms and lay slumped over the desk. "Leave the money," he said in a low voice.

As Rand departed with a cheerful: "Thanks, Dunc', I'll see you next week," Duncan lay there scarcely realising what he had done. This had to come, he thought; it is the beginning of the end for me.

He arose, took a few of the notes from the bundle, and placed the remainder in the drawer. He put on his hat, left the house, and walked slowly in the direction of his favourite hotel.

Six weeks later, Dr. Jenner arrived in Chirraboo. In his pocket he carried a telegram from the Minister for Mines, instructing him to report on an application from George Rand, lessee of the Lady Joan and Gilowell Mines, for a Government subsidy of ten thousand pounds.

The train trip had fatigued him. He was accustomed to travel on horseback in his wanderings around Queensland and the Northern Territory, probing the earth for minerals. The train was uncomfortable and the line of narrow gauge. He was glad when the slow, jolting journey ended.

Dr. Jenner was a very tall man – over six feet three – and slightly stooped. He wore a grey suit, and its long coat and narrow-legged trousers accentuated his height. He was lean and gaunt looking; his stride was measured and purposeful. His features were pointed, and his penetrating blue eyes looked neither to the right nor left. His manner indicated diligence, resoluteness, and a determination to be dutiful and just in all things.

Doctor Jenner was about forty years of age. His parents had brought him to North Queensland from Denmark when he was six. As their shack was twenty miles from the nearest school, he was aged ten before his education began. Later he worked his way through the Sydney University. After a brilliant scholastic career, he decided to concentrate on Geology. He joined the New South Wales Department of Agriculture as Soil Investigator. In 1912, he became Chief Geologist and Director of Mines in the Northern Territory. There he received his first taste of the dishonesty which often accompanies the mining business. After fighting unsuccessfully against grafters among officials and mine-lessees, he resigned and joined the Queensland Mines Department.

Dr. Jenner had been in Chirraboo on several occasions. The area interested him: he was convinced that it was one of the world's richest mineral fields. The deserted aspect of the town disturbed him: he had seen so many mining fields deteriorate into ghost towns, sometimes because the area had "cut out," sometimes because the speculators had made their fortune and left the remainder of the ore neglected in the earth.

Doctor Jenner had heard the Labor Government was considering taking over the Smelters; he had recommended that they do so. He had heard, too, that a syndicate had been granted the lease of the Lady Joan and Gilowell mines, after the Mulgara Company had failed to pay its rent. The decision incensed him, but when he complained he was told that the Minister and his officials were quite capable of administering the department without his assistance. He had heard that the lessees had been granted a subsidy of £3000 to de-water the mines; he came to Chirraboo determined to investigate how Rand had spent that money.

He carried his baggage to one of the hotels and booked in for the night. After a bath he felt less dusty and grubby, ate a plain meal with gusto, then sat on the hotel verandah smoking his beloved pipe. The bar was still open, and sounds of talk and laughter wafted to him through the door. Through an open window of the parlour he could hear a card game in progress. He decided to take a walk in the fresh air.

He felt lonely. Temperamentally, Dr. Jenner was a family man. Leaving his wife and six young children always affected him this way. His wife had always said that he was a bigamist as he was married to his work as well as her. Dr. Jenner *was* wedded to the soil. Probing the earth and reading its secrets by studying the surface soils and rocks held a deep fascination for him. To assist man to wrest rich treasure from the soil was his life's work. This loneliness will be over in a few days, he thought. His thoughts turned to the task he was to begin on the morrow. He considered the forfeiture and the granting of the lease to Rand to be a blatant piece of claim-jumping – an unsavoury decision unworthy of Duncan. He had been puzzled when the Melbourne company made only mild complaints, and amazed when the Government granted Rand a subsidy to de-water the mines.

He approached Rand's application for a further subsidy with the deepest suspicion. He resented wasting time from research to investigate this application, nevertheless he would investigate it thoroughly.

He turned slowly to his hotel room, lit the lamp and sat at the little dressing table to do some writing. He always carried pen and writing paper with him, writing copious reports back to the department. A prolific writer, he was author of textbooks on soil and minerals, and regularly wrote articles on economics and politics for various radical and Socialist papers in Queensland.

His pen soon began to move quickly. Flies, moths and other

insects flew around the light and flopped on to the paper, but he ignored them. Presently he heard a voice outside the door saying: "Here's Dr. Jenner's room," and then someone knocked crisply.

"Come in," Dr. Jenner said without ceasing writing. His voice was resonant with a tendency to be guttural, but not harsh.

The door opened and Jenner looked up to see a short man of sandy complexion dressed in open-necked shirt and light grey trousers. It was George Rand.

"Dr. Jenner, I presume," Rand said jocularly.

Jenner put down his pen. "Yes. What can I be doing for you?"

The short man approached with hand extended. "Rand is me name, Doctor, lessee of the Lady Joan and Gilowell Mines." They shook hands as Jenner rose and towered over his visitor. "I understand you are here to report on my application for a subsidy of ten thousand pounds from the Government."

"I am doing that, yes." Jenner had trouble with his syntax, and sometimes spoke quaintly. His speech was clipped and his voice rose and fell rhythmically.

"Well, Doc, I hope you'll give me a good go," said Rand, nonchalantly sitting on the single bed in the corner, ruffling the mosquito net which was slung above it.

"As an employee of the Government, I will be reporting in the interests of the people."

"Ar yer don't want to worry about the Government, Doc. Nothing wrong in robbing the Government." Unaware of his complete lack of finesse, Rand leaned towards the Doctor confidentially. "Tell yer what I'll do, Doc. There's a syndicate running the mines – me and a certain two other people who are in the Government. I've been saving a fourth share. Give a favourable report and the fourth share is yours."

Dr. Jenner drew himself erect indignantly. "Are you attempting to bribe me?"

"Ar, I wouldn't put it that way, Doc. Just a business offer, that's all."

"Business, you say. I will report justly on your application. But seeing you haf come talking this way I will tell you that I did not approve even of the other subsidy before. However, I shall call on you in my official capacity in the morning. I think you had better be leaving now, Mr. Rand."

Rand made to protest and try further persuasion, but Doctor

Jenner moved to the door and stood restraining himself with difficulty. "Going you'd better be, Mr. Rand. I am losing my temper, yes."

George Rand hesitated, then walked past Jenner, who slammed the door and returned to his writing. He could not concentrate. He sensed there was something even more crooked about this whole business than he could yet fathom. He determined to probe deeply into it.

When John West received a trunk line telephone call from his manager in Perth, he was confronted with a big problem. The Western Australian Government was going to bring down a Bill to wipe out proprietary, profit-making control of race-courses, whether for trotting, pony racing or galloping. Among other interests there, John West owned two racecourses in Western Australia. He could relinquish his control of the racecourses at a fair price, but ownership of racecourses meant power. He was now interested in money only when it was the measure of power. He told his manager to stand by for instructions; he would send someone over immediately.

Frank Lammence suggested that Sugar Renfrey should be sent, but John West rejected Sugar on the grounds that he was a bloody fool at times.

John West knew that the Bill represented an attempt by his rivals in Perth to drive him out. They were a well-organised gang and worked on similar lines to himself. The trip to Perth was a dangerous, delicate job.

"What about Bob Scott?" Lammence suggested.

"Don't be silly. Can't have politicians doing work like this. We must use each man in his own field. I wonder ... Where's Barney Robinson these days?"

"Oh, he's around. Writing boxing notes for THE HAWKLET last I heard of him."

"I wonder would he go? Very popular fella, Barney. Good mixer. I wonder would he go?"

"Hardly likely, after the Darby affair."

"Ar, ol' Barney wouldn't keep harping on that. He's a weak man. I think he'd come back, if he's doing badly elsewhere."

"I hear things are bad with him."

"See if you can get him to come and see me."

Barney Robinson had to walk to the city: he had not the price of his fare. His suit was shabby, his boxer-hat dented, he wore no watch chain, for he had long since pawned his watch, and his boots were down-at-heel. He had lost weight; his clothes hung loosely.

Florrie was working three days a week: Barney didn't like that, but his wages as a boxing writer for the impecunious sporting journal, THE HAWKLET, were insufficient. Yet he felt that Florrie was more content than when he had been earning ample wages from John West.

Barney had been puzzled when told that J.W. wanted to see him.

Before he left home, he became aware of a vague feeling of expectancy and excitement. Now, as he neared the city, this feeling had crystallised: he was hoping that John West would offer him a job. He felt a little ashamed, but the hope persisted and he found himself rationalising it. Barney loved boxing. The standing he had held before his resignation had been a source of great satisfaction: making the announcements from the ring, writing the advertisements, discovering new pugilists, advising the "prelim boys," taking up grievances of fighters with John West and Lamb, doing the rounds of the "Gyms." – everywhere a welcome for "ol' Barney," the pugilist's friend. Writing boxing for THE HAWKLET was a poor substitute, and the boys weren't getting as good a go since he had resigned. If he went back he could again offset some of the worst effects of the West control. There were no rival promoters to approach.

Barney was not one to harbour a grudge for long: what was the use of continuing to revive the Darby episode? Lou Darby now belonged to the world of legend.

But what of Florrie? When Barney had told her about the circumstances of Darby's death, she had said: "What do you expect from West? He is rotten to the core, and you know it." She had stuck to a man through many a tough period, but she wouldn't tolerate him returning to West. Barney shrugged his shoulders and grinned; a man's counting his chickens before they're hatched, anyway. West hadn't offered him a job yet.

"You wanted to see me, Jack."

"That's right, Barney. How are things?"

"Not bad – could be worse."

"How would you like a trip to Western Australia?"

"I couldn't afford a trip across the bloody Yarra."

"I'll pay all expenses. I want you to do a job for me over there. We started off together; why not come back? Tell you what I'll do: I'll give you fifty quid for a week or two's work in Perth; then when you come back, I'll give you your old job back. There's a good offer. Why not let bygones be bygones?"

John West didn't really want Barney back in his employ. Barney's ideas were old-fashioned; he was an agitator, and John West had never forgiven him for the Darby affair. He was offering him his job back as a lever to force him to go to Perth.

"The offer's all right, Jack; but, well, it's a bit difficult. What's the job in the West?"

John West outlined the plan, going shrewdly into the possibilities: who to see, what to do, what not to do, who to trust and who not to trust.

Barney hesitated. A rash idea crossed his mind. "Tell you what I'll do," he said. "I'll do the job in the West if I can take the missus with me. But we mustn't let her know what I'm doing over there. We'll see about the rest when I get back."

"All right. I'll be the mug, as usual. Make you keep your mind on your work, anyway. I'll give you five thousand quid for, er, influence money. You'd better carry a gun. We are up against a tough mob."

On the next afternoon Frank Ashton sat in his study in the front room of his home. The little table at which he worked and the floor around it were littered with notebooks, newspaper cuttings, and scraps of paper. He had been halfway around the world to gather the material.

When the second conscription campaign ended he had been broken in health and pocket. He had flung himself into the fight with abandon. He toured the Commonwealth speaking at meetings; wrote pamphlets against conscription; faced with censorship, he organised illegal distribution, sending them to the far corners of the country packed in cases with two or three rows of apples or pears above the bundles. For a few months he had forgotten his unhappy home life, his growing band of impatient creditors. He had no time to drink much or to make his weekly trip to gamble at the races. He slept where he found himself, saw little of Martha and the children, and less of Harriet.

When the Referendum was defeated, his unsolved problems come back to him with even greater force. His financial position was desperate, so he borrowed ten pounds and lost it at the races in an endeavour to turn it into a few hundred.

Martha complained interminably. One scene followed another while the bewildered children listened. Frank Ashton's love for Martha had turned to pity. Cold, practical, unintelligent Martha wanted to be a good mate for him and didn't know how. Her mind and soul were buried in the household and its everyday needs.

He felt ashamed, remaining in Parliament. Yet where would he go if he resigned? He needed the salary and social status.

The Russian revolution stirred his emotional temperament and gave him a justification for running away from his problems. He devoured the news of the fighting and endeavoured to read between the distorted lines in the daily press. To him one thing became clear: the Russian workers were throwing off the yoke of the exploiters. He began to picture the workers of all Europe rising like lions out of sleep to end the war and the system which caused the war.

Speaking to an enthusiastic Socialist meeting he said:

"I hope we can accomplish the emancipation of the working class by the intelligence of the masses, but I am not h'oblivious of the fact that many a time in the 'istory of the world, it 'as been necessary for blood to be shed in order that people may be free."

He began speaking enthusiastically about Lenin and the Bolsheviks, telling everyone that that kind of relationship was required in Australia. He even mentioned his opinions to Martha, who replied: "If you go around talking like that you'll lose your seat; then what will happen to me and the children?"

He contacted Harriet. Over luncheon in the city he told her he was going to Europe to see for himself.

'I'll come back and tell the Australian workers all about it."

He had no money, that was the problem, but he managed to borrow a small sum and book the cheapest passage available as far as America: from there he would have to get to Europe as best he could. Then he received a shock: the Commonwealth

Government refused him permission to leave. Annoyed, he went straight to Prime Minister Hughes.

Hughes, a little wrinkle-faced man, a small bundle of energy, grinned and said: "I'm going to England myself, Frank. Do you think I am bloody fool enough to have you barking at my heels when I'm trying to impress them over there? You're stopping right here."

Frank Ashton was not to be denied. He had worked his way around the world once, and he could do it again! He got himself a job as assistant purser on a merchant ship bound for America. "You only want to get away from me and the children. You'll never come back," Martha sobbed.

He went to see Harriet. He told Martha he intended to do so, and took the two boys with him as a sign of good faith. Harriet farewelled him calmly, but he sensed her sorrow.

As the ship passed through the heads, Frank Ashton felt an overpowering sense of relief. The first night out he leaned over the side watching the moonlight shimmering on the calm sea. Always he felt that a ship was a world of its own, moving across the waters which cut one off from the mundane cares of life. Now, Australia and his troubles seemed far away. At sea a man could think. Life was simple. A man was free!

He had sixteen pounds in his pocket.

Arriving in America, he was contacted by a Finnish Socialist, a refugee from Mannerheim, "the Butcher of Helsinki." This man gave him a little money and some documents to deliver to Maxim Litvinoff, the Ambassador for Soviet Russia in England.

In London, Frank Ashton met Maxim Litvinoff, the Ambassador for Soviet Russia in England. He suspected that Litvinoff was a little dubious about this member of a Labor Government which had betrayed the workers to the militarists. Ashton waxed enthusiastic about the Russian Revolution, Litvinoff replied: "The greatest task of any revolution is to change the social order. That task still lies ahead. It will only be achieved after great struggle and sacrifice."

Next Frank Ashton hastened to see his mother and half-brother in Devon. His mother wept with joy and kept saying: "My boy has come home again." He found her old and shrivelled, but happy, and proud of her eldest son.

She had married again, happily enough in spite of the advanced age of herself and her third husband. Frank Ashton found his stepfather a fine old fellow. They went walking together through the lanes of old Devon, and sometimes they went in the evenings to an old inn to drink a pint or two.

One evening he told them of his enthusiasm for the Russian Revolution. They responded with hostile silence. They were conservative English country folk, who took their politics from the London TIMES. He decided not to spoil his joy and theirs by any further reference to politics. He consented to attend church in the village with his mother, suspecting that she was anxious to show off her successful son.

Soon he received a cable from the acting Prime Minister of Australia, asking him to join the Australian Press Mission going to France. He now had additional money to supplement the small share of his parliamentary salary left after Martha drew most of it in Melbourne.

In September, 1918, he went to France. He insisted on going to the front. The horrible, futile butchery of war nauseated him as he watched the fighting at Lens from the safety of Vimy Ridge, as close as he was allowed to go.

He studied a French-English dictionary and gained a smattering of French.

He stayed on in Europe after the other members of the mission had returned to Australia. To many people he became known as 'the long-haired Bolshevik,' but sympathisers of the Russian Revolution suspected his association with the reactionary Australian Press Delegation.

Everywhere he talked, and listened, He collected newscuttings, inside stories about Finland and the new Russia, and the facts of the treachery of most of the Labor leaders in Europe.

He would become drunk with his fervour and rush back to his room, where his pen would scratch far into the night.

The war ended, but he continued his frantic search for information. Then in February, 1919, the English press carried reports that he had been appointed by the Australian Labor Party as delegate to the International Socialist Conference at Berne.

Instead, he went to Russia.

He could not get near Petrograd or Moscow, but in the south he saw enough of the war of intervention to make his Socialist blood boil. The armies of Germany, England, Austria, France and many other countries, after four years at each other's throats, were now united against Soviet Russia. He saw evidence of brutality and torture, of treachery and hypocrisy, but he saw that the new-born Red Army would triumph. He gathered notes and facts, photos of Lenin and Trotsky, photos of Japanese and American troops assembling at Vladivostock to make an onslaught on the Soviets' rear, photos of the Red Army in action, maps of fighting zones. Then he went to Finland to confirm for himself what a Finnish Socialist had told him in America about Mannerheim's regime. He witnessed how Mannerheim was throwing Finland open as a jumping-off ground for the armies of the world against Russia.

Then reluctantly back to Paris and so to London before returning to Australia.

In London he met Tom Mann.

Mann came up from his chicken farm in Kent. Mann had aged. He was not yet seventy, but to Frank Ashton he looked like a man who had worn himself out, who had no fight left in him. His clothes hung loosely; the old strength and erect bearing seemed to have deserted him, his cheeks were pale and drawn, his hair and moustache snow white. Over a meal, Ashton waved his arms and shouted his support for Bolshevism. He told Mann of the anti-conscription fight in Australia. Then they reminisced about the days when they had spoken together at so many meetings.

Mann said quietly: "Since then, Frank, I have been in South Africa, Europe and here in England, speaking and organising the workers, while you have sat back on your Parliamentary salary. What we need now, Frank, is a Communist Party in every country on earth. That is the workers' only hope. It will grow all over the world if enough of us work hard enough for long enough."

He was all for it, Ashton declared, but Mann made no reply. He knew Frank Ashton too well. He liked him and appreciated his value as a propagandist, but he knew his weaknesses. He knew that Ashton had not the theory, the patience, or the political integrity required.

"I s'pose you wonder why I became a chicken farmer, Frank?" Mann said, changing the subject.

"I did until I saw you, Tom."

"Well, my health has improved. I am coming back to London,

to re-enter the fight. We live in the period of the revolution; I don't want to be out of it. I am going to help form the Communist Party of England."

Back in Melbourne, Frank Ashton was welcomed with a dinner at the Trades Hall. He found much lip service to the new Soviet Government, many Communists in name, but none of the change of policy and tactics which he considered essential. They sang the Red Flag, but weren't prepared to hoist it in battle.

He ran enthusiastically to the old I.W.W., but found that one-time fighting organisation on its death-bed. He went to the Socialists, told them about Tom Mann and the Russian situation, and found them groping towards some understanding. But most of them were confused.

Everyone found him a changed man: a man possessed of a reborn revolutionary spirit. Even Martha noted the difference, but she wisely remained silent, reasoning that he would get over it.

Harriet heard he was back and waited for him expectantly, but he did not call. Absence had resolved Frank Ashton's conflict in favour of his legal wife; Martha had triumphed over Harriet, temporarily at least. He had to think of the children, and, anyway, making a break would cause fuss and scandal.

He lectured nearly every night, using maps and illustrations. His oratory was inspired; he swayed large audiences towards Socialism.

Harriet would not fade from his life: she often attended his meetings. She sometimes spoke to him after a meeting in the presence of others, and he knew that the old passion was not dead. Martha chided him that he had been away for over a year, and the least he could do was pay her and the children some attention.

Occasionally, his youngest son would come into the room before going to bed and ask: "What are you writing, Dad?" Frank Ashton would answer: "I am writing a book to tell everyone that this is a wicked world and that they must fight to change it." The lad, scarcely eleven years old, would answer: "Why is this a wicked world, Dad?" and that was a difficult question to answer one so young.

Arriving back in Australia, Frank Ashton had a little money, but not enough to satisfy his creditors. He was displeased and shocked when Martha told him that John West had given her sufficient money to pay them all. He reasoned that West would view the gift as payment in advance for services to be rendered. He remonstrated with Martha, but she replied that he should be grateful to Mr. West: they were out of debt now and she would see that they stayed that way.

But now, sitting in his study, Frank Ashton was not thinking of John West. His book was finished. He had decided to call it RED EUROPE. He was seeking a revolutionary, passionate end. Suddenly it came. He grabbed the pen.

> *Capitalism listens with quaking soul to the drum beats of the Armies of Revolution. Those beats grow louder and louder – they draw nearer and nearer.*

He scrawled the words in his ornate hand, wrote *Finis* across the bottom of the page, slumped back and lit a cigarette.

The dying sun glowed through the window. As he flicked the match into the fireplace, and sat fingering the thick manuscript, the front door knocker banged sharply. He arose distractedly, opened the door, and was surprised to see the short figure of Percy Lambert silhouetted against the setting sun. Frank Ashton had been associated with Lambert in what were now referred to as the "old Tom Mann days," but they had not met since, except officially during the anti-conscription campaigns.

"Good afternoon, Frank," Lambert said, in a resonant voice. They shook hands warmly.

"Glad to see you, Percy," Ashton said. "Come in. Come in."

Lambert walked past him into the study. His gait was slightly aggressive. He wore a plain, well-fitting suit but no hat.

"I heard two of your lectures, Frank," he said, when they were seated. "Great stuff. We must do everything we can do to offset the lies in the press. We must tell the workers the truth about the Bolsheviks. This is the beginning of the world revolution."

Ashton held up his manuscript. "I am writing a book with the material I've been using in the lectures plus some excellent photos and maps. I finished it today. I'm calling it RED EUROPE. The last paragraph will give you an idea of the contents, I think. Listen . . ."

He read, then looked up with pride and ran his hand through his hair self-consciously.

"That is the position," Lambert answered, "but there is a lot of organising to be done here in Australia. That's why I've come to see you. We are calling a conference of the Socialist Parties and other interested organisations and individuals with a view to forming a Communist Party in Australia. A branch of the Communist International. The Labor Party has failed, the Socialist Parties are no more than propaganda sects. We must have a new kind of party linked with the international, revolutionary movement. That Party will need you, Frank. Can we count on you as a foundation member?"

"I am with you all the way, you know that, Percy."

"It will mean a lot to have you in the Party from the outset."

"Well, you see, Percy, there are difficulties. You are asking a lot . . . I would lose my seat . . . Not that that matters two hoots to me, but . . ." Ashton stammered. He was saying things he did not want to say.

"Who's to say you wouldn't hold your seat, even as a Communist? You have a big personal following. Besides, you could remain in the Labor Party for the time being."

"Oh, it's not the seat that's worrying me, Percy. You see, I, that is, the political situation is very calm in Australia. The Wobblies are finished, the Socialists can't agree among themselves. The Labor Party is a big party, well established, with a big following. We must work through the Labor Party. Make it a real Socialist Party. When I arrived back I thought a Communist Party was possible, but now I'm sure the Labor Party can be made to do the job."

"What? End capitalism under the leadership of the likes of Hughes, the rat? The Labor Party has failed the workers and will fail them again and again."

"Yes, but that can be altered. I am determined to alter it. Have Socialism made its objective. Who knows, I may even become Party leader. Australia is different from Europe. To form a Communist Party here would be premature. It would take generations to build it up. It's a superhuman task."

"To make the Labor Party a real worker's party is an impossible task."

Frank Ashton dearly wanted to say: "I will come in, Percy." But visions of the privilege and status he enjoyed as a member of Parliament crowded out his true feelings. And if he went with

340

Lambert along the path of struggle? If he lost his seat, he would return to the dread battle for existence of his early life. The idea that Harriet would approve came to his mind, but he swept it out. It would all be of no avail. The Australian workers were not ready. Lambert and the others were no Lenins. No, he had to refuse. There was no alternative.

They sat in awkward silence until Lambert said: "I take it, then, Frank, that you do not believe in what we are going to attempt, and therefore will not take part in it."

Ashton perceived that he was being given a chance to refuse gracefully. "I would prefer to put it this way, Percy. You are asking too much. You are asking me to make a greater sacrifice than I am capable of."

Lambert arose. "In a way, I don't blame you, Frank. But I feel certain that, at heart, you know the Labor Party will continue to let the workers down whatever you try to do."

Through the front window, Frank Ashton watched Lambert's figure swinging along the street towards the tram line. Lambert appeared to him like a soldier going into attack, leaving behind a comrade who had deserted.

Then a motor car halted in front of the house. Who would be calling on him in a new motor car? He recognised Sugar Renfrey at the wheel. Beside him, he saw John West.

Ashton hesitated. He didn't like this. These two were again very active behind the scenes in the Party. West hadn't paid his debts out of the goodness of his heart, that was certain. He walked slowly to the door and opened it.

"Oh, good day, Mr. West."

"How are you, Mr. Ashton?" John West said, affably, proffering his hand. "I heard you were back. Can I come in?"

"Yes. What about Renfrey?"

"Oh, he can wait in the car."

"'Ow are yer, Frank?" Sugar shouted, waving boisterously.

Inside, Ashton sat at the table and John West on the couch. The sun went suddenly and the room darkened. Frank Ashton switched on the electric light. John West sat nursing his hat.

"How did you get on in Europe?"

"I learned a lot."

"I hear you're writing a book."

"That's right."

"You've come a long way since I put you into Parliament."

Frank Ashton did not answer. What's he leading up to, he thought, fingering his manuscript.

"What have you come to see me about, Mr. West?"

John West hesitated. "Well, I would like you to stand down for Real. I am anxious for him to win a Federal seat."

"You mean Archbishop Malone is anxious."

"I said *I* am anxious for him to win a Federal seat."

"Why, Malone has been going up and down the country telling the world that Real is the only honest man in Australian politics. And everyone knows why. Sectarianism is ruining the Labor Movement."

"Perhaps it is, but I want Real in. I want you to stand down. I'll see you don't suffer. I'll set you up in business until you can find another seat. I've done a lot for you. I suppose your wife told you I fixed things up while you were away."

"I didn't ask you to. I can't be bought, Mr. West. Not even with a tip for a racehorse or with a settlement of my debts."

"Don't be unreasonable. I'll pay you a lump sum, if you like. It's merely a gesture. I will give you five thousand pounds to stand down for Real. You can win another seat later."

Ashton's mind ran over the things he could do with five thousand pounds. He could build a house. He could send his sons to the best schools. He could be financially secure for the first time in his life. He could easily win another seat. Martha would cease complaining.

Then he thought of Europe. He looked up at John West and met his gaze. He would oppose this man for what he was: a millionaire and an enemy of the Australian workers.

"I wouldn't stand down for five million pounds. I am opposed to the Catholic influence in the Party – and it seems to me that they are behind this move."

"You seem to forget what I have done for you, Mister Ashton."

"I've forgotten nothing. I opposed the move to invite Real to resign as Premier of Queensland and enter Federal politics, because I don't think he is the man to lead, and I'm certainly not standing down for him."

"Real is a genius. He ought to suit your book. He opposed

conscription and started the government enterprises in Queensland.''

"That is a lot different to what I want. I want Socialism.''

"You mean you want revolution, like in Russia.''

"That's right, Mr. West. Like in Russia.''

"Nothing like that will ever happen here.''

"The fact remains, Mr. West, that I'm not standing down for Real. Even if you and Malone buy him a seat, I'll see to it that he never becomes leader of the Party.''

"I suppose you have ideas of becoming leader yourself.''

"Perhaps I have. Real won't, anyway!''

John West lost his temper. "I say Real will lead! And he will, you see. You seem to forget that I picked you up out of the gutter and put you into politics.''

Frank Ashton stood and faced him. "You helped put me in, Mr. West. But you can't get me out. That is the difference: you can't get me out!''

Barney and Florrie Robinson had a grand trip. It was Florrie's first sea voyage and she made the most of it. The sea in the Bight and beyond was unusually calm. They played deck tennis, drank a little beer, sang in the quiet of the evening with the other passengers, Barney invariably obliging with a recitation from Henry Lawson or Banjo Patterson. Once he sang a parody he had written about Lou Darby:

> Way down in Tennessee
> They murdered Lou Darby.
> They had no hope with him,
> They had to dope him
> In a land called Tennessee ...

The crowd responded to Barney's deep emotion.

The meals were excellent. Florrie said the fact that someone else was cooking them added to her relish. Florrie needed tutoring in table manners in such company: she said there were more knives and forks and spoons than were needed. Barney, an experienced traveller and diner-out, was about to advise her on her choice of cutlery.

A man had forgotten how to appreciate ol' Florrie, Barney

thought more than once, but getting her away alone like this he remembered all she meant to him. She had always wanted children; he hadn't – well, maybe it wasn't too late . . . She's going to be annoyed if ever she finds out that this trip is being paid for by West. Wonder she didn't wake up when I told her THE HAWKLET were paying for it: they can't even pay a man's fare down to the Stadium on Saturday nights. Let her enjoy the trip; worry about other matters after.

They could not remember when last they had been so happy. They were like a honeymoon couple; going to bed was like a new, vital experience. Barney reckoned that they were old enough to have better sense, what with him over fifty and Florrie older than she cared to admit, but their joy was unbounded until the ship neared its destination. Then Florrie noticed that Barney became restless and silent.

"Florrie."

"Yes, Barney."

"If anything should happen to me in Perth, how would you get on?"

"Nothing's going to happen to you."

"Oh, I don't think so either, but just supposing."

"Well, just supposing. I'd marry again the next week: a man with plenty of money. A millionaire, maybe."

"Is that insurance policy of mine lapsed, Florrie?"

"Yes, I'd collect nothing on that."

"All I'll leave you is a bundle of bills."

She pressed his hand in the darkness. "Nothing's going to happen to you, Barney. You'll live to be a hundred and one, fair dinkum. But I do wish I knew what this trip is all about."

He grasped her hand urgently. "I've got a feeling something's going to go wrong on this trip. I'm over here for Jack West. Oh, I know I shouldn't have deceived you. I should never have gone back to West. But it's the boxing. He says if I do this job, he'll give me the old job back."

"You know what I think, Barney. Why did you lie to me?" Florrie was both disappointed and angry, but sensing Barney's distress, she decided to postpone argument.

"He said I should carry a gun, as if he expected shooting."

Florrie managed to say with a display of flippancy: "Surely this is not Barney Robinson getting the wind up?"

344

"I have got the wind up, all of a sudden. I've got a feeling something is going to happen. Tell you what, we'll go back to Melbourne on the next train, and I'll tell West I've changed my mind."

"I think it would be better, Barney. After all, that West has done, I think we should have nothing more to do with him."

As the ship came alongside the wharf, they joined the other passengers waiting to disembark. They collected their scanty luggage and walked down the gang plank, arm in arm. They clung tightly to each other. Barney elegantly dressed in striped trousers, long black coat and boxer-hat; Florrie attractive in her best dress and coat and a hat big with feathers and imitation fruit.

When they got clear of the noisy, bustling crowd of passengers and welcoming parties, Barney said: "We'll get a taxi."

As they walked towards the cab stand, Florrie saw a man emerge from the shadows and move towards them. He approached so quickly she had no time to speak. He came to within five paces of Barney, then Florrie heard a revolver shot split the night, then another, and yet another. She felt Barney shudder and sag, then sink to the ground, and she saw blood streaming from his mouth.

Nearby, a woman screamed and a taxi driver exclaimed: "Jesus Christ, someones's shot!"

The man who fired the shots ran into the night, followed by another. Florrie knelt beside Barney, speaking to him in a hysterical whisper: "Oh, Barney! Barney! What have they done to you?"

His face showed chalky white in the night. His shirt was soaked with blood. He spoke to her urgently, his voice a gurgling sob. "Florrie. The money! The money! I'm done up bad. The money! West's money. Take it!"

A crowd began to gather. No one seemed to know what to do. They stood around looking at the couple on the ground, as though hypnotised.

"You'll be all right, Barney darling," she whispered leaning over him, her face and clothes stained with his blood. Then she looked up at the crowd and screamed: "Don't stand round gaping! Get a doctor! Get a doctor!"

Barney seemed to sink into unconsciousness, but he rallied and spoke again: "I'm done for. The money, Florrie! Get the money and go away! Don't go back near West. Go away. Sorry, Florrie. I love yer, Florrie, ol' girl.''

With a tremendous effort, Barney raised himself on one elbow, and felt in his inside pocket, but he slumped back again saying: "The money, Florrie. In me inside pocket. Five thousand quid. Take it and go away. Don't go back near West.'' His head slumped sideways. Florrie felt his pulse and guessed that her husband was dead. Tears streamed down her face. She kept repeating: "Oh, Barney, my darling. Darling ol' Barney.''

Without thinking what she was doing, she opened Barney's coat with blood-stained hands, while the crowd milled around, jostling and open-mouthed. She felt the wallet. It was soaked in blood and was embedded with its contents in Barney's flesh in the region of the heart. She left it there.

Sobbing, she took off her blood-stained coat and folded it under Barney's head as a pompous man carrying a small, black bag pushed his way through the crowd and knelt at Barney's side.

"This man is dead,'' he pronounced.

Florrie stood as if petrified, looking at Barney's ashen, blood bespattered face. Then, as though making a sudden decision, she pushed through the crowd and melted into the night. A stubborn resolve to achieve something Barney had not achieved thumped through her brain, ringing out the words: "Don't go back near West!''

Three months had passed since Barney Robinson had been murdered, and his photo had joined the footballers and racehorses on the wall of John West's office. News of the crime reached John West through the brief announcement in the Melbourne press: a passenger off such and such a boat, named Jackson, had been murdered on the wharf and detectives were puzzled by certain aspects of the crime. They believed that the dead man was travelling under an assumed name. His woman companion – allegedly his wife – had disappeared.

No sense of guilt or remorse came to John West. His reactions were complex, but unemotional. Should he send Snoopy Tanner to Perth to avenge Barney or would it be wiser to concentrate on having the murder hushed up? Should he send someone else to Perth to negotiate the defeat of the Bill? After the inevitable discussion with Frank Lammence, he reached a quick decision. This was a time to retreat a little; John West had learned that he must accept defeat in an occasional skirmish in order to win his battle for power.

Contact with leading Melbourne detectives through Frank Lammence led to the Melbourne police being most unhelpful to the Perth detectives. The murderers were not apprehended.

John West allowed the course of events in Perth to proceed without his influence. The Bill was passed and he sold one of his racecourses and leased the other on most favourable terms.

He had expected Florrie to call to give further details and, perhaps, return his £5,000. He didn't trust women, and he knew Florrie's deep attachment for Barney. She had to be located and silenced. As she did not call, he sent Lammence to her home. Lammence was told that Mr. and Mrs. Robinson had gone to some unknown place for a holiday.

"No doubt she's taken my five thousand quid – just what I'd expect. Anyway, it'll keep her from talking," John West said to Lammence.

When anyone asked after Barney, John West would turn to the photo and say: "You wouldn't think old Barney had a bad heart, would you? Died suddenly in South Australia. Fine fella, Barney; a real wit and a great personality."

Having to modify his plans in Perth rankled a little, but there were many matters to take up his attention; matters of business and politics. The Federal elections had resulted in a defeat for Labor, but to John West it represented a great victory, for the campaign had increased his influence in the Labor Party. John West bought Real a seat in New South Wales and Real won it easily.

During the campaign, the press missed no opportunity to denounce Labor for having truck with the notorious Sinn Fein agitator, Archbishop Malone. The official organ of the Protestant Federation called on electors to vote for Protestantism and Loyalty lest the Jesuits gain control of the country. The sectarian issue reared up everywhere and Labor lost, largely as a result of it.

John West watched the controversy in the Labor Party with interest. Maurice Blackwell wrote in the LABOR CALL that the lesson Labor must learn from the defeat is that it must adopt religious neutrality as a principle. Archbishop Malone was enraged. He hit back heatedly at a public function, denouncing Blackwell and the section of Labor which did not appreciate the great benefit Catholic support brought the Party. He threatened to withdraw Catholic support unless grants for Catholic schools became part of Labor's policy.

John West had played his cards cleverly. The Catholic Federation was pouring members into the Labor Party branches. By co-operating with the Archbishop, he was winning their support. Now the task would be to mould his own pre-war machine and this new machine into one body.

He was bringing his theories into line with his plans and needs. This had become typical of his thought processes: he did it unconsciously. He would begin a campaign, or a venture, for purely selfish motives, then rationalise his opinions to justify his actions.

Before long, he had convinced himself and nearly everybody else, that he was a thoroughgoing Sinn Feiner, that more than anything else he wanted independence for Ireland and education grants for Roman Catholic schools. He was often heard whistling *The Wearing of the Green* through unpractised lips. He remembered his mother saying once that she had descended from the Irish Kings, and that her family had a crest of arms to prove it. He had treated the matter as a joke then, but now he took it as gospel truth. He began telling certain people that his ancestors were Irish kings, and that his family crest bore an arm with scimitar and a lion rampant, above which was inscribed the family motto, "West to Victory."

When the Archbishop had requested financial aid to defray the large expenses in organising the Saint Patrick's Day Procession scheduled for late in March, 1920, John West signed a substantial cheque. He would not stop at financial assistance, he had told His Grace; he would help organise the procession.

Meanwhile, there was something of a revolt in the sporting world against proprietary control. In case the Victorian Government should introduce a similar Bill to that passed in Western Australia, John West decided to place his racing clubs beyond its reach.

He called again at Levy's emporium.

Confronting Levy Junior across the table, John West was struck with the fact that he was growing more like his dead father every day. He seemed to be shrinking up. He looked more like a greedy, predatory bird than a man.

John West was anti-Semitic: he liked to believe that Levy was typical of the Jewish people.

John West explained the purpose of his visit. The move in Western Australia against proprietary racing clubs was likely to spread to other States and must be met in advance.

"Well, Mr. West, what do you propose to do?"

"I propose to form a non-proprietary club to control trotting and pony-racing in Victoria, and, if possible, to get permission to conduct galloping meetings."

"What? Lose all the profits?"

"Don't be silly," John West replied. "We'll form an association that will appear to be non-proprietary, and ask the Government to appoint a president. You and I will lease the courses to this body at a rate that will mean we still get all the profits. I am consulting you because you must appoint nominees as members of the club. Of course, seeing that I hold the biggest shares in the properties and do all the work, I will have the largest number of nominees."

"Very clever. Very clever. But I think you and I are a bit suspect, Mr. West."

"But we won't figure in the Association. The Government will nominate as President, Bennett, an experienced trotting and racing man, and a member of the Upper House."

"And a friend of yours."

"... and a friend of mine, because he knows that I have cleaned-up the sport of pony-racing and revived trotting."

"All right, Mr. West. I'll nominate one or two of the officials who worked for me in the old days, and some of my shop managers, and people like that. You go ahead. Go ahead. Who's going to convene this, er – non-proprietary Association?"

"Godfrey Dwyer. Formerly Chief Recruiting Officer of Victoria, and now President of the Returned Soldiers' Association."

"He will make it very respectable, Mr. West." Levy sat round-shouldered, leaning over the table with his hands clasped in front of him. "I suppose you still own a lot of horses under someone else's name and run half the book-makers, and print the race-books and run the pie-stalls and the drink-bars, and that kind of thing. Eh, Mr. West?"

"Naturally."

Levy studied John West. No doubt about these Catholics, these Irishmen; you can't trust 'em, he thought. He was forced to admit that pony-racing and trotting had prospered under John West's control, but he had heard stories of corruption in the sports – stories he liked to believe. One owner had told him that he was convinced that the ponies were "measured at Mass" so often did a Catholic owner get a "fourteen-two" horse in a "fourteen-one" race. He had heard tales of horses being rung-in, of horses being deadened by the book-makers.

Levy was more than mildly anti-Catholic: he was willing to believe such stories as proof of the inherent dishonesty of all Catholics, especially Irish Catholics.

These two men despised each other, yet their search for wealth and power bound them together.

Presently Levy said: "I often wonder, Mr. West, why you bother to run race meetings at all. Wouldn't it be much simpler if you just sent your gang out knocking people on the head and stealing their money?"

John West was angry, but refused to be ruffled. "You should talk! You've been robbing the public all your life. I've cleaned up the sports since I took over from you. Everyone says they are cleaner. The stakes are higher, the crowds are larger, and horse-breeding has gone ahead."

"From what I hear there is a lot more cleaning up to be done, Mr. West."

"I know there are still a few things going on. But Dwyer is just the man to clean them up. I'm going to insist that he puts a man on full-time checking the bona-fides of horses entered, and checking their clearances from interstate. You leave the running of these courses to me, Mr. Levy, and stick to your furniture business."

Next afternoon Godfrey Dwyer was surprised to receive a phone call from Frank Lammence. "Mr. John West has a proposition that will interest you. Could you call at two o'clock?"

Dwyer was a tall, erect man, brisk in his movements. Though discharged from the Army and placed on the officers' reserve, he wore his civilian clothes stiffly like a soldier, and, when walking, affected the gait of a soldier on the march. He put on his hat carefully, and, tucking his walking stick under his arm as though it was an officer's cane, told his secretary he would not be back that day.

"Very well, Captain Dwyer," the girl said.

He smirked with satisfaction at the use of the military title. The Army had been the making of him. As a youth before the war broke out, he lived in a country town where he was employed by an auctioneer. He had been fed up with the routine of his poorly-paid duties – with sweeping out, with posting mail, with attending sales and holding up poultry or chasing a cow round the ring while his employer called: "What am I offered?"

He hailed the outbreak of war as if it were the arrival of the second Messiah; at last he could get away from the drudgery, the fowls and the cows. He pleaded with his parents and, gaining their reluctant consent, was the first recruit from his home town for the Australian Imperial Forces. Soon whisked away to Gallipoli, he was wounded with shrapnel in the legs as soon as he hit the bloody beach. While recuperating in hospital, he was promoted to the rank of Lieutenant, and on his return to Australia he was made Captain, and appointed Chief Recruiting Officer for Victoria. What better man for the job than one of the first wounded veterans from Gallipoli?

He had met John West in 1915: spoke from the same platform with him. He wasn't impressed with West: not a true soldier, never saw a shot fired. But this was different. Godfrey Dwyer was not well pleased with his financial status. His position as President of the Returned Soldiers' Association gave him prestige, but not sufficient money. If West had a good position to offer, he would accept.

He found West friendly, but the silent, unintroduced Frank Lammence disconcerted him a little. The duties outlined by John West appealed to him. He would be able to introduce military efficiency as secretary of the proposed non-proprietary Racing and Trotting Club. It seemed that he was to negotiate with the Government regarding the formation of the new Club. It seemed there were certain malpractices going on which he was to eradicate. He was to be more inclined to fine an offender than to disqualify him – fines being an excellent method of swelling the club's profits. Seven hundred pounds a year salary; and he could carry on his present job as well; in fact, John West would insist that he did so.

"I'm glad you will accept, Mr. Dwyer," John said finally. "We will admit ex-servicemen free to all courses, and advertise that we will employ only former soldiers as gatekeepers, barmen and the like. We must do all we can for the soldiers who saved the country."

Yes, Godfrey Dwyer thought, and do our best especially for John West. As he took his leave, Dwyer made a resolution that he would carry out this little man's every wish, expressed or unexpressed. He would serve West as he had served the King, efficiently and without question.

"Er, yes, Dr. Jenner. It's about this adverse report of yours on the application of Rand for a subsidy of £10,000 to develop the Lady Joan and Gilowell Mines," Ted Thurgood said. "Though I've been Premier for some weeks now, I've only just found time to consider it."

Dressed in a white suit and nursing his hat, Dr. Jenner sat opposite Thurgood in the Premier's office of Queensland Parliament House.

Thurgood's red hair was cut short and neatly combed back, his face smooth-shaven, his grey suit impeccable.

A different figure to the legendary Red Ted Thurgood of the North, Jenner mused. "Red Ted can raise a champagne laugh on beer or wine," an old gouger had informed Jenner on one occasion; but now, close inspection revealed little humour in the hard, close-set eyes, and none at all around the thick-lipped, sensual, cruel mouth.

Jenner replied quietly: "Premier Real considered it before he resigned. I rather thought he accepted it."

"A new broom sweeps clean, you know, Doctor," Thurgood replied suavely, picking up the thick typed report from the polished top of the table. "The party line remains much the same, of course. You see, Real told me he hadn't had time to fully consider this report."

"When I discussed it with him, he seemed quite familiar with its contents, and agreeing with its proposals."

"Well, Doctor, I want to congratulate you on the way the report is set out, and on the correct assessment of the great value of the Chirraboo field. I know that field very well, Doctor. I lived there for many years, and it is in my electorate."

Jenner was puzzled. Thurgood was interested in the two mines. He expected an attempt to cajole or bully him into withdrawing the report.

"Thank you," Dr. Jenner said without pride or enthusiasm. "I am aware that you know all about Chirraboo field, Mr. Thurgood."

Thurgood looked up sharply as though trying to gauge what lay behind Jenner's remark. "Frankly, Doctor," he said, "I am in favour of granting Rand the full subsidy asked for."

"I have no doubt you are, but I am not. Convinced I am that there is no justification for the subsidy. There is nothing to show for the £3,000 subsidy Rand has already received, to say nothing of the fact that he got the mines for nothing, plus £8,000 worth of ore which was in the bins at the time. The Lady Joan and Gilowell Mines are essential to the Government smelters and should be taken over by the State for the money owing by Rand. I am convinced, yes! But all these things are in my reports."

"I appreciate your sincerity, Dr. Jenner. But the Government may have over-reached itself by becoming involved in too many State-owned enterprises."

"But it is the aim of the party to which you and I both belong to end capitalist exploitation, yes?"

"Yes, of course, but we must crawl before we can walk. You are a very important man to this Government, Doctor. We are very satisfied with your work. I'm going to recommend higher status and a higher salary for you. I will arrange for you to win a safe Labor seat. We need men like you here, but I would like you to withdraw this report."

Dr. Jenner flinched as if he had been struck a blow. This attempt at bribery was almost as clumsy as Rand's at Chirraboo a year before. "Is higher status and salary all you offer? Why, George Rand was more generous, yes. He offered me a fourth share in your little syndicate if I submitted a favourable report."

Thurgood blanched. "What do you mean my little syndicate? Rand holds the lease to those mines. I have nothing to do with them."

Jenner arose. "Further talk here is no good," he said, smoothing his hat brim. "I am emphatically opposed to the subsidy being granted. I have given my reasons."

Thurgood dropped his mask. He stood and confronted Jenner.

"I am Premier of this State, and what I say goes," he shouted. "And I say that Rand is to get that subsidy. I order you to withdraw this report."

"Do not try to be bullying me. My report stands."

Thurgood was livid. "You will withdraw this report or get out of the Mines Department!"

"Nothing will make me withdraw my report. I have no reason to reconsider my recommendations, which are in line with Labor policy."

"What do you know about politics? I will decide Labor policy." Thurgood tapped his deep chest. "Me, Ted Thurgood."

"You may, but you will not grant that subsidy."

"Why, surely you don't think this rambling document will stop me?"

"No, but the Treasurer will not approve of the subsidy!"

"Oh, so now you are telling me what the Treasurer will do!"

"Yes. He has informed me that the subsidy will never be granted while he's Treasurer ..."

'So you go behind my back to disaffect members of my cabinet."

"I discussed this matter with the Treasurer before you were Premier. Friends we are, and members of the same Party. Real referred my report to him. There was nothing irregular about our discussion."

Thurgood walked around the desk. Mr. Jenner thought for a moment he was going to assault him, but he merely opened the door. "Listen, Jenner," he said in low, menacing tones, "I say that subsidy will be granted. Unless you withdraw this report, you'll be out of a job. Now get out!"

Jenner put on his hat and walked towards the door where Thurgood confronted him. "And I'd advise you not to go around slandering me. I have nothing to do with the mines, do you hear?"

The Doctor brushed past him. "I am not a gossiper, but when sure of my facts I will talk at the right time and place."

After he had gone, Ted Thurgood paced the room for some minutes punching the palm of his hand, then walked to the inter-office telephone.

"Give me Mr. MacCorkell, please! That you, Bill? Listen, I've just had Jenner in here. He won't co-operate ... and listen,

Rand's been wagging his long tongue, as usual. You better come over to my office."

John West kept his promise to help organise the procession. Time and money were no object. Archbishop Malone soon learned that he had a genius for organisation and an appetite for intrigue.

One morning, the Archbishop was walking down the hill towards Jackson Street, thinking of the coming procession. As Saint Patrick's Day drew nearer, he was being subjected to opposition as bitter as any he had suffered during the war. The Protestant Federation was using the Press and pulpit to scream "Jesuit Conspiracy" and to demand that "The Monster from Maynooth" be deported or imprisoned, and the procession banned as disloyal.

Malone met them with logic and withering scorn. He developed a tremendous mass movement in the face of their hysteria and disclaimers from influential Catholics. He missed no opportunity to expound the Irish cause, and carried the Church and its press behind him. Under his influence, the Church still spoke with tolerance of the Russian Revolution. Catholic papers tentatively defended the Bolsheviks and hinted that the Vatican might soon be able to re-establish the Church in Russia where it had been savagely suppressed by the Czar on behalf of the Greek Orthodox breakaway.

"Good morning, Your Grace," John West's voice interrupted Malone's thoughts.

"Good morning, Mr. West. Sure and it's a pleasure to be alive on such a fine morning."

They walked across the bridge.

"I have an idea that will stop the Lord Mayor and the police from interfering with the procession," John West said, "Supposing we invite every Victoria Cross winner in Australia to lead the procession, as your guard of honour, mounted on white chargers."

"And how in the name of God and his Holy Mother can that be arranged?"

"Easy. I'll write to them all and offer the pay their expenses and give them fifty pounds each as well. Most of them are short of money."

"If it could be arranged, permission for the procession could not be withheld. Sure and it's a broth of an idea. The poltroons from the Protestant Federation and the Freemasons would have to cease their talk about disloyalty then, and drop their demand that the procession be banned."

"Yes, Your Grace, and even if they ban the march, we could defy them. The police wouldn't dare to interfere. The crowd would be on the side of the V.C.'s."

"It's wanting no brawl in the street that we are, but if the V.C.'s or some of them, agree to march, then the procession will be above board."

"I'll write to every V.C. in Australia. As you know, Dwyer, the President of the Returned Soldiers' Association, works for me. I'll get a list of names from him. I'll send the letters today and ask them to reply by return mail. Then we'll approach the Lord Mayor again."

They walked past what had once been Cummin's Tea Shop. It was now an undertaker's shop. The Jesuits had seen to it that the Archbishop was not unaware of John West's past. They were not happy about the open friendship that was developing between the pair.

"It's somewhere here that you used to run the – what do you call it – tote shop, isn't it?"

John West wondered how much the Archbishop knew about him. "Er . . . Yes. Somewhere here."

The Archbishop chuckled slyly. "Sure and it's a pity it's not still running; you could get all the V.C.'s to guard it."

John West looked up sharply, but did not answer.

The response from the Victoria Cross winners was more than satisfactory: twelve of them would ride on St. Patrick's Day.

John West then called a meeting of Catholic ex-soldiers, and invited non-Catholics to attend it. Archbishop Malone spoke at the meeting, saying that he was delighted that Australia's fighting men were going to give their support to the Irish cause. John West requested all present to march in the procession, and to get their friends to do the same. This would answer those who said that Catholics were disloyal. He was proud to be a Catholic and proud that he had descended from a race of Irish Kings. The announcement that Mr. West had royal blood flowing through his veins brought loud cheers. The meeting ended on a high note of enthusiasm.

The Lord Mayor of Melbourne and his Councillors were driven on to the devensive, and finally had to permit the procession.

Daniel Malone was well pleased.

John West surpassed all other Catholics in his admiration of Malone, "the great Irish patriot and great Australian." Lacking intellectual achievement himself, John West admired it in others. He had bestowed gifts of shares on one of his medical advisers, a surgeon son of the late Sergeant Devlin. Secretly, he respected Frank Ashton most of all his political acquaintances. "I put Ashton into politics," he would say proudly. When old David Garside died before the war, he was deeply moved. To him, Garside was not a crooked lawyer, but a clever man, a great orator, a man who was "well read." But no one he had ever met impressed John West so much as Archbishop Malone. This intellectual Irishman with his sly humour, courage, academic and theological attainments he endowed with almost supernatural qualities.

When Malone informed him that he had received a directive to proceed to Rome after the Saint Patrick's Day procession, John West determined to offer the Archbishop some token of his undying esteem. His thoughts turned naturally to money. He would start a fund and make the Archbishop a large cash present at the Exhibition Grounds at the rally after the procession.

When the idea first struck him, Sugar Renfrey happened to call one night to discuss tactics in the Labor Party in view of the approaching Victorian elections. Sugar still helped look after John West's interests in the Labor Party in Carringbush and elsewhere. Though unpopular with most people, he wielded great power because his was the delegated power of J.W. In recent years John West had leaned more on Bob Scott and others than on Sugar; Sugar lacked finesse.

Renfrey hadn't changed much except to squint more and to grow fatter. He looked like a flashily-dressed rag doll. Sugar's two sons had grown past school age, but his wife Agatha had never grown up: she had become known in their street as "First with the latest Aggie," because, it was said, she was one of the most gossipy, scandal-mongering women that ever God put breath in.

"I'm going to begin a fund to give Archbishop Malone a send-off present," John West told Sugar. "I'll call a special meeting, and invite several wealthy Catholics. I'll start the fund off with five thousand, and I want you to give a thousand, if you've got it."

"Break it down, Jack. I'll come to the meetin'. Me and Arty are doin' a bit for 'em out at the local church, but I ain't got no thousand quid. Not even a thousand shillings."

"What do you do with all your money? Gamble it on the horses, I suppose. You can't lay 'em and back 'em, Sugar – you ought to know that. All right, then, I'll give you a present of a thousand, and you donate it. Be good for our prestige in the Labor Party."

Daniel Malone sat in the beautifully furnished study of his mansion. He was puzzling over the directive from Rome. What could it mean? Were his actions contrary to Vatican policy? That Jesuit who went to Rome; what did he tell the Pope and the College of Cardinals?

Anyway, he could not retreat now – at least, not until he had been to Rome.

He turned his attention to a meeting which John West had presided over on the previous evening. After a fiery and adulating speech, Mr. West had donated a cheque for £5,000 to start a subscription of £50,000 to be presented to the Archbishop of Melbourne before his departure. £20,000 was collected in the hall.

Daniel Malone sat down, took a pen from the ornate silver inkstand, and began writing a letter to John West, refusing the gift. He would mail a copy to the Catholic Press, just to be sure that his whole flock knew he had not accepted.

He finished the letter and read it over:

My dear Mr. West,

I wish to convey to you, and through you to those associated wity you at last night's meeting, the expression of my deep and lasting gratitude. Your generosity humbles me and makes me wish that I had indeed been able to render you some notable service. What you did at that meeting and what you propose to do are the outcome of the unrivalled generosity of my friends rather than

*the measure of any claim I have upon them. For I have been
repaid a hundredfold for anything I have done or have tried to
do as an Archbishop or as a citizen.*

*At all events I have made it a rule for myself not to accept any
such personal gift as you propose to offer. I am more grateful
than words can tell, but at the risk of seeming ungracious and
unresponsive, I must ask this added favour of being allowed to
have my own way in a matter on which my mind is quite made
up.*

I trust that you accept and convey my grateful thanks.

> *Believe me, my dear Mr. West,*
> *Sincerely yours,*
>
> *Daniel Malone.*

That should clear the matter up. West can't be as bad as the
Jesuits say. Take his money, but don't associate with him in
public, to be sure; they'd have their own Archbishop do a fine
layman an injustice. Well, with the help of God and his Holy
Mother, I'll reverse the process for once: I'll associate with him
in public, and not take his money.

If what was said about West was true, then he belied his own
history. The poltroons of the Protestant Federation seem to think
that he's all but a murderer, but how often they tell lies! They
and their articles reprinted from the LONE WOLF! Couldn't a man
repent his ways? I wish he'd come to Mass and the Sacraments
sometimes; then I could answer the Jesuits. I wouldn't be putting
it past them to report West to the Holy Father.

A young Priest tiptoed into the room. "Mr. John West would
like to see you, Your Grace."

"Speak of the devil, it's just writin' him a letter that I am.
Send him in."

John West came in briskly.

"Sit down, Mr. West."

"I've come to tell you, Your Grace, that I've arranged to have
a film, a real moving film, made of the procession."

"That will be fine, Mr. West. We're sure doing things in
style."

"Yes. And I've arranged also to obtain an imported film on
the Irish rebellion itself. It's called Ireland Will Be Free – a real
movie. Great propaganda for the old country!"

359

'Fine, Mr. West. Strange you should call. I had just finished penning you a letter. It's in regard to your kind gesture of last evening."

John West read the letter. "But surely, Your Grace . . ."

"I'm sorry, Mr. West. The letter states my attitude. I am profoundly grateful, but . . . Perhaps you could give the money to the Church . . ."

"Does the Church own this building?" John West interrupted, gazing around the quietly luxurious room.

"No, we pay rent for it. Why?"

"Supposing I used the money to buy this building? What would it be worth?"

"More than a gold mine, if one can judge by the rent."

"Probably about twenty thousand. I'll hand back the cheques that Mr. Renfrey and others have given, and I'll buy this building for you. Allow me to do so. Your Grace, as a small gesture of my esteem."

"I would accept that, Mr. West. And God Bless you. However, I will still send a copy of that letter to our Press, Mr. West, if you don't mind."

One evening in the week before the St. Patrick's Day procession, Nellie West was tucking her baby into the high-sided cot beside her bed. She kissed the child and said softly: "You must go bye-byes now, Xavier. Mummy is going downstairs to eat tonight."

"Daddy kiss nighty-night," the child lisped. Mrs. Moran often said tactfully that the child was "the image of its mother," but Xavier bore traces of the physical charm of his father, Bill Evans.

"You're always asleep before your Daddy comes home," Nellie lied. "But perhaps pretty soon you will be able to stay awake a little later, if you're a good little boy." The child's belief that John West was its father embarrassed Nellie at first, but now she was resigned to living the lie, and determined that the child would never know otherwise.

Nellie and Xavier were virtual prisoners. The child never left the house, Nellie only to attend Mass on Sundays. For months now, Mrs. Moran had been requesting that Nellie come downstairs for the evening meal, at least. This afternoon the old woman had informed her daughter that John West was of the same mind.

Nellie had decided to face the ordeal. Dressed in white, she looked her attractive best, but she carried a sad, almost sullen expression. She sat in front of the mirror of her dressing-table and inspected her face and hair.

At last, she thought, the seige has ended. The whole household is now to pretend that all is well. She thought of months of anguish and humiliation when Bill's baby was growing in her. Time could never heal the scars which those first months left on her mind and heart. The children came bewildered to her room asking questions: "You're sick, Mummy?" "When will you be better, Mummy?" "Our Daddy must be sick, too; he never speaks to us." "Daddy never seems to come in here to see you."

John West spoke to no one in the house. She rarely saw him, but could sense when he entered or left. If they met in a corridor or on the stairs, neither would speak, but he would gaze at her with hatred and recrimination. What would she have done if Mama had not come? Amid unrestrained weeping she had told her mother everything, and Mother understood. Mama said that she owed it to the children to forget Bill Evans, and somehow make it up with John.

She would never forget the night the child was born – never in a hundred years. By then, Bill Evans was but a bitter-sweet memory, yet his child was coming to remind her of him for the rest of her days. The agony of the downward dragging of the child was submerged in the turmoil of her thoughts while her mother stood by assisting, coaxing, advising. In the next room, she could hear the measured tread of John's feet as he paced the room, with what thoughts she could but guess. Did he share the desperate hope that came to her near the end of the pains – that the child would be born dead?

The birth of the child brought a new longing for Bill Evans, and a realisation of what her husband was suffering, but she mastered her feelings as the weeks passed. What had either of them brought her? Nellie asked herself. Nothing but anguish and care and a broken heart. John did not come to see her, but her mother reported a worsening in his humour and his demeanour.

She turned her attention to the baby. Xavier reminded her cruelly of Bill, and the child's winsome ways captured her heart. The other children came to her before and after school, and before going to bed. Interested in the new baby and loving their mother, but wondering, asking questions with their eyes.

And then the passage of nearly two years, with time measured only by the growth of the child, her weekly visits to Mass, the rising and setting of the sun, and the sprouting and falling of the leaves on the branch of the tall tree whose twigs tapped and scraped on her window. The child was christened when six months old. While at the Church, Nellie dragged herself to the confessional box. The priest gave the same advice as her mother: she must expiate her sins by resuming her rôle as wife and mother.

As Nellie arose from her chair in front of the dressing-table and walked to the door, she noticed that she was trembling and her knees were threatening to cave under her. She imagined she felt a sharp pain at the base of her spine; ever since that day she had suffered these twinges; after the baby was born she had complained of them so persistently that her mother had called a doctor. The spine had been bruised but should give no further trouble, the doctor had said, but Nellie still complained. Only imagination, Mrs. Moran had decided; but it was more than that: Nellie West's mind had seized upon that injury as a symbol of her recriminations against her husband.

With a tremendous effort she braced herself, opened the door and walked towards the top of the stairs.

As she slowly descended the wide carpeted stairway, those in the dining-room were tense with a rigid expectancy. The meal had not begun, but all were seated.

John West sat at the head of the table, his hands resting on its edge, his face an impassive mask, his eyes staring straight in front. Mrs. Moran sat on his left at the side of the table facing the door, her white hair tied in a bun behind her head, a woman growing old with dignity. Beside her sat the eldest child, Marjorie, approaching her seventeenth birthday – a short, stockily built girl very much like her father, but studious and musically talented – sitting with her eyes glued on the door awaiting this desired yet dreaded moment, guessing a good deal of what lay behind the tension. At the other side of the table sat the three younger children. Mary, now nearly fifteen, and flowering into womanhood – a red-haired beauty, tall and slim but well developed; clever, sympathetic and admired already for her striking beauty, Mary was the apple of her father's eye. He spoke of her as would a connoisseur of a beautiful painting, but her sensitive nature revolted against his cold, unbending personality. Next to

Mary sat the two boys, John, eleven years, and Joseph, eight. Joseph, like his Uncle Joe, after whom he had been named, was quiet, easy-going, negative. John, by nature and intellect, resembled his sister Mary. He was like his father physically but in no other way.

At the end of the table stood a vacant chair – Nellie's chair.

She entered the room, walking steadily, her head held high. The children stared transfixed by her haughty beauty and her desperate efforts at composure.

John West did not look up, did not move. Confusing emotions flooded over him: self-pity, humiliation, and, strongest of all, hatred and impotent rage. Nellie had escaped. She had won after all. She retained her place as his wife and the mother of his children, and was on her way to winning back her self-respect. She had defied and betrayed him; he had determined she would not escape the consequences, yet it seemed that she would. And he had made a rule never to admit he was wrong, to do so was a sign of weakness. Allowing Nellie to come downstairs was tantamount to admitting he was wrong . . .

When Nellie sat down, facing him over the long table, the children seemed to relax.

Mary said: "Mummy, it's good that you have come back! It is good, Mummy!" Tears flooded her eyes and trickled down her cheeks.

The other children hung their heads. Nellie gripped the table and bit her lip, determined not to break down.

"This is no time for tears," Mrs. Moran said. "Your mother has regained her health and can come downstairs again. We should all be very happy. Your mother is well again."

John West looked searchingly at his mother-in-law. She is clever, he thought, she has worked and waited for this moment for two years. She always knew that I would one day find it convenient to agree. He found himself granting her involuntary admiration.

Nellie knew she should express some appropriate sentiment, but she could think only of her spine. Her mind seemed to fix on it, and again she imagined the twinge of pain.

She looked defiantly at her husband and said: "My spine still troubles me. Sometimes the pains are terrible. I am sure it shall cripple me one day."

John West raised his eyes and studied her searchingly. He had heard that they had summoned the doctor because her spine was sore, but that was a long time ago. Why had she said that?

An oppressive silence crowded into the room, and all were relieved when the maid entered and served soup to the others and a glass of fruit juice to John West. The maid had been hired that day together with a cook, as part of John West's agreement with Mrs. Moran.

The meal proceeded slowly and quietly. Only necessary words were spoken, except by Mrs. Moran, who did her best to make conversation. No word passed between John and Nellie West.

The meal over, John West left the table first. "I would like to see you in the music-room in a few minutes, if you don't mind, Nellie?" he said stiffly, and walked out and upstairs to the bathroom, to wash his hands and take his medicine.

Five minutes later Nellie entered the music-room and sat under a photo of Chopin, near the piano.

John West entered the room and stood staring fixedly at her. "I hope you realise that it was I who suggested that you should be allowed to come downstairs for your meals," he said aggressively.

"I thought Mother arranged it," she said softly, almost indifferently.

"Well, she didn't! Ever since . . . that – that business, I have been determined that you would be punished and then forced to carry out your obligations to your children."

She remained silent, her hands resting on her lap.

"Well, what have you got to say?"

"I don't need to be forced to love my children. Any trouble in this house has been of your making."

"My making? I suppose it's my fault that you had that child upstairs, whose father was my bricklayer. Why, if it weren't for the children, my children, I would have sent it to a home for waifs and strays long ago. And don't be so sure that I won't yet!"

After a pause, John West continued, in more placatory tones: "It's up to you now to shoulder your responsibilities. I want you to attend a reception to the V.C. heroes at the Archbishop's residence next week and another one here on the night of the procession. Many important people will be in attendance. You are my wife; they will expect you to be there."

"All right," she said. "I will do whatever you say. But remember, John, I will never love you again – never."

"From your behaviour, it would seem that you never have loved me."

She arose and walked towards the door. "I must go and lie down," she said. "My spine is troubling me. It has troubled me ever since that day, that day when you pushed me. I'm sure it shall cripple me eventually."

Near the door she turned and fixed her eyes upon him. She did not speak. He flinched from her recriminating gaze. From that moment he knew that as long as she lived she would persistently hate him.

John West welcomed the Victoria Cross winners at a banquet in one of his city hotels. He sat at the head of the table.

Toasts were drunk to Mother Ireland, to Archbishop Malone, to the success of the procession. John West did not like intoxicants – they upset his stomach – but so important was the occasion that he drank the toasts in wine. Proposing the toast to the Victoria Cross winners, he said that the people of Australia and the Irish race would be eternally indebted to them for coming such long distances to attend the celebrations. It was owing to the great sacrifice of the soldiers that Australia was a free country!

It was an extraordinary thing that so many of the V.C. men were still privates. Every one of them was entitled to a colonelcy. They had gone to the war to fight for the protection of Belgium. Now they had come to Melbourne to show sympathy with another small nation which was not yet free. In this last statement, John West was echoing a remark often made in recent weeks by Archbishop Malone.

John West concluded with an advertisement for his racecourses by announcing that returned soldiers were admitted free and that only returned soldiers were chosen to fill staff vacancies.

After the prolonged applause had ceased, other speakers supported the toast, the last of these being Councillor Robert Renfrey, who arose to his feet rather unsteadily.

Mr. Renfrey's manner of speaking was rather crude and out of keeping with the occasion. He dropped his g's and h's. His speech was thick and, at times, unintelligible, due to over indulgence in whisky earlier in the day, and to the cigar in the corner of his mouth. He listeners gathered that he believed the V.C.'s to be "bloody heroes, but that there was one man who deserved the V.C. yet didn't get it – Jack West!"

Councillor Renfrey concluded by stating that "the Government should be kicked to death for not payin' all V.C.'s a tenner a bloody week pension." If he were Prime Minister, he stated magnanimously, they would "git that and a bloody sight more with it." He spat the frayed end of his cigar on to the floor and flopped back into his chair.

The V.C. heroes responded in turn. Most of them confined their remarks to thanking Mr. West and the St. Patrick's Day committee, but one, who had been a member of the Sportsman's Thousand, stated that he and his confreres would come any distance to meet the wishes of their old General, John West.

The last V.C., a pale-faced young fellow who had lost a leg in France, asked John West to respond on his behalf.

"It was a disgrace that the Government gave a man who had lost one leg the paltry sum of 30 shillings a week!"

Robert Scott then moved a vote of thanks to John West, replete with table-thumping. Mr. West was always ready and willing to help along every movement having for its object the welfare of the people, but it was in the genuine works of charity that he worked unostentatiously, not letting his right hand know what his left hand was doing.

"Everyone knows," Scott concluded, pointing dramatically at John West, "that our host today is a real white man!"

That evening at Archbishop Malone's residence the same people were present. The Archbishop himself was there, and made a fiery speech against the British Empire.

Nellie West also attended. She sat next to her husband, smiling and charming, but pale-faced. The V.C. winners made a great fuss of her, as did all present.

As the evening progressed, Nellie found that she was enjoying herself, and determiend that she would, next evening, entertain the V.C.'s as they had never been entertained before. John West cast a searching glance at her occasionally. She was good at this sort of thing; he must see that he made full use of her in future.

*

At dawn on St. Patrick's Day, John West was awakened by the sun, which promised a fine autumn day. He arose immediately and dressed. He felt excited. He had planned this march on a mammoth scale. What a spectacle it would be!

Arriving in the city at nine o'clock wearing a large shamrock on his coat, he found that people were already gathering for the beginning of the procession that was not timed to begin until two o'clock. He busied himself with last-minute organisation, directing his marshals in the work of arranging the huge procession at its starting point in Bourke Street. By midday it was clear that the crowds participating and watching would be the biggest ever at any march in Melbourne's history. People thronged, blocking the traffic in four city blocks.

There seemed a million things to do, but he did them with all his energy and determination. Then the great moment came: the Archbishop's car arrived, nosing its way slowly through the milling, cheering crowd.

At last the great procession was on its way. It began, as planned by Archbishop Malone, with a bewhiskered, shabby, down-at-heel individual, carrying a small Union Jack. He was followed at a respectable distance by the Archbishop's car and his guard of Victoria Cross winners, all in uniform and mounted on sleek, grey chargers; then came the committee group with John West himself in the front row. It contained many leading Catholic laymen, including one millionaire of a more respectable variety than John West, and Councillor Robert Renfrey.

Behind the committee came thousands of returned soldiers: in rows of four they marched to the bands and cheering.

Sixty former army nurses followed the soldiers. Then, some in uniform, came thousands of boys and girls from Catholic schools; and lastly the great mass of the marchers. Australian and Sinn Fein flags were everywhere, but only one Union Jack, the one carried by the shabby man in front.

It was estimated later that in all 25,000 people marched and 100,000 lined the route. Here and there the crowd burst the rails which had been erected, but it was kept in order by the swarms of policemen on duty. Dotted among the watchers were "Loyalists" and "Orangemen," angry and defeated hoping for a disturbance, but afraid to provoke one.

The atmosphere was electric with fervour and enthusiasm –

never before or since had Melbourne's staid buildings flanked such a procession. Movie cameras here and there created much interest. Thousands fainted in the cheering crowds along the way. Everywhere people displayed badges, shamrocks, buttons, harps, green flags.

The derelict in front responded to the good-natured plaudits of the crowd in an unexpected manner. He bowed and scraped on either side as he led the mammoth stream up the hill towards Parliament House, waving his diminutive flag. He had the animated walk of a "plonk" drinker. As his excitement rose he danced and jigged along, bowing and doffing his battered hat. Never before had an opportunity come his way to perform for 100,000 people, and he seemed determined to make the most of it. Once he fell over, and then endeavoured to walk on his hands, but he found this task beyond him. However, next to the Archbishop and a legless soldier who rode in a car with a Sinn Fein flag held aloft on his crutches, the man with the little flag was the most popular figure in the procession.

John West marched with a swaggering jaunty gait, acknowledging with a wave of his hand occasional shouts of approval and clapping along the way. He felt exultant: this day would bring him wide fame and goodwill.

When the head of the procession reached the top of Bourke Street, Archbishop Malone alighted from his car and took the salute on the steps of Parliament House. He stood erect, his heart athrob with emotion. This was a grand day, the answer of Australian Catholics to their enemies – a display of strength which had drawn his flock around him and struck a blow for Mother Ireland. After the returned soldiers' column had at last passed by, he stepped into the car again and was driven to the Exhibition grounds a few hundred yards away. The Exhibition was packed out long before the end of the procession had left the rallying point, the tens of thousands could not obtain admission to the speech-making, the singing and the display of athletics and dancing.

Daniel Malone added a sarcastic final touch to his day of triumph: "We were instructed by the Melbourne City Council to carry a Union Jack at the head of the procession. I could not get an Irishman to carry it, so I paid an Englishman two shillings to do the job."

John West had won for himself great admiration and respect

from the vast majority of Catholics who supported Archbishop Malone. His name was joined with that of the Archbishop in the attacks on the Irish Movement in the ARGUS and the official organ of the Protestant Federation. Their names were similarly linked in the replies of the Catholic Press to these attacks, and in the wide publicity given to the St. Patrick's Day procession and the subsequent departure of the Archbishop for Rome and Dublin, via America.

John West's photo appeared in the 1920 edition of the Catholic Almanac, and with that of the Archbishop, the V.C. heroes and leaders of the Irish rebellion in a souvenir publication devoted to the St. Patrick's Day celebrations. He figured prominently in the film on the procession, and in the farewell to the Archbishop.

At the farewell the choir sang a song called *Come Back to Australia*, which, it was announced, was "dedicated to the Archbishop by Mr. John West." It was a trite, sentimental ditty to the tune of *The Wearing of the Green*. John West could not have written a song if he had been flayed alive. A penniless song-writer had written the words. John West bought them from him for fifty pounds, and had the sheet-music printed. The song was sung at the farewell and on occasions since then. John West did not attempt to disillusion those who believed he had written it.

On the eve of his departure the Archbishop called at the West home. John West noticed that he was ill at ease; he had been ever since he was summoned to Rome.

In his farewell speech, Malone had said: "I go at the call of duty to give an account of my stewardship during the few years I have been in Australia, especially the years since the death of my late lamented and revered predecessor. If the Holy Father has any fault to find with my career or administration my first reply to him will be that I did not seek the position, that I was sent here without being consulted, that I have done the best I could, that I am prepared to stand or fall by the judgment of the Bishops and Clergy and the people of Australia. If there are any short-comings in my career they are only those he should have been prepared to expect because I did not seek the position, and when it fell to my lot, I knew that I was unequal to its responsibilities."

John West thought he detected fear amid the apparently defiant words.

Before leaving Melbourne, Malone promised to write to John West, and asked him to make every endeavour to prevent the deportation of a priest named Jesper, who had been interned since 1917, and was to be deported by the Federal Government. The Archbishop had explained that he had been in touch with Father Jesper, and was convinced that he was guiltless of the crime of which he had been convicted without a trial – that of having supported the German cause during the war.

Jesper had been born in Germany, but moved with his parents to Switzerland while still a child. Later he studied for the priesthood and came to Australia. During the war he had openly opposed conscription, and supported the Irish rebellion. Another Catholic priest who was stationed in the same parish, a supporter of conscription, had violent disagreements with Jesper, and finally wrote to the Mayor of the locality exposing Jesper's activities. Jesper was immediately interned. He was not a naturalised Australian, and efforts to obtain his release failed.

The priest who denounced Jesper had been disciplined. Daniel Malone told John West, but the task of preventing Jesper's deportation remained.

John West promised to prevent the deportation at all costs. At first, his efforts appeared likely to meet with success, but then two dangerous opponents emerged: Percy Blackwood, Labor member for Broken Hill, and Jock Somerton, Victorian Secretary of the Seamen's Union.

After public rallies at which a few Trade Union leaders and several Labor politicians had spoken with him, John West concentrated his efforts on having the Seamen's Union and Wharf Laborers' Union executives pass a resolution refusing to work any ship on which Father Jesper was to be deported. He could not get the Watersiders' leaders to make a definite decision, but paid Walsh, the Australian Secretary of the Seamen's Union, £1,000 to put a resolution to his Executive, the majority of whom supported it, because Jesper had been an anti-conscriptionist. But the Seamen's Annual Conference, which inconveniently took place at this time, rescinded the decision, largely through the efforts of Jock Somerton. The conference resolved that, by involving itself in the Jesper case, the Union could achieve no good purpose. It should remain neutral in the matter.

John West rang Walsh and stormed and raged. Wash anxious

not to lose his £1,000, suggested that John West should see Somerton.

John West found Jack Somerton in a small, plainly furnished office.

Somerton feigned to be busy. He was a short man of some forty-five years, but very thick-set with a bull neck, sloped shoulders and deep chest.

"Sit down," Somerton said, without looking up.

John West obeyed, disconcerted by the off-handed manner.

Somerton continued to study some papers. After fully three minutes, he looked up and said: "Well?"

"My name is West – John West. I . . ."

"What can I do for you, Mr. West?"

"I want to talk to you about the Jesper case."

Somerton reached behind him, took a leather-bound book from a shelf, and began fingering through its pages.

"Jesper, Jesper," he murmured. "Not in the G's, must be under the J's. Jesper, no.

"There must be some mistake, Mr. West. There's no Jesper listed in the membership of our Union."

"You know who I mean – Father Jesper."

"Oh, Father Jesper," Somerton spoke gruffly, with just a trace of a Scotch accent. His face was inscrutable, but John West sensed that he was laughing at him. "I remember now. Well, the Victorian section of our Union will be taking no action in the matter."

"I happen to know that *you* caused the Union to change its mind about Father Jesper."

"At the recent Annual Conference, I moved that the Union shouldn't commit itself to support Jesper. In my view, our members'ud be foolish to start a fight from which they and the working class movement can benefit nothing."

"There is a principle at stake. Jesper had been convicted without a trial. Trial by jury is part of the Magna Charta."

"Yourself and Archbishop Malone should be the last to mention the Magna Charta. The Roman Church bitterly opposed its introduction."

John West's rage was mounting. "You are supporting Hughes against Father Jesper, because you hate the Catholic Church. I've heard all about you."

371

Jock Somerton believed the Catholic Church was humanity's greatest blight; that Archbishop Malone was as dangerous an enemy of the working man as the biggest capitalists. He contended that Malone had opposed conscription because he was not only pro-Irish but pro-German as well, in line with Vatican policy.

Somerton was unabashed. "I'm not supporting Hughes; but I am opposing the interference of the Roman Church in union affairs and politics."

"I've never interfered in union affairs, but I have helped many Unions, including this one."

"This Union won't seek any more of the kind of help you have given it."

"Speak for yourself! Walsh and the Central Executive were quite willing to support Jesper at my request."

"If I know Tom Walsh he would be well paid for his – er – co-operation."

"Walsh would support Jesper on principle – and he's a militant, as well as you are."

"Walsh pretends to be a militant. He talks like a militant to hold his job, but at heart he's an opportunist. And he takes bribes. In fact, I happen to know that he has been paid to support Jesper."

"You'd better be careful what you're saying."

"He was paid to support Jesper by you, Mr. West."

John West fastened his rapier eyes on Somerton. He was out of his depth when confronted with various forces at work in the Labor Movement. With a cunning that was almost instinctive, he made use of many individuals in the Movement, but he did not understand it and would never learn to understand it. To him, Somerton was a riddle, as were Ashton, Thurgood and many others. He could not differentiate between them; he could not analyse the political and social forces influencing them. He knew that some could be bought and some intimidated, but could not understand why many could neither be bought nor intimidated. The Trade Union leaders puzzled him even more than the politicians. As far as he could make out, Walsh was a similar type to Bob Scott, who talked like a militant and a Socialist, in order to get votes, but could be bought; yet Somerton talked the same but could not be bought or even intimidated. John West put this

372

down to Somerton being anti-Catholic, but there was more than that to it.

Somerton was the last of the Wobbly Trade Union leaders. The IWW had lived long enough to change the old set-up in the Australian Unions. Its class-conscious propaganda, vigour and crude militancy had paved the way for the more scientific and better organised Communists who were to rise in the next decade.

John West's influence in the Trade Union Movement was on the wane. He attributed this to the fact that he could not influence voting in Union elections to anything like the degree he could in Labor pre-selection ballots. He consoled himself with the thought that the Unions were not, in the long-run, essential to his plans.

But he was very annoyed with Somerton. "Do you realise," he cried irately, "that the Victorian section, your section, of the Union, still owes me a thousand of the three thousand pound loan I gave it during the strike?"

"I realise that, but we are up to date with our instalments. You'll get yer money. If I'd been secretary at the time of the strike the money would never have been borrowed. Between your loans and tips for racehorses, many Unions and Union leaders are in debt. I'm not a betting man, and this Union will not need any more of your money."

"The banks won't give you loans during strikes."

"Then we'll do without loans."

"I'll beat you and Blackwood yet."

"Percy Blackwood is barnstorming the country. And the workers take a lotta notice of Percy."

"I'll fix him. I'll drive him out of Parliament! Anyway, if Jesper's ship leaves from any other port but Melbourne, the Unions won't man it."

"I hear the ship is to leave from Melbourne."

John West stood up and leaned across the table. "Listen, Somerton, if you stand in my path in this matter, I'll smash you. I'll get you out of this job if it costs me a fortune."

"No doubt. Tom Walsh will be interested in that. He's been anxious to get me out, and he'll be all the more anxious if there's a few quid in it for him."

John West raised his fist threateningly. But for Somerton's forbidding physique, he would have received a punch on the nose.

"If you lay hands on me, you bandy little bastard, I'll tear you apart," Somerton said, changing his manner suddenly.

John West lowered his hand and walked to the door, saying lamely: "You'll be sorry for this, and so will Blackwood."

By a stroke of ill-judgement, the Government decided to deport Father Jesper from Adelaide.

John West went there with Walsh, who organised a mass meeting of Seamen and Wharf Laborers, which decided to refuse to man the *Nectar* on which Jesper was to sail. The crew of the *Nectar* received £500 between them as a present from John West.

But the authorities tricked them. Jesper was transferred to an English boat which sailed in the night.

Realising too late that he had been checkmated, John West boarded the train for Perth, where he organised a huge demonstration, including 2,000 returned soldiers, to greet the ship, but the vessel had loaded attitional coal in Adelaide to avoid stopping in the west.

On his journey back to Melbourne, John West was in a seething rage against those who had defeated him. He cursed Jock Somerton, he cursed Percy Blackwood.

On the afternoon after his arrival in Melbourne, John West addressed a meeting of 5,000 indignant workers in front of Parliament House. He was becoming adept at fiery speech-making; he would have made a good Labor politician had he chosen to enter politics.

He opened by saying that he had just completed a journey of 4,000 miles in an attempt to prevent an injustice to a wronged and innocent man. Using terms such as "The solidarity of the working classes," and speaking of the sacredness of the Magna Charta and the principle of trial by jury, he raised his audience to a fever of wrath. He outlined his version of the case, contending that the priest, although admittedly an anti-conscriptionist, was certainly not disloyal, and, in any case, should not have been found guilty without proper trial.

The huge assembly gave three cheers for Labor, for Solidarity, and for John West. The meeting broke up to the strains of *Solidarity Forever* and *Mother Ireland*.

Next day, John West told Frank Lammence to investigate the possibility of driving Blackwood out of the Broken Hill seat, and to tell the boys to "teach Somerton a lesson." Snoopy Tanner and Arty West were only too willing to oblige, but their gang found Somerton an adept in the art of self-protection. Their men desisted after they received two hidings from the band of protectors who stayed at Somerton's side day and night. John West had to content himself with financing a campaign to oust Somerton from office. He spent nearly £2,000 before Somerton was finally defeated in a rigged ballot two years later.

John West was saved the trouble of dealing with the Labor member for Broken Hill – Percy Blackwood was accidentally shot dead by a lunatic. Jock Somerton and others wrongly believed that John West was behind the murder.

One evening six months later, John West sat in the reception room waiting for Archbishop Malone, who had arrived back in Melbourne the day before.

He arose and inspected the chair in which he had been sitting. Its upholstery was an ermine ground on which an emblem was skilfully embroidered: the emblem bore the crest of an open arm with raised scimitar and lion rampant with an inscription in Gaelic. He stood back inspecting the chair critically. He stepped forward and moved the chair to cause the light to fall more favourably upon it, inspected it further, then sat down again.

The chair had been embroidered by Nuns from the Convent of the Good Shepherd, and presented to John West by a gathering of Catholic citizens. In making the presentation, Mr. T. J. Real, newly elected Deputy-Leader of the Australian Parliamentary Labor Party, had traced Mr. West's ancestry from a race of Irish Kings, and explained that the inscription, broadly translated, meant "West to Victory." Mr. Real said that this was the original coat-of-arms of Mr. West's ancestors, and added that Mrs. West, who was a Moran, had descended from Brian Boru himself. Real described John West "an all-round sport," "a bountiful giver to charity," and "a fearless defender of freedom and justice."

John West was very proud of the chair. He intended to use it in his city office, but had kept it here to show the Archbishop first.

He was looking forward to seeing Malone, who would, no doubt, be pleased with his efforts in the Jesper case and other matters.

John West sat down again. Nellie entered. He did not look up and no word passed between them. She must help entertain the Archbishop as part of her duties, but no conversation was necessary while awaiting their guest.

Meanwhile, Archbishop Malone was preparing to leave his mansion to visit John West. He was dressed in his long, black, frock-coat. He put on his top hat as he walked out of the house.

The five years since the Irish rebellion had left their mark on him. Previously well preserved, he now looked his sixty years: his hair was turning grey, his long eyebrows were wispy white, his eyes were sunken and narrowed, and his face was deeply lined. He was more gaunt than formerly, but he still carried himself proudly erect.

Archbishop Malone was uneasy about the impending interview. He would have to be quite frank with West about the Vatican's instructions. West would have no inkling of what had transpired: Malone had corresponded with him, even sent him a photo, but the letters had been uninformative.

Arriving at the Vatican City after a tour of America, Daniel Malone had found the College of Cardinals, and the Holy Father himself, anything but pleased with developments in Ireland and their repercussions in Australia. The Vatican wanted hostilities in Ireland to end, and end quickly. The Catholic Church, he was told, had nothing to gain and everything to lose by supporting the rebels. The Irish clergy were divided on the issue. There were elements among the revolutionaries who would undermine the power of the Church as well as the power of the English land-owners. A stable government must be formed in the south which would agree to partition, and negotiate with England. When Archbishop Malone arrived in Ireland he must use his influence to this end, he was told.

In an interview with the Pope, Daniel Malone stated that he had rallied great support among Australian Catholics. The Pope expressed pleasure, but said that some grave errors had been made in Australia on the Irish question and other matters. The Irish question was to be quietly relegated to the background where Archbishop Conn had left it until Easter 1916, His Holiness insisted. It had repelled many of Australia's richest Catholics. It had been handled in a way contrary to Vatican policy.

But other and more serious errors were being made by the Australian arm of the Church. Its Press, especially in Victoria, was taking the wrong attitude towards the Russian Revolution. Contrary to what had been believed earlier, there was no possibility of the new regime opening the road for the return of the Vatican to Russia, the Holy Father said. Lenin represented the most dangerous threat to the Church since Martin Luther. Socialism, or Communism as it was becoming known, must be resisted in Australia as elsewhere. A series of articles on the subject by the famous Catholic writer, Hillaire Belloc, were being sent to all countries and must be widely published. Communism aimed to remove the power of the so-called capitalist class: for good or ill, the Pope pointed out to Daniel Malone, the power of the Vatican was now largely dependent upon the power of the capitalist class, so Socialism or Communism must be fought tooth and nail as being atheistic and opposed to the Christian concept of the family and the sanctity of private property.

This new attitude towards Socialism and Communism would presuppose, the Pope demanded, a change of tactics by Archbishop Malone. He must cease associating with the Socialists and the IWW, who might well become the basis for the spread of world revolution to Australia. Also, steps must be taken to prevent the Australian Labor Party from becoming socialistic.

His Holiness then summoned the Cardinal who had studied the Australian scene with the aid of the Australian Jesuit Priest who had recently visited Rome. Further long discussion ensued. In Australia, the Church should turn to the Labor Party as the main basis of its political influence. It should cease to contest elections through the Catholic Federation, and should, for the time being, allow the agitation for Government grants for Catholic schools to fade into the background. Daniel Malone pointed out that he had already begun to implement this policy. His Holiness and his Cardinals were aware of this, he was told.

There was just one other little matter, the Cardinal intervened tactfully. Archbishop Malone must cease his open association with a certain notorious man named – what was his name? West, that was it, John West! To accept West's money was quite in order, to use his political influence was laudable, but to associate his name with that of an Archbishop in public affairs was going too far. The Church could not afford to be particular about its allies, but must avoid scandal.

377

After further discussions on the situation in Australia and the troubles in Ireland, Daniel Malone left Rome for England. The English authorities would not grant him permission to visit his beloved land, even when he insisted that he merely wished to see his mother who was so old and failing in health that she must surely die very soon. So eventually Daniel Malone had "Come Back to Australia," as the seven-day-wonder song dedicated to him by John West had implored. Though he had failed to get into Ireland to help implement Vatican policy it was now plain to him that the new Government under De Valera was successfully doing so.

Nellie West opened the door to the Archbishop, took his hat and invited him in with servile enthusiasm. John West greeted Malone and remarked that he seemed fagged out. Talk turned to Malone's trip, while Nellie sat knitting. Then the Archbishop brought the conversation round to the Irish question. He was surprised when John West agreed that the matter should be allowed to subside, so far as circumstances would permit except for the annual procession. The Irish question had served its purpose for John West, and he was losing enthusiasm for it.

After John West had proudly displayed his chair, he outlined his vast efforts on behalf of Father Jesper, and was a little disappointed when His Grace merely said: "A grand effort, Mr. West! May God bless you! But Father Jesper is gone now, and there is not much we can do but await the news that he has been satisfactorily placed overseas."

Looks as if the Vatican has rapped him over the knuckles, John West mused; feeling for the first time that he could dominate even this holy and intelligent man.

Daniel Malone then mentioned the Vatican's attitude towards Socialism, Communism and the Labor Party. John West said he had read Belloc's recent articles in the Catholic ADVOCATE and thoroughly agreed with every word of them. The Labor Party was his party, he explained. He believed in White Australia, in the Arbitration Court and in a fair day's pay for a fair day's work, but he had opposed the Russian Revolution right from the outset and would oppose that sort of thing in Australia.

John West was more than pleased when informed the Catholic Federation was to cease being an instrument of politics, that the idea of forming a Catholic Workers' Association was to be abandoned, and that the Church intended to rely on the Labor Party for its political influence.

More than an hour had passed since Daniel Malone's arrival and he felt a heavy tiredness fall upon him. Only by a great effort could he prevent his eyes from folding shut and his head from drooping. In his tired state he felt an urge to postpone the main purpose of his visit, but when Nellie went to order supper he rallied his dwindling resolve.

"The Holy Father is well pleased with the grand work you have done in these past two years, Mr. West," he said.

"The Holy Father and Cardinals could not speak too highly of you. At the same time," Daniel Malone spurred himself to continue: "At the same time, He and the Cardinals were a little disturbed . . ."

John West's eyes narrowed.

". . . they were a little disturbed . . . you see, the Jesuit who preceded me to Rome reported the libellous, savage attacks that the Protestant Press has made upon you . . ."

Malone waited for John West's reaction.

If John West felt any anger, he did not betray it. After a silence, he said in a voice that was rather quieter than usual: "Go on, Your Grace. In my rise from poverty, I made many enemies. In fighting for Mother Ireland and Father Jesper I have made many more. I have often wondered what you and the Holy Father might think about the way the Press has sought to discredit you by raking up the old lies that have been told about me for donkey's years."

"You are a strong, courageous man," the Archbishop said, much relieved. "It has been decided that, though the Holy Father and the Cardinals have nothing but admiration for you, you and I should not associate together openly or bracket our names in public affairs. We can remain friends, and I trust we shall, always. But the Holy Father will be better served, I feel, if we do as he has willed. We can achieve much more together in this way. It will suit my purpose better – and yours, too."

Though John West had been hoping to be recognised by the Vatican with a Papal knighthood, he suppressed his great disappointment and humiliation. No one else would know that the Vatican had more or less insulted him. Ever since he had emerged again into the public light he had realised that he must return to the shadows when his purpose was achieved.

Power becomes more mighty and satisfying when exercised by remote control. He did not want glory, he wanted power – power without glory.

"I think this way will suit my purposes very well, Your Grace," was all he said.

CHAPTER NINE

It is a world of money, all other powers deposed, all other standards a shell without life inside . . .

UPTON SINCLAIR

Nearly four years had passed when four men filed out of John West's office in the late afternoon. All of them were Victorian Labor politicians.

One of them, W.J. Bennett, The Gentleman Thief himself, said to Fighting Bob Scott: "Well, that fixes that. We'll get control this year with an ounce of luck."

Behind them came a lanky man, six feet six inches tall, named Ned Horan. His hair grew in a black mass to fully five inches above his forehead – his boxer-hat seemed to balance on top of it. His eyes were big and round, their pupils were small and blue.

"We'll win," Horan replied to Bob Scott. "I'll tell yer for why." Ned Horan was always telling someone "for why", and used other quaint sayings hardly fitting for a man bent on becoming Premier of Victoria, but neither he nor his backer, John West, seemed perturbed by this fact.

After Horan came a short man, who lagged behind as the others began descending the stairs. His name was Tom Trumbleward. Trumbleward had a round face. His twinkling eyes and dimpled cheeks gave him a permanent smile. He tried to offset his babyish expression by wearing a big, black walrus moustache. The others had descended to the floor below while Trumbleward was slowly measuring four steps, when as though making a sudden decision, he retraced his way quickly.

Going to the door of John West's office he knocked gently.

"Come in."

"Sorry to trouble you again, Jack," Trumbleward said nervously, "but I was wanting to ask you something."

"What is it, Tom?"

"Er, well. It's about the leadership of the Party, Jack. Er, I was wondering whether, after the election, there was any chance of your supporting me for the leadership of the Victorian Labor Party when caucus votes on it."

"Ned Horan will be leader, Tom," John West said.

"Yes, but, I thought when I stood for Carringbush you said . . ."

"Sorry, Tom. Ned Horan will be leader."

Trumbleward hesitated a moment before walking out.

John West saw nothing incongruous in his being able to decide who would lead the Victorian Labor Party. Had he not striven for twenty-five years to achieve the power to do so?

In the conference just concluded, he and Frank Lammence had hammered out with Scott, Bennett, Horan and Trumbleward final plans to capture the annual conference of the Victorian Labor Party. He was confident of success.

The methods by which John West would exert his corrupting influence in the Parliaments had now assumed a definite pattern. He played politics like a game of chess, planning his moves in advance, moving his men, marshalling them for victory. Always, the tall sinister figure of Frank Lammence stood at his right hand.

From this shabby suite of offices, tentacles of the West octopus reached out to grip all manner of men: sportsmen, judges, gangsters, councillors, Trade Union leaders, and, most important of all, politicians. John West used the ability of other men, sucking out their brains, harnessing their influence with a shrewd, unerring insight. The politicians were mainly Labor men, but John West was determined not to respect party barriers which he believed were more apparent than real: he had added quite a few Country Party and Nationalist politicians to the ranks of the West men.

The basis of his political power was the Labor Party in which his relentless manoeuvring had for him fascinating pleasure: he thirsted for it like a man addicted to alcohol. None knew better than he the machinations of the Party. He studied the prospects of Labor in every electorate and ran a man in the pre-selection ballot only in electorates where Labor had some chance of winning, and especially in safe Labor seats. His grip was strongest in industrial areas, especially in and around Carringbush. He did not always decide whom he would run in a pre-selection ballot until he surveyed the contestants and chose one who was both likely to win and capable of being bought or intimidated if he entered Parliament. Then, whether his man won or not, the winner would receive a telephone call from Frank Lammence offering "a coupla hundred quid for expenses in the coming campaign and an ample supply of cars and helpers." Usually the offer was accepted.

The helpers were thugs and hangers-on, members of Snoopy Tanner's gang or the mobs with which Sugar Renfrey, Ron Lassiter and others had surrounded themselves. They distributed election manifestos and leaflets, and sometimes intimidated electors or opponents: occasionally this intimidation took the form of physical violence. In pre-selection ballots for safe Labor seats these men were always active. They had developed some interesting techniques. Their motto was "Vote early and vote often."

The Labor Party constitution allowed union members to vote in pre-selection ballots whether they were party members or not. This provision was exploited by the West men to their own ends. Union membership cards were obtained from the dwindling band of West Trade Union officials. Votes were then cast in the names of absent union members, living or dead. If this precaution failed, the ballot box was, if the opportunity arose, stuffed, as Sugar Renfrey termed it. This entailed the addition of as many more bodger votes as possible. As well as his own machine, John West had the support of the majority of Catholics in the Party; and the illusion that he was a generous supporter of the working man still persisted.

John West already called the tune in the Queensland Labor Party, which was well entrenched in office. In other States his influence was small. But the Victorian and the Australian Federal Parliaments, both of which sat in Melbourne, were his main concern.

John West had no real political philosophy. He had not been interested when Horan and the others discussed Labor Policy. Other millionaires and the Church were worried about the so-called Socialist Plank which had been introduced into Labor's platform, and was ostensibly aimed at the socialisation of production, distribution and exchange, but John West knew so many Labor politicians so well that he did not take it seriously.

He sat at his desk dreaming of power. He was fifty-six years of age now and his hair was turning grey, but his neat appearance offset his age, and he had the energy and virility of a man of forty. He felt that the best years of his life lay ahead.

When Thomas Trumbleward, the Honourable Member for Carringbush in the Victorian Legislative Assembly, left John West's office, he knew that his destiny was held in the palm of John West's hand. The realisation shocked him a little, though he should have known that this situation would arise.

As he slowly descended the three flights of bare, creaky stairs, a great wave of self-pity swept over him. All the tireless work and idealism which he had expended in the Labor Movement had gone for nothing. There was no way out. To attempt to extricate himself meant losing the Carringbush seat, and to Tom Trumbleward that was unthinkable.

As he boarded a tram, he thought of how he had been relentlessly drawn into the West machine. Entering Parliament after winning a country seat, he had found that the Labor politicians were of three varieties in their relations with John West: some, led by Bennett and Scott, supported West absolutely, if at times secretly; others, led by Maurice Blackwell, opposed West vigorously; the rest did not support West, but were more or less intimidated by his power. Trumbleward managed somehow to stand between the latter two varieties until he had lost his seat. The newly-formed Country Party ran a candidate named Davison against him. Davison conducted a vigorous campaign in which money was obviously no object, and won easily. Trumbleward would never forget the shock when the first figures were released, or the dwindling of his hopes as the progress totals continued. He knew he could never win the seat back; the mines were played out and the electorate was being stripped of its working class vote. He knew he would find it difficult to gain another endorsement: defeated candidates are taboo in any party. He had saved no money, below him yawned the gulf of poverty. He had climbed out of that gulf once; he did not want to fall into it again.

Fear of poverty was strong in Tom Trumbleward: as a child he had seen it warp a whole household. His experience of poverty had turned him to the Socialist movement; he joined the Socialist Party and the Labor Party and worked tirelessly. He was a brilliant pamphleteer. Some of his writings, such as *Successful Socialism*, and *The Problem of Poverty*, were famous among radicals. He worked in the boot industry at Carringbush, but did not know the West boys, who, by then, had left the trade. He devoted his spare time to the Labor Movement, and soon got his chance to run for Parliament.

He won his seat at the first try, soon left the Socialist Party, and concentrated on building a political career. He purchased the boot shop formerly owned by the defunct Labor Co-operatives, but, finding it unprofitable, sold out and based his security on his ability as a politician.

After his defeat he returned to Melbourne to seek employment. He found the prospect irksome, not to say humiliating. His young wife, whose sister had married Percy Lambert, did not help matters when she expressed her pleasure at his defeat; she told him she secretly wished he had never abandoned his revolutionary ideals for a plush seat in Parliament.

Hard work and small wages in the boot trade reduced Tom Trumbleward to a shadow of a man. Though he retained his party membership at Carringbush, he abandoned political activity. He yearned helplessly for the social standing and the sense of strength which Parliamentary membership meant to him. He returned to his former study of the poets, and found some consolation reading Shelley, Keats, Adam Lindsay Gordon and a host of others. He did his best to suppress his expensive tastes and his interest in horse racing, in order to support his wife and two young children.

Then suddenly, within a year, came the silver lining. An election was forced prematurely. One day, Tom Trumbleward came home to find a message requesting him to call on Mr Frank Lammence. He had never met Lammence but knew who, and what, he was. He hardly dared to hope that Lammence would offer him, a political reject, support for a come-back. Lammence brought him face to face with John West.

It appeared that the Labor Member for Carringbush had somehow managed to win the last pre-selection ballot without West support. He apparently thought so little of his political future as to oppose not only John West, but Archbishop Malone as well. Displaying foolhardy courage he had joined Maurice Blackwell against the Catholic influence in the Party.

John West informed Trumbleward that he wanted this iniquitous man removed, and had chosen him to do the job. Without stopping to consider the consequences, Trumbleward agreed. He had known the member well in the old Socialist days, but this did not deter him.

As he left John West's office, he had been called back. "Eh, Mr Trumbleward, I suppose you know I ran Davison against you. Sorry, I wanted him in Parliament, and your seat was his home ground. I decided at the time that I would get you another seat."

Tom Trumbleward said nothing. So West had deliberately brought about his defeat in order to force him into line!

He won the pre-selection and the seat. He knew that if he did West's bidding he had a job for life. His conscience pricked him, but he insulated himself against it by becoming cynical about life, about politics, about Socialism and the struggles of the working man.

West had, it was true, made very few demands on him; but he knew, as all Labor members knew, that West was planning for the day when the Party would become the Government of Victoria. Then West would make many demands.

Tom Trumbleward felt very sorry for himself. He would soon have to consummate the betrayal of his ideals, without ever achieving his ambition of becoming Party leader.

Fancy preferring that Irish ignoramus Horan to Tom Trumbleward, the writer, the orator, the cultured reader of the poets. Sheer bigotry it was. West knew he was an atheist. West preferred Catholics. Oh, well, I suppose I should be thankful that he had me in his camp at all.

Tom Trumbleward decided that he would not go home. Instead he would ring Marion, his actress friend, whom he had obtained since his return to politics. He squared his shoulders, drew in his ample girth and retraced his steps with a more buoyant gait. They would wine and dine together, and then in her arms he would forget the cares which befell a man of culture and ideals in the hurly-burly game of politics.

Meanwhile, Arthur West had entered his brother's office. He looked like a church lay-preacher, with his white hair combed straight back, his white moustache, his white celluloid collar a size too large, and his plain black suit, until the observer looked into his expressionless eyes.

Arthur West valued the protection from the law his brother gave him, and, on occasions, still hovered near him as bodyguard.

The urge to violence was still strong in him, and found outlet in his duties as John West's contact with Tanner's gang, and as chief intimidator in election campaigns. But his life was really devoted to Richard Bradley. Arthur West had never forgotten those words of comfort uttered so long ago in Pentridge Jail: "Never mind, son. It will soon be over."

Bradley was in "smoke" and John West was reluctantly "putting in" to keep him there. The crime which had made Bradley a fugitive was a cold-blooded one, and could have had serious consequences for John West, though it was committed without his sanction.

Bradley had no sooner completed his sentence for the Trades Hall robbery than he began to plan with Snoopy Tanner a daring daylight hold-up. The Victorian Police, driven to desperation by bad conditions and low pay, had gone on strike. The time was ripe to take risks! One day a bank manager, carrying a bag containing £2,000 up the ramp of a suburban railway station, was confronted by two men – Bradley and a young newcomer to Snoopy's gang named Martin. Bradley must have been a fearful sight to the little bank manager: a scar ran from behind his left ear along his cheek and jaw, a wide-brimmed hat was pulled low over his uneven face and his relentless eyes menaced even more than the gun that showed in outline through his coat pocket.

"Give us that bag," he muttered, and Martin stepped forward. The bank manager resisted Martin's efforts to take the bag. Bradley fired three shots into his body without compunction, and he and Martin fled to Snoopy's car nearby.

As Tanner swiftly drove the car away, Arthur West, who sat beside him, shouted to Bradley: "What happened? Did you have to plug the bastard?" Bradley made no reply.

Martin, wild-eyed and pale, shouted: "There was no need to, either. I had the bag. I never carried a gun in me life. Now what'll happen to me?"

Tanner said: "Shut yer bloody trap and nothin'll happen to yer."

There was no pursuit. They dropped Arthur West in the city and the car sped them to a prearranged hideout.

Next day the Press screamed the story and demanded an end of the wave of violence by organised gangs. John West sent for Arthur and told him that he was fed up with Tanner and Bradley.

387

Arthur took good care not to say that he was on the scene of the crime, and asked for money to finance the fugitives. At first John West refused, then he relented. Arthur was not worried about Martin: but Bradley must not be captured.

The bank manager had said to the man in whose arms he breathed his last: "The little man with the limp fired the shots." Not even the power of John West could save Bradley if he were caught, but the cunning of his brother and Tanner could make an attempt to prevent his capture. Tanner moved Bradley and Martin from place to place, but they were hard pressed. The detective force was not on strike, and the hue and cry of the Press and the defenceless populace drove it to all-out efforts. The hunted men would not escape capture for long!

Arthur West, remembering how Piggy had been sacrificed to save Bradley in 1915, then conceived a diabolical plan. If one of the men were caught before the other, that man would be hanged, and so the public conscience would be placated. Snoopy Tanner was only too willing to co-operate to save himself, and incidentally, Bradley, from imprisonment or worse. He separated Bradley and Martin, then rang a friendly detective arranging that he himself should be picked up with Martin, then released, to allay suspicion.

Martin was duly captured, tried and sentenced to death, without suspecting that he had been betrayed. Then the leader of a rival gang visited Martin and told him the truth – Tanner and Arty West had shelved him.

Martin's lawyer informed Frank Lammence through Arthur West that Martin would 'blow' what he knew of Snoopy Tanner's gang, its connections and its protectors. John West was angry and nonplussed. But Snoopy Tanner soon conceived a solution: they would 'spring' Martin from the Melbourne jail. When Arthur related the plan, John West observed that it would be suicide: Martin would be too well guarded, he would be dead before he reached the outside wall. With quiet deliberation Arthur West had replied: "Snoopy says that doesn't matter. That would shut Martin's mouth all the tighter."

By prearrangement, a friendly warder had a number of prison towels tied together. Martin obtained this crude rope at the selected time, but checked its length before making the suicidal dash for the wall. The rope was not long enough! Suspecting a plan to have him shot while attempting to escape, Martin ran to a warder and demanded to be locked in his cell.

Then fate stepped in, in the form of the Catholic religion, and silenced Martin forever. He had been brought up a Catholic, and was now driven back by conscience and fear of death to the religion of his early years. He confessed his sins, set his mind and soul at rest, and calmly waited the hangman's noose.

John West began to think that his criminal arm was becoming an embarrassment. But such associations are easier to form than to break. Anyway, he still needed Tanner. He told Arthur that no such risks should be taken again, not even if the miracle of the police strike should be repeated. Since then gang feuds had led to shooting affrays, but nothing happened to embarrass John West.

Today he had summoned Arthur to inform him that he had a new plan to use Tanner and a few of his most trusted henchmen.

He related the plan to his brother. In America, prohibition continued. He, John West, controlled a large distilling business in Australia which manufactured large quantities of gin and whisky. Of inferior quality, the spirits were selling poorly in Australia. His company was on the rocks, but in America they would buy anything with alcohol in it, even Austral gin and whisky. He wanted Arthur to arrange with Tanner to ship bootleg spirits to Mexico, from where it would be transported across the border to the U.S.A. Getting shipping would be difficult, but he would pay well for the work if it could be organised.

Arthur West listened eagerly, his eyes shifting in his head. The scheme could be organised easily, he said.

"Yer could buy a ship yourself, if necessary."

"Perhaps I will, but, remember, this must be a well-kept secret."

"Don't worry."

"See Tanner, then make all arrangements through Frank Lammence. I want nothing to do with this. You can go. Let Frank know."

"Er, all right. But can I get some more dough for Dick Bradley?"

"What do you think I am, the Bank of England? I gave you fifty quid a week or two ago!"

"Yair, but it costs a lot. There's food and drink for him and

389

his niece who's been lookin' after him, and there's money for payin' orf flatfoots. Sometimes a lag gets on to where Dick is and pays a visit. Just says: 'How are yer, Dick?' first time, see? Then he calls again, see; and asks for a loan of twenty quid. Just a loan, see. That's what happens when you're in smoke – the vultures find yer. We bashed up the last bastard who came that caper; teach him not to try again."

"Very clever," John West said, sarcastically. "Listen! You keep away from bashing parties. Remember, you're my brother. You can do me a lot of harm. Keep behind the scenes, that's the way to work. How often do you go to see Bradley?"

"Nearly every night. Why?"

"Well, don't go so often. There are still flatfoots looking for him; be nice for me if they pick you up with him, wouldn't it?"

"Aw, they'll never catch Dick. Long as we have dough. He don't spend nothin' on himself; only leaves the house late at night to get some exercise."

"How long is this going to go on? Why don't you get him out of the country? I can't keep this up forever." As John West spoke he took a roll of ten pound notes from a drawer in the table and handed five to his brother. "Here's another fifty, and don't make it too hot in future. Get him out of the country; that could be arranged."

"Dick won't go," Arthur said hastily. "And I don't blame him. Better off here. Doesn't need to run away." Arthur West would not have permitted Bradley to leave the country.

"Well, don't hang around him so much. I think I'll have to see Frank about getting the money to him some other way. Let it go for now, and don't forget about that bootlegging job. Let Frank know."

About this time Marjorie, John West's eldest daughter, returned home from Italy, where she had been studying the violin for three years.

As the day of her arrival approached, the household reached a pitch of excited expectancy. Mrs Moran buzzed about like a busy bee preparing the house, planning the welcome. Mary, who was very much attached to her sister, invited a few friends to a celebration dinner on the evening of Marjorie's arrival, and purchased a present, a fine portrait of Beethoven, Marjorie's favourite composer. John Junior, whom Marjorie had always adored, was perhaps the most excited of all. Margo was coming home, good old Margo. He found it hard to think of her as the famous virtuoso of the violin which her father hoped she would become; rather he liked to think of her as his rollicking play-mate, a tomboy who climbed the big pine trees in the grounds and was happy in the days before the family came to know their father's history and to realise that their parents hated each other. Even easy-going Joe seemed to stir himself from his round of muddling through school, reading penny dreadfuls and munch-ing lollies.

Nellie West joined Mary and Mrs Moran in the excited prep-arations. Nellie had slowly entered again into her role of mother but not of wife. She still slept in the spare bedroom with her son Xavier, who was now more than eight years old; a beautiful child, the image of the father, but with a dreamy, almost morose tem-perament. He sensed that he was different to the other children, that he did not belong here. Only his mother seemed to care for him. His father repulsed all his childish advances: he seemed to hate him. Apart from his mother, only Gran and Mary were kind to him. He could scarcely remember Marjorie, but did his best to join in the prevailing excitement.

After his own fashion, John West himself loved Marjorie, and was looking forward to her return. At first he had been uninter-ested in her musical studies: he could not understand and did not appreciate classical music. There was no chord in his soul that music, literature or painting could strike, except when he might respond sentimentally to the singing of Mother Machree or some such ballad which reminded him of his mother or of some other person or thing he had once cherished. But when well-informed people began to say that Marjorie might become a great violinist who would play in the concert halls of the world, he had changed his attitude. His daughter might become famous and make a lot of money. So interested did he become that he prevailed upon the manager of a theatre circuit he controlled to organise a tour of Australia for the virtuoso Fritz Kreisler. The tour was a great success, artistically and financially. During his stay, Kreisler visited the West home several times and heard Marjorie play. On his advice John West sent Marjorie to Europe to finish her studies. Now Marjorie was coming home, he hoped as a fully fledged violin virtuoso ready to take the cities of the world by storm.

Marjorie approached John West after the celebration dinner on the first evening and said she wanted to marry immediately. His name was Paul Andreas. She had met him at the conservatorium where he, too, had been studying the violin. He had followed her to Australia as a buyer for a German firm of wool importers. She had invited Paul to dinner on the next night, she told her father. He would formally ask permission to marry her.

John West was disappointed, not to say angry. The welcome home had been a huge success. Never before had there been so much joy in the family, but now yet another conflict had arisen. With laudable self-control he said little to Marjorie: let her lover come, meantime he would think the matter over.

In contrast to the previous evening, the atmosphere during the meal was strained and depressing. From his position at the head of the table, John West kept gazing critically at Paul Andreas, and he took an immediate dislike to his would-be son-in-law. From Andreas' accent it was plain that he was a German, and that in itself prejudiced John West against him.

Andreas was ill at ease. He had difficulty with the language, and seemed under some great strain. He discussed the weather with Mrs Moran, and when that topic lapsed, Nellie did her best to begin a conversation about music which also failed to develop. Then Mary, vivacious and self-assured, guided the conversation from topic to topic, and soon everyone was more at ease, except the guest.

John West continued to study Andreas' aesthetic yet sullen face. His dislike grew: this weak-chinned fiddler was after Marjorie's money, his money, there was no doubt about that. He was obviously a lady's man; see how he looked at Mary – think it was she, not Marjorie, he wanted to marry. Won't look you in the eye. Surely Marjorie wouldn't give up her career for this overdressed fop.

John West turned his attention to Marjorie. She was obviously infatuated with Andreas, but what did this flash lady-killer see in her? She was plain with her bobbed hair cut to a severe fringe and coming to a point like a sideboard whisker over each round cheek; and, in these days of skirts above the knee, her chubby legs would hardly attract him. No, Andreas was after Marjorie's money, but he would not get it. No German would become heir to any of the West millions.

After the meal, John West excused himself, and said softly: "Marjorie, could I speak to you for a moment in the music room?"

"Yes, Father, right away."

He sat on a chair near the piano.

"Take a seat," he said.

"Why do you want to give up your career to marry that . . . to marry Andreas?"

"Because I love him."

"Love him? You don't know what . . . But does he love you?"

"Of course he does; he wants to marry me."

"Have you stopped to think that he might be wanting to marry you for your money?"

Marjorie West was stung by this, to her, mean remark. She hesitated.

She knew a good deal of the story behind her parents' estrangement, and was glad when her trip to Europe had released her from the atmosphere of conflict. She had loved her mother very deeply until she had pieced together a version of the story of the infidelity and the parentage of Xavier; then her love had changed to resentment and pity, and an invisible barrier began to separate them. Always she had been repulsed by her father's personality. She had paid him a respect born of a vague fear, that was all. She had never felt she could go to him with any problem. She might have known he would talk like this. But he could not keep her from Paul.

She sat tensely, avoiding her father's eyes. Presently she tossed her head, then rose and faced him defiantly.

"Paul wants to marry me because he loves me. You should not say such mean things."

Paul Andreas held an irresistible charm for women, and Marjorie had fallen desperately in love with him the very first week of his arrival at the Conservatorium. At first he had not reciprocated, but as they came to know each other better, he eventually declared his love and asked for her hand. She was elated and a little surprised: there were many far more attractive girls whom Paul could have had if he wished, she felt sure of that.

"But he is a German. Why didn't you tell me that last night?"

"It never entered my head. His nationality makes no difference."

"The Germans are an evil race. You don't remember the war, that's the trouble. No daughter of mine will marry a German!"

"The Germans are a fine race. Look at the great musicians and scientists they have given the world. Paul has explained that all the propaganda during the war was a pack of lies. Anyway I am over twenty-one, Father. If I want to marry Paul, you can't stop me!"

"Don't you talk to me like that. I say that no daughter of mine will marry a German."

"Suppose I defy you?"

"Then I would cut you off with a shilling. Andreas is after your money, but he won't get it!"

"Paul is not interested in money. He is in love with me. And I don't want your money, if that is the way you feel about it."

John West stood and stepped towards her. His manner was placatory, his voice softer. "But don't you see, child, he is only after your money. Why give up your career for him? In another year or two your studies will be completed. You have a great future. You will become famous and make a lot of money. Marry him and you will miss all that."

This line of argument did not have the desired effect on Marjorie. Since she had met Paul she had abandoned her ambition for a career as a violin virtuoso. She knew that she was an outstanding violinist, one of the best at the Conservatorium, but a virtuoso must have just that extra self-discipline and genius which she came to believe she lacked. She began to neglect her studies; her whole being consumed by this her first love. Marjorie was a religious, romantic girl, who carried out the tenets of the Catholic Church on sex to the letter. Until she met Paul she had sublimated her sex impulses and emotions in music. When Paul started to pay attention to her, a great emotional flood was released that seemed to wash away some of her love and talent for music.

"I will give up anything for Paul. I want to marry right away, and have children. That is every woman's right. I will not give up my music, but I want more than anything else in the world to be Paul's wife."

John West felt a desire to place his arm around her, to speak softly to her, giving her fatherly advice, imploring her to heed his mature judgment, to tell her that he loved her and thought only of her future happiness and success, but it was not in him to do so. He was no longer capable of intimacy even with his own children. He could not tolerate defiance even from them.

He said irately: "You don't know what you're doing. You can tell Andreas that he needn't bother approaching me. No German will marry my daughter. Think this over, and come to your senses before you go back to Europe. I have spent a lot of money on your music, and I won't allow you to throw away your career on this ... this fortune hunter. Think it over. If you defy me, neither you nor Andreas will get another penny from me."

He turned on his heel and walked out.

John West went into the reception room and sulked over the evening paper while waiting for Sugar Renfrey, who was coming to discuss Labor Party business.

The family went to the music room. On the way Marjorie whispered to Paul that her father did not wish to speak to him tonight. She would tell him all about it later.

Pieces from Dvorak which Marjorie played at John's request pulsated with plaintive longing. Mary sensed that something was wrong and guessed what it might be. Later they played the gramophone: a Beethoven symphony, and some Kreisler recordings.

Meanwhile, Councillor Renfrey was engaged in earnest conversation with John West. The topic was a forthcoming by-election. The Labor candidate, Maurice Blackwell, had come in for particular reference. Every effort must be made to drive Blackwell from politics, John West informed Sugar.

"Turn it up, Jack. Blackwell's too popular. He won the pre-selection and the workers in Fitzroy would vote Labor if Billy the Blackfeller was the candidate."

"He'd be beaten if we could prove he was a Communist, and force the Party to cancel his nomination and run another pre-selection ballot."

The decision made at a recent Annual Conference to expel all Communists from the Labor Party placed a new weapon in the hands of John West. He wanted Blackwell out, and so did Archbishop Malone. He had discussed Blackwell's victory in the pre-selection ballot with the Archbishop. John West had hastened to inform Malone that he had done everything possible to defeat Blackwell, and had a plan that might still succeed.

Achbishop Malone had been impressed with the plan.

Sugar exclaimed: "That's a bloody good idea, Jack. How can we work it?"

"Well, I don't know exactly. It might be possible to get one of the local Reds to say publicly that Blackwell is a secret member of the Communist Party, which he probably is, anyway. The Reds have no money; they'll have a price like everyone else. Think you can arrange it?"

Sugar lit a big cigar, thrust out his chest and puffed vigorously. "Might at that. That fella Morton, Jim Morton, not a bad bloke for a red, they tell me. Poor as Job's turkey. Might listen to reason. I could see him if you like, Jack."

"All right, but be careful, I don't trust these Communists. We'll run an Independent Labor Candidate against Blackwell, just in case our scheme fails. Try to get this Morton to say that Blackwell is a Communist, member number so and so, give details, make it look good. I'll give Morton, say, fifty quid. Try him with less first. I don't want too much of my good money going into the pocket of a red-ragger."

Pretty soon John West sent Sugar home, and himself went to bed, after changing clothes in his dressing-room and placing his revolver under the pillow. He lay awake for nearly an hour listening to the light wind murmuring in the pine trees, puzzling over his conversation with Marjorie and its implications. From downstairs he could hear music, voices and occasional laughter.

A little later he heard Nellie enter her room. He heard her speak to *that* child, her child, whose father had been his bricklayer, and whom he felt sure she loved more than *his* children, *their* children. What a mess things were in this home! Sometimes he felt a hungry desire for love and passion, for Nellie's companionship, but always he suppressed it. She had wrecked his house, and she must be punished. He would be just, but above all he would be strong. He would hold his house together, guiding and ruling its members, all but *that* child, who was not his responsibility. His conscience was clear, he was giving it food and shelter and an education; it could expect no more, nor could Nellie. He was being more than fair. But Marjorie was a problem. The silly child wanted to throw away her career on a fop, and, what was worse, a German. Well, he would just have to force her to see reason, that was all.

He pondered over the matter until he became drowsy. It was past his usual time of sleep, which was before ten o'clock except on Saturday nights, when he went to his stadium.

Deep sleep promised to envelop his mind, when he became conscious of a murmur of voices downstairs, out of doors, apparently on the verandah. He roused himself and listened. There were two whispering voices – a man's and a woman's. Marjorie and the German, no doubt. Don't they think anyone wants to sleep? His keen ears could not distinguish what was being said, but soon he thought he heard Marjorie weeping softly and the German trying to console her.

He got out of bed, tip-toed to the balcony in his bare feet, and listened.

"Paul! Paul! You do love me, don't you, Paul? You won't let this make any difference between us, will you, Paul?"

It was Marjorie's voice, torn with emotion, raised now loud enough to be heard clearly. He could not hear Andreas' murmured reply, but Marjorie's weeping still wafted up to him. Then he heard sounds of their kissing and Marjorie murmuring: "Oh Paul, Paul darling, I love you. You must never leave me, Paul."

Suddenly a bitter hatred of Paul Andreas welled up in John West, in the starless, black night. This German was tampering with his daughter's love and wrecking her career, just because he wanted her money. Over my dead body, you German bastard!

John West heard them breathing heavily and sighing. They were embracing and kissing in the darkness below. He was aware of rising anger not unmixed with a queer form of jealousy. For the first time he realised that his daughters had grown up, and that they were women who would attract physical attention from men. The thought shocked him strangely.

Suddenly, his voice cracked the night: "For goodness' sake Marjorie, go to bed. Do you want to wake the whole household?"

A tense moment of absolute quiet on the verandah below, then Marjorie's voice: "Sorry, Father. I didn't know you were awake."

"Well, you know now. And it's a pity some people didn't know better than to abuse hospitality!"

John West went back to bed, and heard no more from the verandah below. His nerves were taut, and bitter thoughts wrenched his mind. He lay awake for over an hour thinking, not of the Labor Party or Maurice Blackwell, but of how he could frustrate Paul Andreas' designs on his daughter's love and *his* money.

If appearances were any criterion, no one could be less worthy of the importance placed upon him by John West and Sugar Renfrey than Jim Morton, as he walked down Bourke Street hill a few days later. It was a fine spring morning, but the warm sun could not cheer him, because he was tired, and, what was much worse, he was hungry. Morton was tall and erect, but thin and sallow-looking. His clothes – odd coat and trousers – were clean enough but threadbare. His shoes were down at heel and he limped: a hole in the sole of his right shoe exposed his foot to the asphalt footpath. He needed a shave, too.

Jim Morton did not feel satisfied with the progress the Communist Party was making in Australia. A year after Percy Lambert and others formed it, the Party had fallen apart through lack of united policy, but had been reformed. Lambert did not rejoin, he had come to believe the move to be premature, but he remained the unofficial leader of the dozen or so men who made up the membership of the Victorian Branch.

Jim Morton was beginning to believe the struggle to be a hopeless one. He was no Tom Mann, but a competent enough organiser and speaker. Apart from routine jobs such as selling pamphlets, speaking on the Yarra Bank, and agitating among the unemployed and the organised workers, his official task was to lead the Party's Trade Union work.

The task consisted of exerting whatever influence he could among the more militant Trade Union leaders on the major issues of the day. His job was an uphill one; his influence slight indeed.

He limped along fingering his last solitary sixpence, holding it in his hand as if afraid it might somehow leap from his pocket and be lost.

How long ago was it that he had fled the dingy house in New Zealand where his parents had brought him as a child from Ireland? How long ago had he run away to sea, working his way around the world? It seemed a long time ago, a long road to come down-hill to this.

How long ago had he been jailed for leading a mutiny aboard ship? How long ago had he walked off a ship in Melbourne, sick to death of the sea? He got an odd job here and there, and found his land legs. How long since he had wandered to the Yarra Bank on Sunday for the want of something better to do, and heard the irrepressible Joe Shelley exhorting a large audience to organise and work for the day when the poor and the downtrodden would rise up and throw the hated "Master Class" from their backs? How long since the name of Lenin had flamed in his mind? How long since he had been drawn into the Communist Party?

He stopped on a corner outside a hotel and hesitated. He suspected that the sinking pain in his innards was due as much to lack of nicotine as to hunger. When had he last had a smoke? When we have tobacco we smoke it to the stage of nausea, but when we haven't got it, we hanker after it hungrily and bestow upon its use far greater value than it deserves. What he wouldn't give for a smoke right now! How long ago did he reluctantly yet hungrily smoke his last butt? Only the day before yesterday! Seemed years ago!

He collected his wits. Spend fivepence on a cup of tea and a meat-pie at that cheap cafe over the road, then with a penny in his pocket so he would not be completely broke, go to the AGE office, look up the situations vacant column and find himself a job. He must have money with which to bring the room rent up, for food and for soles and heels for his shoes. It would mean that his political work would become only a spare-time activity. A man couldn't do wonders; he had to live. Collections from meetings wouldn't keep a man in cigarettes. Give up, Jimmy boy. What do the workers care that you are stony broke, that your rent's behind, your clothes and shoes worn out? He shrugged his shoulders; perhaps I'll feel better when I get that pie and tea under my belt.

As he stepped off the kerb to cross the road, a big motor car swerved towards him. He leapt back. The car stopped at the kerb with a grind of brakes, and a man got out. Jim Morton was annoyed.

The man swaggered towards him. He wore a boxer-hat and a big cigar protruded from a corner of his mouth. Jim Morton knew him by sight and repute. It was Sugar Renfrey.

"You're Jim Morton, ain't yer?"

"Yeh. Is that any reason to try and run me down like that?"

Sugar slapped him on the back heartily. "Missed yer be a mile. Me son there in the car, he was drivin'. Bit reckless. I been lookin' for you, and we're drivin' along and he says 'There's Morton there on the corner.' 'Speak of the devil,' I says. My name's Renfrey. Yer know me, I s'pose.''

"I know of you," Morton said, still annoyed, but too weak to persist in his anger.

"Have a drink?"

Morton hesitated. Was it Henry Lawson who said that people will often offer a hungry man a drink, but rarely a feed? "All right," he said. And Sugar took him by the arm roughly. They went into the bar.

"What'll yer have?"

"A whisky and soda." Morton reasoned that he couldn't keep a beer down, and that a whisky would do him good.

Morton knew Sugar to be a powerful figure behind the scenes in the Labor Party: a representative of the mysterious John West. Sugar ordered two whiskies and leant on the counter, squinting and twirling an unlit cigar from one side of his mouth to the other.

No doubt about Darwin's theory, thought Morton. Wonder what this ape wants.

'Y'know, it's a bloody shame to see a clever young fella like you lookin' as poor as a fourpenny rabbit; walkin' about with the arse outta his trousers," Sugar said confidentially.

As he spoke, Morton gingerly took a sip from his whisky; it seemed to punch him in the stomach, then in the head, and he became dizzy and sick. When his head cleared a little, he said: "They're not worn right through yet."

"A young fella like you would get along well in business. You're a good speaker and well-read. I could get you a job in a clothing factory. One of Jack West's. I'm a director." Sugar preened himself and poked a chubby thumb into the armhole of his waistcoat.

Morton made no answer.

"Why don't yer give up all this red-raggin' business? Where's it gettin' yer?"

"Not gettin' me very far, I'm afraid."

"Course it ain't. Why don't you get into the Labor Party? Work in with me, and I'll get yer that job I was tellin' yer about. And I'll get you into Parliament. I'll get Jack West to work you in."

Morton sipped his whisky. It seemed to stimulate him now that its first effects had cleared away, and he felt better. This is interesting. To Morton, as to most other people in the Labor Movement, Jack West was a mysterious power behind the scenes. He had been told that West owned stadiums and race-courses, and God knew what else, and had made his money out of a tote shop in Carringbush in the early days.

Morton decided he must find out what this was all about. "Is it as easy as that?"

"Yair. Jack West has the final say in most pre-selections. And, if anything goes wrong, we rig the ballot." Sugar held his cigar in his hand and roared with laughter, hitting Morton on the back, nearly spilling his whisky.

"But surely you are not going to do all this for me for nothing."

"Well, no, not exactly. There's a bloke who gives money to the Communist Party who calls hisself Member Number Nine. He's in the Red paper, the WORKERS' WEEKLY, nearly every issue. D'yer know who he is?"

"No, I don't, as a matter of fact."

"Wouldn't be Blackwell, would it? He opposed the Labor Party ban on Communists."

"No, Blackwell's not a member of the Communist Party."

"Well, we think he is."

"Who's we?"

"Me and Jack West."

"Well, you're wrong."

"Even if we are, if you said he was he'd lose the election."

The plot thickens, thought Morton. Trying to prove poor old Morrie is a Red, eh. "What d'yer want me to do?"

"Well," Sugar leaned towards him, and looked around the deserted bar with a conspiratorial air. "I'll give yer fifty quid if you put it in writin' that Blackwell's Member Number Nine. He beat our man in the pre-selection, see. If we can prove he's a member of the Communist Party, his endorsement'll be cancelled, and our man will get it and win the seat. The endorsed Labor candidate is sure to win."

"Fifty quid's a lot of money. You must be anxious to beat Blackwell."

"Yair, he stands in our way."

"And he'll continue to, if I refuse to do this?"

"I wouldn't say that. If we can't show Blackwell's a Red we're going to run our man against him as an independent. And we're going to use Snoopy Tanner's gang in the campaign."

What a loud-mouthed fool you are, thought Morton. I'd have thought the great West would have a shrewder man than you on the job.

"Here, have another drink," Sugar continued, convinced he was doing a good job. "You do this, and you'll never look back. The workers don't give a damn. They're like a lotta sheep. You come in with me. Fifty quid and a good job. An executive job. Not many men get an offer like it."

Jim Morton gulped his drink down. He'd heard enough. He could use the money, but not this kind of money. Better get away and have a yarn to Morrie Blackwell and Percy Lambert.

"It's a big decision," he said. "I must have time to think it over."

Sugar began to argue but finally said: "All right. I'll give you till tomorrer. Tell yer what, you meet me outside the Carringbush Town Hall tomorrer night at ten o'clock. I'll have the fifty quid with me and the document to sign."

Morton watched the car depart up the hill, then crossed the road and entered the cafe. He ate a pie ravenously, casting envious glances at a steak and eggs being devoured by a fat woman opposite him. Then he left the cafe and walked down the hill to a theatrical supply shop at which Percy Lambert worked. The wall of the shop was lined with weird masks, and the shelves strewn with theatrical equipment.

He found Lambert serving a customer with some false moustaches, trying them on and gesticulating.

When the customer left, he approached the counter and said: "Can I see you a minute, Percy?"

"Yes, Jim. Come round."

Morton followed Lambert into a small room behind the shop. He told him what had transpired. Lambert whistled softly then went to the phone in the shop. Morton heard him ring Blackwell.

Lambert came back. He was a little stouter now, and his thinning hair was greying. He was still a force in Communist Party circles, and, in his position on the Trades Hall Council, worked closely with Morton.

402

"Morrie is coming down right away."

"Good. What do you think we should do?" answered Morton.

"I think you should keep the appointment and stall him along. I can see a chance here not only to ensure Morrie of re-election, but to isolate and perhaps expel Renfrey. You meet Renfrey and pretend you'll do what he asks, but remain undecided for a few days. Then we'll bring out a leaflet near election time exposing Renfrey and West and give the story to the papers. Leave it till the last minute. Give them no time to reply."

Jim Morton now realised more clearly that he had begun something dangerous. He didn't like the sound of Tanner's gang coming into the picture. He began to have misgivings.

"It's a good scheme, Percy; we'll see what Morrie thinks."

Lambert was enthusiastic: "This is a chance of a life-time to bring Renfrey and the West gang into the open, and strike a blow against them. They are destroying the movement; here's our chance to destroy them politically. The bulk of the movement, even some of those intimidated by West, will support Morrie. Renfrey said he was going to use Tanner's gang, eh? We'd better carry guns. Have you a licence?"

"No."

"Perhaps you'd better carry one, anyway."

"I won't bother, Percy."

"I might. This will be a bitter fight."

They heard footsteps in the shop. Lambert peeped around the door. "Oh, come in, Morrie."

Maurice Blackwell entered the little room, took off his black hat, and accepted a chair proffered by Lambert. Blackwell was a man of medium height and build; a lock of hair fell over one side of his wide forehead. He had a round, good-humoured face. His clothes were black and plain, and very old-fashioned. Blackwell stood to the left of the Labor Party, and bitterly opposed the influence of John West and Archbishop Malone. He had unsuccessfully led the fight against the exclusion of Communists from the Labor Party at a recent conference. He looked what he was: a quiet family man from the professional class, but those who knew him best realised that he possessed reserves of energy and courage, and an adherence to principle.

"What's wrong, Percy?" Blackwell asked. He listened while Morton and Lambert related the story.

"Yes, we'll fight them, Percy. I can't say I altogether agree with your scheme to fool Renfrey; he's a violent and irresponsible man. I'll prefer to fight him and West with political weapons only. But, still, I can see the possibilities, and will not interfere." Blackwell then addressed Morton: "You realise that this is dangerous, Jim, I suppose."

"I realise that, Morrie, but I think Percy's plan is a good one," Morton said, without enthusiasm.

"And you're prepared to go ahead with it? It's you who will take the main risk, you know."

"I'll go through with it, I s'pose. I'll have to meet Renfrey tomorrer night, anyway."

Blackwell arose. Lambert said to him, somewhat jocularly: "You'd better get yourself a gun, Morrie."

"No. I don't believe in violence, you know that. I will fight them my way."

The next night, Jim Morton waited in front of the Carringbush Town Hall. He started involuntarily as the big clock in the tower tolled the first stroke of ten. He was as nervous as a cat.

No sooner had the last chime pealed out than a car pulled up and Sugar Renfrey alighted. He looked around in all directions, then came over to Morton.

"Come on, we'll talk in the car," he said.

Morton hesitated, then followed. They sat in the front seat. Morton noticed that there were two men in the back seat. Even in the gloom, he recognised Renfrey's son, a solid youth with a round, unintelligent face. He turned and looked at the other man. His hat was over his eyes: he wore a white moustache and his hands were in his coat pockets. Morton didn't know him, but it was Arthur West. He held a revolver in his pocket and it was pointing at the back of Morton's head.

The tense atmosphere frightened Morton. How on earth could he extricate himself from this dilemma?

"Well, have yer thought the matter over?" Sugar asked.

Morton had to clear his throat before he could speak. "Well, yes, but . . ."

"Holdin' out for more dough, are yer?"

"Well. It's unsavoury work."

"Wot's unsavoury about it? Blackwell's no good. You'd do

404

the movement a good turn if you help to git rid of 'im.''

Morton was stung by this remark, but controlled his feelings. ''Anyway,'' he said, ''I want more money. At least a hundred quid.''

Morton heard the man with the white moustache stir in his seat. Never know what these men would do if he antagonised them too much. He must get away as quickly as possible.

Sugar hesitated. ''Well,'' he said. ''I'll tell yer what I'll do. As well as sayin' that Blackwell is member nine, you sign a letter sayin' that he's been a member of the Communist Party for years. If you do that I'll give you a hundred quid. There y'are. That's fair enough, and if you take my advice you'll do it. There's more ways of killing a goose than by wringing its neck.''

''All right. I'll do it, but . . .''

''That's the bloody spirit. And you give these Reds away. You'll always have the arse outta yer trousers if you stay with them. You meet me tomorrer night and I'll have everything ready.''

''No. I can't tomorrer night. I've got a meeting. Better make it Friday night.''

Sugar Renfrey gave Morton directions where to meet him and the car drove away, leaving a very worried Jim Morton to walk slowly towards the city.

Percy Lambert stood in the darkness near the wall watching Jim Morton, who waited for Sugar Renfrey under a street light on the opposite side of the road. Lambert felt the revolver in his pocket. Morton had misgivings about this appointment and Lambert did not blame him.

It was a sinister area. The address given to Morton was that of a sweet shop – a ''screen'' used by Snoopy Tanner's gang.

The day after Jim Morton's interview outside the Carringbush Town Hall, a hurried meeting was held between Morton, Blackwell and the President of the Victorian Labor Party.

Morton assured the President that Blackwell was not ''No. 9'' and was certainly not a member of the Communist Party. The President said that he, for one, would not tolerate Renfrey running a ''West man'' against the endorsed candidate, Blackwell. It was then agreed that Morton should keep the further appointment, and that Lambert should act as witness, and, if necessary, protector.

Car lights approached down the narrow street. Lambert saw Sugar Renfrey alight from the car, and speak to Morton; then they walked into a lane beside the sweet shop. Lambert crossed the road, walked past the lane fingering his gun. He saw Morton, Renfrey, and two others speaking in the light of the opened side door.

He heard Morton say: "I'm not signing until I get the money." He heard Sugar answer: "Don't trust me, is that it?"

Lambert walked past the lane and stood listening tensely. He heard the voices of Renfrey and Morton and another raised in argument. He wondered whether he ought to intervene. Anything might happen now. After a while, he heard footsteps coming up the lane, so he hurriedly returned to the other side of the road. Morton came out of the lane, walked past the shop, and turned the corner towards the city. As arranged, Percy walked in the opposite direction around the block.

When they met, Morton said huskily: "No more of this for me, Perc'. There was three of them. They had guns in their pockets. I think one was Snoopy Tanner."

"What did you arrange?"

"I've arranged to meet Renfrey at the Clifton Hill railway gates on Sunday afternoon at five o'clock; said I wanted time to think it over. I don't mind admitting that I was bloody scared."

"I think we have all we need. You'd better not turn up, Jim. I'll go with a few witnesses, just to see who they send."

One evening in the week after the Fitzroy election, John West paced up and down the music room in a towering rage. Sugar Renfrey sat full of fear in a chair near the piano.

"I told you to be careful," John West was saying. "I told you not to trust Morton. But what do you do? You give him a copy of the typed letter; and you blow off your silly mouth."

"No, I never, Jack. I never told him nothin'; God's honour, I didn't," replied Sugar. "I didn't trust him, like you told me not to."

"You didn't trust him! Oh, no!" John West confronted Sugar aggressively. "Well, where did they get all the information that's in this leaflet?" He read aloud extracts from a leaflet he held in his hand.

LABOR'S TAMMANY

Is Labor Party To Be Tool For "Sports"?

BLACK HAND AT FITZROY

Blackwell's victory in the Fitzroy by-election is more than a victory over an allegedly independent candidate, it is a victory over the Black Hand Gang of Victorian politics.

Once in this organisation's power, a man becomes a mere tool. Oppose them, thwart their wishes, and the general opinion is that you are lucky if you have a licence to carry a gun. Against this organisation, Maurice Blackwell fought an historic battle and won!

"Historic battle! I'll give them historic battle!"

"Ar, yer don't want to take much notice of this, Jack. This was all published in the Commo paper, THE WORKER'S WEEKLY. All made up outta their bloody heads, like the things they wrote about what I said to Morton," Sugar intervened, hopefully using a device that was to become popular in later years, especially among politicians – that of attacking the Communists in order to conceal one's own misdeeds.

John West wasn't impressed. "If it's all lies, how do you account for this – "

In one of his conversations with Morton, Renfrey said that Snoopy Tanner's gang was at his service for certain work in election campaigns . . .

"And how do you account for this – "

This organisation has interfered more or less successfully with Labor pre-selection ballots and is headed by the well-known book-maker Renfrey, behind whom stands a sinister and comparatively silent figure, one who is commonly understood to be one of the richest men in Melbourne, and who has contributed to political campaign funds for many years."

"That's you, Jack."

"Yes, that's me," John West answered, savagely. "And this

407

is you, *a bouncing braggart, a vain-glorious, conceited, boastful lump of ferment*. At least they are right about you; except they don't say straight out that you are a bloody fool!"

"Aw, turn it up, Jack!"

"You're the one that's going to turn it up. They say you're going to be expelled; well, you won't be."

"Why, can yer fix it up, Jack?"

"I'm not going to try to fix it up. You're going to get in first and resign. Then I'll arrange for you to be readmitted before you come up again for election to the Carringbush Council. And from then on, you confine your work to the Carringbush area. This is the last big job you'll do for me."

"Aw, don't be hard, Jack."

"I'm not hard. You've made a fortune out of me – and spent it, no doubt – yet nearly every job you do you mess up."

"Ar, I wouldn't say that, Jack."

"Instead of beating Blackwell, you helped him to win. The reports of this campaign in the papers did me a lot of harm; and it's all your fault. Now they've brought out their leaflet! I warned you after you first saw Morton that it might be a trap; yet you let him make a fool of you. Listen." He read again from the leaflet in an irate voice.

It must be remembered that many members of this gang are members of Labor Party branches, and that in the large, thickly populated area surrounding Carringbush, their word is law . . .

"And this is even worse – "

Speaker after speaker, politician after politician, whom the boasting book-maker declared to be under his thumb, appeared on Blackwell's platform. The attempt to bribe Jim Morton figured much in Blackwell's last two election speeches. Resenting the crooked tactics of the Sports, the Labor Movement rallied behind Maurice Blackwell. Tammany has not control!

John West read in mincing tones, but already his rage was subsiding. He found it difficult to sustain anger against Sugar, for whom he had a contemptuous affection.

He knew that he should have ceased using Sugar for important work years ago. This would teach him never to do it again.

"Anyway, Morton won't get away with this," John West continued. "We offered to help him if he helped us. We'll know better than to trust these bloody Communists in future. They're a menace to the community. We'll teach Morton to lie to us. Oh, let it go, Sugar, I'll see Frank Lammence about it."

"Ar, I'll fix it, Jack. I got a score to settle with him."

"No, Sugar, leave it to Frank. You lie low for a while."

Marjorie West stood near the piano in the music room playing her violin. She was playing *Liebeslied*. Grief sang in the strings and in her heart.

She wore a short navy blue skirt and a white blouse – her bobbed hair hung over one side of her face. A tear trickled down her cheek and fell upon the violin. Before she had finished playing Mary came in and sat in a chair in the shaft of the dying sunlight that was shining through the tall window.

Mary had been playing tennis, and was wearing a daringly-short white skirt. She sat with her shapely legs outstretched; wisps of her flaming red hair had fallen loose from the pins and decorative combs with which she kept it up in "basin crop" style.

When the violin sobbed and was quiet, Mary, oblivious of Marjorie's grief, said: "What a life. Tennis, dinner, a dance, then bed, breakfast, and more tennis or perhaps a church bazaar. My God!"

Marjorie made no reply, as she endeavoured to compose herself.

"What a life," Mary repeated, with an air of exaggerated boredom. "If you tire of tennis you may go riding and to be daring, you don't ride side-saddle. Tennis and riding and dancing. Why, it's as bad as huntin', shootin' and fishin'. What a curse to be born a member of the idle rich. It wouldn't be so bad if a girl had a respectable banker or something for a father. The way these old dears look down their noses!" She arose to illustrate her discourse – with a clever imitation. " 'Yes, she's attractive, but her father, my deah, made his money out of a tote shop – of all things, a tote shop, my deah!' If only I could do something useful like work in an office, or a factory. Imagine Father's reaction." She stood erect in passable impersonation of John West.

" 'Mary, I know what is best for you. If you defy me in this matter I will cut you off with a shilling. You just continue to look beautiful, then people will say: *That's John West's daughter. Isn't she lovely?*' My God, what a life!''

Mary flung herself on a couch near the wall in an abandoned fashion, then sat up pensively, with her knees under her chin; while Marjorie stood, leaning against the piano.

Their mother came in. Not having given way to the fashion, she wore a long skirt. Now in her late forties, her beauty was clouded with a sullen air of self-pity.

Nellie West had been in bed all morning, complaining of pains in her back. She still persisted with her ailment, though no one else in the house took it seriously.

"For goodness' sake, Mary, how often must I tell you not to sit with your knees up? You're a grown woman now, not a schoolgirl.''

"Oh, all right, Mother,'' Mary answered, changing posture.

Nellie had entered the room intending to speak to Marjorie, whom she believed to be alone. She knew that Marjorie was most unhappy because her father was persisting in his refusal to countenance "any daughter of mine marrying a German.'' Deciding not to mention Marjorie's problem in Mary's presence, she said: "Time you two changed for dinner.''

Nellie was disappointed that Marjorie had so far refused to discuss her problem with her. She knew that she had failed to regain the confidence of her daughters.

Mary noticed her sister's extremely downcast aspect. "Cheer up, Margo,'' she said. "It's not as bad as all that, surely.''

"Yes, it is,'' Marjorie answered, and her body quivered in a deep sob.

Mary joined her and placed a sympathetic arm around her shoulders.

"You've been brooding, Margo. You haven't been eating, and I can see you haven't been sleeping, either. Why not have a good heart-to-heart talk about the whole business? Come and sit on the couch with me.''

Marjorie allowed herself to be led to the couch, where they sat in the falling dusk.

Marjorie's pent up anguish flooded in convulsive weeping. "Oh, whatever will I do, Mary?''

Mary held her close and allowed her to cry until the sobs became less convulsive, then she took a tiny handkerchief from her skirt pocket and handed it to her sister. "Here, Margo, blow your nose. Nothing like a good cry to put things right."

"Nothing can put things right for me, ever again, Mary. I'm sure I shall kill myself."

"Oh, Margo! Don't be so melodramatic!" ejaculated Mary, shocked by her sister's earnestness. "What is so desperately wrong that you should talk like that?"

Suddenly Mary felt her sister stiffen as though she were steeling herself.

"Mary, do you believe that it is really sinful, if you love a man, love him desperately, I mean, with true love, to give yourself to him, though you are not married to him?" As Marjorie spoke she evaded her sister's gaze by burying her head in her shoulder.

"No, Margo, I don't really. Our religion seems very hard sometimes. I know that when I meet my man, the man I love, I shall, well, I shall love him. You really mustn't torture yourself. Only your heart knows what is true love; and true love cannot be sinful."

"Oh, I love him, Mary. I do love him, and I don't care what the Church says. But, Mary . . . Oh, how can I tell you? Mary, I'm going to have a baby!"

"Oh, my poor Margo. Are you sure?"

"Yes, I think so. Oh, Mary, whatever is to become of me now? It's Father's fault. I resisted Paul until Father refused permission for us to marry."

Mary was shocked by her sister's disclosure, but quickly pulled herself together: Margo needed someone to lean on now, as never before. Mary hugged her close, and said: "It is not so hopeless as it may seem. You love him; you have done nothing wrong. You can marry him right away, and return to Europe. No one there will know. You say he wants to marry you; he must return your love."

"He says he does, but Father is sure he only wants my money."

"Oh, take no notice of Father. Money is his god. He thinks *everyone* is after his money." Mary, herself, held some misgivings about the genuineness of Andreas, but dared not mention

411

them now. Paul must be made to face up to the dilemma which he had created for Margo.

"Does Paul know?" Mary asked. "About the baby, I mean."

"Yes, I told him last night. Oh, Mary, do you think he loves me?"

"Of course I do, sweet. But don't tell Father, not yet. You can write to him from Europe, afterwards."

"I thought I might have a talk to Mother, perhaps."

"I have a better idea. We'll have a talk to Gran' this very night. Gran' will understand, and she will help, too, I'm sure. Oh, darling old Margo, how worried you must have been, keeping this to yourself. Everything will work out right in the end, you see. We'll go up to Gran's room tonight."

Marjorie felt relieved, though a little dazed. She wiped her eyes, and they walked up the stairs.

The day before she was to leave for Europe, Marjorie West married Paul Andreas. They were married secretly in the vestry of a suburban Catholic Church.

That evening she sat with the others on the verandah.

The pale summer night was tranquil, but her mind was agitated and confused. Where had all her sorrow begun? Where would it all end? How disappointing, how terribly sorrowful and harrowing had been her four months at home, to which she had looked forward so much.

True to her religion and her idealistic dream of perfect love, she had resisted all her experienced lover's attempts to consummate their love before it had been blessed with a Christian marriage. Her body and soul had cried out "let our desires be fulfilled!" but she had desperately pursued her efforts to remain true to her faith and her dreams. But when her father had refused to allow her to marry Paul she had given herself up to the passion for which she longed. That very night on the verandah couch their love was sealed forever, and later, in bed, she wept for shame and self-recrimination. She had sinned against her religion and her ideal of love.

If Father had been reasonable this would not have happened. Now everything was spoiled. Yet she was happy in an irresponsible way – happy and defiant – but misgivings about Paul kept persisting.

There were many things she didn't understand about Paul. Paul could have made his choice from many women, yet he had chosen her – slowly and deliberately. Surely Father could not be right in his insinuation that Paul was a fortune-hunter! Yet Paul's people were poor; they hadn't always been poor, but the war had reduced them to poverty, so they could scarcely afford to have him continue his studies.

The Versailles Treaty had reduced Germany to ruin, Paul used to say, but Germany would rise again and destroy her enemies. When she said to Paul that there had been many lies in war propaganda on both sides, he had insisted that only the British had lied, the Germans had told the truth. When she said that she believed the Germans to be just as good as the British, he always replied that the Germans were the greatest race on earth, an Aryan race. There was a man named Hitler whom Paul's father, who had been an officer in the German Army, knew. This Hitler would some day lead Germany out of its chaos forward to domination of the world. When Paul talked of these things he frightened her with his intensity. He seemed to have an inferiority complex about the poverty of his country and his own family, and this kind of talk seemed to placate his resentment. He was determined that Germany would again be rich. Was he determined that he and his family would again be rich? – determined enough to become a fortune-hunter? Always she dismissed the thought as treacherous and unworthy.

Dear Paul, with his sentimental love talk, his brittle and not-very-good musicianship, his quotations from Nietzsche and Spengler. She was upset, that was all. Father was a miser who would automatically think that anyone who wanted to marry herself or Mary was after his money.

Paul loved her, it must be so!

Would she ever forget how the weeks brought the terrible realisation that she was pregnant? After the initial anguish came defiance; she would have the baby, it was a child of love. Why had Paul suggested so callously that they should arrange to prevent the birth, then later, so eagerly agreed to her proposal that they should be secretly married?

How far short of her dreams her wedding had been. Paul was not a Catholic, so according to the rules of the Church they were married in the vestry. What a drab ceremony, how disappointing, how terribly humiliating! The young priest knew or guessed the situation, and though he tried hard to be considerate, he only succeeded in being patronising. He obviously thought she was in some way unclean. Mother was there, and wept throughout the brief ceremony. Young John was best man and made jokes; even pretended he had lost the ring. Joe and Mary were quiet, kindly observers, and Mary brought a camera and took photos afterwards. Gran' was there, practical and jolly, doing her best to alleviate some of the suffering.

Marjorie West had dreamed of a grand church wedding, a Nuptial Mass, with the organ playing "Oh, Promise Me," with "something old and something new, something borrowed and something blue," with flowers and candles, relatives and friends, and Father bringing her up the aisle to Paul, and lovely speeches at the breakfast afterwards. Instead, this small ceremony, this anguish and deceit.

Coming out of the church Paul had said softly: "Cheer up, everything will be all right. But I wish we had your father's permission."

They would spend their wedding night apart; she would have to sleep here and Paul at his hotel, but tomorrow they would be reunited aboard ship.

Conversation on the verandah was most desultory. Mrs Moran and Mary were doing their best to be cheerful, and to draw Marjorie out of herself. Marjorie noticed her mother wiping her eyes in the gloom, then said flippantly: "I do hope Father doesn't invite that terrible man, Renfrey, to supper. I'm sure I shall burst out laughing in his face if I have to sit through supper with him ever again, with his vulgar talk and his silly cigars."

"I don't think you'll be troubled with Mr Renfrey tonight," Mrs Moran said. "He is getting the rounds of the kitchen, or rather the music room, if I can judge by the angry voices I heard earlier. Personally I find him most amusing."

"Sugar's all right," said young Joe, absent-mindedly. He was sitting against a verandah pillar looking into the gathering night as though seeking some answer there to the tragedy of recent events. "Bit of a crank, that's all."

"He's more than a crank if you can judge by the papers the other week. I don't know why Dad has anything to do with him," Mary said.

"Oh, your father has employed Sugar since the days of the tote in Carringbush. Went to school together, I suppose," Mrs Moran replied. "I think your father invites him to supper just to embarrass us. His idea of a joke."

Silence resumed control until they heard footsteps crunching slowly along the gravel path, and Paul Andreas emerged from the darkness. He came on to the verandah diffidently, as though he feared that something may have occurred since earlier in the day to create for him a hostile reception. Greetings were exchanged. He sat beside Marjorie. Mrs Moran suggested they should retire to the living room as the air was becoming chilly.

Sugar Renfrey came out the front door, lit a cigar and walked off down the gravel path, mumbling to himself, oblivious of their presence.

As they walked indoors, they met John West in the hall. "Marjorie," he said quietly, "I would like to see you in the music room for a moment."

The others retired to the living room, and Marjorie followed him, her heart thumping. Could she resist the relentless cross-examination which undoubtedly awaited her?

He switched on the light, sat at a round table near the centre of the room, and moved the vase of flowers nearer the edge of it.

"Sit down, Marjorie."

She pulled up a chair hurriedly and sat opposite him. She was self-conscious about her condition, fearing that people might notice the almost imperceptible bulge in her stomach.

"Marjorie, here is a little money for extras on your way over," he said, passing a small roll of ten-pound notes to her.

She took the money without replying.

"You seem unhappy. What is the trouble?"

She thought before answering. She must lie as she had never lied before: cleverly and convincingly. "I want to marry Paul, Father. That is why I am unhappy."

His sharp eyes menaced her resolution. "Are you sure you haven't already married him?"

"I don't know what you mean."

"I mean that there is something going on in this house that I know nothing about, and it concerns you, and Andreas."

She could think of nothing to say. He leaned towards her. "If you defy me in this matter, you will regret it. I am trying to protect your interests, your career, your happiness, from this penniless German fortune-hunter. Forget about him. When you return and begin your career, there will be plenty of time to get yourself a good husband with wealth and position.''

"You place too much store on wealth and position, Father," she said, then she bent forward entreatingly. "Oh, Father, can't you see? I love Paul, and I must marry him. Race and creed and wealth are not everything. Can't you be reasonable, please?"

"I am being reasonable. I'm your father and I know what is best for you. You marry this man over my dead body."

The irony of the situation struck her. She could almost have burst out laughing, and taunted him with the truth; but she resisted the impulse. "I will obey my true feelings, Father."

He rose to his feet, gripping the edge of the table with both hands. She answered his gaze, studying him. The neat appearance, the greying hair: he looked friendly enough except for his eyes and mouth. For a moment she felt like exclaiming: "Oh, Father, I am your daughter. I need your help. I will tell you everything, and you can help me," but she knew it to be useless to do so.

John West was sharing the fate of all men who rule with the iron rod of domination: his attitude often forced people to deceive him. At the beginning of the interview, he had wanted to be placatory, to talk the matter over as between father and daughter, but he was being defied: that meant that he must browbeat and threaten reprisals. He leant towards her and spoke slowly and with emphasis. "There's something going on! There's been a conspiracy against me in my own house for weeks! I can tell from the manner of your mother and Mary and your grandmother. There is something going on, and I don't like it! If you have defied me, or do defy me, I shall cut you off with a shilling and you shall never darken the door of this house again!"

The bitter finality of his tones struck her. After tomorrow she might never see this man, this house, or her family again. Oh God! was any of this her fault? Oh, Paul, you must love me; you must be good to me!

Dr Jenner sat in the lounge of the new Atlantic Hotel, in the seaport town of Cairns, Queensland. The oppressive, wet-season night had fallen – heavy and still. Though accustomed to northern weather and sensibly dressed in white shirt and trousers, Dr Jenner felt stifled and depressed.

No longer employed by the Queensland Goverment, he was using Cairns as a base for some survey work for private mining interests. His refusal to capitulate before the cajoling and threats of Premier Thurgood had long ago cost him his job.

The local secretary of the Miners' Union had just left Dr Jenner. After requesting the doctor to lecture at a meeting before his departure inland, the secretary had related some disquieting stories about Chirraboo. He contended that Thurgood, Rand and MacCorkell lived in constant fear of exposure and would stop at nothing to suppress the criticism against them that was growing. There were three men most outspoken against the scandal: one of them was dead, the second was in a lunatic asylum, and the third was Dr Jenner himself.

"Your life may be in danger," the miners' leader had said before leaving. "Don't move about here at night alone."

Within a year of his interview with Red Ted Thurgood, Dr Jenner had been replaced by another geologist, who not only reported favourably on Rand's application, but later recommended that the Government buy the Lady Joan and Gilowell mines for forty thousand pounds, and work them in conjunction with the Chirraboo Smelters.

After the State purchased the mines, a man named Garrardi, an old friend of Premier Thurgood, Dr Jenner had been told, became the manager of the Chirraboo Smelters.

As far as Dr Jenner could gather, Thurgood and MacCorkell had each received a big parcel of shares in rich mines at Mt Isa in return for installing a Government Railway to that centre; and later, financed by Mr John West of Victoria, they had purchased other mines at Mt Isa. Then ore began to stream from Mt Isa to the Chirraboo Smelters, where all of it – the good, the bad, and the indifferent – was paid for at top prices. George Rand also found Garrardi useful: George began obtaining loads of inferior ore, burned bricks from old blast furnaces and any other rubble he could lay his hands on, and sent them to the smelters to receive top price from Garrardi.

Garrardi later recommended to the Government that, as the smelters used a lot of timber, it should allow a company to be formed to supply timber exclusively to the smelters from a nearby Government forestry reserve. Premier Thurgood consulted Treasurer MacCorkell and a company was formed. This time, Mr Duncan, who still drank too much and worked too hard, was given shares.

Dr Jenner could not help being sorry for Duncan. He had great respect for his ability and for the years of excellent service he had given to Queensland mining before he got into the clutches of the Chirraboo swindlers. He had confronted Duncan and demanded that he get out before it was too late, only to receive the crestfallen reply: "It is already too late, Doc. It hurts to lose my self-respect and your esteem, but there is no hope for me now. I'm headed for trouble and I can blame the bottle."

Garrardi thought of another bright idea. He decided to embark with Thurgood, MacCorkell and Rand on yet another business venture which could be largely financed with Government money. He appointed his brother to the position of manager of the Government Store at Chirraboo. This store supplied the general needs of the working men of Chirraboo. Soon (the miners' leader had just informed Dr Jenner) merchandise hitherto unknown in Chirraboo began to appear in the store: expensive crockery and cutlery, table linen and table decorations, and gaudy furniture and furnishings of all kinds. These goods, lying as they did outside the simple tastes and limited purses of the miners, remained unsold. Garrardi then approached the Premier, stating that the Chirraboo store contained large stocks of unsaleable goods which he craved approval to sell by auction. This was readily granted.

It appeared that this very hotel, the Atlantic, had been built, though the owners' names were kept secret, on behalf of Messrs Rand, Garrardi, Thurgood and MacCorkell, the timber, cement, steel and other materials used having been supplied by the Chirraboo Smelters, the Government Forestry Reserve and the State Railways. At the auction sale at the Chirraboo store, the unsaleable goods were disposed of at bargain prices, and in some manner best known to Mr Garrardi himself, found their way into the Atlantic Hotel, which became generally acknowledged as the "flashest hotel in the North."

But the Atlantic was popular only with drinkers and gamblers. Tourists and boarders preferred premises where one could sleep at night without being disturbed by merrymakers and card players.

Judging by noises emanating from the next room and somewhere upstairs, it seemed to Dr Jenner that the reputation given the hotel by his informant was by no means unjust. This was his first trip to Cairns since the hotel had been built. He had been attracted by the modern exterior, but next time he would return to his usual hotel. Not only the beginnings of the nightly orgy had formed this resolution in the doctor's mind. His friend, the Union Secretary, whose word he did not doubt, had informed him that a man had been murdered here only a few months ago, allegedly because he had been writing to politicians and the press with information about the *Swindles of the Mulgara Mining Company and the Management of the Chirraboo Smelters*. The man had once been an accountant at the Smelters.

After being relieved of his duties by Garrardi, he had begun to talk. Lately he had been boarding at the Atlantic Hotel and frequented one of its poker schools. One morning his body had been found on the footpath below the balcony. His back was broken. He was dead. No one seemed to know what had happened to him – perhaps there had been a fight and he had fallen from the hotel balcony.

Rumours spread like wildfire that he had been murdered because he had spoken 'out of his turn' on the Chirraboo scandals. The Miners' Union demanded a Government inquiry, but the coroner recorded a finding of accidental death and the matter was hushed up.

Dr Jenner went to his room early, locked the door, changed, and stretched his long figure on the sheets under the mosquito net; but sleep would not come. Not the noise but his agitated thoughts kept him awake.

Jenner's whole life was being blighted by Thurgood and his gang. Gathering evidence against them had become an obsession with him. His sense of justice revolted against the cheap trickery which was reducing Australia's richest mineral fields to heaps of rubble and waterlogged holes in the ground. His long cherished hope that the Australian Labor Party would introduce Socialism had been an idle dream. His scientific career was ruined. His work as a consulting geologist was being done for private speculators seeking quick profits.

He had been expelled from the Labor Party. If ever a man had seemed assured of election to Parliament it was he. He had contested a Queensland State seat in 1919; and in 1925 had been a member of the Labor Senate team. He had polled well. His friends told him he would live to become a member of the Federal Parliament, but Red Ted Thurgood had other ideas. Thurgood's chance came only six months ago. The so-called anti-Communist pledge arose in the Labor Party. Dr Jenner refused to endorse it on principle, contending that the Communists were a Socialist group like the Labor Party, and that all Socialists should be united.

He would never forget the look of triumphant hatred on Thurgood's face when he moved for his expulsion at the last Party conference, and the motion was carried.

Dr Jenner had always placed great importance on his regular articles in the weekly journals published by the Labor Party, and the powerful Australian Workers' Union. Their columns were immediately closed to him. He saw more ironic significance in the fact that he was, at the same time, black-listed from the columns of the two Brisbane daily papers which formerly had welcomed his regular scientific articles. John West, sinister figure behind Thurgood and MacCorkell, owned one of the dailies. West's connection with the whole affair was rather obscure, but Dr Jenner knew that West had made a fortune recently when he sold the Mt Isa mines at a huge figure to an English company.

Weirdly fantastic was the story of the man who had been declared insane. It appeared that he was a member of the Labor Party who often got hold of queer ideas, but who had been agitating lately for an inquiry into the behaviour of certain Labor leaders in relation to the Mulgara Mining Company and the Chirraboo Smelters. Before long he had been sent to a lunatic asylum.

The great riddle of the Queensland mining rackets puzzled Dr Jenner's brain; the murmur of the ocean and sounds of shouting, laughter, thumping and footsteps elsewhere in the hotel combined with it to keep him awake until the early hours.

Once footsteps seemed to approach his door and he rose on his elbow listening tensely in the darkness, but nothing happened. At last he slept heavily.

After breakfast he packed his bags and was the first customer in the bar.

"This is a fine hotel, yes," he said to the barmaid.

"Glad you like it. It's real modern, there's no doubt about it. The swankiest hotel in the North, they say. The furniture and the curtains and crockery and all, are the very best, and real flash, I must say."

"Its owners must be really enterprising. Tell me, who does own it?"

"Er . . . I couldn't say. I mean, I don't know."

"Surely you – the head barmaid – would know who it is that employs you. But, still, it doesn't matter."

The woman looked around the bar, then leaned across the counter towards him. Her big breasts flopped on to the polished bar.

"It's supposed to be a secret," she said, "but the Mulgara Mining Company owns this place."

"But there is no Mulgara Mining Company now. The Government have taken it over."

She eyed him a little suspiciously. "You seem a nice feller," she said, "but you shouldn't ask so many questions."

She forced a coquettish smile. "Ask no questions and you'll be told no lies. Understand?" she said.

Then she studied him as though trying to sum him up. He sipped his whisky nonchalantly.

"I'm not really interested; just making conversation with a pleasant lady, I am, that is all," replied the doctor, with a rather unconvincing effort at flirtatious conversation.

He was a tall, handsome man: she was pleased and a little flattered.

"Do you know who used to own the Mulgara Mines?"

"No, I'm sure I do not."

"Well, for being a good boy. I'll tell you who owns this hotel. The people who used to own the Mulgara Mines own this hotel; but I'd advise you to forget it."

As John West stepped on to the tram for home, the Post Office clock struck midnight. This was a late hour for him to be abroad; even on a Saturday night. Tonight he had missed the boxing matches to attend the posting of progress figures in the Victorian

421

State Elections. He felt elated. The Labor Party had won. It was assured of an absolute majority over the Nationalist and Country Parties.

Soon Ned Horan would be Premier of Victoria, Tom Trumbleward Chief Secretary, Bob Jolly and others among his men would be in the Cabinet. His great enterprises could now be protected and extended!

He must make certain that Trumbleward became Chief Secretary. For all his radical talk, Tom was the easiest to handle of all: he had the capacity for the job, and the popularity among Labor supporters. And Chief Secretary was the most important post. The Chief Secretary allotted racing dates, he controlled the Police Force, the penal laws and the prisons. If a man could have nominated the Chief Secretary in those days, the tote would still be operating, and the V.R.C. would not have beaten him. Bit different now, with Tom Trumbleward instead of that hypocrite old Gibbon.

John West never forgot a rebuff or a defeat. The V.R.C. had warned him off for life! True they had lifted their ban after the war, and allowed him to race at Flemington and other galloping courses, but they still prevented him from entering the members' enclosure or the birdcage. They treated him with disdain, just because he had made his wealth from an illegal totalisator, because he conducted the cinderella sports of pony racing and trotting. Well, they would be made to sit up and take notice now! Soon he would enter the galloping world. He'd have as many galloping dates as the V.R.C.; he'd teach them to rub him out for life.

The tram clattered on towards Carringbush. Though electric trams had replaced the old cables on most routes, this route was still served with the self-same cable trams that had carried customers to the tote in the nineties.

It was a warm summer night, so John West had seated himself on the side of the open front car.

Victoria was safe. Now he must redouble his efforts to ensure a Labor victory in the Federal Elections which might fall next year, and juggle the right men into the Cabinet. The Federal Parliament was moving from Melbourne to Canberra before the end of the year. That would make it harder to control, but if he got enough of his men in, it would be all right. Somehow he must get a Federal seat for Ted Thurgood. With Real dead Thurgood must become Prime Minister.

Just as well Labor had won in Victoria. There was talk of revolt among the trotting men. They were demanding non-proprietary control. In the boxing game, things weren't much better. There was talk of a Government-appointed Boxing Commission. Well, they could talk as much as they liked now. Jack West was boss!

Presently Sugar Renfrey boarded the tram at the other end. He had been celebrating Labor's victory. Seeing John West, he precariously negotiated the journey along the rocking tram on to the front car.

" 'Ow are yer, Jack?" he shouted. "Heard the figures? What a bloody victory!"

His cigar fell from his mouth, and in his effort to catch it he would have fallen off the tram, had not John West grasped him by the coat.

"Great victory, all right, Bob. I told you we would win," John West answered benignly.

Sugar took out another cigar and lit it with difficulty, then his face assumed a scowl as he said: "I see Blackwell won easy, the bastard!"

John West did not reply. He had again tried to defeat Blackwell in the pre-selection ballot, and then run an independent candidate against him. Sugar Renfrey had insisted on helping this candidate, vigorously assisted by his usual gang of thugs.

They distributed leaflets, intimidated scrutineers, and, where possible, voted for the absent, the sick and the dead. During the campaign, several members of the Timberworkers' Union, which was engaged in a bitter strike against wage cuts, assisted in Blackwell's campaign. Sugar had ordered a few of Snoopy Tanner's men to teach the bastards a lesson. Forthwith three timberworkers were attacked by several men while pasting up Blackwell's election posters. One of them was bundled into a waiting car, while the other two fled towards a moving tram. They were overtaken, felled from behind, and dragged to join their mate in the car.

The three of them were taken to Sugar Renfrey's house, where they were severely beaten up. Their eyes were blackened, their clothes torn, their bodies bruised. They were tied up and told they would not be released until they gave an undertaking to cease working for Blackwell and to tell their friends to lay off also.

News of the kidnapping reached the Union office. Two very tough Union organisers, one of them an illegitimate son of Richard Bradley, were sent out to rescue the victims. Eventually their inquiries led them to Carringbush.

Arriving at Sugar's home, the rescuers thumped on the door several times.

Before Sugar could speak, the biggest man jammed his foot against the door and said: "Where's them timberworkers, Sugar?"

"Timberworkers! There ain't no timberworkers 'ere."

"We'll take a look!"

Sugar resisted their entry. He received a blow across the face with the revolver for his trouble, and fell to the floor.

They released their bound and gagged mates and departed without any protest from Sugar, who was sitting on the front step holding his swollen face.

The event received some publicity in the press, and further confirmed John West's opinion that Sugar's efforts should be confined to Carringbush.

John West and Sugar discussed the election figures, then the former asked: "Did that Commo, Morton, work on Blackwell's campaign?"

"No. Jack. He's gorn away like I told yer. Hasn't been heard of for a long time."

Jim Morton *had* gone away. A few weeks after Blackwell's first victory over the West machine he had been warned by the local police that his life was in danger. They also suggested that, as they didn't like Communists anyway, he should change his address immediately.

Jim Morton soon discovered that they were not bluffing. After a meeting on the following evening he went to a cafe and found four evil-looking individuals seated watching him surreptitiously. He recognised one of them as a member of Snoopy Tanner's gang. So he was to be bashed up or murdered for defying Sugar Renfrey and John West!

Fear gripped him. He must keep calm. Perhaps he could bluff his way out. Their plan would be to follow him when he left, and waylay him in a secluded spot.

The old Greek proprietor came to take his order. Feigning to speak thickly as if he had been drinking, Jim Morton said to him: "Where's the lavatory, Nick? Must go to the lavatory."

He rose and unsteadily followed the Greek through the kitchen into the backyard, where he said: "Listen, Nick. I think those fellas in there are after me. Can I get out the back way?"

"Well, you might. If you can climb that wall there, and over the roof into the lane."

With difficulty and urgent haste, he succeeded in using a window ledge and a drainpipe as stepping stones to the roof.

On the other side, he made a thirty foot jump into the lane and sprained his ankle. Hobbling away with difficulty, he slept the night on the Yarra Bank, and next day jumped the rattler to Sydney.

"Jees. I've gorn past me stop!" Sugar exclaimed. He swayed for a moment holding the upright rail of the tram, then leapt off to be hurtled through the air and roll in an undignified ball in the gutter.

John West abandoned himself again to his dreams of power. No feeling in all the range of human emotion could be so satisfying to him as this. The gambler's elation after a successful plunge, a man's elated expectancy as he bent over the trembling, submissive body of a lovely woman: these could not, no feeling could, compare with this sense of power.

The tram passed 136 Jackson Street. How vastly his power had grown since he had bribed Constable Brogan! And how its machinations had changed! In the old days he had only one source of income, the tote; he could protect his power only by bribing a few policemen; now he was worth millions and could control the whole Victorian Police Force through the Chief Secretary. Then he had depended for protection on a few strong men like Piggy, Hope and One-Eyed Tommy; now the whole power of the State would protect him.

He no longer needed direct influence over the criminal world. Bradley and Arty, Snoopy Tanner and his gang had outlived their usefulness and had become an embarrassment. It was still costing him a mint of money to keep Bradley in 'smoke.' Arty didn't seem to care much for his wife and daughter, he seemed to live only for Bradley. Arty had to revert to the expensive and dangerous procedure of bribing detectives. How absurd the position would now become! His good money would continue to be paid to detectives whom he could influence when necessary through the Chief Secretary and the Chief of Police, for the purpose of protecting a murderer who was not, and never could be again, of any use whatsoever.

The new Chief of Police had been appointed with John West's approval. He was a former Army Officer with a reputation as a lady's man and a racketeer. Rumour had it that he had established lucrative rackets in brothels and motor insurance.

Whatever became of Bradley, John West would never again employ Tanner unless in case of desperate need. He admired Tanner's daring and cleverness, but Tanner had double-crossed him, so Tanner was finished. Tanner's downfall had resulted from an indiscretion connected with 'bootlegging' John West's spirits to America. Not satisfied with the good money he and his gang were making from the work, Snoopy had decided to earn a bit on the side. He had organised a series of robberies of rival wine and spirit stores and exported the proceeds to U.S.A. Finally, the police caught him. He absconded from bail and for a while lived in the cellars of a city theatre, then moved about Australia disguised as a woman. His exploits created nation-wide interest; on one occasion he wrote to the press telling of his movements. But finally he was run to earth and sentenced to two years' imprisonment. He would be out next year, but Jack West was finished with him. The bottom had fallen out of the liquor smuggling racket, costs were too high and there were too many rivals nearer, and in, America. There were other avenues of contact with strong-arm men.

John West alighted from the tram at the terminus, crossed the river, and walked briskly up the hill.

He would reorganise his empire. Nothing could stop him now. If he played his cards correctly he would soon control, for his own purposes, the Government of Australia. His great day was near at hand.

CHAPTER TEN

The Australian Labor Party degenerated into a machine for capturing political power, and when it got that power it did not know how to use it except for the benefit of individuals.

PROFESSOR V. G. CHILDE

The following months were arduous and difficult for John West. Men in Victorian trotting were on the verge of revolt. There were moves to form a Government commission to control boxing in Victoria. As part of preparations to control the Federal Parliament through the Labor Party, he purchased a Federal seat for Ted Thurgood for eight thousand pounds – and bought trouble with it.

Though preoccupied, he was also troubled by the drift of affairs in his household. He was now positively convinced that Marjorie had married Andreas in defiance of his wishes. He discovered that Nellie was exchanging letters with Marjorie and sending her money, so he cut off every channel through which Nellie could obtain money. He then saw his solicitors and altered his will, carrying out his threat to cut Marjorie off with a shilling. But even this did not satisfy him. Marjorie's defiance rankled: this was unfinished business; he didn't like unfinished business. He told Nellie he knew she and the others were corresponding with Marjorie; while they were on the job, he said, they could tell Marjorie that he had cut her off with a shilling and that she could never again set foot in the house unless she deserted Andreas.

He was worried, too, about Mary. She was going around with some amateur theatrical crowd. He had been to see her in two plays. Mary was quite an actress, but she was in bad company, staying out late, drinking, and changing her boyfriend almost weekly. She was neglecting her religious duties, too, he had heard – and he believed that religion was good, especially for women.

427

One night she came home very late, and judging by the row on the verandah below both she and her escort were tipsy. Enraged at being awakened, John West impetuously took the revolver from under his pillow and fired a shot in the air from the side of the balcony. Mary's lover had departed in haste; but Mary became even more restless in the weeks that followed, and more resentful of her father.

John junior was also a problem to his father. He showed no interest in preparing himself to take control of the West empire after his father's death. He was working in the office of one of John West's brokers, but was making little progress. Joe worked for one of his father's solicitors and seemed quite content to draw his salary with as little effort to earn it as possible. Like his uncle, he took for granted that he was entitled to an easy living out of the West empire without contributing anything to it.

Relations with Nellie had not changed. They hardly met except at meals, where they spoke to each other as little as possible. She still lived with Xavier in the room upstairs.

Yet the household was perhaps happier now than ever before. The children, especially Mary, had attracted friends who came on some evenings and every Sunday afternoon and night. They played tennis on a court recently laid in the grounds, they played billiards on a new table purchased for them, they went riding and swimming in season, they laughed and talked and played music. John West found himself welcoming their presence, especially on Sundays – Sunday's dinner was an enjoyable experience.

Mrs. Moran was fading a little. More than seventy-seven years old, and weighed down at last by the years, she still managed to play her part in the household. Her hair was snow-white and her skin wrinkled like old leather, but John West often marvelled at her vigour and cheerfulness, and the deference she commanded from Nellie and the children.

John West would have liked to enjoy the new friendly atmosphere, but he had lost all idea of mixing socially and his affairs kept him more than busy. Although approaching sixty he worked as never before. Work and interviewing which could not be completed in a long day at the office were carried on at home. He had a great incentive to work: soon, he believed, he would be the most powerful man in Australia.

*

In the spring of 1928 John West conducted three important inter-views. The first was with Red Ted Thurgood, who presented a worried expression across the office table to John West.

Thurgood had just arrived by train from Sydney. He had good cause to be worried. He was to be one of the central figures in a Royal Commission established to investigate charges that a Labor politician had been bribed to resign his seat in favour of Thurgood.

"It's up to you to help me out," said Thurgood, flourishing a Sydney newspaper. "You've read all about it, I suppose."

John West surveyed him in silence, studying his face – the thick lips being licked nervously, the Roman nose, the high eyebrows arching up towards the grey-flecked temples, the heavy folds of flesh puffed around the hard, slanted eyes. The eyes were ruthless, but now John West saw fear lurking there. He is scared, John West was thinking, and that is good. Thurgood will be Prime Minister – Thurgood will be pliable because he is capable of real fear.

Ted Thurgood was frightened, not because he seriously believed that the bribery charge would be sheeted home to him, but because it might reopen the Mulgara scandal in Queensland.

At John West's request, Thurgood had resigned as Premier of Queensland to seek a Federal seat. His chance soon came: a Labor member died and Thurgood won the pre-selection ballot. But he lost the seat. His unpopularity among the workers, indi-cated by his defeat, shocked him greatly.

Thurgood would have moved to Federal politics years before but, like a clerk who has misappropriated funds and knows that his absence could lead to exposure, he felt that he must remain on the spot – ever vigilant.

After his defeat, Thurgood moved with his wife and grown-up family to Sydney, where he won wide support by opposing Lane, the demagogic leader of the New South Wales Labor Party. For the second time in his career, people began to think that his nick-name referred as much to his politics as to the colour of his hair. He rose to a position of leadership in the left wing of the Labor Party, all the time keeping his eye out for a safe seat in the Commonwealth Parliament.

Almost two years passed before a seat could be found. Seats in Parliament are valuable property: trading in them is rare, their price high. A Conservative politician who is asked to stand down for an aspirant whom the capitalists are anxious to put into Parliament often emerges as director of some big enterprise. A Labor politician usually settles for cash, as did the man who stood down for Thurgood. Through an intermediary, John West had paid £8,000 in notes to a retiring member who used some of the money to purchase a hotel, and hid the rest under the carpets in his house.

John West continued to study Thurgood, then said: "Someone must have talked out of turn for all this to come out."

"Yes. One of the men we approached last year who has since lost his seat. This is bad. You'll have to do something about it."

"Don't worry. I won't let you down. Anyway, I've been called as a witness myself."

"You have!" Thurgood exclaimed as though he could not credit that anyone, even a Nationalist Prime Minister, would have the audacity to arraign John West before a Royal Commission.

"Yes. I have, and so has Ashton. They must know he was approached, too. We must move to make sure nothing serious comes of this. But old Davie Garside used to say that Royal Commissions are appointed to whitewash people."

"He wasn't far out, either, but this one might be different. They might start probing into my business affairs. That does a Labor man a lot of harm. The workers seem to think a Labor member should remain a pauper all his life."

A ghost of a smile haunted John West's sullen mouth for a moment. "You mean that you're worried about the Mulgara business?"

"You're in that, too."

"My name isn't. I didn't sell the mines to the Government."

"Anyway, you know the Queensland business is dangerous. Jenner is still talking. Questions are being asked in Parliament. Mt. Isa may come up as well, and you made a tidy fortune there."

"MacCorkell is Premier. He's there to see they don't do anything. It doesn't matter what they say in Queensland. You're in New South Wales now."

"If anything happens to me, it might reflect on you," Thurgood persisted.

"The difference between you and me is that I don't have to be elected to power," John West said. "Anyway, most people know little or nothing about me."

"They're learning about you up in Queensland," Thurgood persisted, rankled by John West's apparent unconcern. "There's a paper out called the WEEKLY MIRROR – a sporting paper. It's had cartoons and articles about how you got control of the DAILY MAIL, and it exposed the fact that you and Levy control the racecourses for profit, and . . ."

John West interrupted him tersely: "I know all about it . . ."

"Well, what are you going to do? They'll be talking Mulgara next. And after Mulgara, Mt. Isa!"

"I've already closed up the MIRROR. Gave its two proprietors a job on the MAIL. Always remember, every man has his price. I was telling you about old Davie Garside. He always said that the odds are with the accused, if he has enough money. If a man cannot bribe or intimidate the judge, the jury or some of the witnesses, then he deserves to be convicted. With a good lawyer and plenty of money, we should be all right."

Thurgood said: "This is just an attempt by the Nationalists to discredit me on the eve of Labor coming to power. They know that I've got great plans to keep the workers, so they're trying to defeat me in advance, but they will fail. I'll fight back."

"I have already consulted my legal advisers and worked out a plan," said John West. "Tell this fellow you bought the seat from – Maloney or whatever his name is – to say that he won the money at the races. Make it a good while ago, so that they can't check the book-maker. He was over here for the Melboune Cup carnival last year; that's when he got the money. Say he backed Spearfelt – say he backed the card. It's happened before. I once knew a fellow who walked on to one of my pony courses with a pound and walked off with a thousand. I'll quote that at the Royal Commission. Even if the story sounds a bit tall, they can't prove it's not true. That's the point."

Thurgood pondered momentarily, then laughed louder and longer than usual. He leaned forward, resting his hand on the table and laughed until tears rolled down his cheeks.

"Haw! Haw! Haw!"

"What's so funny?" John West interrupted impatiently.

"Just the idea of Maloney winning eight thousand pounds at the races." Thurgood replied, suppressing his laughter with difficulty. "He wouldn't bet an even shilling that the sun will rise tomorrow."

431

"Well, you see him and tell him what to say."

"What about Ashton? What's he likely to say?"

"I've already seen Ashton. He'll be all right. He will refuse to divulge who made the offer to him. He will say that trafficking in seats is not unusual and that the Nationalists do more of it than Labor. He's a director of one of my gold mines now, you know."

"Frank Ashton is! How did that come about?"

"Well, before I approached him about standing down for you, I gave him a parcel of shares. He was in financial difficulties, so he accepted. You know what he is: he lives above his means, gives money away, drinks, gambles, and so on."

"Then had the cheek to refuse to stand down."

"Doesn't matter, anyway. You've got a seat. I have great respect for Ashton. I picked him up out of the gutter and put him into politics. He is a self-educated man and the best orator in Australia."

"Well, why don't you make him Prime Minister, then?"

"He's a very sick man at the moment. Anyway, he's too much of an extremist. I said I'd make you Prime Minister, and I will, if you can out-manoeuvre Summers."

"Going to be hard. He's got the Catholic vote."

"Well, why don't you spread around the fact that you've joined the Church?"

Ted Thurgood *had* spread around the fact of his turning a Catholic. His wife and children were Catholics. His wife had endeavoured to convert him, but he had steadfastly refused, saying that his grandfather had been a patriarch in the Greek Orthodox Church in Roumania. He must respect his ancestors' wishes. When recently he had announced his intention of turning Catholic, his wife was delighted at Ted's change of heart, little suspecting his real motives. Red Ted needed Catholic support in the Party, and he needed John West's support. He knew that West was extremely Catholic-minded, even though he didn't practise his religion. Furthermore, Thurgood's relations with his wife had been strained for many years by his unfaithfulness. Red Ted was well built, handsome, and well dressed, and the fair sex were much attracted to him. He, in turn, liked a pretty face and a trim figure, though he was too clever to involve himself in any affair that might wreck his career.

"I don't believe in playing on people's religious susceptibilities," Thurgood lied.

"It's not a question of that. Catholics must stick together like the Freemasons do."

"Oh, I agree. I just don't like playing on it, that's all."

Not much, you don't, John West thought. He both admired and disliked Thurgood. Of all the politicians over whom he had influence, Thurgood was perhaps the most suitable. He was reputed to be the best organiser in Australian politics; he was an able speaker and debater, very shrewd, extremely close-mouthed and utterly unscrupulous. Yes, Thurgood would be the ideal Prime Minister. Of course, the Archbishop would prefer Summers, because Summers was a Catholic first and a Labor man second, but Summers was not susceptible to the bribe.

"To get back to the Commission," John West said. "Leave Ashton to me. You attend to Maloney and the other witnesses in Sydney. When the name of the Judge is announced, see if anything can be done with him. We'll beat this case, then I'll teach the bloody Nationalists to call me before a Royal Commission."

Later they had lunch – John West contenting himself with a glass of orange juice. They decided whom they should try to get into the Cabinet if Labor won the elections the following year.

The second interview, a few days later, was with Godfrey Dwyer, who arrived on time to the minute.

As Secretary of John West's racing club, Dwyer was like a temperance advocate compelled to manage a low-class hotel. The office was run with military thoroughness, records were scrupulously kept, but the racing had got out of control. Pony racing was bad enough, but trotting was the biggest problem.

Under John West's control trotting had declined as a sport and an industry. So ruthlessly did the club bleed profits from it, that stakes for races became miserably low, breeding deteriorated, and attendances dropped.

Godfrey Dwyer, a soldier without imagination or flexibility, was surrounded by officials whose only interest was to make an honest or dishonest shilling from the sport.

John West, concerned at the decline in profits, told Dwyer to "clean the sport up," but his officals made this impossible.

As quickly as Dwyer stamped out one malpractice another

arose. He was quite unable to cope with the situation. Matters were made worse by the Owners' and Breeders' Association which had Frank Lammence as secretary and an executive that did his bidding. The Association was supposed to be the channel through which the trotting men could air their grievances, but here again they were helpless. Attempts to change the secretary or the executive at the annual elections were frustrated by methods similar to those used by the West machine in politics.

The sport had not become a big man's game, like galloping: the majority of trotting men owned, trained and drove one or two moderate horses. With stakes small and rackets rampant, they could not earn sufficient to stay in the game. When they won a race, their horses soon ate the stake. Though most trotting men have a great love for their sport for its own sake, many of them began to resort to shady methods.

"Everybody will want to back your horse today," a bookmaker might say. "I'll give you fifty quid to put it in the peter with me, and some tickets to cover you if the stewards ask questions."

One driver might say to another: "Your horse will be at a good price today. My fellow will be favourite. What about we put our heads together and make a boat race of it?"

A horse could be pulled with impunity providing stewards were bribed, or at least told when the horse was trying. For a small fee the starter would give a signal to be on the move for a flying start when he released the barriers.

Not the least dishonest of the officials was the President and Stipendiary Steward, Mr. Bennett, who in his spare time was Labor Party Leader in the Upper House of the Victorian Parliament. The situation had become impossible. The Gentleman Thief, like his employer, John West, owned horses under the name of a leading trainer-driver, and Godfrey Dwyer soon learned that this man was immune from punitive action.

In best army style, Dwyer obeyed John West's orders. He conducted inquiries which were often abortive because most of the other officials, except a few of Benjamin Levy's nominees, seemed bent on frustrating his efforts. He imposed fines with monotonous regularity. There had been a few cases of ringing in a well-performed horse under a false name. Dwyer impounded one such horse in the Police Barracks pending an inquiry – the horse disappeared overnight and was neither seen nor heard of again.

He began to impose suspensions, usually of short duration; these seemed to have a salutary effect for a while, but soon the game declined again, and more of its members and supporters left it.

In desperation, Dwyer decided to make an example of someone. He disqualified a man named MacDonald for life, and refused him permission to sell his horses or to take them out of the country. MacDonald was unpopular with John West for his part in the current agitation for a change of control.

MacDonald had immediately set about organising a new trotting League, which now threatened the very existence of John West's club. Dissatisfaction of the majority of trotting men with John West's control and with the Owner's and Breeders' Association made MacDonald's task easy.

So successful were his efforts that the trotting men had gone on strike! To the surprise and chagrin of John West, the strike was making it impossible for him to conduct trotting meetings. One Monday only fifteen horses were nominated.

Bennett was chosen as a particular object of MacDonald's hostility. The trouble happened to coincide with an election in the Upper House. MacDonald campaigned against Bennett. Assisted by a committee of trotting men and returned soldiers he swamped the electorate with leaflets carrying the report from a New Zealand paper of the ringing in by Bennett's brother of the mare, Nellie W, in 1903. They attended meetings and flung accusations at a most embarrassed Bennett. Bennett recoiled from his attackers. At one meeting he wept on the platform. Eventually, unable to face his tormentors, he cancelled his last three meetings.

Worst of all, he lost his seat.

The strike was now four weeks old, and though some of the trotting men were weakening, still not enough nominations were being received to make meetings possible. Refused permission to race in the city, the new trotting League conducted a £1,000 meeting at a provincial track. Members approached the Chief Secretary with their grievances. Mr. Tom Trumbleward had given a polite hearing, but no promises and no action. They approached the Lord Mayor of Melbourne for permission to run a charity meeting. He refused and told the deputation that they could never hope to beat John West because the Chief Secretary and other politicians were "in his pocket," and the Premier, Horan, and the Labor Leader in the Upper House, Bennett, were on the Committee of his bogus Trotting and Racing Club.

At first John West had treated the trouble lightly. Trotting men could not live without him, he believed; they would soon learn where their best interests lay; but now he was worried and determined to smash the strike.

"I thought I told you to quieten MacDonald?" he said gruffly when Godfrey Dwyer had seated himself.

Dwyer spread his hands with a gesture of bewilderment. "But, Mr. West, the only way to quieten him is to lift his suspension. That would be fatal. If we are to have discipline, then we must be firm. We cannot give way now."

"If we pacify MacDonald, the whole move will collapse. The trouble with you military men is that you work by a book of rules. By refusing to recognise that MacDonald is dangerous you have cost us hundreds of pounds. Bennett has lost his seat in Parliament. The racecourses are idle. The employees are being paid for doing nothing. If Labor should lose the State elections next month our control of trotting and pony racing would be threatened. That's no way to clean up the sport. Lift MacDonald's suspension, and next time you make an example of someone, pick a man who won't make so much trouble!"

Dwyer was still prone to defy his employer. His regimented mind, accustomed to acting and reacting along clearly defined lines, revolted against these subtle, unscrupulous methods.

"Mr. West, let me clean the sport up my way: let me punish those who break the rules without exception or partiality; otherwise I must ask you to accept my resignation."

Dwyer had been on the verge of blurting out this little speech more than once since the strike began, but his need of salary, power and influence had restrained him. Now, having said it, he cocked his head to one side like a frightened bird, as if expecting John West to draw a revolver and shoot him stone dead.

John West leaned forward, resting his hands on the table, studying Dwyer's face quizzically as though unable to believe his ears.

The silence grated on Dwyer's frayed nerves. "It's no use, Mr. West," he said. "It's no use. Law and order can only come from the severest discipline. I must have freedom to carry out the rules of the club without fear or favour.''

Still John West made no reply. He was annoyed but he did not show it. Dwyer figured largely in plans to expand his racing interests. He needed time to think and to test Dwyer's resolve.

Very much to Dwyer's relief John West's tone was placatory when at last he spoke.

"The strain of the last few weeks has played on your mind, Captain. You need a rest. We'll clear this matter up and then you take a few weeks' holiday.''

Complimented by John West's use of the cherished military title for the first time, Dwyer replied: ''I have endeavoured to carry out your wishes, but I cannot continue to do so unless I have freedom to see that the rules are obeyed to the letter.''

"Captain, you can't make a silk purse out of a sow's ear. Trotting men are a shrewd, scheming lot. They'll find loopholes no matter how strict you may be. Always bear in mind, Captain, that this pony and trotting club is only a means to an end. I've lost interest in trotting and pony racing, but I must keep my courses, my licences and my organisation, because one day I will enter the galloping field. That's where the money is, Captain. I have a score to settle with the V.R.C. I will bring them to their knees. I will conduct galloping races at Flemington, you see if I don't. My day is near at hand. And my day in racing will be your day. You'll grow with me. You will be the most important public figure in the racing world. Think of it!''

Godfrey Dwyer had concluded long ago that for John West nothing was impossible. The vision of sitting in the Secretary's office at Flemington flashed vividly before his mind, until he remembered his resignation. I must climb down gracefully, he told himself.

Dwyer tapped his cane on the palm of his hand nervously.

"Oh, I realise, Mr. West, that you have great plans, and that your prospects of carrying them out increase daily; but I really feel that . . .''

"Do you realise, Captain, that I will soon be the most powerful man in Australia?'' John West interrupted, raising his eyes and leaning forward, tapping the table with his knuckles. "Do you realise that no Government will be game to oppose my wishes? And I won't forget my friends. Take yourself, for instance. You were wounded fighting for your country; you are President of the Returned Soldiers' Association; and one day you will be the most important public figure in the racing world. Yet, will the Government give you a title?''

Quite nonplussed, Godfrey Dwyer replied rather coyly: ''Well, I hardly think that I warrant knighthood. Such recognition by the King is reserved for great public figures. I must admit I hadn't thought . . . but, of course when you put it that way, I . . .''

''Left to themselves, they would not give you a title; but I will see to it that they do. I give you my word on that.''

John West was never more serious in his life. If he could influence the policy of governments, he could influence their annual recommendations for Royal honours!

''Thank you, Mr. West,'' Dwyer stammered. ''I appreciate this very much. But I really must repeat . . .''

John West continued as if Dwyer had never threatened to resign. ''This matter has got out of hand. I'll have to get Bennett another seat; I need every vote I can get in the Labor Party and the Upper House. Besides, the club is getting too much bad publicity. Frank Lammence has been busy among our best supporters, and says that if we silence MacDonald the bottom will fall out of this strike. Trotting men are beginning to realise that they can't defy Jack West and get away with it. I picked their sport up out of the gutter and put it on the map. I'd starve them into submission, if it weren't that I want this thing ended quickly. We must learn to give ground in order to gain further ground later. I suggest you call MacDonald in and suggest that he appeals again. This time uphold the appeal. Then Frank Lammence can persuade the majority of trotting men to leave their case in the hands of the Chief Secretary. They'll get no change from Tom Trumbleward.''

''Very well, Mr.West, whatever you suggest: but I would like to be allowed to proceed with a clean-up. You suggested it yourself. And we must offer the men something when racing begins again.''

''Clean the game up just sufficiently to ensure a rise in attendances. They are complaining that the system of handicapping on times run is causing much of the trouble. They reckon that if a horse wins a race in fast time, he is handicapped so that he can never win another one. I believe they are right. Well, change the handicapping system to automatic handicapping on races won. Say, twelve yards for each win, like in the old days. They say stakes are low. All right, raise them a little. They say that book-makers are deadening horses. All right, cancel some of the book-makers' licences. They say that Snoopy Tanner and his gang are urging punters, financing crooked book-makers and using standover tactics. All right, warn Tanner and his gang off for life.''

"But I thought . . .''

"Never mind what you thought. I hold no brief for Tanner. Warn him and his gang off!''

The third interview took place one evening a fortnight later at John West's house. John West and an American wrestler named Tinn sat in the reception room awaiting the arrival of Richard Lamb and a sports writer named Parker.

"You see, J.W., we don't have sports writers criticising the game in the States,'' Tinn was saying, in a drawling voice. "We have 'em all on the payroll.''

Tinn was gross, cauliflower-eared, evil-looking. He wore a grey suit with wide stripes; there were gold rings on two of his fingers and a gold pin in his ostentatious tie; his shoes were tan and white, and a big cigar lolled in his mouth.

"I know, Ted,'' John West answered impatiently. "*We* have all of them on the payroll except Parker. He's a smart lad. If he were as easy to shut up as you think, we'd have shut him up long ago. As I told you, I wish you hadn't made this appointment. The paper he works for is going to be bought out by the Murkett chain. Murkett is my partner in the MAIL in Brisbane.''

"Don't be a piker, J.W.,'' Tinn replied, with exaggerated heartiness. "Come to the point with him. We Americans call a spade a spade. I come from Chicago, a tough city.''

John West studied him for a moment. More brawn than brains, he thought. I'll have to watch this interview closely.

Tinn and John West were partners in a huge wrestling enterprise covering Australia, New Zealand and the Philippines. As a sideline they had, with the assistance of Snoopy Tanner and Arthur West, shipped bootlegged liquor from Australia to America until hazards increased and profits fell.

Tinn was a good wrestler, and a better business man. With a cunning developed as a "dead-end kid'' in the slums of Chicago, he had cleaned up a small fortune. Tinn had taken up wrestling at an early age, and soon learned that the promoters and managers made the money while the mugs on the mat took all the knocks; so as soon as he had made a name he turned to promotion, and now had a team of wrestlers working for him on wages. His theory was that the art of wrestling was the art of advertising. The public didn't want skill, he contended, they wanted brutality – blood and thunder – and you had to convince them they were getting it.

Tinn arrived in Australia with all the tricks of the American wrestling trade. First of all, you had to have "goodies" and "badies," game little men with skill and brutal big men without skill. The winner of each contest was decided in advance with future box-office takings as the deciding factor. When a goodie and baddie met, the goodie struggled hard to win by dint of skilful wrestling, while the baddie bit his ears, poked his thumb in his eyes, kicked him in the face, threw him out of the ring and generally behaved towards him in a most violent manner. When two baddies met, they vied with each other for unpopularity. Just to add a little variety, the referee was occasionally attacked by one of the baddies and thrown out of the ring after his shirt had been torn from his back. From all this pretended but convincing brutality, no eyes were gouged out, no ears were bitten off, no bones were broken.

Tinn's team of wrestlers were all Americans, but they arrived in Australia at intervals under various *noms de plume*. One was billed as an Apache Indian Chief, and entered the ring replete with feathers and moccasins, greeting the crowd with an ear-piercing tribal call. Another was champion of Wales, though he had been born in Tennessee, and had never been in Wales in his life. Another who hailed from New York, was publicised as champion of the British Empire. Yet another, a native of Chicago, was presented to a bewildered public as Count Sogoloski, Champion of Russia. No wrestler was billed under his right name. One had a beard and was said to be a Mormon. Those who lacked the glamour of hailing from some foreign land were compensated with ferocious nicknames, like Killer or King Kong, or even given credit for having invented some new hold capable of breaking a man's leg or his neck.

Tinn himself was billed as the heavy-weight champion of the

world, while a man named Chapman laid claim to the light-heavy-weight title. To sell this racket to an unsuspecting Australian public, Ted Tinn had at his disposal John West's influence over the sporting journalists and the man who broadcasted over the radio from the Stadium.

At first, all went well. The crowds thronged to John West's stadiums to see the gladiators mutilate each other, and tens of thousands tuned in on the radio. Only one paper exposed the game as a sham and a burlesque, a Melbourne morning paper for which a young fellow named Clive Parker worked as a sports writer. Parker's exposures consisted of satires on the bouts, lampoons on the identity of the wrestlers, humorous and sarcastic reports, including one which printed word for word the broadcaster's lurid description, ending with the comment: *But no one was hurt!*

Takings rose to record levels until a wrestler named Sandow landed in Victoria and claimed through Parker that he was light-heavy and heavy-weight champion of the world. Sandow was, in fact recognised in some States of America as dual world-title holder, whereas Ted Tinn and Chapman were recognised only by John West and Richard Lamb. Sandow was welcomed by Parker, who gave clever publicity to his statements. Within a few more weeks several more wrestlers arrived in Melbourne, and bouts were arranged at the Exhibition grounds in opposition to John West. So superior was the standard there that the wrestling public began to desert Mr. Tinn's gladiators in favour of the Exhibition team.

Sandow proved himself a worthy champion. It was clear that Tinn and Chapman had no doubts about his prowess: they evaded persistent challenges to wrestle him. They preferred to be humiliated by him and ridiculed by Parker.

Finally, Sandow offered to put up both of his titles, and wrestle Tinn and Chapman on the one night, but still they remained silent. And all the time Parker taunted them. Small attendances caused the Monday night bouts to be abandoned, and vaudeville items were staged before the wrestling each Saturday as an added attraction. Still crowds dwindled.

In desperation, John West demanded that Tinn or one of his team accept Sandow's challenge. Tinn replied shamelessly: "Look, J.W., he would beat me and Chapman and three or four more of my boys on the one night. He's sure good; he's only playin' with those mugs he's wrestling up at the Exhibition."

Finally, Tinn agreed to stage a bout between two of his best men, the winner to accept Sandow's challenge. So determined to avoid meeting Sandow were these two, that they wrestled fifteen rounds without either obtaining a fall, and the referee by pre-arrangement declared the bout a draw. Parker wrote a facetious report of the bout, and all Melbourne laughed.

John West was very angry, but in recent years his impulse to take immediate reprisals had been curbed. He could no longer afford to act rashly. Ted Tinn, a man of savage nature, had been advocating violence against Parker, but John West had restrained him. Now Tinn had precipitated this appointment.

"We've been too lenient with this smart little bastard, J.W.," Tinn said presently. "If he won't play tonight, then I'll deal with him in good old Chicago fashion."

Meanwhile, Lamb and Parker were on their way in a taxi. Their mutual dislike kept them silent until they arrived at their desti-nation. John West himself opened the door and ushered them into the reception room.

Parker looked like a newspaper reporter as typified in Holly-wood films. He wore a well-cut grey suit. He entered the room with his hat tilted on the back of his head.

I'll let them do the talking, he thought as he sat down. He looked around the room with a reporter's eye. The polished wood floors, the expensive rugs, the photos on the wall. Probably his old woman, that one; and West and his two brothers. Poor woman, what a trio she brought into the world. The old-fashioned furniture and the antimacassars on the backs of the chairs. All in bloody bad taste.

Parker took off his hat and lit a cigarette. They sat around him in a circle. Tinn, huge and pugnacious – a tough baby, this. Lamb, rugged featured and solid, of medium height; hard eyes, thin lips and square jaws denoting ruthlessness. And John West himself, the spider, looking straight at me with those steely-grey eyes. Gives a man the feeling he can read your mind.

Tinn spoke first, coining a nickname for Parker: "Snowy," he said, "how much pay do you get?"

"Seven quid, but I'll be on a quid more when Murkett takes over the STAR."

"That's mighty poor pay for a man of your ability. How would you like to get a few quid a week more?"

"Doing what?"

Tinn looked at John West uncertainly. His gaze was not returned. John West kept his eyes on Parker, trying to sum him up.

Lamb leaned forward impetuously. "Laying off the wrestlers," he said.

"Nothin' doin'. Havin' too much fun. Just written an article called, *Sam, where art thou?* about Chapman running away from Sandow."

"Don't be a mug all yer life, Snowy. Back in the States all the sports writers get a rake-off from the promoters. Nothin' crook about it, boy; just good business."

"Supposing I prefer to be a mug; an honest mug telling the public the truth."

John West spoke. They all turned to him.

"You say you will soon be working for Murkett. Do you realise that Murkett and myself are partners in the Brisbane MAIL, and that I have shares in his papers in Melbourne? He won't permit his business partner to be attacked the way you're attacking my stadium."

"I've checked the share register. You may be Murkett's partner in Brisbane, but your holdings in Melbourne are very small. Murkett told me that I could attack the wrestling so long as I didn't overdo it."

"He'll say differently after I've seen him."

"Well, I'll carry on until I hear from him."

Tinn laughed cynically: "A man of principle! Don't be a fool all yer life, Snowy. They're all on our payroll. Every boxing and wrestling writer. And the broadcaster, he gets eight quid a week. And most of the other sports writers and editors. Here's your chance to make some hay, real hay. Tell you what: we'll give you three quid a week, and raise it to double when you show you mean business."

Parker lit another cigarette off his butt, stood up with swift movements, and walked to the open fireplace. He threw the butt into it, then turned and confronted them.

"Listen, gentlemen. You are playing the public for suckers. And you get away with it, because you have made sugar-bags of the men who should expose you. Well, here's one darky you can't buy off." Parker tapped his chest with his right forefinger, pursed his lips and squinted his eyes. I'll run Tinn and his circus clowns out of this country! Then I'll clean up the sport of boxing. There'll be a Boxing Commission appointed before very long. Then look out!"

John West made to interrupt, but Parker continued, pointing his hat at him. "Every sport you've ever handled has been corrupted. Trotting, the ponies, cycling, wrestling, and, worst of all, boxing."

Tinn leaned forward in his chair menacingly. "Listen here, smart guy. We've tried to help you, but you won't play. Well, all right; if your health declines suddenly, don't blame us."

"If I got Sandow as a bodyguard, you wouldn't be game to come near me!"

Tinn's eyes dilated with rage and he leapt to his feet. Lamb grabbed him helplessly by the shoulder.

John West said: "Sit down, Ted! Don't let him egg you on."

Tinn sat down sullenly.

Parker put his hat on and walked briskly towards the door. John West arose and followed him. As he let Parker out, John West said: "You're very foolish. These Yanks are tough nuts. You're bashing your head against a brick wall, Parker. Anyway, you'll have to lay off after I see Murkett."

"We'll see about that," Clive Parker said. As he walked along the path, he saw two shadowy figures behind a shrub.

"You shoulda let me punch the little smart guy on the jaw," Tinn snarled when John West returned.

"You might get your chance," John West said quietly. "I'll see Murkett first."

John West accompanied Tinn and Lamb to the door. He stood on the verandah until they had gone, then called softly to the two figures lurking in the grounds.

One of them appeared from the darkness. It was Arthur West. The brothers exchanged words softly, then John West returned to the reception room, where he took his revolver from his pocket and examined it.

He had been uneasy during the interview with Parker. He would have handled Parker differently, but for two days he had lost his grip of things.

John West was under sentence of death: Snoopy Tanner had threatened to murder him!

After Godfrey Dwyer warned him and his gang off, Tanner burst into John West's office and demanded that the ban be lifted. Tanner had been drinking and was in violent mood. John West threatened to call the police.

"So the great J.W. will call the coppers! Well, the coppers won't save you! Either yer lift the ban or yer die!"

White with rage and fear, John West repeated:

"I said you're warned off! Now, get out!"

Next day, up the grapevine from the underworld came to Frank Lammence the news that Tanner was on a drinking bender and bragging that he would murder John West.

To answer the taunts of his followers and their lowered respect and fear, Tanner was talking big. John West knew Tanner and his kind only too well. Tanner would talk this way until he would force himself to suit actions to his words. Snoopy Tanner was a coward! But he was also an exhibitionist. Alone with a man he would quake with fright at a threat, yet in front of a crowd of his followers he would take daredevil risks. Being warned off meant more than financial loss to Tanner. It meant loss of prestige. It meant the scorn of his gang. To redeem himself, Tanner might feel impelled to carry out his threat.

For two days and nights Arty West and another gunman hovered close to John West.

Rumours from the underworld became more ominous. The inner circle of Tanner's gang was sticking to him. Sinister plans were being hatched. "Jack West will be dead before the end of the week," Tanner was saying.

Even Frank Lammence, usually sceptical about threats from larrikins, became convinced that Tanner was mad enough to try it.

Lammence sent Arthur West to see Tanner, but Tanner had gone into smoke.

"The bastard's mad," Arthur West told his brother. "His pride's been 'urt, yer might say. Apt to do anything. Get in first, Jack. Get in first!"

John West sat thoughtfully for a while caressing his revolver. Presently he arose and peered through the window and drew the curtains more closely.

A man could shoot through the window from that angle, he thought. He shifted his chair to the corner and sat down again.

After a while he went upstairs, undressed and got into bed, after placing a revolver under his pillow.

For an hour he lay tense and far from sleep.

What if Tanner or one of his gang eluded Arty and the other bloke? He could climb one of the pine trees! Might be lurking there now, peering at me in the darkness. Waiting! Waiting to kill!

Pull yourself together!

Why should he be afraid? Why should Jack West, the most powerful man in Australia, live in fear of a syphilitic little bastard like Tanner?

Arty was right. Get in first. Kill Tanner, and let it be a lesson to all. Jack West was boss. Tanner was of no use any more. Tanner had overstepped the mark. John West began to contemplate the problem more calmly. Any idea of squaring off with Tanner was repulsed. There were men who would shoot it out with Tanner for a hundred pounds. Tanner must be killed and buried with all proof that he had ever worked for John West.

Arty would tackle Tanner, but that wouldn't do. Tanner would be too clever for Arty and too quick on the draw. Tanner had enemies; there were men he had shelved who would have murdered him long ago except for fear.

What about the police? The C.I.B. detectives were sick of Tanner. Supposing the Chief of Police declared open season on Snoopy? That was the idea. Open season! A nice, neat murder and no questions asked.

A plan crystallised in John West's mind. He got out of bed, went downstairs to the wall phone in the hall, and rang Frank Lammence.

"That you, Frank? Come over right away. I'll tell Arty to let you through."

Clive Parker stood under a shop verandah in a shabby, suburban street. The collar of his overcoat was pulled round his ears and his hat down over his eyes. The gutter at his feet was strewn with his cigarette butts. He had been there for nearly two hours. In the house on the opposite side of the road, "Slasher" Cutting, aptly named for vicious use of the razor, lay ill in bed. At half past two this afternoon, two men should have arrived by car and entered the house. They were an hour late. One of them, Snoopy Tanner, was to be murdered in there. How or by whom Parker did not know.

Clive Parker was married to Ronald Lassiter's grand-daughter. "Old Ron" was proud of his reporter grandson-in-law, and had more than once put him on to a scoop story in the trade union, criminal or sporting world. This was the biggest story yet – if it came off. First on the scene of the death of Snoopy Tanner!

Snoopy was likely to be bumped off at a certain time and place – old Ron would say no more.

When Parker informed the editor, he was told to tell the police. He refused, saying the police probably knew all about it and would be pleased to see the last of Tanner, who had worked "too hot" and knew too much about the criminal activities of the Chief of Police and certain detectives. What a scoop! What a pity it would appear only in the last issue of the STAR.

Suddenly a yellow taxi turned into the street and Parker stiffened and moved back into the doorway. The taxi stopped in front of Cutting's house, and Parker saw two men alight from it. No mistaking the little dapper bloke with the Charlie Chaplin moustache, Parker thought, it's Tanner all right. The other bloke is a stranger. Parker heard Tanner tell the taxi driver to wait. Sounds as if he's been drinking.

Tanner and the big man went into the house. As they went down the side path, they crouched low as though trying to avoid being seen through the window. His heart pounding, Parker watched and listened. The taxi driver looked at him suspiciously. Leaning against the shop window, Parker assumed a nonchalant attitude, and lit another cigarette.

Presently, the air was shattered by a revolver shot which echoed along the street. It was followed by another and yet another. The deserted street became alive with people, looking this way and that, gesticulating and asking questions. Then three more shots rang out in quick succession.

Parker moved from the doorway and signalled to another who stood a hundred yards down the street. This man was a STAR photographer who had wisely refused to come any closer until the shooting was over. The photographer waved back but did not move nearer.

At that moment the front door of Cutting's house commenced to open slowly. Then a man appeared. He was bent double, with his arms folded across his stomach. It was Snoopy Tanner, groaning horribly. From the house to the car a trail of blood followed his staggering body. He leaned against the back of the taxi. His face was white as a pillow-case, a thin trickle of blood flowed from the corner of his mouth, his eyes were dilated and he spat on the ground into the blood which seemed to be flowing down his legs.

The taxi driver, who had watched Tanner's approach with a terrified expression, suddenly came to life and started his motor, apparently intending to flee, leaving his wounded fare on the roadside. The sound of the motor roused Tanner from his near oblivion. With a tremendous effort of will he roused himself to action. He straightened up, drew a gun from his pocket and staggered up to the driver's side just as the vehicle began to move. He menaced the taxi man with his revolver.

"Don't leave me, you bastard," he said. His voice gurgled, spluttering blood in the driver's face. "Don't leave me or I'll blow your bloody brains out!"

The car stopped. Parker watched the scene, transfixed. Other people stood at a safe distance. No one knew what to do, or knowing, dared not act.

"The Melbourne hospital," Tanner said weakly, swaying beside the car.

He swayed perilously, his boots squelching in his own blood. He staggered against the passenger's door and gripped the handle. He let out a scream of pain as his hands exerted pressure to open the door. The taxi-driver watched fear-frozen, incapable of either aiding or hindering the injured man.

Tanner succeeded in opening the door. He fell forward on to the floor and lay still. The car sped away, the door swinging dangerously open. Tanner's feet protruded. Blood dripped from the toes of his shoes.

Pulling himself together, Parker rushed across the street. People gathered on the blood-stained roadside.

"Stand back, please," Parker said. "Police here!"

He entered the house through the open front door, and walked cautiously down the gloomy passage. His feet struck something and he almost fell. It was the body of an old woman who lay stunned. She moaned and opened her eyes. She mumbled something, but he could not distinguish the words.

Stepping over her prostrate body Parker walked a few more trembling paces and came to an open door on the right of the passage. He looked into the room cautiously. There was a bed across the far corner. Lying in it was a man. His brains were blown out and had splashed on the pillow, the bars of the iron bedstead and the wall. Parker knew it was Slasher Cutting, because one side of his face had not been blown away and it was hideously scarred. Cutting's right arm hung limply over the side of the bed and in the hand a revolver was clenched tightly. The pillow was red, and blood had seeped through the bedclothes in the region of Cutting's heart.

Gripped by an urgency of excitement and fear, Parker surveyed the sparsely furnished room. Mirrors were set on an angle on the wall – one at each side of the bed. One gave a view of anyone coming down the passage from the front, and the other of anyone approaching down the side path from the front. The position of the bed would enable Cutting to see through the door and window towards the back of the house. Slasher had been expecting visitors. That's why they crouched as they passed this window, Parker thought.

There were framed pictures on the wall. A photo of a woman with a baby in her arms, another of a young man. Parker recognised the latter as Cutting in his youth before he had been slashed with a razor. The other was a coloured print of Jesus Christ, crowned with thorns.

Good material, Parker thought, taking the two photos from the wall and putting them in his pocket. He made to take the print, hesitated, then left it untouched. Then he turned swiftly to see the old woman leaning against the doorway. Ignoring Parker, she stared at the body in the bed, as though hypnotised by the one-eyed brainless skull.

Suddenly she came to life and swayed towards the bed.

"Oh, my boy," she screamed. "They have killed my boy. May God and His Holy Mother curse them."

She knelt by the bed and flung her wizened arms around the body, weeping uncontrollably, ignoring the blood which stained her face, hands and clothes.

Parker watched her, torn between compassion and his desire

449

to escape with the story. He walked over to her and laid his hand on her shoulder.

The old woman looked up at him, her face cob-webbed with wrinkles and soggy with tears and blood.

"Get a priest," the woman screamed, without querying his presence. "Get a priest and a doctor! Get a priest! My boy hasn't been to church for years. He mustn't die without confessing."

"Who killed your son?" Parker asked. "The little man, Tanner?"

"No, the big man! He shot both of them. I tried to stop him but he knocked me down. He ran out the back way," she answered, then wept again.

Parker ran from the house into the street. A large crowd was milling around the gate. Standing on the verandah Parker saw the photographer, and called him. "What are you waiting for? Get in and get pictures."

The photographer entered hesitantly, carrying his camera. Parker walked to the gate. "Stand back! Stand back! Police here," he said commandingly.

From the house he heard a scream, a crash and a scuffle, and the photographer appeared. His face was scratched, his clothes were dishevelled, the camera was damaged and its flashlight broken.

"The old bitch went mad," he explained to Parker. "Bloody near tore my eyes out and I dropped the camera."

"You bloody fool," Parker muttered. "Come on. We'd better get away from here!"

They pushed their way through the excited, inquiring crowd. Parker broke into a run. "Come on. Get back to the office and get another camera. I'll ring the police. Meet me at the Melbourne Hospital casualty room as soon as you can. Go on, hurry!"

Parker ran in the direction of a telephone box. As he did so, a police car turned into the street, its bell ringing. Someone else had rung the police, he thought, or maybe the police knew the day and the hour!

John West's plan to dispose of Snoopy Tanner had succeeded. Tanner was dead when he reached hospital.

At Frank Lammence's request, friendly detectives had spread the word through their pimps in the underworld, that Tanner could be murdered and no questions asked. A Sydney gunman, who had been shelved by Tanner five years before had done the rest for five hundred pounds.

The gunman took Tanner to Cutting's house ostensibly to murder Cutting, who had been threatening to slash Tanner with a razor.

The police denied Parker's story, which appeared in the last issue of the MORNING STAR, that there had been a third man present at the dual murder. At the inquest the coroner found that Tanner and Cutting had shot each other dead.

The murder was a seven-day wonder. Snoopy Tanner was dead and no one cared. As for Slasher Cutting, only his old mother mourned his passing.

By the end of 1928, John West had once again triumphed over his enemies.

The revolt of the Victorian trotting men had fizzled out: under-currents of discontent still existed, but the situation was under control. Jack West had shown them he was boss. The Royal Commission which investigated the circumstances in which Thurgood had obtained a seat in the Federal Parliament proved inconclusive.

At the Royal Commission, Maloney swore that he won the money at the races, mainly on the redoubtable steed, Spearfelt. Thurgood denied any knowledge of how Maloney came by the eight thousand pounds.

Asked if Mr. John West, of Melbourne, had bought the seat for him, Thurgood replied: "I don't know why Mr. West should interest himself in me. I have only met him once or twice on business matters."

Red Ted refused point blank to discuss his business interests at the inquiry: "My possession of wealth has often been used against me politically. A Labor man is not supposed to make any money," he explained. Finally, he agreed to allow the Judge to inspect his bank accounts confidentially.

John West opened his evidence by saying that he had no interest in getting Thurgood into Parliament. "In fact," he added, "I take very little interest in politics." After denying that he had any hand in paying Maloney, he was asked: "Then how do you think Maloney came into possession of such a large sum of money, all at once?"

"Well," John West replied, "he says he won it at the races and I have no reason to doubt his word."

"But," the Commissioner interjected, "surely it is surprising for a man, especially a temperate man like Mr. Maloney, to win thousands of pounds on a racecourse."

John West then told them the story of the man who had walked on to one of his courses with a pound and turned it into a thousand. This seemed to impress the Commissioner.

Frank Ashton's behaviour in the box puzzled John West. Looking haggard and hobbling as though crippled with arthritis, Ashton did not deny that he had been approached to stand down for Thurgood. In fact, he said, the same man had approached him to stand down for T. J. Real in 1919.

He is going to betray me after all I have done for him, John West thought. But Ashton continued, saying he had given his word to treat the matter as confidential, and the Commission hadn't the power to compel him to break his word. Stood down and later recalled, Ashton persisted in his refusal. He then made an impassioned speech. There was nothing unusual about trafficking in seats, he declared. The Nationalists were past masters in the art of bribery. Men who deserted their comrades and ratted from the Labor Movement, invariably received monetary rewards from the Nationalists. Hughes had received twenty-five thousand pounds to rat on Labor. Then he shouted prophetically: "There are other rats still in the movement who will sell out one day!"

He said that he did not know whether Maloney had been paid to resign his seat for Thurgood. If he had, then at least he sold out to a Labor man. The Nationalists, who represented big business, had corrupted the whole of Australian society with their rotten system. They ought to talk about bribery and graft. At this stage, Ashton broke down and wept in the box.

John West watched with puzzled interest while this sick and white-haired man wept uncontrollably. Was he acting? He didn't seem to be; then what the hell was he crying about? Must be really sick. Needs a holiday. I must ask his wife if he has enough money to have a holiday.

John West could not have judged that the passion in Ashton's speech was born of shame – shame at his own weakness.

The Commission lasted for weeks. The Judge seemed puzzled

and not very determined to probe fully into the matter. He did, however, delve deeply enough to reveal that Maloney had resigned his seat for reasons of ill-health when, in fact, his health was apparently quite good.

The finding was a foregone conclusion. After summarising the evidence, the Judge gravely announced that Maloney had been paid to resign his seat by a person (or persons) unknown.

Speaking to John West after the Royal Commission, Thurgood said Labor was certain to win the Federal elections to be held before the end of 1929. John West had been shocked recently when the Victorian Labor Government was defeated. Were his hopes to be dashed? He had faith in Thurgood's judgement. Thurgood argued that Labor's defeat in Victoria was a symptom of the economic situation. Unemployment was becoming widespread.

During his frequent walks up Jackson Street to and from the city, John West had noticed that more people spoke to him by name than for many years. Previously he had attributed the decline in greetings to unfamiliarity; fewer people in Carringbush knew him by sight since his empire had spread. Now it dawned on him that more greetings meant more requests for financial assistance. Often lately, a shabby man or woman would sidle up to him with a direct or veiled request for money. Once even, an old woman had revived the practice of "showing Jack West the rent book." It seemed that bad times were once again coming to Carringbush.

The thought disturbed John West, but his reaction to the coming of bad times was different now. As memories of his own days of poverty stirred in him he quickly repulsed them. The old impulse to give seemed blunted. The beggars were dead-beats who would spend money on drink, he told himself; no need for anyone to be in want these days. Anyone who was out of work, didn't want work!

"We'll win the Federal elections, all right," Thurgood repeated. "The people are becoming dissatisfied and will kick out all sitting governments irrespective of party. There is going to be a depression."

"All Australian Governments now in office will be defeated within a year," Thurgood prophesised, and time was to prove him right.

"But," John West said, "that means MacCorkell will be defeated in Queensland!"

"Yes!" Thurgood answered. "And that's what is worrying me."

John West reassured Thurgood: "If MacCorkell is defeated and the Nationalists bring you to trial, I will protect you. I give you my word on that."

Thus fortified, Thurgood fell to discussing plans for the future. "Summers will retain the leadership of the party," he said. "He's won up to now, but I'll beat him yet."

"Keep trying," John West replied. "I had a discussion with the Archbishop last night. He is very confident. Summers told the Archbishop that you will be Treasurer."

"Just as well," Thurgood replied. "If a depression comes, as I am sure it will, then I have a financial plan to save the country."

John West then mentioned for the first time a scheme that would make him a million pounds.

"Summer's policy is protection. He plans to raise a tariff wall against imported goods in order to develop Australian industry. Well, I have the biggest wine and spirit company in Australia. I have absorbed many of the smaller companies recently. I want you to arrange for a high tariff on imported wine, whisky and gin."

Thurgood raised no objection. "That could be arranged when the time comes," he said.

The defeat of the Victorian Labor Ministry occurred at the height of the trouble in the trotting world. It had been replaced by a Nationalist Ministry which took office precariously with the support of Alfred Davison's break-away party which had left the Country Party with a programme for the small farmer.

Horan's fall from office had taught John West one thing: he could exercise a lot of influence on the Victorian Parliament even with Labor out of office, provided Davison's so-called Progressive Country Party held power, or the balance of power.

The trotting men received as little help from the new Chief Secretary as they had from Tom Trumbleward. He was a member of Arthur Davison's group. Davison instructed the Chief Secretary to assist John West, then saw John West afterwards. No mention of bribes, no requests for favours. Just an announcement of what had been done, and a hint that he wanted to become

Premier. A coalition with Labor was his ultimate aim. Could Mr. West assist him to get the support of Labor?

John West agreed. If Labor could not get back with an absolute majority, then they could rule with the support of Davison; and perhaps the Nationalists could never rule without Davison's help. Davison was a key man in Victorian politics – more important now to John West than any of the Labor men.

Meanwhile John West had continued his efforts to silence Clive Parker. Shortly after the abortive attempt to bribe Parker, John West called on Kenneth Murkett, Australia's most powerful newspaper owner.

John West felt at a disadvantage; he could not dominate this man. Instead of his usual shrewd manoeuvres, he bluntly stated his business and surveyed Murkett sullenly.

Murkett was in his forties. Suave, and self-assertive, he spoke to John West patronisingly, and John West hated him for it.

"My reporters are expected to give our readers a fair, authoritative and objective report of all news. Parker has, I believe, been attacking your wrestlers in the STAR. I have made it clear to him, Mr. West, that he must not make personal attacks or take sides in my columns – that he must report the wrestling at both venues with complete impartiality. I have made it clear to young Parker that I will not tolerate the vicious tone of some of his STAR articles; but I have promised him a free hand to say that he believes Sandow to be superior to your wrestlers, if he believes that is the case."

John West saw in a flash the thought processes of Murkett. He had insisted for so long that his papers were impartial that he was beginning to believe the lie himself.

On the tip of John West's tongue were several points he had intended to make.

"Why not sack Parker?" Murkett wouldn't sack Parker, because Parker was a brilliant all-round journalist. Of course, he would say that he did not sack staff except for some professional misdemeanour. "I am your partner in Queensland." Murkett would say that he could not alter the policy of his paper merely to please a business associate. Of course, the real reason would have been that Jack West had been too clever for him when the partnership was formed. Each was to appoint an equal number of directors and control an equal number of shares with Murkett as Chairman of Directors, but John West had tricked him by paying a member of the staff to become a Murkett director, then sell out to John West. Murkett had never forgiven him for that.

John West knew it was no use mentioning his shares in Murkett's Melbourne companies either, because his holdings were small, and there were no more shares for sale. Murkett controlled these papers on behalf of more respectable millionaires than Jack West. No use to mention that he had been a consistent advertiser, because Murkett would say that his papers reported the truth without considering advertisers. More bull-dust!

Murkett was typical of the respectable rich; John West hated, despised and envied the respectable rich. They excluded him and his family from their social circle. He was not respectable. He had made his money out of an illegal tote. He had heard Nellie amusing the children with stories of their women's stupid snobbery and hypocritical self-righteousness. The menfolk were just as bad. The did not invite John West to Parliament House functions (not that he would go, anyway!). They had banned him from their respectable clubs (not that he wanted to be a member, anyway!) They were proud that they had not made their money from the "nefarious side of life." Well, they still made millions! What difference how they made them?

John West raised none of these points. Instead he demanded: "Parker is trying to organise extremists into a Boxing Commission. At least you can stop him from interfering with private enterprise."

Murkett followed John West to the door with disarming friendliness. "I assure you, Mr. West, that Parker will not be permitted to form a Boxing Commission, nor will I allow him to make personal attacks or to be unfair in any way. He will be somewhat curtailed. I think everything will work out all right."

Work out all right! It was too late to undo the harm Parker had done. Chapman left the country, but not before he told Parker that he was not an Englishman, and had never been world light-heavy-weight champion.

Tinn himself left the country, when the season ended prematurely. His parting words to John West were: "If ever I come back, J.W., and I will if things look better, I'll murder this guy Parker!"

456

Tinn came back, all right, bringing his team with him. This time, Parker's welcome was not flattering, but it was mild in comparison to his stories in the STAR at the beginning of the previous season. Takings were fair; Parker could not stop the public from coming in sufficient numbers to make the game pay.

Then, Tinn and Lamb made a serious error.

John West was furious. Arriving at the office one morning, he summoned the two offenders.

"Who gave Parker that cheque?" he demanded.

"Why, I did," Lamb began to explain, "you see, he said that he had decided to co-operate this season."

"You did!" John West said savagely, then turned to Ted Tinn. "And I suppose you agreed to it!"

"Sure, Jack, sure. All our worries are over; we'll clean up a fortune now that guy's off our back!"

"Oh, we'll clean up a fortune, will we? You make me laugh! Do you know that Parker took that cheque straight back and put it on the editor's table?"

"What!" Lamb exclaimed.

"I'll murder that god-dam, snowy-headed bastard for this," Tinn shouted, rising to his feet and swaying aggressively as if he were coming into the referee's hold with Parker.

"Fancy letting him put that across you!" John West continued. "The most obvious trap imaginable, and you fall for it. He's demanded the right to publish the whole story with a photo of the cheque in tomorrow's paper."

"If he publishes that, we might as well shut up shop," Tinn said. "How do you know all this?"

"You needn't worry; it won't be published. I've fixed that. But I can do little to stop Parker now. If you hadn't allowed him to use this cheque to prove to his editor and Murkett that we are in the habit of paying out cheques to reporters, I could have convinced Murkett that Parker was being vindictive for no reason. You must admit that his articles have been less troublesome since he's been with Murkett; but houses won't be much better this season than last, unless we can stop him altogether. You blokes have got to learn never to under-estimate an enemy!"

"I'll murder the little bastard," Tinn repeated, still pacing the room. Suddenly he stopped. "Why didn't I think of it last season? Listen, you guys. Ted Tinn's got a bright idea to fix Mister

Smart-guy Parker. Supposing my opponent throws me out of the ring, first time I wrestle, right in front of Parker on the press table. Be just too bad if I accidentally kicked him in the face, now, wouldn't it. We've done it in the States many a time.''

"That's right; its been known to happen," John West said. He chuckled, then added: "Mind you, I know nothing about it.''

Clive Parker was in the ringside press seats as usual, the night Ted Tinn had his first wrestle for the 1929 season.

Parker had been reporting football that afternoon and had spent a good deal of time at the bar; he felt listless now, but noted with satisfaction that the stadium was barely half full.

The Melbourne Stadium could accommodate ten thousand people. It looked, from inside, like a huge barn. It was a suitable building, but badly in need of repairs. Its roof was high, and wooden seats and steps rose steeply from the upraised square in the centre towards the walls and roof on all sides.

Clive Parker was not pleased with recent developments in his war with John West. West's talk of influence with Murkett was not all eye-wash. The incident of the cheque proved that. They had asked for proof, and he had produced it, but they had refused to use the evidence. Every second article he submitted was being mutilated with the blue pencil, and Murkett had ordered him to abandon his efforts to have a Boxing Commission set up to control the sport. West must have seen Murkett, all right.

He was disappointed in Murkett. "The Stadium's interests are big advertisers . . . Wrestling is good entertainment . . . The public is not expected to take it seriously . . . Boxing is a brutal sport at any time, and will not be improved by a Boxing Commission.'' Wouldn't be improved! Struth! Clive Parker could think of a few improvements. Higher pay for preliminary boys. Medical supervision by an independent panel of doctors, instead of by the Stadium doctor, who would pass a crippled pensioner as fit, if it suited Dick Lamb.

Pensions for disabled fighters. And no favouritism to be shown to certain managers and boxers. And no victimisation of boys who stood up for their rights. Murkett talked every year at the annual meeting of the Company about freedom of the press, Parker mused ruefully; a bit of a joke!

Anyway, he had managed to get in a few cracks at the wrestlers again this season. Parker chuckled at the thought of his first article. *The "Razzlers" are back. Wait till Sandow hears about it. If he comes to Melbourne, I know one "World Champion" who will take the next boat home to God's own country.* His musing was interrupted by a roar of thousands of voices. The crowd was on its feet, booing and catcalling. Ted Tinn was swaggering up the aisle towards the ring.

Tinn had expected this sort of reception after the events of last season. He was a good showman. There was some consolation in being unpopular with the fans. They would come to jeer you, to see you beaten. He played up to their feelings. He shook his fist at them and vaulted over the ropes, glaring at Clive Parker, who grinned cheekily.

A burst of clapping and cheering arose as Tinn's opponent, an unknown wrestler named Wylie, walked briskly down the aisle to the ring.

"Another Englishman from New York, I suppose," Parker said to the reporter next to him.

"Oh, I don't know," replied the other, remembering the cheque with Richard Lamb's signature on it which was folded in his pocket.

Around the ringside there were as many women as men. Strange the charm of men's naked bodies wrestling has for some women, Parker mused; a sort of second-hand sexual experience.

Above the mumble of five thousand voices could be heard the calls of the drink and lolly boys with their trays earning a few shillings for themselves and a few more for John West, and the shouts of men near the ringside betting.

"Three to one on Tinn!"

"Three to one against Wylie!"

The broadcaster came into the ring and announced the wrestlers. Boos and shouts of "Look out, Ted, Sandow is here," greeted Tinn, and wild cheering greeted the littler man. Tinn shook his fist and snarled; Wylie arose and bowed gracefully.

The bell clanged. Wylie moved from the referee hold and cleverly brought Tinn down in a leg scissors. Tinn writhed and grimaced, threshing his legs and dragging his opponent towards the apron of the ring. The crowd was wild with excitement.

"He's not hurting him," Parker shouted. "Tinn's up to his old tricks."

"Oh, I don't know," his fellow reporter answered, again remembering the cheque. "Wylie's clever with his legs, they tell me."

The other reporters tapped away at their typewriters or wrote brisk shorthand in long notebooks, but Parker just sat thinking.

So this is the stunt tonight. The game Englishman is clever with his legs, and Tinn is in such pain that he is forced to use his superior strength to crawl from the ring. The Englishman knows the leg-holds all right – nice body scissors. But he's not strong enough to hurt Tinn.

Again and again, Tinn crawled from the ring to avoid leg-holds. As the round drew into its last few seconds, Tinn returning again to the ring amid howls of disapproval, was grabbed by Wylie in a crutch hold and thrown to the mat. In a flash, Tinn was caught in a body scissors and press. The referee on his belly beside the two men began counting.

"One! Two! Three!" The crowd was beside itself in a frenzy of joy. The hated Tinn was being given a wrestling lesson!

Parker shook his head in disgust. He was a keen student of the sport. Whatever else Tinn was, he was a forceful and aggressive wrestler. His skill was limited, but he was as strong as an ox. Clive Parker knew that he could have wriggled loose from these puny holds and countered with one of his excruciating toe holds or a head lock. This was all part of the circus, Parker reasoned; Tinn was playing his part well.

Tinn's price lengthened: the gamblers began betting even money each of two. Here was a chance for a clean-up. He noticed John West, who was sitting opposite at the ringside, back Tinn for fifty pounds. Hungry old bugger! There's a lead.

"I'll have an even fiver on Tinn," he shouted to the other press men, but there were no takers; they'd been coming here too long to fall for this. Bad enough having to report the bout seriously, without losing money on it.

The wrestlers came into the referee's hold for the second round. The crowd was on its feet, yelling for Wylie. Clive Parker sat leaning on his elbows. Tinn will probably get the equaliser soon, he reflected, then carry this bloke for a few more rounds before putting an end to it.

Above the ring the broadcaster was working himself up into a frenzy: "Wylie has Tinn in a side headlock. He can't get out of it! He's in great pain, he's tugging and weaving. But he can't get out of it. He can't get out of it!''

All over the State people sat listening to the radio, wondering whether he would "get out of it." Like most people present, they were convinced Tinn was in terrible agony.

"This game little Englishman is giving the champion more than he bargained for tonight," the broadcaster continued.

"Tinn is dragging him towards the ropes. The crowd is shouting its disapproval at Tinn's tactics. He's trying to get out of the ring again. He can't get out of it! He's trying to drag Wylie through the ropes. He can't get out of it! But he's out of it. He dragged Wylie out of the ring and broke the hold. They've fallen on to the press tables!''

Clive Parker looked up and two bodies fell on to the table in front of him. Next thing he knew, Tinn's face was close to his. It was dirty and sweating. And its mouth moved and said in a low but violent whisper: "Cop this, you bastard!" And Ted Tinn's mighty fist smashed into Clive Parker's face.

The crowd was in a pandemonium of uproar. Wylie was standing on the press table protesting to the referee, who was looking over the ropes calling for the wrestlers to come back into the ring.

For Clive Parker there were stars. Then his head swam and blackness came over his vision, but he was conscious of being dragged from his seat and rolled on the floor with a heavy body on top of him. The ushers, normally quick and violent in suppressing a melee, were not yet on the scene. Tinn had Clive Parker's unconscious body under the ring, knocking its snowy head on the floor.

John West sat impassively. It had all happened in about a minute. Pressmen and ushers crowded around as Tinn climbed back through the ropes. Under the ring they saw the prostrate figure of Clive Parker. His face showed chalky white in the shadows, and blood trickled from his mouth.

A gentle knocking on the door and Mrs. Moran's voice saying: "Are you awake, Mary?" awakened Mary West. She opened her eyes and they were gritty as if filled with dust. She looked around the room, smacking her lips, grimacing at the taste of her coated tongue. Consciousness came slowly in a muddle. The weak

461

autumn sun was high. She reached for her watch on the dressing table. It had stopped. Must be nearly lunch time.

"Are you awake, Mary?" she heard her grandmother saying again.

"Yes, Gran'," she said wearily. "Come in."

Mrs. Moran entered carrying a breakfast tray, which she placed on the dressing table. Mary sat up yawning and running her fingers through her hair, then sat nursing her head, her titian locks falling over her face. Her right breast, round and firm, protruded unashamedly from her low-cut nightdress. Mrs. Moran took a glass from the tray and mixed a drink of fizzling fruit salts which she handed to Mary.

"Here, drink this. It will settle your stomach. And by the look of you, it needs settling. And, for goodness' sake, put on a wrap, you look positively indecent."

Mary drank the fruit salts, then adjusted her nightdress, threw a bedjacket around her shoulders, and sank back wearily.

"How my head throbs!" she exclaimed.

"I can't say that I have any sympathy for you, but there are Aspros and water on the tray with the tea. Help yourself."

"Thanks."

While Mary washed the tablets down, Mrs. Moran flung up a window, murmuring something about the place smelling like a wineshop, then she sat on a chair beside the bed. Her hair was as white as the purest white enamel, her face was lined as a spider's web, her shoulders were rounded and her finger joints swollen with arthritis, but she was still alert and energetic.

Mary picked up the cup of steaming tea and a piece of toast and began eating without enthusiasm.

"Whatever is the time?" she asked, stiffling a yawn.

"It's after midday; but you'd better not go downstairs for lunch. You look like a hag; and your mother is preparing to have a good heart-to-heart with you. We both heard you come in last night, or rather, this morning. Your mother is very worried about you, and I can't say I blame her."

"Can't say I do, either. But I just couldn't stand another of Mother's heart-to-heart talks. Not today, anyway."

"I told your mother that I would talk to you. And you're going to listen to me, young lady. Wherever do you think you will end up?"

462

"Oh, I'll be all right, Gran'. I'm not really important anyway," Mary said distractedly, sipping her tea.

"Important or not, you'd better look out if your father finds out the way you are going on. Just as well he is a sound sleeper, and hasn't heard you come in since that night he fired his revolver."

"I don't care what Father thinks. He's the last person in the world for me to worry about."

"God forgive you, child! How can you be so hard?"

"Maybe because I'm my father's daughter. Anyway he doesn't care, so long as I look beautiful at functions he attends; so he can say: *Isn't she lovely?* Oh, Gran', you can't imagine how sick I am of being a useless person – a parasite. I have talent and I'm not allowed to use it. Why can't I take a job? Oh, but Father would never allow that!"

"No, I'm afraid he wouldn't; but you really must pull yourself together, Mary. You have everything that most young women would give their right arm for. Money, a home, leisure, pretty clothes . . ."

"That's not everything, Gran'."

"No one knows that more than I, Mary, but there is another life to remember. We all must one day face our Maker."

Mary looked at the old woman inquiringly.

"Mary, how long is it since you have been to confession and communion?"

"A long time, Gran'. I'm afraid I can't remember exactly," Mary answered, pecking at a piece of toast and marmalade.

"More than a year, I'll bet, and the Church obliges us all to receive the Sacraments at least once a year. And you only go to Mass when you can't get out of going. God knows, I'm not a prude or a wowser, but you really must pull yourself together, child." She rested her hand on Mary's arm. "By all means, have your fun, Mary, but don't forget your religion; it will help you through the troubles of this world."

"Sometimes I wonder, Gran'. Remember, you are old now. You might live for years, but your mind has turned towards the next world. Religion doesn't seem so important when you're young – at least, it doesn't to me."

"But surely you believe . . ."

"I don't know what I believe, Gran'. Life is empty and meaningless. I used to believe all the Church taught. Now I don't

463

know. The confessional frightens me; and about the rest, I don't know.''

"The confessional frightens you because you have drifted for so long. That's what's wrong with you . . .''

"No more today, Gran', please. My mind is not working too well.''

"I am speaking to you for your own good, young lady. I must tell you this. Last night, the Archbishop called to see your father. As he was leaving, your mother called him aside. I could not hear all they said, but I think you were the topic discussed. Your mother has been worried . . .''

"Trust her to bring the Archbishop into it. No one less than the Archbishop would do for Mother!''

Mrs Moran smiled vaguely.

"If Mother thinks that I am going to discuss my private affairs with the Archbishop, then she's mistaken. The old boy is all right, but . . .''

"What worries me, Mary, is that Archbishop Malone may discuss the matter with your father. You know how thick they are.''

"Well, there's nothing I can do to stop them putting their heads together if they choose,'' said Mary, with feigned indifference – she dreaded a showdown with her father.

Mrs. Moran stood up and grasped Mary's hand. "Mary,'' she said earnestly, "if your father speaks to you, don't defy him. In the name of God and his Holy Mother, don't defy him.''

Without waiting for a reply she departed, leaving Mary with her thoughts. They stirred slowly in her mind, oppressing it with a sense of guilt. She dreaded this sense of guilt which had crept into her thinking this past year or two. She usually combated it with rationalisations and a forced devil-may-care attitude, but now she could not dispel it.

She had come to believe that her sense of guilt was a legacy from the Catholic religion – from the confessional. The practice of Catholicism, she reasoned, was a succession of sins committed, confessed and then forgotten. When she ceased to confess her sins – minor transgressions as they were – she could not forget them; and her inability to forget them had led to sins of greater magnitude.

Many of her sins were now mortal sins. She often ate meat on

Friday when lunching with non-Catholic friends; occasionally at a party she would get drunk as she had done last night; she would relate lewd stories in mixed company; and there had been lovemaking. At first it had been just kissing and cuddling in parked cars, but soon her passionate vitality could not be contained. Her beauty attracted men, and her body often cried out for love. And so she had begun a desultory affair with the leading man in a play in which she had been acting. At first, she had pretended to herself that she loved him, but soon she had to admit that she did not; but while it lasted it had been a gay, exhilarating affair. There had been others since, until she sometimes thought she must be licentious and depraved.

Mary arose from the bed, put on a pair of slippers and walked to the dressing table.

"Ugh! What a face! What an old witch!"

As she combed her long hair, she pondered her problems: facing up to them, analysing them as never before.

Her doubts about her religion had begun with a fear of the confessional: she could not bring herself to utter her sins even to a strange priest in the dark secrecy of the box where none could hear. Once even she went to a church prepared to go to confession. She made an examination of her conscience in the prescribed way, but when her turn came she could not direct her footsteps into the box; instead, she fled from the church. Was it fear born of embarrassment that caused her to flee? Or was it that she no longer believed that the man there in the gloomy box was God's representative with power to forgive sin?

Previously, she had believed explicitly in the confessional. She had often wondered how other Catholics she knew could treat it in such a cavalier fashion. She knew Catholic girls and men who sinned like heathens all the week in the expectation of being able to cleanse their soul in the confessional on Saturday night. It hadn't seemed right to her; the confessional was surely not intended to be used in that manner.

Other things about her religion aroused doubts in her. The Church was too interested in money. Take Father, for instance. He hadn't been to church for years, yet the Archbishop deferred to him, visited the house to discuss church business and politics.

The Archbishop did not visit the poor across the river in

Carringbush. Why? Because they had no money, and Father was a millionaire who gave generously to the Church and advised the Archbishop about church property and finances.

"Blessed are the poor," the Church said, but the Church was rich. It wasn't so long ago that the rich could buy indulgences: for money they could escape the wrath of Christ. This still applied. Though the Church now said that indulgences could not be bought, the rich could have Masses said for the living and dead in return for money, and those Masses carried indulgences. The Church said divorce was not permitted, yet rich people had obtained divorces in return for veiled donations to the Church.

In the friendly warmth of a well filled bath, Mary wondered if her heretical doubts arose from her own moral decline or whether she was genuinely discovering that her religion was a falsehood and a mockery? Of late she had mixed with more non-Catholic than Catholic people. Had she been influenced by their arguments against Church dogmas such as the Virgin birth and the changing of bread and wine into the body and blood of Christ? She must face up to these questions and make up her mind as soon as possible!

She felt certain that her quandary was in no small measure due to her idleness. Her round of dancing, tennis, riding and amateur theatricals had led her to boredom and a conviction that she was a social parasite. She was of no use in the world. She had no career, not even a job. She could write quite well, she could play the piano, "dance divinely," "act like Sybil Thorndike," yet she was a parasite. Her life was empty and useless. She felt a twinge of conscience that she could not analyse or understand.

Somewhere, in the shadows of her life, the sinister figure of her father lurked. Many of her friends, Catholics and Protestants alike, had been warned against coming to the house because of her father's reputation. Not that she worried much about that: she had always had a tremendous capacity for enjoying herself until lately, and friends who came to the house always came again and again. But her father was shrouded in mystery and the household was always tense with strange cleavages.

She knew something of the reason for the estrangement of her mother and father, and in the back of her mind lurked a suspicion that Xavier was not her father's child. Father hated Xavier: he did not ever speak to him or of him. Sometimes she had seen him secretly studying Xavier, and his implacable eye had been frightening.

Then the incident about the piano. Xavier was studying music at school. He had natural ability, but had no instrument to practise on, because John West had sold the grand piano as a reprisal against Marjorie. Afraid to approach her father, Mary purchased a piano on time-payment.

One evening a week later, Mary and Xavier were seated at the piano practising a duet when John West entered the music room. They each sensed his presence, ceased playing and turned swiftly.

They flinched from his savage gaze.

"Where did that piano come from?"

"I bought it at Myer's," Mary answered. "I'm paying it off out of my allowance."

"It will go back in the morning!"

John West did send the piano back. Mary was convinced that his action was aimed at Xavier.

He was not like other fathers: she could not remember a single instance of any member of the family approaching him for fatherly advice or of him offering it. He and Mother did not live as man and wife, and spoke to each other only when conversation was unavoidable. He had ruined Mother's life. Perhaps she had erred once, but why didn't Father either break with her or forgive her?

Mary sometimes thought that her father had mapped out a life of punishment for Mother. Mother was a little queer at times. The pains in her back of which she complained interminably, and which often kept her in bed, were, it seemed, quite imaginary. Mother's strange fixation on her spine seemed to be aimed at Father. She mentioned it in his presence as if she expected to hurt him. What lay behind it? And what lay behind the hushed conversations which Father held with ill-assorted visitors at night? What lay behind the rumours that her father was a mysterious leader of the underworld who had once ordered a bomb to be thrown into a policeman's house? Bad enough to be the idle daughter of a millionaire; worse still if your father should have an unsavoury reputation. Surely the Archbishop knew her father's reputation; then why did he cultivate Father? There could be only one answer to that question – and the answer was money!

Having dressed, Mary went downstairs to the music room and

sat by the big window reading a book. She could not absorb her mind in the story and fell again to pondering. What was she to do? The only answer her spirit could give was defiance. They could all go to blazes: Mother and Father and old Dan Malone. She would defy them all! But she knew defiance was no solution.

If only she could unburden herself to someone. No use to go to Mother, because Mother had been completely cowed by Father. No use to go to Joe, because Joe would pass the matter off as a joke. No use to go to Gran' or John: they would be sympathetic, but both were deeply religious and were always shocked when she betrayed doubts or disrespect of the Church. And no use to go to Father.

The showdown to Father would come all right. Gran' may have heard more of the conversation between Mother and the Archbishop than she pretended; and, anyway, Gran's instinct was never wrong in such matters. The Archbishop would be almost certain to mention the matter to Father. Look out for trouble, Mary West!

She would defy him, she decided. He might browbeat Mother and John and everybody else, but not Mary West.

Mary stretched out on the couch and returned to her book, but soon weariness enveloped her; the hand which held the book slid slowly to her lap, then the book dropped to the floor and her eyes closed in deep sleep in which she dreamed unintelligibly. The sun was low when she was awakened by her mother.

Nellie West had grown old. Though not yet sixty, she looked almost as old as her mother. She had become a neurotic mixture of religious fervour, imaginary sickness and quaint wit. She shook her daughter roughly by the shoulder. "Wake up, Mary! Wake up!"

Mary stirred drowsily, and sat up rubbing her eyes. "Whatever time is it? I must have fallen asleep!"

"If you would come home at a respectable hour you would not fall asleep, young lady. Dinner will be ready in half an hour. But first of all I want to talk to you."

Mary yawned exaggeratedly. "Oh, Mother, not again."

"Oh, it's all right for you to pout and say 'not again.' God knows I don't believe in wrangling, but I intend to be firm with you in future."

"Mother, please. If you don't mind."

"If I don't mind! Well, if you won't listen to me, perhaps you'll listen to someone else," Nellie said, suggestively stressing her last two words. Then, apparently believing she had won a moral victory she flounced out of the room.

In the twelve-year battle between John and Nellie West neither had triumphed. John West had not broken Nellie's spirit; Nellie had not regained the love and confidence of her children. Only Xavier acted towards her in the intimate manner of a child towards its mother. The others remained aloof, though outwardly friendly. How much they knew about Bill Evans and Xavier she could only guess; certainly they knew enough to feel an involuntary revulsion towards her.

To Nellie, the affair with Bill Evans had been relegated to the limbo of the regretted past. He had not been seen nor heard of since he left Melbourne, and the years had healed her regret and sorrow. Only Xavier and the tension of the household remained to remind her that once she had sinned against God and her husband. She had maintained her threat to hate John West, but now her hatred was a fire without flame.

John West had robbed Nellie of love, but now she was old and the stream of love had dried up in her. She had sought to punish him with her ridiculous pretence of being crippled, but she had succeeded only in turning herself into an imaginary invalid. Slowly John West had been forced to restore the servants, though she had not purchased another car. His ban on Nellie leaving the house had slowly crumbled and she occasionally went out, mainly to Church functions. The question of whether Xavier should be allowed a room of his own was never raised between them: to mention it would have been to make an open wound out of a fester. Mrs. Moran once suggested the idea to John West; but, as she said to Nellie afterwards: "He just gave me one of the looks of his that froze the words on my lips."

Nellie West was deeply disturbed about Mary, but was quite unable to help her. When in desperation she had asked the Archbishop to intercede with Mary, she realised immediately that the Archbishop might tell her husband. God knows what would happen now!

After her mother left, Mary West went upstairs to her room. She hadn't been there long when her brother John tapped on the door and said: "You in there, Ginger?" Joe had nicknamed Mary "Ginger."

"Come in, John."

He flung the door open and burst into the room. He was very much like his father, though taller and broader. The same sloping head and low ears, the same unruly lock of hair. But his legs were not bandy, and he had not his father's unfathomable grey eyes. He had his mother's blue eyes.

"You're in for it, Ginger. The Archbishop is talking to Father at the gate and I heard your name mentioned. Gran' told me this morning that she expected this, and she's never wrong."

Mary, who was powdering her face in front of the dressing-table mirror, turned swiftly.

"I'm not trying to frighten you. Just thought I should warn you, that's all."

"Thanks, John," she said, recovering her composure. "But don't worry, I can look after myself."

"Now don't say anything rash, Mary. You know what the old man is. Don't say or do anything that will make things worse. Don't ruin your life."

"Ruin my life? I should care! It's ruined already!"

John came over behind her and draped his arms around her shoulders.

"You mustn't talk like that, Mary. Whatever's come over you lately?"

"If I want to defy Father, I will! You secretly defy him, but you haven't the courage to do it openly."

She felt his hands fall away from her, and watching him in the mirror she saw him bite his lip, turn his back, and bow his head. She walked to his side.

"I'm sorry, John. No offence meant."

"You're right, I'm a coward. I want nothing to do with Father's plans for me, yet I know I will obey him. I don't want to take over the reins of his butcher's waggon. I know more of his life story and business methods than you do, Mary. He is a ruthless, evil man. And may God forgive me, for thinking so of my own father!"

John stood in front of the mirror, holding his fist behind his back. "I haven't told you about my music room interview with him, the night before last, have I?"

"No."

"Well, his latest plan is to send me all round Australia to manage various of his enterprises in turn; and so prepare myself to step into his shoes later on."

"And what did you say to that?"

"Nothing. I said I'd rather not, but if he really wanted me to . . ." Suddenly John turned and gripped Mary by the shoulders. "Oh, I know I'm weak, Mary. I hate business, especially his kind of business. I don't want his money – not a penny of it. I just want a job and a little happiness, that's all. I'm not cut out to be a business tycoon. I always mean to tell him straight, but he's too strong-willed for me. Last night he demanded, then cajoled; at one stage he became almost friendly like a father should be. I just couldn't resist him. He is the most dominant person I have ever known and I am afraid of him."

John was right. Mary *was* in for it.

Their father had been driven home by a new business associate, named Patrick Cory. Pat Cory was rivalling Frank Lammence as John West's right-hand man. His late father had been associated with John West in his wine and spirit business. Patrick Cory had inherited his father's share, and soon proved to John West that he could not be pushed around as his father had been. In the battle of tactics for control during the buying out and incorporation of the smaller vineyards and distilleries he had proved a worthy partner.

Pat Cory had been a broker and an accountant before inheriting his father's business interests. He knew all the tricks of modern business. He was ruthless, sly and clever. He was out to make money; and if need be he would make it with cynical disregard for the interests of others. John West soon learned to admire him. They became joint controllers of the Australian distilling industry, and, at Cory's suggestion, formed a holding company which had already begun to stretch its tentacles into all manner of enterprises throughout the Commonwealth.

John West had found lately that he was too tired at the end of the day to tackle the walk home, so he had fallen into the habit of being driven home by Cory. Tonight, as they sat for a moment in front of the West mansion chatting, Archbishop Malone had strolled by dressed in the formal top hat and frock coat, having walked home from the Cathedral as was his practice. He had joined them and questioned Cory, who he knew well as a wealthy church layman, about some matter of business procedure.

Eventually, Cory said in his rich Irish voice: "Well, Your Grace and Mr. West, I must be on my way. My little lady is fussy about punctuality at meal times."

John West got out of the car, and Cory drove away with a cheerful farewell. Archbishop Malone lingered chatting idly. His bushy eyebrows and the wisps of hair which rose from his temples and fringed the inner rim of his hat were snow white, but his erect figure belied his sixty-seven years.

"There is a little matter I'd like to mention, Mr. West, if you'll pardon my making so bold. It concerns Mary. Not that I condemn the girl. I know there is no great harm in her, but I've been hearing a few tales of her drinking and staying out late and mixing with bad companions. Worst of all, she is neglecting her religious duties."

John West studied the Archbishop's face in the fading light, but made no reply.

"I hope you will accept this news in the spirit in which it is imparted. I feel a personal interest in Mary. Many's the time, long ago, that I nursed her on my knee. I have watched her grow up into the beautiful woman she is. Like you, I am proud of her talents; but she needs guidance. In truth, I must say that I had heard disquieting rumours even before your good wife raised the matter with me last evening. I think, perhaps, if you were to have a little talk to her, Mr. West."

"Very well, your Grace. I have been a little concerned . . . but being so busy of late I have not . . ." John West was embarrassed, and annoyed with Mary.

"I thought it best that you, rather than I, should speak to the child. No need to be hard with her, she's just a little head-strong, that's all," the Archbishop advised as they turned to depart.

When they had each walked a few steps, the Archbishop said over his shoulder: "And remember, Mr. West, the main thing is to get her to begin attending Mass regularly, and the Sacraments. In that regard, example is the best teacher."

John West turned swiftly, but Malone's tall figure had already melted into the gathering dusk.

The evening meal was eaten in silence. All seemed to feel the tension. As he left the table, John West said: "Mary, I would like to speak to you in the music room."

Mary followed him obediently. He switched on the light, sat at the table, and indicated the chair opposite.

He focused his unblinking eyes upon her. "What's this I hear about you not carrying out your religious duties?"

She raised her head defiantly. "You should care. You haven't been inside a church for years."

Involuntary, he admired her. She was her father's daughter all right. And beautiful, very beautiful, sitting there defying him. But for her own good, he must be strict.

"What do you mean, talking to me like that?"

She did not answer.

"You have neglected your religion, you have been drinking, and keeping late hours until the Archbishop himself is talking about your behaviour. What do you mean by it?"

"You wouldn't understand."

"Oh, wouldn't I? Well, it must cease!"

"I refuse to be browbeaten, Father," she said. Her voice had fallen to a whisper and her lips quivered a little.

"Oh, do you? Well, you will do as I tell you. You will go to confession and communion immediately. I will see to that! And I will see that you go to Mass each Sunday in future, too!"

Oh, Father, she thought, if only I could tell you of my troubles, my doubts! If only I could sit on your knee and stroke your grey hair and ask your advice! She imagined what would happen if she did and she almost burst into hysterical laughter at the thought.

Can't you see, girl, he thought, I know what is best. You must cease this loose behaviour and practise your religion. He wished that it was in him to speak softly to her, to tell her she was the apple of his eye, that he thought only of her welfare. But his personality was incapable of melting even when confronted with his favourite child in trouble.

"Well?" he demanded.

"Supposing I defy you?"

"You will not defy me! Why should you defy me? You know that I am speaking for your own good. I've given you everything you need. A good home, an excellent education, an ample allowance. Why should you bring disgrace on this house?"

The hypocrisy of his words suddenly enraged her. "I refuse to

473

be spoken to in this way, Father. I am very unhappy for a number of reasons, but I refuse to be treated like a child. I'm a grown woman. I'm capable of living my own life.''

He leapt to his feet and leaned across the table. "And what a life it is! You're acting like a drunken harlot. No daughter of mine will go on as you're going on. You'll do as I say or get out of this house!''

She began to sob and hot tears rolled down her cheeks.

He stood gazing at her, aware that his cruel words must have hurt her. He wanted to apologise, but felt that if he did, her courage to defy him would be renewed. Instead, he followed up his assault, though less savagely.

"You will do as I say, Mary. And you will keep earlier hours; you will be indoors by midnight. And you will get out of that theatrical company; they're a bad lot.''

Mary choked her sobbing. Until she was prepared to leave this house forever, she must obey this man, she thought.

"All right, Father I'll do as you say. But one day, we shall see.''

She ran from the room across the hall and up the stairs. Arriving in her room, she flung herself on the bed and sobbed herself to sleep.

John West remained standing like a statue, his face set like a sullen, wax mask. Why could he not ever let Mary see that he worshipped her, and wanted her to be happy?

Mary West woke in the early hours of the morning frozen stiff. She undressed and got under the bedclothes, but she did not sleep again until the cheerless autumn morning greeted her through the window.

On the next night, Saturday, she went to the confessional, determined to see whether it could console her: to check whether she believed in the priest's powers.

The result shocked her. Irrevocably she was convinced that the confessional was a sham. The priest was a young man, a callow youth with no knowledge of the world. How could he help her? Try as she would to find consolation and revive her flagging belief, she could not. Next morning she fasted and went to Mass and Communion. The result was the same: try as she would to believe that the wafer was the body and the blood of Christ, she just could not.

474

Mary West had lost her faith, and her mind began to search for something to replace it, or else her personality would disintegrate.

Sometime in the early hours of the morning after Tinn had assaulted him, Clive Parker awakened in the Melbourne Hospital. He could not open his mouth. His head was swathed in bandages and seemed on the verge of exploding.

The doctors told him that he was suffering from concussion and a broken jaw. They kept him in hospital for six weeks. His wife, Jeannie, who was three months with child, came to visit him each day and tried hard to cheer him up and have him resign himself to the inactivity of a hospital bed. After they had wired up his jawbone, and the effects of the concussion had worn off, he was permitted to have other visitors. Old Ron Lassiter was one of the first of these, but apart from the comment that "the stadium mob are tough boys," he refused to discuss the matter. West certainly had his men well trained, Parker thought.

Meanwhile the West machine had gone into action to hush the affair up.

The Journalists' Association held an inquiry into the incident; but it was inconclusive because the other pressmen who had been present did not positively testify that the injuries were inflicted deliberately. They did not know, they said; it might have been an accident.

After a week Parker began to think seriously about action to fight back against John West. He thought of suing Tinn and West, but a lawyer summoned to his bedside seemed doubtful that the case could be proven.

At last he was released from hospital, and after a few days' rest returned to work. That afternoon Murkett interviewed him. It was clear that Murkett's reaction was one of retreat. "Remember that you are working for me," he had concluded. "You're too valuable to risk your neck over wrestling. Have a crack at them occasionally, if you like, but don't overdo it."

Parker did not protest. What was the use?

He felt embarrassed by the fact that the nerves on the left side of his face were permanently affected by his injuries. His facial muscles twitched intermittently, causing him to move his head jerkily every now and then. This lowered his morale.

That same afternoon, he received a message from Richard Lamb. Could he meet him in the back of a certain hotel at 3 o'clock! Curious, Parker presented himself. As he walked in the door, Ted Tinn himself rushed forward and grasped his hand. A flashlight popped. They had photographed him shaking hands with Tinn.

Parker rushed at the photographer, but Tinn and Lamb restrained him gently. "Better beat it, Snowy," Tinn said. "That photo of you and me shaking hands will be in the papers this week!"

Back at the office he had interviewed Murkett again. "No, no, Parker, it's better to let the matter drop. We have paid your salary while you were off. We will pay your medical expenses. Take my advice, lad, let the matter drop. If you don't, you only risk further expense and injury."

Half an hour later Parker received a message to call on John West. He went immediately.

"Well, Parker," John West said, benignly: "I tried to warn you that these Yanks were tough boys, but you wouldn't be told. I had nothing to do with all this, but I want to help you. Here is a cheque for five hundred pounds, to cover your medical expenses and incidentals."

Parker arose abjectly. Temporarily his spirit was broken. Tears welled into his eyes, but he blinked them back. He took the proffered cheque and tore it to shreds with savage movements.

"I can't be bought, West," he said. "I will get you yet!"

John West merely smiled vaguely. It was as though he could foretell that Parker would spend the rest of his career in a fruitless endeavour to have the inside story of the West empire published, and in vainly moving from one job to another seeking a paper that would give him permission to attack West-controlled sports.

In October, 1929, John West was in the huge crowd that thronged to the Spencer Street railway station to farewell the Right Honourable James Summers, Prime Minister of Australia.

Labor had swept the polls in the most sensational election since Federation. So wide was the swing of the political pendulum that the Nationalist Prime Minister himself had lost his seat.

For James Summers, this was the greatest moment of his life.

He was to hold the highest position in the land. The Right Honourable James Summers, Prime Minister of Australia! Little had he dreamed years ago when he had left his little shop in the country, stony broke, to throw himself into the Labor Movement in the city, that one day he would be Prime Minister. His whole career was capped with this great triumph. He was a man of destiny: the man who would pull Australia out of the crisis.

The dingy, sleepy station had come to life to farewell the new Prime Minister. The Governor-General was travelling on the same train, but the huge crowd that waited was not interested in him. They were here to farewell Jimmy Summers.

In the crowd were men who had not voted Labor before in their lives: business men large and small who saw in Summers the only hope of recovery. But mainly they were Labor Party members or working men who believed that the Labor Party would serve only their interests. Jimmy Summers was their idol. Now he was Prime Minister; this was something to celebrate. He would solve the unemployment problem, and increase wages and social services. Don't worry, the big heads are going to learn that they can't rule the roost with Jimmy Summers in office.

As he alighted from the car and pushed his way through the crowd, wild cheering echoed along the platforms of the old building. Then came the loud singing of the workers' song:

Solidarity forever!
Solidarity forever!
Solidarity forever!
For the union makes us strong.

There were men in the crowd who had never heard the old song before, and wondered what connection it could have with the proceedings. John West, who had heard it sung last when he addressed the crowd outside Parliament House after Father Jesper had been deported, turned towards those who were singing as if to say: "Don't sing that song! Only reds sing that song!"

Summers smiled and waved towards the singing throng. He was a small man of sixty years and his hair was grey-flecked. He reached the train with difficulty, answering congratulations. He stood waving, as the cheering and singing increased.

Summers was a devout Catholic and a devoted family man.

He was an inspiring orator in a period when oratory still played a major part in politics. As he waved to the crowd, his eyes filled with tears. They had faith in him; he would not fail them.

Dusk came down like a dark cloud. The whistle shrilled; slowly the train began to move away. Summers took his seat and the singing and cheering faded until he could hear it no more. His tired body relaxed.

The great reception moved him to thoughts of his own worthiness. He was worthy of the great trust that had been placed in him. Had he not fought in the movement since he was a boy? Had he not played a great rôle in the defeat of conscription? Had he not fought tooth and nail in an effort to save the Commonwealth Shipping Lines? And had he not fought this election to save the Arbitration system? Had he not introduced the socialisation objective, the great resolution in 1922?

The socialisation resolution! That was a long time ago. The workers were not ready for socialisation. The Constitution would not allow it, anyway. The hostile Senate would block any socialisation measures.

No need for socialisation, anyway. Raise the tariff wall, and stop the flow of cheap labor from overseas: that was all that was needed to solve the unemployment problem, then prosperity would be restored. The Communists advocated Socialism, which was more extreme than socialisation, and they lost their deposits at the elections. They were alarmists, running up and down the country saying that we were on the eve of the greatest and most terrible depression of all time. There would be no depression, Jimmy Summers would see to that. All right for the Communists to talk Socialism and depression, they were not in office. Anyway, the workers had shown what they thought of the fellow at Port Melbourne. Howled him down, threw vegetables and shouted that they were putting Jimmy Summers in to look after them.

No, if he had gone round yelling socialisation he would not be here today; then where would the workers be with the Nationalists still in office?

His tired mind could not contain his swirling thoughts. His head ached, his throat had been rasped raw by a hundred inspiring speeches. His head began to nod, and soon sleep came: a restless sleep where crowds cheered and carried him to a great marble throne.

At Albury he was awakened by cheering and shouting. His head still ached and his joints were stiff. He changed trains after moving through another cheering crowd with difficulty. He went to his special sleeping berth and slept as the train sped through the night.

Next morning he arrived at Canberra, the new capital of Australia. Far from the sea, far from the great centres of industry. The home of politicians and public servants. A neat, soulless miniature city. Here, another large crowd awaited the new Prime Minister. So dense was it that the Governor-General could not reach the Vice-Regal carriage. Jimmy Summers took ten minutes to reach his car. He was driven to the Hotel Canberra. Jimmy Summers, the workers' Prime Minister, would not live in the luxurious Prime Minister's lodge.

At the hotel he received news of the first great Wall Street crash from his secretary, and he was troubled. Was he to be faced, not by a passing phase of unemployment, but by a great crisis like that of the nineties? Was he to rule a land whose economy was on the verge of collapse?

As he bathed and retired to his comfortable bed, he had a premonition that this crash in stocks at Wall Street, New York, might be an ominous sign that the world was plunging headlong into a terrible pit. The working men of Australia might be faced with starvation and despair; could he, Jimmy Summers, prevent this?

John West often said in the years following 1929, that it had cost him £25,000 to put the Summers Government in office. Of course, Labor would have won had he never been born, but like all men smitten with the lust for power, he attributed to his influence events that would have occurred in the normal course.

For several days after the elections John West could not work; for several nights he could not sleep. He had reached the zenith of his power. The exultation that took possession of him was like an opium smoker's dream: it was at the same time vivid and confused.

He saw himself as the most powerful man in Australia. The jumbled pattern of his power flashed before his mind's eye, but its vagueness troubled him. Why was he disturbed? After a few days he realised why. He was troubled because he did not quite know what to do with his power now that he had achieved it! He had in mind the plan for a prohibitive tariff on imported spirits that would make him a million. He could protect and extend his empire, but what else?

He had not previously cared much what policy a politician or government pursued, so long as his wishes were obeyed in matters affecting his interests. Perhaps he should this time form definite ideas on policy, then he could use his power to the full. At least, he determined finally, he must see to it that the Summers Government pursued a policy that would end the depression. Business was bad; profits must be restored to their former level in all enterprises. Here Ted Thurgood would again come in handy. This idea consoled him.

One day he met Archbishop Malone and discussed the matter. He found Malone concerned about ending the depression quickly, but worried that the general unrest and the miners' strike in New South Wales might lead to revolution. He was struck when the Archbishop stated that it was just as well Labor lacked power in the Senate, because the Conservative Senate would act as a brake on the Cabinet if extremists like Ashton forced even partial implementation of the Labor Party's socialisation objective. Malone had certainly become conservative in recent years, John West reasoned; but he was right: there must be no interference with the sanctity of private property.

A few days later Ted Thurgood came to Melbourne to see John West. He was full of his fiduciary issue to save the country. John West gathered that the plan proposed to revive trade by the issue of up to sixty million pounds in new currency through the Commonwealth Bank. So forcefully did Thurgood state his ideas that John West became fully convinced of their validity, but for the time being he was more interested in his own plan for making a million out of the pending Tariff Bill which was to be introduced by Summers before Christmas.

John West rang Cory, who came promptly. After John West had introduced him to Thurgood, they got down to details.

"As you know," John West said to Thurgood, "my plan to develop the Australian spirit industry in line with Labor policy, is to be made law. I mentioned it to Summers before the elections, and he was agreeable. He said he intended developing all Australian industries in this way."

As John West continued talking to Thurgood across the polished table, Patrick Cory sat under the photo of Barney Robinson. He had taken off his spectacles and was massaging the bridge of his nose meditatively with forefinger and thumb. His face was thin and angular, a fold of lean flesh ran straight from his nose to his jaw on either side and his thin lips curved upwards to meet it at its centre. Cory remained silent during an interview, only intervening with a few well-chosen words at the appropriate moment. Now, polishing his glasses with a handkerchief, he gave a false impression that he was hardly listening.

Importations of Scotch whisky were restricting the Australian industry, John West explained to Thurgood. If the tariff were increased steeply, the imported product would become prohibitive in price. "An immediate increase in production and employment will result. But I have a further suggestion."

"Haw! Haw! Haw!" Thurgood laughed, and Cory ceased his polishing and eyed him disapprovingly.

"Excuse my cynicism, gentlemen, please," Thurgood said, "but Canberra is alive with lobbyists asking for protection. If it's not wine and spirits, it's razor blades or silk stockings, or God knows what. 'Tariff Touts' we call 'em. They nearly all get what they want."

"The attitude towards lobbying in this country is stupid," John West interrupted. "I've just been reading an article in the LITERARY DIGEST about lobbying in America. Over there they have registered lobbyists who interview politicians officially. Lobbyists put the views of business men and others to the politicians. That's how it should be."

"Yes, I suppose there's something in that, too. But you see, Mr. West, Summers and some of the others have a pathetic faith in this Tariff Bill. I believe that only a fiduciary issue can save the country ..."

Cory replaced his glasses and adjusted them to his satisfaction. "Mr. Thurgood," he said quietly, "our plan is bigger now than it was when Mr. West last mentioned it. Don't you think it would be a fine thing for Australian industry if a clause were inserted in the Tariff Bill compelling the Scotch company to mix a percentage of our – I mean the Australian – product with theirs?"

"I daresay it would," Thurgood said, somewhat puzzled; "but I'm afraid I can't see ..."

"Well, then, supposing another clause were included in the Bill, increasing the length of time that spirits had to mature before sale to – say – ten years?"

"No reason why not, but I still can't see . . ."

"Well, we have ample supplies of matured spirits. The Scotch people have opened a distillery in South Australia, but have only just begun production . . ."

"Haw! Haw! Haw! What a scheme! Now I can see why you and Mr. West work so well together. Easily arranged, I should think, though the Customs Minister and his assistant may need some – er – inducement."

"That can be arranged," John West said. "What about Summers?"

"Oh, you just keep away from Summers. Jimmy doesn't do business that way," Thurgood said jovially. "What about Ted Thurgood? That's more to the point. Haw! Haw! Haw!"

"If you stand by me, you'll end up a millionaire," John West said in emphatic prophecy.

"Will I tell Mr. Thurgood about the plan for amalgamation, Mr. West?" Cory said with a gravity that was so emphasised as to sound mocking.

"I don't see why not."

"Well, Mr. Thurgood."

"Ted's the name. Everybody calls me Ted. Red Ted. Haw! Haw!"

"Well, Ted, when the Bill has gone through the House, I will approach the Scotch people with a proposition that we form a joint company to control the production and importation of spirits in this country within the terms of the law. I think they may accept, even though we intend asking for a parcel of shares in their overseas company as part of the deal."

"They'd have no alternative but to accept," Thurgood said in astonishment. "This scheme is worth a million!"

"At least a million," John West said. "At least a million in the long run, and I won't forget those who help me to implement it."

Cory departed and John West asked Thurgood about the situation in Queensland State politics. Thurgood's prophecy had been vindicated: the MacCorkell Government had been defeated at the polls and the Nationalists were in power again after fourteen years.

482

Thurgood told John West that he did not think the Nationalists would act yet to inquire into the Chirraboo mining deals. Jenner had ceased his clamouring, apparently loth to give the Nationalists ammunition to shoot at the Summers Ministry, and the Queensland Government was strangely silent on the matter.

"Perhaps they have forgotten all about it, or maybe they will wait until I bring down my Fiduciary Bill. Then they will appoint a Royal Commission to inquire into Chirraboo. They have nothing on me, Mr. West, but they may try to discredit me at the crucial moment. If they do, I will need your influence to prevent a political assassination."

"I gave you my word that I would protect you, and I am a man of my word," John West reassured him without seriously believing that he would be called on to honour his promise.

A few days later John West met Frank Ashton in the street, and congratulated him on Labor's victory. Ashton looked fitter than when they had last met at the Royal Commission into the Maloney affair, but to John West's surprise, he responded without enthusiasm.

"Yes, Labor has had a victory, yet thousands of people are without work. We must do something for them quickly. The situation calls for extreme measures and we cannot get extreme measures through the Senate. I am returning to Canberra tomorrow to campaign for a double dissolution and an immediate election. That way, we will win power in both Houses and be able to implement our policy."

"But surely you can solve the problem without an election," said John West.

"We must force an immediate election, Mr. West. There is no other way out. Prosperity is not just around the corner as the papers say, and as Summers and some of the others believe. This depression will get worse as the months go by, unless we get control of the Senate."

"What about Thurgood's fiduciary plan?"

"No financial reform short of the nationalisation of banking will be of any use."

"Nationalisation of banking! But that's socialisation!"

"That's right, Mr. West. Apparently you, like a lot of Labor politicians, have forgotten that socialisation is the first plank of Labor's platform."

With that he was gone, before John West could tell him that the mining company in which he had shares was about to declare its first dividend.

Next day, Ned Horan, leader of the Victorian Labor Party, Bob Scott and Tom Trumbleward called to see John West and Frank Lammence. Labor had forced an election in the Victorian Parliament and they were confident of success.

"I'll tell you for why," Ned Horan said. "I'll tell you for why, Mr. West. The people are dissatisfied because of the bad times, and the Nationalists here will 'folley' the Nationalists at Canberra and the Labor Party in Queensland into the political wilderness."

John West instructed Frank Lammence to make available the usual cars and money for the campaign and to study the pre-selection candidates in the various electorates.

Before the end of the year, the Tariff Bill was law, incorporating all the clauses requested by John West, and Ned Horan was again Premier of Victoria. Before the end of the year, also, there were more than 300,000 unemployed men in Australia and even the Christmas period failed to stimulate business.

And so 1930, the most terrible year in Australia's history, dawned with such a promise of poverty and ruin that even into the mind of multi-millionaire John West crept a vague dread of the future.

CHAPTER ELEVEN

The Australian Labor Party is a liberal capitalist party and
the so-called Liberals in Australia are really Conservatives.

V. I. LENIN

In January, John West announced that the Prime Minister was to
pay a visit. Nellie and Mrs. Moran would have set about preparing a sumptuous feast, but he insisted that all he required was a
simple tray of afternoon tea on the following Sunday for
Summers and the Archbishop, who would also be present.

Archbishop Malone arrived first and Nellie ushered him into
the reception room where John West waited.

When they were alone, the Archbishop said to John West: "As
I mentioned previously, Mr. West, it is essential that Summers
should resist the extremists in the Party and refuse to force
another election. The anti-Labor Senate will ensure that Ashton
and Thurgood don't run wild with socialisation schemes and
encourage the workers to revolt."

"Oh, I don't think you need worry about Thurgood, Your
Grace. His bark is worse than his bite."

"Musha, you might be right, Mr. West. After all, didn't he run
from one end of the country to the other during the election campaign saying like a parrot that if Labor were returned he would
open the mines within a fortnight; and the strike or lockout or
whatever it is, still goes on. I tell you, Mr. West, this country faces
great trouble, perhaps revolt, unless sanity prevails at Canberra."

"I agree, Your Grace. Business is stagnant and – "

John West was interrupted by the entry of the Prime Minister.
Summers' face was pasty and pale, and his hair, grey a few
months ago, was now snowy white. He was ill at ease, embarrassed as though anticipating instructions that he might resent yet
feel impelled to comply with. He seemed overawed by the
presence of the Archbishop like a child beside a department store
Santa Claus. Conversation was stilted while Nellie and the maid
served afternoon tea.

When the table had been cleared, all three sensed the tension. Summers most of all: he knew that his invitation was not of a social nature. West wanted something – he'd done all right out of the Tariff Bill and would get no more – or, more likely, His Grace had something in mind. But why bring West into it? West was a strange friend for the Archbishop to cultivate, though there was no denying that he was most generous to the Church.

"Mr. Summers, what is the situation at Canberra?" Malone demanded. "Is there any substance at all in the rumours of a double dissolution?"

"The question of an election is being actively canvassed in caucus, mainly by Frank Ashton."

"And, pray, what is your attitude?"

"I am undecided, Your Grace. I think we can solve the nation's problems in spite of the Nationalist Senate. I have faith in the tariff wall and in financial reform. But I must admit financial reform would be easier if we had the Senate."

"I think the tariff wall will work," John West intervened. "Take the spirit industry, for instance. Negotiations between the local distilleries and the Scotch interest have been made possible by the increased duty. That will lead to increased employment."

"For a few hundred men, Mr. West, but God knows there are tens of thousands already workless and their numbers increase daily."

"But," John West persisted, "if the same thing happens in other industries, it will go a long way towards solving the unemployment problem."

"That is what I hope, Mr. West," Summers said wearily. "I go on my knees every night and pray that it will."

"Meantime," the Archbishop said sceptically, "the situation steadily worsens. The miners and police have clashed again. There are symptoms of unrest everywhere. You will need strength and Christian sanity, Mr. Summers. May God and His Holy Mother help you. Can you end the trouble at the mines? That seems to be the most dangerous point."

"It is a terrible business, Your Grace. The workers have been foolish – waging strikes against the crisis. First the wharfies, then the timberworkers. They were utterly smashed before we came to office. The miners have been out for nearly a year. Thurgood has seen the mine owners, but they will not give way. The Constitution does not permit us to take action against them or the strikers. All we can do is force the dispute into the Arbitration Court, and we hope to achieve that soon. The miners are hungry and despairing. Their leaders are extremists, and there are Communists on the coal-fields encouraging them. They are trying to turn the men against my Government. But they will fail. I am hopeful that the dispute will soon end, and that prosperity will be restored."

Summers spoke without conviction, like a man confronted with a problem too vast for his powers, who hoped against hope that it would solve itself.

"What financial reforms do you envisage?" Malone asked sharply. His hands were folded on his lap, his long face expressionless.

Summers sighed wearily. "There are many plans. Ashton and others want to nationalise the banks. Thurgood has a plan for a fiduciary issue to stimulate production. I'm opposed to Ashton's plan, but if the tariff wall fails I will support Thurgood. But then we would need the Senate. As well, the Bank Board has suggested that Thurgood and I invite Sir Otto Niemeyer to come from England to suggest economies. But there would be uproar in the Party and the Trade Unions if we did. Niemeyer would be sure to suggests pension and wage cuts."

"Perhaps economy is the only way out of this terrible depression," Malone replied, "And if Niemeyer came here, no one need know that *you* invited him."

John West was out of his depth, and he felt drowsy after his late night at the Stadium.

"But Ashton is moving now for an election. Will he succeed?" Malone asked.

"It's hard to say. I think the matter will be decided when the caucus meets next week. I have remained neutral."

"If Ashton succeeds in forcing an election it will mean that his influence would be strong enough to force socialisation measures like the nationalisation of banking. Would that be true, Mr. Summers?"

"Partly, Your Grace."

"I do not wish to speak officially. It is not the place of the Church to interfere in politics; but the Church is opposed to all forms of Socialism, because Socialism is against the Christian concepts of the inviolability of private property. If Ashton triumphs, socialisation will follow, and the workers will turn their backs on humility and prayer, and place their reliance on material things."

John West was pleased to note that Malone seemed to have lost all vestiges of the radical outlook of the days of anti-conscription and the Irish Rebellion.

Suddenly, Malone drew a pamphlet from his pocket. It was obviously old, for the paper had faded to a dirty yellow. He handled it gingerly as if it were sacred.

"At a time like this we Catholics should refresh ourselves on the views of the Holy See on these matters. Some of us have forgotten (I must admit that I forgot during the stormy years of the war) that His Holiness Pope Leo XIII issued this Encyclical. It is called Rerum Novarum and states the Church's attitude towards Socialism, poverty and private property. It is, God knows, a holy and wise statement."

He began to read in singsong voice, like a priest reading a gospel text, selecting passages that he had apparently marked beforehand. His voice droned on, penetrating John West's consciousness in vague snatches, while Summers listened with fervent attention.

... It is impossible to reduce society to one dead level. Socialists may in that intent do their utmost, but all striving against Nature is in vain ...

... The consequences of sin are bitter and hard to bear, and they must accompany men as long as life lasts. To suffer and endure, therefore, is the lot of humanity ...

... Nothing is more useful than to look upon the world as it really is – and at the same time to look elsewhere for the solace to its troubles ...

... It is ordained by Nature that these two classes should dwell in harmony and agreement ... Each needs the other. Capital cannot do without Labor, nor Labor without Capital. Religion teaches the laborer and artisan to carry out honestly and fairly all equitable agreements freely entered into, never to injure the property nor to outrage the person of an employer; never to resort to violence in defending their own causes, nor to engage in riot and disorder ...

488

From time to time Malone raised his head towards heaven as though calling the testimony of the Almighty to back the arguments in the pamphlet.

... and to have nothing to do with men of evil principles who work upon the people with artful promises of great results and invite foolish hopes which usually end in useless regrets and grievous loss ...

"The most significant point in the pamphlet," Malone concluded, "especially now, is this one. *The first and most fundamental principle, if one would undertake to alleviate the conditions of the masses, must be the inviolability of private property.* We should bear in mind that this Encyclical was written in 1891 during a terrible depression, and it has equal application to today's conditions. The Australian Hierarchy is most concerned about the present situation in Europe. We must never forget that the most Godless manifestation of Socialism – Communism – controls Russia, and is gathering great strength throughout Europe – and here in Australia. We have news that the Holy Father will prepare another Encyclical on this subject. Ashton may not be a Communist, but he is an atheistic Socialist and his policy plays right into Communist hands."

"Ashton is only asking for nationalisation of banking," Summers replied. "Perhaps he realises that the Constitution will not permit any more, if that."

"The Constitution must not be violated," Malone replied. "I do not wish to interfere, but I really believe – and here I have the support of the other Archbishops and the Apostolic Delegate – that the double dissolution should be resisted by all Catholics at Canberra."

"I can see you're right, Your Grace," Summers said humbly. The extracts from the pamphlet seemed to have had a profound effect upon him. "I have lost my perspective a little. I, too, once forgot our Holy Father's Encyclical. In fact, it was I who moved the socialisation resolution in 1922. Since then I have changed my outlook, but the adoption of the socialisation objective had one good effect, Your Grace."

"And what effect was that, pray tell me?"

"It cut the ground from under the Communists' feet. They

489

were growing powerful then: because of the revolution in Russia, the workers were turning a little socialistic. My resolution helped keep the Australian workers behind us.''

"And don't you think that was a dangerous way to retain support?'' Malone said with a smile. "But I must agree that your good name among all sections of the workers will stand you in good stead now in your hour of stress.''

"I believe I have the support of the vast majority of them,'' Summers replied proudly.

"I believe I can defeat Ashton. While I am leader we will have sanity and not Socialism. Thurgood is not Socialist, though many seem to think he is, because of the radical way he talks. He opposed the resolution in 1922, you know. I think I can persuade him to oppose Ashton. And Lyons, as you know, Your Grace, is a Catholic and a man of conscience and stability. He'll oppose Ashton, too.''

Malone and Summers continued to discuss the situation at Canberra. John West looked from one to the other. This conversation was a little beyond him, and he was aware of a prickling of resentment that Malone and not he should be speaking thus to the Prime Minister.

Presently, Malone looked at his watch. "Goodness me, gentlemen, it approaches five o'clock. I really must go, Mr. West. Do not trouble to call the good lady, I can find my way out.''

Turning to Summers, he said: "May God bless you in your great task, Mr. Summers. I shall offer up prayers and masses for you. Good-bye.''

"I must leave, too, Mr. West,'' Summers said, "I am expected for dinner. Good-bye and thank you.''

Frank Ashton faced the caucus meeting during the following week with a puzzled frown. A few days before he would have wagered that his advice would be taken, but now doubts had entered his mind.

He would know soon, he told himself as he stood sipping a whisky and water in the Parliament House bar waiting for the Labor members to assemble.

In October, the news of Labor's victory had been bittersweet to Frank Ashton. It sent no exultant spark through his aching body. Politically and physically he had gone to seed. He had, like most people, been lulled by the apparent permanence of the period of prosperity.

Two years ago, a terrible paralysis had crept over his body, leaving him bedridden for months, and still it affected him, sending excruciating pains to every joint and limb. He had difficulty in dressing himself, and could barely hobble about. He had cured the worst effects of the disease in an extraordinary manner. A specialist had told him that if he were to go to the Islands and be bitten by the malarial mosquito, he might get well. The opportunity to go to the Islands came unexpectedly. John West had called to see him, ostensibly to inquire after his health. When told what the specialist had said, West answered quietly: "I will give you some shares in one of my big mining companies, and you can go and inspect the mines at the company's expense when you're well enough."

Frank Ashton accepted the offer. He was desperately in debt.

As he made to depart, John West had inquired: "Will you be resigning the deputy leadership owing to your health?"

So that's what West was after. Ashton had intended to resign anyway. He had not been in Canberra for months. His health would not permit him to carry on. He was not selling out. This was not a dishonest thing; so bad was his health that he had contemplated getting out of politics altogether. But if he had not been so terribly ill these two years, and if West had not come that day, he might have been Prime Minister of Australia now!

Frank Ashton did not like the situation much. The Labor Party was only a nominal Government; it had power only in the House of Representatives. The Conservative Senate would baulk all progressive measures. Unemployment had grown alarmingly during the year; already charitable institutions were distributing meagre relief. Summers naively expected to solve the problem by raising tariffs to encourage local industry, and by stopping immigration of Southern Europeans.

And Thurgood, with his fiduciary plan. Thurgood, a fellow director in the mining company, Ashton thought bitterly. Thurgood with his reputation as a "grafter". Thurgood, John West's right-hand man, who had fought the socialisation plank bitterly in 1922, and had since brought the Queensland Labor Party into disrepute. Frank Ashton had approached Thurgood in Sydney before the elections and asked if he would support the national-isation of banking. Thurgood had parried the question.

Then there was Lyons, the little man from Tasmania, no more a Labor man than most of the Opposition, with his small-town ideas and his ambitious wife hovering in the background seeking fame and power for her Joe. And the Lane group from New South Wales, likely at any moment to create fatal disunity. Then the old Victorian anti-conscription, and mainly Catholic, group around Summers. Who would constitute a left-wing group? Frank Ashton alone? Frank Ashton, half-paralysed still, and a director of a gold-mining company exploiting slave labor. He had seen the black men working in the mines with his own eyes, and com-plained to West about their conditions. "They are better off than they were," West had said.

Had he struggled for over thirty years in the Labor Movement to end like this?

He had grown "respectable" these recent years. His period as deputy leader of the Party for six years from 1922 had been a period of boom, and he had done nothing to prepare the workers for the coming crisis. He knew there was no hope of Socialism, but he felt it imperative to remove the big-business control of the Commonwealth Bank. Only power in the Senate would make this possible. An election was essential.

His first dividend from the gold mine had come to hand. For the first time in ten years he could face his creditors, but he couldn't face his conscience. The only thing that could restore his self-respect was to fight now to force the Party to go to the people for a mandate to implement its financial policy.

What a paradox was this Labor Party! It claimed to support Socialism, yet most of its members were not Socialists. Its first plank was the socialisation of production, distribution and exchange; the Constitution would not permit socialisation, yet the party was not prepared to rewrite the Constitution. Perhaps the Communists were right. Perhaps the Labor Party was, in effect, merely a disguised representative of the big business. Yet it could ease the burden of poverty from the workers if only he could win the fight today. He must win it!

Martha was hopeless. In her desperate hatred, her jealousy of Harriet, and her all-absorbing desire for security, she had become unbalanced in mind. Poor Martha, how hard he had tried to

492

convince her that he was a representative of the workers and should not be rich, but should devote his life to helping them. How empty his arguments sounded now! A fine representative of the workers he was!

Martha was more satisfied since he had received the shares from West. Well, let her have them. He had given up Harriet in order to remain true to his responsibilities. The boys were being well educated, her debts were now paid, he was faithful to her. She should be content, but she wasn't. She was forever complaining. She imagined she was ill, and when the doctor said otherwise, she said he was mad and would let her die. She had taken to telling everyone she met lately that she was sick of her husband being a politician, too many cadgers at the door, too many begging letters. Her husband was a director of a big mining company now, and she hoped he would get out of politics. He tried to prevail upon her to cease this kind of talk. What would his electors say if she went on like this? He didn't want his holdings in the mines made public. She had said: "Huh. If you are ashamed of them, why did you take them? You are not the only one who can hurt. I can hurt! I can hurt!"

Was Martha mad? He gently suggested she should consult a nerve specialist. "You mean one of those psychologists," she had screamed. "You beast. You are trying to get rid of me so you can go to that woman! You are trying to put me in a lunatic asylum!"

Since then he had been more than gentle with her, but she refused to be pacified. He might be imagining it, but he sensed she was trying to poison the boys' minds against him.

At times he was tortured with the thought that his affair with Harriet had played so much on Martha's mind that largely as a result of it, she had been reduced to her present state. Yet, could he help his love for Harriet? Was it not the only beautiful and worthy thing in his life? But again, sometimes, he was oppressed by the thought that he should have left Martha long ago and gone to Harriet. Would not that have been better for all concerned?

Harriet was wonderful in her unselfish love. When he told her their relationship must cease, or at least become merely an intellectual, platonic friendship, a tear had flowed down her smooth cheek, but she had soon pulled herself together with affected flippancy.

493

The matter had never been mentioned between them since, and that was four years ago now. They met often at Labor Party meetings, and at each election she was active on his campaign committee. Strangely, their affection for each other had grown more intense – in some ways more satisfying – as if it thrived, he liked to believe, because it was no longer sullied by physical passion, of which he was becoming incapable.

During his illness, she had not seen him, but several letters awaited him when he returned to Parliament House. He wrote and arranged a luncheon appointment in Melbourne. She was standing at the door of their favourite Chinese cafe; still, at 45, looking petite and attractive. When she saw him hobbling along on his walking stick, she ran to him and exclaimed: "Oh, Frank, you have been very ill. Let me help you. You look haggard. You're not being looked after properly."

"I'm all right," he said, "Martha does her best and I have a nurse occasionally. After all, I have got arthritis and I'm getting old. White hair now." He took off his hat. "I'll have you know, dear lady, that I'm fifty-seven years of age."

Since then he had seen her only at meetings and during his campaign in October, yet he knew that she would carry out her vow never to marry, never to love anyone but him. She lived with her parents and worked in an office. Her spare time was devoted to Labor Party work in his electorate, and to charitable work on hospital committees and the like. Her presence and her devotion lurked in his mind always, and he felt certain that she knew this.

Since his return from New Guinea his health had steadily improved. The only evidence that remained of his illness was his enlarged joints, which ached when the weather changed. He could walk quite well and his mind retained its alertness and penetration.

But now he realised that his private affairs must be pushed into the background. He had a fight on his hands and he was in the mood for fight for the first time in years.

The bar began to fill with pressmen and politicians. He moved from group to group, dropping a word here and there, testing the feelings of the Labor members. Many of them avoided the issue, hastening to change the subject and buy a drink. Men who had pledged their support only a few days before were now non-committal. Something had gone wrong! He saw Ted Thurgood come to the door, then turn on his heel quickly.

When the meeting assembled he asked for the floor. The room was tense as if enemies were gathered there instead of comrades in the Labor Movement.

He called on his brilliant oratory in an endeavour to save the day. At times he thought he had swung the majority.

"As we gather here, nearly 400,000 Australian working men are walking the streets looking for employment. Daily the plight of the worker worsens. Those in work are having their wages slashed. Poverty and despair stalk the land. They have put us in office to save them from this plight. Are we going to betray them?"

Thus he began, and for half an hour he continued, rising to heights of impassioned oratory. Some of his listeners were attentive, others shifted uncomfortably in their chairs.

Their position was unsound, he told them. The tariff wall was not enough. It had taken only a few weeks for that myth to be exploded.

"Our objective is socialisation; we are ashamed of it. Our real policy is to nationalise the banks, to smash the money power of big business and to create credit to lift the country out of this terrible depression. The hostile Senate will protect big business by throwing out our most important legislation. Smash their grip on the Senate! Let us go to the people and demand a mandate in both houses. Assuredly we will get it. The great victory in the Victorian elections last month shows clearly that the workers are still right behind us.

"Politics is warefare!" he shouted. "In warfare, the initiative must be gained and held. We have the initiative, now let us smash the enemy's crumbling defences. We can win the Senate now. Later we may not be able to, because we will meantime be ineffective and the people may turn against us."

So he persuaded and argued as a man who believed that calamity would result from his failure to convince.

"The destiny of the great Australian Labor Movement, and the welfare of the workers, depend on your decision today," he concluded. "Comrades, I appeal to every man here to forget his own personal interests and to think only of the working men and women of this country. In their despair and poverty their eyes

495

turn towards us, watching for confirmation that we will not let them down. In this room are the ghosts of our pioneers of the Labor Movement. Men in overalls and dungarees accompanied by their haggard women lurk in the corners watching us. Our hour of destiny has struck. Don't let us fail!''

He sat down amid a heavy silence. No one clapped, no one spoke, no one coughed, no one even smoked.

Ashton brushed his locks of grey hair away from his forehead and sat erect, his lower lip and chin thrust forward aggressively, his hands on his lap, waiting.

At last the Chairman found words.

"The matter is open for discussion."

Speaker after speaker skirted the question, made excuses, but ended by obliquely opposing the forcing of an election. One new member said that he had spent his last shilling on his campaign and could not possibly afford another one so soon. Someone else said that by remaining in office Labor could at least half the wage-slashing that was going on.

Frank Ashton found anger and contempt rising in him. Summers, Thurgood and other leading lights in the Cabinet are silent. They have pushed the lesser lights forward, but they are behind this.

Suddenly he found himself blaming the Catholics. All the Catholics are against me. No doubt, Malone or one of the other Archbishops had been at Summers. Jimmy's first loyalty lay with the Church; Ashton had known that since the early days. Once he had asked Summers: "If you had to choose between loyalty to the Party or the Church, which would you choose?"

"I hope I never have to make that choice," Summers had answered. Well, you've made it now, Jim, Ashton thought. You have betrayed the Party!

But Frank Ashton knew that this betrayal was not attributable to Catholic opposition to socialisation alone. The betrayal arose, he found himself admitting, from the weakness, corruption and lack of united policy of the Labor Party. These men were not Socialists; they were merely politicians, many of them basking in the sunshine of Government office for the first time, who looked upon politics as a career. They were determined not to risk going to an election until the laws of the country forced them to do so.

A wave of cynical contempt swept over Ashton and his face reflected it, so that each speaker avoided his gaze, until one new member said: "It is all very well for Ashton to talk about another election. He has a safe seat. I won a blue ribbon seat from the Nationalists by a few votes. For years I have been the Labor candidate in a seat that everyone thought we could never win. I will go out at the next election, and I don't think it's fair that I should be forced to give up my seat as soon as I have won it. In every political landslide seats are won that cannot be held, and this is no exception. Others will lose their seats. Since the elections things have got worse; the people will blame us for that. Let us stay in office. Even with the Senate against us, we can achieve a good deal. If we go before the people now, we may be voted out of power, then what would happen to the workers with the Nationalists in office?"

What would happen to the workers with the Nationalists in office? The words re-echoed in Ashton's mind. What will happen to them now that they have pinned their faith in these unworthy men? These men had just come from an election in which they had slated the Nationalists, the bankers and big business, and the workers had swept them into office. They had ridden to power on the backs of the workers, and now they would betray them, sell them out. And they would get away with it where the Nationalists could not.

Curtin supported him, speaking ably. Young Curtin was worth all of them put together if he would lay off the booze!

The Trade Union leaders were just as bad. "Better a bad Labor government than any Nationalist government," they said. They would bask in the reflected glory of the politicians and depend on them to prevent further wage cuts and so keep the workers quiet.

Momentarily, Ashton's contempt turned inwards on himself. At least he knew better!

The ballot was to be taken at last. Get it over. A man would be lucky to get four or five supporters.

"The noes have it. Thirty-eight to three!"

One of his supporters was a Lane man from New South Wales. He was in strange company. Ashton vaguely distrusted Lane. Lane was ambitious. Lane wanted control of the Federal Party, and might be prepared to create a split to get it.

As soon as the vote was announced, Ashton leapt to his feet.

"Traitors!" he shouted. "Traitors! One day the workers will realise that they have been betrayed!" He walked quickly to the door and slammed it behind him.

In the lobbies he met a member of the Opposition, who said: "Heard the news? A miner has been shot dead by the police at Rothbury. Wouldn't there be a stink if we were in office and that happened!"

He sought out Thurgood.

"Don't blame Summers for this. Blame the Nationalist Government of New South Wales."

That was all Thurgood said.

One afternoon in mid-winter, 1930, the Honourable Edward Thurgood, Treasurer of the Commonwealth of Australia, received a phone call at his Sydney flat. A newspaper man rang and asked if he had any statement to make on the fact that the Royal Commission to "Inquire into certain matters relating to the Mulgara, Chirraboo Mines, etc.," had found him and the others guilty of "fraud and dishonesty."

Mr. Thurgood *would* like to make a statement: "This is a dastardly piece of partisanship by the enemies of Labor to assassinate me politically. I am innocent of these infamous charges. I refused to appear before the Nationalist Royal Commission, because I knew it was biased against me. But now I demand a trial by jury to clear my name."

Thurgood obtained an evening paper.

FEDERAL TREASURER GUILTY OF FRAUD the headline screamed. He read the article. He, MacCorkell, Rand and Garrardi had all been branded guilty!

Since the Royal Commission had been quietly appointed some weeks ago, he had lived in dread of its findings. That the result was expected did not lessen its impact. Ted Thurgood was greatly shaken, but he would fight back. He had powerful friends.

All day long the telephone rang. He told variations of the same story to reporters and friends. His face was a stern mask, his wide jaws were set, but occasionally he laughed without mirth, pooh-pooing the charges.

The Prime Minister rang: "This is a terrible thing to happen at a time like this, just when I'm going overseas. Do you still say there is no substance in the accusations?''

"Substance? Haw! Haw! Haw! That's lovely. It's coming to something when my own leader falls for the Nationalist propaganda.''

Thurgood made his explanation. Summers seemed unconvinced. "Oh, well, the caucus will have to meet on this immediately. You may have to resign your portfolio until your name is cleared.''

His eldest son rang from Melbourne and readily accepted his father's explanation. His wife remained silent. He had long since lost all interest in her. She had become very fat and ungainly. She listened to his phone conversations and interviews with sly amusement. He avoided her gaze. Now he knew why they were still together only nominally, why he resented and sometimes hated her; she alone knew him; she could see right through him; she was laughing at his heroics!

At the evening meal she said: "Well, Ted, just as well you have big business interests. This is the end of your political career.''

"Don't be stupid! This is a plot to destroy me because they are afraid of me. Big business is trying to get rid of me.''

"Why should they get rid of one of their own number? You're a pretty big business man yourself these days, Ted. There's nothing wrong with that, but why delude yourself?''

"That's lovely. Even a man's own wife falls victim to Nationalist propaganda.''

"I haven't fallen victim to propaganda, Ted. This is a dangerous situation, and you know it! You are trying to bluff it out, but you're worried, all right. But I'll stand by you whatever happens, you can rest assured of that.''

He walked around to her side. "Thanks," he said. "This may go bad with me, I know. But I'll fight them. I'll fight to the bitter end!''

"I know you will, Ted." She placed a fleshy arm around his waist as he stood with his head beside hers.

"I'd have been Prime Minister before the end of the year," he said. "The job is too big for Summers. I'd have deputised while he was away. I had him beaten if this hadn't happened. I always said I'd be Prime Minister one day.''

"I know, Ted. What a fool you've been! You know, when I first knew you at Chirraboo, I couldn't understand how you could lead every fight on behalf of the miners and gougers and, at the same time, run the two-up school and take their money from them. Since then I have watched the two-up king and the underdogs' leader fight it out within you. The two-up king has won, Ted."

She felt him wince. He went back to the other end of the table, and they finished the meal in silence.

As Mrs. Thurgood finished clearing the table, the front door bell rang, and she heard her husband say: "Oh, it's you, Bill. Come in."

Thurgood returned, accompanied by Big Bill MacCorkell, who had come post haste from Brisbane by plane.

No one would have believed that this big, round-faced man had been known throughout his career as a jovial fellow; Big Bill MacCorkell, bluff, hearty, everybody's friend; for here was a badly frightened man with his mask off, a thief caught in the act. He sat down nursing his hat, haggard after a sleepless night.

Mrs. Thurgood took his hat with a quiet greeting and left the room, closing the door. He hardly noticed her. "I s'pose you've heard the news, Ted. What are we going to do?"

Thurgood forced a loud laugh. "Don't tell me Big Bill has got the wind up. This is an attempt to assassinate me politically. We'll treat it as such."

"Never mind about politics. What about me and Rand and Garrardi? We're in it too, you know. I'm leaving the country as soon as I can."

"Where are you going?"

"Somewhere! Anywhere! I've got money. Might even go to Russia."

"Haw! Haw! Haw! You don't think the Bolshies will welcome the man who tried to break the rail strike, do you? Better go to England, you'll be safer there!"

There was a pause. MacCorkell sat with hunched shoulders staring at the floor, his bulbous eyes dilated behind his thick glasses. He had no fight left in him, but Thurgood had.

"It didn't matter how well we smothered things up, Bill; we were convicted in advance by the Nationalists. But we'll beat them in the Courts, you see."

"I wish I thought so. Could I have a drink?"

Thurgood poured two whiskies sprinkled with a little soda. MacCorkell gulped his down. Thurgood paced the floor, sipping his with a meditative air.

"It might be better if you go away. I'm going to Brisbane as soon as possible to see the Premier. He might listen to reason. While I'm there I'll try to silence a few people."

MacCorkell wrung his hands. "We might be charged with murder! God! Why did we bother about those mines at all?"

"What do you mean, murder? Listen, Mac, I didn't tell them at Cairns to throw that bloke off the balcony! I just told them to shut him up. Remember, we know nothing about that business! For Chrissake, pull yourself together, man! This is merely a political charge. By the way, I thought you said Jenner was loth to testify because he believed the Commission would be used politically?'

"He said that before the Commission, but I saw him yesterday and he said he had been subpoenaed. Said we should have thought of this being used against Labor before we did it."

Thurgood snarled. "Jenner is trying to get his revenge on me for driving him out of the Party for being a Commo. He's against Labor just like the Nationalists are." He lowered his voice as though speaking to himself. "If you want more fight, Doctor Jenner, you will get it! And don't be so sure that I won't win again!"

Thurgood sat down, elbows on knees, holding his half-filled glass in his fists. MacCorkell poured himself another drink with trembling hands. He drank it and poured another before resuming his seat.

For nearly ten minutes they sat in a silence so deep that to MacCorkell the gentle ticking of the ornate mantel clock sounded like the chimes of some great bell.

He sat staring at Thurgood. Thurgood, who had been his idol in the old days, and his leader and corrupter in latter years. Even now, in serious trouble, when he could see that Thurgood thought only of himself, MacCorkell could not help admiring this relentless man opposite, and pondering on the tremendous potential for good that had been in him. Thurgood, sitting in front of his book shelves, where lay worn working class books, even Marx and Engels, not read for many years; newer books of poetry and plays, including Shakespeare, little read; brand new classical novels, never opened. Thurgood, the strange mixture of good and evil, the genius who could not go straight.

Suddenly, Thurgood said dramatically: "You want to run away, Bill! All right, run. But Red Ted will stay behind to fight ... To take arms against a sea of troubles ..."

"Quoting poetry won't help," MacCorkell interrupted. "I'm going overseas. And you've got to help Rand and Garrardi."

"Let Rand and Garrardi and Duncan look after themselves; but for their bungling this would never have happened. I'm the important man. Not that I care for myself, but I have a duty to the workers. I have a plan to end the depression. The Nationalists are doing this to prevent me from implementing my fiduciary issue scheme, but they'll fail – Red Ted Thurgood won't be bluffed."

MacCorkell poured himself another drink. "I haven't got accommodation," he said. "Can I stay the night here?"

"You're welcome to, but if you're seen, you may not get away. Go and book in at a pub under an assumed name, then leave the country at your first opportunity."

"That's a good idea. Get my hat, Ted. I'll be going."

When Thurgood returned with MacCorkell's hat, Big Bill put it on and grasped the hand of his life-long friend.

"Good luck, Ted. Good luck, ol' timer. We've come a long way to end up like this."

MacCorkell's voice was broken; he was on the verge of tears.

"Haw! Haw! Haw! Don't take it too hard, Bill. Yer can come back when the coast is clear. They haven't beaten me yet. Not by a long chalk. I'm going to Melbourne to see Jack West. He made a fortune when we jumped the claim off his company. He's promised to help me. He won't let me down."

He slapped MacCorkell on the back heartily. "How are yer off for money?"

"Not too bad, Ted. I've got all the ready I could lay me hands on."

"Just a minute!"

Thurgood went to the bedroom adjoining and returned with a roll of ten pound notes enclosed by a rubber band. "Here, take this! I won it at the races on Saturday. It's all yours, Bill, for old times' sake. Should old acquaintance be forgot ..."

502

"Thanks, Ted. You always were a good mate. Hope you don't mind me running out on you like this."

"Don't be silly, Bill. I feel like running away myself, but I've got the workers to think of. I can't let 'em down . . ."

"No, that's right, Ted. Good luck, Ted. Good luck to yer, mate." A maudlin tear trickled from under MacCorkell's glasses. He walked towards the front door.

Next day at Canberra Thurgood faced a hostile caucus. Next afternoon he faced the hushed Parliament. The press and public galleries were crowded to capacity. Thurgood rose to speak. His resonant, well-modulated voice trembled with real and feigned emotion as he asked the Speaker's permission to make a statement.

"All the charges laid against me are damnably false. The evidence at the Royal Commission was tainted. I have not been treated with ordinary British fair play. Not only in my own name but in the name of this honourable House, I say that if I am guilty of a tittle of these charges, I am not worthy to be a member of this Parliament. If I am not guilty, I am entitled to clear my name of every tarnish that these charges can attach to it. I have resigned my portfolio. My Party has given me two months to clear my name. Given the opportunity, I shall clear my name of this political charge."

There was no clapping, no booing, no interjection, only silence. Everyone was puzzled, undecided. Even some of the Nationalist members who had co-operated with the Queensland Government to use Thurgood's past as a weapon to destroy this vacillating Government, wondered if this man was indeed innocent.

The following day Thurgood went to Brisbane and saw the Premier. Thurgood was told that if he did the bidding of Sir Otto Niemeyer, who was coming here soon, the Government would not proceed against him, except perhaps in a civil action to recover some of the money involved.

Ted Thurgood's thick lips were spread in a disdainful smile of relief as he left the Premier's office.

Two men sat by the stove in the little kitchen. One, in the wooden chair on the left, a white haired, round shouldered little man caressing his white walrus moustache with a restless hand, was

Arthur West. The other man was Richard Bradley. He wore a dressing gown over shabby dark trousers and a woollen jacket. His slippered feet were stockingless. He was reading a book. During his years in hiding Bradley had become fatter, pasty faced and flabby. His face was heavily jowled. His grey beard hid the scars on his neck, but nothing could hide those cold expressionless eyes.

The kitchen was spotlessly clean, homely and tidy. The mantelshelf and table were draped with patterned oil cloth, the tall dresser with white lace curtains. The prints on the wall included one of Ned Kelly, another of the film star, Ramon Novarro. Outside the wind leapt out of the darkness, howling around the weatherboard cottage, accentuating the warm comfort of the room. A pair of woollen socks hung on the opened stove door.

As always when Arthur called – which was three or four evenings a week – the two men sat for a long time in silence. They did not feel the need for conversation. Whatever judgement the world placed on these men, a deep friendship that needed no embellishment of words existed between them. Theirs was a strange fellowship, its emblem weals on the back.

Arthur West shoved a piece of wood into the fire. "What're yer readin'?" he asked.

"Just a book about the early history of the Maoris. Very inter-*esti*n'. Early history is very inter*esti*n'."

"Never read a book in me life," Arthur West replied. "Don't seem to be able to concentrate on 'em."

"Didn't read meself 'til I went into hiding. Started for somethin' to do. Like history books."

Bradley read avidly, almost exclusively books of early Australian and New Zealand history, aboriginal folklore, and a little early European history. It was as though he wished to steep himself in the world that existed before his time, before he had been flogged.

"Where's Pat to-night?" Arthur West asked.

"Gone to the pictures."

"What? That's risky, Dick! You're takin' risks lately, and I keep tellin' yer, they're really after yer now. Been following me and ol' Ron and Paddy. Gone to the pictures! Jees!"

"Ar, the kid gets lonely. She's growin' up, yer know. Seven-

504

teen now, and as pretty as a picture. Gets restless sometimes, and lonely. Got a crush on that Novarro bloke up there; cut his picture out of the paper. She's been good, Arty, real good. Think she was me daughter, not me niece.''

"You've gotta shift from here, Dick," Arthur West said urgently, his eyes darting and staring wildly. "I got a place. Nice little place." He leant over and placed his hand on Bradley's shoulder. "They'll get yer, Dick, the way you're goin' on!" Bradley returned to his book without replying, and they fell silent again for a while.

"How're yer off for money?"

"Gettin' low."

"What did you do with the fiver I brought last Friday?"

"Gave it to Pat to get some clothes."

"Money's gettin' tight, Dick. A lot of the boys have stopped kickin' in. Only for ol' Ron and young Col. Lassiter and Jack we'd be battlin'. Just as well the coppers and stool pigeons don't know where you are now, or we wouldn't have enough to buy 'em off."

"Next time they find me, they'll come and get me. From what I see in the papers there's a bit of an outcry against corruption in the Police Force. If they catch me, it'll be a good smother for their rackets, the bastards."

As he mentioned the police, Bradley's voice reverted to its old harsh tones. "The bloody police are crook, especially the detectives. If things was dinkum half the bloody dicks at Russell Street'd be in jail!"

"You're takin' things too easy, Dick. You orta shift again. Been here too long."

"I'm sick of running away. No more shifts for me. If they get me, they get me. Read a book about Ned Kelly. He got sick of running away. Sick of being hunted. That's why he fought it out at Glenrowan."

Bradley began reading again. A long silence followed, measured by the old-fashioned clock on the mantelpiece, until suddenly a heavy hand knocked on the front door. The sound was a clear, slow five knocks. The two men sat upright, and Arthur West drew a revolver from his pocket.

"I'll go," Bradley said, putting his book on the table. "Don't get excited, it was the code knock."

505

"How do you know the bloody copper won't discover the code? Where's your gun?"

"In the bedroom."

"Jees!"

Bradley walked out into the dark passageway. He had a decided limp; a result of the gun battle in the Trades Hall. Arthur West heard him switch on the light in his bedroom, then came the sound of a revolver being cocked. Arthur West stood, revolver pointed towards the passage door, listening intensely. At last, he heard Bradley open the door.

"Hullo Dick, me boy," a distinctly Irish voice said. "Put that toy away and let a man in be the fire. That wind'd freeze the cods orf a brass monkey."

Arthur West relaxed, put his revolver in his pocket, and resumed his seat.

Presently, Bradley returned, followed by a red-faced, bandy-legged individual named Paddy Ryan. Paddy had a rich Irish voice and humour. In his youth, as a leading pony jockey, he had brought home many winners for John West. It had been said of Paddy that he rode even more skilfully when not trying than when trying, and that he couldn't lie straight in bed, but he was well liked for his brazeness and good spirits. Becoming too heavy for riding, he disappeared for some years, only to turn up again penniless to approach John West for help. For old times' sake, he was granted ten pounds a week to run messages and carry bags for his master, and feed and train one of his racehorses. It was said that Paddy fed himself (mainly out of a bottle) much better than the horse, which had not won a race in twelve months under his care.

Paddy pulled up a chair and sat in front of the fire between the other two.

"Well, gents," he said, "I brought a little of the necessary, with the compliments of ol' J.W."

"How much?" Arthur West asked.

"Twenty quid."

"Jees, twenty quid. Think he was peelin' 'em off his arse?"

"Business is bad, yet know," Paddy defended. "J.W.'s losing dough hand over fist."

"Must be down to his last three million," Bradley said, chuckling mirthlessly.

Ryan handed an enevelope to Bradley, who placed it carelessly on the mantelpiece and resumed his reading. Arthur West stared moodily at the stove.

"Why don't yet carry your gun in your pocket?" Arthur West asked Bradley. "If they came, you wouldn't have a chance."

"If you've got a gun in your pocket you're on edge all the time; if you have a gun under your pillow, you wake at the slightest sound, so I leave the guns in the dressing-table drawer. I'll get 'em soon enough to kill a few of the bastards, if they come."

After a while, Paddy said: "What about a cuppa tea?"

"The kettle's boilin', and you know where the other things are. Make it yourself!" Arthur West snapped. He resented Ryan's occasional visits to interrupt his evenings with Bradley, and the fact that the Irishman was trying to supplant him as John West's lackey.

Paddy Ryan made some tea, and they had a light supper. While he talked without pause, they remained silent. Soon afterwards, Arthur West and Ryan departed, leaving Bradley to clear the table, wash the dishes, and begin again to read by the fire.

Half an hour later, Bradley sat upright, alert as a lyre bird. The wind had dropped. He could hear the sound of soft voices in front of the house. He crept slowly to the bedroom, got a revolver, and went to the window. Raising the curtain he saw a girl and a young man standing kissing on the verandah. The girl was Pat, his niece. A sharp twinge of emotion caused him to shudder. Pat was a young woman now, and her natural desire to mix with other young people had become a danger to his freedom. Arty was right!

He went back to the kitchen, but did not take up his book again. He sat deep in thought. Pat was a menace, but Pat was a good kid. With Pat, first in Carringbush and later here, Dick Bradley had found feelings in himself that he had never known before. If Pat stayed they might catch him through her. She liked to get out of doors lately; even went to the city a couple of times. She brought a girl she had befriended to the house one night without his permission. He had enjoyed talking to them, but after the girl left he remonstrated with Pat and she cried and said: "Forgive me, Uncle Dick, I knew I shouldn't have done it, but I get terrible lonely sometimes."

He almost shed a tear for the first time in his life. Poor Pat. This was no life for her. For her sake, as well as his own, he should send her back to her mother; but he felt he could not face the years ahead without her. He was old now, getting on for seventy, and had lost the hard strength that had made him the sinister lone wolf of the Melbourne underworld. He needed Arty and, most of all, he knew he needed Pat.

He got up again and went to the front door. Speaking through it, he said: "You'd better come inside now, Pat. It's very late."

"All right, Uncle Dick, open the door."

He opened it and the girl entered. He followed her into the kitchen, and sat again by the stove.

The girl was dark-haired and pretty in an unsophisticated way. She took off her coat, revealing a pretty floral dress around a robust figure. She watched her uncle as he sat slumped, gazing at the stove.

"You're angry with me, Uncle Dick, aren't you?"

"No, Pat," he said softly. "I'm not angry with you. I'm angry with myself for keeping you here. This is no life for you, Pat."

For months after Pat had agreed to look after her uncle, provided her mother was cared for by the gang, she had been afraid of this silent, brooding man, but as time passed he seemed to become more kind. Slowly she had learned to love him. Their attachment had grown stronger in this friendly house, and, though she didn't realise, she had come to give him all the love she would have given her father who had died when she was a baby.

"You mustn't talk like that, Uncle Dick."

She went to him and placed her arm around his shoulder, and whispered sobbingly: "I love you. I don't care what you have done or what they say about you, I'll stay with you and look after you."

He reached up and patted her hand. "You're a good girl, Pat, a good girl." Then he pulled himself together and wiped alien tears from his eyes with the back of his hand. "Off to bed now, lass, it's nearly midnight."

She hesitated at the door. "Uncle Dick. I know I shouldn't have brought Jim home to the gate. I – I won't do it again. He's really very nice. I met him with Mary, a few weeks ago. But I won't let him come right home any more."

508

"We'll see, lass, we'll see. We'll have a talk about it in the morning."

She smiled, much relieved, and came back and kissed his brow.

"Good night, lass. I'll go for my walk now."

"Good night, Uncle Dick."

Soon she was in bed and all was silent except for the howl of the wind which had grown fierce again.

Bradley sat brooding for a while, then bestirred himself and put on the pair of socks that had been airing on the open stove door. Going to the bedroom he donned his shoes, overcoat and hat, and put a revolver into his pocket. Listening at the door opposite his room he heard the even breathing of his sleeping niece, then let himself out quietly.

At the front gate he paused, peering either way into the murky night. Outside the gate the wind swept against him, almost blowing off his hat. He ventured out of doors only late at night before going to bed. He looked forward to these walks now, having lost his fear of being recognised. But tonight his mind was troubled. He found himself thinking of Pat and her boyfriend; not worrying about the danger to himself in the friendship, but worrying like a father about Pat's welfare. Should he talk to her explaining the facts of life? Poor kid had been isolated from life; she was innocent and emotional, and young fellows today knew more than their prayers.

He felt inclined to laugh at himself. The killer, the toughest man in the Australian underworld, hard-bitten Dick Bradley, the 'staunch' man who had been through the 'mincer' torture at Russell Street three times without 'squealing,' indulging in loving concern for a slip of a girl! He, who had two illegitimate children and hadn't seen or thought of them or their mothers since they were babies!

All through his unusually long walk he went on brooding. That she should seek a boy friend was natural. That lads should be interested in her was natural. By the time he got back to the house he had determined to talk to Pat in the morning. The prospect worried him; never before had he faced such a delicate task.

Back in the kitchen he took off his overcoat, hat and shoes, put another log on the stove and planned what he would say. He sat thus for an hour until the clock showed two o'clock. He began to nod and fell asleep.

He slept for an hour. He was awakened by a loud bashing on the front door. He leapt to his feet, wide awake instantly like a soldier in a battle area. They had come for him at last! After eight years they had found him! In a moment, Bradley the kindly old man disappeared, and he became again Bradley the hunted animal, who would fight desperately when cornered.

With amazing agility he leapt across the room and switched off the light. He crept quickly into the passage. Already they had broken in the door and were in front of him, silhouetted against the faint glow of the night. If he had a gun he could kill every one of them!

Pat screamed from the bedroom: "Uncle Dick. Oh, God, they have come!"

They were proceeding cautiously. They knew that Dick Bradley, a desperate man and a deadly shot, was lurking somewhere in the darkness. They now stood between him and the bedroom door, intimidated by this unseen presence, afraid to show a light.

He must get into the bedroom!

"Back! Back, you dirty, copper bastards, or I'll blow your bloody brains out."

As he spoke he shifted across the passage quickly and soundlessly in his stockinged feet. A shot rang out, then three more. They had fired at the sound of his voice and missed him. Involuntarily they moved back a little.

Becoming accustomed to the darkness and having the advantage of their being silhouetted against the open door, he crept to the bedroom door and brushed past one of them.

Suddenly a trembling voice said: "There he is. He's unarmed. Get him!"

Someone flashed a torch and three burly detectives overpowered Bradley. His niece came from her room.

"Leave him alone. He's a good man. He's my Uncle Dick and I love him!"

Bradley struggled violently, finding demoniacal strength. He dragged himself clear only to run out to the kitchen into the arms of three more detectives who had smashed in the back door. Seeing his position was hopeless, he slowly raised his hands and they placed hand-cuffs on his wrists.

"Well, we've got you at last, Bradley," said the giant of a

man in charge of the ten detectives, smugly. "It's been a long search."

He omitted to mention that the police had been able to capture Bradley only with the aid of a paid informer. The secret information had cost them five hundred pounds.

"If I'd had my gun, I'd have killed the lot of you," Bradley snarled.

He looked as if in disbelief at his manacled wrists. His face had become hard and frighteningly evil again. The girl came into the room trembling with cold and fear. She went to Bradley, placed her arms around his waist and sobbed pitifully, but he ignored her.

"The kid's mother lives at 31 Cooper Street, Carringbush. Take her there," he said curtly.

A detective led her gently to the kitchen door, where she turned her anguished face. "Good-bye, Uncle Dick."

"Good-bye, girl," Bradley said, and she turned from his gaze with an expression of fear and wonder in her reddened eyes.

It had all taken only a minute or two, but during that time Richard Bradley had reverted to type. He began to think of his reputation in the underworld and regret that he had not had a revolver in his pocket and shot it out with the hated police, killing a few of them or being killed himself.

As they led him up the passage he thought of his shabby clothes. Dick Bradley had always been well turned out. There might be a crowd at Russell Street; there would be visitors at the watch-house, and lawyers.

"I can't go like this. Can I change my clothes?"

"Nothing doing, Bradley. None of your tricks. We've got a nice suit all picked out for you."

They surrounded him in the garden and escorted him to one of the waiting cars. A crowd had gathered, mainly people in their pyjamas with coats or dressing gowns thrown on hastily. There was a buzz of excitement and speculation among them. This quiet old man who lived with his niece arrested at the point of the gun in the early hours of the morning! Who was he? Could he be Richard Bradley?

Bradley was charged with the murder of the bank manager for which Martin had already been hanged. Arthur West went berserk when he heard the news.

The press blazoned the story for a week or two with fantastic accounts of the man-hunt. The public was told that detectives had twice found Bradley's bed still warm when they raided two of his former hideouts; and that in recent months, two detectives, one of them disguised as a woman, had frequented underworld haunts until finally they discovered Bradley's whereabouts. The public believed the stories and temporarily forgot the scandals surrounding the Victorian Police Force, but the underworld was sceptical; they suspected an informer.

Richard Bradley was soon tried. He was defended by the best criminal lawyer in the land, whose fees were paid by several friends of the accused, mostly by John West. He was sentenced to death, but this was commuted to life imprisonment.

Richard Bradley was soon forgotten by all but his bewildered niece, Pat, and Arthur West.

One afternoon in the Spring of 1930 John West sat in his office reading the first bound book he had ever purchased. It possessed a quaint title: "The Culture of the Abdomen." It claimed to illustrate how perfect health and long life could be achieved by scientific attention to diet. John West occasionally allowed himself the luxury of reading it in slack moments at the office.

Presently he was interrupted by a gentle knock on the door. The tall, gaunt figure of Frank Lammence entered.

"Miss West would like to see you, Mr. West."

Time hadn't altered Lammence much, although he was slightly stooped and his hair was turning grey. He had worked for John West for nearly 25 years, yet John West scarcely knew him. Lammence was married and had a family, but John West had never seen his wife and children; Lammence sometimes gambled on galloping and trotting, but he never discussed whether he won or lost; Lammence had business interests outside the West empire, but he mentioned them to no one. So reserved and impassive was Lammence's nature that his employer did not even think of suggesting that the term "Mr. West" could be dropped.

"Send her in."

Mary looked as beautiful as ever in a smart grey costume, but her hair was swept severely into a bun at the back, and her expression had become less vivacious, more sombre.

"This letter came in the mail this morning. It seems to be from John. Gran said to bring it in, as it may be important."

512

"Take a seat," he said pleasantly, intending to begin a conversation more friendly than the rare and cold ones they had had in the past two years.

She sat down and waited while he read the letter.

Mary West had built up a wall of reserve against her father. She gave him no opportunity either to recriminate with her or to become friendly. She attended to her religious duties without interest, kept reasonable hours, and behaved as she believed he expected her to. She was determined that he would never hurt her again.

She studied his face as he read the letter – a face crowned now with close-cropped white hair, and permanently fixed in a scowl. What secrets lay in that long aggressive head, between those two large ears? Was her father as evil as the rumours and legends about him indicated? Had there ever been a time when he had been kind and capable of love? Sometimes she sensed that there had been, and that, at times, perhaps at this very moment, he tried to soften towards her and the world. Suddenly she saw his lips draw into a snarl.

He threw the letter down, drummed the table with his fingers, then picked it up again.

"Is there anything wrong?" she asked.

"No," he said. "You'd better go, I'm busy."

When she had gone he read the letter again.

Dear Sir,

I wish to inform you that the manner in which you obtained control of the business for which I am now responsible has been brought to my notice by one of your victims.

As I do not wish to continue in the invidious position of perpetuating the theft of a valuable business, I request that I be relieved of my duties as soon as possible.

Yours in disgust,

John West, Junior.

The letter infuriated John West. I'll give him relief, the ungrateful young hound!

Young John had given way and taken over the management of a big catering business in Sydney recently acquired by his father. John had begun his task with an obvious lack of enthusiasm which annoyed his father. What a priceless pair of sons he had raised! Joe just didn't care about anything; his laughing, irresponsible nature made it impossible to do anything with him. Just like his useless Uncle Joe. But John had ability. He had been given a chance that many young fellows would have given their right hand for, but he was pig-headedly refusing to take it. Well, stubborn as he was, he would be made to toe the line! Bad enough, him asking to be allowed to resign every time a man saw him, but this impudent letter was the last straw! So they were 'victims' were they? Like hell!

John West was quite proud of this particular business deal. The two brothers who had conducted the business had become bankrupt when the depression began, and he had taken over their liabilities and given them jobs. Not his fault that they couldn't make the show pay! Not his fault they hadn't had the intelligence to extricate the company from insolvency by a clever political move as he had done!

John West's pride in the finesse he had used made his son's sympathy for the former owners all the more unpalatable. The brothers, who had worked for twenty years to build up the biggest catering business in the Southern Hemisphere, had approached him six months before, and he had agreed to take the business over. Shortly afterwards, by a stroke of luck, a moratorium was being put through the New South Wales Parliament by the new Labor Premier, Lane. The Bill was allegedly designed to protect small householders from the banks and the building societies, by postponing payments on houses and farms.

The catering company had two city buildings on which deposits had been paid, but it could not meet the payments from money earned. The buildings could not be sold profitably, because buildings all over the city were half empty and values had fallen steeply.

John West had some influence in Labor circles in Sydney. He approached Lane through an intermediary, and for £5,000 the Premier carried an amendment late in an all-night session of Parliament, widening the Bill to include larger buildings. John West was no longer required to meet the interest and instalments on the buildings, and with his son's efficient management the company began to pay. That was a stroke of business genius if ever there was one, yet his own son called it theft!

He rang for the typist and dictated a letter in reply.

Dear Sir,

In reply to yours of yesterday.

You have obviously been misinformed. Your resignation is not accepted.

I will come to Sydney tomorrow to discuss your insolent letter.

John West, Senior.

When the typist went out, he fell to bitter reflection. It seemed that his whole family was determined to defy him. They all seemed to have found means of keeping their distance from him. Nellie evaded clashing with him, and led a tolerable life. Sometimes, he watched her at the table – she was having her revenge on him; she was once again mistress of her household. The children and their friends admired her wit and imitations of high society. Again, sometimes, he would listen to her talking to the child in her bedroom next to his dressing-room. He could not distinguish the words, but could sense joy and friendliness and love – never sorrow, never fear. Mrs. Moran, full of old age but very much alive, unobrusively contrived to hold the household together against him. If he crashed through the defence lines of the family she would parry the thrust and seal off the gap.

He sat for some minutes in a tension of rage. They would see. He had forced Nellie to shoulder her responsibilities, he had cut Marjorie off with a shilling, he had made Mary mend her ways, now the others would see who was boss! John would be made to toe the mark, anyway. The bloody cheek of him!

Never before had his power been so great, but of late he felt frustrated. The depression was deepening. His accountants estimated that he had lost nearly half a million pounds; and his losses would have been more than doubled but for the success of the scheme which the Tariff Bill had made possible. Business was bad and it was getting steadily worse! Many of the small traders whom he had financed were seeking further help without much prospect of ever repaying. He had begun to refuse some of them. Requests for assistance along Jackson Street and elsewhere were more numerous than ever before. Try as he could to convince himself that all cases were undeserving, he could not blind himself to the deadly poverty that had smitten the land.

From Canberra came a strong rumour that the English banker, Sir Otto Niemeyer, was coming to Australia to enforce economy, especially drastic cuts in Government expenditure on salaries and social services. The sooner he came the better, if he could restore prosperity! Now that Ted Thurgood was out there seemed little hope that the Summers Government would do anything decisive.

The Mulgara scandal did not diminish John West's admiration for Thurgood. On the contrary his admiration was increased by the Treasurer's courage in face of the onslaught. Thurgood had asked him for help in the event of his being brought to trial, and he would get help.

Conscious that his lack of political direction was weakening his power in the Parliaments, John West had determined to study politics. His studies consisted in reading mainly Catholic Truth Society pamphlets and discussing politics and social questions with Archbishop Malone and leading Catholic laymen. His researches led him to become a keen admirer of Mussolini and the Corporate State in Italy. He had taken to saying occasionally: "What Australia needs is a benevolent dictator, and Thurgood is the man for the job," but that hope was now dead.

The bankers and the heavy-industry monopolists had greater power over Summers than he had, even though their party occupied the opposition benches; even more powerful still, as far as he could see, were the English bond-holders. *They* were not losing money, but not all the combined efforts of Frank Lammence, Pat Cory, Dick Lamb and all his managers and accountants could do anything to stop *him* from losing. The crowds attending race meetings and boxing matches had fallen by nearly half. His political influence availed him little. His control of the Victorian Parliament through Ned Horan, 'Artful-Alfie' Davison, Tom Trumbleward and others, and his undisputed say in some suburban councils, had only the negative value of protecting his empire – he could not use them to extend it.

But they would find out yet that Jack West held the big stick and would use it! He would save Thurgood and have him reinstated in the Cabinet – make him Prime Minister.

On leaving her father's office, Mary walked to Collins Street, then up the hill towards her favourite coffee lounge. She was wondering what had been the import of John's letter to annoy her father so obviously, when she became aware of a loud, untuneful singing. She was amazed to see a grreat column of marching people – four abreast – approaching along the intersecting street. Like a huge, headless dragon it straggled back as far as the eye could see in the direction of the Trades Hall. A few of the marchers carried red flags or banners, and all the time the mournful defiant singing. She could read two of the banners: –

Down with the bag system.
Work not charity.

She watched, vaguely excited. As the demonstration reached Collins Street and turned up the hill, two policemen on the corner hesitated, uncertain what to do.

Just then two opulent women came from an exclusive shop and stared aghast at the spectacle.

"Loafers," one of them said to the other. "Loafers being led by the nose by the Communists."

Mary was surprised that she wanted to answer them. She could think of no suitable rejoinder. Instead she moved to the edge of the footpath and stared transfixed in a mixture of fear, excitement and pity. Suddenly, two tattered figures appeared beside her – a man and a woman.

"This is the demonstration they announced at the unemployed meetin' I was tellin' yer about, Liz," the man said. "A bloke oughta be in it."

"Oh, I dunno, Ted. They'll be in trouble again. The police attacked them last time. They'd be better to look for work."

"Look for work? How long have I been lookin'? See that banner. They're out to end the bag system. You're against it, ain't yer? Margarine insteada butter, bulk tea, a candle, cheapest brands of everythin'. Six bobs' worth a week. What do they take a man for?"

Just then an enthusiastic marcher called out: "Be in it, mate," and the man dragged the woman after him. "Come on, Liz. We gotta march with 'em."

They ran out and fell in, extending a row to six until the marchers reshuffled to welcome them. The woman walked listlessly as though she were tired, hungry and a little ashamed. The man marched animatedly and tried to join in the singing, but clearly he did not know the song. Mary noticed that only about half the marchers were singing, and that some of them appeared timid and uncomfortable, as though marching was a new experience. Here and there a mouth-organ tried to assist the singers.

Suddenly the song ended. All was quiet save for the scraping of feet out of step; then the men in front began a new song, which was gradually taken up, until Mary could hear it travel back along the seemingly endless columns of people.

She could not follow the words, except the oft-repeated line: *Solidarity forever!* More of the marchers seemed to know this song, and the singing became louder, more menacing.

Here was proof of the atmosphere of tension; the strange, intangible feeling of uneasiness that she had sensed all about her in recent months. So this was the reply of the poor to the indignities heaped upon them.

Unemployment had meant little more than reports in the press to Mary West, until one night, some months before, she had witnessed a scene that filled her with pity and revulsion. With a group of friends she had left an expensive cafe and walked through an arcade on the way to the theatre. Passing a lane at the rear, she saw a dozen or so silent ragged men outside the door to the cafe kitchen waiting around the scrap bins – waiting, she thought, like Lazarus for the crumbs from the rich man's table. Reluctant to believe the evidence of her own eyes that men had been reduced to this animal state, she took a few steps down the lane. As she did so, the kitchen door opened and a man wearing a white coat came out and emptied a tin of scraps into one of the two big bins on either side of the door. He pretended not to notice the assembled scavengers. In the light of the door she saw in the tin scrapings from the plates of diners: lettuce leaves, fruit peels, part-eaten pieces of meat, and the like churned into a disgusting mess; and then the men surrounded the bin rummaging for it, jostling each other. Hypnotised by the horror of the scene, she moved closer.

A man at the rear, waiting for a chance to obtain some scraps, turned towards her. She could discern that he wore a long overcoat with all the buttons gone, and a shabby hat pulled low over his eyebrows. From under the hat, two terrifying eyes fixed themselves upon her, and a croaking voice said: "What do you want, lookin' here?"

The eyes stared like those of a strangled man. In those eyes lurked humiliation, despair, desperation, perhaps also insanity, and certainly hatred. He hated her because she wore forty pounds' worth of clothes and a hundred pound fur while he wore rags. He did not know her, but he hated her because she was rich and had just eaten a sumptuous meal, and he was poor and was waiting to rummage in a scrap bin.

She turned and ran from the lane just as her escort came back to see where she had disappeared to.

That night she dreamed of the men around the scrap bin, and in a nightmare saw the man with the terrible eyes in an old dirty house feeding little children with disgusting scraps. And all the time his eyes were staring at her.

Since then she had seen and read more evidence of how countless thousands of people had been thrust into the lower depths. She read reports of eviction; of people living in tents or sleeping in railway carriages in the Flinders Street railway yards; travelling the country on foot or in old vehicles seeking employment; eating meals in a cafe then telling the waiter they had not money – let him put them in jail, or better still, see the Premier, Ned Horn, and ask him to pay. Then there was the report of a man throwing a brick through a shop window and calmly asking a policeman to put him in jail, because while there he would be fed and the State would care for his wife and child. She had taken to walking to town through Carringbush, to torture herself with scenes of squalor and suffering. The queues at the soup kitchens, the hopeless women, the groups of hungry men, the rickety, shivering children. Houses empty while people slept out of doors, shops empty and factories closed while people were idle, food thrown away while people starved!

And all the time the tension, the vague menace in the uneasy atmosphere, and now the poor were marching, singing songs of revolt!

There was a small percentage of women in the march; like their men folk they wore old clothes. This was like a rag-tag army of despair, but it pleased Mary because hitherto she had been inclined to ask: "Why do they suffer so and remain passive?"

She saw that the march had ended at the top of Collins Street and crowds swarmed around the Treasury Buildings; yet still tattered columns came, silent now but for a hum of conversation and the tramp of feet, watched by dumb crowds lining the footpaths. The electric trams had banked up in Collins Street and their bells clanged without avail.

She began to make her way slowly along the crowded footpath towards the Treasury Buildings. Unable to move quickly enough, she stepped on to the side of the road and ran holding her hat daintily, her skirts swirling around shapely legs.

She reached the outskirts of the crowd, which now extended around the grey, two-storied building on three sides, and was spreading over the Treasury Gardens. There were police everywhere, hundreds of them, but they had not yet attacked the demonstration.

She stood on tiptoe and saw four men who had led the procession ascending the wide stone steps amid cheering.

"Where are they going?" she asked anyone.

"To see Trumbleward, the Chief Secretary," a lean man answered. He looked incongruous in incredibly shabby clothes and a new pair of cheap, white sandshoes.

"What for?"

"To ask for work, not charity, and stop the bag system."

"Bag system?"

"Yes, bag system," he said, disdainful of her ignorance. "We want to decide for ourselves what we'll spend our miserable few bob on, not have a bag of cheap groceries thrown at us. Not that seeing Trumbleward will do any good. He turned the police on us last time – only does things for John West and such like. And he calls himself a Labor man!"

Trumbleward. He *was* one of Father's men. He'd come to the house several times. Are all Father's men like Trumbleward?

Suddenly her thoughts were interrupted by a scuffle nearby. An angry murmur went up. Mary pushed her way nearer the trouble area. A huge, unkempt individual was abusing a policeman.

"... not so game terday, you flatfoots. Not using yer batons terday. We'll tear you to pieces if you start anythin' terday!"

He was pushing the policeman. Another constable came up behind him and raised his baton to strike. The people in the vicinity were of two minds. Some tried to move towards the scene, others away from it. Just as the upraised baton was about to crash on the big man's skull, a Police-Sergeant pushed through the crowd and knocked it from the constable's grasp.

"Good God, man," Mary heard him shout. "Do you want us all to be kicked to death?"

A diverting shout went up to greet a man who climbed up on to a high window ledge and addressed the crowd which, now that the marchers had all arrived, seemed to Mary to be at least ten thousand strong. The speaker was too far away for Mary to hear any more than isolated phrases:

"... bag system ..."

"Unity is strength ..."

"... Labor Party has betrayed us ..."

The section of the crowd nearest the man cheered.

A man near Mary said: "Communist! Too bloody extreme for my likin'." and an animated argument on politics ensued which, for a while, threatened to develop into a brawl.

For nearly an hour Mary West waited for the return of the deputation, but it did not reappear. Slowly the crowd dwindled to half its size. Isolated singing of the same two songs; here and there an argument or a desultory fight; but finally quietness. The crowd, it seemed, had not eaten well enough of late to maintain its fervour for long.

Mary walked slowly away. Her feet were aching cruelly. She was tired, but no longer felt like afternoon tea. As she walked towards the tram stop she noticed that she was trembling. The spectacle had thrown her mind and nerves into chaos.

That evening at the dinner table, she found herself telling what she had seen, explaining the injustice of the bag system, speaking up for the unemployed. Her mother expressed sympathy for 'the poor wretches': she had heard that at St. Vincent's Hospital they had given away over a hundred cut lunches daily, but the crowds had become so enormous that they had to stop. But what good could come of making trouble, Nellie West concluded.

John West interrupted Mary's answer. "They have been led on by the Communists. The Reds want revolution. I say: send them all to work! Half of them have been out of work so long that they'll never do another day's work while they can get a free hand-out. Put the Reds in jail, and put the others to work!"

"But, Father, you've said yourself that you are employing five hundred less men than you used to. If other employers are doing the same, how can people get work?"

"Wages are too high for employers to employ labor at a profit; wages must be reduced. Not that I want to see wages cut. But we must restore prosperity or the country will go to rack and ruin. Give them any sort of work. Digging holes and filling them in again."

"But, Father, they were only asking for a little more dole and . . ."

"Increase the dole and no one will want to work. Anyway, I won't have this table turned into a forum for communistic talk from my own daughter. What have you got to complain about? You live on the fat of the land. Don't start trying to help the poor. If you do, they'll take your last shilling from you, and I know what I'm talking about."

"Oh, Father, you are like all rich people. You can't understand why the poor complain," Mary said, emotionally.

Mrs. Moran adroitly turned the conversation to prospects for the forthcoming football season, and John West carried it on, declaring that he had been to a practice game at Carringbush; they had several promising recruits, and were likely to win the premiership.

Mary fell silent, but that night she lay awake for hours pondering the events of the day. Less than a fortnight later, she read in the press that the bag system had been abolished and the dole raised by two shillings per week for a married couple and sixpence for each child. She felt a wave of exultation. She had more or less taken part in the demonstration that had forced the politicians to act.

Events in the first half of 1931 increased John West's frustration.

He was unable to bring off the quick-money business coups for which he had been previously notorious, but by harassing his business executives in all States, managed to prevent financial calamity and keep his depression losses under a million pounds. He even resorted to a habit of ringing up his business executives in the middle of the night if an idea came to him.

At home he became crotchety and inquisitive in family affairs. His victory over John compensated him for the decline in his influence in other fields. The interview in Sydney gave him satisfaction bordering on the sadistic. His son had begun like a lion and finished like a lamb. So he didn't like my business methods, thought the former owners of the company had been cheated, would prefer to be relieved of his responsibilities and allowed to lead his own life! Relieved him of his responsibilities, all right! Sent him to manage those milk-bars in Brisbane. Just the man to make them pay. Kidstaked to him a bit at the finish just to sugar-coat the pill. All for his own good. Like the rest of the family, he'd got things too easily.

While he fought desperately to stem his losses, calls for help still came. He began to see himself as a philanthropist, bled by every Tom, Dick and Harry. Political aspirants, the Church, charities and 'meal-bots' alike found him less free with money. He went so far as to walk about without small change. If accosted in the street, he would say to his companion: "Give this man two shillings, I haven't any change." For a while this stratagem succeeded, but eventually Richard Lamb and others became tired of making J.W. popular with their money, and they would declare on such occasions that they "had no change, either."

The period gave birth to the so-called Premiers' Plan. During the discussions and manoeuvring that led to its adoption in the winter, John West tried hard to follow the events and to influence them.

When the Prime Minister returned from England in January, Archbishop Malone and John West had interviewed him. Summers' conversation revealed that his vanity had been well catered for in England. The King said this, the English bondholders said that, the English Prime Minister said the other. When the Archbishop brought him back to pending events in Australia, he declared that he favoured Niemeyer's proposals and would call the State Premiers together to draw up a common plan of economy to balance the budgets. It would call for sacrifices. There would be trouble in the Party, but there were times when the Nation must come before Class and Party. The Archbishop thoroughly agreed and suggested that men like Ashton should be dropped from the Cabinet to prevent trouble.

John West expressed support for Summers' proposals. But he didn't like the drift of events. The bondholders, the Bank Board behind whom stood the bankers and heavy industry magnates, had the biggest say; the Archbishop had some say, but John West, who had put the Labor Party where it was today, had no say! Suddenly he demanded that Summers reinstate Thurgood, as it was obvious the Queensland Government had no intention of taking action against him on the trumped-up Royal Commission finding. To his surprise, Summers agreed. Summers said he believed in Thurgood's innocence and needed his help in the trying months ahead. People looked on Thurgood as a radical, therefore Thurgood could offset the critics of the Premiers' Plan within the Party.

John West determined to back Thurgood and his fiduciary plan. He would make Thurgood Prime Minister yet!

During the months following, the State Premiers met with Thurgood and Summers several times before the Premiers' Plan was adopted. Meanwhile, John West sensed that Thurgood had become lukewarm about his fiduciary plan. He presented it to Parliament as a Bill, but the Senate defeated it; he presented it unsuccessfully to a Premiers' Conference; he took it to the Bank Board at the eleventh hour before the Premiers' Plan was adopted, but again it met rejection. Thurgood seemed relieved. Why?

Political events were sowing in John West's mind seeds of utter confusion.

The Premiers' Conference went from adjournment to adjournment. The Nationalist Premiers whole-heartedly supported drastic wage cuts, but the Labor Premiers and Summers and Thurgood were evasive. Thurgood and Summers pretended they had no plan, then Thurgood consulted the Bank Board's committee of experts and brought down what was, in essence, Niemeyer's plan. Having promised John West that he would force the fiduciary issue plan through, Thurgood raised the matter. Premier Lane, for New South Wales, supported it, then when Thurgood demurred, he brought out a plan of his own – the Lane plan for repudiation of debts to English bondholders. The unaccepted Lane plan was obviously put forward to foster the illusion that Lane was a friend of the working people – an illusion that persisted for many years because Lane continually denied that he voted for the Niemeyer proposals, which were finally adopted by the State Premiers, when he had actually done so – had in fact endorsed a plan opposite in effect to his own.

When the Premiers' Plan became law, the Labor Party split;

the workers and unemployed were angry. Horan implemented the plan in Victoria with the same legislation as the Nationalist Premiers of other States. Lane made a show of proceeding with his own plan and was eventually removed from office by the Governor of New South Wales.

Thurgood passed the necessary legislation in the Federal Parliament. A few weeks later, he and the other culprits in the Mulgara scandals were sued for the return of the money of which they had defrauded the Queensland Government.

Thurgood was shocked, angry, filled with fear, but determined to fight. As he admitted Bill MacCorkell to his Sydney flat, his expression was stern. Big Bill looked haggard and frankly afraid. He had returned to Australia early in the year believing that danger had passed. He had had a grand trip. He even visited Russia, and since his return had delivered a few lectures which were pro, or anti, Soviet according to the audience. Taken to task about this discrepancy by one of his former associates, Big Bill had replied: "You must consider your listeners, mate."

Thurgood believed he had been betrayed. Had he not done all they had demanded of him? Hadn't they held the Mulgara business over his head for over a year to make him carry out Niemeyer's wishes? Pity he hadn't fought harder for John West and the fiduciary plan. West would never betray a man!

Once, Thurgood had revolted against his position. When he submitted the fiduciary plan to Parliament and Premiers' Conference he was only placating West, but the last time, when he presented it to Gibson, the Bank Board Chairman, the last fragments of his Labor principles were uppermost in him. Gibson, dour and domineering, said: "I thought, Mr. Thurgood, that a man such as yourself, whom I have stated to be the best financial brain in Australian politics, would by now have realised the futility of such a scheme."

Thurgood looked at him for a long moment, laughed mirthlessly, and said: "I must keep up appearances with my followers, you know."

At first his own words had shocked Thurgood, but afterwards he knew that his future lay with the rich; that imperceptibly but surely he had lost all semblance of the reformer.

"I'll teach the bastards to betray Red Ted Thurgood!," Thurgood told MacCorkell when they were seated.

MacCorkell mentioned running away again, but Thurgood dissuaded them.

"I planned to leave the country myself while you were away, Mac. I had begun transferring money to America, but was told by a director of Broken Hill Proprietary that I needn't worry. Needn't worry! You can't trust the bastards unless you're as powerful and rich as they are. And one day I will be, you see. You get no thanks for helping the workers."

All evening MacCorkell drank three whiskies to Thurgood's one, and did most of the listening.

Mrs. Thurgood came in and prepared supper for them.

"Well, Mary," MacCorkell said, with a whisky fringe on his voice. "We came a long way from Chirraboo to end up like this."

"Yes, Bill. I sometimes wonder if we weren't happier then, after all."

As Big Bill preened himself to support these sentiments, Thurgood interrupted. "Better off, my eye. I've been sacrificed for the Labor Movement, and the Labor Movement doesn't care a damn. Harking back to the old days won't help us now. We must fight! I'm going to fly to Melbourne tomorrow to see Jack West. He promised to help, and I'm going to keep him to his word."

Next afternoon, Thurgood saw John West.

John West had learned long ago that assistance to people in trouble, whether they were criminals, business men or politicians, or just people looking for a job, was always a source of future support. People who were grateful to him were in his power. But the high cost of saving Thurgood prompted him to say: "Remember that theory of old Davie Garside's I told you about. Well, this case can be defeated, if you have enough money."

Thurgood interrupted quickly. "I have a little money, but if I spend it all on this case what would I do afterwards? After all, I've made several fortunes for you. You made money out of Chirraboo, and a fortune out of Mt. Isa. And Mt. Isa might be brought up in this case; you never know. And I did protect your interests in Queensland for years and so did MacCorkell. Then there was the Tariff Bill. I think that you . . ."

Suddenly Thurgood noticed John West's face. It had no

expression at all; even the scowl seemed momentarily to have gone. Neither spoke for several seconds.

"Listen!" John West broke the silence, his lips scarcely moving as he spoke. "I am tired of being bled. I have lost nearly a million pounds in the past year, yet everyone expects me to have my hand in my pocket all the time. Don't threaten me about Mt. Isa. I'll fix that part of the case. You have money; more than you ever admit. You'll pay half, or I won't raise a finger to help you. I have to go to Brisbane shortly; I've beaten the Nationalist Government over racing. They tried to close up my courses by legislating against proprietary racing, but I've formed a new non-proprietary body like I did in Victoria. While I'm in Brisbane I'll help you and MacCorkell, but you'll have to put up half the money – this may cost thousands. Personally, I wouldn't care if Garrardi and Rand went to jail for life; if they had been more careful this might never have occurred!"

"MacCorkell has a little money, but it's all invested in safe securities to see him through his old age. He spent his ready money on his trip. I'll pay our half."

A week later the trial began. John West was in Brisbane during its first few days. One of his representatives 'squared' the jury in a manner which even David Garside would have thought more than usually effective. No chances were taken. The jurymen had been carefully challenged. They were allowed home at night. The foreman, a man well known to Ted Thurgood, was approached and given £500 for himself and offered £100 for every other member of the jury who would answer a firm Not Guilty.

The Judge, a fat, jovial whisky-drinking fellow who had married a barmaid under the false impression that she was with child to him and who didn't take life or justice very seriously, proved as co-operative as the jury foreman. He knew Thurgood well. Thurgood had had him appointed to the Bench.

Though Thurgood told John West the Judge would "listen to reason," John West had doubts because he believed Judges rarely took direct bribes, but preferred to administer a partial law impartially. However, he called on the Judge in Brisbane.

He would like to help, the Judge told John West, but the evidence had been overwhelmingly against the accused at the Royal Commission. To direct an acquittal would be very risky.

"They are innocent men. This is a political trial," John West said with conviction. "And if they are acquitted I give you my word that you will be appointed Chief Justice."

'That's very nice of you, Mr. West," the Judge said, but having heard that Thurgood was prepared to buy his acquittal at any price, he wanted some more substantial reward for his services. "But you see, unless the lawyers and the accused can find some way of refuting the mass of evidence against them . . ."

"They have the best lawyers that money can buy." John West's eyes were on him, seeking a clue to his real thoughts as he had done when he span the sovereign to Constable Brogan. Suddenly, he pulled a bulging envelope from his coat pocket. "However, the purpose of my visit was not to discuss the trial, but to make a gesture I have had in mind for many years."

He placed the envelope on the table. "As a citizen I wish to make a private presentation to you of £3,000 in recognition of the public-spirited manner in which you have carried out your duties since your appointment to the bench."

The Judge averted his gaze.

"Good day, Your Honour. And, just another little matter. I don't want Mt. Isa mentioned; or the fact that I had an interest in the Melbourne company that got behind with the rent."

"I understand, Mr. West. Tell Thurgood to have his lawyer call her tomorrow night. This is a difficult case, very difficult."

When John West had gone the Judge poured himself a double Scotch, and then another, before opening the envelope and counting the notes twice with infinite care and caressing fingers.

Doctor Jenner approached the civil action with fewer misgivings than the Royal Commission. Then he had been loth to be an instrument in the hands of big business against the Labor Government; now he didn't care if the Government were smashed. He could see no benefit in keeping Summers in office. Summers had done everything the monopolies and overseas bondholders had asked of him, and he'd got away with it where similar action by the Nationalist would have led to little short of revolution.

But now, as at the Royal Commission, Jenner decided to refer only to the alleged fraud: he felt it would be unfair to mention the rumours he had heard from Cairns and elsewhere.

As the trial progressed, he began to suspect a conspiracy. The Judge seemed just a little too anxious to appear impartial on unimportant matters as biased Judges always do, and he seemed to have pre-knowledge of the defence tactics. The facts that led to a scathing adverse finding a year before were made to appear less incriminating.

The Taxation files of the Mulgara syndicate, vital evidence at the earlier inquiry, had disappeared; one of Dr. Jenner's own reports, of which he had not kept a copy, had also disappeared.

Thurgood and MacCorkell refused to enter the witness box. Under the terms of the action this was optional. In written answers to questions, MacCorkell admitted having shares in the mines. He said he had never denied this.

Thurgood admitted receiving cheques of high denominations from MacCorkell, but refused to disclose what they were for. Rand said he gave shares to Garrardi and MacCorkell 'out of friendship,' but didn't know Thurgood had anything to do with the mines.

Outside the court, Thurgood confronted Jenner, sneering: "Well, Jenner, you've tried to destroy me because I drove you out of the Party. You've lined up with the Nationalists, just as I expected; but you and they will fail."

"A cheek you have," Dr. Jenner replied. "You have done the work of big business these last two years."

Called, Dr. Jenner answered questions and referred to his reports to the Government. He noted ruefully that they were given scant attention. He told of Rand's offer of the fourth share and how Thurgood tried to force him to alter his report, and later sacked him.

As long as he lived, Dr. Jenner would never forget the cross examination to which he was subjected by Thurgood's barrister. Brushing aside Jenner's contention that the leases and subsidies had been fraudulently obtained in the first place, the lawyer proceeded to question the doctor about the value of the mines. Dr. Jenner reiterated that the value of the mines was only a potential when Rand had finished with them, and that the real point at issue was the manner in which the Government had been defrauded by Rand and his partners, and by Garrardi as manager of the Chirraboo Smelters.

"But surely the mines were worth £40,000. According to one of your own reports they contained £300,000's worth of recoverable zinc apart from the value of the metal."

"Yes, but the syndicate jumped the claims in the first place, and had already received £13,000 for which it had nothing to show. The Government would have had to de-water and equip the mines . . ."

"What I want to know," the Judge intervened, "is if you can assist me and assist the jury by telling us what the value of the mines was? If you had recommended the Government to buy the mines, what would you have suggested it should pay for them?"

"I did not recommend that the Government buy them."

Thurgood's advocate came into the breach again. "You recommended confiscation as against purchase?"

"That is so."

"Confiscation! The good old Soviet system! You were a keen advocate of the Soviet system of control of mines."

"It was not known as such. At that time little was known of the Soviet system."

"In 1919 you were preaching the co-operative system or the Soviet system of mining."

"I favoured management by the men themselves."

"Is that the Soviet system?"

"Yes."

"I take it that at that time you had great faith in the growing strength of the Soviet system in Russia?"

"I did, and I still have."

"Are you a member of the Communist Party?"

"No. I am sympathetic with its aims, but I do not see what . . ."

"All right, then. You realised at the time that restoring the Chirraboo Smelters would give the great lead field of North Queensland a chance to properly develop?"

"Yes, that was my opinion then and still is."

"And that the foundation of providing supplies of ore for the Chirraboo Smelters must be the Mulgara mines?"

"Yes, but . . ."

"The witness will confine himself to answering questions," the Judge interrupted.

"And you expected that if the Government had resumed the mines they would have been able to work them at a profit?"

"Yes."

"That is all, Your Honour."

The case lasted a few more days. Finally, a list of 25 questions was presented to the jury. The jury answered all in favour of the defendants. A further debt of £18,000, in the form of costs, was added to the price of the Mulgara mines paid by the taxpayers of Queensland. The smelters were silent, the mines lay like two great water holes, their machinery and equipment rusting in the violent northern weather. So they were destined to remain for nearly a decade until George Rand restored his fortune by stripping their metal fittings to be sent to Japan as scrap iron. Eventually, the mines were to be sold at a considerable loss, by a later Queensland Labor Government to a subsidiary of the mighty Broken Hill Proprietary.

The tall, stooped, white-haired figure of Doctor Jenner was to be seen walking around Brisbane, or riding around his beloved North, but he was a man without a mission. Even his own children, much as they loved and respected him, used to say at the finish: "Dad is a bit queer the way he keeps hating Thurgood and talking so much about Chirraboo, the Eldorado of the North."

John West was not surprised when, before the end of the same year, the Summers Government fell. Months before, it had split into factions. Lyons had left the Party, with a few followers, and formed the "All for Australia League." The Lane group peeled off and formed a corner party in the House of Representatives. This group brought about the final collapse. One day they moved an adjournment of the House to discuss an allegation against Thurgood, who had been reinstated again as Treasurer.

Apparently fearing that the Lane machine in New South Wales would defeat him when the elections came, Thurgood set about ensuring his own re-election in a typical manner. He sent a batch of canvassers into his electorate promising unemployment relief work from the £250,000 Federal Parliament grant to men who would support him at the elections. The mover of the motion in the House produced sworn declarations by men who had been approached.

Government members, by now used to the sniping of the Lane group, did not view the move seriously. "Just another Lane bluff."

A division was called. The Opposition Whip ran frantically

around the corridors marshalling votes. The adjournment was carried by 37 votes to 32.

That night James Summers, who had entered Canberra two years before in triumph, secured from the Governor-General a dissolution and faced an election that he knew must inevitably result in crushing defeat.

John West heard that on the eve of the elections Lyons consulted with business representatives in Murkett's newspaper office. Lyons struck a hard bargain with them. He must be leader of the new United Australia Party. He must receive an honorarium of £5,000. In the event of his death, his wife must receive a substantial pension from the Commonwealth. The terms were agreed to. Lyons joined Hughes as a Labor renegade in the ranks of the Tories, the Conservative Party once more changed its name, and, as the U.A.P., won the elections and became the Government.

At the declaration of the poll, Frank Ashton made a very brief speech. "Amid a landslide against Labor," he said, "I am proud that I won on the second preferences of the Communist candidate."

Leaving the hall, he walked slowly along the street. He was grey-haired and slightly stooped, and his steps were restricted in a shuffling gait.

A young member of the local Labor Party joined him. They had walked a hundred yards in the afternoon sun before Frank Ashton became aware of his presence.

"Well, young fella, we got the plurry hiding we deserved."

"Oh, I wouldn't say we deserved it. The worker is now at the bosses' mercy."

"He's been at the bosses' mercy for the last two years; no one knows that better than I do."

"But . . ."

"There's no buts, Les. Listen, Why are you in the Labor Party?"

"Well, I . . . To get Socialism for the workers."

"To get Socialism for the workers, eh? All right then, let me tell you a little story. When the Labor Party first started, the old pioneers were hounded as subversive agitators by the other two parties, the Liberals and the Conservatives, weren't they?"

"Yes."

"All right. The Conservaties were the reactionaries and the Liberals the progressives; then later the Liberals became the reactionaries and Labor the progressives. Is that right?"

"Yes."

"All right. Now, one of these days, probably even in my time, Labor will become the reactionary party and the Communists the progressive party. That's why I'm going to get out of politics as soon as I can."

His companion was silent, as if unwilling to abandon his remaining faith in the Labor Party.

Ashton continued: "You're clinging to your illusions. Don't do it, lad. I did it too long and wasted my life as a consequence. During our fight against the Premiers' Plan and the ban by the Labor Party of the so-called kindred Communist organisations, I talked of a Federation of Labor Organisations to contain the Unions, the Socialists, the I.W.W., the Communists and the Labor Party; well, that was the last of my illusions. I have no more."

"But the Communists have no support."

"There was a time when Labor had no support."

They chatted on a street corner for a while, then Ashton's young friend said: "I have to cross the road here."

"All right," Ashton said, as they shook hands. "Good luck, and remember what I told you. If you want Socialism, not a seat in Parliament, you're in the wrong party. You'd better join the Communists. Cheerio, I'll get a tram here."

"Oh, I work with them in the Unemployed Movement. I'm going over the street to their club-rooms now. There's an unemployed meeting about to start."

"Is there? I'd like to say a few words and thank them for their second preferences."

"Well, I could arrange it," Ashton's friend answered diffidently. "But many of them are Communists, and the Communists didn't give you their second preferences officially, they left it to the voters."

"Well, I got most of 'em, that's the main thing. I'd like to thank them and give them encouragement. Tell them I've always been with them."

"Well," the other said, still hesitating. "I'll see what I can do."

They crossed the street and entered an old building. The younger man led the way into a big room which contained a table, a few chairs and several wooden stools. The walls were decorated with slogans and photographs, including one of Lenin. At the back was a soup kichen. This was the local headquarters of the Unemployed Workers' Movement, which existed to assist and organise the unemployed and to resist evictions.

About fifty shabby people on stools faced the table at which two men were seated.

One of the men at the table said: "We've been waiting on you to make a start, Les."

"Sorry I'm late."

He went to the table and conferred with the two men who seemed for a moment undecided, then one of them stood up and said: "Well, comrades, Mr. Ashton, the local member, would like to address us before we begin. Would you come up to the front, Mr. Ashton?"

A murmur arose as Frank Ashton walked to the table, placed his hat upon it, and confronted them.

He noticed himself trembling: he was more nervous than he could remember being for years.

"Comrades, I asked permission to speak to you, because I'm on your side. I am proud to have won on the Communist second preferences because I believe that Communism is ..."

As he spoke on, he realised with horror that his audience was not responding, that it was hostile.

"... I say that Labor was defeated because it failed the workers, but what was the use of the workers jumping out of the frying pan into the fire by putting the Nationalists in?"

Suddenly, a big-boned, gaunt man at the rear shouted: "At least we know where we stand with the bloody Nationalists."

Frank Ashton's platform technique deserted him. He felt as confused and helpless as a novice speaker. He looked openmouthed at the interjector.

"But, my friend," he managed to grasp. "I am not, that is, what I mean to infer is, that the workers should have ..."

"What do you care about the workers?" the big man persisted.

Ashton's friend was abashed, sorry he had laid his idol open to this humiliation. The chairman hesitated: he had hoped Ashton would receive a polite hearing. The hostility of the interjector transformed the mute distrust of the audience into anger.

"Yes," another man yelled, leaping to his feet. "You're only an exploiter of cheap, coloured labor."

"Yes, and a mate of John West, the millionaire. Go back to New Guinea," one of the few women present shouted shrilly.

These people were in no mood for compromise. Ashton was a Labor man and Labor had let them down. They hurled unfriendly interjections at him. The chairman stood with upraised hand pleading for silence and a fair go for the speaker, but without avail.

Frank Ashton struck a pathetic figure. "You must listen to me," he said. "I know I have too often compromised, but I have learned my lesson. At heart, I always remained true to my socialist principles. And now, I . . ."

"Tell that to John West!"

"Go back to New Guinea, to look after your mines."

"I only went to New Guinea for the good of my health," he shouted fiercely.

This brought a burst of spontaneous laughter. Then someone began to sing *The Internationale* and nearly all joined in:

Arise, you workers, from your slumbers,
Arise you prisoners of want,
For reason in revolt now thunders . . .

After shouting at them again and again, Frank Ashton stumbled towards the door. His young friend tried to speak above the singing. The chairman picked up Ashton's hat and followed him.

"You forgot your hat," he said lamely. "You mustn't take this too much to heart. Most of these people are not Communist Party members. They've suffered a lot . . ."

Frank Ashton took his hat and ran blindly into the street. If only they could understand, he thought! But it was no use, they were a lot of sheep. You could do nothing for them. This was the end! He had given the best years of his life to an illusion, at least now he would get a little rest!

He walked aimlessly towards home. He had been heckled – he, Frank Ashton, who had fought a lone battle against the treachery of Summers and Thurgood, who had moved for the dissolution to get control of the Senate, who had been dropped from the Cabinet because he was the sole remaining leftist, who had fought against the Premiers' Plan tooth and nail. They had heckled him, but not Summers. Seventy thousand workers had cheered Summers at Footscray during the campaign after he had told them that Labor had failed because it had no power in the Senate. The fools – Summers had never wanted the Senate!

The Bank Board had run the Government on behalf of the big capitalists. The evil hand of Niemeyer jerked the strings that made the traitor puppets dance. Summers, priest-ridden and vain, was easy meat. He knew no better. Thurgood knew better, but his crookedness always got the upper hand. At least, the workers kicked Thurgood out and put the Lane man in.

Lane, the demagogue, had fired the last shot! But what did it matter? You don't have to shoot a rotten corpse! Frank Ashton had sometimes supported Lane. Well, he was only one of thousands who had been deceived. The Lane Plan. The Thurgood Plan. This Plan. That Plan. Any plan that did not involve action by the workers. Action by the workers! That was impossible, anyway. For two years he had watched the workers tolerate every indignity. They had been betrayed, yet they remained passive. Frank Ashton's contempt for the Summers Government had, after turning inwards on himself, turned finally down on the worker.

As he walked he bumped into people. His eyes were blinded with tears. They would bot from you. They would accept your health and life in sacrifice, then dump you. The militant workers had heckled him, abused him. This was the finish!

Arriving home, he went to his study. He could hear Martha talking to one of his sons in the kitchen.

He sat down at the little table and took a pen and paper. He would write to Harriet. The pen charged to and fro.

Dearest Harriet,

Well, we got it in the neck. It had to be so. The Labor way is the right-wing way, so what matters? Between the Labor Party today, and the other side, the only difference is the brand.

And the workers are hopeless. I gave my life for a spineless mob. Educational democracy is a myth, Government by the People is a delusion. As much as ever they worship images of rags and wood and stone. They will perish for a king or a priest as in the days of old, and see their children starve. They are hopeless. They have only the instincts of slaves. In them there is no hope and I am finished.

To continue in public life and accomplish nothing is not a pleasure. It is a torture. The next election will not find me in the field. I am getting out as soon as I can. I will stay just long enough to secure my future. I can only do that by getting away from pleaders for help who would leave me bone-dry, then throw me to the dogs.

If I live long enough I may set down on paper thoughts that I have not dared to utter these recent years. All I want now is rest. I am going to live quiet, so plurry quiet that people may think that I am dead, and they wouldn't care.

I am full of old age and pain. In the evening of my life I am without hope. Martha is no better, and the boys are still luke-warm towards me. The three of them together have less Labor ideas than my foot.

Grief and sorrow is all I have, except "the what might have been with you."

Good-bye, darling Harriet.

To you I can say: "Frank Ashton is ashamed of himself!"

He threw the pen aside, addressed an envelope, stuck down the letter and put it in his pocket to post that night.

He walked to the sofa by the window and slumped on it. Here in this room he had interviewed Percy Lambert and John West. That day had decided his fate. Ashton the fence-sitter had refused them both.

Here, also, he had written "Red Europe." He rose and took a copy of the book from the bookshelf. He sat again on the sofa, flicking slowly through its pages to the end, where he read:

Capitalism listens with quaking soul to the drum beats of revolution. They grow louder and louder, they draw nearer and nearer.

He gazed at the photo of his dead mother on the wall.

What would you think of your boy now?

His mind reverted back to the bare room and the sneering, singing crowd at the unemployed meeting. They had hurled *The Internationale* at him, to show their contempt.

537

His face contorted in anguish and he wept. Suddenly he stood up and flung the book savagely into the corner of the room, and his weeping turned to hysterical laughter.

Martha opened the door to find him standing in the middle of the room laughing as one insane.

She was haggard, wrinkled and bent. She looked at him in amazement and anger.

"What's the matter with you? Started drinking again I suppose."

He ceased his laughing and turned to her. His gaze frightened her and she cowered back.

"No!" he shouted. "I'm getting out of politics. I am going to become a capitalist and it makes me laugh. I am going to be a parasite and make plenty of money. Plenty of money, do you hear? I'm old and sick, and I'm selling out to make plenty of money! It makes me laugh!"

She looked at him uncomprehendingly, then went out, closing the door.

He fell on to the sofa and cried without restraint. His bent figure shuddered and he beat his head with his fists.

Presently, the door opened again and his eldest son looked into the room.

"What on earth's wrong with you?"

Frank Ashton looked up.

"Nothing, son," he said, composing himself. "I'm just an old man with no fight left in him."

His son shrugged his shoulders and closed the door.

Labor's defeat left John West with a vague depression. He worked automatically, as if his efforts were without ultimate purpose.

One day, shortly after the elections, was typical: he worked hard but without verve, without satisfaction. Having dealt with his correspondence he sent for his brother, Joe. As usual, Joe was late.

Joe looked much the elder. John West, at sixty-two, was neat and well-preserved; years of self-assurance had kept his personality smooth. Joe, on the other hand, had become indolent and shabby; he was round-shouldered, the years were hitting him hard, his face was flabby and red, his nose bulbous.

"When I say ten o'clock, I don't mean twenty past," John West said curtly.

Joe sat down impassively without replying. He seemed quietly amused at his brother's power, as if he could not credit that the bandy-legged boy who had played with him in the narrow back streets of Carringbush should have lived to be treated with such respect and awe. They viewed each other as casual acquaintances and no social intercourse existed between their families. Richard Lamb often said that Joe was the only man who could 'see through' his brother. John West wondered why he tolerated Joe, for he displayed little talent for, or interest in, his work. Now Godfrey Dwyer had complained that Joe was drinking more heavily and neglecting his work at the racecourse.

John West told Joe that he was not satisfied with his work at the races. He would have to drink less and attend to his duties. "Just because you're my brother doesn't mean that you get paid for doing nothing."

Joe remained smilingly impassive. "I helped you make your first million, boy," he said.

"You got paid."

"Yes, and I'll continue to get paid."

"Not if you don't work."

"Don't put on airs with me, Jack. I know yer too well. You'd never let anyone say yer sacked your own brother."

"Don't try me too far."

"Save your bluff stakes," Joe said.

Joe's calculated indifference rankled John West.

"Listen! You're a sponger and a loafer; and you drink too much. You're satisfied to bludge along while I keep you and your wife and kids. Well, either you give up drinking and do your work, or you get out!"

Joe was suddenly concerned. "Break it down, Jack. I'm gettin' old, yer know."

"You're not as old as I am, and look at me. You drink too much. Give it up and do your job. If I hear of you having another drink, or get any more complaints about your work, you're finished? Understand?"

Joe stood up. He was shaken. He wouldn't put it past Jack to sack him. He knew no trade, had little ability. He turned and walked to the door slowly.

"All right," he said.

John West felt no elation at his domination. A desire to call his brother back came, but he rejected it. Never admit you're wrong! But what did it matter if old Joe just pottered along?

That afternoon John West had a mysterious appointment. A younger member of one of Australia's most powerful families, the Bainetons, had rung, asking to see him. What could he want?

Baineton proved to be a youngish man, very well dressed.

"Well, Mr. West," he said jovially, "you must be wondering why I've come."

John West eyed him coldly without answering.

"Mind if I smoke? Thanks! Well, Mr. West, I am more or less the black sheep of our family. The crisis has hit me hard and I'm short of ready money. Frankly, I am seeking liquid credits. A hundred thousand pounds' worth."

The words amazed John West, but he showed no reaction.

After a long pause, during which Baineton momentarily lost some of his poise, John West said: "A hundred thousand is a lot of money, Mr. Baineton. Surely you can get accommodation from your banker?"

"You know what the banks are today."

"Well, what about your people, your father, your uncles or brothers? Surely they'd help."

"I wouldn't like them to know my position, Mr. West, unless it becomes absolutely necessary. I would rather make my own arrangements. I shudder to think what they would say if they knew I'd come to you."

Baineton gulped, as if trying to bite back his last sentence.

"What's wrong with me?" John West snapped. "My money's clean and I'm worth millions. Oh, I know they wouldn't have me in their exclusive clubs or at their official functions, but I have more power than all of them put together."

"Oh, I wouldn't say that, Mr. West. You're one of the richest and most powerful men in Australia. That is individually. But it's the big financial combines that have the real power. Believe me, I know."

"I put men into Parliament, and they do my bidding," John West persisted like an obstinate schoolboy. "I control the Labor Party."

"They put men into Parliament, too, Mr. West, and they rule

whichever Party is in office. The past two years proved that, surely. They control the banks and the heavy industries. They are the power in the land."

"The Jews control the banks!"

"Don't believe a word of it, Mr. West. The really big men in this country are respectable Presbyterians. Why, they won't even allow Jews into the Melbourne Club."

John West's scowling expression caused Baineton to switch the conversation. "But all this is a matter of conjecture, Mr. West. Anyway, you can take it from me you're often discussed. The mysterious John West. The man who came from the Carringbush tote to the world of big business."

Unusually, John West was softened by flattery. "A man who has come up the hard way is always more sympathetic," he said. "What's your proposition?"

They discussed the details. John West called in one of his accountants, and a deal was made on the spot. Baineton had excellent security. He was worth nearly a million.

John West was surprised that he got from the interview no thrill of power. Baineton would repay easily when business improved.

After a busy afternoon, John West felt tired and depressed. He rang Pat Cory and arranged for a lift home. Often lately he had felt the walk home in the evening beyond him. At sixty-two, he was beginning to feel he might be getting old. The last two years had taken their toll. He had not taken a holiday since his honeymoon thirty years before. Cory had suggested a trip around the world, but John West answered: "I wouldn't know what to do with myself if I left all this."

They drove home in silence. John West ate the evening meal quickly and retired to the reception room. He was expecting visitors.

He read the evening paper. A rape. A murder. A suicide. Trouble with the unemployed. Someone saying that prosperity was just around the corner. New Prime Minister restoring confidence ... He turned to the sporting pages, but was soon interrupted by the front door bell.

In came Sugar Renfrey, who was now Mayor of Carringbush. Sugar was pathetically proud of his position, not realising he cut such a ludicrous figure that he was a standing joke. However, his aptitude for graft and his native cunning enabled him to serve John West quite well.

Sugar lit up a cigar and said: "Jest come up to discuss a few council matters, Jack. There's an election in the North Ward next month, and a few other things."

John West listened, and indifferently advised Sugar.

John West later escorted him to the music room, where Nellie, Mrs. Moran, Mary and Joe were gathered in desultory conversation. He occasionally foisted Sugar and other uncouth characters on his family. He took pleasure from the belief that this offended the family's middle-class susceptibilies, but Joe and Mrs. Moran, at least, found Sugar amusing.

Tonight, John West felt impelled to play the old joke that Mick O'Connell used to perpetrate on Sugar in the old days. It was the only joke John West had played in his life. He had played it once before, years ago, and the children had been greatly amused.

"Your glasses are crooked, Sugar," John West forced himself to say.

Sugar, credulous as a child, took off his glasses and replied: "No they ain't, Jack; it's just the way they're made . . ."

The joke fell flat, only Joe was amused. Rebuffed, John West returned to the reception room.

He tried to study the paper, but he felt tired and depressed. Disillusionment had crept up on him since the elections. He was concerned not so much by the defeat of the Federal Labor Government as by his inability to control it. The life of the Summers Government had revealed the limits of his power. Why, it had even appointed Isaac Isaacs Governor-General – Isaacs who had drafted the first bill against the tote! The Premiers' Plan, he believed now, would set the country on the road to recovery, but other men, more powerful than he, had forced it through.

He lolled back in the deep chair. Tiredness seemed to seep through his bones. An alien feeling of remorse crept over him. Where had the long road led him? Was power an illusion? All his life he had protected himself from remorse by refusing to indulge in introspection; but now, though he would not admit to himself that his power had passed its zenith, a mood of was-it-worth-while afflicted him.

John West had dreamed of power greater than, and apart from, class power of the capitalist class. Such power was impossible of achievement. Because he did not gain control of heavy industries like steel, coal, shipping or of banking or effective control of the press, he could not achieve even membership of the inner sanctum of the few big families who really controlled Australia.

He had picked up men in the dustbins of society and placed them in high places; he had won power over many men already in high places. He was powerful, but the respectable rich were more powerful. They held direct or remote control over all Governments and the State.

John West had set out to become the most powerful man in Australia, but had finished up as the black sheep of the family of millionaires.

Why did he bother to go on? Where was the ceaseless struggle getting him?

Surely with all his money and power he should be happy. Had he been too ruthless and unbending?

Suddenly he felt, as never before, the need for the more intimate, human things in life. He looked up at the photo of his mother. She seemed to gaze reprovingly at him. He looked at the photo of himself, Joe and Arty. If she were alive now, what would she think? Joe despised him; Arty was mad. Between the three of them there was not one ounce of affection left. Among his associates there was not one person he called a friend.

He heard Sugar Renfrey leave. He felt drowsy. Bestirring himself, he went upstairs.

Here in this very house were the people who should love him – his own family. Yet young Joe didn't seem to care, Mary avoided him, Nellie's mother conspired against him, John was in Queensland resenting being forced to follow in his father's steps, and Marjorie was in Germany, rearing German children, disowned by her father. He switched on the light in his dressing-room and began to undress. He heard Nellie enter the next room. A dagger of hatred stabbed his soul. Why had Nellie done this to him? Why had his family taken everything he gave them, yet offered no affection in return?

After changing into his pyjamas, he took the revolver from the drawer of the dressing table and walked to his lonely, open-air bedroom. He placed the revolver under the pillow, then got into the large double bed and turned off the lights.

He no longer felt sleepy. His mind would not relax. He

switched on the light again and picked up a pamphlet from the bedside table. It was a copy of the Pope's latest Encyclical, *Quadragesimo Anno*, which Archbiship Malone had given him recently. He had tried unsuccessfully to digest it on several occasions.

He began to read in a desultory manner:

Although there are evils in the modern society, Socialism is not the cure . . . Quite right, too.

. . . *No one can be, at the same time, a sincere Catholic and a Socialist properly so called* . . . *We perceive* . . . *a few of our children* . . . *have deserted the camp of the Church and passed over to the camp of Socialism.* He's right! Communism is spreading like a flame right here in Melbourne. Even my own daughter seems to be sympathetic with it, the way she talks sometimes.

John West's mind would not absorb the sentences fully.

. . . *The apostasy of many working men from the Catholic Faith.* . .

. . . *We must gather and train* . . . *auxiliary soldiers of the Church, men who well know their mentality and aspirations* . . . *the first and immediate apostles of the working men, must be themselves workingmen, while the apostles of the industrial and commercial world should themselves be employers and merchants.* That's the part the Archbishop seemed most interested in: the formation of groups of laymen to win back the world to Christ and the Church, especially to combat Communism . . . *Revival of Catholic Action all over the world.*

He tried to read on, but his mind failed to concentrate, so he switched off the light again.

The night was warm and still. He could see the stars blinking through the pine trees. Unusual feelings of remorse and self-pity again entered his mind. The grandfather clock downstairs had struck midnight before he drove them out and began to speculate on the future.

As the States had power to legislate in the sphere in which he was interested, power over State Parliaments was all he needed. Must keep some power in the Federal Labor Party, of course, but in future the States counted most, especially Victoria. In Victoria his position was complicated. Labor could easily lose office again. Ned Horan and a few lesser lights were likely to be expelled from the Party for enforcing the Premiers' Plan.

The Nationalists, now the United Australia Party, were in office, but Alfred Davison's group held the balance of power, and John West could probably prevent the Government from doing anything hostile to him. Besides, Davison and Ned Horan had agreed to work towards an alliance between Labor and the Country Party eventually.

Business was still bad, but he had succeeded in halting his own decline: though many of his enterprises were losing money, his overall profits now exceeded losses. Soon things would improve and he could fulfil his unachieved aims in business, sports promotion and politics.

His mind swarmed with scraps of plans, old and new, until at last sleep came. It was disturbed by a dream.

He dreamt he was alone in a vast desert. His mother and brothers, his wife and family appeared and beckoned to him. In his dream he ran after them, but they faded away in the distance and were gone.

Next morning he was in his office at the usual time and threw himself into his work with his usual well-directed vigour.

PART THREE

1935–1950
DECLINE OF POWER

Power that can be defied with impunity is drawing to its end.

HONORÉ DE BALZAC

CHAPTER TWELVE

Where is the man in hot pursuit of wealth and power who has been known to stop?

HONORÉ DE BALZAC

John West could say that, as far as he was concerned, the economic depression was over by 1935; but the mood of depression engendered by the fall of the Summers Government did not pass away.

Since it is not difficult for a millionaire to make money, except in times of deepest economic crisis, John West had recouped his depression losses and made an additional million.

Several people had helped. Ted Thurgood had stumbled on to the richest gold mine in the Southern Hemisphere: when a fossicker, seeking capital for a rich seam of gold in Fiji, approached him, Red Ted formed a company with himself. John West and Pat Cory as principal shareholders, organised a survey party and unearthed a bonanza of fabulous riches. Already a million pounds had been made from the mines.

Frank Lammence, Patrick Cory and other executives had also helped. Frank Lammence saved John West fifty thousand pounds in one swoop by arranging the theft of certain files from the Taxation Department.

John West's men in the Victorian Parliament were of assistance, especially Alfred Davison. Davison's group held the balance of power in the House, and shared the ministerial benches with the conservative United Australia Party. Through Davison, through West men in the Labor Party and men with a price among the Conservatives, John West achieved his ambition to conduct galloping meetings in opposition to the Victorian Racing Club. A pseudo inquiry instituted into racing was followed by a Bill to abolish pony racing, which John West had controlled, and close two of John West's race-courses. The courses closed down were not owned but merely leased by John West and Benjamin Levy from local municipal councils, and had lost their usefulness; they were too small for galloping events, and pony racing had lost public support because it was even more corrupt than trotting under John West or galloping under the V.R.C. In spite of all this, John West was given galloping fixtures to replace the pony dates, and was paid compensation of a hundred thousand pounds.

On his remaining racecourse, John West ran galloping meetings on nineteen Saturdays each year, and trotting every Monday. A new club – the Melbourne Galloping and Trotting Association – was formed, with Godfrey Dwyer as Secretary, Bennett as President, and Ned Horan a member of the West-controlled Committee.

John West had also made a lot of money out of sheep and cattle stations. His interest in these began in the twenties when Ted Thurgood had suggested that he purchase properties adjoining the state-owned sheep and cattle stations in Queensland. The idea was to herd livestock from the Government stations and change the brands. John West had taken to rewarding his associates with partnerships in station properties. His partner in one in the Northern Territory was Archbishop Malone, who said he accepted the share on behalf of the Church. In another, Thurgood was his partner; in another, Alfred Davison; in yet another, a friendly U.A.P. politician from the elite suburb of Toorak – and so on. His entry into the ranks of the squatters was most profitable, but not without problems. Satisfactory managers were hard to get, and one had nearly landed himself in jail for flogging an aboriginal who worked on the property. John West's influence saved the manager from the authorities, and he retained his job because he had made the station pay.

Though there was still widespread unemployment, dole work payments had been raised after several dole strikes. More people were working and business was slowly reviving. Attendances at race meetings, boxing and wrestling matches had increased, and takings in most of John West's other businesses were higher. Also, he had begun again to buy controlling interests in any good businesses offering.

As well, his interest in matters of health had led him to make profitable investments. After reading in *The Culture of the Abdomen* that certain breakfast foods were good because they introduced "roughage" into the diet, he bought into firms which manufactured these foods, began to eat them himself and instructed the others at home to do the same. Similarly with yeast: his health bible insisted that yeast was a wholesome food, so he began to eat it and bought up some yeast factories.

Politically he was concentrating on State Parliaments, especially in Victoria. Labor was in the political wilderness at Canberra and seemed likely to remain there. In Victoria he still had much influence in the Labor Party, but was no longer purely a "Labor" man; he had done well with the U.A.P. in office through the agency of Davison. There was now an unofficial fourth party in the Victorian Parliament – the West party – comprising men from all the other parties.

In the election of March, 1935, the Country and Labor Parties gained seats, and John West's old plan for a coalition between them came about with Davison as Premier.

But the idea that money and power were not everything kept niggling at the back of John West's mind. He felt dissatisfied and lonely. He was vaguely aware that this was because his aim to win all power had fallen short, and because of the disintegration of his family life. Yet still he pursued wealth and power – he could not help himself, his every thought process was directed to this quest. Never able to feel or admit he was wrong, he could not brook defiance in politics, business or family life.

And there were growing signs of defiance. The manager of John West's cycling promotions, Cameron, had left him and started on his own at the Exhibition arena. Cameron had taken all the best riders. Cameron was also conducting boxing at the Exhibition, and was getting the bigger crowds. When listening on the radio to a fight at the Exhibition between an Australian champion and an American importation, John West had stamped with rage and savagely switched off the set.

Defiance had also broken out in the Ralstone City Council, for more than thirty years a West stronghold. The position became so bad that John West issued orders that the Mayor, Colin Lassiter, old Ron's son, was to be defeated in the Labor pre-selection, and driven off the Council.

One night after his defeat, Colin Lassiter had called on John West. They talked in the reception room. Colin Lassiter was an extraordinary character. Tall and dressed impeccably, he was an impressive figure until he spoke. Then his speech would give the impression that a ventriloquist was hidden nearby. Though dressed like a prosperous business magnate, he talked like a Carringbush larrikin.

Colin Lassiter had had a chequered career. As a youth, he entered a Jesuit monastery, but left after three years because his behaviour displeased the authorities. He went from the monastery into Snoopy Tanner's gang, and became the blight of the Catholic Young Men's Society, being expelled from that organisation when he shot the lights out at a church dance with well-aimed revolver shots. After Snoopy's death, Lassiter had joined the Labor Party to seek political honours. He was readmitted to the Church after making a special general confession to Archbishop Malone, and won a seat for Labor on Ralstone Council.

Nursing his Homburg hat, he appeared ill at ease as he sat opposite John West. Behind his pince-nez glasses his eyes turned from the little man's gaze. His face was at first glance even-featured and handsome, but his upper lip curved slightly over the lower, likening the mouth to the beak of a predatory bird. He was generous and very witty in a cynical way, but at times ruthless and quite without conscience – a strange mixture of good and evil.

"What's this I hear about you holding a street meeting and saying that I run the Ralstone Council? That if you want anything in Ralstone, you have to see Jack West?"

"Well, it's true, isn't it?"

"I don't like men who can't keep their mouths shut."

"I kept mine shut, Jack, till you dumped me."

"You went too far. You were jeopardising my position."

"You work hot yerself – hot as steam. Don't come the high toby with me."

"I'll come the high toby if I like. I don't interfere with my men unless they overdo it. I didn't mind you making a little on the side like the others, but the Ralstone Council became the talk of Melbourne, and there were worse things going on that people didn't know about: such as burning criminal evidence in the incinerator. I have ways and means of finding these things out."

"If I get my seat on the Council back, I'll hold my tongue."

"Don't try to blackmail me or I'll put you where you belong," John West said in a menacingly quiet voice.

The Ralstone Council had always been a centre of graft. Tenders for Council contracts were faked, ballots rigged, monies expropriated. With Lassiter as Mayor, it became even worse; and John West was left out of most of the proceeds.

John West was now seeking a way to pacify Lassiter, who was a dangerous man, with the courage to talk or blackmail with the threat of talking. He might resort to violence, even against John West.

"You've been boss cocky so long, Jack, that yer think if a man is once under your thumb he becomes your property for life. Here's one darky yer can't bluff. Unless I get back, I might have a few things to say. The mighty Jack West has stable secrets. Get what I mean?"

"Listen, you've had your chance, and you abused it. Don't start threatening me. I've struck your type before."

"And I've woke to your form, very lively. There's a lot of donkeys around who would murder you if they were game. But I'm not going to be brushed off. If I am, I'll be just another reason why you should carry a gun and sleep with it under your pillow. See what I mean?"

John West eased the strain. He guessed that Lassiter was bluffing. "Listen, Colin, I know you're a shrewd man, and you have ability. Tell you what I'll do. I'll tell them down at the Ralstone Town Hall to give you a job – an easy job with nothing to do."

"That's better, Jack. All right. Tell you what I'll do. I'll settle for a lifetime job at a tenner a week."

"Righto, Colin. I had this in mind all the time. You should know that Jack West never forgets his friends."

Lassiter smiled knowingly. "Just thought I'd jog yer memory, Jack. Workin' hot becomes a habit, sometimes."

"You haven't met my family, have you?" John West evaded. "Better stay and have a bit of supper."

Lassiter followed him, hat in hand. John West was thinking: I'd better be careful of this fellow.

Mary had gone to bed, but they found Nellie, Mrs. Moran and Joe in the music room. John West introduced Lassiter to them with exaggerated formality.

Joe said: "How are you?" Mrs. Moran said: "Do sit down, Mr. Lassiter, I'll take your hat." Nellie looked at Lassiter as if she expected him to draw a revolver and blow the lights out.

Lassiter greeted them with a courtesy so heightened as to be mocking. He bowed elaborately to the ladies and shook Joe's hand stiffly. A grin hovered round his mouth. "So I meet the family of the notorious J.W." he said ironically.

Sensing that John West was trying to use him to embarrass the others, Lassiter played his part so well that even John West was relieved when he departed.

In the West home, the situation had changed in one respect only: the child Xavier was dead.

When Xavier had contracted pneumonia in 1933, Nellie, frantic with worry, called a local doctor. It was left to Mrs. Moran to tell John West.

All night, while the child was gasping for breath, with Nellie and Mrs. Moran at its side, John West lay awake. Let it die and end this terrible episode! He should have sent it to a home long ago, anyway! Why should he give food and shelter to a bastard son of a bricklayer? Why should he worry if it got sick and died?

Yet everyone believed it was his child. It was part of his family, in a way; and it was dying in there. It would be expected of him that he would try to save it.

After a night of troubled indecision, he got up early and asked Mrs. Moran how the child was. No better, she told him; the crisis had not passed, the doctor would call again at eight o'clock.

"Perhaps this doctor doesn't know his business; I'll ring Devlin and get him to come immediately. And get a nurse, woman; you can't sit up all night."

Sensing her gratitude, and resenting it, he added gruffly: "I wouldn't care, if *it* died this minute!"

In spite of Devlin's unremitting skill the child died the next evening.

John West felt relief surge through him. Fate had removed from his household its most shameful blemish!

The family mourned deeply for the child, especially Nellie, who hardly stirred from her room for weeks afterwards. The death was never mentioned between her and John West, but the child's existence had left an indelible mark. The tension was not relieved by its passing. A new, deeper cleavage, subtler and more disturbing than the old, brooded over the household.

Since then John West had, at times, to resist an urge to seek smoother, more intimate terms with Nellie and his family. Instead he sought relief from the loneliness that harassed him sometimes, in a platonic affair with a middle-aged married woman.

She was Veronica Maguire. Vera was a well-preserved woman, very much a "sport", who could discuss football, racing and boxing with enthusiastic intelligence.

John West had been attracted to her since they had met two years before. She was the sort of woman he should have married, he told himself. She appreciated and admired him. He was more at ease with her than with anyone he had known.

To Vera Maguire, John West was a strong, silent man. From the beginning, she determined to break through his forbidding outer reserve to the inner human being. She delighted in chaffing him, as no one else would have thought of doing, and he liked it. She believed all the stories of his generosity, courage, shrewdness and strength; she was impressed by the legends of his rise from poverty.

At first they met only in the company of her husband or other people; but soon John West jovially suggested that she should have a car, as well as her husband. He bought her one, and she often drove him to and from the city.

They talked mainly about sport. He found her company stimulating. He looked forward to seeing her. Though he was sexually impotent, she aroused passion in him. He tried to kiss her in the car in front of his home one night. She rebuffed him gently: "Naughty boy; we're getting too old for that sort of thing."

John West asked her to accompany him to the Stadium. She did so, and soon it became a weekly outing. Sometimes Vera's husband went with them. He did not object to the strange affair. He knew Vera could handle the situation.

Nellie West became suspicious. Some evenings from an upstairs window she would catch them sitting talking in the car in front of the house for a few minutes. At first she felt a pang of jealousy, but dismissed it. Why should she care? He was nothing to her. She did not mention the matter to him or anyone else, and thought little of it.

John West came to value Vera as his only real friend. Moments with her were relaxed and happy. He even took to discussing business problems with her, and she proved an attentive and helpful confidant.

Vera Maguire knew the kind of friendship she wanted, and felt confident she could get it. She set a platonic seal on it; and John

West, who for a time had vague ideas of forcing it further, resigned himself.

However steep the decline in his power in other fields, John West's influence over the Victorian Parliament remained very strong.

One day, shortly after the 1935 elections, several politicians called at his office.

The first was Ned Horan.

Horan's high mass of hair had grown thicker and turned grey, as had his moustache. His tall, gangling frame was spare, but he looked healthy and prosperous.

Horan has been expelled from the Labor Party in 1932 for his part in the Premiers' Plan, but held his seat as an independent, and later joined the Country Party. "It doesn't worry me, Jack," he told John West at the time. "I'll tell you for why: my seat is in the country. I might lose it one day as a Labor man. I'm better off in the Country Party."

Ned quickly came to the point. He wanted John West to intercede with Premier Davison on his behalf. Horan had asked Davison to appoint him Chief Secretary, but Davison had refused.

"I'm sorry, Ned," John West answered. "Tom Trumbleward will be the Chief Secretary."

John West spoke listlessly. That he had the power to influence Cabinet appointments no longer struck an exultant chord in him. The exercise of power was now merely a habit.

John West's hair, greyed to an even colour, matched his eyes and his suit. Having given up the struggle with his unruly lock, he wore his hair close-cropped in the style of a Prussian officer. His face was set permanently in a sullen scowl, but his gaze was as penetrating as ever; and now at sixty-five he had the air of an alert man of fifty.

Horan departed with a rueful: "Ar, well; no harm in asking."

The next caller was a short, black-haired man under forty with a determined chin and a bullet-shaped head. He was Paddy Kelleher, Victorian secretary of the Labor Party.

"Aaarrr, w-well, Mr. West," Kelleher stammered. "Aaarrr, we're in office again. Even if we do 'ave to play, aaarrr, second fiddle to Alfie Davison."

The impediment in Kelleher's speech prevented him from

speaking much in public, but had not prevented him from winning a safe seat in the Upper House or from being active behind the scenes in the Victorian Labor Party.

Kelleher had been a rank and file member of the Labor Party when he left Melbourne in search of work in 1928, but this did not prevent John West from putting him forward as Party Secretary five years later. Kelleher had gone to Yallourn, where he became active among the electricity plant workers as union organiser, secretary of the Labor Party branch and treasurer of the local football club. Some aspersions were cast on his handling of the football club funds, but no one could deny the effectiveness of his work in the Labor Movement.

Then one of Kelleher's young children fell seriously ill. Paddy rang John West by trunk-line phone. West could get the child a free bed in a Catholic hospital; maybe he would get Paddy Kelleher a high-up job somewhere. Kelleher obtained the hospital bed for his child and an interview with John West.

John West had heard of Kelleher, and on meeting him saw behind his stammer to a shrewd, agile and cynical mind. As was his custom, John West sounded Kelleher out: asked him about his attitude to gambling and liquor legislation. Kelleher gave the answers he thought most likely to please.

In sponsoring Kelleher, John West displayed his usual uncanny ability to pick the right man. Kelleher soon learned more about winning pre-selection and election ballots than even Frank Lammence. He would serve the Party, John West, the liquor interests, the Catholic Church, or anyone else he considered important. With rare agility he skated the thin ice of maintaining party unity between the ''left'' Blackwell faction, the centre faction, and the Catholic and West factions which overlapped. In pre-selection ballots, many members voted twice, once on their Labor Party ticket and again on their Union ticket; non-members voted as well as the absent and the dead. He brought as much skill to bear on preparations for annual conferences to ensure as far as possible that the ''right'' delegates attended. To his other devices he often added the formation of bogus branches which sent proxy delegates of the ''right colour.'' Expediency was his middle name. He would co-operate with the Communists one minute and the Catholics the next. Those party members who were aware of Paddy's methods, shrugged their shoulders; after all, Pat, if a rogue, was a likeable one, and he had certainly infused new life into the organisation.

Kelleher had come to John West to discuss the delicate moves necessary to bring about the proposed coalition Government with the Country Party. Some Labor Party members and supporters would object, he explained to John West, but they could be appeased by pointing out that Davison's policy had included rises in dole work wages and a moratorium on farmer's debts.

John West listened patiently, never helping Kelleher out when a word refused to come, as he had learned that this was embarrassing. They made decisions on policy and Cabinet positions, and John West paid a promised donation to Party funds. Paddy controlled the funds. He would take donations from anyone at all, often keeping a "little for himself" with or without the donor's permission and without the knowledge of his colleagues. In this manner he had purchased three houses and a motor car, and built up a presentable bank account.

John West then asked Kelleher if it would be possible to defeat the Party leader, Carr, when a caucus met. Kelleher temporised. Better to wait until a suitable opponent were available, he suggested.

"What about Tom Trumbleward or Bill Brady?"

"Aaarrr, b-b-brother," Kelleher replied, unintentionally calling John West "brother" as he did everyone else, friend and foe alike. "B-b-brother. You don't want to back a horse that can't win; you should, aaarrr, know that. T-Trumbleward was, aaarrr, leader and got beat, and Brady's not, aaarrr, popular."

"Well, I want Carr beaten."

"Aaarrr, don't kill the, aaarrr, g-goose that lays the, aaarrr, g-golden egg, Mr. West. If we move against, aaarrr, Carr now, we'll split the party in halves."

Kelleher was not a "West" man pure and simple. Somewhere behind his wall of cynical roguishness lay a spark of solidarity; and, anyway, John West was not the only pebble on his beach. Kelleher believed Carr to be the only man capable of keeping tied the mixed bag that constituted the Labor Party membership. A former member of Tom Mann's Socialist Party, but softened by Parliament, Carr was a skilful politician with supporters in all factions of the Labor Party. Though intimidated by John West's power, Carr would not toe the line directly, so John West wanted him out.

John West decided to postpone further action against Carr. It was clear to him that Kelleher was stalling, but what could he do?

Kelleher had not long departed when another "Labor" man came into the office. He was William Brady, a foul-mouthed larrikin, unscrupulous and devoid of humour. Brady was very well-dressed and groomed, but nothing could disguise his sly countenance and thin, cruel mouth.

Brady had won a seat at a recent by-election brought about by the death of Fighting Bob Scott. Near the finish, Scott had become so senile and whisky-sodden that to John West he became merely a vote in the House.

In choosing William Brady as Scott's successor, John West again showed uncanny insight. To Brady, politics was a career. As yet he was a junior member of Parliament, but he had his eyes on the big pickings of politics, and reasoned that to serve John West was the best way "to get on in the game."

Brady had come into politics through the Trade Union Movement. When Secretary of the Tobacco Workers' Union, he had talked like a lion, but acted like a very sly fox when the membership passed any motion of which he disapproved – once he burned the minute books to avoid carrying out a decision of his Union.

On entering Parliament, Brady had himself appointed Justice of the Peace, not because he wished to sit on the Bench, but because he wanted power to witness postal ballot papers.

Today, John West had called Brady to him to set in motion a plan to destroy Jack Cameron's cycling and boxing promotions. For months they had been seeking ways and means to drive Cameron from the Exhibition grounds. Brady had organised a petition by residents who complained about the noise of the motor bikes. Cameron countered the move by cutting out motor-paced races. At John West's suggestion, Brady then prevailed upon the Board of a nearby Catholic hospital to complain also, but still Cameron continued operations, and crowds at John West's stadium remained small.

"Well," John West greeted Brady. "Have you found a way to beat Cameron yet?"

"No, Mr. West; but I'm still trying."

"Well, I have. Read this."

Brady wiped his pince-nez glasses with his handkerchief.

"Um," he said, after gazing at the typed paper handed to him by John West. "But what's this got to do with the matter?"

"Makes it illegal to enclose a public park to make an arena or a stadium, doesn't it?"

"By Christ, so it does. But it's dated eighteen-seventy-five!"

"No difference. It's still in force, my lawyer tells me. I want you to raise this when the House assembles. This will end Cameron's career. I want you to demand that the Government instructs the Exhibition trustees to refuse him the use of the grounds. And I'm going to ask Davison to appoint you to the board of trustees of the Exhibition so you can watch that it is never used again for sports meetings. I'm expecting him in a few minutes. You'd better go."

A few minutes later, the Premier, Alfred Davison himself, was seated in the chair vacated by Brady.

Davison was short, fat and jovial. His face was a cartoonist's dream; he resembled a happy-go-lucky pig. His nose was a snout, his cheeks were puffed, his ears were large and pointed at the top like those of a pig, and his head was bald except at the sides.

He was a little nervous. This was his first visit to J.W.'s office. He didn't like it. He preferred lobbiers to call on him. The cheek of Lammence on the phone: "Mr. West would like to see you." Was Alfred Davison Premier, or John West? There were other powerful pressure groups to consider besides West. The B.H.P. group, the transport group, the breweries; but they leaned more on the U.A.P., worse luck. He had to continue to play ball with West because only West could guarantee Labor's support for the coalition, and, besides, West was generous.

John West observed that Davison was not as many other politicians who called – he was not fawning and servile. He tried to put the Premier in more pliant mood by congratulating him on his victory. Davison brushed the compliments aside. He was not vain; he could not be flattered. Davison depended on commonsense and shrewdness. He proudly boasted that he hadn't read a book in his life. To him, politics was a game. He loved the subtlety of debate, feeling the pulse of the electors, juggling for position and power. Politics was also a career and a business – in politics you didn't need dreams and aspirations, you needed commonsense and powerful backers.

560

Davison's father had been a country town storekeeper. Alfred went on the land, realised the hopeless position of the small farmer, decided to go into politics on a programme for the mortgage-ridden small holder.

When, in 1919, he had decided to oppose Trumbleward, he heard a rumour that the mysterious John West was not well pleased with Trumbleward. He approached West and obtained his blessing. West had ignored him, more or less, for nearly ten years, until he realised that Davison held the key to power in the Victorian Parliament. Davison had led his breakaway group back into the Country Party when promised leadership. Since then West had made his plans around him. Davison knew that – he wasn't called Artful Alfie for nothing. Just so long as West didn't succeed in getting him right under his powerful thumb!

They discussed Cabinet posts. Davison was difficult. He didn't want Trumbleward as Chief Secretary. He had in mind one of his own party – one of the men who had been kicked out of the Labor Party with Horan.

John West couldn't shift him.

"Well," he said, "I want to have Godfrey Dwyer made Sir Godfrey, then appointed Chief of Police in place of Blaire, who, I hear, is to resign after the Royal Commission's findings."

"I'll recommend Dwyer for a knighthood in this year's honours list, but I'm afraid he won't be Chief of Police. I've already written to London to obtain a Scotland Yard man for the job."

John West scowled. Through Davison he had obtained power; but at a price. Davison knew he was indispensable. John West felt like thumping the table and making demands, but thought better of it.

"But surely you can change that . . ."

"I'm afraid not, Mr. West. After Blaire's regime the people are demanding a clean-up. A Scotland Yard man will restore confidence."

"But Dwyer is a man of integrity, surely . . ."

"I'm sorry, Mr. West," Davison persisted. "You must remember: in order to help, I must do my job efficiently, and I must retain power. It will be a long time before the Labor Party can rule again alone. I've been elected on a programme of increased dole work rates and a moratorium on farmers' debts. I shall carry out that programme. I must. Also, I must run the State efficiently."

Davison took his grey hat from the table. "I really must go, Mr. West. Many duties call."

With that he left.

John West sat pondering on his protégé. Davison must be forced further into line. He was going to be difficult, but Jack West held his future in his palm. He'd handle him somehow.

His mind turned to a conversation he had had with his daughter, Mary, earlier that day. He pressed a button behind his desk. A buzzer rang and a young woman entered.

"Send Mr. Lamb in," John West said.

To Lamb, he said: "Listen, Dick. My daughter, Mary, was in here first thing this morning. Asked for the Stadium for a Peace Rally next Tuesday. I told her she could have it. She said you had refused. I rang for you but you were out. What's the strength of it?"

"Well, Mr. West, it's a red organisation: the Movement against War and Fascism, or whatever they call it. This fellow Kisch, that they tried to keep from landing: he's here with a bloke named Griffin, from New Zealand. Some big conference, red-sponsored. You were away in Sydney at the time. I decided to refuse use of the Stadium."

John West really wanted to say: "So you should have. My daughter deceived me." But instead he said: "Um. Well, I reversed the decision. We've no booking for that night. All sorts of people attend the fights. Just as well to keep in with all sections."

When Lamb had gone, John West rang for Frank Lammence.

"Frank. My daughter, Mary, is mixed up in an organisation called the Movement against War and Fascism, or some such name. This fellow Kisch is here to attend some conference. Sounds like a red show. I'd like you to check on Mary's movements. Can you arrange it?"

"Certainly, Mr. West. Perhaps I could get Paddy Ryan to follow her."

"Right. Don't waste any time. Let me know."

Mary West was certainly "mixed up in" the Movement against War and Fascism. She was a member of its executive committee, and had approached her father in that capacity.

Since the unemployed demonstration, Mary had taken more interest in politics and steadily drifted into the left-wing movement. She would have found it difficult to explain the processes through which she had passed.

She knew the controversy over the building of the Shrine of Remembrance in St Kilda Road had had its effect. When work began on the Shrine, she immediately dubbed it a "white elephant". Why should they build a useless monument of stone in memory of the heroic dead? Why not a hospital? Why not a school? Then the Communists had said the same. Why not a hospital? Why not a school? And they had gone further. They asked why should returned soldiers build a memorial to themselves on relief wages? The reds led the strike at the Shrine; the strike that won higher relief rates. They said that if the Shrine must be built, men working on it – largely returned soldiers – should be paid the basic wage.

That was in 1933. Then, early in 1935, Mary had taken a part in a Workers' Art Society play, and met Ben Worth.

Ben Worth had a small part in the play. As an actor he amounted to little, but it was soon clear to Mary that in the Workers' Art Society he amounted to quite a lot! He seemed to be a kind of political leader.

Mary was soon attracted to Ben. He was wide-shouldered and handsome. His face, though inclined to be swarthy, was even-featured. He had that unconscious knack of wearing his clothes carelessly but neatly that appeals to women; his black hair was unruly, tending to fall over his forehead on the left side. He had an air of quiet strength.

Mary, who had not as much as kissed a man for years, soon had to admit to herself that she was head over heels in love with him. She learned that he had been a textile factory worker before getting mixed up in the Labor Party in Sydney, and later in the Communist Party in Melbourne. A revolutionary – how romantic! Was he married? She made inquiries; no, he was not married, but he was hard to get.

When the play finished its short run, Mary was loth to end their association. So was he, she soon gathered. He approached her after the show. Would she care to have supper? She would!

In the coffee lounge he was obviously restless. At last he blurted it out. An anti-war movement had been formed. He was to take a leading part in organising it. The movement against war was the most important work one could do. Mussolini and Hitler, fascists who represented the millionaires, were in power. They were bent on war. They had friends in England, Japan, France and America, even in Australia. The progressive people of the world were mobilising against fascism and war. He, as a Communist, was playing a part in that struggle.

Mary noticed him becoming agitated, intense. He leaned towards her, his coffee becoming cold.

"Hitler has turned Germany into a great torture chamber. The Reichstag Fire was the frame-up which created the mass hysteria, then he arrested Communists, Trade Union leaders, Social Democrats, clergymen – anyone who opposed him. With devilish cunning the Nazis have diverted the wrath of the people away from the capitalist system which reduced them to their sorry plight, on to the Jewish people. Jews are hounded, tortured, murdered! for no other reason than they were born of their parents! Anti-Semitism is a form of cannibalism, once it . . ."

Mary had been watching him closely. As he mentioned the Jewish people's sufferings, his body became taut, his breathing heavy. "Ben, are you a Jew?" Mary found herself asking. She wished she could have bitten the words back.

Ben gazed at her inquiringly, almost suspiciously. "Yes, of course I am. Why?"

"Oh, nothing . . ."

"Surely you're not an anti-Semite."

"Oh, Ben, how could you say such a thing? It was just that I could see that the sufferings of the Jews were a personal matter to you!"

"The sufferings of the Negroes and any other persecuted people are a personal matter to me – the sufferings of the working man, especially. Though I suppose I naturally feel the sufferings of my own people most deeply."

"I can assure you, Ben, that I'm not anti-Semitic. I'm opposed to all forms of racial prejudice. I could easily be anti-Semitic, but I'm not. My father has business dealings with Benjamin Levy, the big furniture man, and reckons he's a miserable old skinflint. Says you've got to be careful of Jews."

"Surely a case of the kettle calling the pot black," Ben replied, instinctively going on to the defensive for a moment.

Mary did likewise: "My father is good to the poor of Carringbush . . ."

"Such charity is only conscience money . . ."

Seeing Mary looked a little resentful, Ben added: "But, of course, your father's right about Levy. My father came out to Australia with Levy's father. They both came from the East End of London where thousands of Jews are among the poverty-stricken slum-dwellers. My father remained poor – a working man, a hawker, a bottle-oh, factory hand, always on the breadline. But Levy, with a cunning developed in the jungle of the East End, became a millionaire. The fact that they were both Jews has little to do with the matter."

"I understand, Ben. You don't have to tell me." She laughed with forced gaiety. "Let's change the subject. And you'd better order more coffee. Yours is stone cold."

"Ugh, so it is. I won't bother with any more. We'd better be catching our last trams. But before we go: the Movement against War and Fascism is drawing in people from all walks of life who want to preserve peace – clergymen, writers, scientists, trade unionists. I want you to join and work for peace and against fascism. Would you, Mary?"

She would, she told him. She believed in the idea. Just because she was John West's daughter was no reason to believe she was on the side of the millionaires. For years she had been fed up with her useless existence. For years she had been on the side of the poor. She had been seeking a cause to give meaning to her life. This was it. What better cause than fighting against war?

As they stood waiting for Mary's tram, she was aware of a wave of elation sweeping over her. Here was a cause to give meaning to her life. Here, beside her, was a man she could really love. She associated the two together. She felt she would be capable of laying down her life for both.

Ben helped her on to the tram. The warm strength of his hand on her arm thrilled her.

"Good night, Mary," he said fondly. "I hope you'll never regret the decision you've made."

"I know I never will. Good night – Ben."

That night in bed, Mary lay awake thinking: thinking of the new meaning that life was taking on. In the play she had taken the part of a worker's daughter. She had lived that character and came out of the play – blatant and badly produced as it was – feeling she had a personal affinity with the poor.

And now she had a cause. She knew little about fascism, but the need to oppose war was obvious, something you could get your teeth into.

But mainly her thoughts were of Ben Worth. This was love! She abandoned herself to wild dreams of Ben. She would give over her love, her body, her very life to this man who stirred all her instincts, sexual, maternal and social. He was great in his selfless life. And he was lonely. He needed a woman to love him, to stand by him. Mary West would be that woman.

Mary threw herself into the work. She took a part-time job at the Movement's offices, refusing wages: she would be proud to donate her services, she told them. For the first time in years she felt she was a useful person. She did clerical work, helped arrange meetings and printing. She took part in organising the anti-war conference and preparing for the visit of Egon Kisch, the writer-delegate from Czechoslovakia. When Kisch arrived Mary was one of more than two hundred people who went aboard the ship on which Kisch was "interned," shouting: "We want Kisch! Kisch must land!"

Over the heads of the crowd she saw him. His bronzed, rugged face suggested toughness and emotional intensity, fierce sincerity and energy. The quizzical eyes glinted with humour; his gaze would penetrate the outer shell of things, she felt.

The crowd was ordered off the boat, but on the wharf they joined hundreds more to shout for Kisch. Mary had never been so excited, so thrilled by indignation.

Next day she was at the wharf again with hundreds of other people. The liner was to sail, taking Kisch to Sydney. As it began to move, Kisch appeared at the deck rail. All eyes turned upwards. Cheering began: even the sailors on the English warships, there for the Melbourne Centenary celebrations, joined in.

"We want Kisch!" the crowd shouted.

"I want you!" Kisch shouted back, raising his fist.

Then the crowd gasped. Kisch had climbed up on to the rail. "God!" someone said. "He's going to jump!"

Suddenly Kisch leapt. He hurtled twenty feet to the wharf, where he lay in a heap. Surely he had broken every bone in his body! Quickly he was surrounded by police and carried on board the ship amid angry shouts from the crowd. Kisch had broken one leg. The ship went on to Sydney with its injured prisoner.

Then the "Kisch must land" meeting.

Richard Lamb refused to allow the Kisch Defence Committee to book the Melbourne Stadium.

"We've also been refused the Exhibition Building," Ben Worth told Mary. "They're the only two buildings that will hold the crowd. Any good you seeing your father about the Stadium?"

Just as easy as that: see your father. Only her belief in Kisch and the anti-war movement enabled her to face the ordeal.

Then the Stadium meeting. Mary arrived early with the other organisers. Their spirits rose as a great stream of people began to enter.

Mary looked back on that meeting as the most dramatic she ever attended. After Maurice Blackwell had spoken, the Chairman rose and asked:

"Is Gerald Griffin in the audience?"

A tense silence. Surely Griffin, the New Zealand delegate to the Anti-War Congress, could not be here! He, too, had been refused permission to land. True, he was reported to have entered the country secretly and spoken in Sydney last night; but . . .

Suddenly a slight man dressed in a black overcoat and hat walked briskly to the platform.

"I am Gerald Griffin."

The newspaper men were astonished. The police were paralysed. The crowd roared its approval. Griffin made a brief speech and vanished unmolested.

Then, a little later, the unforgettable torchlight procession. Carrying lighted torches, thousands of people, Mary West among them, marched through the streets of Melbourne viewed by curious bystanders, to the Yarra Bank.

Kisch was to speak! He had appealed against being declared a prohibited immigrant. His appeal was upheld, but more trouble awaited him. Carried from the boat with his leg in plaster, he was arrested and taken to a prison hospital. Later he was given a language test in Gaelic (one of the few European languages he could not speak); but finally he was released.

At the Yarra Bank, thousands gathered in torchlight to hear Kisch. Mary would never forget that night! In the cool air by the

567

river they sang and heard the speakers. Kisch, on crutches, captured them with his dynamic presence.

"They say in the papers I speak broken English. Yes, my English is broken, my leg is broken, but my heart is not broken, because I am able to fulfil my mission and deliver my message of peace to the people of Australia."

The sentences hushed the tense excitement.

As a survivor of fascist prisons, he told them stories of courage against savage oppression in Germany. He told of the terrible penalties for political apathy. He gave the names of German humanitarians, who had remained passive until too late, who were in the hands of sadistic jailers. He warned that what happened in Germany could happen anywhere capitalism existed. He exhorted Australians not to take lightly the danger of fascism and war.

"Fight them from the first, my comrades, with all your strength!" he shouted.

Sitting beside Mary on the grass, Ben Worth looked from Kisch to her. Silhouetted in the uneven light of the torches, her beautiful face mirrored her deep emotions; her eyes were wide with fervour. He reached and touched her hand. She turned to him slowly, smiled and turned again towards the speaker.

When Kisch had finished, he raised his clenched fist. The torchlight heightened his dramatic, defiant pose.

For a long moment, Kisch stood thus. The crowd was awed and silent. Then some people wept, others sighed, others clapped and cheered. Mary West was one who wept – she wept for a strange joy she could not explain that surged through her.

This man fought in the war, Mary thought, later he learned what fascism meant in Hitler's jails; this man knows what the struggle is all about. While such men as this fought for humanity, the world could hope!

The unmentioned love between Mary and Ben Worth deepened. They saw each other every day, often had meals together, occasionally went to the theatre. Mary knew without being told that Ben returned her love, as all women know when they are loved: by unconscious considerateness, little words and deeds of sympathy and understanding, thrills at a smile or touch of a hand.

When at last Ben declared his love he did so simply and directly, as Mary would have expected. One Saturday night she invited him home. Father, of course, was at the Stadium; Mrs. Moran, full of old age, always went to bed after the evening meal, and Mother and Joe had gone to some church function. They sat in the music room. Mary played the piano. They sang, drank a little beer, and talked politics, literature, organisational problems in the anti-war movement; while all the time Mary wished they would talk of each other, of their love.

At last Ben sat beside her on the couch, buried his face in her titian hair and whispered: "Mary, I'm proud of you. You're a grand girl. I love you. I love you, Mary."

She tilted her head up to him, her red lips parted and moist, her eyes bright: "Oh, God, Ben; I love you, too. I'll always love you!"

They kissed. He held her terribly close, and her lips were sweet and softly resilient.

He held her head in his hands, looking at her searchingly.

"Mary, I know this is a stupid time to mention this – but you see, I'm a Communist. You know what demands that makes on my time. It's a life's work, a life's sacrifice. Sometimes it is dangerous to be a Communist. To share my life would be hazardous. Do you – would you join the Party, Mary; then together we can ..."

"Ben, I've learned a lot about politics lately, as you know, and I've come to believe in Communism. My life is full and useful now and I'm happy. I'll join the Party, if you think I'm worthy."

"Worthy, of course you're worthy."

"Oh, Ben, you can't imagine how you have changed my life. I have a cause to fight for; and someone with whom to fight it."

Suddenly Mary exclaimed: "My God, look at the time! I'm proud of you, Ben, but you mustn't be here when the family get in. My family, especially Father, are very annoyed with me for working in the anti-war movement. They believe all the Bolshevik bogey stories. If they found me kissing a Communist in the lounge, they would have me declared insane, or something. You really must go, darling."

They kissed lingeringly and Ben left. Mary removed the two empty beer bottles and glasses and went upstairs to bed just before Nellie West and Joe came in.

Later, Mary heard a car stop in front, then drive away. Soon afterwards her father entered the house. His girl friend had been to the Stadium with him again tonight.

Though glowing with love and happiness, Mary could not evade the thought that there was now no road back. She had burned her bridges. Soon the final showdown with her father must come.

John West was conscious of a growing dissatisfaction. He was being defied on all sides, and was becoming cantankerous about it.

He was worried, too, about Mary. What was she up to? All Frank Lammence could find out was that she spent a lot of her time working for this Movement against War and Fascism.

One Sunday afternoon he called her to the music room. He came straight to the point. She had deceived him into letting them have the Stadium, he told her. This organisation was Communist-inspired. He wouldn't tolerate his daughter working with the reds. She explained that the organisation was not Communist-inspired. He wouldn't tolerate his daughter working to fight against the danger of another world war, and to expose the menace of fascism which was in power in Germany, Italy and Japan.

"Mussolini is not a menace," he retorted. "This country would be better off if we had a man like him – a benevolent dictator. I have a pamphlet that shows all the good he has done in Abyssinia."

He took a pamphlet from his inside pocket and threw it on the table.

Mary ignored it and said: "Mussolini is bent on war. He has turned Italy into a vast prison at the bidding of the millionaires and the Vatican." The words were no sooner out than she realised her foolhardiness.

"So now you're against millionaires and your own Church! I have devoted my life to rise from poverty to become a million-aire. The Vatican is the home of your religion. Easy to see you *are* working with reds. But will you stop!"

"I won't stop, father."

"You will stop! You marched in the peace procession, but you didn't march in the Eucharistic procession; oh, no! You will do as I say, or get out of this house."

"All right, father, if that's your attitude, I'll leave im-mediately."

He faltered. He loved her. She must stay with him. Why did she choose to do things over which he had to cross her?

"You will stay here in your own home," he said lamely.

He stood, head bowed. When he looked up, she had gone.

John and Joe, too, were defying him. Joe passively sauntered through his work and treated his father's requests to settle down with smiling indifference. John was back in Sydney with the Catering Company. In Brisbane, he had placed the milk bar on a paying basis, but was showing no interest in his work. He had taken to drink. He smelt like a brewery whenever John West visited Sydney, and with Dutch courage up would act defiantly. He didn't want the job, he would say. His father was being robbed right and left by the two brothers who managed his Sydney affairs, he contended, but refused to give details. Well, he would stay on the job. Two could play the game of being pig-headed.

Nellie was still sending money to Marjorie and exchanging letters. John West searched the drawers in her bedroom and found letters. There was a scene. Mrs. Moran stepped in. "Would you like your daughter to starve?" she demanded. "Surely the least that can be done for the poor child is to write to her and send her a little money." The money sent came from the house-keeping allowance, she explained.

Again he faltered. No daughter of his should starve. He had been right about Andreas. Couldn't even afford to keep a wife and two children. Well, let them send a little money to Marjorie, but neither she nor the German would get a penny in his will!

Then there was the flare-up about Nellie's mother.

The old lady, though more than eighty and fading fast, had refused to lie down until she had stumbled on the stairs and broken her leg. The bone would not knit. She became bed-ridden. A nurse came to live in the house. John West decided she must be sent to a home.

Ever since Nellie's affair with Evans, Mrs. Moran had stood between him and the others, endeavouring to parry his every effort to exert his power. He had learned to harbour a secret resentment against her. He found himself welcoming this chance for revenge. Let her die in a pauper's home. He was not obliged to keep her and pay her medical fees. He had kept her for nearly twenty years. She was old. She was dying. Let her go to the

Hospice for the Dying – Caritas Christi – across the road.

She would be well looked after. They could all go to see her there, he told the family at dinner one night.

Nellie wept. Mary thumped the table with her fist. "This is a cruel, heartless thing to do," she said. She would look after Gran', if the cost of the nurse was worrying him. The Hospice was nothing more than a morgue, where poverty-stricken wretches went to die. Joe lost his evenness of temper and offered to "put in" from his wages to pay some of the medical costs.

John West was brusquely adamant. He had said the old woman must go and go she would.

Mrs. Moran was duly taken across the road in an ambulance. She went cheerfully enough, but the family soon realised that she was unhappy at the Hospice.

Years ago, John West had donated the Hospice for the Dying to the Church. It stood beside the Archbishop's residence. It was a grey, forbidding place. The purpose of establishing it, Archbishop Malone told John West at the time, was to supply a place where the aged and incurably sick could spend their last days in comfort. Non-Catholics would be taken as well as Catholics – perhaps some of them would turn to the Church and be converted. Later, John West made an arrangement with the Head Sister that burials from the Hospice would be, as far as possible, by an undertaking firm he controlled. By this means he planned to get back a good deal of the purchase price.

Outside of his household he was also being defied. Bill Brady had raised the old law in the House and had Cameron removed from the Exhibition grounds. This ended Cameron's boxing promotions, but, full of fight, he built a cycling board-track in a northern suburb and retained control over the sport.

And John West's move to get night trotting failed. In Perth and Adelaide, night trotting was "putting the gallopers out of business." If he could get a Bill through the House and conduct night trotting events at Apsom, trotting would begin to pay again and he would give the V.R.C. a jolt. But Davison procrastinated. Later on he would bring down a Bill.

Enraged, John West told Bennett to bring down a Private Member's Bill in the Upper House. The Bill was defeated by one vote, although £2,000 was distributed in bribes.

At the 1936 Labor Party Conference, Kelleher reluctantly

pushed Trumbleward forward against Carr, but when caucus met, Carr easily defeated Trumbleward for the Party leadership.

Dissatisfaction festered in John West like an abscess. He came to lean more on Vera Maguire for consolation. At the office, he lost his finesse and drive; at home, confronted with smouldering resentment because of his action against Mrs. Moran, he became more sullen and aggressive.

One day towards the end of 1936, Paddy Ryan walked into Frank Lammence's office.

"Well, me boy, Detective Ryan has at last got a clue in the case of the mysterious red-haired woman."

Paddy had been shadowing Mary West for months, not very diligently, for Paddy had his racehorse to look after and his drinking to do. The only man who didn't know Paddy drank was John West: Paddy always sucked "breath tablets" when his master was around.

Ryan handed Lammence a decorated invitation card. Lammence glanced at it and went to John West's office.

Lammence handed the card to John West. It was headed: *Welcome Home to Ralph Gibson*. It gave details of a luncheon with musical items. At the foot of the card were the words: *Organising Secretary: Miss Mary West*.

"Thought I'd better draw your attention to this, Mr. West. Gibson is a leading Communist; he's been in jail for political offences. This is obviously a Communist gathering. She – Miss West – must be a member of the party to be organising it."

John West did not reply. His eyes stared frighteningly. His nose dilated as he breathed heavily. Lammence walked out – he knew when to leave his employer alone.

That evening, Mary did not come home for the evening meal. John West, angry and determined to have a showdown, waited up for her. At eleven-thirty he was nodding off to sleep in an armchair in the breakfast-room when he heard her come in.

He opened the breakfast-room door, saw her begin to climb the staircase, and called quietly but tensely: "Mary, I want to speak to you."

She turned sharply. Seeing him silhouetted in the doorway, she said softly: "Oh, Father, I thought you'd be in bed. Is anything wrong?"

"Come in here," he said.

She followed him into the room. She looked a little tired, he thought, and her appearance was not as impeccable as usual. For a moment, she reminded him of his mother.

"What's the meaning of this card?"

She started, took it from him and studied it, as though pretending she had not seen it before. She did not reply.

"Well!" he demanded.

"Well, Father, I am only doing what I think is right."

"Are you a member of the Communist Party?"

She hesitated, then raised her head with a defiant toss.

"Yes, I am."

"No daughter of mine will be a Communist! You'll cease to associate with these people or get out of this house!"

"I'm sorry, Father, but I cannot go back on my principles."

"Principles!" he shouted, pounding the table. "You call it principles. They should all be put in jail! Nothing is sacred to them. They're trying to stir up trouble. They will destroy our way of life."

"Yes, and replace it with a decent way of life."

"Don't stand there arguing with me! You don't know what you're talking about! I've studied this thing up. If you read some of the Church pamphlets about Communism you wouldn't support it. Either give it up, or I'll cut you off with a shilling and throw you out of this house."

"You can't bribe me, Father. And you won't need to throw me out – I'll leave in the morning."

He was beside himself with rage. He raised his fist to strike her, but checked himself. His fist unclenched slowly. He lowered his head and stood in front of her – abject, defeated.

He saw there were tears in her eyes. She walked past him and out of the room. He slumped into the chair and sat there for nearly an hour before going upstairs to bed.

Neither of them slept.

In the morning, Mary did not get up until after her father had left the house. After breakfast, she packed a few clothes into a suitcase, preparatory to leaving the house. Her mother came into the room.

"What are you doing? What were you and your father quarrelling about last night?"

"Never mind the details, mother. You wouldn't understand. I've been ordered out of the house and I'm going. I'll keep in touch with you and the others."

Her mother sat on the bed and began to weep. "But you can't, Mary! Perhaps he doesn't really mean it. He can't do this. What have you been doing? Oh, if only Mother were here."

"Gran isn't here. And even if she were, this is one row she couldn't patch up." Mary went to her mother and put a sympathetic arm around her shoulder. "Please don't cry, Mother. This had to happen. We must face it. You see, I have become a Communist and Father is very annoyed."

"But, Mary ... a Communist! Oh, you must give it up. Oh God, as if I haven't suffered enough!"

Mary comforted her as best she could, closed the suitcase, and left the house with a heavy heart. At the gate she looked back. She had been happy here some of the time, in spite of everything. But things changed and life went on.

All day at the office John West could not concentrate. He speculated on whether Mary would leave the house or not. That evening, when Nellie, pale, red-eyed and sullen, gave him the news, his reaction was complicated. He was shocked and grieved, but determined now not to relent.

Next morning, on arriving at the office, he called Frank Lammence in and said: "I have ordered my daughter out of the house. She'll learn sense and give up all this dangerous nonsense. But she must be taught a lesson. I want you to locate where she is staying. She has very little money. And if she finds employment, let me know."

The weeks that followed were a nightmare for Mary West. The day she left home she had lunch with Ben Worth. He was upset and full of sympathy. He pressed her hand across the table.

"Well, Mary, it's a pity it had to happen, in a way. But it was inevitable. I have often worried about just this. I asked a lot of you when I recruited you to the movement. What will you do? Have you any money?"

"Very little, but I can work. I'll get a room and a job. Make a new woman of me." She smiled bravely, but he sensed that tears were close.

That night after a meeting they walked to the gardens and sat on the lawn.

Suddenly Ben said: "Mary, I've been thinking. They say two can live as cheaply as one. Perhaps . . ."

"Oh, Ben!"

"If there were only us to think of, I would go on my bended knees and plead with you to be my wife. But a Communist in my position has to consider many things before he gets married and perhaps has children. We'll see, darling. With the fighting in Spain and China one never knows what may happen. We'll wait a while and see."

"All right, Ben. Just so long as we're together, that's all I want."

She fell into his arms and wept. He consoled her fondly. Composing herself, she lay with her head on his lap.

"Lying here looking at the stars, Ben, one finds it hard to believe that people hate instead of loving. That there are people starving amid plenty. That men want war."

"Yes, Mary. But we, who know why, must not let humanity down. In us, millions of us, lies man's hope of ending all this poverty and strife. But while capitalism lasts it will be so. Sometimes at night I lay awake for hours, thinking of the Communists, Trade Unionists and Jews in Hitler's horror camps. The Jews, my own people, Mary." She felt his fingers bite into her arm. "And I say to myself, I must work harder to defeat fascism. If only I had the strength of ten. And the news from Spain! The fascists are sharpening their swords on the Spanish people. Sometimes I feel out of the main struggle here in Australia. I ask myself: are my people to be annihilated and the fascists triumph before I strike a direct blow?"

She looked up at him.

"Oh, Ben. Sometimes I'm scared. Oh, darling Ben, I love you."

They kissed. In the early hours of the morning, a chill came into the air and drove them indoors.

Mary West had obtained a comfortable room cheaply. She found it eerie and lonely at first.

Next day, she got a job in a bookshop. This, with her work as an ardent, active member of the Communist Party and Ben's friendship, kept her from loneliness and remorse.

Mary was a member of a unit of the Party in an industrial suburb. She found the meetings strange for a while; she couldn't get used to calling everyone Comrade, but when she did the word became precious to her. The other members were working men and women. They were a little awed with her for a while, and she with them. She idealised these – to her – rather uncouth people who were capable of such learning, such sacrifice and persistent effort.

Mary took part in many campaigns: Spanish relief, the move to boycott Japanese goods to help the Chinese people, work to help the unemployed. Best of all she liked pasting up posters and letter-boxing leaflets at nights – these jobs appealed to her sense of adventure.

A week or two after she left home, Mary called at the house one Saturday night, knowing her father would not be there. Her mother wept again. Joe suggested she should forget her "red bug" and come back.

She wrote to John in Sydney telling him the whole story. Her letter brought a staunch, heated reply. Their father was the most ruthless man he knew, John wrote. Good luck to you, Ginger. I wish I had your courage. Communism was against his religion. He was no Communist, just a broken-down boozer; but it was time the reds or someone else put a stop to crooked businessmen like Dad and his henchmen ruining the country. Soon he'd be down in Melbourne for a few days. He'd look her up. Mary wrote to Margo in Germany, then she went to see her Grandmother at the Hospice. The place smelt of decaying human flesh – of death.

A nun showed Mary where Mrs. Moran lay. "The old lady is sinking fast; you mustn't stay very long. She is not much longer for this world. She may die this very night, God rest her soul. I have sent for Mrs. West."

Mary found Mrs. Moran saying the rosary, fondling her beads with bony, crooked fingers. Mary was shocked at the decline in the old woman. She had shrivelled up. Her skin was webbed with folding wrinkles. Her nose was shiny, her cheeks, eyes and mouth sunken.

"Oh, it's you, Mary," Mrs. Moran said weakly. "What's this I hear about you leaving home? God, what troubles that white mansion has seen! I knew when I left something terrible would happen!" She began to ramble. "Forty years ago I met him first. Him and his tote shop. God have mercy on him, and my poor Nellie. I've loved you children like you were my flesh and blood. I tried to do everything for the best. God and His Holy Mother help us all. God forgive you, Mary. Communism, oh, Mary. But you're a good girl, I know. I know. Mother-o'-God, watch over her."

Mary held the wrinkled hands and sobbed. Just then Nellie West came in on tiptoe.

"Nellie, Nellie," the old woman said in a gurgling whisper. Nellie stooped over and kissed her mother on the brow.

"I have prayed for you all," Mrs. Moran said. "God help us all. The priest has been. I am ready to go."

Her poor, withered old body sagged. Her eyes turned up in her head.

A Sister came in and looked at her. Mrs. Moran was dead.

John West attended the funeral with the others. When the coffin was laid low and the priest had finished the service, he thought of the old woman with a tinge of regret and remorse. His mind turned back through the years to their first meeting at the Church bazaar – she had been tolerant then and cheerful, but . . . He shrugged his shoulders.

He had noticed Mary in the background before the service, weeping. He turned now to speak to her but she had gone.

On the day Mrs. Moran died, Frank Lammence had discovered Mary's whereabouts and place of employment. After the funeral, John West went to the city, interviewed the proprietor of the bookshop, and demanded that he dismiss Mary. "Give her the sack for her own good, but don't tell her I've been to see you." It was agreed.

During the next three months, John West did not see Mary; but each time Frank Lammence reported from Paddy Ryan that she had a new job, he contacted her employer and each time had her sacked. A few times his task was made easier by the fact that, unknown to Mary, he had an interest in the firm concerned.

When Mary lost her job at the bookshop she had been puzzled. She liked the work. She felt certain she had been giving satisfaction. Her employer was polite but definite. He gave her an excellent reference.

After she lost three more jobs, Ben Worth suggested that the sackings might be inspired. She agreed, and they soon obtained proof. She had been at a new job in an office only a few days when the manager called her in. He was very nice about it. He was quite satisfied with her work, but her father was a big share-holder in the company and had instructed him to dismiss her.

Whatever was she going to do?

"This settles it," Ben said. "I'm proposing."

They were married quietly in a registry office. Two party com-rades acted as witnesses. Mary shed a tear afterwards. None of her family present, no wedding dress, no music, no flowers. Only a cheap ring, and a certificate. But Ben was beside her, and that was the main thing.

There was a small reception. A few friends of Mary's – old and new, Catholic and Communist. A few of Ben's friends and his mother. Ben's mother, a faded Jewish woman, held Mary's hands in hers, wept, and said: "He is a strange, head-strong boy, but a good boy. I'm glad my Ben has married a nice girl."

John turned up just as the brief wedding ceremony finished. Mary was amazed at his physical decline. He was obviously drunk. His eyes were bloodshot and bagged, his skin pasty. At the reception he ate nothing, but drank much wine and spirits. He tried to be friendly with all, but only succeeded in making a fool of himself.

"I don't hold with commos," he told Mary for all to hear. "But I wish I – hic – had the gutsh to defy the old man, like you have."

"My father's a bastard!" he shouted, then collapsed on a couch and went to sleep.

The honeymoon in the hills was brief, but full of ecstasy. They were good together in every way. They matched each other's violent passion.

After the honeymoon, they settled happily into a small flat. Mary furnished it on time-payment – cheaply, but tastefully. On occasional evenings when neither had a meeting, they sometimes entertained friends, mainly sons and daughters of middle and upper class families who had joined the left wing movement. Mary sensed that they grated on Ben a little – Ben preferred the company of workers.

Ben had an old gramophone and a selection of good recordings gathered over the years with money spared by cutting down on smokes or even food; their happiest evenings were alone listening to music, to which they both responded deeply.

They had an extensive library of good books in which they also shared an interest. Mary was amazed that Ben, an uneducated working man, had such a deep knowledge and appreciation of music and literature.

Mary worshipped him. She admired his incisiveness, his courage, his dry sense of humour, his quiet self-confidence, his patient confidence in the inevitable triumph of Communism. His mental and physical strength bolstered her in moments of depression, gave her a feeling of security.

The events of the past year or two had left Mary bewildered, whenever she stopped to think of them; but now she could push them behind her. She would build a new life with Ben. She loved him; she would be worthy of him.

Physically, he excited her. She responded to his caresses with eager delight. She could tolerate frugal meals, lack of nice new clothes, being cut off from her home and family, so long as she had Ben.

She lived for Ben. Ben's life was devoted to the struggle. To her, Ben and the struggle were one.

She sensed, sometimes, that Ben was concerned lest what he termed her "bourgeois background" would lead her to errors. Sometimes he chided her good-naturedly about it, but she had soon convinced him she was "solid", as he termed it.

Mary was given a full-time job with the anti-war movement. She received three pounds a week, which, added to Ben's two pounds as an organiser for the Communist Party, enabled them to live in reasonable comfort.

Mary noticed that Ben was intensely aroused by the Spanish fighting; he viewed it as a test of strength between the fascists and the forces of freedom.

"The fascists are testing their claws and fangs," he told Mary. "If they win in Spain they will eventually tackle the Soviet Union. Unless Franco is defeated another world war is inevitable. Japan will tackle Australia. The movement may be crippled for many years, everywhere in the world. Our comrades will die; Australia will be invaded; the Jewish people will be exterminated."

Mary held similar views, but not so strongly. Ben's preoccupation with Spain worried her at times. He scanned the papers daily and talked excitedly about the news of the fighting. At meetings, his speeches were more fiery and emotional when he spoke on the Spanish conflict. Once when a comrade returned from a tour of Spain, Ben invited him to the flat and talked until the early hours. Ben asked question after question while Mary studied him, troubled by a vague fear.

The visitor had brought back anonymous poems and songs writtem by Republican fighters. Ben and Mary endeavoured to learn the songs. They drank wine and sang. One song about a German Jewish Communist who had been killed gripped Ben's imagination. He learned it quickly. In bed, after their friend had left, Ben sang the song again, loudly, with pathos. The way he sang the last verse frightened Mary:

> *With heart and hand I pledge you,*
> *While I load my gun again;*
> *You never will be forgotten,*
> *Nor the enemy forgiven.*
> *Hans Beimler, our Commissar.*
> *Hans Beimler, our Commissar.*

In the weeks that followed, Ben became restless. Observing him, Mary realised it was as if every wound inflicted on a Republican soldier was inflicted on him. In spirit he cheered every victory – mourned every defeat. His heart and soul were in Spain. Mary came to view the Spanish conflict almost as a rival for his affections. She could see, too, that he was deeply conscious of the threat to the Jewish people from fascism.

Then one evening at tea, Ben was more than usually quiet. Normally a good eater, he picked at his food. He seemed far away – he didn't answer her when she spoke sometimes.

"Penny for them, Ben. What's the matter?"

"I don't know how I'm going to tell you, Mary. It'll be a shock. For the first time in my life, I have made a big decision without being sure of myself."

"Ben, what is it? What have you done?"

He reached across the table and held her hand. "I've joined the International Brigade. I'm going to Spain. The boat leaves next week."

Though for months she had been pushing the possibility out

of her mind, the news shocked her. Her body stiffened, tears filled her eyes and she bit her lip. Visions of her new happy world collapsing filled her with terror.

"Oh no, Ben! You can't leave me! You're all I have!" She gripped his hand, her long finger nails digging into his flesh. "You mustn't go, Ben. It isn't fair!"

"Mary," he said softly, "you must be brave. In times like these we mustn't think only of ourselves. Oh, Mary, I don't want to leave you. I have the most wonderful wife in the world, and I'm happy; but it would be selfish for me to let that stop me."

They travelled home on the tram in silence.

As soon as he had closed the door of the flat behind them, he took her in his arms. He showered her with kisses. She wept and he kissed her wet eyes.

"Oh, Mary, my darling! I will come back; but I must go. You have no idea how I've been called to Spain. I can resist no longer!"

They clung to each other. A variety of conflicting reactions swarmed through Mary's mind; uppermost came resentment and self-pity cloaked in various disguises.

They sat on the bed, holding hands. She expressed her thoughts in a distraught manner: "The party shouldn't let you go, Ben, you are too valuable here. Anyway, if you really loved me, you wouldn't go and leave me all alone."

He held her chin in his fingers and thumb and looked into her eyes. "You must never doubt that I love you, Mary. You are the most beautiful, wonderful person I have known; but we are involved in a life and death struggle. I want to be in the front line. I have discussed it with the party and they finally agreed."

Her anguish prevented any other consideration than stopping him from going: "But it's wrong, Ben! The Spanish workers must fight their own battles, we can help them in other ways, but we shouldn't send soldiers. Besides, the fighting will be all over when you get there. Anyway, why should you, a Jew, help the Spaniards, who have in the past tortured your people?"

"You don't know what you're saying, Mary. The Spanish workers did not torture my people. Today they are fighting the fascists, the gangster anti-Semites. Oh, darling, please understand. I didn't discuss my decision with you beforehand, because I feared you might take it like this."

He knelt in front of her and held her hands on her lap. "Mary, darling, you mustn't make it more difficult for me – please don't. As for the Spanish workers fighting their own fight – they are, and magnificently, but this is not a purely Spanish fight. The fate of the international working class is being decided in Spain – the Spanish war is very much the business of workers of all countries. Only a strong International Brigade can turn the scales in our favour." He spoke persuasively, almost pleadingly. "Mary, darling, I know there are two sides to the question of my going, but I've made up my mind. Oh, darling, be brave. We shall beat them. I'll come back all right; then we can begin again."

He stood up and began to pace the floor, talking with intense feeling. "The millionaires of England and America are helping to finance the fascist countries' war preparations. The bestial hirelings of Franco, Hitler and Mussolini have the equipment, they have been trained like robots, but they have no morale – they will beat in vain against the wall that the international working class will erect against them in Spain, Chamberlain's blockade can't keep us out. Just let me get at grips with these beasts. I know how to handle a rifle. I'll soon learn to handle more complicated weapons."

He flexed his muscular frame and stood, legs apart, alert as if about to go into a bayonet charge.

Watching him, Mary realised that only now did she know the depth of her husband's hatred of fascism and devotion to Communism. Only now could she see that he had reached the stage where only physical contact with the enemy could assuage his hatred. This was the man she had married acting typically.

"I can lead men. I'll study military tactics and strategy. I'll lead a battalion into battle against the fascist bastards . . ." Ben was saying.

He was the man she loved – for better or worse. In a more peaceful age they could have been blissfully happy; they could continue to be happy in this age only if she matched his fierce courage and devotion. Suddenly she rose, rushed to him, and flung her arms around him.

"Oh, Ben," she said, "take no notice of anything I've said. I love you and I'll be proud to have my husband a soldier in the International Brigade."

"This is *my* Mary speaking. We won't take long to drive them out of Spain, then I'll come back to carry on the fight here, with you. From then on we'll be together – always together."

When Paddy Ryan discovered that Mary was married, he reported to Frank Lammence.

"Well, me boy, Detective Ryan will get promotion and a rise in pay. J.W. will be mighty pleased to hear that his daughter was married yesterday to a commo in a registry office. And they tell me the bridegroom is a 'five-to-two,' a member of the ancient Jewish faith."

John West was further enraged when he heard the news. This was the last straw. He told no one. While he had been able to prevent Mary from holding a job, he had felt like a cat playing with a mouse: he was teaching her a lesson; he would eventually force her to give up her silly, dangerous ideas and come running back. But now he knew he could not prevail upon the Movement against War and Fascism to dismiss Mary. She had defied him and he could do nothing about it. At least, he could cut her out of his will. He saw his lawyers and did so, but it gave him little satisfaction: he wished to force Mary to do his bidding, but also he loved her, as far as he was capable of loving anyone, and wanted her to come home and be happy. The house was lonely without her. This contradiction in his attitude left him quite unable to solve the problem. To approach Mary in an attempt at reconciliation was out of the question – he could never admit he was wrong.

The "yellow press" did not help when it reported: *Titian-haired beauty, Mary West, daughter of millionaire Jack West, has become a commo. They saw her father's face is redder than Mary's hair and politics.*

Nellie occasionally raised the subject, but he brusquely rebuffed her pleas to let bygones be bygones. Mary had deserted her religion and, worse still, become a Communist, he said; until she came to her senses she must be treated as an outcast. Nellie hated, or perhaps more truly, feared Communists; she believed all that the Church and the daily papers said about them. She agreed Mary had acted badly.

His son John, home from Sydney on holidays, made an emotional plea for Mary. His father sternly rebuked him.

"Don't try to tell me my business. She must be taught a lesson. And unless you cut out drinking and attend to your work you'll be put out without a penny as well."

Feeling the need to tell someone his true feelings, John West chose Vera Maguire. She was sympathetic, but offended him by saying she admired Mary's courage. Vera suggested he should compromise. Young people often got the red bug. Mary would get over it if he was reasonable. But John West couldn't bring himself to compromise. At times, fires of self-recrimination flared up in him, but he promptly quelled them. Mary was at fault. He had acted only in her interests and she had defied him. Now that she had married this Communist and become so deeply involved with these people as to work for them full time, it seemed to him that little could be done except punish her for her folly and disobedience.

One day he saw her in the street. She was about to board a tram alone. She appeared to him to be thinner and her clothes much shabbier. What a fool she was! For a fleeting moment, a pall of sadness enveloped his spirit. Should he approach her, speak kindly to her? He stood on the footpath undecided, until the tram moved off, Mary with it.

That afternoon, Paddy Ryan reported that Mary's husband had gone to Spain. Just like the commos! He had ruined her life, John West thought, then deserted her. That night he lay awake, pondering the problem. Now was his chance. He would send a message to her asking her to come and see him.

After Ben Worth departed for Spain, Mary's life lost its zest and charm. Though her new friends were very kind, she became desperately lonely and depressed. She went about her work without enthusiasm. She tried hard to play the rôle of a hero's wife struggling on while her husband went to fight the foe, but alone in the flat at night she wept for Ben and her body ached for his caresses.

One day Paddy Ryan accosted her in the street outside the office and gave her a note from her father. *It would be to your advantage to call and see me*, the note read.

"Is there any answer, Miss?" Ryan asked.

In her loneliness, she was tempted.

After a moment's indecision, she raised her chin defiantly and said: "Yes, there is a reply. Tell Father – tell Mr. West I have nothing to discuss with him."

As Ryan walked away, she called after him: "And I'd ask you to stop spying on me."

She received a letter from Margo, a strange letter, written as if the writer were afraid to record her deepest feelings on any subject, yet expressing sympathy, love, loneliness; and a letter from Ben full of love for her and enthusiasm for his self-imposed task. She shed tears over it, carries it everywhere with her, and slept with it under her pillow at night. Other letters came; she treasured them similarly. He had arrived in England, and said he expected to go to Spain, via France, within a few days.

A premonition that Ben would be killed began to haunt her, after she read a poem by William Morris, in which the lines recurred:

> Hear a word, a word in season, for the time is
>   drawing nigh,
> When the cause shall call upon us, some to live and
>   some to die.

Somehow, the words would not leave her mind. *Some to live and some to die!*

The next news she received was the announcement of Ben's death. He had been killed in action near Madrid.

Something of Mary died with him and lay buried in the blood-stained city of sorrow. Her friends could not quiet her grief or ease her dreadful hopelessness. Neither they nor her own reason could convince her spirit that she had anything to live for. She believed in Communism and the campaign for peace; but alone, without Ben, nothing, it seemed, could suffice to make life seem worth living. People said that Ben would have liked her to be brave and carry on the fight. She knew this was so, but she could not yet face the struggle without Ben. The thought kept insisting: Why should her love have been smashed for an ideal?

She lost all interest in her work, in life itself. She ate little. She neglected her clothes. She twisted her hair carelessly into a bun at the back. Her skin became rough. She wore no make-up. The idea of going away – perhaps to England – occurred to her. Trouble was, she had no money. She knew no one to whom she could turn for money. But somehow she must get away from scenes and people that tortured her with memories of Ben, yet could offer her no consolation.

A desperate solution came to her.

One evening she went to a phone box and rang her father's home number.

Joe's voice answered.

"Is Mr. West, senior, there?" she asked coldly. Her heart was thumping. She was trembling.

"Is that you, Ginger?" Joe answered cheerfully. "Well, well. The prodigal returns. Bury the hatchet, Ginger. This place is a morgue without you. I think he'll be reasonable."

"I want to speak to Father," she answered sharply.

Her father came to the phone.

"Hullo," he said.

"I want to see you, Father. Could I call this evening?"

"Yes."

"I'll be there in half an hour."

John West waited for her in the reception room. He was nervous, excited. He could not analyse his feelings. She was coming back. He was pleased he had beaten her and also because, he believed, soon her bright presence would grace this melancholy house.

He answered the door when she came and took her to the music room. When he switched on the light and saw her clearly, he was shocked at her drab appearance and pale cheeks. She wore a brown costume and shoes and a light green jumper; she carried an old brown handbag. She had lost weight. She was ill!

He drew up a chair for her. She sat down and he sat opposite her behind the table. She sat erect and very tense. Proud, he thought; she doesn't like to admit I've beaten her.

To him, her very presence in the room seemed to revive its pleasant atmosphere. She and Marjorie had made this room their very own, and brought to it laughter, music and friendliness. Marjorie was gone, it seemed forever; but Mary was coming back to bring with her the old gaiety, her old friends, and his pride in her beauty.

"What do you want?" he asked, and was shocked at his stern tone.

"I want to go to England, and I want a thouand pounds to take me there," she answered, holding her head high.

587

He straightened and his scowl deepened.

"Don't be ridiculous!"

"I'm not being ridiculous, Father. I need a thousand pounds and you're going to give it to me."

"I'm going to do nothing of the kind! You have a cheek, coming here demanding money, after all you have done."

"Well, I'm demanding money, father, and I'm going to get it."

Rage got the better of John West. He clenched his fist and thumped the table.

"I won't tolerate you talking like this. I suppose your commo friends have sent you here to get money by a trick. Well, you won't get it! And if this is all you have to say, you can get out and stay out!"

He noticed that she was on the verge of tears and biting her lip.

She braced herself. "Don't worry, Father, I will get out, and stay out. But you'll give me a cheque for a thousand pounds first."

"Oh, will I?" He rose to his feet and pointed to the door. "Get out! You'll get no money from me, now or ever. I have already cut you out of my will."

She took a piece of foolscap paper from her handbag and, rising, confronted him. She handed him the paper.

"Read this! Then write out a cheque," she said in a voice low and tremulous, but bitterly determined.

He took the paper. His eyes skimmed over it. "What does all this mean?" he demanded.

"It means that I'm worth the best part of two hundred and ten thousand pounds in shares in some of your companies."

"Where did you get this list?"

"I got it from the Titles Office. I paid to make a search of share lists of companies in which I knew you were interested."

He was abashed.

Mary continued: "For years you have got me to sign forms which you covered with blotting paper. I guessed they were to put shares in my name to save taxation. I'll claim the lot, unless you make me out a cheque for a thousand pounds."

"But you couldn't."

He sat down again, thinking quickly. The list was by no means complete, but it was accurate, Mary could claim the best part of half a million if she searched further.

"You wouldn't have a leg to stand on," he said lamely.

"Wouldn't I? I've had expert advice."

"Who from?"

"From Mr. Cory. He said I have every legal right to the shares."

"Oh, he did, did he?"

He sat confused and hesitant. This was a lot of money! She might get away with it! Anyway, he didn't really want to fight with her.

"Now listen, Mary. Sit down and we'll talk this over. Why should we wrangle over a thousand pounds? Why, I'd give you all those shares. I intended you to have them all along if you hadn't run away to the commos."

"I'm not really interested in the shares. I want a thousand pounds."

"Be reasonable, girl! I'll tell you what. You come back home and give up all this political nonsense and I'll give you two thousand pounds to do what you like with, and . . . and I'll leave these shares in your name. When I die you can have them and the profits from them."

"I'm not interested, Father. And I'm not coming back home."

"Why are you doing this?"

"Because I'm hard and ruthless. Because I'm your daughter!"

"Well, what are you going to do now your Jew-commo husband has deserted you and left you to starve?"

"My husband is dead. He was killed in Spain fighting against Hitler and your famous Mussolini. I am proud to have been his wife. He died for humanity."

"Serve him right. And the sooner a few thousand more commos are killed off the better," John West snarled.

Mary lunged forward. Her little fist struck him a stinging blow in the face. She stepped back, as pale as death.

"I'll trouble you to write out the cheque, or I'll claim those shares in the morning," she said deliberately.

He fingered his cheek gingerly. "Just what I'd expect from a guttersnipe commo!"

He took a fountain pen and a cheque book from his pocket and wrote with a savage hand. He ripped the cheque out and handed it to her.

"Here," he said. "Now get out! And if ever you come back to this country I'll hound you out again."

"Don't worry, I shan't come back."

His eyes followed her until she melted into the gloom of the hallway.

He stood leaning on the table. What had he said? What had he done? Why had she done this thing to him?

Mary returned to her lonely flat. She picked up Ben's photo and looked at it. What would you think of your Mary now?

She went to bed but could not sleep. The whole of her adult life seemed to pass before her mind's eye. She had been tossed by the storms of time and thrown up on the beach of despair. Oh Ben, darling, why did you leave me all alone? I will try hard to continue the fight, darling; but it's going to be hard, terribly hard!

She booked her passage – the cheapest steerage – and announced at the office and the party branch that she was going to England. She would contact the movement there. Everyone was extremely nice. They understood, they said. Understood! God, could they or anyone else ever understand what life had done to her?

She visited her mother one morning at the house. Her mother wept and implored her to stay, to come back to the Church and to her home.

"It's no use, Mother, I've made up my mind. I will write. And perhaps some day I'll come back."

"God forgive me for saying it," her mother said, "but your father has a lot to answer for. He will burn in hell."

Mary was startled at the hatred concentrated in her mother's words. "Poor mother, how you have suffered!"

They wept, they kissed, then parted. On her way out she met Joe at the gate. She told him she was going to England.

Joe exclaimed: "Don't do it, Ginger; don't go!"

Throughout Mary's battle with her father, Joe had been casual, a little amused; but now Mary could see he was upset.

"Ginger – Mary – don't. By Christ, our father has a lot to answer for!"

He kissed her tenderly. "Think it over. At least, see me before you go."

On the brow of the hill, Mary paused on the road and looked

back at the big white mansion. What sorrow and sinister things it had seen; yet at times what happiness some of its members had managed to win! The tragic house of John West!

Next day she went to Sydney by plane to see John. He was not at his office. They brought him from a hotel. He was drunk. They went and had coffee, which steadied him a little. She told him the story.

"God, Ginger," he exclaimed. "Our father is the most ruthless man in the world! He has scattered us like straws in the wind."

When Mary's sailing time came, she was farewelled by a small group of friends from the movement. They exhorted her to keep up the good work in England, to write and to come back soon.

On board the ship, she was told that she had been shifted from steerage to one of the best cabins up on deck. Her father had arranged it.

Why had he done it? Mary asked herself. Because somewhere deep in his twisted soul was love for her? Or because he didn't want it known that a daughter of his travelled among the common herd in the steerage?

Even her father could not have answered her question.

After Mary had gone that night, John West sat in the music room, prey to a convulsive clash of emotion, a violent shake-up of the soul. He had been proud of her, he had loved her, he had been generous to her – why had she treated him so callously? Again and again the question arose in his mind. Had he been too hard? No, he told himself, at last; Mary was in the wrong. The commos had corrupted her.

By the time he dragged himself upstairs to bed he was smarting under a feeling of enraged frustration: she had defied him and succeeded, she had bluffed him into giving her a way out of her dilemma.

Arriving at the office in the morning, he rang Patrick Cory and upbraided him for advising his daughter that she had a legal right to the shares. Cory said he hadn't really believed she meant to claim them. Patrick Cory was, as usual, undeterred by John West's rage: "I admire her pluck, anyway," he said.

John West told Pat Cory, Richard Lamb and Frank Lammence that he had sent Mary overseas until she "got some sense into her head".

All morning, John West hovered on the verge of stopping payment of the cheque; but, somehow, he could not bring himself to phone the bank. In the afternoon, he had Frank Lammence ring all the shipping companies to discover if and when she was sailing. When he learned the details, John West found himself impelled to change Mary's booking.

His conflicting reactions to Mary's departure brooded over him for weeks until one evening Paddy Kelleher and Bill Brady arrived with trouble that was to divert his attention.

When John West ushered them into the reception room, Kelleher flourished a newspaper under his nose.

"Aaarrr, Mr. W-W-West. Have you, aaarrr . . ." Kelleher was clearly agitated and, as usual, his stammer worsened as a consequence.

Brady intervened: "TRUTH carries a story on the Milk Bill. There'll be a terrific scandal."

John West took the paper.

IF MONEY TALKS, TRUTH WILL TALK, the front page headlines brazenly declared. John West sat down and began reading.

The article inferred that money had been talking in the Victorian Parliament for too long. It had been openly stated that theatre interests, sporting interests, liquor interests, money-lending, and other big business interests had made money talk, the paper contended. Now TRUTH would talk about rumours that certain politicians had accepted bribes to oppose the passage of the Milk Supply Bill.

"Well," said John West, looking up, "how did they get on to this?"

"Aaarrr . . ." Kelleher began.

"The commo paper, the SENTINEL, has been dropping hints for weeks," Brady interposed, "but nobody takes any notice of those dirty animals. I think Ned Horan told the TRUTH."

"Why should Horan tell them?"

"Because a Labor candidate is to oppose him at the next elections. He's bloody savage – knows he'll lose his seat."

"I said Horan was no to be opposed! He saw me about it." John West turned to Kelleher. "I asked you to fix it up."

"Aaarrr, yes, Mr. W-W-West,' Kelleher replied. "But I couldn't. Carr is determined to have him opposed. Aaarrr, he says, the p-p-party must endeavour to rule without the aaarrr, Country Party, m-m-must win seats from the aaarrr, Country Party.''

''Never mind what Carr says, I say that Horan mustn't be opposed.''

''Aaarrr, I did my best, but the, aaarrr, majority of the Executive and branches support Carr on this issue – and really – they're right, you know. Anyway, I, aaarrr, must do my job, or I w-won't keep it.''

John West glared at Kelleher distrustfully. Kelleher rarely came near him lately. Kelleher was secretly keeping a foot in all camps, often co-operating with Carr.

''So you must do your job, whatever I want; but you come running to me when there's trouble.''

Brady was obviously in a complete funk. ''But this is very serious. Jack. Davison is talking about a bloody Royal Commission.''

''Davison is!'' John West said testily. ''We'll see about that!''

He walked into the hall, switched on the light, went to the phone and spoke to Davison.

''What's this I hear about a Royal Commission over this TRUTH article?''

''What else can I do? There are some pointed rumours going about.''

''I told you not to go on with the Milk Bill in the first place.''

''I had to. I'm supposed to represent the farmers, including the cow cockies, you know. We've been over all this before, Mr. West. This could bring the Government down. The U.A.P. is demanding an inquiry. I've made up my mind to appoint a Royal Commission into this – if I don't there might be trouble over a lot of other things. I'm sorry, Mr. West. Your boys should be more careful. Anyway, I'll see to it that your name is not mentioned. And you know what these Royal Commissions are; nothing ever comes of them.''

John West then rang Ned Horan.

''Did you give this story to TRUTH?'' he demanded, without preliminaries.

Horan's voice came over flustered.

''No – no, not me, Mr. West. I'll tell yer for why: I wouldn't do such a thing, you know that.''

"Oh, wouldn't you?" John West replied, and slammed down the receiver.

Back in the reception room he said: "Horan did it. He didn't admit it, but he did it all right. Put him out. Put the boots right into him at the elections."

"Aaarrr . . ." Kelleher began.

"Don't worry, Jack," Brady intervened venomously. "We'll put the boots right into the lanky bastard, but what's going to happen to us?"

"No doubt you two and Trumbleward, at least, got your share of the Milk Distributor's fighting fund."

"Aaarrr. I only got a b-b-bloody hundred, aaarrr, quid out of it. W-w-wish to C-C-Christ I'd left it alone."

Brady did not commit himself. He was trusting no one with an admission that he had received two hundred pounds to vote against the Bill.

John West felt tired. "Who else is in it?"

Brady averted his gaze. He was here to get protection, not to admit complicity.

"Aaarrr, T-Tom. T-Tom . . ."

"Trumbleward," John West prompted him. "Wouldn't be a show without Punch. Who else?"

"Aaarrr, that's all."

John West sighed: "All right. I suppose I'll have to be the mug and save your bacon. Better sleep on it. I'll contact you to-morrow."

This was a serious situation, John West thought, when they had gone. Never before had he felt less like fighting a difficult defensive battle. He had contributed £200 when the Milk Distributors' Society decided to collect a fund to fight the Milk Supply Bill, but took little interest in developments. Apparently they had used the fund, more than a thousand pounds in all, mainly to bribe politicians, and, because of his lack of attention, they had bribed men who would have done as he told them, anyway.

Though he usually did John West's bidding. Davison had introduced the Milk Supply Bill. The main provisions were to raise the wholesale price paid to the farmers without raising the retail price, to prevent adulteration and watering of milk, and to break the monopoly tendency in the sale of dairies and transfer of licences.

594

As in all other industries, retail milk distribution was monopolised, and ownership was concentrated mainly in the hands of a few powerful firms. Davison soon discovered that, secretly, John West was a powerful owner of dairies, but he refused the latter's request to withdraw the Bill.

A most astute politician, Davison calculated that the Bill would get him the support of farmers and housewives, while the recent wage increases to milk carters would please the workers. Davison needed support. He was hard-pressed to retain Labor's co-operation. This Bill would please Labor voters.

Slumped in his chair, John West pondered over the matter until nearly eleven o'clock. He felt tired and very old. Where were his dreams of power now?

He found himself taking stock of his position. His household had fallen to pieces. He could not deny that his political power was shrinking, even in Victoria. In the Trade Union Movement, the Communists were winning election after election, and were even threatening the position of old Ron Lassiter, his one remaining direct nominee, as secretary of the Builders' Laborers Union. John West held that vague fear and hatred of the Communists common to millionaires, but he had found that power in the Trade Union Movement was of no use in his plan, so he did not raise a hand to intervene. Only in the Carringbush and Ralstone Councils did he hold complete power, and since his racecourses in those areas had been closed, the power was of little real value.

He was being defied right and left, and he felt that each time he failed to take effective reprisals he laid himself open to further defiance. True he was making money. He was worth nearly five million pounds. But he wanted more than money: the lust for power had not waned in him. He would never tire of pursuing it.

As before, when he fell victim to occasional feelings of remorse and reverie, he quelled them with renewed determination to fight on.

CHAPTER THIRTEEN

Wealth keeps out only one of life's evils, and that is poverty.

DR. SAMUEL JOHNSON

As John West walked up the steps of the Catholic Hospital his mind was as much absorbed in the threat of war as in the Milk Supply Royal Commission. He felt certain that war would break out over Poland; he could not sort out his reactions to the prospect. His thoughts turned to the turbulent years of the first world war and could find no parallel: this war would be different somehow, he thought; and he had no enthusiasm for it, just a vague regret that it had to be.

"You wish to see Mr. Trumbleward, Mr. West?" the voice of a bustling, plump sister interrupted his thoughts.

"Yes, sister. How is he?" John West replied, a little embarrassed at being recognised.

"Oh, there's nothing much wrong with him. Not as young as he was. Old ticker a little weak."

The day before, embarrassed by cross-examination at the Royal Commission, Trumbleward had collapsed, clutching his hands over his heart. "Don't let my wife go to the wash-tub," he had exclaimed as he was carried out. Tom sometimes suffered from palpitations of the heart, and now found them convenient to avoid being convicted by his own words.

Ushered to Trumbleward's bedside in a private ward, John West found him drinking a glass of his favourite white wine.

"What do you think you're doing?" John West asked.

Trumbleward smiled, raised his glass as if to some secret toast, and drained it with a flourish.

"Just having an appetiser, Jack."

Ignoring him, John West went to the locker beside the bed and took out a wine bottle. "Hm, it's nearly empty. You can finish it, but no more."

A nurse approached with a tray containing a piping hot meal.

"I'm sorry, sister," John West intervened. "Mr. Trumbleward says he is too ill to eat."

She hesitated unbelievingly, then walked out.

"Break it down, Jack. I'm not sick, you know that," Trumbleward replied with the air of a chastised schoolboy.

"You're not sick, but you will be if they send a doctor from the Commission to examine you. You're going to eat little or nothing – then you'll be sick from lack of food. You don't seem to realise the danger you're in. You'll go to jail unless you think up a better story than the one you were telling when you collapsed."

With an abject expression, Trumbleward placed his glass on the top of the locker and lay with his hands folded on the bedclothes in front of him. Years under the thumb of John West had reduced him to a docile, cynical fool. He did John West's bidding, abandoning all his earlier principles and ideals on the pretext that it was no use trying to help the workers, who were a helpless rabble. He was little active in party affairs and visited his electorate only at election time to tell small meetings of workers of the glories of Socialism to be achieved in some unspecified time in the distant future.

"You're not going back into the box until they've heard Kelleher and Brady. I'll see the lawyers about some way out," John West continued.

"How did you get on with Archbishop Malone?"

"He said that, although the Judge is a Catholic, he had no influence over him. Says the Judge's father was one of the Catholic laymen who branded him a traitor during the anticonscription campaign."

"Ah, the anti-conscription campaign!" Trumbleward said rapturously. "There was a fight. I remember one night . . ."

He was about to embark on one of his stories of the good old days when the workers would fight, with which he sought to excuse his own failure and inactivity, but John West interrupted brusquely:

"You'd better forget anti-conscription. We have another war coming. I won't tolerate you opposing conscription this time. The Archbishop has sent a Jesuit priest to see the Judge – he's a friend of his, but Malone reckons you can expect little quarter unless you put up a good case for yourself – that may win the day."

597

"What's that, Jack? I knew you'd fix things up."

"I'm going to see young Watty, and get him to take the blame. I think he'll do the right thing at a price."

John West summoned Jim Watty to his office next morning. Watty was secretary of the Milk Distributors' Association, and had paid out the bribes that caused the Royal Commission to be established.

Watty was a tall, neatly dressed young man with a handsome but weak face. He had been secretary of the Food Preservers' Union until he went over to the direct service of the employers in the milk industry.

His usual swaggering confidence was absent as he placed his hat on the table and faced John West.

"How do you think this inquiry is going?" John West asked, following his time-honoured method of beginning with a question.

Watty's reply was mirrored in his downcast demeanour. "No good, Mr. West," he said. "Someone's going to go to jail, the way things are going."

"No one will go to jail if you do as I ask. How would you like to earn five hundred pounds?"

"Always on the market to make money, Mr. West. Depends on what you want done."

"I want you to switch your evidence. I want you to go into the box and deny that you gave this bloke Gilbert the money to give Trumbleward and the others."

"But I've already said I gave him the money, but didn't know what he did with it. If someone's going to jail, it's not going to be me!"

"You won't go to jail. If they send you to trial, I'll square the jury. Anyway, Royal Commissions never send anyone to jail."

John West then repeated David Garside's theory on Royal Commissions and frustration of the law by the rich. This seemed to give Watty little satisfaction. He had great faith in the power of John West, but it took half an hour of argument and cajolery, and finally £1,000 in notes to convince him that he should become a scapegoat for the three politicians.

John West then carefully outlined what he wanted him to say: he would say there was a secret fund, that he had approached Trumbleward and Kelleher, but they had refused to help,

598

suggesting he should approach the Country Party or U.A.P.

Having reached agreement, they fell to discussing a topic on which the whole world had become one great debating society. Would there be war? Would England declare war on Germany over Poland? Watty expressed the opinion that Chamberlain and Hitler would not go to war except together against Russia. England had built Germany up to fight Russia. Chamberlain had let Hitler have Austria and Czechoslovakia, because Hitler was moving east towards Russia. Chamberlain would let him have Poland for the same reason. John West was not so sure. If England believed Hitler would fight only Russia, then England was mistaken. You couldn't trust the Germans. Hitler had to be fought and beaten eventually; if they didn't make a stand soon, he would eventually attack England. Finally, they agreed that the best possible result would be for Germany and Russia to fight each other to a standstill.

On the following Sunday, John listened with the rest of the English-speaking world to Chamberlain's announcement that a state of war existed between England and Germany.

The news found John West unresponsive, calm. The patriotic fervour and excitement with which he had greeted the outbreak of the 1914–18 war were absent; he was too old for heroics, and the events which led up to this war were far too complex for him to fathom. He still hated Germans because of their alleged atrocities in the "war to end war," and because a German had led his daughter to defy him; but he sensed that Hitler represented interests similar to his own, and he hated and feared Soviet Russia.

But war fever slowly crept over him: he talked and speculated about events and pored over the papers.

The war overshadowed the Royal Commission in the Victorian press and in John West's mind.

Watty gave evidence as instructed. He threw the inquiry into confusion. The Counsel assisting the Commissioner exclaimed: "Mr. Watty, are you offering yourself to a holocaust? Are you being a martyr to help other people?" Watty answered shakily: "No, I am not."

The Commission continued, eventually going to Thomas Trumbleward's beside for further evidence and crossexamination.

Few would have recognised the stooped, white-haired old man who shambled to the graveside, as Frank Ashton, one time famous Minister of the Crown. He stood head bared, hat in front of chest, as the coffin was lowered and the clergyman read the burial service. His overcoat and shoes were shabby and a faded scarf was folded untidily around his neck.

Two days before, death had come mercifully to his wife, Martha, who for three years had been an inmate of a lunatic asylum near Sydney. With Frank Ashton at the graveside were his two sons, their wives and two of his grandchildren. No tears were shed; though an air of desolation and gloom pervaded the proceedings, none seemed to feel sorrowful enough to weep. Even before death, insanity had destroyed the personality of its victim so that those closest to her could never feel the same attachment for Martha again.

Martha had been mad; now she was dead and her death was a happy release from insanity and recurring violent fits: that is what Frank Ashton tried to tell himself as the last clods fell into place, forming the mound on which a tombstone and flowers would be placed and weeds would grow. But, as the mourning car sped away, he could not dispel melancholy and remorse. If he had been able to foresee the future forty years ago, would he have walked to the altar as an enthusiastic bridegroom? If he could have foreseen the loneliness, disillusion and remorse of recent years would he have stayed in England rather than come here to win fame and eventually to be forced to answer "No" to the eternal question: "Was it worth while?"

That evening, his sons, their wives and children departed on the train for Melbourne, where they lived, leaving Ashton alone in his two-roomed flat on the edge of the great harbour. He owned the block of flats. He lived on the rents and had saved a little money. He had built the flats from dividends on the gold mining shares given him by John West. He rarely went to Melbourne these days, and seldom saw West, though they were quite friendly when they did meet.

Here he had lived since before Martha had been taken away. He tried hard to convince her that they could spend their aged years happily together, but her mind had been warped by bitterness – violent insanity followed. He hesitated to have her certified, but eventually had to do so. After that he adhered even more steadfastly to his promise to live "plurry quiet." But one person who had not forgotten him was Harriet. She continued to write letters from Melbourne even after Martha had gone to the asylum, but when he did not reply she eventually ceased.

When Frank Ashton first moved into the block of flats he had been content to spend most of the time sitting at home "scribbling" as he called it – writing his memoirs. He completed the story of his early life in England, his travels at sea and his political career up to his return from Russia. This revived in him the call of the sea and a desire to go to Russia again. Impetuously he satisfied both: he purchased a small seaworthy craft, got a crew together, and went north to the Islands, to China, and eventually to Vladivostock. He returned convinced that his earlier prophecies of the success of the Russian Socialist experiment were correct, and very conscious of the danger of war. Much of his "scribbling" in the following months was taken up with his observations on the Axis Pact between Germany, Italy and Japan, and its danger to world peace. Especially was he concerned with the betrayal of Czechoslovakia by France and England, and the menace of Japan's growing militarism.

In the months prior to Martha's death, his health, which had shown improvement for many years, declined seriously, and he was constantly in pain and under the doctor. His arthritis became worse, and a cancerous sore developed on his side. He wanted to complete his memoirs, especially he wanted to write the inside story of the "Starvation Scheme" called the Premiers' Plan, to expose Thurgood, Summers and the rest; and to set on paper the infamous influence of John West and the Catholic Church over the Labor Party. But his sight and concentration were impaired now, and he wrote with difficulty and without his old colour and fire.

Sitting in his lonely armchair that night, Frank Ashton's thoughts turned to Harriet. Throughout Martha's confinement, though Harriet was constantly in his thoughts, he had not been able to bring himself to write to her; now, lonely and dejected, he was free to go to her if she still wanted him! Free? Old and full of aches and pains, he needed a nursemaid more than a mistress, he told himself ruefully. He was nearly seventy years old. And Harriet? Why, Harriet would be over fifty, easily! What strange tricks life plays! Yet he could have gone to Harriet years ago, had he had the courage. Now he could not escape the recriminating thought that he should have done so, that such a course would have been better for all concerned, including poor Martha. Yes, his life had been a miserable failure! He had been weak on principles, not only in politics, but in his relation with these two women. All he had succeeded in doing was to hurt both of them. And now, in his twilight years, when Martha's tragic end made it possible to go to Harriet, he would go, if Harriet would have him, with a twinge of conscience, a broken heart and diseased body.

For three weeks he pondered, then suddenly making up his mind, he went by plane to Melbourne. Getting a taxi from the aerodrome he was driven direct to the little cottage in his former electorate where Harriet lived with her married sister.

He hobbled to the gate on a walking stick.

Harriet opened the door. At first she scarcely recognised him. She said breathlessly: "Oh, Frank, it's you! Do come in."

She assisted him to the little lounge room and they sat on the sofa. He noticed that her hair was flecked with grey, but she was well preserved, smooth of skin and as attractive as ever.

"Harriet," he began, "I couldn't bring myself to write. Martha was . . . she is . . ."

"I know, Frank. I met your son. He told me enough for me to realise the position. I understand."

"I was wondering . . . you see, I am lonely and ill . . . I . . ."

She placed her hand on his. "There is a detached flat at the back here. A nice sun room and a little living room with a fireplace. Since Mother died I have always kept it furnished and clean. I think you would find it very comfortable, and I'd have great pleasure in looking after you."

She forced a smile, but he noticed that her eyes were filled with tears.

Meanwhile, John West, his attention divided between the war and the Milk Scandal, was prey to frustration and loneliness.

Vera Maguire became an even greater source of consolation. She often drove him to and from work and to the Stadium each Saturday night. They went to the pictures occasionally at a theatre owned by John West. One night, when the war and the Royal Commission were a few weeks old, Vera drove him home from the office. John West did not speak during the journey.

602

Though over fifty now, Vera Maguire, well corsetted and with skilful beauty care, had the arresting appearance of an attractive woman of forty. Her dark costume set off by a lace blouse and tastefully-chosen hat, her grey hair lending dignity, she held a rare charm for John West.

At the gate, she said: "Cheer up, John, they'll get out of it all right."

"Get out of it?" he asked sharply. "Who? I have nothing to do with this Commission."

She placed her hand on his arm. "Oh, I'll bet you've got a finger in the pie somewhere; even if only to step in and save Trumbleward and Co. And you really will have to tell them to be more careful." She spoke lightheartedly, seeking to calm the fears she knew he held but could never admit.

"They acted without my authority," he said; and then surprised himself by telling her the full story, simply and straightforwardly.

Her sympathy could melt the steel-like barriers around his spirit. How different from Nellie! If she had been by his side always, things would have been different. "Why do you trouble with it all, John?" she said. "Why don't you get some peace, some happiness?"

He touched her hand as he got out of the car. "It's too late for me," he said. "I only know one way to live."

She watched his slightly stooped, bow-legged figure disappear down the sweeping gravel path to the verandah of the great white mansion, shrugged her shoulders, and drove away.

At the dinner table, John West found Joe, but not Nellie.

"Where's your mother?" he said, without looking up from his vegetable salad.

"She's upstairs. She's very upset. She's had a letter from Mary."

"What kind of letter?"

"Don't know. Some sort of bad news. She said she'd be down shortly. I tried to console her, to get her to tell me, but you know what she is."

John West left the table and walked briskly towards the stairs. He saw Nellie slowly descending, an envelope in her hand. Her eyes were red from weeping; though regally dressed, she looked harassed and sad.

Since war commenced, Nellie's main concern had been for Marjorie's safety. She had begun to feel the absence of her daughters more deeply since Xavier's death, and was worried about them now, especially Marjorie. Several times lately, she had mentioned her fears to her husband, to whom she had scarcely spoken since her mother's death, except to complain that her spine kept her in bed much of the time.

At dinner the previous evening she had said: "Poor Marjorie what will become of her? Those Germans might put her in one of those horrible concentration camps."

"Why should they?" he had replied. "She's a German now, just like her husband and kids."

John West went to Nellie at the bottom of the stairs. "You've heard from Mary," he said. "What's the matter?"

She leaned on the banister, one hand on her spine as if in pain. She handed him the letter. She began to weep.

"It's poor Marjorie. Oh, it's terrible, and it's set my spine laying me low again."

"Your spine! Are you ever going to realise that there is nothing wrong with your spine?" he said impatiently.

He opened the envelope. The letter was addressed to Nellie. It was from Mary. He read it hastily, taking in only the important passages.

... a few weeks before the war broke out, I went into Germany by plane to see poor Margo. I managed to convince her that war was imminent, and to get her to come back to England with me.

Admiration for Mary's action glowed in John West's mind, but he repressed it.

... we had to act without telling her husband, Paul, who is a member of the Nazi Party, and a terrible, drunken fascist. We were unable to bring the children out.

Poor Margo was pathetic. She lives in fear of her husband and the Nazis. She told me that, since she has been receiving little or no money from home, her fascist husband has neglected her.

I was right about the German bastard! John West thought.

604

She only stayed in England a few days. She spoke English with
a very noticeable German accent, and fretted after the children.
She went back to Germany. She said she was a German now and
could not desert her children. I could not stop her. Now that war
has broken out, goodness knows what will happen to her. We
may never see her again . . .

John West skimmed the rest of the letter.

"Well," Nellie said, "what can we do? Oh, my poor Marjorie.
You shouldn't have been so hard."

"Me be so hard! What have I to do with her troubles? I tried
to prevent her from marrying Andreas. The rest of you conspired
to get her away to Germany."

"Yes, but you drove her out. You cut her out of your will."

"Don't you accuse me. She has made her own bed – let her
lie on it!"

John West handed back the letter, and, without finishing his
meal, went to the reception room. He sat there until bedtime,
unable to stifle the remorse that troubled him. Next day he felt
impelled to tell Pat Cory that he was very worried because his
daughter Marjorie was in Germany, probably in a concentration
camp.

The Royal Commission continued to create great interest in spite
of competition from war news. Britain was dropping leaflets on
Berlin. The newspaper outcry against the Russo-German
non-aggression pact continued, and the march into Poland was
headline news.

Tom Trumbleward denied everything. A man named Gilbert
had called on him but he had told him he could not help him.
"Practically nothing that Gilbert said is true!" Asked how he
obtained £200 shown as being banked in his account at the time
of the alleged bribe, Trumbleward stated that he had drawn £100
to send his wife on a holiday, but she didn't go; the other £100
was the return of a sum lent to his son-in-law. The fact that his
son-in-law's bank account showed no such withdrawal appeared
not to perturb Trumbleward.

Paddy Kelleher denied the allegations against him with as
much vigour and succinctness as his impediment permitted.

Bill Brady was also asked to account for a bank deposit of

£200. His explanation was much more ingenious than Trumbleward's, if none the less a perversion of truth. He had earned the money doing secretarial and organising work at night. His wife entered the box to substantiate his story. Her husband did not trust banks, she explained, so had kept the money in the house until it amounted to £200. This she said with great conviction.

Asked for whom he did the work, Brady declined to name the person. The work had been spread over ten weeks at £20 per week. Asked by the Commissioner to write the name on a slip of paper, he did so hesitantly. Sitting in the court room, John West felt his heart skip a beat. He rightly believed that Brady had written down his name.

"Um," the Commissioner said gravely, "after seeing the name, I can understand your reticence. I am not going to insist on the gentleman being called, because there is no question of his being implicated."

During this period, John West had several discussions about the war with Archbishop Malone. The Archbishop was not anti-German. He told John West he believed that the Western Powers and Germany should unite against Bolshevik Russia, which, he contended, was the main enemy of the Christian world. Malone pointed to Russia's occupation of half of Poland and the new attack on Finland as examples that Western diplomacy was playing into Stalin's hands. He favoured Chamberlain's plan to send an expeditionary force to aid the Finns. Though from John West's point of view these sentiments were sound, he could not abandon his ingrained hatred of everything German. "No," he told Malone, "though Hitler will fight Russia eventually, he is bent on dominating the world, and will probably attack France and England first. If England sends a force to Finland that will mean war with Russia, while Hitler waits to pounce on the winner."

Malone replied that if England sent a force to Finland an alliance with Hitler against Stalin could be arranged, and this seemed to be what Chamberlain had in mind. John West remained unconvinced: Germany had tried to beat the world once, and she would try again, he believed.

When at last the Royal Commission presented its findings, John West felt the exultation of victory for the first time in years. The men accused of accepting bribes in connection with the Milk Supply Bill were exonerated. Of Trumbleward, the Commissioner reported: "You have on the one hand Gilbert's story of what took place, corroborated to some extent by his subsequent conduct: and on the other hand, you have Trumbleward's more or less bald denial of the story. Such a charge is so loathsome and so grave that, if it were established against any public man, the community would insist on his being hounded out of public life for ever afterwards, and that being so, the degree of proof you would require is the same as the degree of proof you would require in a criminal trial. Therefore, I give Mr. Trumbleward the benefit of any doubts I have in my mind."

A few weeks later, Ted Thurgood called on John West. They talked of the war situation and matters of business, but John West soon sensed that Thurgood had something else on his mind.

Thurgood had prospered sensationally since leaving politics. He had achieved his ambition of becoming a millionaire, he told John West. The years had not impaired his physique or sapped his drive and shrewdness. His sandy hair was speckled with grey, but, dressed expensively, he seemed a decade younger than his sixty odd years, and looked the part of a prosperous business executive.

"There's another matter, Jack, we'll have to do something about. Frank Ashton's up to something."

"Ashton? How is he? I haven't seen him for months. Last time I saw him I gave him tickets for the Stadium, but he didn't use them."

"He's sick. Wonder he hasn't died years ago. Got cancer and arthritis. And he's living with that old flame of his."

"Yes I know. What's he doing that's worrying you?"

"Worry you, too, when you hear what it is. He's written his memoirs; and I hear he's attacking you and me in them."

"Is he? He's got a bloody cheek, after all I've done for him. What can we do about it?"

"I'm going out to see him. They tell me he's lonely. He can't get about much. In politics, he's offended everybody – left, right and centre. Hasn't got a friend left in the world, except his woman, and he wouldn't be much use to her. Haw! Haw! Haw!"

"What good will you do going to see him?"

"Make a good fella of myself. Eventually I'll ask him about his memoirs, and ask him in fairness to soft-pedal on us."

"Good idea. Must go and see him myself, anyway. He's apt to pass on any time, poor devil."

Next afternoon – Saturday – Frank Ashton was sitting, his dressing gown over his clothes, by the fire, when Harriet came and announced Mr. Thurgood.

As Thurgood entered, Frank Ashton tried to rise.

"Don't get up, Frank, old-timer."

Thurgood wrung Ashton's hand vigorously, sending excruciating pain up his arm.

Ashton's face wrinkled. "Careful, Ted. My old hands won't stand such friendly handclasps these days." He held out his hands, displaying the swollen, deformed joints.

"Sorry, Frank. Just didn't think for a moment. So pleased to see you."

Ashton introduced Thurgood to Harriet, and she departed.

Thurgood sat at the other side of the fire and they chatted.

The room was the smallest of the three small rooms in the flat. Lenin gazed down from a large frame on the opposite wall.

Red Ted was at his heartiest best. Frank Ashton was soon lifted out of his depression. They fell to reminiscence, Thurgood channelling the conversation into old occasions dearest to Ashton's heart, and conjured up scenes of Ashton's triumphs.

Later, Harriet brought afternoon tea, which was eaten amid laughter and warm friendliness. Ashton had always liked Thurgood personally, and admired his ability. In his memoirs he had scathingly exposed Thurgood's treachery during 1930, but, in a series of pen pictures of prominent politicians, he had featured Red Ted's charm and drive, and struck the note of what Thurgood might have been.

When Thurgood left, with a promise to call again when next in Melbourne, Ashton was left with crowds of old memories – rich memories of worthwhile actions in his life that had lain buried under a mountain of remorse and disillusionment. The full extent of the self-imposed loneliness of his old age became clear to him. He was a social being: he needed friends, many friends. The months with Harriet had soothed his loneliness, but now it broke out afresh.

Since coming here, he had continued his writings in a stimulating atmosphere, but his failing sight and health made progress slow, and results, to him, unsatisfactory. Reading back over his manuscripts, the writing of which had been spread over eight years, he found they had become more scrappy and less clearly written as time passed, the recent ones being, he considered, thoroughly bad. Before leaving Sydney, he had passed from his incomplete memoirs to historical sketches dealing mainly with political struggles of Popes and Kings in the Middle Ages and Renaissance period. These subjects had interested him as a young man in the Working Men's College days; he felt impelled to revert to them when his memoirs seemed, as they often did, unimportant, even boring.

The "phoney war" nauseated, yet intrigued him. He read the morning and evening papers avidly. The crocodile tears shed by the press over the suffering of the "brave little Finns" filled him with disgust. Surely they knew, as he knew, that Finland under Mannerheim was to be a base for an attack on Russia by Germany, or England, or both. The Russians were obviously determined to remove the threat to Leningrad represented by the Mannerheim line. His conclusions about Finland in *Red Europe* were, he believed, proving correct, and the Russians understood the situation well.

Now and then, Frank Ashton would reflect on his strange reunion with Harriet. She nursed him and looked to his comfort with tender kindness. She seemed happy. They rarely referred to the past; if it cropped up inadvertently, the subject was changed as if by common consent. Harriet had told her sister, her sister's husband, and anyone else who asked, that he was boarding there, which was true, for he paid board.

An hour after Thurgood left, the doctor came on his daily visit. Sometimes Frank Ashton wondered if he should seek specialist opinion, at least about the growth on his side, which was growing larger and more malignant, but he could not be bothered.

The doctor chided him for having become excited. "As well as your other ailments, you'll have to watch your ticker, Mr. Ashton. And there's always the danger of a stroke."

During the next week, Frank Ashton was surprised to receive a visit from John West, who said: "Ted Thurgood told me you could not get about much. Thought I'd drop in for a chat."

Ashton had no real idea of the extent of John West's activities, and had no antipathy for him. There was a relentless strength of character in West that he admired. Ashton's attack on the West machine and the Catholic Church in his memoirs was purely political: there was no personal spleen in it. Really, Ashton was forced to admit, he would have died a pauper but for West. But their conversation was stilted and unfriendly. They had nothing in common.

Observing John West, white haired, but well preserved for his years, Frank Ashton could not help musing on his personality. The man had no idea of literature, music or art, no interest or hobbies outside of his business and political empire. John West was but the total of things he had had to know and do in furtherance of his ambitions.

Before John West left, he said he would arrange for Doctor Devlin to call on Ashton to diagnose and perhaps treat his illnesses.

"Won't cost you a penny," John West said. "He's a genius. He'll fix you up."

Devlin duly called, but after examining Ashton told Harriet on his way out that he had been consulted too late. Twelve months ago he could have cut the growth away – now it had gone too deep.

John West called again the next morning and, in the afternoon, Archbishop Malone paid a visit.

Frank Ashton was puzzled.

"I am being embarrassed by the friendly attentions of my political enemies," he told Harriet later.

Harriet, whom he had found to be susceptible to the charm of meeting well-known people, said: "It's nice of them to call, Frank. After all, your old friends of the left have deserted you."

"You mean, I've deserted them."

"Oh, I don't know. Frank, don't you think you should . . . well, maybe there's a hereafter, you know. I've never been an atheist, Frank, and really, you . . ."

"Aha, so the old Archbishop is trying to convert me, eh?"

"Well, no-o-o, but Mr. West said that any religion is better than none. He said this morning on his way out that he had asked the Archbishop to call because he wouldn't like to see you die like the animals of the field, without a soul or a God."

"I do believe you're turning religious. But I'm not. That's one principle I'll never break. Religion is the opiate of the people – it teaches them to obey their exploiters. I'm a Rationalist, and I don't believe in God or heaven or hell – even now when I know I haven't long to go, I don't believe in them. 'Do good, for good is good to do; spurn bribe of heaven and threat of hell,'" Ashton concluded, light-heartedly quoting. "That's the Rationalist attitude. Anyway, West should talk. He breaks the ten commandments every day. Must be getting a guilty conscience in his old age. Still, I must admit I enjoy having a visitor occasionally, even an Archbishop."

Ashton received regular visitors in the next few weeks. John West called twice, Frank Lammence once, and Ted Thurgood, in Melbourne again on business, called nearly every day for ten days.

At last Thurgood mentioned Ashton's memoirs. "Hope you're not going to roast your best friends, Frank. No good can come from muck raking."

So cleverly had Thurgood led up to the subject that Ashton suspected no ulterior motive in his recent friendliness.

"Oh, my scribbling doesn't amount to much. It's very scrappy. I'm not really confident that enough will be thought of it when I'm gone for it ever to be published. I have raked up some muck, I'm afraid. I may tone it down, if I ever get enough energy."

Noting that Ashton had reacted favourably, Thurgood did not press the matter further that day, but mentioned it again at a subsequent visit.

Later on the next Saturday afternoon, Harriet returned from a visit to a sick friend to find Frank Ashton burning papers in the incinerator in the backyard. When she left the house, Frank Ashton had been in jovial conversation with Thurgood.

"Frank, what are you doing?"

"Burning some of my scribbling."

"But why, Frank? After all the work you've put into it."

He did not reply.

"But, Frank, you keep impressing on me to be sure to arrange for publication after you . . ."

"Look, Harriet. I am burning the parts that expose Thurgood and West. I owe my financial security to them, especially West.

611

And if it's good enough for them to befriend me in my sickness and old age, then it's good enough for me to spare them this.''

While Harriet stood gripped in indecision, he threw the last of the papers into the drum, and stood watching them burn, poking them with a stick to ensure their utter destruction.

A gust of wind blew, picked up the last burning page and blew it over the back fence. They watched it rise high in the air and disintegrate.

"There goes my last bit of guts," Frank Ashton said, and Harriet noticed that there were tears in his eyes.

She sighed. He threw away the stick and picked up his walking cane. She held his arm as he shambled back to the house.

Frank Ashton was quite excited as he said farewell to Harriet and left the house with Maurice Blackwell to attend an X Club meeting. Blackwell had discovered Ashton's presence in Melbourne when they met in the street a few days before, and had suggested to his old comrade that he accompany him to the meeting.

Ashton had been a member of the X Club before going to live in Sydney. The club held monthly meetings. Frank Ashton had dubbed it "the society for the retention of Socialist opinions long since departed from." Many of its members were former supporters of the Tom Mann Socialist Party who had got on in the world and the club gave them an opportunity to express radical and Socialist opinions without fear of their remarks being published. But Frank Ashton had forgotten these facts as he walked to the tram leaning on Blackwell's arm and his own walking stick. This was his first social outing in months. He was going against doctor's orders, but reckoned he might as well be dead if he couldn't have an intellectual discussion occasionally.

He liked Blackwell, whom he viewed as one of the few honest men left among the Labor politicians. Blackwell still held the seat formerly occupied by Ashton. Ashton had never regretted his efforts to ensure that Blackwell "beat the Catholics" in the pre-selection after he had resigned from Parliament.

On the tram, Ashton did most of the talking, as was his wont when excited. At the meeting, he was welcomed with open arms by old friends. They made a fuss of him. They were genuinely pleased to see him. He was not forgotten.

The speaker, a man whom Ashton did not know, took the war situation as his subject. His speech developed into an attack on Soviet Russia for its war with Finland just successfully concluded. He said little of the menace of German Fascism and nothing of Japanese militarism, but accused Stalin of being an imperialist, and advocated by inference an alliance with Germany for an attack on Russia.

The speech took all of the pleasure out of the evening for Frank Ashton. As it progressed a seething indignation rose in him and the answers to the speaker flashed vividly in his mind.

When the speech had ended amid half-hearted applause, the chairman invited discussion, asking each of the twenty odd people present in turn if they wished to participate. Ashton was the third person asked. He was at that pitch of excitement in which all the great speeches of his career had been made. He was attempting to rise to his feet when his doctor's oft-repeated warning came to his mind: "No excitement. If you become over-excited you'll have a heart attack or a stroke. No excitement!"

He shook his head. "No, thanks. I don't wish to speak."

Surely someone else will answer this man, he thought. The old ticker is pounding. Better not start speechifying at my age.

Several people made short speeches. Most skirted around the main theme of the speaker; a few, including Blackwell, lamely defended Russia. Frank Ashton's indignation and excitement rose to fever pitch. He knew exactly what he wanted to say; he could tear this man to pieces with extracts from *Red Europe* and material he had gathered from recent reading.

The last man in discussion had finished speaking. The chairman was about to close the meeting with a vote of thanks.

Frank Ashton rose to his feet with difficulty. No excitement! No excitement!

"Mr. Chairman. I would like to speak if I may."

"Yes, Mr. Ashton."

All present sensed the still-vital personality of the bent old man in the shabby suit, with the old scarf around his neck.

"Mr. Chairman: it is a great pity that our Club has so degenerated as to permit such a speech as we have heard this evening. We are all Socialists, at least, there was a time when we were Socialists. I have always contended that a man who says he is a

Socialist, and is not a friend and supporter of the land of Socialism – Russia – is either a fool or a knave."

He brushed wisps of white hair back from his forehead with the characteristic gesture of old. The meeting was already hushed under the spell of his oratory.

"During my long career in the Labor movement I was at times guilty of weakness and error – even the strongest tree will sometimes bend before the storm – but on one principle I have never wavered. In Russia the workers are building a Socialist society. I have always declared my support for their great experiment and studied it avidly.

"I have been in Russia twice, the last time as recently as three years ago. What I saw convinced me that the defence of Soviet Russia is the greatest task confronting progressive humanity. The Finnish war, gentlemen, was fought in defence of Soviet Russia. The Mannerheim Line was built for offence, not defence. It was built with German and English money as an attacking base against Russia. Mannerheim is one and the same with "Mannerheim the butcher," about whom I learned a good deal during my European trip. May I humbly advise you one and all to read again my little book, *Red Europe*. There you will see the truth about Finland and its fascist ruler, Mannerheim. There you will see the lengths to which the capitalist world went in its first desperate efforts to destroy the Soviet Union."

Ashton was trembling with excitement. His heart was pounding, but his head was clear. He seemed to find his old vigour.

"Britain and France have declared war on Germany; not a shot has been fired in that war, yet the British War Council, a few weeks ago, before Finalnd capitulated, decided to send an expeditionary force of at least 100,000 men to Finland via Sweden. There has been talk of attacking the Baku oil wells, as was done during the wars of intervention when the arms of the world beat against the colossus of the workers' state in vain. Now Chamberlain admits that British planes and guns were sent to Finland.

"What brand of insanity is this? Britain is ill-equipped, yet she sends arms to Finland. There can only be one answer! Chamberlain would like even now to make an alliance with Hitler against Russia. Cast your mind back over the events leading up to this war! Don't be deceived by the millionaire press when it screams now because Stalin has signed a non-aggression pact with Hitler. British and French diplomacy left him no alternative if he is to save the Workers' State.''

Ashton ran his hands through his hair. As he traced the course of events leading up to the war, his bent body straightened. His face was as red as raw meat.

"I have seen war; and I hate war. I value human life, but I cannot shed one tear for the poor little Finns. Rather do I weep for the victims of fascism. And if ever I pray again, I will go down on my knees to thank God that the Russian leaders had the foresight and courage to remove the Mannerheim line, and I will pray that the common people of the western world will demand an alliance with the Soviet Union against the scourge of fascism. This is a matter of urgency to Australia because Japan is a member of the Axis Powers and is preparing to attack – believe me, I have been in the East and I know.''

When Frank slumped into his seat he was grasping for breath and holding his heart. There was a long moment of deep silence, then enthusiastic applause.

The man who had delivered the main address was obviously embarrassed. The chairman closed the meeting and those present adjourned as usual to a nearby cafe for supper. Frank Ashton was sweating and trembling. He could not eat.

On the tram going home, Blackwell said: "A great speech, Frank. One of your best.''

The journey continued in silence. When the tram stopped at Ashton's street, Blackwell said: "You don't look too good, Frank. The excitement has been too much. I'll walk down to the house with you.''

"No, it's all right, Morrie, old-timer. I'll be all right.''

Alighting, he began hobbling up the side street. As he neared the railway gates, having covered about half the hundred and fifty yards or so to the house, he stopped, leaning heavily on his stick, holding his heart.

A quarter of an hour later, Harriet, who had waited up, was startled by a loud thumping on the front door. She opened it to see two strange men supporting a gasping Frank Ashton between them.

"We found him near the railway gates.''

They helped her get him to bed, then they went for the doctor.

Frank Ashton had had a stroke. Within a fortnight he died. His death-bed request for a Rationalist funeral and cremation was carried out. It was attended by his two sons and their wives, Harriet, Blackwell, John West and Frank Lammence. The only tears were shed by Harriet.

Harriet offered Frank Ashton's manuscripts to his eldest son, who refused to have anything to do with them after his Catholic wife read the ones attacking the Popes. She went to the city and asked Frank Lammence about publication, but he said there was no market for such communistic material. She then took them to the Labor Call office. They were interested; they would publish them. She was overjoyed. A week later they sent for her and said they were sorry; the papers were largely composed of attacks on the Labor Party; she could not expect them to publish them.

Defeated, Harriet packed the papers tidily away in an old trunk. From time to time in the years that followed she tried unsuccessfully to obtain a publisher for them.

After Frank Ashton's death, John West often said, proudly: "I put Ashton into politics. He was the greatest of the Labor men; and the best orator this country ever saw."

Though of late his team of racehorses had been small, he sent Paddy Ryan to the yearling sales and purchased a colt which he named "Ashton." The horse was destined never to win a race while in his stables.

Meanwhile, John West followed the startling events of 1940 with a growing conviction of the invincibility of Hitler's armies. Holland! Denmark! Norway! France! The British armies swept into the sea at Dunkirk! The bombing of Britain! What force on earth could stem the savage tide? Some consolation that Churchill had replaced Chamberlain!

When Mussolini declared war on a beaten France, John West was thrown into some confusion. Though politically he was a fascist himself, his old hatred of all things German had led him to oppose Hitler, but as a keen supporter of Mussolini's corporate state he did not know what attitude to take now. One Sunday afternoon he met the Archbishop, who said: "I agree with Marshal Pétain. I'd rather have Hitler than the Communists."

"I think Mussolini has made a mistake entering the war on Hitler's side," John West replied. "If the Germans win, our homes and families are in danger."

"Mussolini is a clever man. He must be convinced that Hitler will win, and, God knows, it does look as if he will," the Archbishop persisted.

John West was pleased when the Menzies Government banned the Communist Party after the fall of Paris. This reminded him of Mary. He demanded to know if Nellie had received further letters. Mary had written once, several weeks back. She had married again, but there was no news of Marjorie.

Nellie wept and complained: "Poor Marjorie might be dead or in a concentration camp, and Mary will be killed any day by a bomb."

John West was as deeply concerned as his wife but he could never admit it. "They have made their own beds; let them lie on them," he said.

The house was desolate these days, with only himself, Joe, Nellie and three servants engulfed in forty quiet rooms. He and Nellie hardly ever spoke to each other. Joe treated his father as a stranger, and laughed at his suggestions that he should join the army. On the odd occasions when John came home from Sydney, he was often drunk, always sullen, and he avoided his father by getting up late and staying in the city for the evening meal.

Early in 1941, John joined the army as a private, without consulting his father. At first, John West was annoyed, but then his patriotism stirred, and he became proud of his son's uniform. Home on leave, John told his mother he was playing the cornet in the regimental band. Obeying an impulse, John West ordered a complete set of instruments and donated it to the unit. However, all this only gave John West further reason for annoyance, for John was soon discharged as medically unfit, having behaved so badly that the authorities were pleased to be rid of him.

John West found the war good for business: there was no unemployment, plenty of money about; many firms in which he held shares had lucrative war contracts; he was making money faster than ever before, but was often oppressed with a feeling of uneasiness – a vague dread of the future. The war situation worried him. He knew that his power and wealth were inseparably bound up with British and Australian big business; he feared and hated the Germans almost as much as he had during the first world war.

His direct political power narrowed as it had done during the first world war; and the war's end seemed far away, victory unlikely. Premier Davison, though dependent on the support of West men in the Labor Party, was just as prone to do the bidding of other strong pressure groups as he was to obey John West. In the Labor Party, his direct influence was confined now to Victoria, though in other States, especially Queensland, he still donated to Party funds, and obtained legislative immunity for his sporting enterprises. Catholic Action groups had become active in the Labor Party. He favoured their crusade against Communism and the socialisation objective of their own party, but they were not *his* men; they were *the Pope's* men, and they were manoeuvring to win pre-selection ballots – in some electorates they seemed likely to defeat *his* men. His plan, first conceived during the "Irish" battles in 1920–21, to unite for his purpose the old West machine with the younger generation of Catholic Labor men would, he feared, prove a rod for his own back. Besides, after Russia came into the war in 1941, there was a leftward swing in the Party which displeased him. As well, there were signs of revolt among some of his own men.

During this period, a political crisis developed in the Victorian Parliament. Artful Alfie Davison weathered the storm, but before the crisis passed the Labor Party conducted its pre-selection ballots. The results shocked John West. A few left-wingers won, though in electorates where he held little sway. Several Catholic Action men won, and, though some of them were West men, many of them were fanatics who would serve only themselves and the Church. Worst of all for John West, right in the "West belt" near Carringbush, old Ron Lassiter and his son Colin ran a candidate in one electorate and defeated a West man, Cotton by name, who had held the seat for over twenty-five years. The Lassiters had become disgruntled. Old Ron and his gang had been defeated by left-wing candidates at the last elections in the Builders' Laborers' Union in spite of ballot-rigging in the best West manner. Old Ron, a reckless spender and nearly seventy, had no money. Ron Lassiter approached John West for financial assistance and met a curt refusal; though Colin Lassiter still "worked" for the Ralstone Council, he had never forgiven John West for dumping him; so Colin and his father had set about building a political machine of their own – right in John West's backyard.

On the evening of the ballot, Paddy Kelleher came stammering to John West in the reception room: "The – aaarrr – b – bloody

618

Lassiter mob have rigged the – aaarrr – ballot against Cotton!''

"Didn't you use Union tickets to beat them?''

"Yes, but – aaarrr – they had more than I did.''

"Well, take the ballot box to Party headquarters like you always do. You should be able to change the result.''

Kelleher laughed cynically. "Aaarrr – if I put any more – aaarrr – tickets in, there'll be more – aaarrr v – v – votes than people in Ralstone. But if I could get the box I'd fix it for – aaarrr – Cotton to win by one vote.''

"Get the box, then.''

"I – aaarrr – tried; but they w-w-won't hand it over. They've g-got it down at the Ralstone Club.''

"Well, go and get it.''

Gripped by foolhardy courage, Kelleher drove alone to the Ralstone Club, which was a "blind'' for after-hours drinking. Entering the bar, he found Colin Lassiter, his brother Jim, old Ron and some cronies drinking and gloating over their victory.

Seeing the ballot box lying on a sofa, Paddy dived on it and departed with it under his arm after stammering something about it being "a b-b-bloody – aaarrr – disgrace to leave a ballot box about in such a place!''

As he ran from the room he heard Colin Lassiter say: "It's worth a fiver to get that ballot box back.''

Kelleher dashed headlong from the building, climbed into his car and placed the ballot box beside him on the front seat. He heard running steps behind him. As he started the motor, a large man climbed into the back seat and slammed the door behind him.

As the car sped away, Kelleher said: "Aaarrr – no b-b-bloody funny – aaarrr – b-b-business!''

"You'll get funny business, if you don't hand that box over, Pat. We've beat you at your own game this time.''

As Kelleher stopped at a red light, he felt the cold muzzle of a revolver on the nape of his neck.

"Give us that box, Pat,'' a menacing voice said, "or I'll blow your bloody brains out.''

"B-b-break it down – aaarrr – b-brother,'' Kelleher began as he let out the clutch when the light changed.

"Well, cop this,'' said the man in the back seat. Kelleher felt a blow on his skull and saw stars before his eyes. His attacker grabbed the wheel and switched off the motor while Kelleher lay

619

slumped on the seat. Having steered the car to a standstill near the kerb with difficulty, the man got out, put his gun away, took the ballot box, and fled through the nearby park.

Next morning the press featured the incident. Kelleher declared that the ballot box had been stolen by an unknown man and that the pre-selection was to be declared invalid. Police investigations revealed nothing. John West sent for Col Lassiter and threatened to have him sacked from the Ralstone Council job if he interfered again. A new ballot was held, and Cotton won easily, due to the superior ballot-rigging skill of Paddy Kelleher.

Later in the year, the Labor Party took office in the Federal Parliament, and John Curtin became Prime Minister. John West was pleased; he saw Curtin as the best available wartime leader; but he had none of the grandiose schemes of 1929 when Summers had taken office. His influence in this Parliament was confined to a handful of men, mainly Victorians; he was a millionaire, so this Government would defend his interests as it would those of other millionaires – he no longer expected more from the Federal Parliament.

Meanwhile, he had become an armchair war strategist.

When Russia was attacked, he joined the prophets who said she would not last six weeks, but when Russia lasted six months and began driving the Germans back he became an admirer of the Red Army, and shocked Archbishop Malone by remarking: "The Russians must think their system is all right; they're defending it well." Malone's reply: "They must fight or be shot" did not convince him.

John West's feeling for Russia was like that of a man saved from drowning by an irreconcilable enemy: he was thankful, he admired Russia's courage, but would revert to the old animosity when all the water was pumped from his lungs.

Widespread opposition in the Labor Party to the coalition with Davison and the Country Party, led the Party Conference of 1942 to resolve to withdraw support from Davison. West men, notably Brady, Trumbleward and Bennett, refused to carry out the decision at John West's demand, but were unable to hold out for long. Later, Party leader Carr became Premier for a week only, to see the U.A.P.'s swing to Davison's support and return him to the Premier's office.

John West's attention was diverted by Japan's southward march after her attack on Pearl Harbor. "Nothing matters now but winning the war!" he exclaimed to Frank Lammence.

Defeats in the Pacific were compensated for by victories elsewhere. Montgomery's men, including the 9th Australian Division, smashed the Germans at El Alamein, and at Stalingrad, Timoshenko's column came down the Volga to surround and annihilate the German attackers who had been held by the city's defenders.

In Melbourne, fevered digging of air-raid shelters, testing of air-raid sirens and sand-bagging of city buildings were ominous signs that war might come to Australia's shores. John West had his office building sand-bagged, an air-raid shelter was built in its cellar, and another in the cellar of the mansion. Then the Japanese raids on Darwin! Rumours of invasion of the Northern Territory or Queensland! John West watched with bated breath. Then the Japs were eventually halted in New Guinea and the Coral Sea, and he sighed with relief.

In the meantime, political considerations raised by the Archbishop and other Catholic acquaintances could not shake John West from his belief in unity with Russia for duration of the war. "We might have to fight against Russia later, but we must fight with her now," he would say.

He even became an advocate of the Second Front in Western Europe. Frank Lammence and Dick Lamb under-estimated the genuineness of his sentiments by refusing to rent the Stadium to the Australia-Soviet Friendship League. When informed of the decision, John West said quietly: "Let 'em have it. Let 'em have it for nothing. I'll write them a letter myself. Bad for business to refuse it at a time like this."

When the Second Front was opened, John West could see that final victory was only a matter of time. But he could not look to the post-war future, as he had done in 1918, with excited expectations of continuing his drive for power. In his middle seventies now, he was feeling his age; he was tired and no longer believed that he could extend his empire.

John West had always lived for the future, but now he was beginning to think he had no future; and he could not turn to the past, as other old men did, because he feared remorse and self-recrimination.

CHAPTER FOURTEEN

*I commit my soul into the hands of my Saviour, in full
confidence that having redeemed it and washed it in His
precious blood He will present it faultless before my
Heavenly Father . . . the blessed doctrine of the complete
atonement for sin through the blood of Jesus Christ . . .*

JOHN PIERPOINT MORGAN, in his will.

*We have got to organise ourselves against Communism.
We must keep the worker from red literature and red
ruses. We must see that his mind remains healthy.*

AL CAPONE

Early in the morning of New Year's Day, 1946, the insistent
ringing of the telephone penetrated John West's slumbers. He sat
up slowly. Yes, it was the phone! Who on earth would be ringing
up at this hour?

Sleepily he switched on the bed lamp, flung back the blankets
and got out of bed. He pulled on his slippers, switched on the
dressing-room light and walked to the top of the stairs. He made
his way slowly down the stairs in the half light, thinking of the
night he had done so when One-Eyed-Tommy had come at this
hour to tell him O'Flaherty had occupied the tote.

His heart was beating fast – too fast. The doctor had said:
"Watch your old ticker, Mr. West. Nothing serious yet; but no
temper, no exertion, no shocks or excitement."

Still the telephone kept up its strident call. Who could it be?
What was wrong?

At the foot of the stairs, he groped for the electric switch and
welcomed the light. He picked up the receiver with a trembling
hand.

"Hullo!"

It was his Sydney manager.

"Sorry to disturb you at this unearthly hour, Mr. West: but I

622

thought I should call. It's young Jack – John – he ..."

"What's he done now?"

"He's – er – he fell from the balcony of his flat an hour ago. He's dead!"

John West did not reply. He was seized by an excruciating pain in the chest; he began to sweat, yet felt icy cold. The pain paralyzed him – had he been able to move, he would have been afraid to, for fear his heart would stop beating.

This was the pain Devlin had said to be aware of – the angina pain! The shock of the news of his son's death passed away – only the pain in his heart remained, the fear of it and a sense of impending doom.

"Hullo! Are you still there, Mr. West? Hullo!"

The pain left John West as quickly as it had come.

"Yes, I'm still here."

"I hope I haven't upset you. I thought I should ring."

"That's all right. Make arrangements for the funeral. I'll come over by plane before lunch."

"And – Mr. West, I don't quite know how to say this, but someone must tell you. There – there seems some doubt whether he, young Jack, I mean, fell or jumped."

After the conversation had finished, John West slowly ascended the stairs. Nellie's voice came from her bedroom door above: "Someone rang you. Is something wrong?"

Reaching the top of the stairs, he walked slowly towards her; he was shivering, yet beads of sweat showed on his brow and his hands were clammy.

"Whatever's wrong?" she exclaimed when she saw him.

Standing there, with a wrap hastily thrown over her night-dress, her white hair straggling around her wrinkled face, she looked to him like a haggard old witch.

"It's John. He's dead. They think he committed suicide," he said with cruel simplicity and acceptance of the suicide theory.

She sobbed, sagged and stumbled weeping to her bed. He made to follow her, but decided not to – he had never entered that room since ... He never would!

"We'll go over by plane in the morning," he called out, then went back to bed.

Uppermost in his mind was the terrible agony he had experienced. Should he ring Devlin? He decided to wait until the

623

morning. He lay for a long time listening to his heart beating. His mind turned to John. Had he suicided? The booze was his trouble. He had been an unworthy son; yet hadn't he said to Cory recently: "The old man has mellowed; we get along better."

The fear of death, grown strong in John West since his heart trouble had begun, harassed him now. Death was everywhere around him. Vera had died. When Vera Maguire was killed instantly in a motor accident a year before, John West had wept. Only then did he realise that she had become his sheet anchor, his most effective barrier against loneliness, fear and remorse.

Then Arty had died. A few hours before his death, Arthur West had called his brother to his bedside. The conversation had been stilted and tentative until Arthur said imploringly: "Get Dick Bradley out of there, Jack. You've gotta get him out. Meantime, get Paddy Ryan to send in cigarettes and that. I've told Paddy about it. Start tryin' to get Dick out!"

"But Bradley's in for life," John West had replied. "How can I get him out?"

"He's been sick lately, got goitre and cancer. Won't live many years. His niece Pat, who looked after him when he was in hiding, will care for him again, she says. You got influence with the Jail Governor and the Chief Secretary. Get him out, Jack. You've gotta promise to try to get Dick Bradley outta there."

Arthur West lived long enough to hear his brother utter an uncertain promise.

Then news had come that Marjorie West had died in a German concentration camp during the war. The shock sent Nellie West to bed for months; she began to complain more than ever of pains in her spine. She had Joe ask his father to endeavour to get Marjorie's children out of Germany, but John West refused.

At first, Marjorie's death had left him with only renewed anger against his unwanted son-in-law, Paul Andreas, but in recent months he had occasionally found himself pondering over the circumstances of her marriage: had he been in any degree at fault then or since? He could not combat a feeling of guilt or of self-pity that his only grand-children had been fathered by a German who, as far as he knew, still had custody of them.

John West felt under his pillow in the darkness and found his rosary beads there beside the revolver. He drew the beads out and began to pray silently. *Our Father, Who art in Heaven, hallowed be Thy name . . . Hail Mary, full of grace, the Lord is with thee . . .*

For more than a year, John West had been practising the Catholic religion with an intensity born of his fear of death. After Doctor Devlin diagnosed heart trouble, John West had, for the first time in his life, seriously considered the tenets of the Catholic religion and the possibility of life after death, of punishment for sin in hell-fire. He discussed the matter with Archbishop Malone and began to take religious instruction. He read *Jackson's Apologetics* and various books and pamphlets, including the Pope's Encyclical on Communism. Then he made a general confession to the Archbishop. The confession was not profound or searching; it did not reveal John West's biggest sins, but it did set his mind turning to the past.

One day, John West told Daniel Malone he was worried because the Bible history quoted Jesus as saying that it was easier for a camel to pass through the eye of a needle than for a rich man to enter Heaven. The Archbishop chuckled and replied that such a statement should not be taken literally; providing a rich man was generous to the Church, practised charity and humility, and carried out his religious duties, he could enter Heaven just as easily as anyone else. Reassured, John West joined the Men's Sodality of the Sacred Heart at a nearby church. Attracted by the Church's promise to wipe out sin and win immunity from eternal punishment, he began to attend Confession and Communion each week.

But just as his heart trouble had brought fear, the confessional brought a sense of guilt – these two crashed through the barriers he had built around his spirit and would torment him for the rest of his days.

More than a year later, Nellie West, stooped and withered, ushered Archbishop Malone and two other men into the reception room to see her husband.

Malone, at eighty years, had sunken, black-ringed eyes; his lips had receded, his hair and eyebrows were wispy and white, his shoulders rounded; he had lost weight and his wrinkled skin clung tightly to his bony frame; yet he still walked with brisk dignity and his mind retained much of its sly alertness.

The three visitors greeted John West and sat in a half-circle around him as he reclined in his easy chair looking his seventy-seven years and feeling very tired.

625

When Nellie had gone, Archbishop Malone introduced the other visitors.

"Mr. West, this is Mr. Parelli, Secretary of Catholic Action."

Parelli, who gave an effusive greeting, was tall, thin, effeminate in his bearing; his small, restless eyes, and his thin, cruel lips, indicated a fanatic who would stop at nothing in the service of his cause.

"And, of course, Mr. West, you know Mr. Cregan."

John West *did* know Mr. Cregan. He had been endeavouring for several years to push Cregan forward as leader of the Victorian Parliamentary Labor Party. To John West, Cregan was the best and most useful of the young Catholic Action politicians, the one who would as often serve J.W. as the Catholic Church.

Cregan was extremely fat and, dressed in a grubby black suit, he looked like a Protestant representation of a Jesuit priest. He sat bulging out of his clothes, his fat, boneless hands folded on his ample lap.

"Yes, Mr. West and I know each other," he said through thick, sensual lips.

"As I told you, Mr. West," Archbishop Malone said, "I have brought these two friends along tonight to discuss the work of Catholic Action in the Labor Movement. I'll let Mr. Parelli do the talking – he's good at it."

John West made no reply. He was suspicious that tonight he would be asked to finance Catholic Action, which had become a menace to his political empire; already a leading member of Catholic Action named Michael Kiely had won a pre-selection ballot from one of John West's men.

The pre-selection for Ralstone, won by Kiely, had been a contest between Cotton backed by John West, Jim Lassiter backed by old Ron's gang, and Kiely backed by Catholic Action. Of the five Labor Party branches in the electorate, Kiely controlled two, West men two, and the Lassiters one. Before the war all the branches had been controlled by John West; but due to the split with the Lassiters and the rise of Catholic Action, he had lost ground.

The ballot was rigged by all three candidates, but least effectively by doddering old Cotton. The absent and the dead voted, and bogus Trade Union tickets were used by all candidates. An unofficial scrutiny an hour before voting finished revealed that

Jim Lassiter led narrowly from Cotton, with Kiely lagging behind. Then five minutes before the ballot closed, three hundred Kiely voters arrived in charabancs. They were all young people, members of Catholic Action, The Holy Name Society or The Children of Mary. A check of their bona fides revealed that they had all been secretly enrolled in Kiely-controlled branches months before.

The other candidates had no time to fight back. Kiely won easily. Cotton ran last. John West swore vengeance!

"Well, Mr. West," Parelli began, taking a thick document from his brief case, "I have here the most recent report of The Movement which, as you know, is the arm of Catholic Action in the Trade Unions."

John West nodded uninterestedly. Parelli proceeded, quoting from the report to illustrate his points.

. . . For obvious reasons we cannot work publicly as members of a Catholic Action organisation, but working anonymously as The Movement we do the highest work of Catholic Action.

Parelli outlined the work of The Movement in combating Communism, strikes and militancy in the Trade Union Movement. He referred to the Papal Encyclical that John West had read some time before, in which the Pope called for organisations of Catholic workmen to put the Catholic point of view to workers and to combat Socialism and Communism.

"In each diocese or suburb we have set about establishing cells of The Movement and in many factories and Trade Unions we have similar groups. We have gathered lists of non-communists, especially anti-communists, who are not Catholics, with a view to drawing them into The Movement, or at least into co-operation with us. In Union elections we have run candidates against Communist and militant leaders. Already we have had some success – we expect more success, providing we can carry on."

Yes, John West thought bitterly; and you're also running candidates against my men in Labor Party pre-selection ballots. But you won't mention that. Oh, no!

Apparently sensing John West's hostility, Parelli said: "I want to make it clear, Mr. West, that this is a fight to protect private property against Godless Communism. We are co-operating with the employers to root out the Communists and militants and to stamp out socialistic ideas among the workers. Though we cannot

627

come out openly against wage increases, we are spreading the idea that higher wages lead to higher prices. The Communists are trying to use their power in the Union Movement to unite the workers around their programme for even higher wages, ultimately for Socialism, which will divert the workers from the path of Christ. You and I know how dangerous this is, don't we. Mr. West?''

Parelli spoke such sentiments with the conviction of one who had never been a working man: his father had made a fortune from a chain of shops which sold Catholic prayer books, statues, rosary beads and the like. Parelli had been a member of the Young Nationalist Association until his interest in church politics turned him to the Labor Movement, then he had joined the Labor Party and the Clerks' Union.

"As you know, Mr. West, the Labor Party Conference last month decided to form A.L.P. Industrial Groups. This will soon be adopted by the Federal Executive – we have the numbers now – then The Movement will be able to work under the cover of the Labor Party all over Australia.''

Parelli paused to insert a cigarette in a pink holder. Having lit the cigarette, he held the holder effeminately with his little finger curved.

Cregan sat impassively. He had decided not to commit himself until he saw how John West reacted.

Now he's coming to it, John West thought. They'll get no money from me!

Parelli continued: "Catholic Action members will be the core of the Industrial Groups. Already we control many Labor Party branches and we will have control of the whole Party in Victoria by next year's conference.''

John West, who had been sitting with his eyes half-closed, stirred and gazed fiercely at Parelli. Control the Labor Party! So they're going to control the Labor Party in Victoria, are they? We'll see about that!

"You'll control the Labor Party?'' he shouted. "We'll see about that! I'll ...''

Malone interrupted: "I wouldn't use the word control, Mr. Parelli. You mean you will be in a position to see the Party follows Catholic Action policy against Communism, socialisation, nationalisation of banking, free medicine and the like.''

"Quite so, Your Grace,'' Parelli compromised. "We have

demanded again and again that the Federal Labor Goverment take action against the Communists, yet it has done nothing. Even many Catholic Labor politicians will not come out openly for a ban on the Communist Party or in support of The Movement. As the report says here: *Until The Movement is so powerful that it has to be placated and until its membership is able to educate the Catholic workers in the danger of giving undivided loyalty to any political party, it will be impossible for us to expect any different behaviour from the Federal Labor Government.* You see, Mr. West, most Catholics in Australia are workers, Labor supporters. Most of them support Chifley's Bank Nationalisation and the Free Medicine Bill.'' Parelli pouted: "It's most distressing for The Movement, Mr. West.''

"Well, why don't you form a separate Catholic Party like the centre parties in Europe?" John West asked.

Old West is being very difficult, Parelli thought.

"I myself favoured that course, but His Grace . . .''

"It couldn't be done, Mr. West, desirable and all as it is; at least not yet,'' Daniel Malone intervened. "Labor traditions go deep among Catholics here. We would cut ourselves off from many of our own people. Similarly with separate Catholic Trade Unions. These exist in some European countries; but most Australian Catholics would stay in the present Unions.''

Cregan widened his fish-like eyes and said: "The Movement, against my wishes, formed two break-away Unions last year, and lost much ground as a consequence. We must work within the existing Unions.''

John West persisted. "I see Archbishop O'Connell says that Catholic Labor politicians should oppose the Bank Nationalisation Bill, then when they are expelled from the Labor Party, form a Catholic Party.''

The Archbishop chuckled slyly. "Musha, Mr. West, Archbishop O'Connell has been wiser than everyone else all his life. Why, he even supported conscription.''

Malone gulped as if trying to swallow his words, then added: "I assure you, Mr. West, that the other Archbishops and the Papal Delegate don't favour such a proposal. For the moment, we must concentrate on getting our own men to Canberra, and put pressure on the older Catholic Labor men to come out more strongly against Communism.''

629

I don't want a Catholic Party formed anyway, John West admitted to himself. They say get *our* men to Canberra, they mean get *their* men to Canberra!

Parelli went on: "As the report says, we must educate Catholics. In this regard, His Grace's public statements against Communism, the Bank Bill and Free Medicine have been of immense value. But as His Grace has pointed out to me, these statements lay him open to the accusation of directing the politics of the laity. Catholics with socialistic tendencies are accusing him of this already. That will only stop when The Movement is strong enough to force its policy on the Labor Party and the Unions, and to educate Catholics out of the idea of giving undivided loyalty to the Labor Party. For example, Mr. West . . ."

What's he driving at now? John West thought wearily.

". . . for example, as you no doubt read in the papers, His Grace called a Communion breakfast of Catholic tramway workers on the morning of the mass meeting, to warn them not to vote for the Communist-controlled executive's motion for a tram strike in support of the metal trades strikers. If Catholic Action, that is, the A.L.P. Industrial Groups, had been stronger in the tramway union, His Grace would have been spared the need to make such a delicate statement."

John West gazed at Parelli quizzically. Why has he come to tell me all this? There's a catch in it somewhere, all right.

"We have not forgotten the youth," Parelli said. "We have already recruited 3,000 from the Young Catholic Workers' Association. We are conducting schools for them and other members, training them in methods of work. From them came the idea of reporting Communists to the employers. Where a Communist is active and popular in a factory, they report him to the foreman or manager and endeavour to get him sacked. Sometimes this succeeds, but some employers have a false sense of fairness because there is a shortage of labor. We are at work in other organisations besides the Unions and the Labor Party, notably the Returned Soldiers' League; there we are pushing forward the idea of patriotism, calling the commos Russian agents."

Malone chuckled again. "Even I would become a British flag-waver to beat the Communists, Mr. West."

"We have problems, Mr. West. Many of our own people support the Communists and militants in the Unions – they vote for them at Union elections. The report has something to say on this problem: *There are 10,000 members of the Ironworkers' Union in Victoria, but years of effort have only been able to disclose six reliable Catholics.* The position is similar in Sydney, Mr. West, and all our experience shows that the more unskilled the trade, the more rapid is the decline of religious faith.

"The fact is that many Catholics object to The Movement's activities, but we hope to overcome this opposition now that we have the A.L.P. Industrial Groups as a front for our work. I'll leave a copy of this report with you, Mr. West. It gives details of the position in all Unions. And now I come to the most important point: Where's the money coming from?"

John West raised his head and gazed at Parelli. So I was right, he thought; I'm to foot the bill!

"The only financial assistance The Movement has obtained, apart from membership fees, came from His Grace, who made a personal donation of £5,000. This enabled us to start our paper, FREEDOM. But we have reached the end of our tether. Through shortage of paid staff our leaders are cruelly overworked. Mr. Cregan here, for instance, works day and night, and his health is in a bad state. In the last year, Mr. West, no less than four key-men on the executive have had to be given long leave of absence on doctors' orders. If this situation continues for another year, The Movement will cease to exist because its leadership will be destroyed. At the moment, the brunt of the work in Victoria is being done by myself, Mr. Cregan here, and Michael Kiely, the member for Ralstone."

Parelli placed his hand over his mouth, as though trying to stifle Kiely's name.

John West exclaimed: "Kiely! He's an imposter! He's a professional Catholic sponging on his religion! He's . . ."

Cregan stirred in his chair and grimaced at Parelli. The Archbishop forced a chuckle and said: "Mr. West and young Michael Kiely don't hit it off, Mr. Parelli. But we must forget personalities. The point is, Mr. West, that The Movement needs money, a large sum. Knowing your hatred of Communism and your long-standing generosity to the Church, I suggested that our friends see you."

John West's resentment melted into confusion. He was to be the mug who put up the money! He would take no part; obtain no power. Catholic Action was challenging several of his Labor politicians. Kiely and some other members of The Movement were agitating against him in the Labor Party. Kiely was a leader of The Movement, yet they wanted him to finance it. But Catholic Action was fighting Communism: the Communists had taken his daughter away from him, ruined her life; they were a threat to his religion and his hard-won wealth.

He eyed them silently. *A rich man who is generous to the Church can enter Heaven . . .*

"How much do you want?"

"A lot of money, Mr. West," Parelli answered. "Fifty thousand pounds."

"Fifty thousand! You must think I'm the Bank of England!"

They sat in deep silence, then John West said: "I'll put up the money – on one condition. Your men are fighting my men – that's no good to either of us. None of my men are communistic. If you agree not to oppose my men in pre-selection ballots in future, I'll give you a cheque."

The Archbishop opened his mouth to speak, but refrained. Cregan stirred in his seat but said nothing. At last, Parelli said: "I'm afraid, Mr. West, that I can't give such an undertaking. Many of your men are not Catholics, and some of those who are, are not openly fighting Communism or helping Catholic Action. However, most of them are all right, in our view. I can assure you that we will not oppose those of good-will, and that our men are free to help you in Parliament if their conscience dictates. It is the Church that matters, Mr. West. Catholic Action is most grateful for the fact that you have often used your influence in Parliament to help the Church. We agree with you that Davison, although not a Catholic, is a key-man for the Church in Victorian politics. We don't like Carr and his group any more than you do. I think we can carry on our work without cutting across your plans, Mr. West."

After a pause, John West said: "All right, I'll put up the money."

When they had gone, he sat brooding. Tonight he had surrendered much of his influence in the Labor Party. Whereas he had vowed for more than a year that he would defeat Kiely in the next Ralstone pre-selection, if it cost him a million, now he had given £50,000 to the organisation that had enabled Kiely to beat his man, Cotton.

Although the Labor Party was now the Government of Victoria, with Carr as Premier, John West's men, led by Bill Brady and Cregan, were a minority in the Cabinet and caucus. With Maurice Blackwell dead, there was no longer a left wing among the Victorian Labor politicians, but the best endeavours of Frank Lammence could not get rid of Carr. The last time John West had run Cregan against Carr for the Party leadership and Brady for the deputy leadership against a young Catholic politician who was neither a West man nor a member of The Movement, £1,000 had been distributed in bribes, but John West's men were defeated. The Deputy leader told caucus that money had changed hands, that he would talk if he were defeated, so some politicians who had accepted bribes changed their votes to avoid exposure.

John West sat reflecting on his position until a late hour. After all he had done for the Church, they had forced him to finance his political enemies. Hadn't he saved the Church hundreds of thousands of pounds by forcing Davison to introduce the Church Rates Bill? Why hadn't he thought to remind Parelli 'and the Archbishop of that?

When Davison's coalition Government with the U.A.P. was tottering, John West and Daniel Malone had manoeuvred the Premier into passing a Bill exempting Catholic Church properties from paying rates to local Municipal Councils.

When first approached, Davison had refused; but when John West got Paddy Kelleher to cancel the Labor pre-selection in a pending by-election, and appointed a 'weak' Labor candidate to run against Davison's man, the Premier said: "I'll tell you what. I'll do it, providing I can exempt all churches from rates. Most of my colleagues are Protestants; they'd never agree unless I do it this way."

Davison pushed the Bill through Parliament and his man won the by-election. After Parliament was next disbanded, Labor went back with an absolute majority over the Country Party and the U.A.P.; but the Carr Government was, from John West's point of view, the worst Victoria had had for twenty years.

Sensing the decline in John West's power, and seeking to win country seats for the Labor Party, the Carr group had decided on a showdown over trotting. Revolt had broken out anew in the trotting world, and Carr was threatening to introduce night trotting after transferring control from John West's bogus club.

The hall clock had struck midnight before John West aroused himself wearily and walked slowly to the foot of the stairs. He consoled himself with the thought that his money would be used to fight Communism; the reds missed no opportunity to write up his influence in the Labor Party; now he'd have revenge.

Half-way up the stairs a heart pain gripped him. He stood rigidly in a cold sweat, afraid to move. The agonising pain, the sense of doom! He stood as if petrified, holding the banister, until the pain eased.

For the first time since the Gaming Suppression Bill of 1906, legislation aimed against John West was introduced into the Victorian Parliament. A Bill was passed to hand over Apsom racecourse, which had been occupied by the Army during the war, to the Housing Commission. Then a Bill was introduced to legalise night trotting and transfer control of the sport to a board of Government appointees.

Brady, Trumbleward, Cregan and Kelleher led opposition to the measure; Michael Kiely supported it. Paddy Kelleher had told a deputation of trotting men's representatives: "If old J.W. wants to keep – aarr – trotting, he can as far as I'm c-c-concerned. When one of my kiddies was sick years ago, the old aaarrr – fellow saved its l-life by getting a-aaarrr – hospital b-bed and the best m-medical attention."

While the second reading debate on the bill raged, John West himself lay in a hospital bed. Devlin had recommended that he risk an operation to rid himself of the dread angina pains.

"The operation won't cure the complaint, Mr. West, but it will remove the pain. And – here's good news – I have arranged to import from America a special new drug to treat the complaint. They are getting wonderful results, putting years on to people's lives. I strongly advise the operation. You have an astonishing constitution – you will survive it. People with hearts often live longest, Mr. West. With this operation and the drug, you may live for years."

John West took Communion and Extreme Unction before going under the anaesthetic. As consciousness faded he felt impelled to shout out: "No! No! I might die!" But unconsciousness claimed him before he could speak.

The operation was successful, and after a few weeks' treatment with the new drug he felt better than he had for two years. He recovered some of his old drive. He amazed everyone with his vigour.

Dick Lamb said to Frank Lammence: "Old J.W.'s a marvel; he's as good as he ever was."

Bennett told Trumbleward: "Ol' J.W.'s back in harness. They'd better look out now. If he'd been fit when the fun first started, this Bill would never have got to Parliament."

John West went into action against his enemies, working out shrewd last-minute moves against the Trotting Bill.

The forces arrayed against him were formidable. The trotting men had found a new leader named Fleming, a former trotting journalist. At the initial protest meeting, Fleming attacked Frank Lammence as "a stooge of John West," the Melbourne Galloping and Trotting Association as a bogus club, "a front to hide the profiteers, notably West, who have bled trotting white for forty years."

When the new trotting men's Association had been formed with Fleming as secretary, less than twenty of two thousand men remained faithful to the old regime. Then lobbying began. Premier Carr and his Chief Secretary agreed to introduce a Bill. Like a rudderless ship without J.W., the West machine could not cope with the situation.

After a narrow victory in the Cabinet, the Bill went to the Labour caucus. Bennett, The Gentleman Thief, attacked Fleming as a 'Johnny-come-lately,' and made an impassioned plea for John West. After all West had done for the Party, surely he was entitled to keep trotting. Bennett actually shed tears. "Why," he said, "West saved certain men here from the shadow of prison." But to no avail.

After Premier Carr had given caucus a pep talk on the need for unity, the Bill was adopted by a large majority. The Chief Secretary introduced it into Parliament. Tom Trumbleward, old and feeble, left his sickbed to oppose his own Party on the issue. He saw Lammence, then he and Bill Brady canvassed support but found that Cregan was the only other Labor man in the Lower House prepared to go against the caucus decision.

They turned to the Country Party. Davison agreed to help. Then Fleming organised a mass meeting in Artful Alfie's electorate. Next day Davison received more than 200 telegrams demanding that he and his Party support the Bill. Knowing the Bill had wide support in the country and fearful for his political future, Davison voted for the Bill, which was carried by a clear majority.

When John West threw himself into the fight, the measure was due to be debated in the Upper House. He summoned Kelleher, Bennett, Cregan, Brady and Trumbleward to his office. Trumbleward, ill in bed and not expected to live, could not come, but the other four arrived on time.

"Well, gentlemen, we're going to beat this Trotting Bill yet."

"Aaarrr, b-b-brother, I'm afraid its t-too late," said Kelleher, who viewed John West's position as tragic.

"No, it's not! I've got a scheme."

John West, whose face was almost as white as his hair, looked alert. In his eyes was much of their old penetration. He turned to Bennett.

"The Honourable Member, Bennett," he said jovially, "is going to turn wowser tomorrow when the House meets."

Bennett was puzzled. "How do you mean?"

John West related how Bob Scott had almost tricked Premier Bent in 1906, then continued: "We'll pretend that we oppose the Bill because it will encourage gambling. There are several wowsers in the Upper House and a few others who will oppose the Bill on behalf of the V.R.C. If you and Paddy oppose it, we'll nearly toss it out."

"Aaarrr – Mr. West, I fought against the Bill in the Party room, b-but, we'll split the Party if we g-go too far."

"Split the Party! Has the Party considered me? Listen. I'll smash Carr's Government and I'll get rid of our smart Chief Secretary and Deputy Leader; I'll end Kiely's career, too, if it costs me a million! After all I've done for the Party and for trotting, they take control off me. There'll be a fortune in night trotting. I tried to get a Bill through years ago, and if I can't have night trotting, then Fleming and his mob of impostors won't run it."

The others fell uncomfortably silent.

John West addressed Bennett again: "Play the wowser; then you and Paddy move a few amendments. Frank Lammence has got them ready. Even if the Bill passes the Upper House, some of the amendments will be carried."

He turned to Cregan and Brady. "Now, Bill, when the amendments are considered by Labor caucus, I want you and Bert to say: 'Send 'em back. We won't accept any amendments.' "

Cregan gazed quizzically at John West. Brady uttered a harsh laugh and said: "Jesus wept! You might get away with it at that. It's a smart scheme."

John West grinned. "Yes, we might. You rally all the support you can for all or nothing on the Trotting Bill."

When they had completed arrangements the politicians departed. Kelleher lagged behind the others. When they had entered the lift, he returned to John West's office.

"Aaarrr – excuse me, Mr. W-West."

"Yes?"

"I – aaarrr – that is, b-b-brother, I c-can't do what you asked in the House tomorrow. As Secretary, I c-can't go against a P-Party decision. But I'll – aaarrr – oppose accepting the amendments when the Bill comes back to us. I'll help you get rid of – aaarrr – K-Kiely and one or two more. I know you'll understand. Mr. W-West. I know how you must feel. The b-bastards have bitten the hand that fed 'em. I'll help in future. Aaaarrr – I . . ."

Whatever else Kelleher had intended to say was frozen on his lips by John West's expression. John West's face was set in a snarl of contempt and suppressed rage. He stared at Kelleher, who shifted uncomfortably, then turned on his heel and was gone.

When the debate began next day in the Upper House, Bennett soon got the floor. He pleaded that the change of control by broadening trotting facilities would bring thousands of working men "under the pernicious influence of the gambling mania." Apparently hoping that people would forget that he had been profitably associated with gambling sports all his life, Bennett asked the Council to consider how "a wage-earner's wife would feel if she knew her husband was a regular attendant at the night trots, and risking his week's wages which perhaps he had in his pocket."

"I make no apologies for opposing my own Party on this issue. Behind closed doors in the Cabinet room they sharpened the dagger to stab the Association of which I am President in the back."

637

He spoke at great length, concluding with a eulogy of John West, who, he said, had stepped in forty years ago and saved trotting from bankruptcy. He declared that the Melbourne Galloping and Trotting Association was not a profit-making body. Its profits went to pay Mr. John West and the estate of Benjamin Levy back for money loaned and property leased.

In spite of Bennett's eloquence, the Bill passed through the Upper House, but not before three of Lammence's amendments had been accepted, including a rather vital one removing the right of appeal to an independent tribunal against stewards' decisions.

When Cabinet considered the amendments, Brady demanded that they be rejected and the Bill sent back to the Upper House. Carr became suspicious and adjourned the meeting to consult Fleming, the trotting men's leader. Fleming said: "I think it's a trap to delay the Bill until after the elections in the hope that your Government will be defeated. I suggest you accept the amendments. They're not fundamental. We can perhaps change the Bill again later."

When caucus reassembled, Carr moved that the amendments be accepted. The motion was carried.

And so, after forty years, control of trotting passed out of John West's hands. He smarted under the defeat. He would smash this Government! Under his urge for immediate reprisals he sent Frank Lammence to see Premier Carr with two demands.

Lammence, in his late sixties with his hair greying, looked younger by many years. As he faced Carr in the Premier's office, the usual unfathomable expression hid his true feelings.

"Mr. West asked me to see you, Jack," Lammence began. "He thinks the least you can do is to ensure that his club will be allowed to continue with galloping meetings."

Carr was a smooth fifty-five years. Well dressed in grey, he had developed the self-confident bearing of the successful politician. Today he was a little nervous; placatory but firm. He had learned that the West machine was not by any means a spent force. In future he would leave West's enterprises strictly alone. He told Lammence that galloping was a matter for the V.R.C.; as that body had allowed John West's club to use its courses while the Army had been in occupation of Apsom, he saw no reason why that situation should not continue when the Army handed over to the Housing Commission.

Suddenly, Lammence said: "Mr. West wants Richard Bradley released from prison immediately."

Carr gaped in astonishment. "What? But Bradley is a murderer, Frank. He's in for life. It's impossible!"

"Nothing's impossible, Jack. The point is, Bradley was a great friend of Mr. West's brother, Arthur, who made a death-bed request for Bradley's release."

Carr laughed nervously, then hesitated.

John West had forgotten Richard Bradley's existence until his desire to make demands on Carr had reminded him of Arty's wish.

Carr found words: "But, it just can't be done, Frank. There'd be an outcry. Interested parties have tried before to get Bradley out, but it's impossible."

"Mr. West said to say that if you don't release Bradley and leave his galloping meetings alone he will bring your Government down if it costs a million."

Carr studied Lammence's impassive face. This man was deadly serious. Paddy Kelleher had said that old J.W. was savage and would seek revenge.

A month later, Richard Bradley hobbled out of Pentridge Jail a free man. He was sick, old and bent. His niece Pat and her husband took him to their home in a taxi.

For John West it was a hollow victory. At times when he felt well and energetic enough, he planned the downfall of the Carr Government; told Brady and Davison to work to revive the Country Party-Labor Coalition.

One evening, in the winter of 1948, John West had just retired to bed when the telephone rang. He put on a dressing gown and slippers and went slowly downstairs, shivering with cold.

"Hullo."

A newspaper reporter answered. "Mr. Kiely, the Member for Ralstone, has just made a bitter attack on you, Mr. West, during the debate on the Racing Reform Bill in the Victorian Parliament."

"Kiely's an impostor! What'd he say?"

"Among other things, he said: 'The new racing club to be formed under the Bill will be as much a creature of West as the V.G. & T.A. The same technique will be used. Those who can

639

be bought will be bought, and those who can be intimidated will be intimidated'.''

"Kiely's a liar!" John West shouted.

"He also said that you helped to defeat the Carr Government; that when Sir Alfred Davison was Premier he called on you nearly every day; and that you financed the Country Party. He went on to say that you have corrupted every sport with which you have been connected. I am ringing to give you a chance to reply, Mr. West.''

John West was nonplussed. He had not the energy to devise a hasty answer. He fell back on evasion and the power of money. "Say that I said I'll give £1000 to the Children's Hospital if Kiely can prove that I have ever given money to the Country Party; providing he'll give £100 if he can't prove it. There you are. I'll pay him ten to one! Put that in, and also that Kiely is an unmitigated liar.''

When the reporter had rung off, John West was cold, yet sweating. Though he felt no pain, his heart seemed to have seized. He was afraid to move until the turn passed. He sometimes wondered if he had been wise to undergo the operation to remove the angina pain; at least the pain had been a warning signal ...

John West's health had steadily declined in the past year. He seemed to grow visibly older every day. His mind had lost much of its clarity. He walked about with bent back; his legs were more bandy. His grey eyes, which had once been inscrutable, able to hold men in awe, intimidate them, were now weak, their feverish oily gleam betraying his mental stress.

Though Devlin had said nothing directly, John West sensed from his constant warnings against excitement and effort, that the doctor had detected a serious worsening in his heart condition.

Fear of death dominated John West in spite of his regular attendance at the Sacraments. Though he felt he would escape Hell, he sometimes pondered on the nature of Purgatory and constantly sought indulgences by paying to have Masses said; he inserted in his will a provision that money be set aside for Masses for the repose of his soul. Meanwhile, he must cheat death as long as he could. He allowed Frank Lammence and Pat Cory to vie for many of his duties. He carried out Devlin's instructions to the letter, rested at the prescribed times, took his digitalis tonic with scrupulous regularity and avoided excitement and worry as much as possible; on his rare visits to the football, races or boxing he tried to remain unexcited, calm. On his way to and from the office, Paddy Ryan was his constant companion. They travelled by fourpenny bus. A scene enacted almost daily was the source of some amusement. When John West left the office, Paddy would accompany him to the bus stop, buy an evening paper, assist his master on to the bus. If the bus were crowded Paddy would say: "A seat for the old gentleman, please." Few passengers knew the frail old man was the legendary, notorious John West.

He often pondered on the past. His mother and Mary were the people he liked to remember. His conscience often smote him when he thought of his mother, and when he probed his memories of Mary he had to resist a desire to write inviting her to come back.

As John West left the telephone, it rang again: another newspaper reporter asking for a statement. After repeating his challenge to Kiely, he left the receiver off the hook and returned to bed. He could not sleep; he lay awake counting his heartbeats. In his weariness, he could not face up to plans to combat Kiely's outburst. He would get Frank Lammence on the job in the morning. Why couldn't they leave him alone?

The Liberal Party had won the recent elections and took office in coalition with the Country Party which had replaced Davison with a new leader. But Kiely was still member for Ralstone. Kiely had consolidated his position in spite of Paddy Kelleher. Paddy, true to his promise to John West, and himself fearing the growing power of Catholic Action, had moved to run a famous Ralstone footballer against Kiely in the pre-selection ballot. Kiely tricked his potential opponent into becoming unfinancial and expelled him from the branch. Paddy could have fixed the matter, but the footballer, disgusted, abandoned his political ambitions.

Kiely's only remaining opponent was Colin Lassiter's brother, Jim, who accepted John West's support. Only expediency caused the Lassiters to help John West: Old Ron had died in poverty on the old age pension, and Colin had been sacked from the Council job. Disgruntled, Colin Lassiter had threatened to expose Ralstone Council rackets in property sales, tenders, charity carnivals, gaming prosecutions and the like. Calling Lassiter's bluff, the Mayor had approached John West and obtained permission to sack him.

The local Labor Party branches were now "packed" with Catholic Action members, so Kiely strenuously argued that John West and the Lassiters were a disgrace to the Church, and easily defeated Jim Lassiter.

John West had more success with the Chief Secretary and the Deputy Leader of the Labor Party: they held "border-line" seats. Paddy Kelleher told John West at the time: "The only way to beat them is to cause them to lose their b-bloody – aaarrr – seats. Then next time we'll beat them at the pre-selection." That Labor would lose two votes as a consequence did not seem to worry Paddy. To get rid of these two men, Kelleher co-operated with Catholic Action which was bitterly hostile towards the Chief Secretary because they considered him a leftist, and towards the Deputy Leader who, though a Catholic, was strongly opposed to Catholic Action's political interference. Controlling many branches in the two electorates, Catholic Action spread damaging rumours, said the candidates were working with the reds to nationalise the banks, and generally sabotaged the campaigns. Both men were defeated.

Although John West had several contacts in the new Liberal Government, the Victorian Racing Club had more influence; it induced the Premier to bring down a Bill to wipe out John West's racing club.

Under John West's direction, Godfrey Dwyer, Bennett, Lammence and Bill Brady organised resistance. As another club had, like John West, no course on which to race, Dwyer tried to arrange a merger of the two clubs. To assist the plan, John West purchased a disused racecourse, proposed to spend a fortune to prepare it for racing, and offered it to the new club.

Finally, the merger was arranged, and though John West could not hope to make profits from the new club, he felt he had saved his face. Now Kiely had used the debate on the Racing Reform Bill to attack him.

Next morning, John West's office buzzed with activity. Politicians and press reporters were interviewed by him and Frank Lammence. At Alfred Davison's suggestion, John West wrote a letter to Parliament denying Kiely's allegations. The Liberal Premier being conveniently ill, the letter was read in the House by the acting Premier, the new leader of the Country Party, who said: "The Victorian Parliament has suffered a complete loss of prestige. I hope Mr. Kiely will give me sufficient grounds to enable me to appoint a Royal Commission so that the matter can be investigated in every detail."

Few indeed were the politicians in the Victorian Parliament who wanted to see John West's political activities investigated. The scandal created turmoil in the Party rooms. Several members of all parties, especially the Labor Party, were in a panic. A gentleman's arrangement was made to hush the matter up. Kiely was agreeable: he had achieved his purpose.

Bedridden and wandering in mind, Thomas Trumbleward died, oblivious of the threatened exposure. For months before Trumbleward's death, Paddy Kelleher had made frequent visits to his bedside to get him to resign.

"The b-bloody – aaarrr – C.A.'s are organising in your electorate," Kelleher said. "If you don't resign they'll win the b-bloody seat, T-Tom."

But Trumbleward was adamant: he would not resign.

Kelleher of late had secretly gone over to the Carr group. He distrusted Catholic Action, which he knew would try to brush him aside eventually.

A few days before Trumbleward died, his wife rang John West. "Mr. West, I don't want to worry you, but Mr. Kelleher's asking Tom to resign. He says you want Tom to resign."

"I haven't told Kelleher to see Tom. Tell Tom not to resign. I'll come and see him tomorrow."

Driven to the house in a taxi, John West found Trumbleward delirious, his big eyes rolling, his pasty face covered with beads of sweat.

John West could make out scattered phrases from the sick man's ramblings. *Strike action is essential. Socialism is the only answer. I am an innocent man, nothing Gilbert says is true.* As he raved, Trumbleward writhed in the bed, at times threshing his arms as if trying to ward off an attack. *I got that washing machine for the last job I did for West. I am an innocent man. The poor shall feed the birds. The anti-conscription campaign – there was a fight. It is all lies. I must have something to eat. Life is mainly froth and bubble. I am innocent.*

Trumbleward's voice trailed off into unintelligibility. The doctor came and John West left.

Trumbleward died next day. His will contained a request for cremation and a Rationalist funeral. John West attended, after obtaining the Archbishop's permission.

In the pre-selection ballot for Trumbleward's seat, John West and Paddy Kelleher backed a Labor member of the Carringbush Council. Catholic Action also put a candidate in the field.

During the campaign, Parelli rang John West and asked him to support the Catholic Action man. Determined this time to defy the Church, John West replied: "I am keeping out of this campaign, and I suggest you do the same. Your interference in Labor Party pre-selections is doing the Church a lot of harm."

John West's man won easily. But his elation was shortlived; he soon sank again into a depression that deepened to melancholy when, a month later, he received news that his brother Joe had died suddenly.

Joe's death brought a flood of bitter-sweet memories of the distant past, and a strong regret that he and Joe had drifted apart. Through the mist of the years, John West remembered what good friends they had been as schoolboys; he remembered, too, that Joe had given him the idea to start the tote on which his millions had been built, that Joe had often tried to prevent him from hurting his mother. He parried remorse with the thought that, after all, he had paid Joe £10 a week right to the end, even after he had become too old to work.

During the Requiem Mass, John West speculated on how long he, himself, would live. After the service, as he followed the coffin up the centre aisle, he cast his eyes on either side. The Church was full, mostly with Joe's own friends; but John West resented the presence of "West men' of many varieties.

Brady, Davison, Cregan and other politicians – they were only here to crawl, he thought. Godfrey Dwyer, who had never ceased complaining when old Joe was working at the race-course – what he was doing here? Cory and Lammence too were only here to keep in his good books; both had visions of controlling the West empire after his death! They were already jockeying for position!

Suddenly he despised them all. Impostors! Flatterers! Hypocritical humbugs! What did they care for Joe! Joe had been worth all of them put together.

As John West stepped into his waiting taxi, Bill Brady approached and said: "I wish to offer my sincere condolences . . ."

"Why? Why should you? You didn't know Joe."

At that moment, John West fully realised that power of the kind he had gained surrounds a man with insincerity – that everything his associates said or did was motivated by self-interest.

On a Saturday afternoon two months later, John West strolled among the crowd in the members' reserve at Flemington racecourse for the first time since he had been warned off all V.R.C. courses after his colt Whisper had won the Caulfield Cup in 1905.

He seemed to have straightened a little; there was an air of quiet contempt about him. He had beaten the V.R.C., he told himself. They had warned him off, but today he had come back.

With typical irony, John West had taken a reprisal against the Victorian Racing Club. The new Club formed by order of the Racing Reform Bill had for its Vice-President W. Bennett; one of its committee members was Ned Horan. Through these two, John West had arranged today's triumph. While the shortage of building materials prevented the new club from preparing its course for racing, it was permitted to conduct its meetings at Flemington. John West was a member of the new club; his member's ticket entitled him to enter the "birdcage" and enclosure.

He flaunted himself embarrassing V.R.C. committee members with hearty greetings, making bets "on the nod" with rails bookmakers. But half-way through the afternoon he became very tired and left for home in the hire car he had come in. Lolling wearily in the comfortable seat, he realised the futility of today's episode. The only way he could have hurt the V.R.C. was to have gained control of night trotting, which was attracting up to 30,000 people each Saturday night and was adversely affecting attendance at the gallops, boxing and wrestling.

The very thought of night trotting brought anger and self-pity. John West had hoped that night trotting would fail, but strictly controlled racing and high stakes had led to good attendances and a boom in breeding. Out of spleen, John West had spread rumours, got newspaper men to report trotting unfavourably, and placed agents in the trotting men's association to disrupt it and attempt to discredit Fleming, its secretary and representative on the Trotting Control Board. But trotting still prospered, though it was fast approaching the state reached by galloping, in which rich owners and breeders were squeezing the "little man" out.

Trotting men in general were convincing even John West that, given strict and efficient control, they would race fairly, honestly and with great enthusiasm.

"Did you back a winner, Mr. West?" the taxi-driver's voice interrupted his thoughts.

"Er – me? No, not today. Don't follow the gallops much these days. Rather go to the football."

That evening Joe brought his fiancee home for the evening meal. She was a bright girl, exuding good humour and charm, intelligently interested in sport. She and Joe had accompanied John West to the boxing and football a few times. To John West, her occasional visits were the only bright spot at home.

Tonight, conversation alternated between football and racing. Joe, who was a rabid Carringbush barracker, told his father excitedly that Carringbush had won by two goals.

The meal reminded John West of meals long ago when the children were all here – when Mary, Marjorie, John and their friends brightened this big house with their chatter and laughter. He would give all his wealth to recapture those days, he told himself. Marjorie and John were dead, but Mary was alive – if only she were here now!

Nellie West was confined to bed, attended by a nurse and a maid. Though she still complained about her spine, Dr Devlin had told John West: "Your wife is merely suffering from old age; she'd be all right – but she's lost all interest in life."

John West and Nellie scarcely ever exchanged words except when others were present. An insidious hatred existed between them. Looking at her vacant chair, John West thought of her now. She had helped wreck his household: but for her affair and that child, the family might still be here to console him in his old age.

When the two young people had left to go to a movie, John West sat by the fire in the breakfast room. The front door bell rang. It was a newsboy with the late sporting paper. John West tried to read, but soon put the paper aside and went wearily to bed.

A reference to John West in a popular column in the daily press, in the spring of 1949, indicated how little was officially known of his career.

Although John West, sportsman and business tycoon,
has been in ill-health for some time, he is still very

much a man of action. Last week he went to Sydney
by plane, returned next day, then went to Perth. His
associates say his judgment is as keen as ever. Mr.
West was a good footballer in his youth and is still
a keen supporter of the Carringbush Club. He has
not had much luck with his racehorses in recent
years, but he won the Caulfield Cup with Whisper
in 1905 and the Doncaster with Garbin in 1924. Mr.
West is Managing Director of Boxing Ltd., and
rarely misses a big fight at the Stadium. Mr. West's
recent philanthropic gestures are typical of him –
his name has been a byword for generosity for fifty
years.

Seated in the embroidered "West for Victory" chair in his office,
John West read the paragraph. Lately he had found the need to
seek a little limelight; the old impulse to give, which he had
harnessed to his drive for power, he allowed rein, giving when
no gain could accrue. He paid cheques to cricketers making
centuries, to footballers for kicking goals; he donated to other
charities as well as the Church. But he was getting little satisfaction; nothing could divert him from loneliness and remorse.
His heart trouble was worse, and his body had begun to wilt. His
hands trembled now, and his sight was failing. He had become
gluttonous, too, and had difficulty in keeping to his diet; occasionally at lunch time he would go to a cafe he owned, and eat
much and ravenously.

Though Richard Lamb told the reporters that "Old J.W. was
as good as ever," behind John West's back he was calling him
a "contrary old nuisance." John West had lost his grip, but he
wouldn't admit it. He resented Lamb, Cory and Lammence
because they insisted on taking over his duties, on telling him to
take it easy, to watch his heart. He became suspicious of them.
He often questioned their actions, disagreeing with them cantak-
erously. Lammence and Lamb were glad each working day when
four o'clock came and Paddy Ryan called to "see J.W. home,"
as he termed it.

John West *had* gone to Sydney on the previous Monday. He
risked the plane trip with Richard Lamb because of serious
trouble in the boxing world. A Trade Union of boxers had been

647

formed months before and, just when John West thought he had crippled the organisation, it was given new life by the strange case of Ron Redmond.

When in his hey-day Redmond had held the middle and light heavy-weight championships of Australia. He had soundly defeatd an American who later became a contender for the world heavy-weight crown. Boxing Ltd. had netted £98,000 in gate receipts from Redmond fights. The experts dubbed Redmond "the greatest fighter since Lou Darby," but after ten years in retirement he was a pitiful punch-drunk, suffering pains in the head, loss of memory, semi-blindness. People were saying that if Redmond had not been permitted to make several comebacks after he was 'over the hill,' he would not be in such a condition.

Redmond had been arrested as a vagrant. He told police he could not keep a job because of his health; that larrikins were knocking him down in the street so they could boast they had 'beat Ron Redmond.'

Meeting Redmond face to face in the Stadium office in Sydney, John West was deeply shocked. Redmond's head rocked from side to side, his eyes were glassy and swam upwards, his eyebrows were scarred where stitches had been inserted, his great torso was flabby and his shoulders stooped.

Richard Lamb had said to John West before the interview: "He was always a malcontent. Went through his money like water, then turned sour on everyone in the fight game. They've got no brains, these half-castes."

Redmond was wearing a new suit that Boxing Ltd. had purchased for him the day before. He sat sullenly silent as though resentful of the charity he was receiving.

John West said: "The Aboriginal Board of Queensland has offered to look after you, Ron. I'll pay your fare to Brisbane and all expenses. Does that suit you?"

"I guess I'll be better off among my own people," Redmond replied. "But the Boxers' and Trainers' Association reckons there should be pensions for sick fighters. What d'yer say to that, Mr. West?"

"Ar, they're only a lot of commo agitators," Richard Lamb intervened. "You must admit, Ron, you made a packet out of the game and threw it away."

"Yeh, I made a packet. So did you – a bigger packet."

The interview quickly ended. It was agreed that Redmond would leave next day for Brisbane. As he shambled towards the door John West said: "Here's your train ticket and expenses, Ron."

Redmond turned and took the proffered envelope, then John West handed him a cheque for £100. "And here's a little nest-egg for old times' sake."

Redmond took the cheque, studied it thoughtfully, then handed it back. "No, thanks, I guess I got no use for money now," he said.

That same night, at the Sydney Stadium, the Australian light-weight champion was knocked out by his challenger. Next day he died! There were rumours that he was a sick man and should not have been permitted to fight. Disturbed, John West started a fund for the champion's widow and child with a cheque for £1000. The Boxers' and Trainers' Association renewed its propaganda for boxing reforms; it began to attract more members in spite of the fact that Boxing Ltd. had stated that none of its members would get fights. Before leaving Sydney, John West and Richard Lamb had arranged for the formation of a rival association which all boxers and trainers must join – that would beat the urgers, Lamb reckoned.

But the incidents distressed John West. When, in the past, many similar tragedies had occurred, he had not given them a second thought, but now they left him conscience-stricken and sad. The most recent issue of the Catholic Action paper, FREEDOM, had consoled him a little by defending his control of boxing and exhorting all sport lovers to ignore "the commo urgers" who were seeking to discredit Boxing Ltd.

. . . his name has been a byword for generosity for fifty years. John West read the columnist's comment again, then turned the pages idly. His new pince-nez glasses hurt him; he took them off, massaged his nose, cleaned them with his handkerchief. He turned to the front page and scanned the news of the coal strike. The paper stated that the miners were to hold mass meetings at which strong back-to-work moves would be made. John West was pleased. What the Archbishop had said about Catholic Action helping to defeat the strike from within the ranks of the miners was coming true. The report brought relief from a fear of the working class that had pestered him lately.

John West's profits were not as directly threatened by strikes as those of other millionaires who owned coal mines, shipping lines, steel factories, etc., but he had been disturbed since the war by strikes for higher wages, shorter hours and on political issues. He felt, as other millionaires felt, that the Communist Trade Union leaders were planning ultimately to use the Trade Union Movement to take economic and political power from the big capitalists. Though he had financed Catholic Action in its endeavours to disrupt the Trade Unions and defeat the Communists, he felt isolated from the field of battle. The Employers' Federation and the Chamber of Commerce, which he had always disdained to join, were leading the fight, helping the Liberal Party and the Labor Party Industrial Groups, using the daily press to mould public opinion and influence Governments.

He turned to the State political news. The paper reported that Labor Party pre-selection ballots were being held for the Federal Elections, which were to take place in December. There were likely to be some sharp contests, the report said: especially between Kiely and Cregan, for the seat vacated by James Summers, former Prime Minister, who had announced his retirement. Only the division of the seat into two electorates under the Chifley Government's Redistribution Bill would prevent a battle royal between rival factions.

Hearing that Kiely intended resigning the Ralstone seat to contest the Federal seat vacated by Summers, John West had asked Cregan to do likewise. Cregan had reluctantly agreed. The two erstwhile friends became bitter enemies. Kiely had been platonically courting Cregan's sister because this was 'good for votes' – he broke off the liaison. Cregan began to go to Mass in parts of the electorate where Kiely held sway; Kiely began doing his religious duties in Cregan-West strong-holds. Membership of Labor Party branches in the electorate increased steeply as the two contenders 'joined up some votes.' Having the support of John West and the Lassiters who hated Kiely, Cregan was being tipped as the likely winner.

Putting the paper aside, John West decided to have lunch. He took a dose of medicine, then produced from a drawer of his desk a bottle of milk and an orange. He ate the orange without relish, then rang for the typist and asked her to boil the milk.

The current epidemic of poliomyelitis had struck fear into John

West. Informed by Devlin that goat's milk was less likely to carry germs, he had purchased a goat and now milked it himself each morning. He took the further precaution of having the goat's milk boiled before drinking it.

A fortnight later, Michael Kiely called by appointment to see Archbishop Malone in his study.

He informed Daniel Malone that, in spite of the fact that Summers' electorate had been divided into two seats under the Redistribution Bill, Cregan had nominated for the same seat as he had. John West was behind the move. It was in the best interests of the Church for both Kiely and Cregan to go to Canberra.

Malone hesitated thoughtfully. Kiely sat with his eyes averted. He was sly, never looking anyone in the face or doing or saying anything without motives of personal gain or gain for the cause of political Catholicism. Recently he had introduced a private member's Bill into the Victorian Parliament aimed at suppressing criticism of the Catholic Church; the Liberal Government, seeking Catholic support, had taken up the measure but had had to withdraw it because of public outcry. Another of Kiely's private Bills had been one to ban the sale and distribution of contraceptives, but this was also defeated.

Colin Lassiter reckoned that Kiely should have been a Jesuit, that his mother, when carrying him, had wanted a girl, not a boy. Michael Kiely had never given way to a sexual urge in his life. Fervent suppression of his sexual desires had led to inhibitions – he was uncomfortable in the presence of young women, and had developed a restless, intense, sadistic personality. He found outlet for his repressions in his religion, his career, and especially in his hatred of Communism. He would exterminate the Communists physically. He had read with glee of the torture of Communists in Spain and Germany – that was the way to deal with them!

Malone studied Kiely. He didn't like him much, but realised his value.

"Sure and this is a difficult situation, Mr. Kiely. It is easy to understand Mr. West's attitude. He has had the say in these electorates for a long time. And, after all, he's been generous to the Church and has practised his religion in recent years."

"He's a disgrace to the Church! Your Grace, I demand that the Church step in and tell Cregan to run for the other seat, so

651

we can both go to Canberra. Why should we let an old scoundrel like West ruin the plans of Catholic Action?''

"Ah, now, we mustn't be too hard, Mr. Kiely. Mr. West's past is between him and his Maker. Who's to say you won't beat Cregan, anyway?''

"Cregan will win, because West and the Lassiters are helping him; but he'll always know that I'm working to undermine him. He'll never be safe. But this feud is undermining Catholic Action in the Labor Party. We can end it by getting Cregan to agree to take one half of Summers' electorate and me the other.''

Malone sighed wearily. "I see your point, Mr. Kiely. I'll see Mr. West and see what I can do.''

"Tell him that I won't attack him publicly again if he agrees.''

Kiely departed. As he started his car, he rubbed his hands and smirked with satisfaction: "Old Dan'' would make West see reason!

While John West awaited Archbishop Malone, Sugar Renfrey called. John West welcomed Renfrey's occasional visits. Sugar was the one man who had stood by him from the beginning. Also, Sugar had, since the war, used his position on the Carringbush Council to make vast sums for John West and a little for himself; from records at the Town Hall Sugar would discover properties for sale, get the money from John West to buy them, then arrange resale at a higher figure.

Sugar was eighty-two – three years older than John West. They both looked their years now. Sugar had gone almost bald, his eyes were red-rimmed and sunken behind his thick glasses, and his rotund body was sagging.

Sugar had another property in mind, he told John West. Then he related the story of how he had defeated a rival candidate for a Labor Party pre-selection ballot for the Carringbush Council.

"See, Jack,'' he concluded. "I was on one side of the road, writin' out Tobacco Union tickets for our man, and Tom Smith was on the other writin' out Tanners' Union tickets for the other fella. Our bloke won by five votes. I always was a faster writer than Tom!''

Sugar laughed uproariously; John West managed a faint smile. Just then the maid announced Daniel Malone. When the Archbishop entered, Sugar said: "I was just leavin', Your Grace.''

"Don't go on my account, Mr. Renfrey. How are things in Carringbush, pray tell me."

"Ar, we're givin' the commos some hurry-up out there. We refused 'em use of the Town 'All, too."

Though Colin Lassiter reckoned, "Sugar wouldn't know a commo from an Eskimo," Renfrey saw himself as Australia's number one red-baiter.

When Sugar had gone, the Archbishop sat opposite John West. Malone came straight to the point. He told John West that he had seen both Kiely and Cregan, that they believed they should contest different seats in the Labor Party pre-selection ballots.

"I'm afraid I must say I agree with them, Mr. West. I know how you feel, but we all must consider the best interests of Catholic Action and the Church. Could you see your way clear to reconsider your attitude?"

"It's nothing to do with me, if Cregan wants to oppose Kiely," John West evaded.

"But Cregan says he would rather not, but that you had insisted."

John West felt embarrassed. He did not know what to say.

Malone continued in a weary monotone: "After all, Mr. West, Kiely is a good Catholic and a tireless worker against Communism. I admit I share your dislike for him, but we must be realistic. What harm could it do to let them both go to Canberra where they can serve the Church best?"

John West remained silent. He knew Malone was right, but was finding the effort of admitting it too great. Of late, John West had begun to think that he should support the Liberal Party because only Menzies wanted to deal vigorously with the Communists. True, Chifley had jailed the leaders of the Miners' Union during the strike and had jailed Sharkey, the Secretary of the Communist Party, for sedition, but only a ban on the Communist Party would allay John West's fears, and Chifley had refused time and again to impose the ban. But for John West to swing right over to the Liberals now was an admission that nearly fifty years of effort to gain decisive influence in the Labor Party had been wasted.

Malone gazed inquiringly at John West. Several times in the past he had been puzzled at West's attitude towards Communism. When the Communist leader, Miller, had been framed on a charge of rape, West had said that he knew positively that Michael Kiely and others had framed Miller. When Cecil Sharpley had left the Communist Party to write for the HERALD newspaper and become chief witness in a Royal Commission into Communism, West had said: "No doubt, Sharpley will be valuable, but you can't trust a paid informer." Malone could not fathom what lay behind these remarks.

Interpreting John West's silence as opposition, Malone persisted: "Catholic Action has made great headway in carrying out the Holy Father's wish that Communism be destroyed. They are gathering lists of Communist Party members and supplying the Security Police with names and addresses – they have a retired detective in charge of this difficult but important work. Last year they drew up a list of all Catholic Trade Unionists in every Australian Diocese, then the local branch of Catholic Action contacted each person suggesting that they should attend their Union meetings. Though the response was disappointing, this led to increased membership of the Movement. As well, the newspaper FREEDOM is doing good work; and anti-communist leaflets are often brought out."

John West straightened up. "Yes, and I often see how they alter signs that the commos put up on walls and fences. For instance, if the commos write 'Release Sharkey' they change it to 'Hang Sharkey.' Very clever."

Malone chuckled: "Just the sort of thing Kiely and Parelli would think up."

"Well, Your Grace, I am prepared to step out of this battle between Kiely and Cregan on one condition: Kiely will cease attacking me." John West spoke as if each word were burning his tongue.

"I know he is agreeable to do that, Mr. West."

They discussed politics for a while. Malone said he thought the Liberals would win the elections. Parelli had seen Menzies. Menzies was going to fight the elections on the Communist issue. He would ban the party and make it illegal for a Communist or a suspected Communist to hold office in a Trade Union. Parelli had agreed that, if the Liberals won, The Movement would encourage the Labor-controlled Senate not to oppose this legislation.

"You see, Mr. West, Catholic Action is striking much

opposition in the Unions, even from many Catholics. The Communists still control most of the big Unions. If Menzies goes into office and removes the Communists from the Unions, our men will win many leading positions. Meanwhile, Catholic Action will work to transform the Labor Party into a party resembling the Catholic centre parties of Europe – I remember you suggested that to Mr. Parelli two years ago – then when Labor gets back to office the position will be most favourable for the Church. That's the general plan. It seems to me, Mr. West, that you have made a fine gesture tonight, in the best service of Almighty God and the Church.''

In December, 1949, the Liberal Party won the Federal elections and R. G. Menzies became Prime Minister. John West had given £10,000 to the Liberal Party's campaign and only £1,000 to Labor. He told Frank Lammence that Menzies was the man to lift price controls, end rationing and deal with the commos.

Yet the result brought no elation to John West: only the state of his heart, his fear of death and his conscience interested him now – and the terrible loneliness of his life.

Joe had married and had shifted into a house purchased by his father in a distant suburb. Now John West was left alone with Nellie, a maid and a nurse, in his huge eerie house whose walls creaked and wept as if in grief at the scenes it had witnessed during the past half-century.

John West's fear of death had led to neurotic behaviour. He still milked his goat early each morning and carried a bottle of goat's milk about with him for fear he might have to drink cow's milk and get the dread polio. He bought fresh bullets for his revolvers out of fear that some enemy, known or unknown, might try to murder him. He would not eat food except that cooked at the house, for fear someone might try to poison him.

He became even more deeply religious. He fervently attended Mass and Communion every morning at the Chapel nearby; he carried his rosary beads and prayer book with him constantly.

Sometimes he lay awake at night, praying, counting his heart-beats, listening to every breath he drew. Devlin was clearly convinced that he had not much longer to live. The idea of dying pulverised him: though he had, he believed, cleansed his soul, he could not face the dread prospect of judgment.

When free of his fears, he was gripped by a gnawing loneliness; in such moments his thoughts would turn to Mary. She was the only person alive he could love, who could console him now in his hour of need. Reviewing the past, as he often did with remorse, he would sometimes blame himself for her departure: he had been a little harsh with her. He wondered what she was doing. She had married again; had she any children? Was her second husband a Communist? Perhaps she had married a respectable chap – he was supposed to be a doctor. Perhaps she herself had changed her views. Speaking to Nellie for the first time in weeks, he asked if she had received letters. Nellie replied coldly that Mary had written once in a while but there was nothing in the letters that would interest him.

When Ted Thurgood, Alfred Davison and Sugar Renfrey all died within a fortnight, he felt a terrible conviction that he would soon follow.

As Christmas approached, John West thought of the grand Christmas parties Mary and the others used to organise. If only she could be here this Christmas . . .

When the nurse said on Christmas Eve that word had come that Mary would ring by radio telephone from England that night at eight o'clock, he trembled with excitement. He could not eat his dinner. He sat in the reception room waiting for the telephone to ring. When at last it did, he had to resist a desire to get to it first; but the nurse answered it and handed the receiver to Nellie, who had hovered nearby in her dressing-gown.

John West stood in the hall breathless and impatient, while Nellie spoke stiltedly to her daughter in a quavering, mournful voice.

At last, Nellie said: "Yes, your father is here. Do you want to speak to him?"

He took the receiver from Nellie, who was weeping softly. He could scarcely speak.

"Hullo – Mary," he said, and the tenderness in his voice surprised him.

"Hullo, Father. How are you?"

"Oh, n-not the best – er – not too bad, you know. How are you?"

"Oh, I haven't been well. Sometimes I feel like seeing good old Australia again."

There was a pause. He could think of nothing to say. In spite of himself he blurted out: "Mary, are you still, still a, a commo?"

"Yes, Father, but surely . . . Oh, Father . . ."

"Your time has expired," a precise female voice interrupted them. "Are you extending?"

"I can't afford an extension, Father," Mary said, as though hinting that he should pay for one.

He stood gasping for breath, his heart pounding, his head aching cruelly, a mist swirling before his eyes.

"I'm sorry," the operator said. "You will have to finish now."

John West caught his breath and shouted: "No. I'll extend!" but the line was dead.

He thumped the phone with his fist. "I'll extend, I said!" but no voice answered. Slowly he replaced the receiver.

In the first weeks of 1950, John West thought constantly of Mary. She would think he hadn't wanted an extension, but he had wanted one – he just couldn't collect his thoughts, he'd had a heart attack. Once he thought of obtaining Mary's address from Nellie so he could write a letter of explanation, and ask why she had said she wasn't very well.

His loneliness, his desire to have Mary with him, dominated even his fear of death, his sense of guilt and his hatred of Communism. One day in March he made up his mind. He would get Mary's address. He would write to her explaining about the extension, and – yes, he must do it! – he must ask her to come home! She had said she wanted to see Australia again. He could write that he was willing to supply the money to fulfil her wish. She could even bring her husband if she wanted to.

All day at the office, he planned what he would write, thought up excuses for his action. He would tell Nellie that Mary seemed lonely; he would tell the Archbishop that he was bringing her home to try to win her back to the Church; he would tell Frank Lammence that Mary had written begging his forgiveness . . .

He took a taxi home. On the way he rehearsed what he would say to Nellie.

At the dinner table he found Nellie, red-eyed, her bony frame convulsed in weeping, tears trickling down her wrinkled cheeks. He stood leaning on the table, gazing at her. Could she ever have been the beautiful girl he had kissed in her mother's kitchen when they were young and life was good?

"What's wrong with you? I thought you were sick! Why are you down for dinner?"

"It's Mary," she croaked. "A cable from her husband ... she's – she's dead!"

He stood like a statue, his face contorted, his eyes staring. He rushed to her, gripped her by the shoulders.

"You're mad, woman! You're mad!"

Her eyes turned to a cablegram form on the table. He released her and picked it up.

> *It is with deep sorrow that I have to inform you that your daughter, Mary, my beloved wife, died of cancer yesterday. She had been ill for some months.*

John West stared as if in disbelief at the cablegram. He crushed it in his hand. Suddenly, a severe heart attack gripped him. He stumbled forward, fell to the floor and lay still.

Nellie screamed weakly. The nurse rushed into the room, and knelt beside John West. "Mrs. West, get the maid to ring Dr. Devlin! Tell him to come immediately!"

When Devlin came they shifted John West with difficulty to the couch in the music room. The maid lit a fire, and they shifted the couch close to it, covering him with rugs. John West rallied. Devlin gave him an injection and some medicine, then sat with him for half an hour.

As he was leaving, he said: 'That was a bad one, Mr. West. You'll have to be very careful. Lie here for a while then get nurse to help you upstairs to bed. And you'd better stay in bed for a few days. I'll call in the morning."

On his way out, Devlin said softly to the nurse: "He may not get over this one. I can't stay; I have an urgent case. Don't hesitate to ring if you need me during the night."

Though John West felt weak and breathless, his mind was clear. Oblivious of the nurse, who sat behind him in the shadows, he lay gazing into the dancing flames. Mary was dead, and with her had died his last faint hope of relief from the torments of his soul.

"Do you feel you could walk up to bed now, Mr. West?" the soft voice of the nurse interrupted him.

"Yes," he said. "Bed is the only place for me now."

Leaning on her arm, he made his way slowly up the stairs. At his bedroom door she said: "Are you sure you'll be all right? Will I help you undress?"

"No," he replied weakly. "I've undressed myself for a long time now. I'll be all right, sister."

"Well, don't hesitate to press the bell if you want me during the night. I suppose you haven't forgotten it's connected to my bedroom."

"No, I haven't forgotten, sister. But I'll be all right. Just the shock."

"Good-night, Mr. West. I've switched on the gas fire in the dressing room and put a hot water bottle in the bed."

"Good-night, sister."

John West undressed slowly. A feeling of weary apathy enveloped him. Where had his wealth and power led him? He could have all the things that money could buy, but the will to possess them, the ability to use them, had deserted him; he wanted things that money could not buy, but they had passed him by, or had been taken from him by others.

He stood in his pyjamas and slippers, the light above him heightening his bandiness, throwing grotesque shadows over and around him. He gazed at the wardrobe which stood against the door of the room where Nellie slept – or did she sleep? If she were awake, what was she thinking? Suddenly, an impulse urged him to go to her, to speak tenderly, to share his sorrow with her. But he could not. She had betrayed him. He had vowed he would punish her . . . The memory of the night when the child, Xavier, was born in there came to him, slashing at his mind. He shuddered, shrugged and walked to his open air bedroom where the bed lamp was alight.

He took the rosary beads from under the pillow and knelt by the bed. He knelt there until he had said a decade on the beads, his lips moving silently, his eyes upraised. He recited the Confiteor:

> *I confess to Almighty God . . .*
> *. . . that I have sinned exceedingly in thought, word and deed . . . May the Almighty God have mercy on me, forgive me my sins, and bring me to life everlasting, Amen.*

He climbed slowly into bed, but immediately got out again. For the first time in fifty years he had forgotten the revolver! He went to the dressing-room, took the revolver from the drawer and put it under his pillow.

He lay in the darkness, thinking distractedly. His heart seemed to be beating weakly and irregularly. Suddenly his mind returned to Mary, and self-pity swamped him. They had taken her from him, the commos! The commos had done it! But Menzies and Catholic Action would fix them – jail them, kill them! He would give Catholic Action another fifty thousand pounds to fight them with!

His body became taut, his heart seemed to stop beating. At last he slumped deep into the bed and a great weariness pressed down on him.

In the half-world between wakefulness and sleep, he imagined he could hear the piano being played downstairs, then laughter wafted up, and Mary's voice seemed to call him. He tried to rise, but could not.

As sleep drew him closer into its web, he dreamed he saw Constable Brogan standing near, as he had done in front of Cummins' Tea Shop so long ago. In his dream, he span the sovereign at Brogan. Brogan caught it but passed it back, saying: "I'm sorry, I have my orders. I'm going to search the shop, then put you out of business. Your mother will be happier if I do."

Then his mother seemed to come to him pleading: "Please, John, for me. For your own mother." He reached out to her but she faded away from him until he could see her no more.

There was no moon, but bright stars twinkled. The autumn wind stirred mournfully in the branches of the pine trees that formed the two outside walls of the sleepout. John West dozed restlessly and fitfully. Now and then he stirred in the bed and cried out in his sleep.